GREAT BOOKS OF THE WESTERN WORLD

GREAT BOOKS
OF THE WESTERN WORLD

ROBERT MAYNARD HUTCHINS, *EDITOR IN CHIEF*

36.

SWIFT

STERNE

GULLIVER'S TRAVELS

BY JONATHAN SWIFT

TRISTRAM SHANDY

BY LAURENCE STERNE

WILLIAM BENTON, *Publisher*

ENCYCLOPÆDIA BRITANNICA, INC.

CHICAGO · LONDON · TORONTO

THE UNIVERSITY OF CHICAGO

The Great Books
is published with the editorial advice of the faculties
of The University of Chicago

GENERAL CONTENTS

....

GULLIVER'S TRAVELS, Page 1

By Jonathan Swift

TRISTRAM SHANDY, Page 191

By Laurence Sterne

GENERAL CONTENTS

GULLIVER'S TRAVELS

BIOGRAPHICAL NOTE
JONATHAN SWIFT, 1667–1745

SHORTLY after the death, in 1658, of Thomas Swift, Vicar of Goodrich, his five sons migrated to Ireland in hope of restoring the family fortunes, lost through their father's support of the losing side during the Civil War. The eldest son, Godwin, gained wealth and, when his younger brother died, leaving a widow and two children without any source of income, he became their support. The second of these children was Jonathan Swift, born in Dublin on November 30, 1667. At the age of six, he was sent to Kilkenny Grammar School and later to Trinity College by his Uncle Godwin. Swift attributed the fact that he was "stopped of his degree for dulness and insufficiency" to his uncle's ill-treatment of him, which, as he put it, caused him to become so "discouraged and sunk in spirits" that he neglected his studies. By a special provision, he obtained his degree from this institution in February 1685.

In 1689, his uncle having died insolvent, Swift went to England and entered the employment of the essayist and diplomat, Sir William Temple, in his retirement at Moor Park. After "growing into some confidence" with his employer and obtaining an A.M. degree from Oxford, his lack of advancement rankled. He left Temple, took orders in Ireland, and was appointed to the parish of Kilroot near Belfast. Two years later he resigned and returned to Moor Park, where he remained until his patron's death.

Swift's ten years' connection with Temple had acquainted him with men and affairs and afforded him the opportunity for extensive reading and writing. "He writ and burnt, and writ again upon almost all manner of subjects," even composing Pindaric poems in the manner of Cowley which elicited Dryden's comment: "Cousin Swift, you will never be a poet." Before Temple's death, Swift had written two satires, *The Battle of the Books* and *The Tale of a Tub*, which, however, were not published until 1704.

After Temple's death, Swift found another patron in the Lord Justice of Ireland, Lord Berkeley, but again he was disappointed in his hope of preferment and forced to content himself with the income from three small parishes. The only one which had a church was Larocor with its congregation of fifteen people, "most of them gentle and all of them simple." Here Swift established himself. To Larocor he invited Esther Johnson, the "Stella" to whom he addressed his Journal, and her companion, Rebecca Dingley. Esther Johnson had been a dependent of Sir William Temple, and Swift had taught her to read and write when they resided at Moor Park together; she had been eight, he, twenty-two.

Swift's life in Ireland did not absorb his energies or satisfy his ambitions. He travelled often to London where he frequented the coffee houses and made the acquaintance of Addison, Steele, Pope, and Congreve. Like them, his sympathies were with the Whig party and his first political pamphlet, published in 1701, was actually attributed to various Whig leaders. Swift's discovery that the Whigs did not intend to use their power to aid the Church was the occasion for a letter and three tracts, the most famous being the *Argument to prove that the abolishing of Christianity in England may, as things now stand, be attended with some inconveniences* (1708).

In 1710, the Tory, Robert Harley, became Chancellor of the Exchequer and shrewdly welcomed Swift "with the greatest respect and kindness imaginable." Soon afterwards Swift became the editor of the Tory weekly, the *Examiner*. His pen made him a power in the State; he warned Harley "never to appear cold" to him; at the Court, he boasted to Stella, "I am so proud I make all the lords come up to me." With the accession of George I, the Tory Ministry fell, and Swift retired to the deanery of St. Patrick's in Dublin, bestowed on him by Queen Anne instead of the English appointment he would have preferred as recompense for his services.

While in London Swift entered deeply into the literary life of the time. He invented Sir Isaac Bickerstaff, who predicted and announced the death of the almanac-maker and astrologer, John Partridge, so convincingly that the man was obliged to issue a special almanac to assure his clients that he was still alive. At the time his political activity was at its height, Swift was treasurer of a society of wits and statesmen, known as the Brothers; a contributor to the *Tatler, Spectator,* and *Intelligencer;* joint founder with Pope and Arbuthnot of the Scriblerus Club. To this period belong a miscellany of works in prose and verse and his *Journal to Stella,* a series of daily letters to the two ladies in Ireland, minutely recording his busy life and his inmost thoughts with an admixture of tenderness, humour, and playfulness.

In 1714 Swift returned to Ireland, where, to his discomfort, he was later followed by Esther Vanhomrigh, a young girl he had come to know in London. Although he undoubtedly preferred the company of Stella, his relations to both ladies remained ambiguous; it is not known whether he ever married Stella or whether he ever saw her except in the presence of Mrs. Dingley. The history of his attachment to Miss Vanhomrigh is preserved in the poem, *Cadenus (Decanus) and Vanessa,* and in their correspondence, later edited by Sir Walter Scott. At length Vanessa, in 1723, took the despairing step of writing to Stella, or to Swift, demanding to know whether they were married. Swift returned the letter and left Vanessa forever without uttering a word. Within a few weeks Vanessa was dead. Stella died five years later.

Swift hated the Irish and always considered himself an "Englishman dropped in Ireland," but, as a "fighter for human liberty," he was outraged by the results of English misrule. Once again he took up his pen to combat the Whigs, this time on behalf of the Irish. Gradually there collected around him the nucleus of an Irish party which gained popular support as a result of the six famous *Drapier Letters* (1724), wherein Swift protested the scandalous patent accorded William Wood for supplying Ireland with a coinage of copper halfpence. His *Modest Proposal for Preventing the Children of Poor People from Being a Burden to their Parents or the Country* (1729), by the expedient of eating them, further aroused the national spirit. Swift became revered as a leading Irish patriot, a reputation he felt he in no way deserved "because what I do is owing to perfect rage and resentment, and the mortifying sight of slavery, folly, and baseness about me, among which I am forced to live." A product of the period of his Irish banishment was *Travels Into Several Remote Nations of the World by Lemuel Gulliver,* published in 1726.

During his last years Swift suffered acute physical torture from an ailment that had long plagued him with giddiness and deafness. In March, 1742, it became necessary to appoint guardians of his person and estate. After a paralytic stroke in September of the same year, he sank into complete mental apathy, which lasted until his death on October 19, 1745. In his will he made provision for his interment in St. Patrick's in the same coffin as Stella "as privately as possible and at twelve o'clock at night," for the disposition of his fortune to found a lunatic asylum in Dublin, for the Latin inscription on his black marble tombstone "in large letters, deeply cut and strongly gilded," commemorating his release from the "savage indignation" that could no longer "lacerate his heart."

CONTENTS

PART III. *A VOYAGE TO LAPUTA, BALNIBARBI, LUGGNAGG, GLUBBDUBDRIB, AND JAPAN*

PART IV. *A VOYAGE TO THE COUNTRY OF THE HOUYHNHNMS*

ADVERTISEMENT

Mr. Sympson's letter to Capt. Gulliver, prefixed to this volume, will make a long advertisement unnecessary. Those interpolations complained of by the captain, were made by a person since deceased, on whose judgment the publisher relyed to make any alterations that might be thought necessary. But, this person, not rightly comprehending the scheme of the author, nor able to imitate his plain simple style, thought fit, among many other alterations and insertions, to compliment the memory of her late Majesty, by saying, That she governed without a chief minister. We are assured, that the copy sent to the bookseller in London, was a transcript of the original, which original being in the possession of a very worthy gentleman in London, and a most intimate friend of the author's; after he had bought the book in sheets, and compared it with the originals, bound it up with blank leaves, and made those corrections, which the reader will find in our edition. For, the same gentleman did us the favour to let us transcribe his corrections.

A LETTER FROM CAPT. GULLIVER, TO HIS COUSIN SYMPSON

I hope, you will be ready to own publickly, whenever you shall be called to it, that by your great and frequent urgency, you prevailed on me to publish a very loose and uncorrect account of my travels; with direction to hire some young gentlemen of either university to put them in order, and correct the style, as my Cousin Dampier did by my advice, in his book called, *A Voyage round the World*. But, I do not remember, I gave you power to consent, that any thing should be omitted, and much less that any thing should be inserted: therefore, as to the latter, I do here renounce every thing of that kind; particularly a paragraph about her Majesty the late Queen Anne, of most pious and glorious memory; although I did reverence and esteem her more than any of human species. But you, or your interpolator, ought to have considered, that as it was not my inclination, so was it not decent to praise any animal of our composition before my master Houyhnhnm: and besides, the fact was altogether false; for, to my knowledge, being in England during some part of her Majesty's reign, she did govern by a chief minister; nay, even by two successively; the first whereof was the Lord of Godolphin, and the second the Lord of Oxford; so that you have made me say the thing which was not. Likewise, in the account of the Academy of Projectors, and several passages of my discourse to my master Houyhnhnm, you have either omitted some material circumstances, or minced or changed them in such a manner, that I do hardly know mine own work. When I formerly hinted to you something of this in a letter, you were pleased to answer, that you were afraid of giving offence; that people in power were very watchful over the press; and apt not only to interpret, but to punish every thing which looked like an innuendo (as I think you called it.) But pray, how could that which I spoke so many years ago, and at above five thousand leagues distance, in another reign, be applyed to any of the Yahoos, who now are said to govern the herd; especially at a time when I little thought on, or feared the unhappiness of living under them? Have not I the most reason to complain, when I see these very Yahoos carried by Houyhnhnms in a vehicle, as if these were brutes, and those the rational creatures? And, indeed, to avoid so monstrous and detestable a sight, was one principal motive of my retirement hither.

Thus much I thought proper to tell you in relation to your self, and to the trust I reposed in you.

I do in the next place complain of my own great want of judgment, in being prevailed upon by the intreaties and false reasonings of you and some others, very much against mine own opinion, to suffer my travels to be published. Pray bring to your mind how often I desired you to consider, when you insisted on the motive of publick good; that the Yahoos were a species of animals utterly incapable of amendment by precepts or examples; and so it hath proved; for instead of seeing a full stop put to all abuses and corruptions, at least in this little island, as I had reason to expect: behold, after above six months warning, I cannot learn that my book hath produced one single effect according to mine intentions: I desired you would let me know by a letter, when party and faction were extinguished; judges learned and upright; pleaders honest and modest, with some tincture of common sense; and Smithfield blazing with pyramids of law-books; the young nobility's education entirely changed; the physicians banished; the female Yahoos abounding in virtue, honour, truth and good sense: courts and levees of great ministers thoroughly weeded and swept; wit, merit and learning rewarded; all disgracers of the press in prose and verse, condemned to eat nothing but their own cotten, and quench their thirst with their own ink. These, and a thousand other reformations, I firmly counted upon by your encouragement; as indeed, they were plainly deducible from the precepts delivered in my book. And, it must be owned, that seven months were a sufficient time to correct every vice and folly to which Yahoos are subject; if their natures had been capable of the least disposition to virtue or wisdom: yet so far have you been from answering mine expectation in any of your letters, that on the contrary, you are loading our carrier every week with libels, and keys, and reflections, and memoirs, and second parts; wherein I see myself accused of reflecting upon great states-folk; of degrading human nature, (for so they have still the confidence to style it) and of abusing the female sex. I find likewise, that the writers of those bundles are not agreed among themselves; for some of them will not allow me to be author of mine own travels; and others make me author of books to which I am wholly a stranger.

I find likewise, that your printer hath been so careless as to confound the times, and mistake the dates of my several voyages and returns; neither assigning the true year, or the true month, or day of the month: and, I hear the original manuscript is all destroyed, since the publication of my book. Neither have I any copy left; however, I have sent you some corrections, which you may insert, if ever there should be a second edition: and yet I cannot stand to them, but shall leave that matter to my judicious and candid readers, to adjust it as they please.

I hear, some of our sea-Yahoos find fault with my sea-language, as not proper in many parts, nor now in use. I cannot help it. In my first voyages, while I was young, I was instructed by the oldest mariners, and learned to speak as they did. But, I have since found, that the sea-Yahoos are apt, like the land ones, to become new fangled in their words; which the latter change every year; insomuch, as I remember upon each return to mine own country, their old dialect was so altered, that I could hardly understand the new. And I observe, when any Yahoo comes from London, out of curiosity, to visit me at mine own house, we neither of us are able to deliver our conceptions in a manner intelligible to the other.

If the censure of Yahoos could any way affect me, I should have great reason to complain, that some of them are so bold as to think my book of travels a meer fiction out of mine own brain; and have gone so far as to drop hints, that the Houyhnhnms, and Yahoos have no more existence. than the inhabitants of Utopia.

Indeed I must confess, that as to the people of Lilliput, Brobdingrag (for so the word should have been spelt, and not erroneously Brobdingnag) and Laputa; I have never yet heard of any Yahoo so presumptuous as to dispute their being, or the facts I have related concerning them; because the truth immediately strikes every reader with conviction. And, is there less probability in my account of the Houyhnhnms or Yahoos, when it is manifest as to the latter, there are so many thousands, even in this city, who only differ from their brother brutes in Houyhnhnmland, because they use a sort of jabber, and do not go naked. I wrote for their amendment, and not their approbation. The united praise of the whole race, would be of less consequence to me, than the neighing of those two degenerate Houyhnhnms I keep in my stable; because, from these, degenerate as they are, I still improve in some virtues, without any mixture of vice.

Do these miserable animals presume to think, that I am so far degenerated, as to defend my veracity: Yahoo as I am, it is well known through all Houyhnhnmland, that by the instructions and example of my illustrious master, I was able in the compass of two years (although I confess with the utmost difficulty) to remove that infernal habit of lying, shuffling, deceiving, and equivocating, so deeply rooted in the very souls of all my species, especially the Europeans.

I have other complaints to make upon this vexatious occasion; but I forbear troubling myself or you any further. I must freely confess, that since my last return, some corruptions of my Yahoo nature have revived in me by conversing with a few of your species, and particularly those of mine own family, by an unavoidable necessity; else I should never have attempted so absurd a project as that of reforming the Yahoo race in this kingdom; but, I have now done with all such visionary schemes for ever.

April 2, 1727

THE PUBLISHER TO THE READER

THE author of these travels, Mr. Lemuel Gulliver, is my antient and intimate friend; there is likewise some relation between us by the mother's side. About three years ago, Mr. Gulliver growing weary of the concourse of curious people coming to him at his house in Redriff, made a small purchase of land, with a convenient house, near Newark, in Nottinghamshire, his native county; where he now lives retired, yet in good esteem among his neighbours.

Although Mr. Gulliver was born in Nottinghamshire, where his father dwelt, yet I have heard him say, his family came from Oxfordshire; to confirm which, I have observed in the churchyard at Banbury, in that county, several tombs and monuments of the Gullivers.

Before he quitted Redriff, he left the custody of the following papers in my hands, with the liberty to dispose of them as I should think fit. I have carefully perused them three times: the style is very plain and simple; and the only fault I find is, that the author, after the manner of travellers, is a little too circumstantial. There is an air of truth apparent through the whole; and indeed the author was so distinguished for his veracity, that it became a sort of proverb among his neighbours at Redriff, when any one affirmed a thing, to say, it was as true as if Mr. Gulliver had spoke it.

By the advice of several worthy persons, to whom, with the author's permission, I communicated these papers, I now venture to send them into the world; hoping they may be, at least for some time, a better entertainment to our young noblemen, than the common scribbles of politicks and party.

This volume would have been at least twice as large, if I had not made bold to strike out innumerable passages relating to the winds and tides, as well as to the variations and bearings in the several voyages; together with the minute descriptions of the management of the ship in storms, in the style of sailors: likewise the account of the longitudes and latitudes; wherein I have reason to apprehend that Mr. Gulliver may be a little dissatisfied: but, I was resolved to fit the work, as much as possible to the general capacity of readers. However, if my own ignorance in sea affairs shall have led me to commit some mistakes, I alone am answerable for them: and, if any traveller hath a curiosity to see the whole work at large, as it came from the hand of the author, I will be ready to gratify him.

As for any further particulars relating to the author, the reader will receive satisfaction from the first pages of the book.

RICHARD SYMPSON

PART I
A VOYAGE TO LILLIPUT

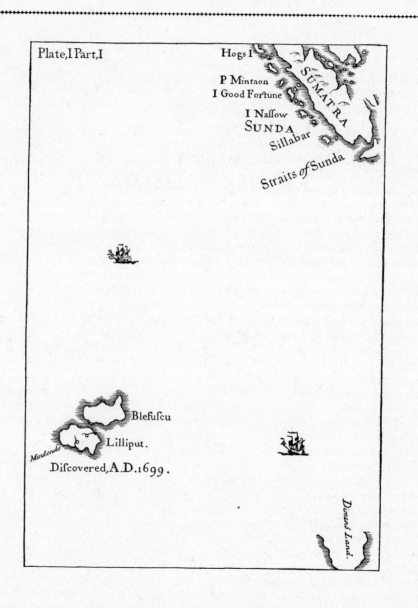

Plate, I Part, I

Hogs I.

P Mintaon
I Good Fortune

I Naſſow
SUNDA
Sillabar

Straits *of* Sunda

SUMATRA

Blefuſcu

Lilliput.

Mendendo

Diſcovered, A.D. 1699.

Dimens Land.

CHAPTER I

The author giveth some account of himself and family; his first inducements to travel. He is shipwrecked, and swims for his life; gets safe on shore in the country of Lilliput; is made a prisoner, and carried up the country.

MY FATHER had a small estate in Nottinghamshire; I was the third of five sons. He sent me to Emanuel-College in Cambridge, at fourteen years old, where I resided three years, and applied my self close to my studies: but the charge of maintaining me (although I had a very scanty allowance) being too great for a narrow fortune, I was bound apprentice to Mr. James Bates, an eminent surgeon in London, with whom I continued four years; and my father now and then sending me small sums of money, I laid them out in learning navigation, and other parts of the mathematicks, useful to those who intend to travel, as I always believed it would be some time or other my fortune to do. When I left Mr. Bates, I went down to my father, where, by the assistance of him and my Uncle John, and some other relations, I got forty pounds, and a promise of thirty pounds a year to maintain me at Leyden: there I studied physick two years and seven months, knowing it would be useful in long voyages.

Soon after my return from Leyden, I was recommended by my good master Mr. Bates, to be surgeon to the *Swallow*, Captain Abraham Pannell commander; with whom I continued three years and a half, making a voyage or two into the Levant, and some other parts. When I came back, I resolved to settle in London, to which Mr. Bates, my master, encouraged me; and by him I was recommended to several patients. I took part of a small house in the Old-Jury; and being advised to alter my condition, I married Mrs. Mary Burton, second daughter to Mr. Edmond Burton, hosier, in Newgate-street, with whom I received four hundred pounds for a portion.

But, my good master Bates dying in two years after, and I having few friends, my business began to fail; for my conscience would not suffer me to imitate the bad practice of too many among my brethren. Having therefore consulted with my wife, and some of my acquaintance, I determined to go again to sea. I was surgeon successively in two ships, and made several voyages, for six years, to the East and West-Indies; by which I got some addition to my fortune. My hours of leisure I spent in reading the best authors, ancient and modern; being always provided with a good number of books; and when I was ashore, in observing the manners and dispositions of the people, as well as learning their language; wherein I had a great facility by the strength of my memory.

The last of these voyages not proving very fortunate, I grew weary of the sea, and intended to stay at home with my wife and family. I removed from the Old-Jury to Fetter-lane, and from thence to Wapping, hoping to get business among the sailors; but it would not turn to account. After three years expectation, that things would mend, I accepted an advantageous offer from Captain William Prichard, master of the *Antelope*, who was making a voyage to the South-Sea. We set sail from Bristol, May 4th, 1699, and our voyage at first was very prosperous.

It would not be proper for some reasons, to trouble the reader with the particulars of our adventures in those seas: let it suffice to inform him, that in our passage from thence to the East-Indies, we were driven by a violent storm to the north-west of Van Diemen's Land. By an observation, we found ourselves in the latitude of 30 degrees 2 minutes south. Twelve of our crew were dead by immoderate labour, and ill food; the rest were in a very weak condition. On the fifth of November, which was the beginning of summer in those parts, the weather being very hazy, the seamen spyed a rock, within half a cable's length of the ship; but the wind was so strong, that we were driven directly upon it, and immediately split. Six of the crew, of whom I was one, having let down the boat into the sea, made a shift to get clear of the ship, and the rock. We rowed by my computation, about three leagues, until we were able to work no longer, being already spent with labour while we were in the ship: we therefore trusted ourselves to the mercy of the waves; and in about half an hour the boat was overset by a sudden flurry from the north. What became of my companions in the boat, as well as of those who escaped on the rock, or were left in the vessel, I cannot tell; but conclude they were all lost. For my own part, I swam as fortune directed me, and was pushed forward by wind and tide. I often let my legs drop; and could feel no bottom: but when I was almost gone, and able to struggle no longer, I found myself within my depth; and by this time the storm was much abated. The declivity was so small, that I walked near a mile before I got to the shore, which I conjectured was about eight o'clock in the evening. I then advanced forward near half a mile, but could not discover any sign of houses or inhabitants; at least I was in so weak a condition, that I did not observe them. I was extremely tired, and with that, and the heat of the weather, and about half a pint of brandy that I drank as I left the ship, I found myself much inclined to sleep. I lay down on the grass, which was very short and soft; where I slept sounder than ever I remember to have done in my life, and as I reckoned, above nine hours; for when I awaked, it was just day-light. I attempted to rise, but was not able to stir: for, as I happened to lie on my back, I found my arms and legs were strongly fastned on each side to the ground; and my hair, which was long and thick, tied down in the same manner. I likewise felt several slender ligatures across my body, from my arm-pits to my thighs. I could only look upwards; the sun began to grow hot, and the light offended mine eyes. I heard a confused noise about me, but in the posture I lay, could see nothing except the sky. In a little time I felt something alive moving on my left leg, which advancing gently forward over my breast, came almost up to my chin; when bending mine eyes downwards as much as I could, I perceived it to be a human creature not six inches high, with a bow and arrow in his hands, and a quiver at his back. In the mean time, I felt at least forty more of the same kind (as I conjectured) following the first. I was in the utmost astonishment, and roared so loud, that they all run back in a fright; and some of them, as I was afterwards told, were hurt with the falls they got by leaping from my sides upon the ground. However, they soon returned; and one of them, who ventured so far as to get a full sight of my face, lifting up his hands and eyes by way of admiration, cryed out in a shrill, but distinct voice, "Hekina degul": the others repeated the same words several times, but I then knew not what they meant. I lay all this while, as the reader may believe, in great uneasiness: at length, struggling to get loose, I had the fortune to break the strings, and wrench out the pegs that fastened my left arm to the ground: for, by lifting it up to my face, I discovered the methods they had taken to bind me; and, at the same time, with a violent pull, which gave me excessive pain, I a little loosened the strings that tied down my hair on the left side; so that I was just able to turn my head about two inches. But the creatures ran off a second time, before I could seize them; whereupon there was a great shout in a very shrill accent; and after it ceased, I heard one of them cry aloud, "Tolgo Phonac"; when in an instant, I felt above an hundred arrows discharged on my left hand, which pricked me like so many needles; and besides, they shot another flight into the air, as we do bombs in Europe; whereof many, I suppose, fell on my body, (though I felt them not) and some on my face, which I immediately covered with my left hand. When this shower of arrows was over, I fell a groaning with grief and pain; and then striving again to get loose, they discharged another volley larger than the first; and some of them attempted with spears to stick me in the sides; but, by good luck, I had on me a buff jerkin, which they could not pierce. I thought it the most prudent method to lie still; and my design was to continue so until night, when my left hand being already loose, I could easily free my self: and, as for the inhabitants, I had reason to believe I might be a match for the greatest armies they could bring against me, if they were all of the same size with him that I saw. But fortune disposed otherwise of me. When the people observed I was quiet, they discharged no more arrows: but by the noise encreasing, I knew their numbers were greater; and about four yards from me over against my right ear, I heard a knocking for above an hour, like people at work; when turning my head that way, as well as the pegs and strings would permit me, I saw a stage erected about a foot and a half from the ground, capable of holding four of the inhabitants, with two or three ladders to mount it: from whence one of them, who seemed to be a person of quality, made me a long speech, whereof I understood not one syllable. But I should have mentioned, that before the principal person began his oration, he cryed out three times "Langro dehul san": (these words and the former were afterwards repeated and explained to me.) Whereupon immediately about fifty of the inhabitants came, and cut the strings that fastened the left side of my head, which gave me the liberty of turning it to the right, and of observing the person and gesture of him who was to speak. He appeared to be of a middle age, and taller than any of the other three who attended him; whereof one was a page, who held up his train, and seemed to be somewhat longer than my middle finger; the other two stood one on each side to support him. He acted every part of an orator; and I could observe many periods of threatnings, and others of promises, pity, and kindness. I answered in a few words, but in the most submissive manner, lifting up my left hand and both mine eyes to the sun, as calling him for a witness; and being almost famished with hunger, having not eaten a morsel for some hours before I left the ship, I found the demands of nature so strong upon me, that I could not forbear shewing my impatience (perhaps against the strict rules of decency) by putting my finger frequently on my mouth, to signify that I wanted food. The Hurgo (for so they call a great lord, as I afterwards learnt) understood me very well: he descended from the stage, and commanded that several ladders should be applied to my sides, on which above an hundred of the inhabitants mounted and walked towards my mouth, laden with baskets full of meat, which had been provided, and sent thither by the king's orders upon the first intelligence he received of me. I observed there was the flesh of several animals, but could not distinguish them by the taste. There were shoulders, legs, and loins shaped like those of mutton, and very well dressed, but smaller than the wings of a lark. I eat them by two or three at a mouthful; and took three loaves at a time, about the bigness of musket-bullets. They supplyed me as fast as they could, shewing a thousand marks of wonder and astonishment at my bulk and appetite. I then made another sign that I wanted drink. They found by my eating that a small quantity would not suffice me; and being a most ingenious people, they slung up with great dexterity one of their largest hogsheads; then rolled it towards my hand, and beat out the top; I drank it off at a draught, which I might well do, for it hardly held half a pint, and tasted like a small wine of Burgundy, but much more delicious. They brought me a second hogshead, which I drank in the same manner, and made signs for more, but they had none to give me. When I had performed these wonders, they shouted for joy, and danced upon my breast, repeating several times as they did at first "Hekinah degul." They made me a sign, that I should throw down the two hogsheads, but first warned the people below to stand out of the way, crying aloud, "Borach mivola"; and when they saw the vessels in the air, there was an universal shout of "Hekinah degul." I confess I was often tempted, while they were passing backwards and forwards on my body, to seize forty or fifty of the first that came in my reach, and dash them against the ground. But the remembrance of what I had felt, which probably might not be the worst they could do; and the promise of honour I made them, for so I interpreted my submissive behaviour, soon drove out those imaginations. Besides, I now considered my self as bound by the laws of hospitality to a people who had treated me with so much expense and magnificence. However, in my thoughts I could not sufficiently wonder at the intrepidity of these diminutive mortals, who durst venture to mount and walk on my body, while one of my hands was at liberty, without trembling at the very sight of so prodigious a creature as I must appear to them. After some time, when they observed, that I made no more demands for meat, there appeared before me a person of high rank from his Imperial Majesty. His excellency having mounted on the small of my right leg, advanced forwards up to my face, with about a dozen of his retinue; and producing his credentials under the signet royal, which he applied close to mine eyes, spoke about ten minutes, without any signs of anger, but with a kind of determinate resolution; often pointing forwards, which, as I afterwards found was towards the capital city, about half a mile distant, whither it was agreed by his Majesty in council that I must be conveyed. I answered in few words, but to no purpose, and made a sign with my hand that was loose, putting it to the other, (but over his excellency's head, for fear of hurting him or his train) and then to my own head and body, to signify that I desired my liberty. It appeared that he understood me well enough; for he shook his head by way of disapprobation, and held his hand in a posture to shew that I must be carried as a prisoner. However, he made other signs to let me understand, that I should have meat and drink enough, and very good treatment. Whereupon I once more thought of attempting to break my bonds; but again, when I felt the smart of their arrows upon my face and hands, which were all in blisters, and many of the darts still sticking in them; and observing likewise, that the number of my enemies encreased; I gave tokens to let them know that they might do with me what they pleased. Upon this, the Hurgo and his train withdrew, with much civility and cheerful countenances. Soon after I heard a general shout, with frequent repetitions of the words, "Peplom selan," and I felt great numbers of the people on my left side relaxing the cords to such a degree, that I was able to turn upon my right, and to ease my self with making water; which I very plentifully did, to the great astonishment of the people, who conjecturing by my motions what I was going to do, immediately opened to the right and left on that side, to avoid the torrent which fell with such noise and violence from me. But before this, they had dawbed my face and both my hands with a sort of ointment very pleasant to the smell, which in a few minutes removed all the smart of their arrows. These circumstances, added to the refreshment I had received by their victuals and drink, which were very nourishing, disposed me to sleep. I slept about eight hours as I was afterwards assured; and it was no wonder; for the physicians, by the emperor's order, had mingled a sleeping potion in the hogsheads of wine.

It seems, that upon the first moment I was discovered sleeping on the ground after my landing, the emperor had early notice of it by an express; and determined in council, that I should be tyed in the manner I have related; (which was done in the night while I slept) that plenty of meat and drink should be sent me, and a machine prepared to carry me to the capital city.

This resolution perhaps may appear very bold and dangerous, and I am confident would not be imitated by any prince in Europe on the like occasion; however, in my opinion, it was extremely prudent as well as generous. For, supposing these people had endeavoured to kill me with their spears and arrows while I was asleep; I should certainly have awaked with the first sense of smart, which might so far have rouzed my rage and strength, as to enable me to break the strings wherewith I was tyed; after which, as they were not able to make resistance, so they could expect no mercy.

These people are most excellent mathematicians, and arrived to a great perfection in mechanicks, by the countenance and encouragement of the emperor, who is a renowned patron of learning. This prince hath several machines fixed on wheels, for the carriage of trees and other great weights. He often buildeth his largest men of war, whereof some are nine foot long, in the woods where the timber grows, and has them carried on these engines three or four hundred yards to the sea. Five hundred carpenters and engineers were immediately set at work to prepare the greatest engine they had. It was a frame of wood raised three inches from the ground, about seven foot long and four wide, moving upon twenty two wheels. The shout I heard, was upon the arrival of this engine, which, it seems, set out in four hours after my landing. It was brought parallel to me as I lay. But the principal difficulty was to raise and place me in this vehicle. Eighty poles, each of one foot high, were erected for this purpose, and very strong cords of the bigness of packthread were fastened by hooks to many bandages, which the workmen had girt round my neck, my hands, my body, and my legs. Nine hundred of the strongest men were employed to draw up these cords by many pullies fastened on the poles; and thus in less than three hours, I was raised and slung into the engine, and there tyed fast. All this I was told; for while the whole operation was performing, I lay in a profound sleep, by the force of that soporiferous medicine infused into my liquor. Fifteen hundred of the emperor's largest horses, each about four inches and a half high, were employed to draw me towards the metropolis, which, as I said, was half a mile distant.

About four hours after we began our journey, I awaked by a very ridiculous accident; for the carriage being stopt a while to adjust something that was out of order, two or three of the young natives had the curiosity to see how I looked when I was asleep; they climbed up into the engine, and advancing very softly to my face, one of them, an officer in the guards, put the sharp end of his half-pike a good way up into my left nostril, which tickled my nose like a straw, and made me sneeze violently: whereupon they stole off unperceived; and it was three weeks before I knew the cause of my awaking so suddenly. We made a long march the remaining part of the day, and rested at night with five hundred guards on each side of me, half with torches, and half with bows and arrows, ready to shoot me if I should offer to stir. The next morning at sunrise we continued our march, and arrived within two hundred yards of the city-gates about noon. The emperor, and all his court, came out to meet us; but his great officers would by no means suffer his Majesty to endanger his person by mounting on my body.

At the place where the carriage stopt, there stood an ancient temple, esteemed to be the largest in the whole kingdom; which having been polluted some years before by an unnatural murder, was, according to the zeal of those people, looked upon as prophane, and therefore had been applied to common use, and all the ornaments and furniture carried away. In this edifice it was determined I should lodge. The great gate fronting to the north was about four feet high, and almost two feet wide, through which I could easily creep. On each side of the gate was a small window not above six inches from the ground: into that on the left side, the king's smiths conveyed fourscore and eleven chains, like those that hang to a lady's watch in Europe, and almost as large, which were locked to my left leg with six and thirty padlocks. Over against this temple, on the other side of the great highway, at twenty feet distance, there was a turret at least five feet high. Here the emperor ascended with many principal lords of his court, to have an opportunity of viewing me, as I was told, for I could not see them. It was reckoned that above an hundred thousand inhabitants came out of the town upon the same errand; and in spight of my guards, I believe there could not be fewer than ten thousand, at several times, who mounted upon my body by the help of ladders. But a proclamation was soon issued to forbid it, upon pain of death. When the workmen found it was impossible for me to break loose, they cut all the strings that bound me; whereupon I rose up with as melancholy a disposition as ever I had in my life. But the noise and astonishment of the people at seeing me rise and walk, are not to be expressed. The chains that held my left leg were about two yards long, and gave me not only the liberty of walking backwards and forwards in a semi-circle; but being fixed within four inches of the gate, allowed me to creep in, and lie at my full length in the temple.

CHAPTER II

The Emperor of Lilliput, attended by several of the nobility, comes to see the author in his confinement. The emperor's person and habit described. Learned men appointed to teach the author their language. He gains favour by his mild disposition. His pockets are searched, and his sword and pistols taken from him.

WHEN I found my self on my feet, I looked about me, and must confess I never beheld a more entertaining prospect. The country round appeared like a continued garden; and the inclosed fields, which were generally forty feet square, resembled so many beds of flowers. These fields were intermingled with woods of half a stang, and the tallest trees, as I could judge, appeared to be seven feet high. I viewed the town on my left hand, which looked like the painted scene of a city in a theatre.

I had been for some hours extremely pressed by the necessities of nature; which was no wonder, it being almost two days since I had last disburthened my self. I was under great difficulties between urgency and shame. The best expedient I could think on, was to creep into my house, which I accordingly did; and shutting the gate after me, I went as far as the length of my chain would suffer; and discharged my body of that uneasy load. But, this was the only time I was ever guilty of so uncleanly an action; for which I cannot but hope the candid reader will give some allowance, after he hath maturely and impartially considered my case, and the distress I was in. From this time my constant practice was, as soon as I rose, to perform that business in open air, at the full extent of my chain; and due care was taken every morning before company came, that the offensive matter should be carried off in wheel-barrows, by two servants appointed for that purpose. I would not have dwelt so long upon a circumstance, that perhaps at first sight may appear not very momentous, if I had not thought it necessary to justify my character in point of cleanliness to the world; which I am told, some of my maligners have been pleased, upon this and other occasions, to call in question.

When this adventure was at an end, I came back out of my house, having occasion for fresh air. The emperor was already descended from the tower, and advancing on horseback towards me, which had like to have cost him dear; for the beast although very well trained, yet wholly unused to such a sight, which appeared, as if a mountain moved before him, reared up on his hind feet: but that prince, who is an excellent horseman, kept his seat, until his attendants ran in, and held the bridle, while his Majesty had time to dismount. When he alighted, he surveyed me round with great admiration, but kept beyond the length of my chains. He ordered his cooks and butlers, who were already prepared, to give me victuals and drink, which they pushed forward in a sort of vehicles upon wheels until I could reach them. I took these vehicles, and soon emptied them all; twenty of them were filled with meat, and ten with liquor; each of the former afforded me two or three good mouthfuls, and I emptied the liquor of ten vessels, which was contained in earthen vials, into one vehicle, drinking it off at a draught; and so I did with the rest. The empress, and young princes of the blood, of both sexes, attended by many ladies, sate at some distance in their chairs; but upon the accident that happened to the emperor's horse, they alighted, and came near his person; which I am now going to describe. He is taller by almost the breadth of my nail, than any of his court; which alone is enough to strike an awe into the beholders. His features are strong and masculine, with an Austrian lip, and arched nose, his complexion olive, his countenance erect, his body and limbs well proportioned, all his motions graceful, and his deportment majestick. He was then past his prime, being twenty-eight years and three quarters old, of which he had reigned about seven, in great felicity, and generally victorious. For the better convenience of beholding him, I lay on my side, so that my face was parallel to his, and he stood but three yards off: however, I have had him since many times in my hand, and therefore cannot be deceived in the description. His dress was very plain and simple, the fashion of it between the Asiatick and the European; but he had on his head a light helmet of gold, adorned with jewels, and a plume on the crest. He held his sword drawn in his hand, to defend himself, if I should happen to break loose; it was almost three inches long, the hilt and scabbard were gold enriched with diamonds. His voice was shrill but very clear and articulate, and I could distinctly hear it when I stood up. The ladies and courtiers were all most magnificently clad, so that the spot they stood upon seemed to resemble a petticoat spread on the ground, embroidered with figures of gold and silver. His Imperial Majesty spoke often to me, and I returned answers, but neither of us could understand a syllable. There were several of his priests and lawyers present (as I conjectured by their habits) who were commanded to address themselves

to me, and I spoke to them in as many languages as I had the least smattering of, which were High and Low-Dutch, Latin, French, Spanish, Italian,
and lingua franca; but all to no purpose. After about two hours the court
retired, and I was left with a strong guard, to prevent the impertinence,
and probably the malice of the rabble, who were very impatient to croud
about me as near as they durst; and some of them had the imprudence to
shoot their arrows at me as I sate on the ground by the door of my house;
whereof one very narrowly missed my left eye. But the colonel ordered six
of the ringleaders to be seized, and thought no punishment so proper as to
deliver them bound into my hands, which some of his soldiers accordingly
did, pushing them forwards with the but-ends of their pikes into my reach:
I took them all in my right hand, put five of them into my coat-pocket; and
as to the sixth, I made a countenance as if I would eat him alive. The poor
man squalled terribly, and the colonel and his officers were in much pain,
especially when they saw me take out my penknife: but I soon put them
out of fear; for, looking mildly, and immediately cutting the strings he
was bound with, I set him gently on the ground, and away he ran. I treated
the rest in the same manner, taking them one by one out of my pocket; and
I observed, both the soldiers and people were highly obliged at this mark of
my clemency, which was represented very much to my advantage at court.

Towards night I got with some difficulty into my house, where I lay on
the ground, and continued to do so about a fortnight; during which time
the emperor gave orders to have a bed prepared for me. Six hundred beds
of the common measure were brought in carriages, and worked up in my
house; an hundred and fifty of their beds sown together made up the
breadth and length, and these were four double, which however kept me
but very indifferently from the hardness of the floor, that was of smooth
stone. By the same computation they provided me with sheets, blankets,
and coverlets, tolerable enough for one who had been so long enured to
hardships as I.

As the news of my arrival spread through the kingdom, it brought
prodigious numbers of rich, idle, and curious people to see me; so that the
villages were almost emptied, and great neglect of tillage and household
affairs must have ensued, if his Imperial Majesty had not provided by
several proclamations and orders of State against this inconveniency. He
directed that those, who had already beheld me, should return home, and
not presume to come within fifty yards of my house, without license from
court; whereby the Secretaries of State got considerable fees.

In the mean time, the emperor held frequent councils to debate what
course should be taken with me; and I was afterwards assured by a particular friend, a person of great quality, who was as much in the secret as
any; that the court was under many difficulties concerning me. They apprehended my breaking loose; that my diet would be very expensive, and
might cause a famine. Sometimes they determined to starve me, or at least
to shoot me in the face and hands with poisoned arrows, which would
soon dispatch me: but again they considered, that the stench of so large a
carcase might produce a plague in the metropolis, and probably spread
through the whole kingdom. In the midst of these consultations, several

officers of the army went to the door of the great council-chamber; and two of them being admitted, gave an account of my behaviour to the six criminals above-mentioned; which made so favourable an impression in the breast of his Majesty, and the whole board, in my behalf, that an imperial commission was issued out, obliging all the villages nine hundred yards round the city, to deliver in every morning six beeves, forty sheep, and other victuals for my sustenance; together with a proportionable quantity of bread and wine, and other liquors: for the due payment of which his Majesty gave assignments upon his treasury. For this prince lives chiefly upon his own demesnes; seldom, except upon great occasions raising any subsidies upon his subjects, who are bound to attend him in his wars at their own expense. An establishment was also made of six hundred persons to be my domesticks, who had board-wages allowed for their maintenance, and tents built for them very conveniently on each side of my door. It was likewise ordered, that three hundred taylors should make me a suit of cloaths after the fashion of the country: that six of his Majesty's greatest scholars should be employed to instruct me in their language: and lastly, that the emperor's horses, and those of the nobility, and troops of guards, should be exercised in my sight, to accustom themselves to me. All these orders were duly put in execution; and in about three weeks I made a great progress in learning their language; during which time, the emperor frequently honoured me with his visits, and was pleased to assist my masters in teaching me. We began already to converse together in some sort; and the first words I learnt, were to express my desire, that he would please to give me my liberty; which I every day repeated on my knees. His answer, as I could apprehend, was, that this must be a work of time, not to be thought on without the advice of his council; and that first I must "Lumos kelmin pesso desmar lon emposo"; that is, "Swear a peace with him and his kingdom." However, that I should be used with all kindness; and he advised me to acquire by my patience and discreet behaviour, the good opinion of himself and his subjects. He desired I would not take it ill, if he gave orders to certain proper officers to search me; for probably I might carry about me several weapons, which must needs be dangerous things, if they answered the bulk of so prodigious a person. I said, his Majesty should be satisfied, for I was ready to strip my self, and turn up my pockets before him. This I delivered, part in words, and part in signs. He replied, that by the laws of the kingdom, I must be searched by two of his officers: that he knew this could not be done without my consent and assistance: that he had so good an opinion of my generosity and justice, as to trust their persons in my hands: that whatever they took from me should be returned when I left the country, or paid for at the rate which I would set upon them. I took up the two officers in my hands, put them first into my coat-pockets, and then into every other pocket about me, except my two fobs, and another secret pocket which I had no mind should be searched, wherein I had some little necessaries of no consequence to any but my self. In one of my fobs there was a silver watch, and in the other a small quantity of gold in a purse These gentlemen, having pen, ink, and paper about them, made an exact inventory of every thing they saw; and when they had done, desired

I would set them down, that they might deliver it to the emperor. This inventory I afterwards translated into English, and is word for word as follows.

"Imprimis, in the right coat-pocket of the great Man Mountain (for so I interpret the words 'Quinbus Flestrin') after the strictest search, we found only one great piece of coarse cloth, large enough to be a foot-cloth for your Majesty's chief room of State. In the left pocket, we saw a huge silver chest, with a cover of the same metal, which we, the searchers, were not able to lift. We desired it should be opened; and one of us stepping into it, found himself up to the mid-leg in a sort of dust, some part whereof flying up to our faces, set us both a sneezing for several times together. In his right waistcoat-pocket, we found a prodigious bundle of white thin substances, folded one over another, about the bigness of three men, tied with a strong cable, and marked with black figures; which we humbly conceive to be writings; every letter almost half as large as the palm of our hands. In the left there was a sort of engine, from the back of which were extended twenty long poles, resembling the pallisado's before your Majesty's court; wherewith we conjecture the Man Mountain combs his head; for we did not always trouble him with questions, because we found it a great difficulty to make him understand us. In the large pocket on the right side of his middle cover, (so I translate the word 'ransu-lo,' by which they meant my breeches) we saw a hollow pillar of iron, about the length of a man, fastened to a strong piece of timber, larger than the pillar; and upon one side of the pillar were huge pieces of iron sticking out, cut into strange figures; which we know not what to make of. In the left pocket, another engine of the same kind. In the smaller pocket on the right side, were several round flat pieces of white and red metal, of different bulk: some of the white, which seemed to be silver, were so large and heavy, that my comrade and I could hardly lift them. In the left pocket were two black pillars irregularly shaped; we could not, without difficulty, reach the top of them as we stood at the bottom of his pocket: one of them was covered, and seemed all of a piece; but at the upper end of the other, there appeared a white round substance, about twice the bigness of our heads. Within each of these was inclosed a prodigious plate of steel; which, by our orders we obliged him to shew us, because we apprehended they might be dangerous engines. He took them out of their cases, and told us, that in his own country his practice was to shave his beard with one of these, and to cut his meat with the other. There were two pockets which we could not enter: these he called his fobs; they were two large slits cut into the top of his middle cover, but squeezed close by the pressure of his belly. Out of the right fob hung a great silver chain, with a wonderful kind of engine at the bottom. We directed him to draw out whatever was at the end of that chain; which appeared to be a globe, half silver, and half of some transparent metal: for on the transparent side we saw certain strange figures circularly drawn, and thought we could touch them, until we found our fingers stopped with that lucid substance. He put this engine to our ears, which made an incessant noise like that of a water-mill: and we conjecture it is either some unknown animal, or the god that he worships: but we are more inclined to the latter opinion, because he assured us, (if we understood him right, for he expressed himself very imperfectly) that he seldom did any thing without consulting it. He called it his oracle, and said it pointed out the time for every action of his life. From the left fob he took out a net almost large enough for a fisherman, but contrived to open and shut like a purse, and served him for the same use: we found therein several massy pieces of yellow metal, which if they be of real gold, must be of immense value.

"Having thus, in obedience to your Majesty's commands, diligently searched all his pockets, we observed a girdle about his waist made of the hyde of some prodigious animal; from which, on the left side, hung a sword of the length of five men; and on the right, a bag or pouch divided into two cells; each cell capable of holding three of your Majesty's subjects. In one of these cells were several globes or balls of a most ponderous metal, about the bigness of our heads, and required a strong hand to lift them: the other cell contained a heap of certain black grains, but of no great bulk or weight, for we could hold above fifty of them in the palms of our hands.

"This is an exact inventory of what we found about the body of the Man Mountain; who used us with great civility, and due respect to your Majesty's commission. Signed and sealed on the fourth day of the eighty ninth moon of your Majesty's auspicious reign.

"CLEFREN FRELOCK, MARSI FRELOCK."

When this inventory was read over to the emperor, he directed me to deliver up the several particulars. He first called for my scymiter, which I took out, scabbard and all. In the mean time he ordered three thousand of his choicest troops, who then attended him, to surround me at a distance, with their bows and arrows just ready to discharge: but I did not observe it; for mine eyes were wholly fixed upon his Majesty. He then desired me to draw my scymiter, which, although it had got some rust by the sea water, was in most parts exceeding bright. I did so, and immediately all the troops gave a shout between terror and surprize; for the sun shone clear, and the reflection dazzled their eyes, as I waved the scymiter to and fro in my hand. His Majesty, who is a most magnanimous prince, was less daunted than I could expect; he ordered me to return it into the scabbard, and cast it on the ground as gently as I could, about six foot from the end of my chain. The next thing he demanded was one of the hollow iron pillars, by which he meant my pocket-pistols. I drew it out and at his desire, as well as I could, expressed to him the use of it, and charging it only with powder, which by the closeness of my pouch, happened to escape wetting in the sea, (an inconvenience that all prudent mariners take special care to provide against) I first cautioned the emperor not to be afraid; and then I let it off in the air. The astonishment here was much greater than at the sight of my scymiter. Hundreds fell down as if they had been struck dead; and even the emperor, although he stood his ground, could not recover himself in some time. I delivered up both my pistols in the same manner as I had done my scymiter, and then my pouch of powder and bullets; begging him, that the former might be kept from fire; for it would kindle with the smallest spark, and blow up his imperial palace into the air. I likewise delivered up my watch, which the emperor was very curious to see; and commanded two of his tallest yeomen of the guards to bear it on a pole upon their shoulders, as dray-men in England do a barrel of ale. He was amazed at the continual noise it made, and the motion of the minute hand, which he could easily discern; for their sight is much more acute than ours: he asked the opinions of his learned men about him, which were various and remote, as the reader may well imagine without my repeating; although, indeed, I could not very perfectly understand them. I then gave up my silver and copper money, my purse with nine large pieces of gold, and some smaller ones; my knife and razor, my comb and silver snuff-box, my handkerchief and journal book. My scymiter, pistols and pouch, were conveyed in carriages to his Majesty's stores; but the rest of my goods were returned me.

I had, as I before observed, one private pocket which escaped their search, wherein there was a pair of spectacles (which I sometimes use for the weakness of mine eyes), a pocket perspective, and several other little conveniencies; which being of no consequence to the emperor, I did not think my self bound in honour to discover; and I apprehended they might be lost or spoiled if I ventured them out of my possession.

CHAPTER III

The author diverts the emperor and his nobility of both sexes, in a very uncommon manner. The diversions of the court of Lilliput described. The author hath his liberty granted him upon certain conditions.

MY GENTLENESS and good behaviour had gained so far on the emperor and his court, and indeed upon the army and people in general, that I began to conceive hopes of getting my liberty in a short time. I took all possible methods to cultivate this favourable disposition. The natives came by degrees to be less apprehensive of any danger from me. I would sometimes lie down, and let five or six of them dance on my hand. And at last the boys and girls would venture to come and play at hide and seek in my hair. I had now made a good progress in understanding and speaking their language. The emperor had a mind one day to entertain me with several of the country shows; wherein they exceed all nations I have known, both for dexterity and magnificence. I was diverted with none so much as that of the rope-dancers, performed upon a slender white thread, extended about two foot, and twelve inches from the ground. Upon which, I shall desire liberty, with the reader's patience, to enlarge a little.

This diversion is only practised by those persons, who are candidates for great employments, and high favour, at court. They are trained in this art from their youth, and are not always of noble birth, or liberal education. When a great office is vacant, either by death or disgrace, (which often happens) five or six of those candidates petition the emperor to entertain his Majesty and the court with a dance on the rope; and whoever jumps the highest without falling, succeeds in the office. Very often the chief ministers themselves are commanded to shew their skill, and to convince the emperor that they have not lost their faculty. Flimnap, the Treasurer, is allowed to cut a caper on the strait rope, at least an inch higher than any other lord in the whole empire. I have seen him do the summerset several times together, upon a trencher fixed on the rope, which is no thicker than a common packthread in England. My friend Reldresal, principal Secretary for Private Affairs, is, in my opinion, if I am not partial, the second after the Treasurer; the rest of the great officers are much upon a par.

These diversions are often attended with fatal accidents, whereof great numbers are on record. I my self have seen two or three candidates break a limb. But the danger is much greater, when the ministers themselves are commanded to shew their dexterity: for, by contending to excel themselves and their fellows, they strain so far, that there is hardly one of them who hath not received a fall; and some of them two or three. I was assured, that a year or two before my arrival, Flimnap would have infallibly broke his neck, if one of the king's cushions, that accidentally lay on the ground, had not weakened the force of his fall.

There is likewise another diversion, which is only shewn before the emperor and empress, and first minister, upon particular occasions. The emperor lays on a table three fine silken threads, of six inches long. One is blue, the other red, and the third green. These threads are proposed as prizes, for those persons whom the emperor hath a mind to distinguish by a peculiar mark of his favour. The ceremony is performed in his Majesty's great chamber of State; where the candidates are to undergo a tryal of dexterity very different from the former, and such as I have not observed the least resemblance of in any other country of the Old or the New World. The emperor holds a stick in his hands, both ends parallel to the horrison, while the candidates advancing one by one, sometimes leap over the stick, sometimes creep under it backwards and forwards several times, according as the stick is advanced or depressed. Sometimes the emperor holds one end of the stick, and his first minister the other; sometimes the minister hath it entirely to himself. Whoever performs his part with most agility, and holds out the longest in leaping and creeping, is rewarded with the blue-coloured silk; the red is given to the next, and the green to the third, which they all wear girt twice round about the middle; and you see few great persons about this court, who are not adorned with one of these girdles.

The horses of the army, and those of the royal stables, having been daily led before me, were no longer shy, but would come up to my very feet, without starting. The riders would leap them over my hand as I held it on the ground; and one of the emperor's huntsmen, upon a large courser, took my foot, shoe and all; which was indeed a prodigious leap. I had the good fortune to divert the emperor one day, after a very extraordinary manner. I desired he would order several sticks of two foot high, and the thickness of an ordinary cane, to be brought me; whereupon his Majesty commanded the master of his woods to give directions accordingly; and the next morning, six wood-men arrived with as many carriages, drawn by eight horses to each. I took nine of these sticks, and fixing them firmly in the ground in a quadrangular figure, two foot and a half square, I took four other sticks, and tyed them parallel at each corner, about two foot from the ground; then I fastned my handkerchief to the nine sticks that stood erected; and extended it on all sides, until it was as tight as the top of a drum; and the four parallel sticks rising about five inches higher than the handkerchief, served as ledges on each side. When I had finished my work, I desired the emperor to let a troop of his best horse, twenty four in number, come and exercise upon this plain. His Majesty approved of the proposal, and I took them up one by one in my hands, ready mounted and armed, with the proper officers to exercise them. As soon as they got into order, they divided into two parties, performed mock skirmishes, discharged blunt arrows, drew their swords, fled and pursued, attacked and retired; and in short discovered the best military discipline I ever beheld. The parallel sticks secured them and their horses from falling over the stage; and the emperor was so much delighted, that he ordered this entertainment to be repeated several days; and once was pleased to be lifted up, and give the word of command; and, with great difficulty, persuaded even the empress her self to let me hold her in her close chair, within two yards of the stage, from whence she was able to take a full view of the whole performance. It was my good fortune that no ill accident happened in these entertainments; only once a fiery horse that belonged to one of the captains, pawing with his hoof struck a hole in my handkerchief, and his foot slipping, he overthrew his rider and himself; but I immediately relieved them both: for, covering the hole with one hand, I set down the troop with the other, in the same manner as I took them up. The horse that fell was strained in the left shoulder, but the rider got no hurt; and I repaired my handkerchief as well as I could: however, I would not trust to the strength of it any more in such dangerous enterprizes.

About two or three days before I was set at liberty, as I was entertaining the court with these kinds of feats, there arrived an express to inform his Majesty, that some of his subjects riding near the place where I was first taken up, had seen a great black substance lying on the ground, very oddly shaped, extending its edges round as wide as his Majesty's bed-chamber, and rising up in the middle as high as a man: that it was no living creature, as they at first apprehended; for it lay on the grass without motion, and some of them had walked round it several times: that by mounting upon each other's shoulders, they had got to the top, which was flat and even; and, stamping upon it, they found it was hollow within: that they humbly conceived it might be something belonging to the Man-Mountain; and if his Majesty pleased, they would undertake to bring it with only five horses. I presently knew what they meant; and was glad at heart to receive this intelligence. It seems, upon my first reaching the shore, after our shipwreck, I was in such confusion, that before I came to the place where I went to sleep, my hat, which I had fastened with a string to my head while I was rowing, and had stuck on all the time I was swimming, fell off after I came to land; the string, as I conjecture, breaking by some accident which I never observed, but thought my hat had been lost at sea. I intreated his Imperial Majesty to give orders it might be brought to me as soon as possible, describing to him the use and the nature of it: and the next day the waggoners arrived with it, but not in a very good condition; they had bored two holes in the brim, within an inch and a half of the edge, and fastened two hooks in the holes; these hooks were tied by a long cord to the harness, and thus my hat was dragged along for above half an English mile: but the ground in that country being extremely smooth and level, it received less damage than I expected.

Two days after this adventure, the emperor having ordered that part of his army, which quarters in and about his metropolis, to be in readiness, took a fancy of diverting himself in a very singular manner. He desired I would stand like a Colossus, with my legs as far asunder as I conveniently could. He then commanded his general (who was an old experienced leader, and a great patron of mine) to draw up the troops in close order, and march them under me; the foot by twenty-four in a breast, and the horse by sixteen, with drums beating, colours flying, and pikes advanced. This body consisted of three thousand foot, and a thousand horse. His Majesty gave orders, upon pain of death, that every soldier in his march should observe the strictest decency, with regard to my person; which, however, could not prevent some of the younger officers from turning up their eyes as they passed under me. And, to confess the truth, my breeches were at that time in so ill a condition, that they afforded some opportunities for laughter and admiration.

I had sent so many memorials and petitions for my liberty, that his Majesty at length mentioned the matter first in the Cabinet, and then in a full council; where it was opposed by none, except Skyresh Bolgolam, who was pleased, without any provocation, to be my mortal enemy. But it was carried against him by the whole board, and confirmed by the emperor. That minister was Galbet, or Admiral of the Realm; very much in his master's confidence, and a person well versed in affairs, but of a morose and sour complection. However, he was at length persuaded to comply; but prevailed that the articles and conditions upon which I should be set free, and to which I must swear, should be drawn up by himself. These articles were brought to me by Skyresh Bolgolam in person, attended by two under secretaries, and several persons of distinction. After they were read, I was demanded to swear to the performance of them; first in the manner of my own country, and afterwards in the method prescribed by their laws; which was to hold my right foot in my left hand, to place the middle finger of my right hand on the crown of my head, and my thumb on the tip of my right ear. But, because the reader may perhaps be curious to have some idea of the style and manner of expression peculiar to that people, as well as to know the articles upon which I recovered my liberty, I have made a translation of the whole instrument, word for word, as near as I was able; which I here offer to the publick.

"Golbasto Momaren Evlame Gurdilo Shefin Mully Ully Gue, most mighty emperor of Lilliput, delight and terror of the universe, whose dominions extend five thousand *blustrugs*, (about twelve miles in circumference) to the extremities of the globe; monarch of all monarchs: taller than the sons of men; whose feet press down to the center, and whose head strikes against the sun: at whose nod the princes of the earth shake their knees; pleasant as the spring, comfortable as the summer, fruitful as autumn, dreadful as winter. His most sublime Majesty proposeth to the Man Mountain, lately arrived at our celestial dominions, the following articles, which by a solemn oath he shall be obliged to perform.

"First, the Man Mountain shall not depart from our dominions, without our licence under our great seal.

"Secondly, he shall not presume to come into our metropolis, without our express order; at which time, the inhabitants shall have two hours warning to keep within their doors.

"Thirdly, the said Man Mountain shall confine his walks to our principal high roads; and not offer to walk or lie down in a meadow, or field of corn.

"Fourthly, as he walks the said roads, he shall take the utmost care not to trample upon the bodies of any of our loving subjects, their horses, or carriages; nor take any of our said subjects into his hands, without their own consent.

"Fifthly, if an express require extraordinary dispatch, the Man Mountain shall be obliged to carry in his pocket the messenger and horse, a six days journey once in every moon, and return the said messenger back (if so required) safe to our imperial presence.

"Sixthly, he shall be our ally against our enemies in the island of Blefuscu, and do his utmost to destroy their fleet, which is now preparing to invade us.

"Seventhly, that the said Man Mountain shall, at his times of leisure, be aiding and assisting to our workmen, in helping to raise certain great stones, towards covering the wall of the principal park, and other our royal buildings.

"Eighthly, that the said Man Mountain shall, in two moons time, deliver in an exact survey of the circumference of our dominions, by a computation of his own paces round the coast.

"Lastly, that upon his solemn oath to observe all the above articles, the said Man Mountain shall have a daily allowance of meat and drink, sufficient for the support of 1724 of our subjects; with free access to our royal person, and other marks of our favour. Given at our palace at Belfaborac the twelfth day of the ninty-first moon of our reign."

I swore and subscribed to these articles with great chearfulness and content, although some of them were not so honourable as I could have wished; which proceeded wholly from the malice of Skyresh Bolgolam the High Admiral: whereupon my chains were immediately unlocked, and I was at full liberty: the emperor himself, in person, did me the honour to be by at the whole ceremony. I made my acknowledgements, by prostrating my self at his Majesty's feet: but he commanded me to rise; and after many gracious expressions, which, to avoid the censure of vanity, I shall not repeat, he added, that he hoped I should prove a useful servant, and well deserve all the favours he had already conferred upon me, or might do for the future.

The reader may please to observe, that in the last article for the recovery of my liberty, the emperor stipulates to allow me a quantity of meat and drink, sufficient for the support of 1724 Lilliputians. Some time after, asking a friend at court how they came to fix on that determinate number; he told me, that his Majesty's mathematicians, having taken the height of my body by the help of a quadrant, and finding it to exceed theirs in the proportion of twelve to one, they concluded from the similarity of their bodies, that mine must contain at least 1724 of theirs, and consequently would require as much food as was necessary to support that number of Lilliputians. By which, the reader may conceive an idea of the ingenuity of that people, as well as the prudent and exact œconomy of so great a prince.

CHAPTER IV

Mildendo, the metropolis of Lilliput described, together with the emperor's palace. A conversation between the author and a principal secretary, concerning the affairs of that empire: the author's offers to serve the emperor in his wars.

THE first request I made after I had obtained my liberty, was, that I might have licence to see Mildendo, the metropolis; which the emperor easily granted me, but with a special charge to do no hurt, either to the inhabitants, or their houses. The people had notice by proclamation of my design to visit the town. The wall which encompassed it, is two feet and an half high, and at least eleven inches broad, so that a coach and horses may be driven very safely round it; and it is flanked with strong towers at ten feet distance. I stept over the great western gate, and passed very gently, and sideling through the two principal streets, only in my short waistcoat, for fear of damaging the roofs and eves of the houses with the skirts of my coat. I walked with the utmost circumspection, to avoid treading on any stragglers, who might remain in the streets, although the orders were very strict, that all people should keep in their houses, at their own peril. The garret windows, and tops of houses were so crowded with spectators, that I thought in all my travels I had not seen a more populous place. The city is an exact square, each side of the wall being five hundred foot long. The two great streets which run cross and divided it into four quarters, are five foot wide. The lanes and alleys which I could not enter, but only viewed them as I passed, are from twelve to eighteen inches. The town is capable of holding five hundred thousand souls. The houses are from three to five stories. The shops and markets well provided.

The emperor's palace is in the center of the city, where the two great streets meet. It is inclosed by a wall of two foot high, and twenty foot distant from the buildings. I had his Majesty's permission to step over this wall; and the space being so wide between that and the palace, I could easily view it on every side. The outward court is a square of forty foot, and includes two other courts: in the inmost are the royal apartments, which I was very desirous to see, but found it extremely difficult; for the great gates, from one square into another, were but eighteen inches high, and seven inches wide. Now the buildings of the outer court were at least five foot high; and it was impossible for me to stride over them, without infinite damage to the pile, although the walls were strongly built of hewen stone, and four inches thick. At the same time, the emperor had a great desire that I should see the magnificence of his palace: but this I was not able to do until three days after, which I spent in cutting down with my knife some of the largest trees in the royal park, about an hundred yards distant from the city. Of these trees I made two stools, each about three foot high, and strong enough to bear my weight. The people having received notice a second time, I went again through the city to the palace, with my two stools in my hands. When I came to the side of the outer court, I stood upon one stool, and took the other in my hand: this I lifted over the roof, and gently set it down on the space between the first and second court, which was eight foot wide. I then stept over the buildings very conveniently from one stool to the other, and drew up the first after me with a hooked stick. By this contrivance I got into the inmost court; and lying down upon my side, I applied my face to the windows of the middle stories, which were left open on purpose, and discovered the most splendid apartments that can be imagined. There I saw the empress, and the young princes in their several lodgings, with their chief attendants about them. Her Imperial Majesty was pleased to smile very graciously upon me, and gave me out of the window her hand to kiss.

But I shall not anticipate the reader with farther descriptions of this kind, because I reserve them for a greater work, which is now almost ready for the press; containing a general description of this empire, from its first erection, through a long series of princes, with a particular account of their wars and politicks, laws, learning, and religion; their plants and animals, their peculiar manners and customs, with other matters very curious and useful; my chief design at present being only to relate such events and transactions as happened to the publick, or, to my self, during a residence of about nine months in that empire.

One morning, about a fortnight after I had obtained my liberty; Reldresal, Principal Secretary (as they style him) of Private Affairs, came to my house, attended only by one servant. He ordered his coach to wait at a distance, and desired I would give him an hour's audience; which I readily consented to, on account of his quality, and personal merits, as well as of the many good offices he had done me during my sollicitations at court. I offered to lie down, that he might the more conveniently reach my ear; but he chose rather to let me hold him in my hand during our conversation. He began with compliments on my liberty; said, he might pretend to some merit in it; but, however, added, that if it had not been for the present situation of things at court, perhaps I might not have obtained it so soon. For, said he, as flourishing a condition as we appear to be in to foreigners, we labour under two mighty evils; a violent faction at home, and the danger of an invasion by a most potent enemy from abroad. As to the first, you are to understand, that for above seventy moons past, there have been two struggling parties in this empire, under the names of Tramecksan, and Slamecksan, from the high and low heels on their shoes, by which they distinguish themselves.

It is alledged indeed, that the high heels are most agreeable to our ancient constitution: but however this be, his Majesty hath determined to make

use of only low heels in the administration of the Government, and all
offices in the gift of the Crown, as you cannot but observe; and particularly,
that his Majesty's imperial heels are lower at least by a *drurr* than any of
his court; (*drurr* is a measure about the fourteenth part of an inch.) The
animosities between these two parties run so high, that they will neither eat
nor drink, nor talk with each other. We compute the Tramecksan, or high-
heels, to exceed us in number; but the power is wholly on our side. We apprehend his Imperial Highness, the heir to the crown, to have some ten-
dency towards the high-heels; at least we can plainly discover one of his heels
higher than the other; which gives him a hobble in his gait. Now, in the
midst of these intestine disquiets, we are threatened with an invasion from
the island of Blefuscu, which is the other great empire of the universe,
almost as large and powerful as this of his Majesty. For as to what we have
heard you affirm, that there are other kingdoms and states in the world,
inhabited by human creatures as large as your self, our philosophers are in
much doubt; and would rather conjecture, that you dropt from the moon,
or one of the stars; because it is certain, that an hundred mortals of your
bulk, would, in a short time, destroy all the fruits and cattle of his Majesty's
dominions. Besides, our histories of six thousand moons make no mention
of any other regions, than the two great empires of Lilliput and Blefuscu.
Which two mighty powers have, as I was going to tell you, been engaged
in a most obstinate war for six and thirty moons past. It began upon the
following occasion. It is allowed on all hands, that the primitive way of
breaking eggs before we eat them, was upon the larger end: but his present
Majesty's grand-father, while he was a boy, going to eat an egg, and breaking it according to the ancient practice, happened to cut one of his fingers.
Whereupon the emperor his father, published an edict, commanding all his
subjects, upon great penalties, to break the smaller end of their eggs. The
people so highly resented this law, that our histories tell us, there have been
six rebellions raised on that account; wherein one emperor lost his life, and
another his crown. These civil commotions were constantly fomented by
the monarchs of Blefuscu; and when they were quelled, the exiles always
fled for refuge to that empire. It is computed, that eleven thousand persons
have, at several times, suffered death, rather than submit to break their
eggs at the smaller end. Many hundred large volumes have been published
upon this controversy: but the books of the Big-Endians have been long
forbidden, and the whole party rendered incapable by law of holding employments. During the course of these troubles, the emperors of Blefuscu
did frequently expostulate by their ambassadors, accusing us of making a
schism in religion, by offending against a fundamental doctrine of our great
prophet Lustrog, in the fifty-fourth chapter of the *Brundrecal*, (which is
their *Alcoran*.) This, however, is thought to be a meer strain upon the text:
for the words are these; "That all true believers shall break their eggs at the
convenient end": and which is the convenient end, seems in my humble
opinion, to be left to every man's conscience, or at least in the power of the
chief magistrate to determine. Now the Big-Endian exiles have found so
much credit in the Emperor of Blefuscu's court; and so much private assistance and encouragement from their party here at home, that a bloody

war hath been carried on between the two empires for six and thirty moons with various success; during which time we have lost forty capital ships, and a much greater number of smaller vessels, together with thirty thousand of our best seamen and soldiers; and the damage received by the enemy is reckoned to be somewhat greater than ours. However, they have now equipped a numerous fleet, and are just preparing to make a descent upon us: and his Imperial Majesty, placing great confidence in your valour and strength, hath commanded me to lay this account of his affairs before you.

I desired the secretary to present my humble duty to the emperor, and to let him know, that I thought it would not become me, who was a foreigner, to interfere with parties; but I was ready; with the hazard of my life, to defend his person and state against all invaders.

CHAPTER V

The author by an extraordinary stratagem prevents an invasion. A high title of honour is conferred upon him. Ambassadors arrive from the Emperor of Blefuscu, and sue for peace. The empress's apartment on fire by an accident; the author instrumental in saving the rest of the palace.

THE empire of Blefuscu is an island situated to the north north-east side of Lilliput, from whence it is parted only by a channel of eight hundred yards wide. I had not yet seen it, and upon this notice of an intended invasion, I avoided appearing on that side of the coast, for fear of being discovered by some of the enemy's ships, who had received no intelligence of me; all intercourse between the two empires having been strictly forbidden during the war, upon pain of death; and an embargo laid by our emperor upon all vessels whatsoever. I communicated to his Majesty a project I had formed of seizing the enemy's whole fleet; which, as our scouts assured us, lay at anchor in the harbour ready to sail with the first fair wind. I consulted the most experienced seamen, upon the depth of the channel, which they had often plummed; who told me, that in the middle at high water it was seventy *glumgluffs* deep, which is about six foot of European measure; and the rest of it fifty *glumgluffs* at most. I walked to the north-east coast over against Blefuscu; where, lying down behind a hillock, I took out my small pocket perspective glass, and viewed the enemy's fleet at anchor, consisting of about fifty men of war, and a great number of transports: I then came back to my house, and gave order (for which I had a warrant) for a great quantity of the strongest cable and bars of iron. The cable was about as thick as packthread, and the bars of the length and size of a knitting-needle. I trebled the cable to make it stronger; and for the same reason I twisted three of the iron bars together, binding the extremities into a hook. Having thus fixed fifty hooks to as many cables, I went back to the north-east coast, and putting off my coat, shoes, and stockings, walked into the sea in my leathern jerkin, about half an hour before high water. I waded with what haste I could, and swam in the middle about thirty yards until I felt the ground; I arrived to the fleet in less than half an hour. The enemy was so frighted when they saw me, that they leaped out of their ships, and swam to shore; where there could not be fewer than thirty thousand souls. I then took my tackling, and fastning a hook to the hole at the prow of each, I tyed all the cords together at the end. While I was thus employed, the enemy discharged several thousand arrows, many of which stuck in my hands and face; and besides the excessive smart, gave me much disturbance in my work. My greatest apprehension was for mine eyes, which I should have infallibly lost, if I had not suddenly thought of an expedient. I kept, among other little necessaries, a pair of spectacles in a private pocket, which, as I observed before, had escaped the emperor's searchers. These I took out, and fastned as strongly as I could upon my nose; and thus armed went on boldly with my work in spight of the enemy's arrows; many of which struck against the glasses of my spectacles, but without any other effect, further than a little to discompose them. I had now fastned all the hooks, and taking the knot in my hand, began to pull; but not a ship would stir, for they were all too fast held by their anchors; so that the boldest part of my enterprize remained. I therefore let go the cord, and leaving the hooks fixed to the ships, I resolutely cut with my knife the cables that fastned the anchors; receiving about two hundred shots in my face and hands: then I took up the knotted end of the cables to which my hooks were tyed; and with great ease drew fifty of the enemy's largest men of war after me.

The Blefuscudians, who had not the least imagination of what I intended, were at first confounded with astonishment. They had seen me cut the cables, and thought my design was only to let the ships run a-drift, or fall foul on each other: but when they perceived the whole fleet moving in order, and saw me pulling at the end, they set up such a scream of grief and despair, that it is almost impossible to describe or conceive. When I had got out of danger, I stopt a while to pick out the arrows that stuck in my hands and face, and rubbed on some of the same ointment that was given me at my first arrival, as I have formerly mentioned. I then took off my spectacles, and waiting about an hour until the tyde was a little fallen, I waded through the middle with my cargo, and arrived safe at the royal port of Lilliput.

The emperor and his whole court stood on the shore, expecting the issue of this great adventure. They saw the ships move forward in a large half moon, but could not discern me, who was up to my breast in water. When I advanced to the middle of the channel, they were yet more in pain because I was under water to my neck. The emperor concluded me to be drowned, and that the enemy's fleet was approaching in a hostile manner: but he was soon eased of his fears; for the channel growing shallower every step I made, I came in a short time within hearing; and holding up the end of the cable by which the fleet was fastned, I cryed in a loud voice, "Long live the most puissant Emperor of Lilliput!" This great prince received me at my landing with all possible encomiums, and created me a Nardac upon the spot, which is the highest title of honour among them.

His Majesty desired I would take some other opportunity of bringing all the rest of his enemy's ships into his ports. And so unmeasurable is the ambition of princes, that he seemed to think of nothing less than reducing the whole empire of Blefuscu into a province, and governing it by a viceroy; of destroying the Big-Endian exiles, and compelling that people to break the smaller end of their eggs; by which he would remain sole monarch of the whole world. But I endeavoured to divert him from this design, by many arguments drawn from the topicks of policy as well as justice: and I plainly protested, that I would never be an instrument of bringing a free and brave people into slavery: and when the matter was debated in council, the wisest part of the ministry were of my opinion.

This open bold declaration of mine, was so opposite to the schemes and politicks of his Imperial Majesty, that he could never forgive me: he mentioned it in a very artful manner at council, where, I was told that some of the wisest appeared, at least by their silence, to be of my opinion; but others, who were my secret enemies, could not forbear some expressions, which by a side-wind reflected on me. And from this time began an intrigue between his Majesty, and a junta of ministers maliciously bent against me, which broke out in less than two months, and had like to have ended in my utter destruction. Of so little weight are the greatest services to princes, when put into the balance with a refusal to gratify their passions.

About three weeks after this exploit, there arrived a solemn embassy from Blefuscu, with humble offers of a peace; which was soon concluded upon conditions very advantageous to our emperor; wherewith I shall not trouble the reader. There were six ambassadors, with a train of about five hundred persons; and their entry was very magnificent, suitable to the grandeur of their master, and the importance of their business. When their treaty was finished, wherein I did them several good offices by the credit I now had, or at least appeared to have at court; their excellencies, who were privately told how much I had been their friend, made me a visit in form. They began with many compliments upon my valour and generosity; invited me to that kingdom in the emperor their master's name; and desired me to shew them some proofs of my prodigious strength, of which they had heard so many wonders; wherein I readily obliged them, but shall not interrupt the reader with the particulars.

When I had for some time entertained their excellencies to their infinite satisfaction and surprize, I desired they would do me the honour to present my most humble respects to the emperor their master, the renown of whose virtues had so justly filled the whole world with admiration, and whose royal person I resolved to attend before I returned to my own country. Accordingly, the next time I had the honour to see our emperor, I desired his general licence to wait on the Blefuscudian monarch, which he was pleased to grant me, as I could plainly perceive, in a very cold manner; but could not guess the reason, until I had a whisper from a certain person, that Flimnap and Bolgolam had represented my intercourse with those ambassadors, as a mark of disaffection, from which I am sure my heart was wholly free. And this was the first time I began to conceive some imperfect idea of courts and ministers.

It is to be observed, that these ambassadors spoke to me by an interpreter; the languages of both empires differing as much from each other as any two in Europe, and each nation priding itself upon the antiquity, beauty, and energy of their own tongues, with an avowed contempt for that of their neighbour: yet our emperor standing upon the advantage he had got by the seizure of their fleet, obliged them to deliver their credentials, and make their speech in the Lilliputian tongue. And it must be confessed, that from the great intercourse of trade and commerce between both realms; from the continual reception of exiles, which is mutual among them; and from the custom in each empire to send their young nobility and richer gentry to the other, in order to polish themselves by seeing the world, and understanding men and manners; there are few persons of distinction, or merchants, or seamen, who dwell in the maritime parts, but what can hold conversation in both tongues; as I found some weeks after, when I went to pay my respects to the Emperor of Blefuscu, which in the midst of great misfortunes, through the malice of my enemies, proved a very happy adventure to me, as I shall relate in its proper place.

The reader may remember, that when I signed those articles upon which I recovered my liberty, there were some which I disliked upon account of their being too servile, neither could any thing but an extreme necessity have forced me to submit. But being now a Nardac, of the highest rank in that empire, such offices were looked upon as below my dignity; and the emperor (to do him justice) never once mentioned them to me. However, it was not long before I had an opportunity of doing his Majesty, at least, as I then thought, a most signal service. I was alarmed at midnight with the cries of many hundred people at my door; by which being suddenly awaked, I was in some kind of terror. I heard the word "burglum" repeated incessantly; several of the emperor's court making their way through the croud, intreated me to come immediately to the palace, where her Imperial Majesty's apartment was on fire, by the carelessness of a maid of honour, who fell asleep while she was reading a romance. I got up in an instant; and orders being given to clear the way before me; and it being likewise a moonshine night, I made a shift to get to the palace without trampling on any of the people. I found they had already applied ladders to the walls of the apartment, and were well provided with buckets, but the water was at some distance. These buckets were about the size of a large thimble, and the poor people supplied me with them as fast as they could; but the flame was so violent, that they did little good. I might easily have stifled it with my coat, which I unfortunately left behind me for haste, and came away only in my leathern jerkin. The case seemed wholly desperate and deplorable; and this magnificent palace would have infallibly been burnt down to the ground, if, by a presence of mind, unusual to me, I had not suddenly thought of an expedient. I had the evening before drank plentifully of a most delicious wine, called *glimigrim*, (the Blefuscudians call it *flunec*, but ours is esteemed the better sort) which is very diuretick. By the luckiest chance in the world I had not discharged myself of any part of it. The heat I had contracted by coming very near the flames, and by my labouring to quench them, made the wine begin to operate by urine; which I voided in such a quantity, and applied so well to the proper places, that in three minutes the fire was wholly extinguished; and the rest of that noble pile, which had cost so many ages in erecting, preserved from destruction.

It was now day-light, and I returned to my house, without waiting to congratulate with the emperor; because, although I had done a very eminent piece of service, yet I could not tell how his Majesty might resent the manner by which I had performed it: for, by the fundamental laws of the realm, it is capital in any person, of what quality soever, to make water within the precincts of the palace. But I was a little comforted by a message from his Majesty, that he would give orders to the grand justiciary for passing my pardon in form; which, however, I could not obtain. And, I was privately assured, that the empress conceiving the greatest abhorrence of what I had done, removed to the most distant side of the court, firmly resolved that those buildings should never be repaired for her use; and, in the presence of her chief confidents, could not forbear vowing revenge.

CHAPTER VI

Of the inhabitants of Lilliput; their learning, laws, and customs. The manner of educating their children. The author's way of living in that country. His vindication of a great lady.

ALTHOUGH I intend to leave the description of this empire to a particular treatise, yet in the mean time I am content to gratify the curious reader with some general ideas. As the common size of the natives is somewhat under six inches, so there is an exact proportion in all other animals, as well as plants and trees: for instance, the tallest horses and oxen are between four and five inches in height, the sheep an inch and a half, more or less; their geese about the bigness of a sparrow; and so the several gradations downwards, until you come to the smallest, which, to my sight, were almost invisible; but nature hath adapted the eyes of the Lilliputians to all objects proper for their view: they see with great exactness, but at no great distance. And to shew the sharpness of their sight towards objects that are near, I have been much pleased with observing a cook pulling a lark, which was not so large as a common fly; and a young girl threading an invisible needle with invisible silk. Their tallest trees are about seven foot high; I mean some of those in the great royal park, the tops whereof I could but just reach with my fist clenched. The other vegetables are in the same proportion: but this I leave to the reader's imagination.

I shall say but little at present of their learning, which for many ages hath flourished in all its branches among them: but their manner of writing is very peculiar; being neither from the left to the right, like the Europeans; nor from the right to the left, like the Arabians; nor from up to down, like the Chinese; nor from down to up, like the Cascagians; but aslant from one corner of the paper to the other, like ladies in England.

They bury their dead with their heads directly downwards; because they hold an opinion, that in eleven thousand moons they all to rise again; in which period, the earth (which they conceive to be flat) will turn upside down, and by this means they shall, at their resurrection, be found ready standing on their feet. The learned among them confess the absurdity of this doctrine; but the practice still continues, in compliance to the vulgar.

There are some laws and customs in this empire very peculiar; and if they were not so directly contrary to those of my own dear country, I should be tempted to say a little in their justification. It is only to be wished, that they were as well executed. The first I shall mention, relateth to informers. All crimes against the State, are punished here with the utmost severity; but if the person accused make his innocence plainly to appear upon his tryal, the accuser is immediately put to an ignominious death; and out of his goods or lands, the innocent person is quadruply recompensed for the loss of his time, for the danger he underwent, for the hardship of his imprisonment, and for all the charges he hath been at in making his defence. Or, if that fund be deficient, it is largely supplyed by the Crown. The emperor doth also confer on him some publick mark of his favour; and proclamation is made of his innocence through the whole city.

They look upon fraud as a greater crime than theft, and therefore seldom fail to punish it with death: for, they alledge, that care and vigilance, with a very common understanding, may preserve a man's goods from thieves; but honesty hath no fence against superior cunning: and since it is necessary that there should be a perpetual intercourse of buying and selling, and deal-ing upon credit; where fraud is permitted or connived at, or hath no law to punish it, the honest dealer is always undone, and the knave gets the ad-vantage. I remember when I was once interceding with the king for a crim-inal who had wronged his master of a great sum of money, which he had re-ceived by order, and ran away with; and happening to tell his Majesty, by way of extenuation, that it was only a breach of trust; the emperor thought it monstrous in me to offer, as a defence, the greatest aggravation of the crime: and truly, I had little to say in return, farther than the common answer, that different nations had different customs; for, I confess, I was heartily ashamed.

Although we usually call reward and punishment, the two hinges upon which all government turns; yet I could never observe this maxim to be put in practice by any nation except that of Lilliput. Whoever can there bring sufficient proof, that he hath strictly observed the laws of his country for seventy-three moons, hath a claim to certain privileges, according to his quality and condition of life, with a proportionable sum of money out of a fund appropriated for that use: he likewise acquires the title of Snilpall, or Legal, which is added to his name, but doth not descend to his posterity. And these people thought it a prodigious defect of policy among us, when I told them that our laws were enforced only by penalties, without any men-tion of reward. It is upon this account that the image of justice, in their courts of judicature, is formed with six eyes, two before, as many behind, and on each side one, to signify circumspection; with a bag of gold open in her right hand, and a sword sheathed in her left, to shew she is more dis-posed to reward than to punish.

In chusing persons for all employments, they have more regard to good morals than to great abilities: for, since government is necessary to man-kind, they believe that the common size of human understandings, is fitted to some station or other; and that Providence never intended to make the management of publick affairs a mystery, to be comprehended only by a few persons of sublime genius, of which there seldom are three born in an age: but, they suppose truth, justice, temperance, and the like, to be in every man's power; the practice of which virtues, assisted by experience and a good intention, would qualify any man for the service of his country, except where a course of study is required. But they thought the want of moral virtues was so far from being supplied by superior endowments of the mind, that employments could never be put into such dangerous hands as those of persons so qualified; and at least, that the mistakes committed by ignorance in a virtuous disposition, would never be of such fatal consequence to the publick weal, as the practices of a man whose inclinations led him to be corrupt, and had great abilities to manage, to multiply, and defend his corruptions.

In like manner, the disbelief of a divine providence renders a man uncapable of holding any publick station: for, since kings avow themselves to be the deputies of Providence, the Lilliputians think nothing can be more absurd, than for a prince to employ such men as disown the authority under which he acteth.

In relating these and the following laws, I would only be understood to mean the original institutions, and not the most scandalous corruptions into which these people are fallen by the degenerate nature of man. For, as to that infamous practice of acquiring great employments by dancing on the ropes, or badges of favour and distinction by leaping over sticks, and creeping under them; the reader is to observe, that they were first introduced by the grandfather of the emperor now reigning; and grew to the present height, by the gradual increase of party and faction.

Ingratitude is among them a capital crime, as we read it to have been in some other countries: for they reason thus; that whoever makes ill returns to his benefactor, must needs be a common enemy to the rest of mankind, from whom they have received no obligation; and therefore such a man is not fit to live.

Their notions relating to the duties of parents and children differ extremely from ours. For, since the conjunction of male and female is founded upon the great law of nature, in order to propagate and continue the species; the Lilliputians will needs have it, that men and women are joined together like other animals, by the motives of concupiscence; and that their tenderness towards their young, proceedeth from the like natural principle: for which reason they will never allow, that a child is under any obligation to his father for begetting him, or to his mother for bringing him into the world; which, considering the miseries of human life, was neither a benefit in itself, nor intended so by his parents, whose thoughts in their love-encounters were otherwise employed. Upon these, and the like reasonings, their opinion is, that parents are the last of all others to be trusted with the education of their own children: and therefore they have in every town publick nurseries, where all parents, except cottagers and labourers, are obliged to send their infants of both sexes to be reared and educated when they come to the age of twenty moons; at which time they are supposed to have some rudiments of docility. These schools are of several kinds, suited to different qualities, and to both sexes. They have certain professors well skilled in preparing children for such a condition of life as befits the rank of their parents, and their own capacities as well as inclinations. I shall first say something of the male nurseries, and then of the female.

The nurseries for males of noble or eminent birth, are provided with grave and learned professors, and their several deputies. The clothes and food of the children are plain and simple. They are bred up in the principles of honour, justice, courage, modesty, clemency, religion, and love of their country: they are always employed in some business, except in the times of eating and sleeping, which are very short, and two hours for diversions, consisting of bodily exercises. They are dressed by men until four years of age, and then are obliged to dress themselves, although their quality be ever so great; and the women attendants, who are aged proportionably to ours at fifty, perform only the most menial offices. They are never suffered to converse with servants, but go together in small or greater numbers to take their diversions, and always in the presence of a professor, or one of his deputies; whereby they avoid those early bad impressions of folly and vice to which our children are subject. Their parents are suffered to see them only twice a year; the visit is not to last above an hour; they are allowed to kiss the child at meeting and parting; but a professor, who always standeth by on those occasions, will not suffer them to whisper, or use any fondling expressions, or bring any presents of toys, sweetmeats, and the like.

The pension from each family for the education and entertainment of a child, upon failure of due payment, is levyed by the emperor's officers.

The nurseries for children of ordinary gentlemen, merchants, traders, and handicrafts, are managed proportionably after the same manner; only those designed for trades, are put out apprentices at seven years old; whereas those of persons of quality continue in their exercises until fifteen, which answers to one and twenty with us: but the confinement is gradually lessened for the last three years.

In the female nurseries, the young girls of quality are educated much like the males, only they are dressed by orderly servants of their own sex, but always in the presence of a professor or deputy, until they come to dress themselves, which is at five years old. And if it be found, that these nurses ever presume to entertain the girls with frightful or foolish stories, or the common follies practised by chamber-maids among us; they are publickly whipped thrice about the city, imprisoned for a year, and banished for life to the most desolate parts of the country. Thus, the young ladies there are as much ashamed of being cowards and fools, as the men; and despise all personal ornaments beyond decency and cleanliness; neither did I perceive any difference in their education, made by their difference of sex, only that the exercises of the females were not altogether so robust; and that some rules were given them relating to domestick life, and a smaller compass of learning was enjoined them: for, their maxim is, that among people of quality, a wife should be always a reasonable and agreeable companion, because she cannot always be young. When the girls are twelve years old, which among them is the marriageable age, their parents or guardians take them home, with great expressions of gratitude to the professors, and seldom without tears of the young lady and her companions.

In the nurseries of females of the meaner sort, the children are instructed in all kinds of works proper for their sex and their several degrees: those intended for apprentices are dismissed at seven years old, the rest are kept to eleven.

The meaner families who have children at these nurseries, are obliged, besides their annual pension, which is as low as possible, to return to the steward of the nursery a small monthly share of their gettings, to be a portion for the child; and therefore all parents are limited in their expences by the law. For the Lilliputians think nothing can be more unjust, than that people, in subservience to their own appetites, should bring children into the world, and leave the burthen of supporting them on the publick. As to persons of quality, they give security to appropriate a certain sum for each child, suitable to their condition; and these funds are always managed with good husbandry, and the most exact justice.

The cottagers and labourers keep their children at home, their business being only to till and cultivate the earth; and therefore their education is of little consequence to the publick; but the old and diseased among them are supported by hospitals: for begging is a trade unknown in this empire.

And here it may perhaps divert the curious reader, to give some account of my domestick, and my manner of living in this country, during a residence of nine months and thirteen days. Having a head mechanically turned, and being likewise forced by necessity, I had made for my self a table and chair convenient enough, out of the largest trees in the royal park. Two hundred sempstresses were employed to make me shirts, and linnen for my bed and table, all of the strongest and coarsest kind they could get; which, however, they were forced to quilt together in several folds; for the thickest was some degrees finer than lawn. Their linnen is usually three inches wide, and three foot make a piece. The sempstresses took my measure as I lay on the ground, one standing at my neck, and another at my mid-leg, with a strong cord extended, that each held by the end, while the third measured the length of the cord with a rule of an inch long. Then they measured my right thumb, and desired no more; for by a mathematical computation, that twice round the thumb is once round the wrist, and so on to the neck and the waist; and by the help of my old shirt, which I displayed on the ground before them for a pattern, they fitted me exactly. Three hundred taylors were employed in the same manner to make me clothes; but they had another contrivance for taking my measure. I kneeled down, and they raised a ladder from the ground to my neck; upon this ladder one of them mounted, and let fall a plum-line from my collar to the floor, which just answered the length of my coat; but my waist and arms I measured my self. When my clothes were finished, which was done in my house, (for the largest of theirs would not have been able to hold them) they looked like the patch-work made by the ladies in England, only that mine were all of a colour.

I had three hundred cooks to dress my victuals, in little convenient huts built about my house, where they and their families lived, and prepared me two dishes a-piece. I took up twenty waiters in my hand, and placed them on the table; an hundred more attended below on the ground, some with dishes of meat, and some with barrels of wine, and other liquors, slung on their shoulders; all which the waiters above drew up as I wanted, in a very ingenious manner, by certain cords, as we draw the bucket up a well in Europe. A dish of their meat was a good mouthful, and a barrel of their liquor a reasonable draught. Their mutton yields to ours, but their beef is excellent. I have had a sirloin so large, that I have been forced to make three bits of it; but this is rare. My servants were astonished to see me eat it bones and all, as in our country we do the leg of a lark. Their geese and turkeys I usually eat at a mouthful, and I must confess they far exceed ours. Of their smaller fowl I could take up twenty or thirty at the end of my knife.

One day his Imperial Majesty being informed of my way of living, desired that himself, and his royal consort, with the young princes of the blood of both sexes, might have the happiness (as he was pleased to call it) of dining with me. They came accordingly, and I placed them upon chairs of state on my table, just over against me, with their guards about them. Flimnap the Lord High Treasurer attended there likewise, with his white staff; and I observed he often looked on me with a sour countenance, which I would not seem to regard, but eat more than usual, in honour to my dear country, as well as to fill the court with admiration. I have some private reasons to believe, that this visit from his Majesty gave Flimnap an opportunity of doing me ill offices to his master. That minister had always been my secret enemy, although he outwardly caressed me more than was usual to the moroseness of his nature. He represented to the emperor the low condition of his treasury; that he was forced to take up money at a great discount; that exchequer bills would not circulate under nine per cent. below par; that I had cost his Majesty above a million and a half of *sprugs*, (their greatest gold coin, about the bigness of a spangle;) and upon the whole, that it would be adviseable in the emperor to take the first fair occasion of dismissing me.

I am here obliged to vindicate the reputation of an excellent lady, who was an innocent sufferer upon my account. The treasurer took a fancy to be jealous of his wife, from the malice of some evil tongues, who informed him, that her Grace had taken a violent affection for my person; and the court-scandal ran for some time, that she once came privately to my lodging. This, I solemnly declare, to be a most infamous falshood, without any grounds, farther than that her Grace was pleased to treat me with all innocent marks of freedom and friendship. I own, she came often to my house, but always publickly, nor ever without three more in the coach, who were usually her sister and young daughter, and some particular acquaintance; but this was common to many other ladies of the court. And I still appeal to my servants round, whether they at any time saw a coach at my door without knowing what persons were in it. On those occasions, when a servant had given me notice, my custom was to go immediately to the door; and after paying my respects, to take up the coach and two horses very carefully in my hands, (for if there were six horses, the postillion always unharnassed four) and place them on a table, where I had fixed a moveable rim quite round, of five inches high, to prevent accidents. And I have often had four coaches and horses at once on my table full of company, while I sat in my chair leaning my face towards them; and when I was engaged with one sett, the coachmen would gently drive the others round my table. I have passed many an afternoon very agreeably in these conversations:

but, I defy the treasurer, or his two informers, (I will name them, and let them make their best of it) Clustril and Drunlo, to prove that any person ever came to me incognito, except the secretary Reldresal, who was sent by express command of his Imperial Majesty, as I have before related. I should not have dwelt so long upon this particular, if it had not been a point wherein the reputation of a great lady is so nearly concerned; to say nothing of my own; although I had the honour to be a Nardac, which the treasurer himself is not; for all the world knows he is only a Clumglum, a title inferior by one degree, as that of a marquess is to a duke in England; yet I allow he preceded me in right of his post. These false informations, which I afterwards came to the knowledge of, by an accident not proper to mention, made the treasurer shew his lady for some time an ill countenance, and me a worse: for although he were at last undeceived and reconciled to her, yet I lost all credit with him; and found my interest decline very fast with the emperor himself, who was indeed too much governed by that favourite.

CHAPTER VII

The author being informed of a design to accuse him of high treason, maketh his escape to Blefuscu. His reception there.

BEFORE I proceed to give an account of my leaving this kingdom, it may be proper to inform the reader of a private intrigue, which had been for two months forming against me.

I had been hitherto all my life a stranger to courts, for which I was unqualified by the meanness of my condition. I had indeed heard and read enough of the dispositions of great princes and ministers; but never expected to have found such terrible effects of them in so remote a country, governed, as I thought, by very different maxims from those in Europe.

When I was just preparing to pay my attendance on the Emperor of Blefuscu, a considerable person at court (to whom I had been very serviceable at a time when he lay under the highest displeasure of his Imperial Majesty) came to my house very privately at night in a close chair, and without sending his name, desired admittance: the chairmen were dismissed; I put the chair, with his lordship in it, into my coat-pocket; and giving orders to a trusty servant to say I was indisposed and gone to sleep, I fastened the door of my house, placed the chair on the table, according to my usual custom, and sat down by it. After the common salutations were over, observing his lordship's countenance full of concern; and enquiring into the reason, he desired I would hear him with patience, in a matter that highly concerned my honour and my life. His speech was to the following effect, for I took notes of it as soon as he left me.

"You are to know," said he, "that several committees of council have been lately called in the most private manner on your account: and it is but two days since his Majesty came to a full resolution.

"You are very sensible that Skyris Bolgolam (Galbet, or High Admiral) hath been your mortal enemy almost ever since your arrival. His original reasons I know not; but his hatred is much encreased since your great success against Blefuscu, by which his glory, as admiral, is obscured. This lord, in conjunction with Flimnap the High Treasurer, whose enmity against you is notorious on account of his lady; Limtoc the general, Lalcon the chamberlain, and Balmuff the Grand Justiciary, have prepared articles of impeachment against you, for treason, and other capital crimes."

This preface made me so impatient, being conscious of my own merits and innocence, that I was going to interrupt; when he intreated me to be silent; and thus proceeded.

"Out of gratitude for the favours you have done me, I procured information of the whole proceedings, and a copy of the articles, wherein I venture my head for your service.

Articles of impeachment against Quinbus Flestrin, (the Man-Mountain)

ARTICLE I

Whereas, by a statute made in the reign of his Imperial Majesty Calin Dessar Plune, it is enacted, that whoever shall make water within the precincts of the royal palace, shall be liable to the pains and penalties of high treason: notwithstanding, the said Quinbus Flestrin, in open breach of the said law, under colour of extinguishing the fire kindled in the apartment of his Majesty's most dear imperial consort, did maliciously, traitorously, and devilishly, by discharge of his urine, put out the said fire kindled in the said apartment, lying and being within the precincts of the said royal palace; against the statute in that case provided, etc. against the duty, etc.

ARTICLE II

That, the said Quinbus Flestrin having brought the imperial fleet of Blefuscu into the royal port, and being afterwards commanded by his Imperial Majesty to seize all the other ships of the said empire of Blefuscu, and reduce that empire to a province, to be governed by a viceroy from hence; and to destroy and put to death not only all the Big-Endian exiles, but likewise all the people of that empire, who would not immediately forsake the Big-Endian heresy: he the said Flestrin, like a false traitor against his most auspicious, serene, Imperial Majesty, did petition to be excused from the said service, upon pretence of unwillingness to force the consciences, or destroy the liberties and lives of an innocent people.

ARTICLE III

That, whereas certain embassadors arrived from the court of Blefuscu to sue for peace in his Majesty's court: he the said Flestrin did, like a false traitor, aid, abet, comfort, and divert the said embassadors; although he knew them to be servants to a prince who was lately an open enemy to his Imperial Majesty, and in open war against his said Majesty.

ARTICLE IV

That, the said Quinbus Flestrin, contrary to the duty of a faithful subject, is now preparing to make a voyage to the court and empire of Blefuscu, for which he hath received only verbal licence from his Imperial Majesty; and under colour of the said licence, doth falsly and traitorously intend to take the said voyage, and thereby to aid, comfort, and abet the Emperor of Blefuscu, so late an enemy, and in open war with his Imperial Majesty aforesaid.

"There are some other articles, but these are the most important, of which I have read you an abstract.

"In the several debates upon this impeachment, it must be confessed, that his Majesty gave many marks of his great *lenity*; often urging the services you had done him, and endeavouring to extenuate your crimes. The treasurer and admiral insisted, that you should be put to the most painful and ignominious death, by setting fire on your house at night; and the general was to attend with twenty thousand men armed with poisoned arrows, to shoot you on the face and hands. Some of your servants were to have private orders to strew a poisonous juice on your shirts and sheets, which would soon make you tear your own flesh, and die in the utmost torture. The general came into the same opinion; so, that for a long time there was a majority against you. But his Majesty resolving, if possible, to spare your life, at last brought off the chamberlain.

"Upon this incident, Reldresal, Principal Secretary for Private Affairs, who always approved himself your true friend, was commanded by the emperor to deliver his opinion, which he accordingly did; and therein justified the good thoughts you have of him. He allowed your crimes to be great; but that still there was room for mercy, the most commendable virtue in a prince, and for which his Majesty was so justly celebrated. He said, the friendship between you and him was so well known to the world, that perhaps the most honourable board might think him partial: however, in obedience to the command he had received, he would freely offer his sentiments. That, if his Majesty, in consideration of your services, and pursuant to his own merciful disposition, would please to spare your life, and only give order to put out both your eyes; he humbly conceived, that by this expedient, justice might in some measure be satisfied, and all the world would applaud the lenity of the emperor, as well as the fair and generous proceedings of those who have the honour to be his counsellors. That, the loss of your eyes would be no impediment to your bodily strength, by which you might still be useful to his Majesty. That, blindness is an addition to courage, by concealing dangers from us. That, the fear you had for your eyes, was the greatest difficulty in bringing over the enemy's fleet; and it would be sufficient for you to see by the eyes of the ministers, since the greatest princes do no more.

"This proposal was received with the utmost disapprobation by the whole board. Bolgolam, the admiral, could not preserve his temper; but rising up in fury, said, he wondered how the secretary durst presume to give his opinion for preserving the life of a traytor: that, the services you had performed, were, by all true reasons of State, the great aggravation of your crimes: that you, who were able to extinguish the fire, by discharge of urine in her Majesty's apartment (which he mentioned with horror) might, at another time, raise an inundation by the same means, to drown the whole palace; and the same strength which enabled you to bring over the enemy's fleet, might serve, upon the first discontent, to carry it back: that, he had good reasons to think you were a Big-Endian in your heart; and as treason begins in the heart before it appears in overt-acts; so he accused you as a traytor on that account, and therefore insisted you should be put to death.

"The treasurer was of the same opinion; he shewed to what streights his Majesty's revenue was reduced by the charge of maintaining you, which would soon grow insupportable: that, the secretary's expedient of putting out your eyes, was so far from being a remedy against this evil, that it would probably encrease it; as it is manifest from the common practice of blinding some kind of fowl, after which they fed the faster, and grew sooner fat: that, his sacred Majesty, and the council, who are your judges, were in their own consciences fully convinced of your guilt; which was a sufficient argument to condemn you to death, without the *formal proofs required by the strict letter of the law.*

"But his Imperial Majesty, fully determined against capital punishment, was graciously pleased to say, that since the council thought the loss of your eyes too easy a censure, some other may be inflicted hereafter. And your friend the secretary humbly desiring to be heard again, in answer to what the treasurer had objected, concerning the great charge his Majesty was at in maintaining you; said, that his Excellency, who had the sole disposal of the emperor's revenue, might easily provide against this evil, by gradually lessening your establishment; by which, for want of sufficient food, you would grow weak and faint, and lose your appetite, and consequently decay and consume in a few months; neither would the stench of your carcass be then so dangerous, when it should become more than half diminished; and immediately upon your death, five or six thousand of his Majesty's subjects might, in two or three days, cut your flesh from your bones, take it away by cartloads, and bury it in distant parts to prevent infection; leaving the skeleton as a monument of admiration to posterity.

"Thus, by the great friendship of the secretary, the whole affair was compromised. It was strictly enjoined, that the project of starving you by degrees should be kept a secret; but the sentence of putting out your eyes was entered on the books; none dissenting except Bolgolam the admiral, who being a creature of the empress, was perpetually instigated by her Majesty to insist upon your death; she having born perpetual malice against you, on account of that infamous and illegal method you took to extinguish the fire in her apartment.

"In three days your friend the secretary will be directed to come to your house, and read before you the articles of impeachment; and then to signify the great *lenity* and favour of his Majesty and council; whereby you are only condemned to the loss of your eyes, which his Majesty doth not question you will gratefully and humbly submit to; and twenty of his Majesty's surgeons will attend, in order to see the operation well performed, by discharging very sharp pointed arrows into the balls of your eyes, as you lie on the ground.

"I leave to your prudence what measures you will take; and to avoid suspicion, I must immediately return in as private a manner as I came."

His lordship did so, and I remained alone, under many doubts and perplexities of mind.

It was a custom introduced by this prince and his ministry, (very different, as I have been assured, from the practices of former times) that after the court had decreed any cruel execution, either to gratify the monarch's resentment, or the malice of a favourite, the emperor always made a speech to his whole council, expressing his *great lenity and tenderness, as qualities known and confessed by all the world.* This speech was immediately published through the kingdom; nor did any thing terrify the people so much as those encomiums on his Majesty's mercy; because it was observed, that the more these praises were enlarged and insisted on, the more *inhuman* was the punishment, and the *sufferer more innocent.* Yet, as to myself, I must confess, having never been designed for a courtier, either by my birth or education, I was so ill a judge of things, that I could not discover the *lenity* and favour of this sentence; but conceived it (perhaps erroneously) rather to be rigorous than gentle. I sometimes thought of standing my tryal; for although I could not deny the facts alledged in the several articles, yet I hoped they would admit of some extenuations. But, having in my life perused many State-tryals, which I ever observed to terminate as the judges thought fit to direct, I durst not rely on so dangerous a decision, in so critical a juncture, and against such powerful enemies. Once I was strongly bent upon resistance: for while I had liberty, the whole strength of that empire could hardly subdue me, and I might easily with stones pelt the metropolis to pieces: but I soon rejected that project with horror, by remembring the oath I had made to the emperor, the favours I received from him, and the high title of Nardac he conferred upon me. Neither had I so soon learned the gratitude of courtiers, to persuade myself, that his Majesty's *present severities acquitted me of all past obligations.*

At last I fixed upon a resolution, for which it is probable I may incur some censure, and not unjustly; for I confess I owe the preserving mine eyes, and consequently my liberty, to my own great rashness and want of experience: because, if I had then known the nature of princes and ministers, which I have since observed in many other courts, and their methods of treating criminals less obnoxious than myself; I should with great alacrity and readiness have submitted to so *easy* a punishment. But hurried on by the precipitancy of youth; and having his Imperial Majesty's licence to pay my attendance upon the Emperor of Blefuscu; I took this opportunity, before the three days were elapsed, to send a letter to my friend the secretary, signifying my resolution of setting out that morning for Blefuscu, pursuant to the leave I had got; and without waiting for an answer, I went to that side of the island where our fleet lay. I seized a large man of war, tied a cable to the prow, and lifting up the anchors, I stript myself, put my cloaths (together with my coverlet, which I carryed under my arm) into the vessel; and drawing it after me, between wading and swimming, arrived at the royal port of Blefuscu, where the people had long expected me: they lent me two guides to direct me to the capital city, which is of the same name; I held them in my hands until I came within two hundred yards of the gate; and desired them to signify my arrival to one of the secretaries, and let him know, I there waited his Majesty's commands. I had an answer in about an hour, that his Majesty, attended by the royal family, and great officers of the court, was coming out to receive me. I advanced a hundred yards; the emperor, and his train, alighted from their horses, the empress and ladies from their coaches; and I did not perceive they were in any fright or concern. I lay on the ground to kiss his Majesty's and the empress's hand. I told his Majesty, that I was come according to my promise, and with the licence of the emperor my master, to have the honour of seeing so mighty a monarch, and to offer him any service in my power, consistent with my duty to my own prince; not mentioning a word of my disgrace, because I had hitherto no regular information of it, and might suppose myself wholly ignorant of any such design; neither could I reasonably conceive, that the emperor would discover the secret while I was out of his power: wherein, however, it soon appeared I was deceived.

I shall not trouble the reader with the particular account of my reception at this court, which was suitable to the generosity of so great a prince; nor of the difficulties I was in for want of a house and bed, being forced to lye on the ground, wrapt up in my coverlet.

CHAPTER VIII

The author, by a lucky accident, finds means to leave Blefuscu; and, after some difficulties, returns safe to his native country.

THREE days after my arrival, walking out of curiosity to the north-east coast of the island, I observed, about half a league off, in the sea, somewhat that looked like a boat overturned: I pulled off my shoes and stockings, and wading two or three hundred yards, I found the object to approach nearer by force of the tide; and then plainly saw it to be a real boat, which I supposed might, by some tempest, have been driven from a ship. Whereupon I returned immediately towards the city, and desired his Imperial Majesty to lend me twenty of the tallest vessels he had left after the loss of his fleet, and three thousand seamen under the command of his vice-admiral. This fleet sailed round, while I went back the shortest way to the coast, where I first discovered the boat; I found the tide had driven it still nearer; the seamen were all provided with cordage, which I had beforehand twisted to a sufficient strength. When the ships came up, I stript myself, and waded until I came within an hundred yards of the boat; after which I was forced to swim until I got up to it. The seamen threw me the end of the cord, which I fastned to a hole in the forepart of the boat, and the other end to a man of war: but I found all my labour to little purpose; for being out of my depth, I was not able to work. In this necessity, I was forced to swim behind, and push the boat forwards as often as I could, with one of my hands; and the tide favouring me, I advanced so far, that I could just hold up my chin and feel the ground. I rested two or three minutes, and then gave the boat another shove, and so on, until the sea was no higher than my arm-pits. And now the most laborious part being over, I took out my other cables which were stowed in one of the ships, and fastning them first to the boat, and then to nine of the vessels which attended me; the wind being favourable, the seamen towed, and I shoved until we arrived within forty yards of the shore; and waiting until the tide was out, I got dry to the boat, and by the assistance of two thousand men, with ropes and engines, I made a shift to turn it on its bottom, and found it was but little damaged.

I shall not trouble the reader with the difficulties I was under by the help of certain paddles, which cost me ten days making, to get my boat to the royal port of Blefuscu; where a mighty concourse of people appeared upon my arrival, full of wonder at the sight of so prodigious a vessel. I told the emperor, that my good fortune had thrown this boat in my way, to carry me to some place from whence I might return into my native country; and begged his Majesty's orders for getting materials to fit it up; together with his licence to depart; which, after some kind expostulations, he was pleased to grant.

I did very much wonder, in all this time, not to have heard of any express relating to me from our emperor to the court of Blefuscu. But I was afterwards given privately to understand, that his Imperial Majesty never imagining I had the least notice of his designs, believed I was only gone to Blefuscu in performance of my promise, according to the licence he had given me, which was well known at our court; and would return in a few days when that ceremony was ended. But he was at last in pain at my long absence; and, after consulting with the treasurer, and the rest of that cabal; a person of quality was dispatched with the copy of the articles against me. This envoy had instructions to represent to the monarch of Blefuscu, the great lenity of his master, who was content to punish me no further than with the loss of mine eyes: that I had fled from justice, and if I did not return in two hours, I should be deprived of my title of Nardac, and declared a traytor. The envoy further added; that in order to maintain the peace and amity between both empires, his master expected, that his brother of Blefuscu would give orders to have me sent back to Lilliput, bound hand and foot, to be punished as a traitor.

The Emperor of Blefuscu having taken three days to consult, returned an answer consisting of many civilities and excuses. He said, that as for sending me bound, his brother knew it was impossible; that although I had deprived him of his fleet, yet he owed great obligations to me for many good offices I had done him in making the peace. That however, both their Majesties would soon be made easy; for I had found a prodigious vessel on the shore, able to carry me on the sea, which he had given order to fit up with my own assistance and direction; and he hoped in a few weeks both empires would be freed from so insupportable an incumbrance.

With this answer the envoy returned to Lilliput, and the monarch of Blefuscu related to me all that had passed; offering me at the same time (but under the strictest confidence) his gracious protection, if I would continue in his service; wherein although I believed him sincere, yet I resolved never more to put any confidence in princes or ministers, where I could possibly avoid it; and therefore, with all due acknowledgments for his favourable intentions, I humbly begged to be excused. I told him, that since fortune, whether good or evil, had thrown a vessel in my way; I was resolved to venture myself in the ocean, rather than be an occasion of difference between two such mighty monarchs. Neither did I find the emperor at all displeased; and I discovered by a certain accident, that he was very glad of my resolution, and so were most of his ministers.

These considerations moved me to hasten my departure somewhat sooner than I intended; to which the court, impatient to have me gone, very readily contributed. Five hundred workmen were employed to make two sails to my boat; according to my directions, by quilting thirteen fold of their strongest linnen together. I was at the pains of making ropes and cables, by twisting ten, twenty, or thirty of the thickest and strongest of theirs. A great stone that I happened to find, after a long search by the sea shore, served me for an anchor. I had the tallow of three hundred cows for greasing my boat, and other uses. I was at incredible pains in cutting down some of the largest timber trees for oars and masts, wherein I was, however, much assisted by his Majesty's ship-carpenters, who helped me in smoothing them, after I had done the rough work.

In about a month, when all was prepared, I sent to receive his Majesty's commands, and to take my leave. The emperor and royal family came out of the palace; I lay down on my face to kiss his hand, which he very graciously gave me; so did the empress, and young princes of the blood. His Majesty presented me with fifty purses of two hundred *sprugs* a-piece, together with his picture at full length, which I put immediately into one of my gloves, to keep it from being hurt. The ceremonies at my departure were too many to trouble the reader with at this time.

I stored the boat with the carcases of an hundred oxen, and three hundred sheep, with bread and drink proportionable, and as much meat ready dressed as four hundred cooks could provide. I took with me six cows and two bulls alive, with as many ewes and rams, intending to carry them into my own country, and propagate the breed. And to feed them on board, I had a good bundle of hay, and a bag of corn. I would gladly have taken a dozen of the natives; but this was a thing the emperor would by no means permit; and besides a diligent search into my pockets, his Majesty engaged my honour not to carry away any of his subjects, although with their own consent and desire.

Having thus prepared all things as well as I was able, I set sail on the twenty-fourth day of September 1701, at six in the morning; and when I had gone about four leagues to the northward, the wind being at south-east, at six in the evening, I descryed a small island about half a league to the north-west. I advanced forward, and cast anchor on the lee-side of the island, which seemed to be uninhabited. I then took some refreshment, and went to my rest. I slept well, and as I conjecture at least six hours; for I found the day broke in two hours after I awaked. It was a clear night; I eat my breakfast before the sun was up; and heaving anchor, the wind being favourable, I steered the same course that I had done the day before, wherein I was directed by my pocket-compass. My intention was to reach, if possible, one of those islands, which I had reason to believe lay to the north-east of Van Diemen's Land. I discovered nothing all that day; but upon the next, about three in the afternoon, when I had by my computation made twenty-four leagues from Blefuscu, I descryed a sail steering to the south-east; my course was due east. I hailed her, but could get no answer; yet I found I gained upon her, for the wind slackened. I made all the sail I could, and in half an hour she spyed me, then hung out her antient, and discharged a gun. It is not easy to express the joy I was in upon the unexpected hope of once more seeing my beloved country, and the dear pledges I left in it. The ship slackened her sails, and I came up with her between five and six in the evening, September 26; but my heart leapt within me to see her English colours. I put my cows and sheep into my coat-pockets, and got on board with all my little cargo of provisions. The vessel was an English merchant-man, returning from Japan by the North and South Seas; the captain, Mr. John Biddel of Deptford, a very civil man, and an excellent sailor. We were now in the latitude of 30 degrees south; there were about fifty men in the ship; and here I met an old comrade of mine, one Peter Williams, who gave me a good character to the captain. This gentleman treated me with kind-ness, and desired I would let him know what place I came from last, and whither I was bound; which I did in few words; but he thought I was rav-ing, and that the dangers I underwent had disturbed my head; whereupon I took my black cattle and sheep out of my pocket, which after great aston-ishment, clearly convinced him of my veracity. I then shewed him the gold given me by the Emperor of Blefuscu, together with his Majesty's picture at full length, and some other rarities of that country. I gave him two purses of two hundred *sprugs* each, and promised, when we arrived in Eng-land, to make him a present of a cow and a sheep big with young.

I shall not trouble the reader with a particular account of this voyage; which was very prosperous for the most part. We arrived in the Downs on the 13th of April 1702. I had only one misfortune, that the rats on board carried away one of my sheep; I found her bones in a hole, picked clean from the flesh. The rest of my cattle I got safe on shore, and set them a grazing in a bowling-green at Greenwich, where the fineness of the grass made them feed very heartily, although I had always feared the contrary; neither could I possibly have preserved them in so long a voyage, if the captain had not allowed me some of his best bisket, which rubbed to powder, and mingled with water, was their constant food. The short time I continued in England, I made a considerable profit by shewing my cattle to many persons of qual-ity, and others: and before I began my second voyage, I sold them for six hundred pounds. Since my last return, I find the breed is considerably in-creased, especially the sheep; which I hope will prove much to the advan-tage of the woollen manufacture, by the fineness of the fleeces.

I stayed but two months with my wife and family; for my insatiable de-sire of seeing foreign countries would suffer me to continue no longer. I left fifteen hundred pounds with my wife, and fixed her in a good house at Redriff. My remaining stock I carried with me, part in money, and part in goods, in hopes to improve my fortunes. My eldest uncle, John, had left me an estate in land, near Epping, of about thirty pounds a year; and I had a long lease of the Black-Bull in Fetter-lane, which yielded me as much more: so, that I was not in any danger of leaving my family upon the parish. My son Johnny, named so after his uncle, was at the grammar-school, and a towardly child. My daughter Betty (who is now well married, and hath children) was then at her needle-work. I took leave of my wife, and boy and girl, with tears on both sides; and went on board the *Adventure*, a merchant-ship of three hundred tons, bound for Surat, Captain John Nicholas of Liverpool, commander. But my account of this voyage must be referred to the second part of my travels.

THE END OF THE FIRST PART

PART II
A VOYAGE TO BROBDINGNAG

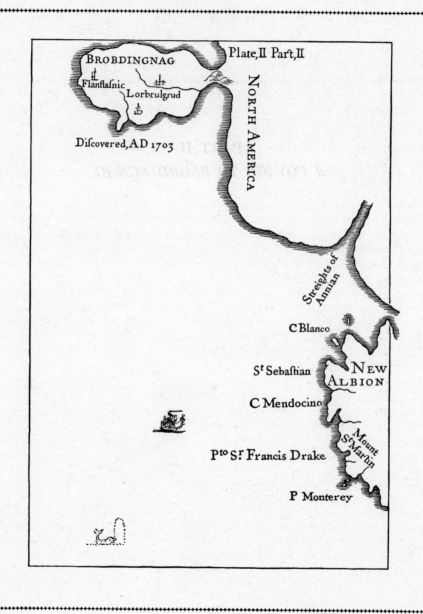

Plate, II Part, II

BROBDINGNAG

Flanflasnic

Lorbrulgrud

Discovered, AD 1703

NORTH AMERICA

Streights of Annian

C Blanco

St Sebastian

NEW ALBION

C Mendocino

Mount St Martin

Pto Sr Francis Drake

P Monterey

CHAPTER I

A great storm described. The long boat sent to fetch water, the author goes with it to discover the country. He is left on shore, is seized by one of the natives, and carried to a farmer's house. His reception there, with several accidents that happened there. A description of the inhabitants.

HAVING been condemned by nature and fortune to an active and restless life, in ten months after my return, I again left my native country, and took shipping in the Downs on the 20th day of June 1702, in the *Adventure*, Capt. John Nicholas, a Cornish man, commander, bound for Surat. We had a very prosperous gale until we arrived at the Cape of Good-hope, where we landed for fresh water; but discovering a leak we unshipped our goods, and wintered there; for the captain falling sick of an ague, we could not leave the cape until the end of March. We then set sail, and had a good voyage until we passed the Streights of Madagascar; but having got northward of that island, and to about five degrees south-latitude, the winds, which in those seas are observed to blow a constant equal gale between the north and west, from the beginning of December to the beginning of May, on the 19th of April began to blow with much greater violence, and more westerly than usual; continuing so for twenty days together, during which time we were driven a little to the east of the Molucca Islands, and about three degrees northward of the line, as our captain found by an observation he took the 2d of May, at which time the wind ceased, and it was a perfect calm, whereat I was not a little rejoyced. But he being a man well experienced in the navigation of those seas, bid us all prepare against a storm, which accordingly happened the day following: for a southern wind, called the southern monsoon, began to set in.

Finding it was like to overblow, we took in our sprit-sail, and stood by to hand the fore-sail; but making foul weather, we looked the guns were all fast, and handed the missen. The ship lay very broad off, so we thought it better spooning before the sea, than trying or hulling. We reeft the foresail and set him, we hawled aft the fore-sheet; the helm was hard a-weather. The ship wore bravely. We belayed the fore down-hall; but the sail was split, and we hawled down the yard, and got the sail into the ship, and unbound all the things clear of it. It was a very fierce storm; the sea broke strange and dangerous. We hawled off upon the lanniard of the wipstaff, and helped the man at helm. We would not get down our top-mast, but let all stand, because she scudded before the sea very well, and we knew that the top-mast being aloft, the ship was the wholesomer, and made better

45

way through the sea, seeing we had sea-room. When the storm was over, we set fore-sail and main-sail, and brought the ship to. Then we set the missen, main-top-sail and the foretop-sail. Our course was east northeast, the wind was at south-west. We got the star-board tack aboard, we cast off our weather-braces and lifts; we set in the lee-braces, and hawled forward by the weather-bowlings, and hawled them tight, and belayed them, and hawled over the missen tack to windward, and kept her full and by as near as she would lye.

During this storm, which was followed by a strong wind west-south-west, we were carried by my computation about five hundred leagues to the east, so that the oldest sailor on board could not tell in what part of the world we were. Our provisions held out well, our ship was staunch, and our crew all in good health; but we lay in the uppermost distress for water. We thought it best to hold on the same course rather than turn more northerly, which might have brought us to the north-west parts of great Tartary, and into the frozen sea.

On the 16th day of June 1703, a boy on the top-mast discovered land. On the 17th we came in full view of a great island or continent, (for we knew not whether) on the south-side whereof was a small neck of land jutting out into the sea, and a creek too shallow to hold a ship of above one hundred tuns. We cast anchor within a league of this creek, and our captain sent a dozen of his men well armed in the long boat, with vessels for water, if any could be found. I desired his leave to go with them, that I might see the country, and make what discoveries I could. When we came to land we saw no river or spring, nor any sign of inhabitants. Our men therefore wandered on the shore to find out some fresh water near the sea, and I walked alone about a mile on the other side, where I observed the country all barren and rocky. I now began to be weary, and seeing nothing to entertain my curiosity, I returned gently down towards the creek; and the sea being full in my view, I saw our men already got into the boat, and rowing for life to the ship. I was going to halloo after them, although it had been to little purpose, when I observed a huge creature walking after them in the sea, as fast as he could: he waded not much deeper than his knees, and took prodigious strides: but our men had the start of him half a league, and the sea thereabouts being full of sharp pointed rocks, the monster was not able to overtake the boat. This I was afterwards told, for I durst not stay to see the issue of that adventure; but run as fast as I could the way I first went; and then climbed up a steep hill, which gave me some prospect of the country. I found it fully cultivated; but that which first surprized me was the length of the grass, which in those grounds that seemed to be kept for hay, was above twenty foot high.

I fell into a high road, for so I took it to be, although it served to the inhabitants only as a foot path through a field of barley. Here I walked on for some time, but could see little on either side, it being now near harvest, and the corn rising at least forty foot. I was an hour walking to the end of this field; which was fenced in with a hedge of at least one hundred and twenty foot high, and the trees so lofty that I could make no computation of their altitude. There was a stile to pass from this field into the next: it had four steps, and a stone to cross over when you came to the utmost. It was impossible for me to climb this stile, because every step was six foot high, and the upper stone above twenty. I was endeavouring to find some gap in the hedge, when I discovered one of the inhabitants in the next field advancing towards the stile, of the same size with him whom I saw in the sea pursuing our boat. He appeared as tall as an ordinary spire-steeple; and took about ten yards at every stride, as near as I could guess. I was struck with the utmost fear and astonishment, and ran to hide my self in the corn, from whence I saw him at the top of the stile, looking back into the next field on the right hand; and heard him call in a voice many degrees louder than a speaking trumpet; but the noise was so high in the air, that at first I certainly thought it was thunder. Whereupon seven monsters like himself came towards him with reaping-hooks in their hands, each hook about the largeness of six scythes. These people were not so well clad as the first, whose servants or labourers they seemed to be. For, upon some words he spoke, they went to reap the corn in the field where I lay. I kept from them at as great a distance as I could, but was forced to move with extreme difficulty; for the stalks of the corn were sometimes not above a foot distant, so that I could hardly squeeze my body betwixt them. However, I made a shift to go forward until I came to a part of the field where the corn had been laid by the rain and wind: here it was impossible for me to advance a step; for the stalks were so interwoven that I could not creep through, and the beards of the fallen ears so strong and pointed, that they pierced through my cloaths into my flesh. At the same time I heard the reapers not above an hundred yards behind me. Being quite dispirited with toil, and wholly overcome by grief and despair, I lay down between two ridges, and heartily wished I might there end my days. I bemoaned my desolate widow, and fatherless children: I lamented my own folly and wilfulness in attempting a second voyage against the advice of all my friends and relations. In this terrible agitation of mind I could not forbear thinking of Lilliput, whose inhabitants looked upon me as the greatest prodigy that ever appeared in the world; where I was able to draw an imperial fleet in my hand, and perform those other actions which will be recorded for ever in the chronicles of that empire, while posterity shall hardly believe them, although attested by millions. I reflected what a mortification it must prove to me to appear as inconsiderable in this nation, as one single Lilliputian would be among us. But, this I conceived was to be the least of my misfortunes: for, as human creatures are observed to be more savage and cruel in proportion to their bulk; what could I expect but to be a morsel in the mouth of the first among these enormous barbarians, who should happen to seize me? Undoubtedly philosophers are in the right when they tell us, that nothing is great or little, otherwise than by comparison: it might have pleased fortune to let the Lilliputians find some nation, where the people were as diminutive with respect to them as they were to me. And who knows but that even this prodigious race of mortals might be equally overmatched in some distant part of the world, whereof we have yet no discovery?

Scared and confounded as I was, I could not forbear going on with these reflections; when one of the reapers approaching within ten yards of the ridge where I lay, made me apprehend, that with the next step I should be squashed to death under his foot, or cut in two with his reaping-hook. And therefore when he was again about to move, I screamed as loud as fear could make me. Whereupon the huge creature trod short, and looking round about under him for some time, at last espied me as I lay on the ground. He considered a while with the caution of one who endeavours to lay hold on a small dangerous animal in such a manner that it shall not be able either to scratch or to bite him; as I my self have sometimes done with a weasel in England. At length he ventured to take me up behind by the middle between his fore-finger and thumb, and brought me within three yards of his eyes, that he might behold my shape more perfectly. I guessed his meaning; and my good fortune gave me so much presence of mind, that I resolved not to struggle in the least, as he held me in the air above sixty foot from the ground; although he grievously pinched my sides, for fear I should slip through his fingers. All I ventured was to raise mine eyes towards the sun, and place my hands together in a supplicating posture, and to speak some words in an humble melancholy tone, suitable to the condition I then was in. For, I apprehended every moment that he would dash me against the ground, as we usually do any little hateful animal which we have a mind to destroy. But my good star would have it, that he appeared pleased with my voice and gestures, and began to look upon me as a curiosity; much wondering to hear me pronounce articulate words, although he could not understand them. In the mean time, I was not able to forbear groaning and shedding tears, and turning my head towards my sides; letting him know, as well as I could, how cruelly I was hurt by the pressure of his thumb and finger. He seemed to apprehend my meaning; for, lifting up the lappet of his coat, he put me gently into it, and immediately ran along with me to his master, who was a substantial farmer, and the same person I had first seen in the field.

The farmer having (as I supposed by their talk) received such an account of me as his servant could give him, took a piece of a small straw, about the size of a walking staff, and therewith lifted up the lappets of my coat; which it seems he thought to be some kind of covering that nature had given me. He blew my hairs aside to take a better view of my face. He called his hinds about him, and asked them (as I afterwards learned) whether they had ever seen in the fields any little creature that resembled me. He then placed me softly on the ground upon all four; but I got immediately up, and walked slowly backwards and forwards, to let those people see I had no intent to run away. They all sate down in a circle about me, the better to observe my motions. I pulled off my hat, and made a low bow towards the farmer: I fell on my knees, and lifted up my hands and eyes, and spoke several words as loud as I could: I took a purse of gold out of my pocket, and humbly presented it to him. He received it on the palm of his hand, then applied it close to his eye, to see what it was, and afterwards turned it several times with the point of a pin, (which he took out of his sleeve,) but could make nothing of it. Whereupon I made a sign that he should place his hand on the ground: I then took the purse, and opening it, poured all the gold into his palm. There were six Spanish-pieces of four pistoles each, besides twenty or thirty smaller coins. I saw him wet the tip of his little finger upon his tongue, and take up one of my largest pieces, and then another; but he seemed to be wholly ignorant what they were. He made me a sign to put them again into my purse, and the purse again into my pocket; which after offering to him several times, I thought it best to do.

The farmer by this time was convinced I must be a rational creature. He spoke often to me; but the sound of his voice pierced my ears like that of a water-mill; yet his words were articulate enough. I answered as loud as I could in several languages; and he often laid his ear within two yards of me, but all in vain, for we were wholly unintelligible to each other. He then sent his servants to their work, and taking his handkerchief out of his pocket, he doubled and spread it on his hand, which he placed flat on the ground with the palm upwards, making me a sign to step into it, as I could easily do, for it was not above a foot in thickness. I thought it my part to obey; and for fear of falling, laid my self at full length upon the handkerchief, with the remainder of which he lapped me up to the head for further security; and in this manner carried me home to his house. There he called his wife, and shewed me to her; but she screamed and ran back as women in England do at the sight of a toad or a spider. However, when she had a while seen my behaviour, and how well I observed the signs her husband made, she was soon reconciled, and by degrees grew extreamly tender of me.

It was about twelve at noon, and a servant brought in dinner. It was only one substantial dish of meat (fit for the plain condition of an husband-man) in a dish of about four and twenty foot diameter. The company were the farmer and wife, three children, and an old grandmother: when they were sat down, the farmer placed me at some distance from him on the table which was thirty foot high from the floor. I was in a terrible fright, and kept as far as I could from the edge, for fear of falling. The wife minced a bit of meat, then crumbled some bread on a trencher, and placed it before me. I made her a low bow, took out my knife and fork, and fell to eat; which gave them exceeding delight. The mistress sent her maid for a small dram-cup, which held about two gallons; and filled it with drink: I took up the vessel with much difficulty in both hands, and in a most respectful manner drank to her ladyship's health, expressing the words as loud as I could in English; which made the company laugh so heartily, that I was almost deafened with the noise. This liquor tasted like a small cyder, and was not unpleasant. Then the master made me a sign to come to his trencher side; but as I walked on the table, being in great surprize all the time, as the indulgent reader will easily conceive and excuse, I happened to stumble against a crust, and fell flat on my face, but received no hurt. I got up immediately, and observing the good people to be in much concern, I took my hat (which I held under my arm out of good manners) and waving it over my head, made three huzza's, to shew I had got no mischief by the fall. But advancing forwards toward my master (as I shall henceforth call him) his youngest son who sate next him, an arch boy of about ten years old, took me up by the legs, and held me so high in the air, that I trembled every limb; but his father snatched me from him; and at the same time gave him such a box on the left ear, as would have felled an European troop of horse to the earth; ordering him to be taken from the table. But, being afraid the boy might owe me a spight; and well remembring how mischievous all children among us naturally are to sparrows, rabbits, young kittens, and puppy-dogs, I fell on my knees, and pointing to the boy, made my master understand, as well as I could, that I desired his son be pardoned. The father complied, and the lad took his seat again; whereupon I went to him and kissed his hand, which my master took, and made him stroak me gently with it.

In the midst of dinner my mistress's favourite cat leapt into her lap. I heard a noise behind me like that of a dozen stocking-weavers at work; and turning my head, I found it proceeded from the purring of this animal, who seemed to be three times larger than an ox, as I computed by the view of her head, and one of her paws, while her mistress was feeding and stroaking her. The fierceness of this creature's countenance altogether discomposed me; although I stood at the further end of the table, above fifty foot off; and although my mistress held her fast for fear she might give a spring, and seize me in her talons. But, it happened there was no danger; for the cat took not the least notice of me when my master placed me within three yards of her. And as I have been always told, and found true by experience in my travels, that flying, or discovering fear before a fierce animal, is a certain way to make it pursue or attack you; so I resolved, in this dangerous juncture to shew no manner of concern. I walked with intrepidity five or six times before the very head of the cat, and came within half a yard of her; whereupon she drew herself back, as if she were more afraid of me: I had less apprehension concerning the dogs, whereof three or four came into the room, as it is usual in farmers' houses; one of which was a mastiff equal in bulk to four elephants, and a grey-hound somewhat taller than the mastiff, but not so large.

When dinner was almost done, the nurse came in with a child of a year old in her arms; who immediately spyed me, and began a squall that you might have heard from Londonbridge to Chelsea, after the usual oratory of infants, to get me for a play-thing. The mother out of pure indulgence took me up, and put me towards the child, who presently seized me by the middle, and got my head in his mouth, where I roared so loud that the urchin was frighted, and let me drop; and I should have infallibly broke my neck, if the mother had not held her apron under me. The nurse, to quiet her babe, made use of a rattle, which was a kind of hollow vessel filled with great stones, and fastned by a cable to the child's waist: but all in vain, so that she was forced to apply the last remedy by giving it suck. I must confess no object ever disgusted me so much as the sight of her monstrous breast, which I cannot tell what to compare with, so as to give the curious reader an idea of its bulk, shape, and colour. It stood prominent six foot, and could not be less than sixteen in circumference. The nipple was about half the bigness of my head, and the hue both of that and the dug so varified with spots, pimples, and freckles, that nothing could appear more nauseous: for I had a near sight of her, she sitting down the more conveniently to give suck, and I standing on the table. This made me reflect upon the fair skins of our English ladies, who appear so beautiful to us, only because they are of our own size, and their defects not to be seen, but through a magnifying glass, where we find by experiment, that the smoothest and whitest skins look rough and coarse, and ill coloured.

I remember when I was at Lilliput, the complexions of those diminutive people appeared to me the fairest in the world: and talking upon this subject with a person of learning there, who was an intimate friend of mine, he said, that my face appeared much fairer and smoother when he looked on me from the ground, than it did upon a nearer view when I took him up in my hand, and brought him close; which he confessed was at first a very shocking sight. He said, he could discover great holes in my skin; that the stumps of my beard were ten times stronger than the bristles of a boar; and my complexion made up of several colours altogether disagreeable: although I must beg leave to say for my self, that I am as fair as most of my sex and country, and very little sunburnt by all my travels. On the other side, discoursing of the ladies in that emperor's court, he used to tell me, one had freckles, another too wide a mouth, a third too large a nose; nothing of which I was able to distinguish. I confess, this reflection was obvious enough; which, however, I could not forbear, lest the reader might think those vast creatures were actually deformed: for I must do them justice to say, they are a comely race of people; and particularly the features of my master's countenance, although he were but a farmer, when I beheld him from the height of sixty foot, appeared very well proportioned.

When dinner was done, my master went out to his labourers; and, as I could discover by his voice and gesture, gave his wife a strict charge to take care of me. I was very much tired and disposed to sleep, which my mistress perceiving, she put me on her own bed, and covered me with a clean white handkerchief, but larger and coarser than the main sail of a man of war.

I slept about two hours, and dreamed I was at home with my wife and children, which aggravated my sorrows when I awaked and found my self alone in a vast room, between two and three hundred foot wide, and above two hundred high; lying in a bed twenty yards wide. My mistress was gone about her household affairs, and had locked me in. The bed was eight yards from the floor. Some natural necessities required me to get down: I durst not presume to call, and if I had, it would have been in vain, with such a voice as mine, at so great a distance from the room where I lay, to the kitchen where the family kept. While I was under these circumstances, two rats crept up the curtains, and ran smelling backwards and forwards on the bed: one of them came up almost to my face; whereupon I rose in a fright, and drew out my hanger to defend my self. These horrible animals had the boldness to attack me on both sides, and one of them held his fore feet at my collar; but I had the good fortune to rip up his belly before he could do me any mischief. He fell down at my feet; and the other seeing the fate of his comrade, made his escape, but not without one good wound on the back, which I gave him as he fled, and made the blood run trickling from him. After this exploit, I walked gently to and fro on the bed, to recover my breath and loss of spirits. These creatures were of the size of a large mastiff, but infinitely more nimble and fierce; so that, if I had taken off my belt before I went to sleep, I must have infallibly been torn to pieces and devoured. I measured the tail of the dead rat, and found it to be two yards long, wanting an inch; but it went against my stomach to drag the carcass off the bed, where it lay still bleeding; I observed it had yet some life, but with a strong slash cross the neck, I thoroughly dispatched it.

Soon after, my mistress came into the room, who seeing me all bloody, ran and took me up in her hand. I pointed to the dead rat, smiling and making other signs to shew I was not hurt; whereat she was extremely rejoyced, calling the maid to take up the dead rat with a pair of tongs, and throw it out of the window. Then she set me on a table, where I shewed her my hanger, all bloody, and wiping it on the lappet of my coat, returned it to the scabbard. I was pressed to do more than one thing, which another could not do for me; and therefore endeavoured to make my mistress understand, that I desired to be set down on the floor; which after she had done, my bashfulness would not suffer me to express my self farther than by pointing to the door, and bowing several times. The good woman with much difficulty at last perceived what I would be at; and taking me up again in her hand, walked into the garden, where she set me down. I went on one side about two hundred yards; and beckoning to her not to look or to follow me, I hid my self between two leaves of sorrel, and there discharged the necessities of nature.

I hope the gentle reader will excuse me for dwelling on these, and the like particulars; which however insignificant they may appear to grovelling vulgar minds, yet will certainly help a philosopher to enlarge his thoughts and imagination, and apply them to the benefit of publick as well as private life; which was my sole design in presenting this, and other accounts of my travels to the world; wherein, I have been chiefly studious of truth, without affecting any ornaments of learning, or of style. But the whole scene of this voyage made so strong an impression on my mind, and is so deeply fixed in my memory, that in committing it to paper, I did not omit one material circumstance: however, upon a strict review, I blotted out several passages of less moment which were in my first copy, for fear of being censured as tedious and trifling, whereof travellers are often, perhaps not without justice, accused.

CHAPTER II

A description of the farmer's daughter. The author carried to a market-town, and then to the metropolis. The particulars of his journey.

My mistress had a daughter of nine years old, a child of toward parts for her age, very dexterous at her needle, and skilful in dressing her baby. Her mother and she contrived to fit up the baby's cradle for me against night: the cradle was put into a small drawer of a cabinet, and the drawer placed upon a hanging shelf for fear of the rats. This was my bed all the time I stayed with those people, although made more convenient by degrees, as I began to learn their language, and make my wants known. This young girl was so handy, that after I had once or twice pulled off my cloaths before her, she was able to dress and undress me, although I never gave her that trouble when she would let me do either my self. She made me seven shirts, and some other linen of as fine cloth as could be got, which indeed was coarser than sackcloth, and these she constantly washed for me with her own hands. She was likewise my school-mistress to teach me the language: when I pointed to any thing, she told me the name of it in her own tongue, so that in a few days I was able to call for whatever I had a mind to. She was very good-natured, and not above forty foot high, being little for her age. She gave me the name of Grildrig, which the family took up, and afterwards the whole kingdom. The word imports what the Latins call *nanunculus*, the Italians *homunceletino*, and the English *mannikin*. To her I chiefly owe my preservation in that country: we never parted while I was there; I called her my Glumdalclitch, or little nurse: and I should be guilty of great ingratitude, if I omitted this honourable mention of her care and affection towards me, which I heartily wish it lay in my power to requite as she deserves, instead of being the innocent, but unhappy instrument of her disgrace, as I have too much reason to fear.

It now began to be known and talked of in the neighbourhood, that my master had found a strange animal in the field, about the bigness of a *splacknuck*, but exactly shaped in every part like a human creature; which it likewise imitated in all its actions; seemed to speak in a little language of its own, had already learned several words of theirs, went erect upon two legs, was tame and gentle, would come when it was called, do whatever it was bid, had the finest limbs in the world, and a complexion fairer than a nobleman's daughter of three years old. Another farmer who lived hard by, and was a particular friend of my master, came on a visit, on purpose, to enquire into the truth of this story. I was immediately produced, and placed upon a table; where I walked as I was commanded, drew my hanger, put it up again, made my reverence to my master's guest, asked him in his own language how he did, and told him he was welcome; just as my little nurse had instructed me. This man, who was old and dim-sighted, put on his spectacles to behold me better, at which I could not forbear laughing very heartily; for his eyes appeared like the full-moon shining into a chamber at two windows. Our people, who discovered the cause of my mirth, bore me company in laughing; at which the old fellow was fool enough to be angry and out of countenance. He had the character of a great miser: and to my misfortune he well deserved it, by the cursed advice he gave my master to shew me as a sight upon a market-day in the next town, which was half an hour's riding, about two and twenty miles from our house. I guessed there was some mischief contriving, when I observed my master and his friend whispering long together, sometimes pointing at me; and my fears made me fancy that I overheard and understood some of their words. But, the next morning Glumdalclitch my little nurse told me the whole matter, which she had cunningly picked out from her mother. The poor girl laid me on her bosom, and fell a weeping with shame and grief. She apprehended some mischief would happen to me, from rude, vulgar folks, who might squeeze me to death, or break one of my limbs by taking me in their hands. She had also observed how modest I was in my nature, how nicely I regarded my honour; and what an indignity I should conceive it to be exposed for money as a publick spectacle to the meanest of the people. She said her papa and mamma had promised that Grildrig should be hers; but now she found they meant to serve her as they did last year, when they pretended to give her a lamb; and yet, as soon as it was fat, sold it to a butcher. For my own part, I may truly affirm, that I was less concerned than my nurse. I had a strong hope which never left me, that I should one day recover my liberty; and as to the ignominy of being carried about for a monster, I considered my self to be a perfect stranger in the country; and, that such a misfortune could never be charged upon me as a reproach if ever I should return to England; since the King of Great Britain himself, in my condition, must have undergone the same distress.

My master, pursuant to the advice of his friend, carried me in a box the next market-day to the neighbouring town; and took along with him his little daughter, my nurse, upon a pillion behind him. The box was close on every side, with a little door for me to go in and out, and a few gimlet-holes to let in air. The girl had been so careful to put the quilt of her baby's bed into it, for me to lye down on. However, I was terribly shaken and discomposed in this journey, although it were but of half an hour. For the horse went about forty foot at every step; and trotted so high, that the agitation was equal to the rising and falling of a ship in a great storm, but much more frequent: our journey was somewhat further than from London to St. Albans. My master alighted at an inn which he used to frequent; and after consulting a while with the inn-keeper, and making some necessary preparations, he hired the *grultrud*, or cryer, to give notice through the town, of a strange creature, to be seen at the sign of the Green Eagle, not so big as a *splacknuck*, (an animal in that country very finely shaped, about six foot long) and in every part of the body resembling an human creature; could speak several words, and perform an hundred diverting tricks.

I was placed upon a table in the largest room of the inn, which might be near three hundred foot square. My little nurse stood on a low stool close to the table, to take care of me, and direct what I should do. My master, to avoid a croud, would suffer only thirty people at a time to see me. I walked about on the table as the girl commanded; she asked me questions as far as she knew my understanding of the language reached, and I answered them as loud as I could. I turned about several times to the company, paid my humble respects, said they were welcome; and used some other speeches I had been taught. I took up a thimble filled with liquor, which Glumdalclitch had given me for a cup, and drank their health. I drew out my hanger, and flourished with it after the manner of fencers in England. My nurse gave me part of a straw, which I exercised as a pike, having learned the art in my youth. I was that day shewn to twelve sets of company; and as often forced to go over again with the same fopperies, until I was half dead with weariness and vexation. For, those who had seen me, made such wonderful reports, that the people were ready to break down the doors to come in. My master for his own interest would not suffer any one to touch me, except my nurse; and, to prevent danger, benches were set around the table at such a distance, as put me out of every body's reach. However, an unlucky school-boy aimed a hazel nut directly at my head, which very narrowly missed me; otherwise, it came with so much violence, that it would have infallibly knocked out my brains; for it was almost as large as a small pumpion: but I had the satisfaction to see the young rogue well beaten, and turned out of the room.

My master gave publick notice, that he would shew me again the next market-day: and, in the mean time, he prepared a more convenient vehicle for me, which he had reason enough to do; for I was so tired with my first journey, and with entertaining company eight hours together, that I could hardly stand upon my legs, or speak a word. It was at least three days before I recovered my strength; and that I might have no rest at home, all the neighbouring gentlemen from an hundred miles round, hearing of my fame, came to see me at my master's own house. There could not be fewer than thirty persons with their wives and children; (for the country is very populous;) and my master demanded the rate of a full room whenever he shewed me at home, although it were only to a single family. So, that for some time, I had but little ease every day of the week, (except Wednesday, which is their sabbath) although I were not carried to the town.

My master, finding how profitable I was like to be, resolved to carry me to the most considerable cities of the kingdom. Having therefore provided himself with all things necessary for a long journey, and settled his affairs at home, he took leave of his wife; and upon the 17th of August 1703, about two months after my arrival, we set out for the metropolis, situated near the middle of that empire, and about three thousand miles distance from our house: my master made his daughter Glumdalclitch ride behind him. She carried me on her lap in a box tied about her waist. The girl had lined it on all sides with the softest cloth she could get, well quilted underneath; furnished it with her baby's bed, provided me with linnen and other necessaries; and made every thing as convenient as she could. We had no other company but a boy of the house, who rode after us with the luggage.

My master's design was to shew me in all the towns by the way, and to step out of the road for fifty or an hundred miles, to any village or person of quality's house where he might expect custom. We made easy journies of not above seven or eight score miles a day: for Glumdalclitch, on purpose to spare me, complained she was tired with the trotting of the horse. She often took me out of my box at my own desire, to give me air, and shew me the country; but always held me fast by leading-strings. We passed over five or six rivers many degrees broader and deeper than the Nile or the Ganges; and there was hardly a rivulet so small as the Thames at London-bridge. We were ten weeks in our journey; and I was shewn in eighteen large towns, besides many villages and private families.

On the 26th day of October, we arrived at the metropolis, called in their language "Lorbrulgrud," or "Pride of the Universe." My master took a lodging in the principal street of the city, not far from the royal palace; and put out bills in the usual form, containing an exact description of my person and parts. He hired a large room between three and four hundred foot wide. He provided a table sixty foot in diameter, upon which I was to act my part; and pallisadoed it round three foot from the edge, and as many high, to prevent my falling over. I was shewn ten times a day to the wonder and satisfaction of all people. I could now speak the language tolerably well; and perfectly understood every word that was spoken to me. Besides, I had learned their alphabet, and could make a shift to explain a sentence here and there; for Glumdalclitch had been my instructer while we were at home, and at leisure hours during our journey. She carried a little book in her pocket, not much larger than a Sanson's Atlas; it was a common treatise for the use of young girls, giving a short account of their religion; out of this she taught me my letters, and interpreted the words.

CHAPTER III

The author sent for to court. The queen buys him of his master the farmer, and presents him to the king. He disputes with his Majesty's great scholars. An apartment at court provided for the author. He is in high favour with the queen. He stands up for the honour of his own country. His quarrels with the queen's dwarf.

THE frequent labours I underwent every day, made in a few weeks a very considerable change in my health: the more my master got by me, the more unsatiable he grew. I had quite lost my stomach, and was almost reduced to a skeleton. The farmer observed it; and concluding I soon must die, resolved to make as good a hand of me as he could. While he was thus reasoning and resolving with himself, a *slardral*, or gentleman usher, came from court, commanding my master to bring me immediately thither for the diversion of the queen and her ladies. Some of the latter had already been to see me; and reported strange things of my beauty, behaviour, and good sense. Her Majesty, and those who attended her, were beyond measure delighted with my demeanor. I fell on my knees, and begged the honour of kissing her imperial foot; but this gracious princess held out her little finger towards me, (after I was set on a table) which I embraced in both my arms, and put the tip of it, with the utmost respect, to my lip. She made me some general questions about my country and my travels, which I answered as distinctly, and in as few words as I could. She asked, whether I would be content to live at court. I bowed down to the board of the table, and humbly answered, that I was my master's slave; but, if I were at my own disposal, I should be proud to devote my life to her Majesty's service. She then asked my master, whether he were willing to sell me at a good price. He, who apprehended I could not live a month, was ready enough to part with me; and demanded a thousand pieces of gold; which were ordered him on the spot, each piece being about the bigness of eight hundred moydores: but, allowing for the proportion of all things between that country and Europe, and the high price of gold among them, was hardly so great a sum as a thousand guineas would be in England. I then said to the queen, since I was now her Majesty's most humble creature and vassal, I must beg the favour, that Glumdalclitch, who had always tended me with so much care and kindness, and understood to do it so well, might be admitted into her service, and continue to be my nurse and instructor. Her Majesty agreed to my petition; and easily got the farmer's consent, who was glad enough to have his daughter preferred at court: and the poor girl herself was not able to hide her joy. My late master withdrew, bidding me farewell, and saying he had left me in a good service; to which I replyed not a word, only making him a slight bow.

The queen observed my coldness; and when the farmer was gone out of the apartment, asked me the reason. I made bold to tell her Majesty, that I owed no other obligation to my late master, than his not dashing out the brains of a poor harmless creature found by chance in his field; which obligation was amply recompensed by the gain he had made in shewing me through half the kingdom, and the price he had now sold me for. That, the life I had since led, was laborious enough to kill an animal of ten times my strength. That, my health was much impaired by the continual drudgery of entertaining the rabble every hour of the day; and that, if my master had not thought my life in danger, her Majesty would not have got so cheap a bargain. But, as I was out of all fear of being ill treated under the protection of so great and good an empress, the ornament of nature, the darling of the world, the delight of her subjects, the phœnix of the creation; so, I hoped, my late master's apprehensions would appear to be groundless; for I already found my spirits to revive by the influence of her most august presence.

This was the sum of my speech, delivered with great improprieties and hesitation; the latter part was altogether framed in the style peculiar to that people, whereof I learned some phrases from Glumdalclitch, while she was carrying me to court.

The queen giving great allowance for my defectiveness in speaking, was however surprized at so much wit and good sense in so diminutive an animal. She took me in her own hand, and carried me to the king, who was then retired to his cabinet. His Majesty, a prince of much gravity, and austere countenance, not well observing my shape at first view, asked the queen after a cold manner, how long it was since she grew fond of a *splacknuck*; for such it seems he took me to be, as I lay upon my breast in her Majesty's right hand. But this princess, who hath an infinite deal of wit and humour, set me gently on my feet upon the scrutore; and commanded me to give his Majesty an account of my self, which I did in a very few words; and Glumdalclitch, who attended at the cabinet door, and could not endure I should be out of her sight, being admitted, confirmed all that had passed from my arrival at her father's house.

The king, although he be as learned a person as any in his dominions, had been educated in the study of philosophy, and particularly mathematicks; yet, when he observed my shape exactly, and saw me walk erect, before I began to speak, conceived I might be a piece of clockwork, (which is in that country arrived to a very great perfection) contrived by some ingenious artist. But, when he heard my voice, and found what I delivered to be regular and rational, he could not conceal his astonishment. He was by no means satisfied with the relation I gave him of the manner I came into his kingdom; but thought it a story concerted between Glumdalclitch and her father, who had taught me a sett of words to make me sell at a higher price. Upon this imagination, he put several other questions to me, and still received rational answers, no otherwise defective than by a foreign accent, and an imperfect knowledge in the language; with some rustick phrases which I had learned at the farmer's house, and did not suit the polite style of a court.

His Majesty sent for three great scholars who were then in their weekly waiting (according to the custom in that country.) These gentlemen, after they had a while examined my shape with much nicety, were of different opinions concerning me. They all agreed, that I could not be produced according to the regular laws of nature; because I was not framed with a capacity of preserving my life, either by swiftness, or climbing of trees, or digging holes in the earth. They observed by my teeth, which they viewed with great exactness, that I was a carnivorous animal; yet most quadrupeds being an over-match for me, and field-mice, with some others, too nimble, they could not imagine how I should be able to support my self, unless I fed upon snails and other insects; which they offered by many learned arguments to evince, that I could not possibly do. One of them seemed to think, that I might be an embrio, or abortive birth. But this opinion was rejected by the other two, who observed my limbs to be perfect and finished; and that I had lived several years, as it was manifested from my beard; the stumps whereof they plainly discovered through a magnifying glass. They would not allow me to be a dwarf, because my littleness was beyond all degrees of comparison; for the queen's favourite dwarf, the smallest ever known in that kingdom, was near thirty foot high. After much debate, they concluded unanimously, that I was only *relplum scalcath*, which is interpreted literally *lusus naturæ*, a determination exactly agreeable to the modern philosophy of Europe, whose professors, disdaining the old evasion of occult causes, whereby the followers of Aristotle endeavour in vain to disguise their ignorance, have invented this wonderful solution of all difficulties, to the unspeakable advancement of human knowledge.

After this decisive conclusion, I entreated to be heard a word or two. I applied my self to the king, and assured his Majesty, that I came from a country which abounded with several millions of both sexes, and of my own stature; where the animals, trees, and houses, were all in proportion, and where, by consequence, I might be as able to defend my self, and to find sustenance, as any of his Majesty's subjects could do here; which I took for a full answer to those gentlemen's arguments. To this they only replied with a smile of contempt; saying, that the farmer had instructed me very well in my lesson. The king, who had a much better understanding, dismissing his learned men, sent for the farmer, who by good fortune was not yet gone out of town: having therefore first examined him privately, and then confronted him with me and the young girl, his Majesty began to think, that what we told him might possibly be true. He desired the queen to order, that a particular care should be taken of me; and was of opinion, that Glumdalclitch should still continue in her office of tending me, because he observed we had a great affection for each other. A convenient apartment was provided for her at court; she had a sort of governess appointed to take care of her education, a maid to dress her, and two other servants for menial offices; but, the care of me was wholly appropriated to her self. The queen commanded her own cabinet-maker to contrive a box, that might serve me for a bed-chamber, after the model that Glumdalclitch and I should agree upon. This man was a most ingenious artist; and according to my directions, in three weeks finished for me a wooden chamber of sixteen foot square, and twelve high; with sash windows, a door, and two closets, like a London bed-chamber. The board that made the cieling was to be lifted up and down by two hinges, to put in a bed ready furnished by her Majesty's upholsterer; which Glumdalclitch took out every day to air, made it with her own hands, and letting it down at night, locked up the roof over me. A nice workman, who was famous for little curiosities, undertook to make me two chairs, with backs and frames, of a substance not unlike ivory; and two tables, with a cabinet to put my things in. The room was quilted on all sides, as well as the floor and the cieling, to prevent any accident from the carelessness of those who carried me; and to break the force of a jolt when I went in a coach. I desired a lock for my door to prevent rats and mice from coming in: the smith, after several attempts, made the smallest that was ever seen among them; for I have known a larger at the gate of a gentleman's house in England. I made a shift to keep the key in a pocket of my own, fearing Glumdalclitch might lose it. The queen likewise ordered the thinnest silks that could be gotten, to make me cloaths; not much thicker than an English blanket, very cumbersome until I was accustomed to them. They were after the fashion of the kingdom, partly resembling the Persian, and partly the Chinese; and are a very grave decent habit.

The queen became so fond of my company, that she could not dine without me. I had a table placed upon the same at which her Majesty eat, just at her left elbow; and a chair to sit on. Glumdalclitch stood upon a stool on the floor, near my table, to assist and take care of me. I had an entire set of silver dishes and plates, and other necessaries, which in proportion to those of the queen, were not much bigger than what I have seen in a London toy-shop, for the furniture of a baby-house: these, my little nurse kept in her pocket, in a silver box, and gave me at meals as I wanted them; always cleaning them her self. No person dined with the queen but the two princesses royal; the elder sixteen years old, and the younger at that time thirteen and a month. Her Majesty used to put a bit of meat upon one of my dishes, out of which I carved for my self; and her diversion was to see me eat in miniature. For the queen (who had indeed but a weak stomach) took up at one mouthful, as much as a dozen English farmers could eat at a meal, which to me was for some time a very nauseous sight. She would craunch the wing of a lark, bones and all, between her teeth, although it were nine times as large as that of a full grown turkey; and put a bit of bread in her mouth, as big as two twelve-penny loaves. She drank out of a golden cup, above a hogshead at a draught. Her knives were twice as long as a scythe set strait upon the handle. The spoons, forks, and other instruments, were all in the same proportion. I remember when Glumdalclitch carried me out of curiosity to see some of the tables at court, where ten or a dozen of these enormous knives and forks were lifted up together, I thought I had never until then beheld so terrible a sight.

It is the custom, that every Wednesday, (which as I have before observed, was their sabbath) the king and queen, with the royal issue of both
sexes, dine together in the apartment of his Majesty, to whom I was now
become a favourite; and, at these times my little chair and table were
placed at his left hand before one of the salt-sellers. This prince took a
pleasure in conversing with me; enquiring into the manners, religion, laws,
government, and learning of Europe, wherein I gave him the best account
I was able. His apprehension was so clear, and his judgment so exact, that
he made very wise reflections and observations upon all I said. But, I confess, that after I had been a little too copious in talking of my own beloved
country; of our trade, and wars by sea and land, of our schisms in religion,
and parties in the State; the prejudices of his education prevailed so far,
that he could not forbear taking me up in his right hand, and stroaking me
gently with the other, after an hearty fit of laughing, asked me whether I
were a Whig or a Tory. Then turning to his first minister, who waited behind him with a white staff, near as tall as the main-mast of the *Royal
Sovereign*, he observed, how contemptible a thing was human grandeur,
which could be mimicked by such diminutive insects as I: "And yet," said
he, "I dare engage, those creatures have their titles and distinctions of
honour; they contrive little nests and burrows, that they call houses and
cities; they make a figure in dress and equipage; they love, they fight, they
dispute, they cheat, they betray." And thus he continued on, while my colour
came and went several times, with indignation, to hear our noble country,
the mistress of arts and arms, the scourge of France, the arbitress of
Europe, the seat of virtue, piety, honour, and truth, the pride and envy of
the world, so contemptuously treated.

But, as I was not in a condition to resent injuries, so, upon mature
thoughts, I began to doubt whether I were injured or no. For, after having
been accustomed several months to the sight and converse of this people,
and observed every object upon which I cast mine eyes, to be of proportionable magnitude, the horror I had first conceived from their bulk and
aspect was so far worn off, that if I had then beheld a company of English
lords and ladies in their finery and birth-day cloaths, acting their several
parts in the most courtly manner of strutting, and bowing, and prating; to
say the truth, I should have been strongly tempted to laugh as much at
them, as this king and his grandees did at me. Neither indeed could I forbear smiling at my self, when the queen used to place me upon her hand
towards a looking-glass, by which both our persons appeared before me in
full view together; and there could nothing be more ridiculous than the
comparison: so that I really began to imagine my self dwindled many
degrees below my usual size.

Nothing angred and mortified me so much as the queen's dwarf, who being of the lowest stature that was ever in that country, (for I verily think
he was not full thirty foot high) became so insolent at seeing a creature so
much beneath him, that he would always affect to swagger and look big as
he passed by me in the queen's antichamber, while I was standing on some
table talking with the lords or ladies of the court; and he seldom failed of a
smart word or two upon my littleness; against which, I could only revenge

my self by calling him brother, challenging him to wrestle, and such repartees as are usual in the mouths of court pages. One day at dinner, this malicious little cubb was so nettled with something I had said to him, that raising himself upon the frame of her Majesty's chair, he took me up by the middle, as I was sitting down, not thinking any harm, and let me drop into a large silver bowl of cream; and then ran away as fast as he could. I fell over head and ears, and if I had not been a good swimmer, it might have gone very hard with me; for Glumdalclitch in that instant happened to be at the other end of the room; and the queen was in such a fright, that she wanted presence of mind to assist me. But my little nurse ran to my relief; and took me out, after I had swallowed above a quart of cream. I was put to bed; however, I received no other damage than the loss of a suit of cloaths, which was utterly spoiled. The dwarf was soundly whipped, and as a further punishment, forced to drink up the bowl of cream, into which he had thrown me; neither was he ever restored to favour: for, soon after, the queen bestowed him to a lady of high quality; so that I saw him no more, to my very great satisfaction; for I could not tell to what extremity such a malicious urchin might have carried his resentment.

He had before served me a scurvy trick, which set the queen a laughing, although at the same time she were heartily vexed, and would have immediately cashiered him, if I had not been so generous as to intercede. Her Majesty had taken a marrow-bone upon her plate; and after knocking out the marrow, placed the bone again in the dish erect as it stood before; the dwarf watching his opportunity, while Glumdalclitch was gone to the sideboard, mounted the stool that she stood on to take care of me at meals; took me up in both hands, and squeezing my legs together, wedged them into the marrow-bone above my waist; where I stuck for some time, and made a very ridiculous figure. I believe it was near a minute before any one knew what was become of me; for, I thought it below me to cry out. But, as princes seldom get their meat hot, my legs were not scalded, only my stockings and breeches in a sad condition. The dwarf at my entreaty had no other punishment than a sound whipping.

I was frequently rallied by the queen upon account of my fearfulness; and she used to ask me whether the people of my country were as great cowards as my self. The occasion was this. The kingdom is much pestered with flies in summer; and these odious insects, each of them as big as a Dunstable lark, hardly gave me any rest while I sat at dinner, with their continual humming and buzzing about mine ears. They would sometimes alight upon my victuals, and leave their loathsome excrement or spawn behind, which to me was very visible, although not to the natives of that country, whose large opticks were not so acute as mine in viewing smaller objects. Sometimes they would fix upon my nose or forehead, where they stung me to the quick, smelling very offensively; and I could easily trace that viscous matter, which our naturalists tell us enables those creatures to walk with their feet upwards upon a cieling. I had much ado to defend my self against these detestable animals, and could not forbear starting when they came on my face. It was the common practice of the dwarf to catch a number of these insects in his hand, as school-boys do among us, and let them out suddenly under my nose, on purpose to frighten me, and divert the queen. My remedy was to cut them in pieces with my knife as they flew in the air; wherein my dexterity was much admired.

I remember one morning when Glumdalclitch had set me in my box upon a window, as she usually did in fair days to give me air, (for I durst not venture to let the box be hung on a nail out of the window, as we do with cages in England) after I had lifted up one of my sashes, and sat down at my table to eat a piece of sweet-cake for my breakfast, above twenty wasps, allured by the smell, came flying into the room, humming louder than the drones of as many bagpipes. Some of them seized my cake, and carried it piece-meal away; others flew about my head and face, confounding me with the noise, and putting me in the utmost terror of their stings. However, I had the courage to rise and draw my hanger, and attack them in the air. I dispatched four of them, but the rest got away, and I presently shut my window. These insects were as large as partridges; I took out their stings, found them an inch and a half long, and as sharp as needles. I carefully preserved them all, and having since shewn them with some other curiosities in several parts of Europe; upon my return to England I gave three of them to Gresham College, and kept the fourth for my self.

CHAPTER IV

The country described. A proposal for correcting modern maps. The king's palace, and some account of the metropolis. The author's way of travelling. The chief temple described.

I NOW intend to give the reader a short description of this country, as far as I travelled in it, which was not above two thousand miles round Lorbrulgrud the metropolis. For, the queen, whom I always attended, never went further when she accompanied the king in his progresses; and there staid until his Majesty returned from viewing his frontiers. The whole extent of this prince's dominions reached but six thousand miles in length, and from three to five in breadth. From whence I cannot but conclude, that our geographers of Europe are in a great error, by supposing nothing but sea between Japan and California: for, it was ever my opinion, that there must be a balance of earth to counterpoise the great continent of Tartary; and therefore they ought to correct their maps and charts, by joining this vast tract of land to the north-west parts of America; wherein I shall be ready to lend them my assistance.

The kingdom is a peninsula, terminated to the north-east by a ridge of mountains thirty miles high, which are altogether impassable by reason of the volcanoes upon the tops. Neither do the most learned know what sort of mortals inhabit beyond those mountains, or whether they be inhabited at all. On the three other sides it is bounded by the ocean. There is not one sea-port in the whole kingdom; and those parts of the coasts into which the rivers issue, are so full of pointed rocks, and the sea generally so rough, that there is no venturing with the smallest of their boats; so, that these people are wholly excluded from any commerce with the rest of the world. But the large rivers are full of vessels, and abound with excellent fish; for they seldom get any from the sea, because the sea-fish are of the same size with those in Europe, and consequently not worth catching; whereby it is manifest, that nature in the production of plants and animals of so extraordinary a bulk, is wholly confined to this continent, of which I leave the reasons to be determined by philosophers. However, now and then they take a whale that happens to be dashed against the rocks, which the common people feed on heartily. These whales I have known so large, that a man could hardly carry one upon his shoulders; and sometimes for curiosity they are brought in hampers to Lorbrulgrud: I saw one of them in a dish at the king's table, which passed for a rarity; but I did not observe he was fond of it; for I think indeed the bigness disgusted him, although I have seen one somewhat larger in Greenland.

The country is well inhabited, for it contains fifty one cities, near an hundred walled towns, and a great number of villages. To satisfy my curious reader, it may be sufficient to describe Lorbrulgrud. This city stands upon almost two equal parts on each side the river that passes through. It contains above eighty thousand houses. It is in length three *glonglungs* (which make about fifty four English miles) and two and a half in breadth, as I measured it my self in the royal map made by the king's order, which was laid on the ground on purpose for me, and extended an hundred feet; I paced the diameter and circumference several times bare-foot, and computing by the scale, measured it pretty exactly.

The king's palace is no regular edifice, but an heap of buildings about seven miles round: the chief rooms are generally two hundred and forty foot high, and broad and long in proportion. A coach was allowed to Glumdalclitch and me, wherein her governess frequently took her out to see the town, or go among the shops; and I was always of the party, carried in my box; although the girl at my own desire, would often take me out, and hold me in her hand, that I might more conveniently view the houses and the people as we passed along the streets. I reckoned our coach to be about a square of Westminster-hall, but not altogether so high; however, I cannot be very exact. One day the governess ordered our coach-man to stop at several shops; where the beggars watching their opportunity, crouded to the sides of the coach, and gave me the most horrible spectacles that ever an European eye beheld. There was a woman with a cancer in her breast, swelled to a monstrous size, full of holes, in two or three of which I could have easily crept, and covered my whole body. There was a fellow with a wen in his neck, larger than five woolpacks; and another with a couple of wooden legs, each about twenty foot high. But, the most hateful sight of all, was the lice crawling on their clothes: I could see distinctly the limbs of these vermin with my naked eye, much better than those of an European louse through a microscope; and their snouts with which they rooted like swine. They were the first I had ever beheld; and I should have been curious enough to dissect one of them, if I had proper instruments (which I unluckily left behind me in the ship) although indeed the sight was so nauseous, that it perfectly turned my stomach.

Beside the large box in which I was usually carried, the queen ordered a smaller one to be made for me, of about twelve foot square, and ten high, for the convenience of travelling; because the other was somewhat too large for Glumdalclitch's lap, and cumbersome in the coach; it was made by the same artist, whom I directed in the whole contrivance. This travelling closet was an exact square, with a window in the middle of three of the squares, and each window was latticed with iron wire on the outside, to prevent accidents in long journeys. On the fourth side, which had no window, two strong staples were fixed, through which the person that carried me, when I had a mind to be on horseback, put in a leathern belt, and buckled it about his waist. This was always the office of some grave trusty servant, in whom I could confide, whether I attended the king and queen in their progresses, or were disposed to see the gardens, or pay a visit to some great lady or minister of State in the court, when Glumdalclitch happened to be out of order: for I soon began to be known and esteemed among the greatest officers, I suppose more upon account of their Majesty's favour, than any merit of my own. In journeys, when I was weary of the coach, a servant on horseback would buckle my box, and place it on a cushion before him; and there I had a full prospect of the country on three sides from my three windows. I had in this closet a field-bed, and a hammock hung from the cieling, two chairs and a table, neatly screwed to the floor, to prevent being tossed about by the agitation of the horse or the coach. And having been long used to sea-voyages, these motions, although sometimes very violent, did not much discompose me.

Whenever I had a mind to see the town, it was always in my travelling-closet; which Glumdalclitch held in her lap, in a kind of open sedan, after the fashion of the country, born by four men, and attended by two others in the queen's livery. The people who had often heard of me, were very curious to croud about the sedan; and the girl was complaisant enough to make the bearers stop, and to take me in her hand, that I might be more conveniently seen.

I was very desirous to see the chief temple, and particularly the tower belonging to it, which is reckoned the highest in the kingdom. Accordingly one day my nurse carried me thither, but I may truly say I came back disappointed; for, the height is not above three thousand foot, reckoning from the ground to the highest pinnacle top; which allowing for the difference between the size of those people, and us in Europe, is no great matter for admiration, nor at all equal in proportion (if I rightly remember) to Salisbury steeple. But, not to detract from a nation, to which during my life I shall acknowledge myself extremely obliged; it must be allowed, that whatever this famous tower wants in height, is amply made up in beauty and strength. For, the walls are near an hundred foot thick, built of hewen stone, whereof each is about forty foot square, and adorned on all sides with statues of gods and emperors, cut in marble, larger than the life, placed in their several niches. I measured a little finger which had fallen down from one of these statues, and lay unperceived among some rubbish; and found it exactly four foot and an inch in length. Glumdalclitch wrapped it up in a handkerchief, and carried it home in her pocket, to keep among other trinkets, of which the girl was very fond, as children at her age usually are.

The king's kitchen is indeed a noble building, vaulted at top, and about six hundred foot high. The great oven is not so wide by ten paces as the cupola at St. Paul's: for I measured the latter on purpose after my return. But if I should describe the kitchen-grate, the prodigious pots and kettles, the joints of meat turning on the spits, with many other particulars; perhaps I should be hardly believed; at least, a severe critick would be apt to think I enlarged a little, as travellers are often suspected to do. To avoid which censure, I fear I have run too much into the other extreme; and that if this treatise should happen to be translated into the language of Brobdingnag, (which is the general name of that kingdom) and transmitted thither, the king and his people would have reason to complain, that I had done them an injury, by a false and diminutive representation.

His Majesty seldom keeps above six hundred horses in his stables: they are generally from fifty four to sixty foot high. But, when he goes abroad on solemn days, he is attended for State, by a militia guard of five hundred horse, which indeed I thought was the most splendid sight that could be ever beheld, until I saw part of his army in battalia; whereof I shall find another occasion to speak.

CHAPTER V

Several adventures that happened to the author. The execution of a criminal.
The author shews his skill in navigation.

I SHOULD have lived happy enough in that country, if my littleness had not exposed me to several ridiculous and troublesome accidents; some of which I shall venture to relate. Glumdalclitch often carried me into the gardens of the court in my smaller box, and would sometimes take me out of it and hold me in her hand, or set me down to walk. I remember, before the dwarf left the queen, he followed us one day into those gardens; and my nurse having set me down, he and I being close together, near some dwarf apple-trees, I must need shew my wit by a silly allusion between him and the trees, which happens to hold in their language as it doth in ours.Whereupon, the malicious rogue watching his opportunity, when I was walking under one of them, shook it directly over my head, by which a dozen apples, each of them near as large as a Bristol barrel, came tumbling about my ears; one of them hit me on the back as I chanced to stoop, and knocked me down flat on my face, but I received no other hurt; and the dwarf was pardoned at my desire, because I had given the provocation.

Another day, Glumdalclitch left me on a smooth grassplot to divert my self while she walked at some distance with her governess. In the mean time, there suddenly fell such a violent shower of hail, that I was immediately by the force of it struck to the ground: and, when I was down, the hail-stones gave me such cruel bangs all over my body, as if I had been pelted with tennis-balls; however, I made a shift to creep on all four, and shelter my self, by lying flat on my face on the lee-side of a border of lemmon thyme, but so bruised from head to foot, that I could not go abroad in ten days. Neither is this at all to be wondered at; because nature in that country observing the same proportion through all her operations, a hail-stone is near eighteen hundred times as large as one in Europe; which I can assert upon experience, having been so curious to weigh and measure them.

But, a more dangerous accident happened to me in the same garden, when my little nurse, believing she had put me in a secure place, which I often entreated her to do, that I might enjoy my own thoughts; and having left my box at home, to avoid the trouble of carrying it, went to another part of the gardens, with her governess and some ladies of her acquaint-ance: while she was absent and out of hearing, a small white spaniel belong-ing to one of the chief gardeners, having got by accident into the garden, happened to range near the place where I lay. The dog following the scent, came directly up, and taking me in his mouth, ran strait to his master, wagging his tail, and set me gently on the ground. By good fortune, he had been so well taught, that I was carried between his teeth without the least hurt, or even tearing my cloaths. But, the poor gardener, who knew me well, and had a great kindness for me, was in a terrible fright. He gently took me up in both his hands, and asked me how I did; but I was so amazed and out of breath, that I could not speak a word. In a few minutes I came to my self, and he carried me safe to my little nurse, who by this time had returned to the place where she left me, and was in cruel agonies when I did not appear, nor answer when she called; she severely reprimanded the gar-dener on account of his dog. But, the thing was hushed up, and never known at court; for the girl was afraid of the queen's anger; and truly as to my self, I thought it would not be for my reputation that such a story should go about.

This accident absolutely determined Glumdalclitch never to trust me abroad for the future out of her sight. I had been long afraid of this resolu-tion; and therefore concealed from her some little unlucky adventures that happened in those times when I was left by myself. Once a kite hovering over the garden, made a stoop at me, and if I had not resolutely drawn my hanger, and run under a thick espalier, he would have certainly carried me away in his talons. Another time, walking to the top of a fresh mole-hill, I fell to my neck in the hole through which that animal had cast up the earth; and coined some lye not worth remembering, to excuse my self for spoiling my cloaths. I likewise broke my right shin against the shell of a snail, which I happened to stumble over, as I was walking alone, and thinking on poor England.

I cannot tell whether I were more pleased or mortified to observe in those solitary walks, that the smaller birds did not appear to be at all afraid of me; but would hop about within a yard distance, looking for worms, and other food, with as much indifference and security as if no creature at all were near them. I remember, a thrush had the confidence to snatch out of my hand with his bill, a piece of cake that Glumdalclitch had just given me for my breakfast. When I attempted to catch any of these birds, they would boldly turn against me, endeavouring to pick my fingers, which I durst not venture within their reach; and then they would hop back unconcerned to hunt for worms or snails, as they did before. But, one day I took a thick cudgel, and threw it with all my strength so luckily at a linnet, that I knocked him down, and seizing him by the neck with both my hands, ran with him in triumph to my nurse. However, the bird, who had only been stunned, recovering himself, gave me so many boxes with his wings on both sides of my head and body, although I held him at arms length, and was out of the reach of his claws, that I was twenty times thinking to let him go. But I was soon relieved by one of our servants, who wrung off the bird's neck; and I had him the next day for dinner by the queen's command. This linnet, as near as I can remember, seemed to be somewhat larger than an English swan.

The maids of honour often invited Glumdalclitch to their apartments, and desired she would bring me along with her, on purpose to have the pleasure of seeing and touching me. They would often strip me naked from top to toe, and lay me at full length in their bosoms; wherewith I was much disgusted; because, to say the truth, a very offensive smell came from their skins; which I do not mention or intend to the disadvantage of those excellent ladies, for whom I have all manner of respect: but, I conceive, that my sense was more acute in proportion to my littleness; and that those illustrious persons were no more disagreeable to their lovers, or to each other, than people of the same quality are with us in England. And, after all, I found their natural smell was much more supportable than when they used perfumes, under which I immediately swooned away. I cannot forget, that an intimate friend of mine in Lilliput, took the freedom in a warm day, when I had used a good deal of exercise, to complain of a strong smell about me; although I am as little faulty that way as most of my sex: but, I suppose, his faculty of smelling was as nice with regard to me, as mine was to that of this people. Upon this point, I cannot forbear doing justice to the queen my mistress, and Glumdalclitch my nurse; whose persons were as sweet as those of any lady in England.

That which gave me most uneasiness among these maids of honour, when my nurse carried me to visit them, was to see them use me without any manner of ceremony, like a creature who had no sort of consequence. For, they would strip themselves to the skin, and put on their smocks in my presence, while I was placed on their toylet directly before their naked bodies: which, I am sure to me was very far from being a tempting sight, or from giving me any other emotions than those of horror and disgust. Their skins appeared so coarse and uneaven, so variously coloured when I saw them near, with a mole here and there as broad as a trencher, and hairs hanging from it thicker than packthreads; to say nothing further concerning the rest of their persons. Neither did they at all scruple while I was by, to discharge what they had drunk, to the quantity of at least two hogsheads, in a vessel that held above three tuns. The handsomest among these maids of honour, a pleasant frolicksome girl of sixteen, would sometimes set me astride upon one of her nipples; with many other tricks, wherein the reader will excuse me for not being over particular. But, I was so much displeased, that I intreated Glumdalclitch to contrive some excuse for not seeing that young lady any more.

One day, a young gentleman, who was nephew to my nurse's governess, came and pressed them both to see an execution. It was of a man who had murdered one of that gentleman's intimate acquaintance. Glumdalclitch was prevailed on to be of the company, very much against her inclination, for she was naturally tender hearted: and, as for my self, although I abhorred such kind of spectacles; yet, my curiosity tempted me to see something that I thought must be extraordinary. The malefactor was fixed in a chair upon a scaffold erected for the purpose; and his head cut off at one blow with a sword of about forty foot long. The veins and arteries spouted up such a prodigious quantity of blood, and so high in the air, that the great *jet d'eau* at Versailles was not equal for the time it lasted; and the head when it fell on the scaffold floor, gave such a bounce, as made me start, although I were at least an English mile distant.

The queen, who often used to hear me talk of my seavoyages, and took all occasions to divert me when I was melancholy, asked me, whether I understood how to handle a sail or an oar; and whether a little exercise of rowing might not be convenient for my health. I answered, that I understood both very well. For, although my proper employment had been to be surgeon or doctor to the ship; yet often upon a pinch, I was forced to work like a common mariner. But, I could not see how this could be done in their country, where the smallest wherry was equal to a first rate man of war among us; and such a boat as I could manage, would never live in any of their rivers: her Majesty said, if I would contrive a boat, her own joyner should make it, and she would provide a place for me to sail in. The fellow was an ingenious workman, and by my instructions, in ten days finished a pleasure-boat with all its tackling, able conveniently to hold eight Europeans. When it was finished, the queen was so delighted, that she ran with it in her lap to the king, who ordered it to be put in a cistern full of water, with me in it, by way of tryal; where I could not manage my two sculls or little oars for want of room. But, the queen had before contrived another project. She ordered the joyner to make a wooden trough of three hundred foot long, fifty broad, and eight deep; which being well pitched to prevent leaking, was placed on the floor along the wall, in an outer room of the palace. It had a cock near the bottom, to let out the water when it began to grow stale; and two servants could easily fill it in half an hour. Here I often used to row for my diversion, as well as that of the queen and her ladies, who thought themselves agreeably entertained with my skill and agility. Sometimes I would put up my sail, and then my business was only to steer, while the ladies gave me a gale with their fans; and when they were weary, some of the pages would blow my sail forward with their breath, while I shewed my art by steering starboard or larboard as I pleased. When I had done, Glumdalclitch always carried back my boat into her closet, and hung it on a nail to dry.

In this exercise I once met an accident which had like to have cost me my life. For, one of the pages having put my boat into the trough, the governess who attended Glumdalclitch, very officiously lifted me up to place me in the boat; but I happened to slip through her fingers, and should have infallibly fallen down forty foot upon the floor, if by the luckiest chance in the world,

I had not been stopped by a corking-pin that stuck in the good gentle-woman's stomacher; the head of the pin passed between my shirt and the waistband of my breeches; and thus I was held by the middle in the air, until Glumdalclitch ran to my relief.

Another time, one of the servants, whose office it was to fill my trough every third day with fresh water, was so careless to let a huge frog (not perceiving it) slip out of his pail. The frog lay concealed until I was put into my boat, but then seeing a resting place, climbed up, and made it lean so much on one side, that I was forced to balance it with all my weight on the other, to prevent overturning. When the frog was got in, it hopped at once half the length of the boat, and then over my head, backwards and forwards, dawbing my face and cloaths with its odious slime. The largeness of its features made it appear the most deformed animal that can be conceived. However, I desired Glumdalclitch to let me deal with it alone. I banged it a good while with one of my sculls, and at last forced it to leap out of the boat.

But, the greatest danger I ever underwent in that kingdom, was from a monkey, who belonged to one of the clerks of the kitchen. Glumdalclitch had locked me up in her closet, while she went somewhere upon business, or a visit. The weather being very warm, the closet window was left open, as well as the windows and the door of my bigger box, in which I usually lived, because of its largeness and conveniency. As I sat quietly meditating at my table, I heard something bounce in at the closet window, and skip about from one side to the other; whereat, although I were much alarmed, yet I ventured to look out, but not stirring from my seat; and then I saw this frolicksome animal, frisking and leaping up and down, until at last he came to my box, which he seemed to view with great pleasure and curiosity, peeping in at the door and every window. I retreated to the farther corner of my room, or box; but the monkey looking in at every side, put me into such a fright, that I wanted presence of mind to conceal my self under the bed, as I might easily have done. After some time spent in peeping, grinning, and chattering, he at last espyed me; and reaching one of his paws in at the door, as a cat doth when she plays with a mouse, although I often shifted place to avoid him, he at length seized the lappet of my coat (which being made of that country silk, was very thick and strong) and dragged me out. He took me up in his right fore-foot, and held me as a nurse doth a child she is going to suckle; just as I have seen the same sort of creature do with a kitten in Europe; and, when I offered to struggle, he squeezed me so hard, that I thought it more prudent to submit. I have good reason to believe, that he took me for a young one of his own species, by his often stroaking my face very gently with his other paw. In these diversions he was interrupted by a noise at the closet door, as if some body were opening it; whereupon he suddenly leaped up to the window at which he had come in, and thence upon the leads and gutters, walking upon three legs, and holding me in the fourth, until he clambered up to a roof that was next to ours. I heard Glumdalclitch give a shriek at the moment he was carrying me out. The poor girl was almost distracted: that quarter of the palace was all in an uproar; the servants ran for ladders; the monkey was seen by hundreds in the court, sitting upon the ridge of a building, holding me like a baby in one of his fore-paws, and feeding me with the other, by cramming into my mouth some victuals he had squeezed out of the bag on one side of his chaps, and patting me when I would not eat; whereat, many of the rabble below could not forbear laughing; neither do I think they justly ought to be blamed; for without question, the sight was ridiculous enough to every body but my self. Some of the people threw up stones, hoping to drive the monkey down; but this was strictly forbidden, or else very probably my brains had been dashed out.

The ladders were now applied, and mounted by several men; which the monkey observing, and finding himself almost encompassed, not being able to make speed enough with his three legs, let me drop on a ridge-tyle, and made his escape. Here I sat for some time, five hundred yards from the ground, expecting every moment to be blown down by the wind, or to fall by my own giddiness, and come tumbling over and over from the ridge to the eves. But, an honest lad, one of my nurse's footmen, climbed up, and putting me into his breeches pocket, brought me down safe.

I was almost choaked with the filthy stuff the monkey had crammed down my throat; but, my dear little nurse picked it out of my mouth with a small needle; and then I fell a vomiting, which gave me great relief. Yet I was so weak and bruised in the sides with the squeezes given me by this odious animal, that I was forced to keep my bed a fortnight. The king, queen, and all the court, sent every day to enquire after my health; and her Majesty made me several visits during my sickness. The monkey was killed, and an order made, that no such animal should be kept about the palace.

When I attended the king after my recovery, to return him thanks for his favours, he was pleased to rally me a good deal upon this adventure. He asked me what my thoughts and speculations were while I lay in the monkey's paw; how I liked the victuals he gave me, his manner of feeding; and whether the fresh air on the roof had sharpened my stomach. He desired to know, what I would have done upon such an occasion in my own country. I told his Majesty, that in Europe we had no monkies, except such as were brought for curiosities from other places, and so small, that I could deal with a dozen of them together, if they presumed to attack me. And as for that monstrous animal with whom I was so lately engaged, (it was indeed as large as an elephant) if my fears had suffered me to think so far as to make use of my hanger (looking fiercely, and clapping my hand upon the hilt as I spoke) when he poked his paw into my chamber, perhaps I should have given him such a wound, as would have made him glad to withdraw it with more haste than he put it in. This I delivered in a firm tone, like a person who was jealous lest his courage should be called in question. However, my speech produced nothing else besides a loud laughter; which all the respect due to his Majesty from those about him, could not make them contain. This made me reflect, how vain an attempt it is for a man to endeavour doing himself honour among those who are out of all degree of equality or comparison with him. And yet, I have seen the moral of my own behaviour very frequent in England since my return, where a little contemptible varlet, without the least title to birth, person, wit, or common sense, shall presume to look with importance, and put himself upon a foot with the greatest persons of the kingdom.

I was every day furnishing the court with some ridiculous story; and Glumdalclitch, although she loved me to excess, yet was arch enough to inform the queen, whenever I committed any folly that she thought would be diverting to her Majesty. The girl who had been out of order, was carried by her governess to take the air about an hour's distance, or thirty miles from town. They alighted out of the coach near a small foot-path in a field; and Glumdalclitch setting down my travelling box, I went out of it to walk. There was a cow-dung in the path, and I must needs try my activity by attempting to leap over it. I took a run, but unfortunately jumped short, and found my self just in the middle up to my knees. I waded through with some difficulty, and one of the footmen wiped me as clean as he could with his handkerchief; for I was filthily bemired, and my nurse confined me to my box until we returned home; where the queen was soon informed of what had passed, and the footmen spread it about the court; so that all the mirth, for some days, was at my expence.

CHAPTER VI

Several contrivances of the author to please the king and queen. He shews his skill in musick. The king enquires into the state of Europe, which the author relates to him. The king's observations thereon.

I USED to attend the king's levee once or twice a week, and had often seen him under the barber's hand, which indeed was at first very terrible to behold. For, the razor was almost twice as long as an ordinary scythe. His Majesty, according to the custom of the country, was only shaved twice a week. I once prevailed on the barber, to give me some of the suds or lather, out of which I picked forty or fifty of the strongest stumps of hair. I then took a piece of fine wood, and cut it like the back of a comb, making several holes in it at equal distance, with as small a needle as I could get from Glumdalclitch. I fixed in the stumps so artificially, scraping and sloping them with my knife towards the points, that I made a very tolerable comb; which was a seasonable supply, my own being so much broken in the teeth, that it was almost useless: neither did I know any artist in that country so nice and exact, as would undertake to make me another.

And this puts me in mind of an amusement wherein I spent many of my leisure hours. I desired the queen's woman to save for me the combings of her Majesty's hair, whereof in time I got a good quantity; and consulting with my friend the cabinet-maker, who had received general orders to do little jobbs for me, I directed him to make two chair-frames, no larger than those I had in my box, and then to bore little holes with a fine awl round those parts where I designed the backs and seats; through these holes I wove the strongest hairs I could pick out, just after the manner of cane-chairs in England. When they were finished, I made a present of them to her Majesty, who kept them in her cabinet, and used to shew them for curiosities; as indeed they were the wonder of every one who beheld them. The queen would have had me sit upon one of these chairs, but I absolutely refused to obey her; protesting I would rather dye a thousand deaths, than place a dishonourable part of my body on those precious hairs that once adorned her Majesty's head. Of these hairs (as I had always a mechanical genius) I likewise made a neat little purse about five foot long, with her Majesty's name decyphered in gold letters; which I gave to Glumdalclitch, by the queen's consent. To say the truth, it was more for shew than use, being not of strength to bear the weight of the larger coins; and therefore she kept nothing in it, but some little toys that girls are fond of.

The king, who delighted in musick, had frequent concerts at court, to which I was sometimes carried, and set in my box on a table to hear them: but, the noise was so great, that I could hardly distinguish the tunes. I am confident, that all the drums and trumpets of a royal army, beating and sounding together just at your ears, could not equal it. My practice was to have my box removed from the places where the performers sat, as far as I could; then to shut the doors and windows of it, and draw the window-curtains; after which I found their musick not disagreeable.

I had learned in my youth to play a little upon the spinet; Glumdalclitch kept one in her chamber, and a master attended twice a week to teach her: I call it a spinet, because it somewhat resembled that instrument, and was played upon in the same manner. A fancy came into my head, that I would entertain the king and queen with an English tune upon this instrument. But this appeared extremely difficult: for, the spinet was near sixty foot long, each key being almost a foot wide; so that, with my arms extended, I could not reach to above five keys; and to press them down required a good smart stroak with my fist, which would be too great a labour, and to no purpose. The method I contrived was this. I prepared two round sticks about the bigness of common cudgels; they were thicker at one end than the other; and I covered the thicker end with a piece of a mouse's skin, that by rapping on them, I might neither damage the tops of the keys, nor interrupt the sound. Before the spinet, a bench was placed about four foot below the keys, and I was put upon the bench. I ran sideling upon it that way and this, as fast as I could, banging the proper keys with my two sticks; and made a shift to play a jigg to the great satisfaction of both their Majesties: but, it was the most violent exercise I ever underwent, and yet I could not strike above sixteen keys, nor, consequently, play the bass and treble together, as other artists do; which was a great disadvantage to my performance.

The king, who, as I before observed, was a prince of excellent understanding, would frequently order, that I should be brought in my box, and set upon the table in his closet. He would then command me to bring one of my chairs out of the box, and sit down within three yards distance, upon the top of the cabinet; which brought me almost to a level with his face. In this manner I had several conversations with him. I one day took the freedom to tell his Majesty, that the contempt he discovered towards Europe, and the rest of the world, did not seem answerable to those excellent qualities of mind that he was master of. That, reason did not extend itself with the bulk of the body: on the contrary, we observed in our country, that the tallest persons were usually least provided with it. That, among other animals, bees and ants had the reputation of more industry, art, and sagacity, than many of the larger kinds. And that, as inconsiderable as he took me to be, I hoped I might live to do his Majesty some signal service. The king heard me with attention; and began to conceive a much better opinion of me, than he had ever before. He desired I would give him as exact an account of the government of England as I possibly could; because, as fond as princes commonly are of their own customs (for so he conjectured of other monarchs by my former discourses) he should be glad to hear of any thing that might deserve imitation.

Imagine with thy self, courteous reader, how often I then wished for the tongue of Demosthenes or Cicero, that might have enabled me to celebrate the praise of my own dear native country, in a style equal to its merits and felicity.

I began my discourse by informing his Majesty, that our dominions consisted of two islands, which composed three mighty kingdoms under one sovereign, besides our plantations in America. I dwelt long upon the fertility of our soil, and the temperature of our climate. I then spoke at large upon the constitution of an English Parliament, partly made up of an illustrious body called the House of Peers, persons of the noblest blood, and of the most ancient and ample patrimonies. I described that extraordinary care always taken of their education in arts and arms, to qualify them for being counsellors born to the king and kingdom; to have a share in the legislature, to be members of the highest court of judicature, from whence there could be no appeal; and to be champions always ready for the defence of their prince and country by their valour, conduct and fidelity. That, these were the ornament and bulwark of the kingdom; worthy followers of their most renowned ancestors, whose honour had been the reward of their virtue; from which their posterity were never once known to degenerate. To these were joined several holy persons, as part of that assembly, under the title of bishops; whose peculiar business it is, to take care of religion, and of those who instruct the people therein. These were searched and sought out through the whole nation, by the prince and wisest counsellors, among such of the priesthood, as were most deservedly distinguished by the sanctity of their lives, and the depth of their erudition; who were indeed, the spiritual fathers of the clergy and the people.

That, the other part of the Parliament consisted of an assembly called the House of Commons; who were all principal gentlemen, *freely* picked and culled out by the people themselves, for their great abilities, and love of their country, to represent the wisdom of the whole nation. And, these two bodies make up the most august assembly in Europe; to whom, in conjunction with the prince, the whole legislature is committed.

I then descended to the Courts of Justice, over which the judges, those venerable sages and interpreters of the law, presided, for determining the disputed rights and properties of men, as well as for the punishment of vice, and protection of innocence. I mentioned the prudent management of our Treasury; the valour and atchievements of our forces by sea and land. I computed the number of our people, by reckoning how many millions there might be of each religious sect, or political party among us. I did not omit even our sports and pastimes, or any other particular which I thought might redound to the honour of my country. And, I finished all with a brief historical account of affairs and events in England for about an hundred years past.

This conversation was not ended under five audiences, each of several hours; and the king heard the whole with great attention; frequently taking notes of what I spoke, as well as memorandums of what questions he intended to ask me.

When I had put an end to these long discourses, his Majesty in a sixth audience consulting his notes, proposed many doubts, queries, and objections upon every article. He asked, what methods were used to cultivate the minds and bodies of our young nobility; and in what kind of business they commonly spent the first and teachable parts of their lives. What course was taken to supply that assembly, when any noble family became extinct. What qualifications were necessary in those who are to be created new lords: whether the humour of the prince, a sum of money to a court-lady, or a Prime Minister; or a design of strengthening a party opposite to the publick interest, ever happened to be motives in those advancements. What share of knowledge these lords had in the laws of their country, and how they came by it, so as to enable them to decide the properties of their fellow-subjects in the last resort. Whether they were always so free from avarice, partialities, or want, that a bribe, or some other sinister view, could have no place among them. Whether those holy lords I spoke of, were constantly promoted to that rank upon account of their knowledge in religious matters, and the sanctity of their lives, had never been compliers with the times while they were common priests; or slavish prostitute chaplains to some nobleman, whose opinions they continued servilely to follow after they were admitted into that assembly.

He then desired to know, what arts were practised in electing those whom I called Commoners. Whether, a stranger with a strong purse might not influence the vulgar voters to chuse him before their own landlords, or the most considerable gentleman in the neighbourhood. How it came to pass, that people were so violently bent upon getting into this assembly, which I allowed to be a great trouble and expence, often to the ruin of their families, without any salary or pension: because this appeared such an exalted strain of virtue and publick spirit, that his Majesty seemed to doubt it might possibly not be always sincere: and, he desired to know, whether such zealous gentlemen could have any views of refunding themselves for the charges and trouble they were at, by sacrificing the publick good, to the designs of a weak and vicious prince, in conjunction with a corrupted ministry. He multiplied his questions, and sifted me thoroughly upon every part of this head; proposing numberless enquiries and objections, which I think it not prudent or convenient to repeat.

Upon what I said, in relation to our courts of justice, his Majesty desired to be satisfied in several points: and, this I was the better able to do, having been formerly almost ruined by a long suit in Chancery, which was decreed for me with costs. He asked, what time was usually spent in determining between right and wrong; and what degree of expence. Whether advocates and orators had liberty to plead in causes manifestly known to be unjust, vexatious, or oppressive. Whether party in religion or politicks were observed to be of any weight in the scale of justice. Whether those pleading orators were persons educated in the general knowledge of equity; or only in provincial, national, and other local customs. Whether they, or their judges, had any part in penning those laws, which they assumed the liberty of interpreting and glossing upon at their pleasure. Whether they had ever at different times pleaded for and against the same cause, and cited precedents to prove contrary opinions. Whether they were a rich or a poor corporation. Whether they received any pecuniary reward for pleading or delivering their opinions. And particularly, whether they were ever admitted as members in the lower senate.

He fell next upon the management of our Treasury; and said, he thought my memory had failed me, because I computed our taxes at about five or six millions a year; and when I came to mention the issues, he found they sometimes amounted to more than double; for, the notes he had taken were very particular in this point; because he hoped, as he told me, that the knowledge of our conduct might be useful to him; and he could not be deceived in his calculations. But, if what I told him were true, he was still at a loss how a kingdom could run out of its estate like a private person. He asked me, who were our creditors? and, where we found money to pay them? He wondered to hear me talk of such chargeable and extensive wars; that, certainly we must be a quarrelsome people, or live among very bad neighbours; and that our generals must needs be richer than our kings. He asked, what business we had out of our own islands, unless upon the score of trade or treaty, or to defend the coasts with our fleet. Above all, he was amazed to hear me talk of a mercenary standing army in the midst of peace, and among a free people. He said, if we were governed by our own consent in the persons of our representatives, he could not imagine of whom we were afraid, or against whom we were to fight; and would hear my opinion, whether a private man's house might not better be defended by himself, his children, and family; than by half a dozen rascals picked up at a venture in the streets, for small wages, who might get an hundred times more by cutting their throats.

He laughed at my odd kind of arithmetick (as he was pleased to call it) in reckoning the numbers of our people by a computation drawn from the several sects among us in religion and politicks. He said, he knew no reason, why those who entertain opinions prejudicial to the publick, should be obliged to change, or should not be obliged to conceal them. And, as it was tyranny in any Government to require the first, so it was weakness not to enforce the second: for, a man may be allowed to keep poisons in his closet, but not to vend them about as cordials.

He observed, that among the diversions of our nobility and gentry, I had mentioned gaming. He desired to know at what age this entertainment was usually taken up, and when it was laid down. How much of their time it employed; whether it ever went so high as to affect their fortunes. Whether mean vicious people, by their dexterity in that art, might not arrive at great riches, and sometimes keep our very nobles in dependance, as well as habituate them to vile companions, wholly take them from the improvement of their minds, and force them by the losses they received, to learn and practice that infamous dexterity upon others.

He was perfectly astonished with the historical account I gave him of our affairs during the last century; protesting it was only a heap of conspiracies, rebellions, murders, massacres, revolutions, banishments; the very worst effects that avarice, faction, hypocrisy, perfidiousness, cruelty, rage, madness, hatred, envy, lust, malice, and ambition could produce.

His Majesty in another audience, was at the pains to recapitulate the sum of all I had spoken; compared the questions he made, with the answers I had given; then taking me into his hands, and stroaking me gently, delivered himself in these words, which I shall never forget, nor the manner he spoke them in. "My little friend Grildrig; you have made a most admirable panegyrick upon your country. You have clearly proved that ignorance, idleness, and vice, are the proper ingredients for qualifying a legislator. That laws are best explained, interpreted, and applied by those whose interest and abilities lie in perverting, confounding, and eluding them. I observe among you some lines of an institution, which in its orginal might have been tolerable; but these half erased, and the rest wholly blurred and blotted by corruptions. It doth not appear, from all you have said, how any one perfection is required towards the procurement of any one station among you; much less that men are ennobled on account of their virtue, that priests are advanced for their piety or learning, soldiers for their conduct or valour, judges for their integrity, senators for the love of their country, or counsellors for their wisdom. As for yourself (continued the king) who have spent the greatest part of your life in travelling, I am well disposed to hope you may hitherto have escaped many vices of your country. But, by what I have gathered from your own relation, and the answers I have with much pains wringed and extorted from you, I cannot but conclude the bulk of your natives, to be the most pernicious race of little odious vermin that nature ever suffered to crawl upon the surface of the earth."

CHAPTER VII

The author's love of his country. He makes a proposal of much advantage to the king, which is rejected. The king's great ignorance in politicks. The learning of that country very imperfect and confined. Their laws, and military affairs, and parties in the State.

NOTHING but an extreme love of truth could have hindered me from concealing this part of my story. It was in vain to discover my resentments, which were always turned into ridicule: and, I was forced to rest with patience, while my noble and most beloved country was so injuriously treated. I am heartily sorry as any of my readers can possibly be, that such an occasion was given: but this prince happened to be so curious and inquisitive into every particular, that it could not consist either with gratitude or good manners to refuse giving him what satisfaction I was able. Yet thus much

I may be allowed to say in my own vindication; that I artfully eluded many of his questions; and gave to every point a more favourable turn by many degrees than the strictness of truth would allow. For, I have always born that laudable partiality to my own country, which Dionysius Hallicarnassensis with so much justice recommends to an historian. I would hide the frailties and deformities of my political mother, and place her virtues and beauties in the most advantageous light. This was my sincere endeavour in those many discourses I had with that monarch, although it unfortunately failed of success.

But, great allowances should be given to a king who lives wholly secluded from the rest of the world, and must therefore be altogether unacquainted with the manners and customs that most prevail in other nations: the want of which knowledge will ever produce many *prejudices*, and a certain *narrowness of thinking*, from which we, and the politer countries of Europe are wholly exempted. And, it would be hard indeed, if so remote a prince's notions of virtue and vice were to be offered as a standard for all mankind.

To confirm what I have now said, and further to shew the miserable effects of a *confined education*, I shall here insert a passage which will hardly obtain belief. In hopes to ingratiate my self farther into his Majesty's favour, I told him of an invention discovered between three and four hundred years ago, to make a certain powder; into an heap of which the smallest spark of fire falling, would kindle the whole in a moment, although it were as big as a mountain; and make it all fly up in the air together, with a noise and agitation greater than thunder. That, a proper quantity of this powder rammed into an hollow tube of brass or iron, according to its bigness, would drive a ball of iron or lead with such violence and speed, as nothing was able to sustain its force. That, the largest balls thus discharged, would not only destroy whole ranks of an army at once; but batter the strongest walls to the ground; sink down ships with a thousand men in each, to the bottom of the sea; and when linked together by a chain, would cut through masts and rigging; divide hundreds of bodies in the middle, and lay all waste before them. That, we often put this powder into large hollow balls of iron, and discharged them by an engine into some city we were besieging; which would rip up the pavement, tear the houses to pieces, burst and throw splinters on every side, dashing out the brains of all who came near. That, I knew the ingredients very well, which were cheap, and common; I understood the manner of compounding them, and could direct his workmen how to make those tubes of a size proportionable to all other things in his Majesty's kingdom; and the largest need not be above two hundred foot long; twenty or thirty of which tubes, charged with the proper quantity of powder and balls, would batter down the walls of the strongest town in his dominions in a few hours; or destroy the whole metropolis, if ever it should pretend to dispute his absolute commands. This, I humbly offered to his Majesty, as a small tribute of acknowledgment, in return of so many marks that I had received of his royal favour and protection.

The king was struck with horror at the description I had given of those terrible engines, and the proposal I had made. He was amazed how so impotent and grovelling an insect as I (these were his expressions) could entertain such inhuman ideas, and in so familiar a manner as to appear wholly unmoved at all the scenes of blood and desolation, which I had painted as the common effects of those destructive machines; whereof he said, some evil genius, enemy to mankind, must have been the first contriver. As for himself, he protested, that although few things delighted him so much as new discoveries in art or in nature; yet he would rather lose half his kingdom, than be privy to such a secret; which he commanded me, as I valued my life, never to mention any more.

A strange effect of *narrow principles* and *short views*! that a prince possessed of every quality which procures veneration, love and esteem; of strong parts, great wisdom and profound learning; endued with admirable talents for government, and almost adored by his subjects; should from a *nice unnecessary scruple*, whereof in Europe we can have no conception, let slip an opportunity put into his hands, that would have made him absolute master of the lives, the liberties, and the fortunes of his people. Neither do I say this with the least intention to detract from the many virtues of that excellent king; whose character I am sensible will on this account be very much lessened in the opinion of an English reader: but, I take this defect among them to have risen from their ignorance; by not having hitherto reduced *politicks* into a *science*, as the more acute wits of Europe have done. For, I remember very well, in a discourse one day with the king, when I happened to say, there were several thousand books among us, written upon the *art of government*, it gave him (directly contrary to my intention) a very mean opinion of our understandings. He professed both to abominate and despise all *mystery, refinement,* and *intrigue,* either in a prince or a minister. He could not tell what I meant by *secrets of State,* where an enemy or some rival nation were not in the case. He confined the knowledge of governing within very *narrow bounds*; to common sense and reason, to justice and lenity, to the speedy determination of civil and criminal causes; with some other obvious topicks which are not worth considering. And, he gave it for his opinion, that whoever could make two ears of corn, or two blades of grass to grow upon a spot of ground where only one grew before, would deserve better of mankind, and do more essential service to his country, than the whole race of politicians put together.

The learning of this people is very defective; consisting only in morality, history, poetry and mathematicks; wherein they must be allowed to excel. But, the last of these is wholly applied to what may be useful in life; to the improvement of agriculture and all mechanical arts; so, that among us it would be little esteemed. And, as to ideas, entities, abstractions and transcendentals, I could never drive the least conception into their heads.

No law of that country must exceed in words the number of letters in their alphabet; which consists only of two and twenty. But indeed, few of them extend even to that length. They are expressed in the most plain and simple terms, wherein those people are not mercurial enough to discover above one interpretation. And, to write a comment upon any law is a capital crime. As to the decision of civil causes, or proceedings against criminals, their precedents are so few, that they have little reason to boast of any extraordinary skill in either.

They have had the art of printing, as well as the Chinese, time out of mind. But their libraries are not very large; for that of the king's, which is reckoned the largest, doth not amount to above a thousand volumes; placed in a gallery of twelve hundred foot long; from whence I had liberty to borrow what books I pleased. The queen's joyner had contrived in one of Glumdalclitch's rooms a kind of wooden machine five and twenty foot high, formed like a standing ladder; the steps were each fifty foot long: it was indeed a moveable pair of stairs, the lowest end placed at ten foot distance from the wall of the chamber. The book I had a mind to read was put up leaning against the wall. I first mounted to the upper step of the ladder, and turning my face towards the book, began at the top of the page, and so walking to the right and left about eight or ten paces, according to the length of the lines, until I had gotten a little below the level of mine eyes; and then descending gradually until I came to the bottom: after which, I mounted again, and began the other page in the same manner, and so turned over the leaf, which I could easily do with both my hands, for it was as thick and stiff as a paste-board, and in the largest folios not above eighteen or twenty foot long.

Their style is clear, masculine, and smooth, but not florid; for they avoid nothing more than multiplying unnecessary words, or using various expressions. I have perused many of their books, especially those in history and morality. Among the latter I was much diverted with a little old treatise, which always lay in Glumdalclitch's bed-chamber, and belonged to her governess, a grave elderly gentlewoman, who dealt in writings of morality and devotion. The book treats of the weakness of human kind; and is in little esteem, except among women and the vulgar. However, I was curious to see what an author of that country could say upon such a subject. This writer went through all the usual topicks of European moralists; shewing how diminutive, contemptible, and helpless an animal was man in his own nature; how unable to defend himself from inclemencies of the air, or the fury of wild beasts; how much he was excelled by one creature in strength, by another in speed, by a third in foresight, by a fourth in industry. He added, that nature was degenerated in these latter declining ages of the world, and could now produce only small abortive births, in comparison of those in ancient times. He said, it was very reasonable to think, not only that the species of man were originally much larger, but also, that there must have been giants in former ages; which, as it is asserted by history and tradition, so it hath been confirmed by huge bones and sculls, casually dug up in several parts of the kingdom, far exceeding the common dwindled race of man in our days. He argued, that the very laws of nature absolutely required we should have been made in the beginning, of a size more large and robust, not so liable to destruction from every little accident of a tile falling from an house, or a stone cast from the hand of a boy, or of being drowned in a little brook. From this way of reasoning, the author drew several moral applications useful in the conduct of life, but needless here to repeat. For my own part, I could not avoid reflecting, how universally this talent was spread of drawing lectures in morality, or indeed rather matter of discontent and repining, from the quarrels we raise with nature. And, I believe, upon a strict enquiry, those quarrels might be shewn as ill grounded among us, as they are among that people.

As to their military affairs, they boast that the king's army consists of an hundred and seventy six thousand foot, and thirty two thousand horse: if that may be called an army, which is made up of tradesmen in the several cities, and farmers in the country, whose commanders are only the nobility and gentry, without pay or reward. They are indeed perfect enough in their exercises; and under very good discipline, wherein I saw no great merit: for, how should it be otherwise, where every farmer is under the command of his own landlord, and every citizen under that of the principal men in his own city, chosen after the manner of Venice by *ballot?*

I have often seen the militia of Lorbrulgrud drawn out to exercise in a great field near the city, of twenty miles square. They were in all not above twenty five thousand foot, and six thousand horse; but, it was impossible for me to compute their number, considering the space of ground they took up. A cavalier mounted on a large steed might be about ninety foot high. I have seen this whole body of horse, upon the word of command, draw their swords at once, and brandish them in the air. Imagination can figure nothing so grand, so surprizing, and so astonishing. It looked as if ten thousand flashes of lightning were darting at the same time from every quarter of the sky.

I was curious to know how this prince, to whose dominions there is no access from any other country, came to think of armies, or to teach his people the practice of military discipline. But, I was soon informed, both by conversation, and reading their histories. For, in the course of many ages, they have been troubled with the same disease, to which the whole race of mankind is subject; the nobility often contending for power, the people for liberty, and the king for absolute dominion. All which, however happily tempered by the laws of that kingdom, have been sometimes violated by each of the three parties; and have more than once occasioned civil wars, the last whereof was happily put an end to by this prince's grandfather in a general composition; and the militia then settled with common consent, hath been ever since kept in the strictest duty.

CHAPTER VIII

The king and queen make a progress to the frontiers. The author attends them. The manner in which he leaves the country very particularly related. He returns to England.

I HAD always a strong impulse that I should some time recover my liberty, although it were impossible to conjecture by what means, or to form any project with the least hope of succeeding. The ship in which I sailed was the first ever known to be driven within sight of that coast; and the king had given strict orders, that if at any time another appeared, it should be taken ashore, and with all its crew and passengers brought in a tumbril to Lorbrulgrud. He was strongly bent to get me a woman of my own size, by whom I might propagate the breed: but, I think, I should rather have died, than undergone the disgrace of leaving a posterity to be kept in cages like tame canary birds; and perhaps in time, sold about the kingdom to persons of quality for curiosities. I was indeed treated with much kindness; I was the favourite of a great king and queen, and the delight of the whole court; but it was upon such a foot as ill became the dignity of human kind. I could never forget those domestick pledges I had left behind me. I wanted to be among people with whom I could converse upon even terms; and walk about the streets and fields without fear of being trod to death like a frog or young puppy. But, my deliverance came sooner than I expected, and in a manner not very common: the whole story and circumstances of which I shall faithfully relate.

I had now been two years in this country; and, about the beginning of the third, Glumdalclitch and I attended the king and queen in a progress to the south coast of the kingdom. I was carried as usual in my travelling box, which, as I have already described, was a very convenient closet of twelve foot wide. I had ordered a hammock to be fixed by silken ropes from the four corners at the top, to break the jolts, when a servant carried me before him on horseback, as I sometimes desired; and would often sleep in my hammock while we were upon the road. On the roof of my closet, set not directly over the middle of the hammock, I ordered the joyner to cut out a hole of a foot square to give me air in hot weather as I slept; which hole I shut at pleasure with a board that drew backwards and forwards through a groove.

When we came to our journey's end, the king thought proper to pass a few days at a palace he hath near Flanflasnic, a city within eighteen English miles of the sea-side. Glumdalclitch and I were much fatigued; I had gotten a small cold; but the poor girl was so ill as to be confined to her chamber. I longed to see the ocean, which must be the only scene of my escape, if ever it should happen. I pretended to be worse than I really was; and desired leave to take the fresh air of the sea, with a page whom I was very fond of, and who had sometimes been trusted with me. I shall never forget with what unwillingness Glumdalclitch consented; nor the strict charge she gave the page to be careful of me; bursting at the same time into a flood of tears, as if she had some foreboding of what was to happen. The boy took me out in my box about half an hour's walk from the palace, towards the rocks on the seashore. I ordered him to set me down; and lifting up one of my sashes, cast many a wistful melancholy look towards the sea. I found myself not very well; and told the page that I had a mind to take a nap in my hammock, which I hoped would do me good. I got in, and the boy shut the window close down, to keep out the cold. I soon fell asleep: and all I can conjecture is, that while I slept, the page thinking no danger could happen, went among the rocks to look for birds eggs; having before observed him from my window searching about, and picking up one or two in the clefts. Be that as it will; I found my self suddenly awaked with a violent pull upon the ring which was fastned at the top of my box, for the conveniency of carriage. I felt the box raised very high in the air, and then born forward with prodigious speed. The first jolt had like to have shaken

me out of my hammock; but afterwards the motion was easy enough. I
called out several times as loud as I could raise my voice, but all to no purpose. I looked towards my windows, and could see nothing but the clouds
and sky. I heard a noise just over my head like the clapping of wings; and
then began to perceive the woeful condition I was in; that some eagle had
got the ring of my box in his beak, with an intent to let it fall on a rock, like
a tortoise in a shell, and then pick out my body and devour it. For, the
sagacity and smell of this bird enabled him to discover his quarry at a
great distance, although better concealed than I could be within a two
inch board.

In a little time I observed the noise and flutter of wings to encrease very
fast; and my box was tossed up and down like a sign-post in a windy day.
I heard several bangs or buffets, as I thought, given to the eagle (for such I
am certain it must have been that held the ring of my box in his beak) and
then all on a sudden felt my self falling perpendicularly down for above a
minute; but with such incredible swiftness, that I almost lost my breath.
My fall was stopped by a terrible squash, that sounded louder to mine ears
than the cataract of Niagara; after which I was quite in the dark for
another minute, and then my box began to rise so high, that I could see
light from the tops of my windows. I now perceived, that I was fallen into
the sea. My box, by the weight of my body, the goods that were in, and the
broad plates of iron fixed for strength at the four corners of the top and bottom, floated about five foot deep in water. I did then, and do now suppose,
that the eagle which flew away with my box, was pursued by two or three
others, and forced to let me drop while he was defending himself against
the rest, who hoped to share in the prey. The plates of iron fastned to the
bottom of the box, (for those were the strongest) preserved the balance
while it fell; and hindred it from being broken on the surface of the water.
Every joint of it was well grooved, and the door did not move on hinges,
but up and down like a sash; which kept my closet so tight, that very little
water came in. I got with much difficulty out of my hammock, having first
ventured to draw back the slip-board on the roof already mentioned, contrived on purpose to let in air; for want of which, I found myself almost
stifled.

How often did I then wish my self with my dear Glumdalclitch, from
whom one single hour had so far divided me! And, I may say with truth,
that in the midst of my own misfortune, I could not forbear lamenting my
poor nurse, the grief she would suffer for my loss, the displeasure of the
queen, and the ruin of her fortune. Perhaps many travellers have not been
under greater difficulties and distress than I was at this juncture; expecting
every moment to see my box dashed in pieces, or at least overset by the
first violent blast, or a rising wave. A breach in one single pane of glass
would have been immediate death: nor could any thing have preserved the
windows but the strong lattice wires placed on the outside against accidents
in travelling. I saw the water ooze in at several crannies, although the leaks
were not considerable; and I endeavoured to stop them as well as I could.
I was not able to lift up the roof of my closet, which otherwise I certainly
should have done, and sat on the top of it, where I might, at least, preserve

my self from being shut up, as I may call it, in the hold. Or, if I escaped these dangers for a day or two, what could I expect but a miserable death of cold and hunger! I was four hours under these circumstances, expecting and indeed wishing every moment to be my last.

I have already told the reader, that there were two strong staples fixed upon the side of my box, which had no window, and into which the servant, who used to carry me on horseback, would put a leathern belt, and buckle it about his waist. Being in this disconsolate state, I heard, or at least thought I heard some kind of grating noise on that side of my box where the staples were fixed; and soon after I began to fancy that the box was pulled, or towed along in the sea; for, I now and then felt a sort of tugging, which made the waves rise near the tops of my windows, leaving me almost in the dark. This gave me some faint hopes of relief, although I were not able to imagine how it could be brought about. I ventured to unscrew one of my chairs, which were always fastned to the floor; and having made a hard shift to screw it down again directly under the slipping-board that I had lately opened, I mounted on the chair, and putting my mouth as near as I could to the hole, I called for help in a loud voice, and in all the languages I understood. I then fastned my handkerchief to a stick I usually carried, and thrusting it up the hole, waved it several times in the air; that if any boat or ship were near, the seamen might conjecture some unhappy mortal to be shut up in the box.

I found no effect from all I could do, but plainly perceived my closet to be moved along; and in the space of an hour, or better, that side of the box where the staples were, and had no window, struck against something that was hard. I apprehended it to be a rock, and found my self tossed more than ever. I plainly heard a noise upon the cover of my closet, like that of a cable, and the grating of it as it passed through the ring. I then found my self hoisted up by degrees, at least three foot higher than I was before. Whereupon, I again thrust up my stick and handkerchief, calling for help until I was almost hoarse. In return to which, I heard a great shout repeated three times, giving me such transports of joy as are not to be conceived but by those who feel them. I now heard a trampling over my head; and somebody calling through the hole with a loud voice in the English tongue: "If there be any body below, let them speak." I answered, I was an Englishman, drawn by ill fortune into the greatest calamity that ever any creature underwent; and begged, by all that was moving, to be delivered out of the dungeon I was in. The voice replied, I was safe, for my box was fastned to their ship; and the carpenter should immediately come, and saw an hole in the cover, large enough to pull me out. I answered, that was needless, and would take up too much time; for there was no more to be done, but let one of the crew put his finger into the ring, and take the box out of the sea into the ship, and so into the captain's cabbin. Some of them upon hearing me talk so wildly, thought I was mad; others laughed; for indeed it never came into my head, that I was now got among people of my own stature and strength. The carpenter came, and in a few minutes sawed a passage about four foot square; then let down a small ladder, upon which I mounted, and from thence was taken into the ship in a very weak condition.

The sailors were all in amazement, and asked me a thousand questions, which I had no inclination to answer. I was equally confounded at the sight of so many pigmies; for such I took them to be, after having so long accustomed mine eyes to the monstrous objects I had left. But, the captain, Mr. Thomas Wilcocks, an honest worthy Shropshire man, observing I was ready to faint, took me into his cabbin, gave me a cordial to comfort me, and made me *turn in* upon his own bed; advising me to take a little rest, of which I had great need. Before I went to sleep, I gave him to understand, that I had some valuable furniture in my box, too good to be lost; a fine hammock, an handsome field-bed, two chairs, a table and a cabinet: that, my closet was hung on all sides, or rather quilted with silk and cotton: that, if he would.let one of the crew bring my closet into his cabbin, I would open it before him, and shew him my goods. The captain hearing me utter these absurdities, concluded I was raving: however, (I suppose to pacify me) he promised to give order as I desired; and going upon deck, sent some of his men down into my closet, from whence (as I afterwards found) they drew up all my goods, and stripped off the quilting; but the chairs, cabinet and bed-sted being screwed to the floor, were much damaged by the ignorance of the seamen, who tore them up by force. Then they knocked off some of the boards for the use of the ship; and when they had got all they had a mind for, let the hulk drop into the sea, which, by reason of many breaches made in the bottom and sides, sunk to *rights*. And indeed I was glad not to have been a spectator of the havock they made; because I am confident it would have sensibly touched me, by bringing former passages into my mind, which I had rather forget.

I slept some hours, but perpetually disturbed with dreams of the place I had left, and the dangers I had escaped. However, upon waking I found my self much recovered. It was now about eight a clock at night, and the captain ordered supper immediately, thinking I had already fasted too long. He entertained me with great kindness, observing me not to look wildly, or talk inconsistently; and when we were left alone, desired I would give him a relation of my travels, and by what accident I came to be set adrift in that monstrous wooden chest. He said, that about twelve a clock at noon, as he was looking through his glass, he spied it at a distance, and thought it was a sail, which he had a mind to make, being not much out of his course, in hopes of buying some biscuit, his own beginning to fall short. That, upon coming nearer, and finding his error, he sent out his long-boat to discover what I was. That, his men came back in a fright, swearing they had seen a swimming house: that, he laughed at their folly, and went himself in the boat, ordering his men to take a strong cable along with them: that, the weather being calm, he rowed round me several times, observed my windows, and the wire lattices that defended them. That he discovered two staples upon one side, which was all of boards, without any passage for light. He then commanded his men to row up to that side; and fastning a cable to one of the staples, ordered his men to tow my chest (as he called it) towards the ship. When it was there, he gave directions to fasten another cable to the ring fixed in the cover, and to raise up my chest with pullies, which all the sailors were not able to do above two or three foot. He said, they saw my stick and handkerchief thrust out of the hole, and concluded, that some unhappy man must be shut up in the cavity. I asked whether he or the crew had seen any prodigious birds in the air about the time he first discovered me: to which he answered, that discoursing this matter with the sailors while I was asleep, one of them said, he had *observed* three eagles flying towards the north; but remarked nothing of their being larger than the usual size; which I suppose must be imputed to the great height they were at: and he could not guess the reason of my question. I then asked the captain how far he reckoned we might be from land: he said, by the best computation he could make, we were at least an hundred leagues. I assured him, that he must be mistaken by almost half; for I had not left the country from whence I came, above two hours before I dropt into the sea. Whereupon he began again to think that my brain was disturbed, of which he gave me a hint, and advised me to go to bed in a cabbin he had provided. I assured him I was well refreshed with his good entertainment and company, and as much in my senses as ever I was in my life. He then grew serious, and desired to ask me freely, whether I were not troubled in mind, by the consciousness of some enormous crime, for which I was punished at the command of some prince, by exposing me in that chest; as great criminals in other countries have been forced to sea in a leaky vessel, without provisions: for, although he should be sorry to have taken so ill a man into his ship, yet he would engage his word to set me safe on shoar in the first port where we arrived. He added, that his suspicions were much increased by some very absurd speeches I had delivered at first to the sailors, and afterwards to himself, in relation to my closet or chest, as well as by my odd looks and behaviour while I was at supper.

I begged his patience to hear me tell my story; which I faithfully did from the last time I left England, to the moment he first discovered me. And, as truth always forceth its way into rational minds; so, this honest worthy gentleman, who had some tincture of learning, and very good sense, was immediately convinced of my candor and veracity. But, further to confirm all I had said, I entreated him to give order that my cabinet should be brought, of which I kept the key in my pocket. (For he had already informed me how the seamen disposed of my closet.) I opened it in his presence, and shewed him the small collection of rarities I made in the country from whence I had been so strangely delivered. There was the comb I had contrived out of the stumps of the king's beard; and another of the same materials, but fixed into a paring of her Majesty's thumb-nail, which served for the back. There was a collection of needles and pins from a foot to half a yard long. Four wasp-stings, like joyners tacks: some combings of the queen's hair: a gold ring which one day she made me a present of in a most obliging manner, taking it from her little finger, and throwing it over my head like a collar. I desired the captain would please to accept this ring in return of his civilities; which he absolutely refused. I shewed him a corn, that I had cut off with my own hand, from a maid of honour's toe; it was about the bigness of a Kentish pippin, and grown so hard, that when I returned to England, I got it hollowed into a cup, and set in silver. Lastly, I desired him to see the breeches I had then on, which were made of a mouse's skin.

I could force nothing on him but a footman's tooth, which I observed him to examine with great curiosity, and found he had a fancy for it. He received it with abundance of thanks, more than such a trifle could deserve. It was drawn by an unskilful surgeon in a mistake from one of Glumdalclitch's men, who was afflicted with the tooth-ach; but it was as sound as any in his head. I got it cleaned, and put it into my cabinet. It was about a foot long, and four inches in diameter.

The captain was very well satisfied with this plain relation I had given him; and said, he hoped when we returned to England, I would oblige the world by putting it in paper, and making it publick. My answer was, that I thought we were already overstocked with books of travels: that, nothing could now pass which was not extraordinary; wherein I doubted, some authors less consulted truth than their own vanity or interest, or the diversion of ignorant readers. That, my story could contain little beside common events, without those ornamental descriptions of strange plants, trees, birds and other animals; or the barbarous customs and idolatry of savage people, with which most writers abound. However, I thanked him for his good opinion, and promised to take the matter into my thoughts.

He said, he wondered at one thing very much; which was, to hear me speak so loud; asking me whether the king or queen of that country were thick of hearing. I told him it was what I had been used to for above two years past; and, that I admired as much at the voices of him and his men, who seemed to me only to whisper, and yet I could hear them well enough. But, when I spoke in that country, it was like a man talking in the street, to another looking out from the top of a steeple, unless when I was placed upon a table, or held in any person's hand. I told him, I had likewise observed another thing; that when I first got into the ship, and the sailors stood all about me, I thought they were the most little, contemptible creatures I had ever beheld. For, indeed, while I was in that prince's country, I could never endure to look in a glass after mine eyes had been accustomed to such prodigious objects; because, the comparison gave me so despicable a conceit of my self. The captain said, that while we were at supper, he observed me to look at every thing with a sort of wonder; and, that I often seemed hardly able to contain my laughter; which he knew not well how to take, but imputed it to some disorder in my brain. I answered, it was very true; and I wondered how I could forbear, when I saw his dishes of the size of a silver three-pence, a leg of pork hardly a mouthful, a cup not so big as a nutshel: and so I went on, describing the rest of his household stuff and provisions after the same manner. For, although the queen had ordered a little equipage of all things necessary for me, while I was in her service; yet, my ideas were wholly taken up with what I saw on every side of me; and I winked at my own littleness, as people do at their own faults. The captain understood my raillery very well, and merrily replied with the old English proverb, that he doubted mine eyes were bigger than my belly; for he did not observe my stomach so good, although I had fasted all day: and, continuing in his mirth, protested he would have gladly given an hundred pounds to have seen my closet in the eagle's bill, and afterwards in its fall from so great an height into the sea; which would certainly have been a most astonishing object, worthy to have the description of it transmitted to future ages: and, the comparison of Phaeton was so obvious, that he could not forbear applying it, although I did not much admire the conceit.

The captain having been at Tonquin, was in his return to England driven north eastward to the latitude of 44 degrees, and of longitude 143. But, meeting a trade wind, two days after I came on board him, we sailed southward a long time, and coasting New-Holland, kept our course west-south-west, and then south-south-west, until we doubled the Cape of Good-hope. Our voyage was very prosperous, but I shall not trouble the reader with a journal of it. The captain called in at one or two ports, and sent in his long-boat for provisions and fresh water; but, I never went out of the ship until we came into the Downs, which was on the 3d day of June 1706, about nine months after my escape. I offered to leave my goods in security for payment of my freight; but, the captain protested he would not receive one farthing. We took kind leave of each other; and, I made him promise he would come to see me at my house in Redriff. I hired a horse and guide for five shillings, which I borrowed of the captain.

As I was on the road, observing the littleness of the houses, the trees, the cattle, and the people, I began to think my self in Lilliput. I was afraid of trampling on every traveller I met; and often called aloud to have them stand out of the way; so that I had like to have gotten one or two broken heads for my impertinence.

When I came to mine own house, for which I was forced to enquire, one of the servants opening the door, I bent down to go in (like a goose under a gate) for fear of striking my head. My wife ran out to embrace me, but I stooped lower than her knees, thinking she could otherwise never be able to reach my mouth. My daughter kneeled to ask my blessing, but I could not see her until she arose; having been so long used to stand with my head and eyes erect to above sixty foot; and, then I went to take her up with one hand, by the waist. I looked down upon the servants, and one or two friends who were in the house, as if they had been pigmies, and I a giant. I told my wife, she had been too thrifty; for I found she had starved herself and her daughter to nothing. In short, I behaved my self so unaccountably, that they were all of the captain's opinion, when he first saw me; and, concluded I had lost my wits. This I mention as an instance of the great power of habit and prejudice.

In a little time, I and my family and friends, came to a right understanding: but, my wife protested I should never go to sea any more; although, my evil destiny so ordered, that she had not power to hinder me, as the reader may know hereafter. In the mean time, I here conclude the second part of my unfortunate voyages.

THE END OF THE SECOND PART

PART III
A VOYAGE TO LAPUTA, BALNIBARBI, LUGGNAGG, GLUBBDUBDRIB, AND JAPAN

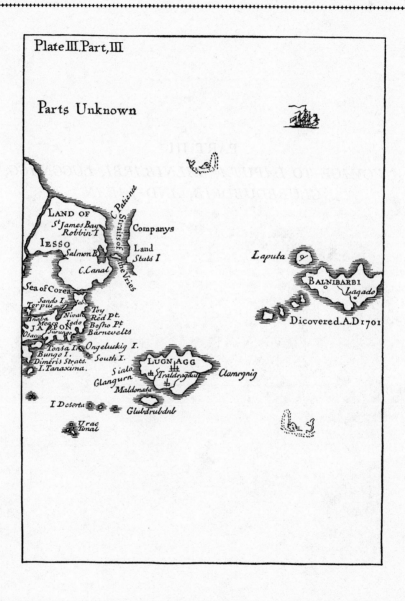

Plate III. Part, III

Parts Unknown

CHAPTER I

The author sets out on his third voyage. Is taken by pyrates. The malice of a Dutchman. His arrival at an island. He is received into Laputa.

I HAD not been at home above ten days, when Captain William Robinson, a Cornish man, commander of the *Hopewell*, a stout ship of three hundred tuns, came to my house. I had formerly been surgeon of another ship where he was master, and a fourth part owner, in a voyage to the Levant. He had always treated me more like a brother than an inferior officer; and, hearing of my arrival, made me a visit, as I apprehended, only out of friendship, for nothing passed more than what is usual after long absence. But, repeating his visits often, expressing his joy to find me in good health, asking whether I were now settled for life, adding that he intended a voyage to the East Indies, in two months; at last he plainly invited me, although with some apologies, to be surgeon of the ship; that, I should have another surgeon under me, besides our two mates: that my salary should be double to the usual pay: and, that having experienced my knowledge in sea-affairs to be at least equal to his, he would enter into any engagement to follow my advice, as much as if I had share in the command.

He said so many other obliging things, and I knew him to be so honest a man, that I could not reject his proposal; the thirst I had of seeing the world, notwithstanding my past misfortunes, continuing as violent as ever: the only difficulty that remained, was to persuade my wife, whose consent, however, I at last obtained, by the prospect of advantage she proposed to her children.

We set out the 5th day of August, 1706, and arrived at Fort St. George, the 11th of April 1707. We stayed there three weeks to refresh our crew, many of whom were sick. From thence, we went to Tonquin, where the captain resolved to continue some time; because, many of the goods he intended to buy were not ready, nor could he expect to be dispatched in several months. Therefore, in hopes to defray some of the charges he must be at, he bought a sloop, loaded it with several sorts of goods, wherewith the Tonquinese usually trade to the neighbouring islands; and putting fourteen men on board, whereof three were of the country, he appointed me master of the sloop, and gave me power to traffick, while he transacted his affairs at Tonquin.

We had not sailed above three days, when a great storm arising, we were driven five days to the north-north-east, and then to the east; after which we had fair weather, but still with a pretty strong gale from the west. Upon the 10th day we were chased by two pyrates, who soon overtook us; for, my sloop was so deep loaden, that she sailed very slow; neither were we in a condition to defend our selves.

We were boarded about the same time by both the pyrates, who entered furiously at the head of their men; but, finding us all prostrate upon our faces, (for so I gave order) they pinioned us with strong ropes, and setting a guard upon us, went to search the sloop.

I observed among them a Dutchman, who seemed to be of some authority, although he were not commander of either ship. He knew us by our countenances to be Englishmen, and jabbering to us in his own language, swore we should be tyed back to back, and thrown into the sea. I spoke Dutch tolerably well; I told him who we were, and begged him in consideration of our being Christians and Protestants, of neighbouring countries, in strict alliance, that he would move the captains to take some pity on us. This inflamed his rage; he repeated his threatnings, and turning to his companions, spoke with great vehemence, in the Japanese language, as I suppose; often using the word "Christianos."

The largest of the two pyrate ships was commanded by a Japanese captain, who spoke a little Dutch, but very imperfectly. He came up to me, and after several questions, which I answered in great humility, he said we should not die. I made the captain a very low bow, and then, turning to the Dutchman, said, I was sorry to find more mercy in a heathen, than in a brother Christian. But, I had soon reason to repent those foolish words; for, that malicious reprobate, having often endeavoured, in vain, to persuade both the captains that I might be thrown into the sea, (which they would not yield to after the promise made me, that I should not die) however, prevailed so far as to have a punishment inflicted on me, worse in all human appearance than death itself. My men were sent, by an equal division, into both the pyrate-ships, and, my sloop new manned. As to my self, it was determined that I should be set a-drift in a small canoe, with paddles and a sail, and four days provisions; which last, the Japanese captain was so kind to double out of his own stores, and would permit no man to search me. I got down into the canoe, while the Dutchman standing upon the deck, loaded me with all the curses, and injurious terms, his language could afford.

About an hour before we saw the pyrates, I had taken an observation, and found we were in the latitude of 46 N. and of longitude 183. When I was at some distance from the pyrates, I discovered by my pocket-glass several islands to the south-east. I set up my sail, the wind being fair, with a design to reach the nearest of those islands; which I made a shift to do in about three hours. It was all rocky; however, I got many birds eggs; and striking fire, I kindled some heath and dry sea weed, by which I roasted my eggs. I eat no other supper, being resolved to spare my provisions as much as I could. I passed the night under the shelter of a rock, strowing some heath under me, and slept pretty well.

The next day I sailed to another island, and thence to a third, and fourth; sometimes using my sail, and sometimes my paddles. But, not to trouble the reader with a particular account of my distresses, let it suffice, that on the

5th day, I arrived at the last island in my sight, which lay south-south-east to the former.

This island was at a greater distance than I expected, and I did not reach it in less than five hours. I encompassed it almost round, before I could find a convenient place to land in, which was a small creek, about three times the wideness of my canoe. I found the island to be all rocky, only a little intermingled with tufts of grass, and sweet smelling herbs. I took out my small provisions, and after having refreshed my self, I secured the remainder in a cave, whereof there were great numbers. I gathered plenty of eggs upon the rocks, and got a quantity of dry sea-weed, and parched grass, which I designed to kindle the next day, and roast my eggs as well as I could. (For I had about me my flint, steel, match, and burning-glass.) I lay all night in the cave where I had lodged my provisions. My bed was the same dry grass and sea-weed which I intended for fuel. I slept very little; for the disquiets of my mind prevailed over my weariness, and kept me awake. I considered how impossible it was to preserve my life, in so desolate a place; and how miserable my end must be. Yet, I found my self so listless and desponding, that I had not the heart to rise; and before I could get spirits enough to creep out of my cave, the day was far advanced. I walked a while among the rocks; the sky was perfectly clear, and the sun so hot, that I was forced to turn my face from it: when all on a sudden it became obscured, as I thought, in a manner very different from what happens by the interposition of a cloud. I turned back, and perceived a vast opake body between me and the sun, moving forwards towards the island: it seemed to be about two miles high, and hid the sun six or seven minutes, but I did not observe the air to be much colder, or the sky more darkned, than if I had stood under the shade of a mountain. As it approached nearer over the place where I was, it appeared to be a firm substance, the bottom flat, smooth, and shining very bright from the reflexion of the sea below. I stood upon a height about two hundred yards from the shoar, and saw this vast body descending almost to a parallel with me, at less than an English mile distance. I took out my pocket-perspective, and could plainly discover numbers of people moving up and down the sides of it, which appeared to be sloping, but what those people were doing, I was not able to distinguish.

The natural love of life gave me some inward motions of joy; and I was ready to entertain a hope, that this adventure might some way or other help to deliver me from the desolate place and condition I was in. But, at the same time, the reader can hardly conceive my astonishment, to behold an island in the air, inhabited by men, who were able (as it should seem) to raise, or sink, or put it into a progressive motion, as they pleased. But not being, at that time, in a disposition to philosophise upon this phænomenon, I rather chose to observe what course the island would take; because it seemed for a while to stand still. Yet soon after it advanced nearer; and I could see the sides of it, encompassed with several gradations of galleries and stairs, at certain intervals, to descend from one to the other. In the lowest gallery, I beheld some people fishing with long angling rods, and others looking on. I waved my cap, (for my hat was long since worn out,) and my handkerchief towards the island; and upon its nearer approach, I called and shouted with the utmost strength of my voice; and then looking circumspectly, I beheld a crowd gathered to that side which was most in my view. I found by their pointing towards me, and to each other, that they plainly discovered me, although they made no return to my shouting: but I could see four or five men running in great haste up the stairs to the top of the island, who then disappeared. I happened rightly to conjecture, that these were sent for orders to some person in authority upon this occasion.

The number of people increased; and in less than half an hour, the island was moved and raised in such a manner, that the lowest gallery appeared in a parallel of less than an hundred yards distance from the height where I stood. I then put my self into the most supplicating postures, and spoke in the humblest accent, but received no answer. Those who stood nearest over-against me, seemed to be persons of distinction, as I supposed by their habit. They conferred earnestly with each other, looking often upon me. At length, one of them called out in a clear, polite, smooth dialect, not unlike in sound to the Italian; and therefore I returned an answer in that language, hoping at least, that the cadence might be more agreeable to his ears. Although neither of us understood the other, yet my meaning was easily known, for the people saw the distress I was in.

They made signs for me to come down from the rock, and go towards the shoar, which I accordingly did; and the flying island being raised to a convenient height, the verge directly over me, a chain was let down from the lowest gallery, with a seat fastned to the bottom, to which I fixed my self, and was drawn up by pullies.

CHAPTER II

The humours and dispositions of the Laputans described. An account of their learning. Of the king, and his court. The author's reception there. The inhabitants subject to fears and disquietudes. An account of the women.

AT my alighting, I was surrounded by a crowd of people, but those who stood nearest, seemed to be of better quality. They beheld me with all the marks and circumstances of wonder; neither indeed was I much in their debt; having never until then seen a race of mortals so singular in their shapes, habits, and countenances. Their heads were all reclined either to the right, or to the left; one of their eyes turned inward, and the other directly up to the zenith. Their outward garments were adorned with the figures of suns, moons, and stars, interwoven with those of fiddles, flutes, harps, trumpets, guittars, harpsicords, and many more instruments of musick, unknown to us in Europe. I observed here and there many in the habit of servants, with a blown bladder fastned like a flail to the end of a short stick, which they carried in their hands. In each bladder was a small quantity of dried pease, or little pebbles, (as I was afterwards informed.) With these bladders they now and then flapped the mouths and ears of those who stood near them, of which practice I could not then conceive the meaning. It seems, the minds of these people are so taken up with intense speculations, that they neither can speak, or attend to the discourses of others, without being rouzed by some external taction upon the organs of speech and hearing; for which reason, those persons who are able to afford it, always keep a flapper, (the original is *climenole*) in their family, as one of their domesticks; nor ever walk abroad, or make visits, without him. And the business of this officer is, when two or more persons are in company, gently to strike with his bladder the mouth of him who is to speak, and the right ear of him, or them, to whom the speaker addresseth himself. This flapper is likewise employed diligently to attend his master in his walks, and upon occasion to give him a soft flap on his eyes; because he is always so wrapped up in cogitation, that he is in manifest danger of falling down every precipice, and bouncing his head against every post; and in the streets, of jostling others or being jostled himself into the kennel.

It was necessary to give the reader this information, without which he would be at the same loss with me, to understand the proceedings of these people, as they conducted me up the stairs, to the top of the island, and from thence to the royal palace. While we were ascending, they forgot several times what they were about, and left me to my self, until their memories were again rouzed by their flappers; for they appeared altogether unmoved by the sight of my foreign habit and countenance, and by the shouts of the vulgar, whose thoughts and minds were more disengaged.

At last we entered the palace, and proceeded into the chamber of presence, where I saw the king seated on his throne, attended on each side by persons of prime quality. Before the throne, was a large table filled with globes and spheres, and mathematical instruments of all kinds. His Majesty took not the least notice of us, although our entrance were not without sufficient noise, by the concourse of all persons belonging to the court. But, he was then deep in a problem, and we attended, at least, an hour, before he could solve it. There stood by him, on each side, a young page, with flaps in their hands; and when they saw he was at leisure, one of them gently struck his mouth, and the other his right ear; at which he started like one awaked on the sudden, and looking towards me, and the company I was in, recollected the occasion of our coming, whereof he had been informed before. He spoke some words; whereupon, immediately, a young man with a flap came up to my side, and slapt me gently on the right ear; but I made signs as well as I could, that I had no occasion for such an instrument; which, as I afterwards found, gave his Majesty and the whole court a very mean opinion of my understanding. The king, as far as I could conjecture, asked me several questions, and I addressed my self to him in all the languages I had. When it was found, that I could neither understand nor be understood, I was conducted, by his order, to an apartment in his palace, (this prince being distinguished above all his predecessors for his hospitality to strangers,) where two servants were appointed to attend me. My dinner was brought, and four persons of quality, whom I remembered to have seen very near the king's person, did me the honour to dine with me. We had two courses, of three dishes each. In the first course, there was a shoulder of mutton, cut into an æquilateral triangle; a piece of beef into a rhomboides; and a pudding into a cycloid. The second course was two ducks, trussed up into the form of fiddles; sausages, and puddings, resembling flutes and hautboys, and a breast of veal in the shape of a harp. The servants cut our bread into cones, cylinders, parallelograms, and several other mathematical figures.

While we were at dinner, I made bold to ask the names of several things in their language; and those noble persons, by the assistance of their flappers, delighted to give me answers, hoping to raise my admiration of their great abilities, if I could be brought to converse with them. I was soon able to call for bread, and drink, or whatever else I wanted.

After dinner, my company withdrew, and a person was sent to me by the king's order, attended by a flapper. He brought with him, pen, ink, and paper, and three or four books; giving me to understand by signs, that he was sent to teach me the language. We sat together four hours, in which time I wrote down a great number of words in columns, with the translations over-against them. I likewise made a shift to learn several short sentences. For, my tutor would order one of my servants to fetch something, to turn about, to make a bow, to sit, or stand, or walk, and the like. Then I took down the sentence in writing. He shewed me also, in one of his books, the figures of the sun, moon, and stars, the zodiack, the tropics, and polar circles, together with the denominations of many figures of planes and solids. He gave me the names and descriptions of all the musical instruments, and the general terms of art in playing on each of them. After he had left me, I placed all my words, with their interpretations, in alphabetical order. And thus, in a few days, by the help of a very faithful memory, I got some insight into their language.

The word, which I interpret the "Flying" or "Floating Island," is in the original "Laputa"; whereof I could never learn the true etymology. "Lap" in the old obsolete language signifieth "high," and "untuh" a "governor"; from which they say by corruption was derived "Laputa" from "Lapuntuh." But I do not approve of this derivation, which seems to be a little strained. I ventured to offer to the learned among them, a conjecture of my own, that "Laputa" was *quasi* "Lap outed"; "lap" signifying properly the dancing of the sun beams in the sea; and "outed" a wing, which however I shall not obtrude, but submit to the judicious reader.

Those to whom the king had entrusted me, observing how ill I was clad, ordered a taylor to come next morning, and take my measure for a suit of cloaths. This operator did his office after a different manner from those of his trade in Europe. He first took my altitude by a quadrant, and then with rule and compasses, described the dimensions and out-lines of my whole body; all which he entered upon paper, and in six days brought my cloths very ill made, and quite out of shape, by happening to mistake a figure in the calculation. But my comfort was, that I observed such accidents very frequent, and little regarded.

During my confinement for want of cloaths, and by an indisposition that held me some days longer, I much enlarged my dictionary; and when I went next to court, was able to understand many things the king spoke, and to return him some kind of answers. His Majesty had given orders, that the island should move north-east and by east, to the vertical point over Lagado, the metropolis of the whole kingdom, below upon the firm earth. It was about ninety leagues distant, and our voyage lasted four days and an half. I was not in the least sensible of the progressive motion made in the air by the island. On the second morning, about eleven o'clock, the king himself in person, attended by his nobility, courtiers, and officers, having prepared all their musical instruments, played on them for three hours without intermission; so that I was quite stunned with the noise; neither could I possibly guess the meaning, until my tutor informed me. He said, that the people of their island had their ears adapted to hear the musick of the spheres, which always played at certain periods; and the court was now prepared to bear their part in whatever instrument they most excelled.

In our journey towards Lagado, the capital city, his Majesty ordered that the island should stop over certain towns and villages, from whence he might receive the petitions of his subjects. And to this purpose, several packthreads were let down with small weights at the bottom. On these packthreads the people strung their petitions, which mounted up directly like the scraps of paper fastned by school-boys at the end of the string that holds their kite. Sometimes we received wine and victuals from below, which were drawn up by pullies.

The knowledge I had in mathematicks gave me great assistance in acquiring their phraseology, which depended much upon that science and musick; and in the latter I was not unskilled. Their ideas are perpetually conversant in lines and figures. If they would, for example, praise the beauty of a woman, or any other animal, they describe it by rhombs, circles, parallelograms, ellipses, and other geometrical terms; or else by words of art drawn from musick, needless here to repeat. I observed in the king's kitchen all sorts of mathematical and musical instruments, after the figures of which they cut up the joynts that were served to his Majesty's table.

Their houses are very ill built, the walls bevil, without one right angle in any apartment; and this defect ariseth from the contempt they bear for practical geometry; which they despise as vulgar and mechanick, those instructions they give being too refined for the intellectuals of their workmen; which occasions perpetual mistakes. And, although they are dextrous enough upon a piece of paper in the management of the rule, the pencil, and the divider, yet in the common actions and behaviour of life, I have not seen a more clumsy, awkward, and unhandy people, nor so slow and perplexed in their conceptions upon all other subjects, except those of mathematicks and musick. They are very bad reasoners, and vehemently given to opposition, unless when they happen to be of the right opinion, which is seldom their case. Imagination, fancy, and invention, they are wholly strangers to, nor have any words in their language by which those ideas can be expressed; the whole compass of their thoughts and mind being shut up within the two forementioned sciences.

Most of them, and especially those who deal in the astronomical part, have great faith in judicial astrology, although they are ashamed to own it publickly. But, what I chiefly admired, and thought altogether unaccountable, was the strong disposition I observed in them towards news and politicks; perpetually enquiring into publick affairs, giving their judgments in matters of State; and passionately disputing every inch of a party opinion.

I have indeed observed the same disposition among most of the mathematicians I have known in Europe; although I could never discover the least analogy between the two sciences; unless those people suppose, that because the smallest circle hath as many degrees as the largest, therefore the regulation and management of the world require no more abilities than the handling and turning of a globe. But, I rather take this quality to spring from a very common infirmity of human nature, inclining us to be more curious and conceited in matters where we have least concern, and for which we are least adapted either by study or nature.

These people are under continual disquietudes, never enjoying a minute's peace of mind; and their disturbances proceed from causes which very little affect the rest of mortals. Their apprehensions arise from several changes they dread in the celestial bodies. For instance; that the earth by the continual approaches of the sun towards it, must in course of time be absorbed or swallowed up. That, the face of the sun will by degrees be encrusted with its own effluvia, and give no more light to the world. That, the earth very narrowly escaped a brush from the tail of the last comet, which would have infallibly reduced it to ashes; and that the next, which they have calculated for one and thirty years hence, will probably destroy us. For, if in its perihelion it should approach within a certain degree of the sun, (as by their calculations they have reason to dread) it will conceive a degree of heat ten thousand times more intense than that of red hot glowing iron; and in its absence from the sun, carry a blazing tail ten hundred thousand and fourteen miles long; through which, if the earth should pass at the distance of one hundred thousand miles from the nucleus, or main body of the comet, it must in its passage be set on fire, and reduced to ashes. That, the sun daily spending its rays without any nutriment to supply them, will at last be wholly consumed and annihilated; which must be attended with the destruction of this earth, and of all the planets that receive their light from it.

They are so perpetually alarmed with the apprehensions of these, and the like impending dangers, that they can neither sleep quietly in their beds, nor have any relish for the common pleasures or amusements of life. When they meet an acquaintance in the morning, the first question is about the sun's health; how he looked at his setting and rising, and what hopes they have to avoid the stroak of the approaching comet. This conversation they are apt to run into with the same temper that boys discover, in delighting to hear terrible stories of sprites and hobgoblins, which they greedily listen to, and dare not go to bed for fear.

The women of the island have abundance of vivacity; they contemn their husbands, and are exceedingly fond of strangers, whereof there is always a considerable number from the continent below, attending at court, either upon affairs of the several towns and corporations, or their own particular occasions; but are much despised, because they want the same endowments. Among these the ladies chuse their gallants: but the vexation is, that they act with too much ease and security; for the husband is always so wrapped in speculation, that the mistress and lover may proceed to the greatest familiarities before his face, if he be but provided with paper and implements, and without his flapper at his side.

The wives and daughters lament their confinement to the island, although I think it the most delicious spot of ground in the world; and although they live here in the greatest plenty and magnificence, and are allowed to do whatever they please: they long to see the world, and take the diversions of the metropolis, which they are not allowed to do without a particular licence from the king; and this is not easy to be obtained, because the people of quality have found by frequent experience, how hard it is to persuade their women to return from below. I was told, that a great court lady, who had several children, is married to the Prime Minister, the richest subject in the kingdom, a very graceful person, extremely fond of her, and lives in the finest palace of the island; went down to Lagado, on the pretence of health, there hid herself for several months, until the king sent a warrant to search for her; and she was found in an obscure eating-house all in rags, having pawned her clothes to maintain an old deformed footman, who beat her every day, and in whose company she was taken much against her will. And, although her husband received her with all possible kindness, and without the least reproach, she soon after contrived to steal down again with all her jewels, to the same gallant, and hath not been heard of since.

This may perhaps pass with the reader, rather for an European or English story, than for one of a country so remote. But he may please to consider, that the caprices of womankind are not limited by any climate or nation; and that they are much more uniform than can be easily imagined.

In about a month's time I had made a tolerable proficiency in their language, and was able to answer most of the king's questions, when I had the honour to attend him. His Majesty discovered not the least curiosity to enquire into the laws, government, history, religion, or manners of the countries where I had been; but confined his questions to the state of mathematicks, and received the account I gave him, with great contempt and indifference, although often rouzed by his flapper on each side.

CHAPTER III

A phænomenon solved by modern philosophy and astronomy. The Laputans great improvements in the latter. The king's method of suppressing insurrections.

I DESIRED leave of this prince to see the curiosities of the island; which he was graciously pleased to grant, and ordered my tutor to attend me. I chiefly wanted to know to what cause in art or in nature, it owed its several motions; whereof I will now give a philosophical account to the reader.

The flying, or floating island, is exactly circular; its diameter seven thousand eight hundred and thirty seven yards, or about four miles and an half, and consequently contains ten thousand acres. It is three hundred yards thick. The bottom, or under surface, which appears to those who view it from below, is one even regular plate of adamant, shooting up to the height of about two hundred yards. Above it lye the several minerals in their usual order; and over all is a coat of rich mould ten or twelve foot deep. The declivity of the upper surface, from the circumference to the center, is the natural cause why all the dews and rains which fall upon the island, are conveyed in small rivulets towards the middle, where they are emptied into four large basons, each of about half a mile in circuit, and two hundred yards distant from the center. From these basons the water is continually exhaled by the sun in the day-time, which effectually prevents their overflowing. Besides, as it is in the power of the monarch to raise the island above the region of clouds and vapours, he can prevent the falling of dews and rains whenever he pleaseth. For the highest clouds cannot rise above two miles, as naturalists agree, at least they were never known to do so in that country.

At the center of the island there is a chasm about fifty yards in diameter, from whence the astronomers descend into a large dome, which is therefore called "Flandona Gagnole," or the "Astronomers Cave"; situated at the depth of an hundred yards beneath the upper surface of the adamant. In this cave are twenty lamps continually burning, which from the reflection of the adamant cast a strong light into every part. The place is stored with great variety of sextants, quadrants, telescopes, astrolabes, and other astronomical instruments. But the greatest curiosity, upon which the fate of the island depends, is a load-stone of a prodigious size, in shape resembling a weaver's shuttle. It is in length six yards, and in the thickest part at least three yards over. This magnet is sustained by a very strong axle of adamant, passing through its middle, upon which it plays, and is poized so exactly, that the weakest hand can turn it. It is hooped round with an hollow cylinder of adamant, four foot deep, as many thick, and twelve yards in diameter, placed horizontally, and supported by eight adamantine feet, each six yards high. In the middle of the concave side there is a groove twelve inches deep, in which the extremities of the axle are lodged, and turned round as there is occasion.

This stone cannot be moved from its place by any force, because the hoop and its feet are one continued piece with that body of adamant which constitutes the bottom of the island.

By means of this load-stone, the island is made to rise and fall, and move from one place to another. For, with respect to that part of the earth over which the monarch presides, the stone is endued at one of its sides with an attractive power, and at the other with a repulsive. Upon placing the magnet erect with its attracting end towards the earth, the island descends; but when the repelling extremity points downwards, the island mounts directly upwards. When the position of the stone is oblique, the motion of the island is so too. For in this magnet the forces always act in lines parallel to its direction.

By this oblique motion, the island is conveyed to different parts of the monarch's dominions. To explain the manner of its progress, let *AB* represent a line drawn cross the dominions of Balnibarbi; let the line *cd* represent the loadstone, of which let *d* be the repelling end, and *c* the attracting end, the island being over *C*; let the stone be placed in the position *cd* with its repelling end downwards; then the island will be driven upwards obliquely towards *D*. When it is arrived at *D*, let the stone be turned upon its axle until its attracting end points towards *E*, and then the island will be carried obliquely towards *E*; where, if the stone be again turned upon its axle until it stands in the position *EF*, with its repelling point downwards, the island will rise obliquely towards *F*, where, by directing the attracting end towards *G*, the island may be carried to *G*, and from *G* to *H*, by turning the stone, so as to make its repelling extremity point directly downwards. And thus by changing the situation of the stone as often as there is occasion, the island is made to rise and fall by turns in an oblique direction; and by those alternate risings and fallings (the obliquity being not considerable) is conveyed from one part of the dominions to the other.

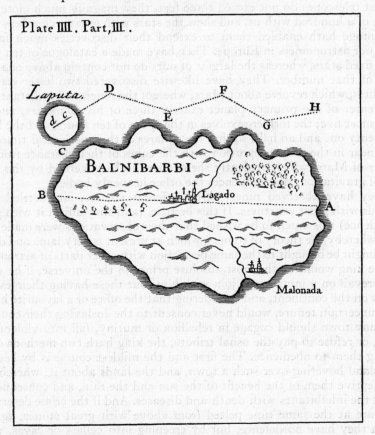

But it must be observed, that this island cannot move beyond the extent of the dominions below; nor can it rise above the height of four miles. For which the astronomers (who have written large systems concerning the stone) assign the following reason: that the magnetick virtue doth not extend beyond the distance of four miles, and that the mineral which acts upon the stone in the bowels of the earth, and in the sea about six leagues distant from the shoar, is not diffused through the whole globe, but terminated with the limits of the king's dominions: and it was easy from the great advantage of such a superior situation, for a prince to bring under his obedience whatever country lay within the attraction of that magnet.

When the stone is put parallel to the plane of the horizon, the island standeth still; for in that case, the extremities of it being at equal distance from the earth, act with equal force, the one in drawing downwards, the other in pushing upwards; and consequently no motion can ensue.

This load-stone is under the care of certain astronomers, who from time to time give it such positions as the monarch directs. They spend the greatest part of their lives in observing the celestial bodies, which they do by the assistance of glasses, far excelling ours in goodness. For, although their largest telescopes do not exceed three feet, they magnify much more than those of a hundred with us, and shew the stars with greater clearness. This advantage hath enabled them to extend their discoveries much farther than our astronomers in Europe. They have made a catalogue of ten thousand fixed stars, whereas the largest of ours do not contain above one third part of that number. They have likewise discovered two lesser stars, or satellites, which revolve about Mars; whereof the innermost is distant from the center of the primary planet exactly three of his diameters, and the outermost five; the former revolves in the space of ten hours, and the latter in twenty one and an half; so that the squares of their periodical times, are very near in the same proportion with the cubes of their distance from the center of Mars; which evidently shews them to be governed by the same law of gravitation, that influences the other heavenly bodies.

They have observed ninety-three different comets, and settled their periods with great exactness. If this be true, (and they affirm it with great confidence) it is much to be wished that their observations were made publick; whereby the theory of comets, which at present is very lame and defective, might be brought to the same perfection with other parts of astronomy.

The king would be the most absolute prince in the universe, if he could but prevail on a ministry to join with him; but these having their estates below on the continent, and considering that the office of a favourite hath a very uncertain tenure, would never consent to the enslaving their country.

If any town should engage in rebellion or mutiny, fall into violent factions, or refuse to pay the usual tribute, the king hath two methods of reducing them to obedience. The first and the mildest course is by keeping the island hovering over such a town, and the lands about it; whereby he can deprive them of the benefit of the sun and the rain, and consequently afflict the inhabitants with death and diseases. And if the crime deserve it, they are at the same time pelted from above with great stones, against which they have no defence, but by creeping into cellars or caves, while the roofs of their houses are beaten to pieces. But, if they still continue obstinate, or offer to raise insurrections, he proceeds to the last remedy, by letting the island drop directly upon their heads, which makes a universal destruction both of houses and men. However, this is an extremity to which the prince is seldom driven, neither indeed is he willing to put it in execution; nor dare his ministers advise him to an action, which as it would render them odious to the people, so it would be a great damage to their own estates that lie all below; for the island is the king's demesne.

But there is still indeed a more weighty reason, why the kings of this country have been always averse from executing so terrible an action, unless upon the utmost necessity. For, if the town intended to be destroyed should have in it any tall rocks, as it generally falls out in the larger cities, a situation probably chosen at first with a view to prevent such a catastrophe: or, if it abound in high spires or pillars of stone, a sudden fall might endanger the bottom or under surface of the island, which although it consist as I have said, of one entire adamant two hundred yards thick, might happen to crack by too great a choque, or burst by approaching too near the fires from the houses below, as the backs both of iron and stone will often do in our chimnies. Of all this the people are well apprized, and understand how far to carry their obstinacy, where their liberty or property is concerned. And the king, when he is highest provoked, and most determined to press a city to rubbish, orders the island to descend with great gentleness, out of a pretence of tenderness to his people, but indeed for fear of breaking the adamantine bottom; in which case it is the opinion of all their philosophers, that the load-stone could no longer hold it up, and the whole mass would fall to the ground.

By a fundamental law of this realm, neither the king nor either of his two elder sons, are permitted to leave the island; nor the queen until she is past child-bearing.

CHAPTER IV

The author leaves Laputa, is conveyed to Balnibarbi, arrives at the metropolis. A description of the metropolis and the country adjoining. The author hospitably received by a great lord. His conversation with that lord.

ALTHOUGH I cannot say, that I was ill treated in this island, yet I must confess, I thought my self too much neglected, not without some degree of contempt. For, neither prince nor people appeared to be curious in any part of knowledge, except mathematicks and musick; wherein I was far their inferior, and upon that account very little regarded.

On the other side, after having seen all the curiosities of the island, I was very desirous to leave it, being heartily weary of those people. They were indeed, excellent in two sciences for which I have great esteem, and wherein I am not unversed: but, at the same time, so abstracted and involved in speculation, that I never met with such disagreeable companions. I conversed only with women, tradesmen, flappers, and court-pages, during two months of my abode there; by which at last I rendered my self extremely contemptible; yet, these were the only people from whom I could ever receive a reasonable answer.

I had obtained by hard study a good degree of knowledge in their language: I was weary of being confined to an island where I received so little countenance; and resolved to leave it with the first opportunity.

There was a great lord at court, nearly related to the king, and for that reason alone used with respect. He was universally reckoned the most ignorant and stupid person among them. He had performed many eminent services for the Crown; had great natural and acquired parts, adorned with integrity and honour; but, so ill an ear for musick, that his detractors reported he had been often known to beat time in the wrong place; neither could his tutors without extreme difficulty, teach him to demonstrate the most easy proposition in the mathematicks. He was pleased to shew me many marks of favour; often did me the honour of a visit; desired to be informed in the affairs of Europe; the laws and customs, the manners and learning of the several countries where I had travelled. He listened to me with great attention, and made very wise observations on all I spoke: he had two flappers attending him for state, but never made use of them except at court, and in visits of ceremony; and, would always command them to withdraw when we were alone together.

I intreated this illustrious person to intercede in my behalf with his Majesty for leave to depart; which he accordingly did, as he was pleased to tell me, with regret: for, indeed he had made me several offers very advantageous; which however I refused with expressions of the highest acknowledgment.

On the 16th day of February, I took leave of his Majesty and the court: the king made me a present to the value of about two hundred pounds English; and my protector his kinsman as much more, together with a letter of recommendation to a friend of his in Lagado, the metropolis: the island being then hovering over a mountain about two miles from it, I was let down from the lowest gallery, in the same manner as I had been taken up.

The continent, as far as it is subject to the monarch of the flying island, passeth under the general name of Balnibarbi; and the metropolis, as I said before, is called Lagado. I felt some little satisfaction in finding my self on firm ground. I walked to the city without any concern, being clad like one of the natives, and sufficiently instructed to converse with them. I soon found out the person's house to whom I was recommended; presented my letter from his friend the grandee in the island; and was received with much kindness. This great lord, whose name was Munodi, ordered me an apartment in his own house; where I continued during my stay, and was entertained in a most hospitable manner.

The next morning after my arrival, he took me in his chariot to see the town, which is about half the bigness of London, but the houses very strangely built, and most of them out of repair. The people in the streets walked fast, looked wild, their eyes fixed, and were generally in rags. We passed through one of the town gates, and went about three miles into the country, where I saw many labourers working with several sorts of tools in the ground, but was not able to conjecture what they were about; neither did I observe any expectation either of corn or grass, although the soil appeared to be excellent. I could not forbear admiring at these odd appearances both in town and country; and, I made bold to desire my conductor, that he would be pleased to explain to me, what could be meant by so many busy heads, hands, and faces, both in the streets and the fields, because I did not discover any good effects they produced; but, on the contrary, I never knew a soil so unhappily cultivated, houses so ill contrived and so ruinous, or a people whose countenances and habit, expressed so much misery and want.

This Lord Munodi was a person of the first rank, and had been some years governor of Lagado; but by a cabal of ministers was discharged for insufficiency. However, the king treated him with tenderness, as a well-meaning man, but of a low contemptible understanding.

When I gave that free censure of the country and its inhabitants, he made no further answer than by telling me, that I had not been long enough among them to form a judgment; and that the different nations of the world had different customs with other common topicks to the same purpose. But, when we returned to his palace, he asked me how I liked the building, what absurdities I observed, and what quarrel I had with the dress and looks of his domesticks. This he might safely do; because every thing about him, was magnificent, regular, and polite. I answered, that his excellency's prudence, quality, and fortune, had exempted him from those defects which folly and beggary had produced in others. He said, if I would go with him to his country house, about twenty miles distant, where his estate lay, there would be more leisure for this kind of conversation. I told his excellency, that I was entirely at his disposal; and accordingly we set out next morning.

During our journey, he made me observe the several methods used by farmers in managing their lands; which to me, were wholly unaccountable: for, except in some very few places, I could not discover one ear of corn, or blade of grass. But, in three hours travelling, the scene was wholly altered; we came into a most beautiful country; farmers houses at small distances, neatly built, the fields enclosed, containing vine-yards, corn-grounds and meadows: neither do I remember to have seen a more delightful prospect. His excellency observed my countenance to clear up; he told me with a sigh, that there his estate began, and would continue the same until we should come to his house: that, his countrymen ridiculed and despised him for managing his affairs no better, and for setting so ill an example to the kingdom; which, however was followed by very few, such as were old and wilful, and weak like himself.

We came at length to the house, which was indeed a noble structure, built according to the best rules of ancient architecture. The fountains, gardens, walks, avenues, and groves, were all disposed with exact judgment and taste. I gave due praises to every thing I saw, whereof his excellency took not the least notice until after supper; when, there being no third companion, he told me with a very melancholy air, that he doubted he must throw down his houses in town and country, to rebuild them after the present mode; destroy all his plantations, and cast others into such a form as modern usage required; and give the same directions to all his tenants, unless he would submit to incur the censure of pride, singularity, affectation, ignorance, caprice; and perhaps, increase his Majesty's displeasure.

That, the admiration I appeared to be under, would cease or diminish, when he had informed me of some particulars, which probably I never heard of at court; the people there being too much taken up in their own speculations, to have regard to what passed here below.

The sum of his discourse was to this effect. That, about forty years ago, certain persons went up to Laputa, either upon business or diversion; and after five months continuance, came back with a very little smattering in mathematicks, but full of volatile spirits, acquired in that airy region. That, these persons upon their return, began to dislike the management of every thing below; and fell into schemes of putting all arts, sciences, languages, and mechanicks upon a new foot. To this end, they procured a royal patent, for erecting an academy of projectors in Lagado: and, the humour prevailed so strongly among the people, that there is not a town of any consequence in the kingdom without such an academy. In these colleges, the professors contrive new rules and methods of agriculture and building, and new instruments and tools for all trades and manufactures; whereby, as they undertake, one man shall do the work of ten: a palace may be built in a week, of materials so durable as to last for ever without repairing. All the fruits of the earth shall come to maturity, at whatever season we think fit to chuse, and encrease an hundred fold more than they do at present; with innumerable other happy proposals. The only inconvenience is, that none of these projects are yet brought to perfection; and, in the mean time, the whole country lies miserably waste; the houses in ruins, and the people without food or cloaths: by all which, instead of being discouraged, they are fifty times more violently bent upon prosecuting their schemes; driven equally on by hope and despair: that, as for himself, being not of an enterprizing spirit, he was content to go on in the old forms; to live in the houses his ancestors had built, and act as they did in every part of life without innovation: that, some few other persons of quality and gentry had done the same; but were looked on with an eye of contempt and ill-will; as enemies to art; ignorant, and ill commonwealthsmen; preferring their own ease and sloth before the general improvement of their country.

His lordship added, that he would not by any further particulars prevent the pleasure I should certainly take in viewing the grand academy, whither he was resolved I should go. He only desired me to observe a ruined building upon the side of a mountain about three miles distant, of which he gave me this account. That, he had a very convenient mill within half a mile of his house, turned by a current from a large river, and sufficient for his own family, as well as a great number of his tenants. That, about seven years ago, a club of those projectors came to him with proposals to destroy this mill, and build another on the side of that mountain, on the long ridge whereof a long canal must be cut for a repository of water, to be conveyed up by pipes and engines to supply the mill: because the wind and air upon a height agitated the water, and thereby, made it fitter for motion: and, because the water descending down a declivity, would turn the mill with half the current of a river, whose course is more upon a level. He said, that being then not very well with the court, and pressed by many of his friends, he complied with the proposal; and after employing an hundred men for two years, the work miscarried, the projectors went off, laying the blame entirely upon him, railing at him ever since, and putting others upon the same experiment, with equal assurance of success, as well as equal disappointment.

In a few days we came back to town; and his Excellency, considering the bad character he had in the academy, would not go with me himself; but recommended me to a friend of his, to bear me company thither. My lord was pleased to represent me as a great admirer of projects, and a person of much curiosity and easy belief; which, indeed was not without truth; for, I had my self, been a sort of projector in my younger days.

CHAPTER V

The author permitted to see the grand academy of Lagado. The academy largely described. The arts wherein the professors employ themselves.

THIS academy is not an entire single building, but a continuation of several houses on both sides of a street; which growing waste, was purchased and applied to that use.

I was received very kindly by the warden, and went for many days to the academy. Every room hath in it one or more projectors; and, I believe, I could not be in fewer than five hundred rooms.

The first man I saw, was of a meagre aspect, with sooty hands and face; his hair and beard long, ragged and singed in several places. His cloaths, shirt, and skin, were all of the same colour: he had been eight years upon a project for extracting sun-beams out of cucumbers; which were to be put into vials, hermetically sealed, and let out to warm the air, in raw inclement summers. He told me, he did not doubt, in eight years more, that he should be able to supply the governor's gardens with sun-shine at a reasonable rate; but, he complained that his stock was low, and intreated me to give him something as an encouragement to ingenuity, especially since this had been a very dear season for cucumbers: I made him a small present, for my lord had furnished me with money on purpose, because he knew their practice of begging from all who go to see them.

I went into another chamber, but was ready to hasten back, being almost overcome with a horrible stink: my conductor pressed me forward, conjuring me in a whisper to give no offence, which would be highly resented; and therefore, I durst not so much as stop my nose. The projector of this cell, was the most ancient student of the academy: his face and beard were of a pale yellow; his hands and cloaths dawbed over with filth. When I was presented to him, he gave me a very close embrace, (a compliment I could well have excused:) his employment from his first coming into the academy was an operation to reduce human excrement to its original food by separating the several parts, removing the tincture which it receives from the gall, making the odour exhale, and scumming off the saliva. He had a weekly allowance from the society, of a vessel filled with human ordure, about the bigness of a Bristol barrel.

I saw another at work to calcine ice into gun-powder, who likewise shewed me a treatise he had written, concerning the malleability of fire, which he intended to publish.

There was a most ingenious architect, who had contrived a new method for building houses, by beginning at the roof, and working downwards to the foundation; which he justified to me, by the like practice of those two prudent insects, the bee and the spider.

There was a man born blind, who had several apprentices in his own condition: their employment was to mix colours for painters, which their master taught them to distinguish by feeling and smelling: it was indeed my misfortune to find them at that time not very perfect in their lessons; and the professor himself happened to be generally mistaken. This artist is much encouraged and esteemed by the whole fraternity.

In another apartment, I was highly pleased with a projector, who had found a device of plowing the ground with hogs, to save the charges of plows, cattle, and labour. The method is this: In an acre of ground you bury at six inches distance, and eight deep, a quantity of acorns, dates, chestnuts, and other maste or vegetables, whereof these animals are fondest; then you drive six hundred or more of them into the field, where in a few days they will root up the whole ground in search of their food, and make it fit for sowing, at the same time manuring it with their dung. It is true, upon experiment, they found the charge and trouble very great, and they had little or no crop. However, it is not doubted that this invention may be capable of great improvement.

I went into another room, where the walls and cieling were all hung round with cobwebs, except a narrow passage for the artist to go in and out. At my entrance, he called aloud to me not to disturb his webs. He lamented the fatal mistake the world had been so long in of using silk-worms, while we had such plenty of domestick insects, who infinitely excelled the former, because they understood how to weave as well as spin. And he proposed farther, that by employing spiders, the charge of dying silks would be wholly saved; whereof I was fully convinced, when he shewed me a vast number of flies most beautifully coloured, wherewith he fed his spiders; assuring us, that the webs would take a tincture from them; and as he had them of all hues, he hoped to fit every body's fancy, as soon as he could find proper food for the flies, of certain gums, oyls, and other glutinous matter, to give a strength and consistence to the threads.

There was an astronomer who had undertaken to place a sun-dial upon the great weather-cock on the town-house, by adjusting the annual and diurnal motions of the earth and sun, so as to answer and coincide with all accidental turnings of the wind.

I was complaining of a small fit of the cholick; upon which my conductor led me into a room, where a great physician resided, who was famous for curing that disease by contrary operations from the same instrument. He had a large pair of bellows, with a long slender muzzle of ivory: this he conveyed eight inches up the anus, and drawing in the wind, he affirmed he could make the guts as lank as a dried bladder. But when the disease was more stubborn and violent, he let in the muzzle while the bellows was full of wind, which he discharged into the body of the patient; then withdrew the instrument to replenish it, clapping his thumb strongly against the orifice of the fundament; and this being repeated three or four times, the adventitious wind would rush out, bringing the noxious along with it (like water put into a pump) and the patient recover. I saw him try both experiments upon a dog; but could not discern any effect from the former. After the latter, the animal was ready to burst, and made so violent a discharge, as was very offensive to me and my companions. The dog died on the spot, and we left the doctor endeavouring to recover him by the same operation.

I visited many other apartments, but shall not trouble my reader with all the curiosities I observed, being studious of brevity.

I had hitherto seen only one side of the academy, the other being appropriated to the advancers of speculative learning; of whom I shall say something when I have mentioned one illustrious person more, who is called among them, 'The universal artist.' He told us, he had been thirty years employing his thoughts for the improvement of human life. He had two large rooms full of wonderful curiosities, and fifty men at work: some were condensing air into a dry tangible substance, by extracting the nitre, and letting the aqueous or fluid particles percolate: others softening marble for pillows and pincushions; others petrifying the hoofs of a living horse, to preserve them from foundering. The artist himself was at that time busy upon two great designs: the first, to sow land with chaff, wherein he affirmed the true seminal virtue to be contained, as he demonstrated by several experiments which I was not skilful enough to comprehend. The other was, by a certain composition of gums, minerals, and vegetables outwardly applied, to prevent the growth of wool upon two young lambs; and he hoped in a reasonable time to propagate the breed of naked sheep all over the kingdom.

We crossed a walk to the other part of the academy, where, as I have already said, the projectors in speculative learning resided.

The first professor I saw was in a very large room, with forty pupils about him. After salutation, observing me to look earnestly upon a frame, which took up the greatest part of both the length and breadth of the room, he said, perhaps I might wonder to see him employed in a project for improving speculative knowledge by practical and mechanical operations. But the world would soon be sensible of its usefulness; and he flattered himself, that a more noble exalted thought never sprang in any other man's head. Every one knew how laborious the usual method is of attaining to arts and sciences; whereas by his contrivance, the most ignorant person at a reasonable charge, and with a little bodily labour, may write books in philosophy, poetry, politicks, law, mathematicks and theology, without the least assistance from genius or study. He then led me to the frame, about the sides whereof all his pupils stood in ranks. It was twenty foot square, placed in the middle of the room. The superficies was composed of several bits of wood, about the bigness of a dye, but some larger than others. They were all linked together by slender wires. These bits of wood were covered on every square with paper pasted on them; and, on these papers were written all the words of their language in their several moods, tenses, and declensions, but without any order. The professor then desired me to observe, for he was going to set his engine at work. The pupils at his command took each of them hold of an iron handle, whereof there were forty fixed round the edges of the frame; and giving them a sudden turn, the whole disposition of the words was entirely changed. He then commanded

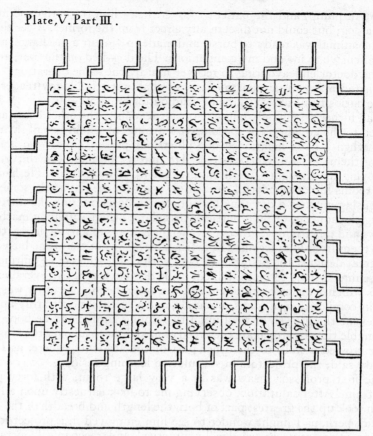

Plate, V. Part, III.

six and thirty of the lads to read the several lines softly as they appeared upon the frame; and where they found three or four words together that might make part of a sentence, they dictated to the four remaining boys who were scribes. This work was repeated three or four times, and at every turn the engine was so contrived, that the words shifted into new places, as the square bits of wood moved upside down.

Six hours a-day the young students were employed in this labour; and the professor shewed me several volumes in large folio already collected, of broken sentences, which he intended to piece together; and out of those rich materials to give the world a compleat body of all arts and sciences; which, however might be still improved, and much expedited, if the publick would raise a fund for making and employing five hundred such frames in Lagado, and oblige the managers to contribute in common their several collections.

He assured me, that this invention had employed all his thoughts from his youth; that he had emptied the whole vocabulary into his frame, and made the strictest computation of the general proportion there is in books between the numbers of particles, nouns, and verbs, and other parts of speech.

I made my humblest acknowledgments to this illustrious person for his great communicativeness; and promised, if ever I had the good fortune to return to my native country, that I would do him justice, as the sole inventor of this wonderful machine; the form and contrivance of which I desired leave to delineate upon paper as in the figure here annexed. I told him, although it were the custom of our learned in Europe to steal inventions from each other, who had thereby at least this advantage, that it became a controversy which was the right owner; yet I would take such caution, that he should have the honour entire without a rival.

We next went to the school of languages, where three professors sat in consultation upon improving that of their own country.

The first project was to shorten discourse by cutting polysyllables into one, and leaving out verbs and participles, because in reality all things imaginable are but nouns.

The other, was a scheme for entirely abolishing all words whatsoever: and this was urged as a great advantage in point of health as well as brevity. For, it is plain, that every word we speak is in some degree a diminution of our lungs by corrosion; and consequently contributes to the shortning of our lives. An expedient was therefore offered, that since words are only names for *things*, it would be more convenient for all men to carry about them, such *things* as were necessary to express the particular business they are to discourse on. And this invention would certainly have taken place, to the great ease as well as health of the subject, if the women in conjunction with the vulgar and illiterate had not threatned to raise a rebellion, unless they might be allowed the liberty to speak with their tongues, after the manner of their forefathers: such constant irreconcileable enemies to science are the common people. However, many of the most learned and wise adhere to the new scheme of expressing themselves by *things*; which hath only this inconvenience attending it; that if a man's business be very great, and of various kinds, he must be obliged in proportion to carry a greater bundle of *things* upon his back, unless he can afford one or two strong servants to attend him. I have often beheld two of those sages almost sinking under the weight of their packs, like pedlars among us; who, when they met in the streets would lay down their loads, open their sacks, and hold conversation for an hour together; then put up their implements, help each other to resume their burthens, and take their leave.

But, for short conversations, a man may carry implements in his pockets and under his arms, enough to supply him, and in his house he cannot be at a loss; therefore the room where company meet who practise this art, is full of all things ready at hand, requisite to furnish matter for this kind of artificial converse.

Another great advantage proposed by this invention, was, that it would serve as an universal language to be understood in all civilized nations, whose goods and utensils are generally of the same kind, or nearly resembling, so that their uses might easily be comprehended. And thus, embassadors would be qualified to treat with foreign princes or ministers of State, to whose tongues they were utter strangers.

I was at the mathematical school, where the master taught his pupils after a method scarce imaginable to us in Europe. The proposition and demonstration were fairly written on a thin wafer, with ink composed of a cephalick tincture. This the student was to swallow upon a fasting stomach, and for three days following eat nothing but bread and water. As the water digested, the tincture mounted to his brain, bearing the proposition along with it. But the success hath not hitherto been answerable, partly by some error in the *quantum* or composition, and partly by the perverseness of lads, to whom this bolus is so nauseous, that they generally steal aside, and discharge it upwards before it can operate; neither have they been yet persuaded to use so long an abstinence as the prescription requires.

CHAPTER VI

A further account of the academy. The author proposeth some improvements, which are honourably received.

In the school of political projectors, I was but ill entertained; the professors appearing in my judgment wholly out of their senses; which is a scene that never fails to make me melancholy. These unhappy people were proposing schemes for persuading monarchs to chuse favourites upon the score of their wisdom, capacity, and virtue; of teaching ministers to consult the publick good; of rewarding merit, great abilities, and eminent services; of instructing princes to know their true interest, by placing it on the same foundation with that of their people: of chusing for employments persons qualified to exercise them; with many other wild impossible chimæras, that never entered before into the heart of man to conceive; and confirmed in me the old observation, that there is nothing so extravagant and irrational which some philosophers have not maintained for truth.

But, however I shall so far do justice to this part of the academy as to acknowledge, that all of them were not so visionary. There was a most ingenious doctor who seemed to be perfectly versed in the whole nature and system of government. This illustrious person had very usefully employed his studies in finding out effectual remedies for all diseases and corruptions, to which the several kinds of publick administration are subject by the vices or infirmities of those who govern, as well as by the licentiousness of those who are to obey. For instance: whereas all writers and reasoners have agreed, that there is a strict universal resemblance between the natural and the political body; can there be any thing more evident, than that the health of both must be preserved, and the diseases cured by the same prescriptions? It is allowed, that senates and great councils are often troubled with redundant, ebulliant, and other peccant humours; with many diseases of the head, and more of the heart; with strong convulsions, with grievous contractions of the nerves and sinews in both hands, but especially the right: with spleen, flatus, vertigoes and deliriums; with scrophulous tumours full of fœtid purulent matter; with sowre frothy ructations; with canine appetites and crudeness of digestion; besides many others needless to mention. This doctor therefore proposed, that upon the meeting of a senate, certain physicians should attend at the three first days of their sitting, and at the close of each day's debate, feel the pulses of every senator; after which, having maturely considered, and consulted upon the nature of the several maladies, and the methods of cure, they should on the fourth day return to the senate-house, attended by their apothecaries stored with proper medicines; and before the members sat, administer to each of them lenitives, aperitives, abstersives, corrosives, restringents, palliatives, laxatives, cephalalgicks, ictericks, apophlegmaticks, acousticks, as their several cases required; and, according as these medicines should operate, repeat, alter, or omit them at the next meeting.

This project could not be of any great expence to the publick; and might, in my poor opinion, be of much use for the dispatch of business in those countries, where senates have any share in the legislative power; beget unanimity, shorten debates, open a few mouths which are now closed, and close many more, which are now open; curb the petulancy of the young, and correct the positiveness of the old; rouse the stupid, and damp the pert.

Again, because it is a general complaint, that the favourites of princes are troubled with short and weak memories; the same doctor proposed, that whoever attended a First Minister, after having told his business with the utmost brevity, and in the plainest words; should at his departure, give the said minister, a tweak by the nose, or a kick in the belly, or tread on his corns, or lug him thrice by both ears, or run a pin into his breech, or pinch his arm black and blue; to prevent forgetfulness: and, at every levee day, repeat the same operation, until the business were done, or absolutely refused.

He likewise directed, that every senator in the great council of a nation, after he had delivered his opinion, and argued in the defence of it, should be obliged to give his vote directly contrary; because if that were done, the result would infallibly terminate in the good of the publick.

When parties in a State are violent, he offered a wonderful contrivance to reconcile them: the method is this. You take an hundred leaders of each party; you dispose them into couples of such whose heads are nearest of a size; then let two nice operators saw off the occiput of each couple at the same time, in such a manner, that the brain may be equally divided. Let the occiputs thus cut off be interchanged, applying each to the head of his opposite partyman. It seems indeed to be a work that requireth some exactness; but the professor assured us, that if it were dextrously performed, the cure would be infallible. For, he argued thus; that the two half brains being left to debate the matter between themselves within the space of one scull, would soon come to a good understanding, and produce that moderation as well as regularity of thinking, so much to be wished for in the heads of those, who imagine they came into the world only to watch and govern its motion: and as to the difference of brains in quantity or quality, among those who are directors in faction; the doctor assured us from his own knowledge, that it was a perfect trifle.

I heard a very warm debate between two professors, about the most commodious and effectual ways and means of raising money without grieving the subject. The first affirmed, the justest method would be to lay a certain tax upon vices and folly; and the sum fixed upon every man, to be rated after the fairest manner, by a jury of his neighbours. The second was of an opinion directly contrary; to tax those qualities of body and mind for which men chiefly value themselves; the rate to be more or less according to the degrees of excelling; the decision whereof should be left entirely to their own breast. The highest tax was upon men, who are the greatest favourites of the other sex; and the assessments according to the number and natures of the favours they have received; for which they are allowed to be their own vouchers. Wit, valour, and politeness were likewise pro- posed to be largely taxed, and collected in the same manner, by every person giving his own word for the quantum of what he possessed. But, as to honour, justice, wisdom and learning, they should not be taxed at all; be- cause, they are qualifications of so singular a kind, that no man will either allow them in his neighbour, or value them in himself.

The women were proposed to be taxed according to their beauty and skill in dressing; wherein they had the same privilege with the men, to be determined by their own judgment. But constancy, chastity, good sense, and good nature were not rated, because they would not bear the charge of collecting.

To keep senators in the interest of the Crown, it was proposed that the members should raffle for employments, every man first taking an oath, and giving security that he would vote for the court, whether he won or no; after which the losers had in their turn the liberty of raffling upon the next vacancy. Thus, hope and expectation would be kept alive; none would com- plain of broken promises, but impute their disappointments wholly to for- tune, whose shoulders are broader and stronger than those of a ministry.

Another professor shewed me a large paper of instructions for discovering plots and conspiracies against the Government. He advised great statesmen to examine into the diet of all suspected persons; their times of eating; upon which side they lay in bed; with which hand they wiped their posteriors; to take a strict view of their excrements, and from the colour, the odour, the taste, the consistence, the crudeness, or maturity of digestion, form a judgment of their thoughts and designs: because, men are never so serious, thoughtful, and intent, as when they are at stool; which he found by fre- quent experiment: for in such conjunctures, when he used merely as a trial to consider which was the best way of murdering the king, his ordure would have a tincture of green; but quite different when he thought only of rais- ing an insurrection, or burning the metropolis.

The whole discourse was written with great acuteness, containing many observations both curious and useful for politicians; but, as I conceived, not altogether compleat. This I ventured to tell the author, and offered, if he pleased, to supply him with some additions. He received my proposition with more compliance than is usual among writers, especially those of the projecting species, professing he would be glad to receive farther information.

I told him, that should I happen to live in a kingdom where plots and conspiracies were either in vogue from the turbulency of the meaner people, or could be turned to the use and service of the higher rank of them, I first would take care to cherish and encourage the breed of discoverers, witnesses, informers, accusers, prosecutors, evidences, swearers, together with their several subservient and subaltern instruments; and when I had got a competent number of them of all sorts and capacities, I would put them under the colour and conduct of some dextrous persons in sufficient power both to protect and reward them. Men thus qualified and thus empowered might make a most excellent use and advantage of plots, they might raise their own characters and pass for most profound politicians, they might restore new vigor to a crazy administration, they might stifle or divert general discontents; fill their pockets with forfeitures, and advance or sink the opinion of publick credit, as either might answer their private advantage. This might be done by first agreeing and settling among themselves what suspected persons should be accused of a plot. Then effectual care is taken to secure all their letters and papers, and put the criminal in safe and secure custody. These papers might be delivered to a set of artists of dexterity sufficient to find out the mysterious meanings of words, syllables, and letters. They should be allowed to put what interpretation they pleased upon them, giving them a sense not only which has no relation at all to them, but even what is quite contrary to their true intent and real meaning; thus for instance, they may, if they so fancy, interpret a seive to signify a court lady; a lame dog an invader; the plague a standing army; a buzzard a great statesman; the gout a high priest; a chamber pot a committee of grandees; a broom a revolution; a mouse trap an imployment; a bottomless pit a treasury; a sink a court; a cap and bells a favorite; a broken reed a court of justice; an empty tun a general; a running sore an Administration.

But should this method fail, recourse might be had to others more effectual, by learned men called acrosticks and anagrams. First, might be found men of skill and penetration who can discern that all initial letters have political meanings. Thus N shall signify a plot; B a regiment of horse; L a fleet at sea. Or secondly, by transposing the letters of the alphabet in any suspected paper, who can discover the deepest designs of a discontented party. So for example, if I should say in a letter to a friend, "Our brother Tom has just got the piles," a man of skill in this art would discover how the same letters which compose that sentence may be analysed into the following words; "Resist,—a plot is brought home—the tour." And this is the anagrammatick method.

The professor made me great acknowledgments for communicating these observations, and promised to make honourable mention of me in his treatise.

I saw nothing in this country that could invite me to a longer continuance; and began to think of returning home to England.

CHAPTER VII

The author leaves Lagado, arrives at Maldonada. No ship ready. He takes a short voyage to Glubbdubdrib. His reception by the governor.

THE continent of which this kingdom is a part, extends itself, as I have reason to believe, eastward to that unknown tract of America, westward of California, and north to the Pacifick Ocean, which is not above an hundred and fifty miles from Lagado, where there is a good port, and much

commerce with the great island of Luggnagg, situated to the north-west
about 29 degrees north latitude, and 140 longitude. This island of Luggnagg stands south eastwards of Japan, about an hundred leagues distant.
There is a strict alliance between the Japanese emperor, and the King
of Luggnagg, which affords frequent opportunities of sailing from one island
to the other. I determined therefore to direct my course this way, in order
to my return to Europe. I hired two mules with a guide to shew me the way,
and carry my small baggage. I took leave of my noble protector, who had
shewn me so much favour, and made me a generous present at my departure.

My journey was without any accident or adventure worth relating. When
I arrived at the port of Maldonada, (for so it is called) there was no ship
in the harbour bound for Luggnagg, nor like to be in some time. The town
is about as large as Portsmouth. I soon fell into some acquaintance, and was
very hospitably received. A gentleman of distinction said to me, that since
the ships bound for Luggnagg, could not be ready in less than a month, it
might be no disagreeable amusement for me to take a trip to the little
island of Glubbdubdrib, about five leagues off to the southwest. He offered
himself and a friend to accompany me, and that I should be provided with
a small convenient barque for the voyage.

"Glubbdubdrib," as nearly as I can interpret the word, signifies the Island
of Sorcerers or Magicians. It is about one third as large as the Isle of Wight,
and extreamly fruitful: it is governed by the head of a certain tribe, who are
all magicians. This tribe marries only among each other; and the eldest in
succession is prince or governor. He hath a noble palace, and a park of about
three thousand acres, surrounded by a wall of hewn stone twenty foot high.
In this park are several small inclosures for cattle, corn and gardening.

The governor and his family are served and attended by domesticks of
a kind somewhat unusual. By his skill in necromancy, he hath power of
calling whom he pleaseth from the dead, and commanding their service
for twenty four hours, but no longer; nor can he call the same persons up
again in less than three months, except upon very extraordinary occasions.

When we arrived at the island, which was about eleven in the morning,
one of the gentlemen who accompanied me, went to the governor, and desired admittance for a stranger, who came on purpose to have the honour
of attending on his Highness. This was immediately granted, and we all
three entered the gate of the palace between two rows of guards, armed and
dressed after a very antick manner, and something in their countenances
that made my flesh creep with a horror I cannot express. We passed through
several apartments between servants of the same sort, ranked on each side
as before, until we came to the chamber of presence, where after three profound obeysances, and a few general questions, we were permitted to sit
on three stools near the lowest step of his Highness's throne. He understood the language of Balnibarbi, although it were different from that of
his island. He desired me to give him some account of my travels; and to let
me see that I should be treated without ceremony, he dismissed all his attendants with a turn of his finger, at which to my great astonishment they
vanished in an instant, like visions in a dream, when we awake on a sudden.

I could not recover my self in some time, until the governor assured me that I should receive no hurt; and observing my two companions to be under no concern, who had been often entertained in the same manner, I began to take courage; and related to his Highness a short history of my several adventures, yet not without some hesitation, and frequently looking behind me to the place where I had seen those domestick spectres. I had the honour to dine with the governor, where a new set of ghosts served up the meat, and waited at table. I now observed my self to be less terrified than I had been in the morning. I stayed until sun-set, but humbly desired his Highness to excuse me for not accepting his invitation of lodging in the palace. My two friends and I lay at a private house in the town adjoining, which is the capital of this little island; and the next morning we returned to pay our duty to the governor, as he was pleased to command us.

After this manner we continued in the island for ten days, most part of every day with the governor, and at night in our lodging. I soon grew so familiarized to the sight of spirits, that after the third or fourth time they gave me no emotion at all; or if I had any apprehensions left, my curiosity prevailed over them. For his Highness the governor ordered me to call up whatever persons I would chuse to name, and in whatever numbers among all the dead from the beginning of the world to the present time, and command them to answer any questions I should think fit to ask; with this condition, that my questions must be confined within the compass of the times they lived in. And one thing I might depend upon, that they would certainly tell me truth; for lying was a talent of no use in the lower world.

I made my humble acknowledgments to his Highness for so great a favour. We were in a chamber, from whence there was a fair prospect into the park. And because my first inclination was to be entertained with scenes of pomp and magnificence, I desired to see Alexander the Great, at the head of his army just after the battle of Arbela, which upon a motion of the governor's finger immediately appeared in a large field under the window, where we stood. Alexander was called up into the room: it was with great difficulty that I understood his Greek, and had but little of my own. He assured me upon his honour, that he was not poisoned, but dyed of a fever by excessive drinking.

Next I saw Hannibal passing the Alps, who told me he had not a drop of vinegar in his camp.

I saw Cæsar and Pompey at the head of their troops just ready to engage. I saw the former in his last great triumph. I desired that the Senate of Rome might appear before me in one large chamber, and a modern representative, in counterview, in another. The first seemed to be an assembly of heroes and demi-gods; the other, a knot of pedlars, pick-pockets, highwaymen, and bullies.

The governor, at my request, gave the sign for Cæsar and Brutus to advance towards us. I was struck with a profound veneration at the sight of Brutus; and could easily discover the most consummate virtue, the greatest intrepidity, and firmness of mind, the truest love of his country, and general benevolence for mankind in every lineament of his countenance. I observed with much pleasure, that these two persons were in good intelligence with each other; and Cæsar freely confessed to me, that the greatest actions of his own life were not equal by many degrees to the glory of taking it away. I had the honour to have much conversation with Brutus; and was told, that his ancestors Junius, Socrates, Epaminondas, Cato the Younger, Sir Thomas More, and himself, were perpetually together: a sextumvirate to which all the ages of the world cannot add a seventh.

It would be tedious to trouble the reader with relating what vast numbers of illustrious persons were called up, to gratify that insatiable desire I had to see the world in every period of antiquity placed before me. I chiefly fed mine eyes with beholding the destroyers of tyrants and usurpers, and the restorers of liberty to oppressed and injured nations. But, it is impossible to express the satisfaction I received in my own mind, after such a manner as to make it a suitable entertainment to the reader.

CHAPTER VIII

A further account of Glubbdubdrib. Antient and modern history corrected.

HAVING a desire to see those antients, who were most renowned for wit and learning, I set apart one day on purpose. I proposed that Homer and Aristotle might appear at the head of all their commentators; but these were so numerous, that some hundreds were forced to attend in the court and outward rooms of the palace. I knew, and could distinguish those two heroes at first sight, not only from the crowd, but from each other. Homer was the taller and comelier person of the two, walked very erect for one of his age, and his eyes were the most quick and piercing I ever beheld. Aristotle stooped much, and made use of a staff. His visage was meager, his hair lank and thin, and his voice hollow. I soon discovered, that both of them were perfect strangers to the rest of the company, and had never seen or heard of them before. And I had a whisper from a ghost, who shall be nameless, that these commentators always kept in the most distant quarters from their principals in the lower world, through a consciousness of shame and guilt, because they had so horribly misrepresented the meaning of those authors to posterity. I introduced Didymus and Eustathius to Homer, and prevailed on him to treat them better than perhaps they deserved; for he soon found they wanted a genius to enter into the spirit of a poet. But Aristotle was out of all patience with the account I gave him of Scotus and Ramus, as I presented them to him; and he asked them whether the rest of the tribe were as great dunces as themselves.

I then desired the governor to call up Descartes and Gassendi, with whom I prevailed to explain their systems to Aristotle. This great philosopher freely acknowledged his own mistakes in natural philosophy, because he proceeded in many things upon conjecture, as all men must do; and he found, that Gassendi, who had made the doctrine of Epicurus as palatable as he could, and the *vortices* of Descartes, were equally exploded. He predicted the same fate to *attraction*, whereof the present learned are such zealous asserters. He said, that new systems of nature were but new fashions, which would vary in every age; and even those who pretend to demonstrate them from mathematical principles, would flourish but a short period of time, and be out of vogue when that was determined.

I spent five days in conversing with many others of the antient learned. I saw most of the first Roman emperors. I prevailed on the governor to call up Eliogabalus's cooks to dress us a dinner; but they could not shew us much of their skill, for want of materials. A helot of Agesilaus made us a dish of Spartan broth, but I was not able to get down a second spoonful.

The two gentlemen who conducted me to the island were pressed by their private affairs to return in three days, which I employed in seeing some of the modern dead, who had made the greatest figure for two or three hundred years past in our own and other countries of Europe; and having been always a great admirer of old illustrious families, I desired the governor would call up a dozen or two of kings with their ancestors in order, for eight or nine generations. But my disappointment was grievous and unexpected. For, instead of a long train with royal diadems, I saw in one family two fidlers, three spruce courtiers, and an Italian prelate. In another, a barber, an abbot, and two cardinals. I have too great a veneration for crowned heads to dwell any longer on so nice a subject: but as to counts, marquesses, dukes, earls, and the like, I was not so scrupulous. And I confess, it was not without some pleasure that I found my self able to trace the particular features, by which certain families are distinguished up to their originals. I could plainly discover from whence one family derives a long chin; why a second hath abounded with knaves for two generations, and fools for two more; why a third happened to be crack-brained; and a fourth, to be sharpers. Whence it came what Polydore Virgil says of a certain great house, "Nec vir fortis, nec fœmina casta." How cruelty, falshood, and cowardice grew to be characteristicks by which certain families are distinguished as much as by their coat of arms. Who first brought the pox into a noble house, which hath lineally descended in scrophulous tumours to their posterity. Neither could I wonder at all this, when I saw such an interruption of lineages by pages, lacqueys, valets, coachmen, gamesters, fidlers, players, captains, and pick-pockets.

I was chiefly disgusted with modern history. For having strictly examined all the persons of greatest name in the courts of princes for an hundred years past, I found how the world had been misled by prostitute writers, to ascribe the greatest exploits in war to cowards, the wisest counsel to fools, sincerity to flatterers, Roman virtue to betrayers of their country, piety to atheists, chastity to sodomites, truth to informers. How many innocent and excellent persons had been condemned to death or banishment, by the practising of great ministers upon the corruption of judges, and the malice of factions. How many villains had been exalted to the highest places of trust, power, dignity, and profit: how great a share in the motions and events of courts, councils, and senates might be challenged by bawds, whores, pimps, parasites, and buffoons: how low an opinion I had of human wisdom and integrity, when I was truly informed of the springs and motives of great enterprizes and revolutions in the world, and of the contemptible accidents to which they owed their success.

Here I discovered the roguery and ignorance of those who pretend to write *anecdotes*, or secret history; who send so many kings to their graves with a cup of poison; will repeat the discourse between a prince and chief minister, where no witness was by; unlock the thoughts and cabinets of ambassadors and Secretaries of State; and have the perpetual misfortune to be mistaken. Here I discovered the true causes of many great events that have surprized the world: how a whore can govern the back-stairs, the back-stairs a council, and the council a senate. A general confessed in my presence, that he got a victory purely by the force of cowardice and ill conduct: and an admiral, that for want of proper intelligence, he beat the enemy to whom he intended to betray the fleet. Three kings protested to me, that in their whole reigns they did never once prefer any person of merit, unless by mistake or treachery of some minister in whom they confided: neither would they do it, if they were to live again; and they shewed with great strength of reason, that the royal throne could not be supported without corruption, because that positive, confident, restive temper, which virtue infused into man, was a perpetual clog to publick business.

I had the curiosity to enquire in a particular manner, by what method great numbers had procured to themselves high titles of honour, and prodigious estates; and I confined my enquiry to a very modern period: however, without grating upon present times, because I would be sure to give no offence, even to foreigners. (For I hope the reader need not be told, that I do not in the least intend my own country, in what I say upon this occasion.) A great number of persons concerned were called up, and upon a very slight examination, discovered such a scene of infamy, that I cannot reflect upon it without some seriousness. Perjury, oppression, subornation, fraud, pandarism, and the like *infirmities* were amongst the most excuseable arts they had to mention; and for these I gave, as it was reasonable, due allowance. But, when some confessed, they owed their greatness and wealth to sodomy or incest; others to the prostituting of their own wives and daughters; others to the betraying their country or their prince; some to poisoning, more to the perverting of justice in order to destroy the innocent: I hope I may be pardoned, if these discoveries inclined me a little to abate of that profound veneration, which I am naturally apt to pay to persons of high rank, who ought to be treated with the utmost respect due to their sublime dignity, by us their inferiors.

I had often read of some great services done to princes and States, and desired to see the persons by whom those services were performed. Upon enquiry, I was told, that their names were to be found on no record, except a few of them whom history hath represented as the vilest rogues and traytors. As to the rest, I had never once heard of them. They all appeared with dejected looks, and in the meanest habit; most of them telling me they died in poverty and disgrace, and the rest on a scaffold or a gibbet.

Among others, there was one person whose case appeared a little singular. He had a youth about eighteen years old standing by his side. He told me, he had for many years been commander of a ship; and in the sea fight at Actium, had the good fortune to break through the enemy's great line of battle, sink three of their capital ships, and take a fourth, which was the sole cause of Antony's flight, and of the victory that ensued: that, the youth standing by him, his only son, was killed in the action. He added, that upon the confidence of some merit, the war being at an end, he went to Rome, and solicited at the court of Augustus, to be preferred to a greater ship, whose commander had been killed; but without any regard to his pretensions, it was given to a boy who had never seen the sea, the son of a *libertina*, who waited on one of the emperor's mistresses. Returning back to his own vessel, he was charged with neglect of duty, and the ship given to a favourite page of Publicola the vice-admiral; whereupon he retired to a poor farm, at a great distance from Rome, and there ended his life. I was so curious to know the truth of this story, that I desired Agrippa might be called, who was admiral in that fight. He appeared, and confirmed the whole account, but with much more advantage to the captain, whose modesty had extenuated or concealed a great part of his merit.

I was surprized to find corruption grown so high and so quick in that empire, by the force of luxury so lately introduced; which made me less wonder at many parallel cases in other countries, where vices of all kinds have reigned so much longer, and where the whole praise as well as pillage, hath been engrossed by the chief commander, who, perhaps, had the least title to either.

As every person called up, made exactly the same appearance he had done in the world, it gave me melancholy reflections to observe how much the race of human kind was degenerate among us, within these hundred years past. How the pox under all its consequences and denominations had altered every lineament of an English countenance, shortened the size of bodies, unbraced the nerves, relaxed the sinews and muscles, introduced a sallow complexion, and rendered the flesh loose and *rancid*.

I descended so low as to desire that some English yoemen of the old stamp, might be summoned to appear; once so famous for the simplicity of their manners, diet, and dress; for justice in their dealings; for their true spirit of liberty; for their valour and love of their country. Neither could I be wholly unmoved after comparing the living with the dead, when I considered how all these pure native virtues were prostituted for a piece of money by their grand-children, who in selling their votes, and managing at elections, have acquired every vice and corruption that can possibly be learned in court.

CHAPTER IX

The author's return to Maldonada. Sails to the kingdom of Luggnagg. The author confined. He is sent for to court. The manner of his admittance. The king's great lenity to his subjects.

THE day of our departure being come, I took leave of his Highness the Governor of Glubbdubdrib, and returned with my two companions to Maldonada, where, after a fortnight's waiting, a ship was ready to sail for Luggnagg. The two gentlemen, and some others, were so generous and kind as to furnish me with provisions, and see me on board. I was a month in this voyage. We had one violent storm, and were under a necessity of steering westward to get into the trade-wind, which holds for above sixty leagues. On the 21st of April, 1708, we sailed in the river of Clumegnig, which is a sea-port town, at the south-east point of Luggnagg. We cast anchor within a league of the town, and made a signal for a pilot. Two of them came on board in less than half an hour, by whom we were guided between certain shoals and rocks, which are very dangerous in the passage, to a large basin, where a fleet may ride in safety within a cable's length of the town wall.

Some of our sailors, whether out of treachery, or inadvertence, had informed the pilots that I was a stranger, and a great traveller, whereof these gave notice to a customhouse officer, by whom I was examined very strictly upon my landing. This officer spoke to me in the language of Balnibarbi, which by the force of much commerce is generally understood in that town, especially by seamen, and those employed in the customs. I gave him a short account of some particulars, and made my story as plausible and consistent as I could; but I thought it necessary to disguise my country, and call my self an Hollander; because my intentions were for Japan, and I knew the Dutch were the only Europeans permitted to enter into that kingdom. I therefore told the officer, that having been shipwrecked on the coast of Balnibarbi, and cast on a rock, I was received up into Laputa, or the flying island (of which he had often heard) and was now endeavouring to get to Japan, from whence I might find a convenience of returning to my own country. The officer said, I must be confined until he could receive orders from court, for which he would write immediately, and hoped to receive an answer in a fortnight. I was carried to a convenient lodging, with a centry placed at the door; however, I had the liberty of a large garden, and was treated with humanity enough, being maintained all the time at the king's charge. I was invited by several persons, chiefly out of curiosity, because it was reported I came from countries very remote, of which they had never heard.

I hired a young man who came in the same ship to be an interpreter; he was a native of Luggnagg, but had lived some years at Maldonada, and was a perfect master of both languages. By his assistance, I was able to hold a conversation with those that came to visit me; but this consisted only of their questions and my answers.

The dispatch came from court about the time we expected. It contained a warrant for conducting me and my retinue to Traldragdubb or Trildrogdrib, (for it is pronounced both ways as near as I can remember) by a party of ten horse. All my retinue was that poor lad for an interpreter, whom I persuaded into my service. At my humble request, we had each of us a mule to ride on. A messenger was dispatched half a day's journey before us, to give the king notice of my approach, and to desire that his Majesty would please to appoint a day and hour, when it would be his gracious pleasure that I might have the honour to *lick the dust before his footstool*. This is the court style, and I found it to be more than matter of form: for, upon my admittance two days after my arrival, I was commanded to crawl upon my belly, and lick the floor as I advanced; but on account of my being a stranger, care was taken to have it so clean, that the dust was not offensive. However, this was a peculiar grace, not allowed to any but persons of the highest rank, when they desire an admittance: nay, sometimes the floor is strewed with dust on purpose, when the person to be admitted happens to have powerful enemies at court: and I have seen a great lord with his mouth so crammed, that when he had crept to the proper distance from the throne, he was not able to speak a word. Neither is there any remedy, because it is capital for those who receive an audience, to spit or wipe their mouths in his Majesty's presence. There is indeed another custom, which I cannot altogether approve of. When the king hath a mind to put any of his nobles to death in a gentle indulgent manner, he commands to have the floor strowed with a certain brown powder, of a deadly composition, which being licked up, infallibly kills him in twenty-four hours. But in justice to this prince's great clemency, and the care he hath of his subjects lives, (wherein it were much to be wished that the monarchs of Europe would imitate him) it must be mentioned for his honour, that strict orders are given to have the infected parts of the floor well washed after every such execution; which, if his domesticks neglect, they are in danger of incurring his royal displeasure. I my self heard him give directions, that one of his pages should be whipt, whose turn it was to give notice about washing the floor after an execution, but maliciously had omitted it; by which neglect, a young lord, of great hopes, coming to an audience, was unfortunately poisoned, although the king, at that time, had no design against his life. But this good prince was so gracious, as to forgive the page his whipping, upon promise that he would do so no more, without special orders.

To return from this digression; when I had crept within four yards of the throne, I raised my self gently upon my knees, and then striking my forehead seven times against the ground, I pronounced the following words, as they had been taught me the night before, "Ickpling gloffthrobb squutserumm blhiop mlashnalt zwin tnodbalkguffh slhiophad gurdlubh asht." This is the compliment established by the laws of the land for all persons admitted to the king's presence. It may be rendered into English thus: "May your cœlestial Majesty out-live the sun, eleven moons and an half." To this the king returned some answer, which although I could not understand, yet I replied as I had been directed; "Fluft drin yalerick dwuldum prastrad mirplush," which properly signifies, "My tongue is in the mouth of my friend"; and by this expression was meant, that I desired leave to bring my interpreter; whereupon the young man already mentioned, was accordingly introduced; by whose intervention I answered as many questions as his Majesty could put in above an hour. I spoke in the Balnibarbian tongue, and my interpreter delivered my meaning in that of Luggnagg.

The king was much delighted with my company, and ordered his *Bliffmarklub*, or High Chamberlain, to appoint a lodging in the court for me, and my interpreter, with a daily allowance for my table, and a large purse of gold for my common expences.

I stayed three months in this country out of perfect obedience to his Majesty, who was pleased highly to favour me, and made me very honourable offers. But I thought it more consistent with prudence and justice to pass the remainder of my days with my wife and family.

CHAPTER X

The Luggnaggians commended. A particular description of the Struldbruggs, with many conversations between the author and some eminent persons upon that subject.

THE Luggnaggians are a polite and generous people, and although they are not without some share of that pride which is peculiar to all eastern countries, yet they shew themselves courteous to strangers, especially such who are countenanced by the court. I had many acquaintance among persons of the best fashion; and being always attended by my interpreter, the conversation we had was not disagreeable.

One day in much good company, I was asked by a person of quality, whether I had seen any of their Struldbruggs, or Immortals. I said I had not; and desired he would explain to me what he meant by such an appellation, applyed to a mortal creature. He told me, that sometimes, although very rarely, a child happened to be born in a family with a red circular spot in the forehead, directly over the left eye-brow, which was an infallible mark that it should never dye. The spot, as he described it, was about the compass of a silver threepence, but in the course of time grew larger, and changed its colour; for at twelve years old it became green, so continued until five and twenty, then turned to a deep blue; at five and forty it grew coal-black, and as large as an English shilling; but never admitted any farther alteration. He said these births were so rare, that he did not believe there could be above eleven hundred Struldbruggs of both sexes in the whole kingdom, of which he computed about fifty in the metropolis, and among the rest a young girl born about three years ago. That these productions were not peculiar to any family, but a meer effect of chance; and the children of the Struldbruggs themselves, were equally mortal with the rest of the people.

I freely own my self to have been struck with inexpressible delight upon hearing this account: and the person who gave it me happening to understand the Balnibarbian language, which I spoke very well, I could not forbear breaking out into expressions perhaps a little too extravagant. I cryed out as in a rapture; "Happy nation, where every child hath at least a chance for being immortal! Happy people who enjoy so many living examples of antient virtue, and have masters ready to instruct them in the wisdom of all former ages! But, happiest beyond all comparison are those excellent Struldbruggs, who being born exempt from that universal calamity of human nature, have their minds free and disingaged, without the weight and depression of spirits caused by the continual apprehension of death." I discovered my admiration that I had not observed any of these illustrious persons at court; the black spot on the forehead, being so remarkable a distinction, that I could not have easily overlooked it: and it was impossible that his Majesty, a most judicious prince, should not provide himself with a good number of such wise and able counsellors. Yet, perhaps, the virtue of those reverend sages was too strict for the corrupt and libertine manners of a court. And we often find by experience, that young men are too opinionative and volatile to be guided by the sober dictates of their seniors. However, since the king was pleased to allow me access to his royal person, I was resolved upon the very first occasion to deliver my opinion to him on this matter freely, and at large by the help of my interpreter; and whether he would please to take my advice or no, yet in one thing I was determined, that his Majesty having frequently offered me an establishment in this country, I would, with great thankfulness accept the favour, and pass my life here in the conversation of those superior beings the Struldbruggs, if they would please to admit me.

The gentleman to whom I addressed my discourse, because (as I have already observed) he spoke the language of Balnibarbi, said to me with a sort of a smile, which usually ariseth from pity to the ignorant, that he was glad of any occasion to keep me among them, and desired my permission to explain to the company what I had spoke. He did so; and they talked together for some time in their own language, whereof I understood not a syllable, neither could I observe by their countenances what impression my discourse had made on them. After a short silence, the same person told me, that his friends and mine (so he thought fit to express himself) were very much pleased with the judicious remarks I had made on the great happiness and advantages of immortal life; and they were desirous to know in a particular manner, what scheme of living I should have formed to my self, if it had fallen to my lot to have been born a Struldbrugg.

I answered, it was easy to be eloquent on so copious and delightful a subject, especially to me, who have been often apt to amuse my self with visions of what I should do if I were a king, a general, or a great lord: and upon this very case, I had frequently run over the whole system how I should employ my self, and pass the time if I were sure to live for ever.

That, if it had been my good fortune to come into the world a Struldbrugg, as soon as I could discover my own happiness, by understanding the difference between life and death, I would first resolve by all arts and methods whatsoever, to procure my self riches: in the pursuit of which, by thrift and management, I might reasonably expect in about two hundred years, to be the wealthiest man in the kingdom. In the second place, I would from my earliest youth, apply my self to the study of arts and sciences, by which I should arrive in time to excel all others in learning. Lastly, I would carefully record every action and event of consequence that happened in the publick, impartially draw the characters of the several successions of princes, and great ministers of State, with my own observations on every point. I would exactly set down the several changes in customs, languages, fashions, dress, dyet and diversions. By all which acquirements, I should be a living treasury of knowledge and wisdom, and certainly become the oracle of the nation.

I would never marry after threescore, but live in an hospitable manner, yet still on the saving side. I would entertain my self in forming and directing the minds of hopeful young men, by convincing them from my own remembrance, experience and observation, fortified by numerous examples of the usefulness of virtue in publick and private life. But, my choice and constant companions, should be a set of my own immortal brotherhood; among whom I would elect a dozen from the most ancient down to my own contemporaries. Where any of these wanted fortunes, I would provide them with convenient lodges round my own estate, and have some of them always at my table, only mingling a few of the most valuable among you mortals; whom length of time would harden me to lose with little or no reluctance, and treat your posterity after the same manner: just as a man diverts himself with the annual succession of pinks and tulips in his garden, without regretting the loss of those which withered the preceding year.

These Struldbruggs and I would mutually communicate our observations and memorials through the course of time, remark the several gradations by which corruption steals into the world, and oppose it in every step, by giving perpetual warning and instruction to mankind; which, added to the strong influence of our own example, would probably prevent that continual degeneracy of human nature, so justly complained of in all ages.

Add to all this, the pleasure of seeing the various revolutions of states and empires; the changes in the lower and upper world; antient cities in ruins, and obscure villages become the seats of kings. Famous rivers lessening into shallow brooks; the ocean leaving one coast dry, and overwhelming another: the discovery of many countries yet unknown. Barbarity over-running the politest nations, and the most barbarous becoming civilized. I should then see the discovery of the *longitude*, the *perpetual motion*, the *universal medicine*, and many other great inventions brought to the utmost perfection.

What wonderful discoveries should we make in astronomy, by outliving and confirming our own predictions; by observing the progress and returns of comets, with the changes of motion in the sun, moon and stars.

I enlarged upon many other topicks, which the natural desire of endless life and sublunary happiness could easily furnish me with. When I had ended, and the sum of my discourse had been interpreted as before, to the rest of the company, there was a good deal of talk among them in the language of the country, not without some laughter at my expence. At last, the same gentleman who had been my interpreter, said, he was desired by the rest, to set me right in a few mistakes, which I had fallen into through the common imbecility of human nature, and upon that allowance was less answerable for them. That, this breed of Struldbruggs was peculiar to their country, for there were no such people either in Balnibarbi or Japan, where he had the honour to be ambassador from his Majesty, and found the natives in both those kingdoms, very hard to believe that the fact was possible; and it appeared from my astonishment when he first mentioned the matter to me, that I received it as a thing wholly new, and scarcely to be credited. That, in the two kingdoms above-mentioned, where during his residence he had conversed very much, he observed long life to be the universal desire and wish of mankind. That, whoever had one foot in the grave, was sure to hold back the other as strongly as he could. That, the oldest had still hopes of living one day longer, and looked on death as the greatest evil, from which nature always prompted him to retreat; only in this island of

Luggnagg, the appetite for living was not so eager, from the continual example of the Struldbruggs before their eyes.

That, the system of living contrived by me was unreasonable and unjust, because it supposed a perpetuity of youth, health, and vigour, which no man could be so foolish to hope, however extravagant he might be in his wishes. That, the question therefore was not whether a man would chuse to be always in the prime of youth, attended with prosperity and health; but how he would pass a perpetual life under all the usual disadvantages which old age brings along with it. For, although few men will avow their desires of being immortal upon such hard conditions, yet in the two kingdoms before-mentioned of Balnibarbi and Japan, he observed that every man desired to put off death for some time longer, let it approach ever so late; and he rarely heard of any man who dyed willingly, except he were excited by the extremity of grief or torture. And he appealed to me whether in those countries I had travelled as well as my own, I had not observed the same general disposition.

After this preface, he gave me a particular account of the Struldbruggs among them. He said they commonly acted like mortals, until about thirty years old, after which by degrees they grew melancholy and dejected, increasing in both until they came to fourscore. This he learned from their own confession; for otherwise, there not being above two or three of that species born in an age, they were too few to form a general observation by. When they came to fourscore years, which is reckoned the extremity of living in this country, they had not only all the follies and infirmities of other old men, but many more which arose from the dreadful prospect of never dying. They were not only opinionative, peevish, covetous, morose, vain, talkative; but uncapable of friendship, and dead to all natural affection, which never descended below their grand-children. Envy and impotent desires, are their prevailing passions. But those objects against which their envy seems principally directed, are the vices of the younger sort, and the deaths of the old. By reflecting on the former, they find themselves cut off from all possibility of pleasure; and whenever they see a funeral, they lament and repine that others are gone to a harbour of rest, to which they themselves never can hope to arrive. They have no remembrance of any thing but what they learned and observed in their youth and middle age, and even that is very imperfect: and for the truth or particulars of any fact, it is safer to depend on common traditions, than upon their best recollections. The least miserable among them, appear to be those who turn to dotage, and entirely lose their memories; these meet with more pity and assistance, because they want many bad qualities which abound in others.

If a Struldbrugg happen to marry one of his own kind, the marriage is dissolved of course by the courtesy of the kingdom, as soon as the younger of the two comes to be fourscore. For the law thinks it a reasonable indulgence, that those who are condemned without any fault of their own, to a perpetual continuance in the world, should not have their misery doubled by the load of a wife.

As soon as they have compleated the term of eighty years, they are looked on as dead in law; their heirs immediately succeed to their estates, only a small pittance is reserved for their support; and the poor ones are maintained at the publick charge. After that period, they are held incapable of any employment of trust or profit; they cannot purchase lands, or take leases; neither are they allowed to be witnesses in any cause, either civil or criminal, not even for the decision of meers and bounds.

At ninety they lose their teeth and hair; they have at that age no distinction of taste, but eat and drink what ever they can get, without relish or appetite. The diseases they were subject to, still continue without encreasing or diminishing. In talking, they forget the common appellation of things, and the names of persons, even of those who are their nearest friends and relations. For the same reason, they never can amuse themselves with reading, because their memory will not serve to carry them from the beginning of a sentence to the end; and by this defect, they are deprived of the only entertainment whereof they might otherwise be capable.

The language of this country being always upon the flux, the Struldbruggs of one age, do not understand those of another; neither are they able after two hundred years, to hold any conversation (farther than by a few general words) with their neighbours the mortals; and thus they lye under the disadvantage of living like foreigners in their own country.

This was the account given me of the Struldbruggs, as near as I can remember. I afterwards saw five or six of different ages, the youngest not above two hundred years old, who were brought to me at several times by some of my friends; but although they were told that I was a great traveller, and had seen all the world, they had not the least curiosity to ask me a question; only desired I would give them *slumskudask*, or a token of remembrance; which is a modest way of begging, to avoid the law that strictly forbids it, because they are provided for by the publick, although, indeed, with a very scanty allowance.

They are despised and hated by all sorts of people: when one of them is born, it is reckoned ominous, and their birth is recorded very particularly; so that you may know their age by consulting the registry, which however, hath not been kept above a thousand years past, or at least, hath been destroyed by time or publick disturbances. But the usual way of computing how old they are, is by asking them what kings or great persons they can remember, and then consulting history; for infallibly, the last prince in their mind, did not begin his reign after they were fourscore years old.

They were the most mortifying sight I ever beheld; and the women more horrible than the men. Besides the usual deformities in extreme old age, they acquired an additional ghastliness in proportion to their number of years, which is not to be described; and among half a dozen I soon distinguished which was the eldest, although there were not above a century or two between them.

The reader will easily believe, that from what I had heard and seen, my keen appetite for perpetuity of life was much abated. I grew heartily ashamed of the pleasing visions I had formed; and thought no tyrant could invent a death into which I would not run with pleasure from such a life. The king heard of all that had passed between me and my friends upon this occasion, and rallied me very pleasantly; wishing I would send a couple of Struldbruggs to my own country, to arm our people against the fear of death; but this it seems is forbidden by the fundamental laws of the kingdom; or else I should have been well content with the trouble and expence of transporting them.

I could not but agree, that the laws of this kingdom relating to the Struld-bruggs, were founded upon the strongest reasons, and such as any other country would be under the necessity of enacting in the like circumstances. Otherwise, as avarice is the necessary consequent of old age, those immortals would in time become proprietors of the whole nation, and engross the civil power; which, for want of abilities to manage, must end in the ruin of the publick.

CHAPTER XI

The author leaves Luggnagg and sails to Japan. From thence he returns in a Dutch ship to Amsterdam, and from Amsterdam to England.

I THOUGHT this account of the Struldbruggs might be some entertainment to the reader, because it seems to be a little out of the common way; at least, I do not remember to have met the like in any book of travels that hath come to my hands: and, if I am deceived, my excuse must be, that it is necessary for travellers who describe the same country, very often to agree in dwelling on the same particulars, without deserving the censure of having borrowed or transcribed from those who wrote before them.

There is indeed a perpetual commerce between this kingdom and the great empire of Japan; and it is very probable, that the Japanese authors may have given some account of the Struldbruggs; but my stay in Japan was so short, and I was so entirely a stranger to the language, that I was not qualified to make any enquiries. But I hope the Dutch, upon this notice, will be curious and able enough to supply my defects.

His Majesty having often pressed me to accept some employment in his court, and finding me absolutely determined to return to my native country, was pleased to give me his licence to depart; and honoured me with a letter of recommendation under his own hand, to the Emperor of Japan. He likewise presented me with four hundred forty-four large pieces of gold (this nation delighting in even numbers) and a red diamond, which I sold in England, for eleven hundred pounds.

On the 6th day of May, 1709, I took a solemn leave of his Majesty, and all my friends. This prince was so gracious as to order a guard to conduct me to Glanguenstald, which is a royal port to the south-west part of the island. In six days I found a vessel ready to carry me to Japan; and spent fifteen days in the voyage. We landed at a small port-town called Xamoschi, situated on the south-east part of Japan. The town lies on the western part, where there is a narrow streight, leading northward into a long arm of the sea, upon the north-west part of which, Yedo the metropolis stands. At landing I shewed the custom-house officers my letter from the King of Luggnagg to his Imperial Majesty: they knew the seal perfectly well; it was

as broad as the palm of my hand. The impression was, "A King lifting up a
Lame Beggar from the Earth." The magistrates of the town hearing of my
letter, received me as a publick minister; they provided me with carriages
and servants, and bore my charges to Yedo, where I was admitted to an
audience, and delivered my letter; which was opened with great ceremony,
and explained to the emperor by an interpreter, who gave me notice of his
Majesty's order, that I should signify my request; and whatever it were, it
should be granted for the sake of his royal brother of Luggnagg. This interpreter was a person employed to transact affairs with the Hollanders: he
soon conjectured by my countenance, that I was an European, and therefore
repeated his Majesty's commands in Low-Dutch, which he spoke perfectly
well. I answered (as I had before determined) that I was a Dutch merchant,
shipwrecked in a very remote country, from whence I travelled by sea and
land to Luggnagg, and then took shipping for Japan, where I knew my
countrymen often traded; and, with some of these, I hoped to get an opportunity of returning into Europe: I therefore most humbly intreated his
royal favour, to give order, that I should be conducted in safety to Nangasac. To this I added another petition, that for the sake of my patron the
King of Luggnagg, his Majesty would condescend to excuse my performing
the ceremony imposed on my countrymen, of *trampling upon the crucifix*;
because I had been thrown into his kingdom by my misfortunes, without
any intention of trading. When this latter petition was interpreted to the
emperor, he seemed a little surprized; and said, he believed I was the first
of my countrymen who ever made any scruple in this point; and that he
began to doubt, whether I were a real Hollander or no; but rather suspected
I must be a Christian. However, for the reasons I had offered, but chiefly to
gratify the King of Luggnagg, by an uncommon mark of his favour, he
would comply with the *singularity* of my humour; but, the affair must be
managed with dexterity, and his officers should be commanded to let me
pass, as it were, by forgetfulness. For he assured me, that if the secret
should be discovered by my countrymen, the Dutch, they would cut my
throat in the voyage. I returned my thanks, by the interpreter, for so unusual a favour; and some troops being at that time on their march to Nangasac, the commanding officer had orders to convey me safe thither, with
particular instructions about the business of the *crucifix*.

On the 9th day of June, 1709, I arrived at Nangasac, after a very long
and troublesome journey. I soon fell into company of some Dutch sailors
belonging to the *Amboyna* of Amsterdam, a stout ship of 450 tons. I had
lived long in Holland, pursuing my studies at Leyden, and I spoke Dutch
well: the seamen soon knew from whence I came last; they were curious to
enquire into my voyages and course of life. I made up a story as short and
probable as I could, but concealed the greatest part. I knew many persons
in Holland; I was able to invent names for my parents, whom I pretended
to be obscure people in the province of Guelderland. I would have given the
captain (one Theodorus Vangrult) what he pleased to ask for my voyage to
Holland; but, understanding I was a surgeon, he was contented to take half
the usual rate, on condition that I would serve him in the way of my calling.
Before we took shipping, I was often asked by some of the crew, whether I

had performed the ceremony above-mentioned? I evaded the question by general answers, that I had satisfied the emperor and court in all particulars. However, a malicious rogue of a skipper went to an officer, and pointing to me, told him, I had not yet *trampled upon the crucifix:* but the other, who had received instructions to let me pass, gave the rascal twenty strokes on the shoulders with a bamboo; after which I was no more troubled with such questions.

Nothing happened worth mentioning in this voyage. We sailed with a fair wind to the Cape of Good Hope, where we staid only to take in fresh water. On the 16th of April we arrived safe at Amsterdam, having lost only three men by sickness in the voyage, and a fourth who fell from the fore-mast into the sea, not far from the coast of Guinea. From Amsterdam, I soon after set sail for England, in a small vessel belonging to that city.

On the 10th of April, 1710, we put in at the Downs. I landed the next morning, and saw once more my native country, after an absence of five years and six months compleat. I went strait to Redriff, whither I arrived the same day at two in the afternoon, and found my wife and family in good health.

THE END OF THE THIRD PART

PART IV
A VOYAGE TO THE COUNTRY OF THE HOUYHNHNMS

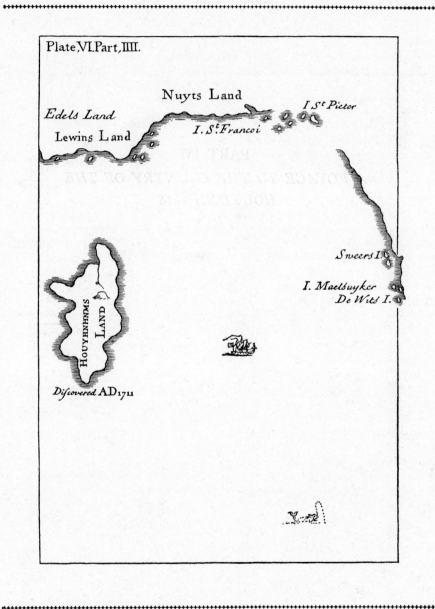

Plate, VI. Part, IIII.

Edels Land

Lewins Land

Nuyts Land

I. S.ᵗ Francoi

I S.ᵗ Pieter

Sneers I.

I. Maelsuyker

De Wits I.

HOUYHNHMS LAND

Discovered AD 1711

CHAPTER I

The author sets out as captain of a ship. His men conspire against him, confine him a long time to his cabbin, set him on shoar in an unknown land. He travels up into the country. The Yahoos, a strange sort of animal described. The author meets two Houyhnhnms.

I CONTINUED at home with my wife and children about five months in a very happy condition, if I could have learned the lesson of knowing when I was well. I left my poor wife big with child, and accepted an advantageous offer made me to be captain of the *Adventure*, a stout merchantman of 350 tuns: for I understood navigation well, and being grown weary of a surgeon's employment at sea, which however I could exercise upon occasion, I took a skilful young man of that calling, one Robert Purefoy, into my ship. We set sail from Portsmouth upon the 7th day of September, 1710; on the 14th we met with Captain Pocock of Bristol, at Tenariff, who was going to the Bay of Campeachy to cut logwood. On the 16th, he was parted from us by a storm: I heard since my return, that his ship foundered, and none escaped, but one cabbin-boy. He was an honest man, and a good sailor, but a little too positive in his own opinions; which was the cause of his destruction, as it hath been of several others. For, if he had followed my advice, he might at this time have been safe at home with his family, as well as my self.

I had several men died in my ship of calentures, so that I was forced to get recruits out of Barbadoes, and the Leeward Islands, where I touched by the direction of the merchants who employed me, which I had soon too much cause to repent; for I found afterwards that most of them had been buccaneers. I had fifty hands on board; and my orders were, that I should trade with the Indians in the South-sea, and make what discoveries I could. These rogues whom I had picked up debauched my other men, and they all formed a conspiracy to seize the ship and secure me; which they did one morning, rushing into my cabbin, and binding me hand and foot, threatning to throw me overboard, if I offered to stir. I told them, I was their prisoner, and would submit. This they made me swear to do, and then unbound me, only fastning one of my legs with a chain near my bed; and placed a centry at my door with his piece charged, who was commanded to shoot me dead, if I attempted my liberty. They sent me down victuals and drink, and took the government of the ship to themselves. Their design was to turn pirates, and plunder the Spaniards; which they could not do, until they got more men. But first, they resolved to sell the goods in the ship, and then go to

Madagascar for recruits; several among them having died since my confinement. They sailed many weeks, and traded with the Indians; but I knew not what course they took, being kept close prisoner in my cabbin, and expecting nothing less than to be murdered, as they often threatned me.

Upon the 9th day of May, 1711, one James Welch came down to my cabbin; and said, he had orders from the captain to set me ashoar. I expostulated with him, but in vain; neither would he so much as tell me who their new captain was. They forced me into the long-boat, letting me put on my best suit of cloaths, which were as good as new, and a small bundle of linnen, but no arms except my hanger; and they were so civil as not to search my pockets; into which I conveyed what money I had, with some other little necessaries. They rowed about a league; and then set me down on a strand. I desired them to tell me what country it was: they all swore, they knew no more than my self, but said, that the captain (as they called him) was resolved, after they had sold the lading, to get rid of me in the first place where they discovered land. They pushed off immediately, advising me to make haste, for fear of being overtaken by the tide; and bade me farewell.

In this desolate condition, I advanced forward, and soon got upon firm ground, where I sat down on a bank to rest my self, and consider what I had best to do. When I was a little refreshed, I went up into the country, resolving to deliver my self to the first savages I should meet; and purchase my life from them by some bracelets, glass rings, and other toys, which sailors usually provide themselves with in those voyages, and whereof I had some about me: the land was divided by long rows of trees, not regularly planted, but naturally growing; there was great plenty of grass, and several fields of oats. I walked very circumspectly for fear of being surprized, or suddenly shot with an arrow from behind, or on either side. I fell into a beaten road, where I saw many tracts of human feet, and some of cows, but most of horses. At last, I beheld several animals in a field, and one or two of the same kind sitting in trees. Their shape was very singular, and deformed, which a little discomposed me, so that I lay down behind a thicket to observe them better. Some of them coming forward near the place where I lay, gave me an opportunity of distinctly marking their form. Their heads and breasts were covered with a thick hair, some frizzled and others lank; they had beards like goats, and a long ridge of hair down their backs, and the fore parts of their legs and feet; but the rest of their bodies were bare, so that I might see their skins, which were of a brown buff colour. They had no tails, nor any hair at all on their buttocks, except about the *anus;* which, I presume, nature had placed there to defend them as they sat on the ground, for this posture they used, as well as lying down, and often stood on their hind feet. They climbed high trees as nimbly as a squirrel, for they had strong extended claws before and behind, terminating on sharp points, hooked. They would often spring, and bound, and leap with prodigious agility. The females were not so large as the males; they had long lank hair on their heads, and only a sort of down on the rest of their bodies, except about the *anus,* and *pudenda.* Their dugs hung between their fore feet, and often reached almost to the ground as they walked. The hair of both sexes was of several colours, brown, red, black and yellow. Upon the whole, I never beheld in all my travels so disagreeable an animal, or one against which I naturally conceived so strong an antipathy. So, that thinking I had seen enough, full of contempt and aversion, I got up and pursued the beaten road, hoping it might direct me to the cabbin of some Indian. I had not gone far, when I met one of these creatures full in my way, and coming up directly to me. The ugly monster, when he saw me, distorted several ways every feature of his visage, and stared as at an object he had never seen before; then, approaching nearer, lifted up his fore paw, whether out of curiosity or mischief, I could not tell: but I drew my hanger, and gave him a good blow with the flat side of it; for I durst not strike him with the edge, fearing the inhabitants might be provoked against me, if they should come to know that I had killed or maimed any of their cattle. When the beast felt the smart, he drew back, and roared so loud, that a herd, of at least forty, came flocking about me from the next field, howling and making odious faces; but I ran to the body of a tree, and leaning my back against it, kept them off, by waving my hanger. Several of this cursed brood getting hold of the branches behind, leaped up into the tree; from whence they began to discharge their excrements on my head: however, I escaped pretty well, by sticking close to the stem of the tree, but was almost stifled with the filth, which fell about me on every side.

In the midst of this distress, I observed them all to run away on a sudden as fast as they could; at which I ventured to leave the tree, and pursue the road, wondering what it was that could put them into this fright. But looking on my left hand, I saw a horse walking softly in the field; which my persecutors having sooner discovered, was the cause of their flight. The horse started a little when he came near me, but soon recovering himself, looked full in my face with manifest tokens of wonder: he viewed my hands and feet, walking round me several times. I would have pursued my journey, but he placed himself directly in the way, yet looking with a very mild aspect, never offering the least violence. We stood gazing at each other for some time; at last, I took the boldness to reach my hand towards his neck, with a design to stroak it; using the common style and whistle of jockies when they are going to handle a strange horse. But, this animal seeming to receive my civilities with disdain, shook his head, and bent his brows, softly raising up his left fore foot to remove my hand. Then he neighed three or four times, but in so different a cadence, that I almost began to think he was speaking to himself in some language of his own.

While he and I were thus employed, another horse came up; who applying himself to the first in a very formal manner, they gently struck each others right hoof before, neighing several times by turns, and varying the sound, which seemed to be almost articulate. They went some paces off, as if it were to confer together, walking side by side, backward and forward, like persons deliberating upon some affair of weight; but often turning their eyes towards me, as it were to watch that I might not escape. I was amazed to see such actions and behaviour in brute beasts; and concluded with my self, that if the inhabitants of this country were endued with a proportionable degree of reason, they must needs be the wisest people upon earth.

This thought gave me so much comfort, that I resolved to go forward until I could discover some house or village, or meet with any of the natives, leaving the two horses to discourse together as they pleased. But the first, who was a dapple-grey, observing me to steal off, neighed after me in so expressive a tone, that I fancied my self to understand what he meant; whereupon I turned back, and came near him, to expect his farther commands; but concealing my fear as much as I could, for I began to be in some pain, how this adventure might terminate; and the reader will easily believe, I did not much like my present situation.

The two horses came up close to me, looking with great earnestness upon my face and hands. The grey steed rubbed my hat all round with his right fore hoof, and discomposed it so much, that I was forced to adjust it better, by taking it off, and settling it again; whereat both he and his companion, (who was a brown bay) appeared to be much surprized; the latter felt the lappet of my coat, and finding it to hang loose about me, they both looked with new signs of wonder. He stroked my right hand, seeming to admire the softness, and colour; but he squeezed it so hard between his hoof and his pastern, that I was forced to roar; after which they both touched me with all possible tenderness. They were under great perplexity about my shoes and stockings, which they felt very often, neighing to each other, and using various gestures, not unlike those of a philosopher, when he would attempt to solve some new and difficult phænomenon.

Upon the whole, the behaviour of these animals was so orderly and rational, so acute and judicious, that I at last concluded, they must needs be magicians, who had thus metamorphosed themselves upon some design; and seeing a stranger in the way, were resolved to divert themselves with him; or perhaps were really amazed at the sight of a man so very different in habit, feature and complexion from those who might probably live in so remote a climate. Upon the strength of this reasoning, I ventured to address them in the following manner: "Gentlemen, if you be conjurers, as I have good cause to believe, you can understand any language; therefore I make bold to let your worships know, that I am a poor distressed Englishman, driven by his misfortunes upon your coast; and I entreat one of you to let me ride upon his back, as if he were a real horse, to some house or village, where I can be relieved. In return of which favour, I will make you a present of this knife and bracelet" (taking them out of my pocket.) The two creatures stood silent while I spoke, seeming to listen with great attention; and when I had ended, they neighed frequently towards each other, as if they were engaged in serious conversation. I plainly observed, that their language expressed the passions very well, and the words might with little pains be resolved into an alphabet more easily than the Chinese.

I could frequently distinguish the word "Yahoo," which was repeated by each of them several times; and although it were impossible for me to conjecture what it meant, yet while the two horses were busy in conversation, I endeavoured to practise this word upon my tongue; and as soon as they were silent, I boldly pronounced "Yahoo" in a loud voice, imitating, at the same time, as near as I could, the neighing of a horse; at which they were both visibly surprized, and the grey repeated the same word twice, as if he meant to teach me the right accent, wherein I spoke after him as well as I could, and found my self perceivably to improve every time, although very far from any degree of perfection. Then the bay tried me with a second word, much harder to be pronounced; but reducing it to the English orthography, may be spelt thus, "Houyhnhnm." I did not succeed in this so well as the former, but after two or three farther trials, I had better fortune; and they both appeared amazed at my capacity.

After some farther discourse, which I then conjectured might relate to me, the two friends took their leaves, with the same compliment of striking each other's hoof; and the grey made me signs that I should walk before him; wherein, I thought it prudent to comply, until I could find a better director. When I offered to slacken my pace, he would cry "Hhuun, hhuun"; I guessed his meaning, and gave him to understand, as well as I could, that I was weary, and not able to walk faster; upon which, he would stand a while to let me rest.

CHAPTER II

The author conducted by a Houyhnhnm to his house. The house described. The author's reception. The food of the Houyhnhnms. The author in distress for want of meat, is at last relieved. His manner of feeding in that country.

HAVING travelled about three miles, we came to a long kind of building, made of timber, stuck in the ground, and wattled a-cross; the roof was low, and covered with straw. I now began to be a little comforted; and took out some toys, which travellers usually carry for presents to the savage Indians of America and other parts, in hopes the people of the house would be thereby encouraged to receive me kindly. The horse made me a sign to go in first; it was a large room with a smooth clay floor, and a rack and manger extending the whole length on one side. There were three nags, and two mares, not eating, but some of them sitting down upon their hams, which I very much wondered at; but wondered more, to see the rest employed in domestick business: the last seemed but ordinary cattle; however, this confirmed my first opinion, that a people who could so far civilize brute animals, must needs excel in wisdom all the nations of the world. The grey came in just after, and thereby prevented any ill treatment, which the others might have given me. He neighed to them several times in a style of authority, and received answers.

Beyond this room there were three others, reaching the length of the house, to which you passed through three doors, opposite to each other, in the manner of a vista: we went through the second room towards the third; here the grey walked in first, beckoning me to attend: I waited in the second room, and got ready my presents for the master and mistress of the house: they were two knives, three bracelets of false pearl, a small looking-glass, and a bead-necklace. The horse neighed three or four times, and I waited to hear some answers in a human voice, but I heard no other returns than in the same dialect, only one or two a little shriller than his. I began to think that this house must belong to some person of great note among them, because there appeared so much ceremony before I could gain admittance. But, that a man of quality should be served all by horses, was beyond my comprehension. I feared my brain was disturbed by my sufferings and misfortunes: I roused my self, and looked about me in the room where I was left alone; this was furnished as the first, only after a more elegant manner. I rubbed mine eyes often, but the same objects still occurred. I pinched my arms and sides, to awake my self, hoping I might be in a dream. I then absolutely concluded, that all these appearances could be nothing else but necromancy and magick. But I had no time to pursue these reflections; for the grey horse came to the door, and made me a sign to follow him into the third room, where I saw a very comely mare, together with a colt and fole, sitting on their haunches, upon mats of straw, not unartfully made, and perfectly neat and clean.

The mare, soon after my entrance, rose from her mat, and coming up close, after having nicely observed my hands and face, gave me a most contemptuous look; then turning to the horse, I heard the word "Yahoo" often repeated betwixt them; the meaning of which word I could not then comprehend, although it were the first I had learned to pronounce; but I was soon better informed, to my everlasting mortification: for the horse beckoning to me with his head, and repeating the word "Hhuun, hhuun," as he did upon the road, which I understood was to attend him, led me out into a kind of court, where was another building at some distance from the house. Here we entered, and I saw three of those detestable creatures, which I first met after my landing, feeding upon roots, and the flesh of some animals, which I afterwards found to be that of asses and dogs, and now and then a cow dead by accident or disease. They were all tyed by the neck with strong wyths, fastened to a beam; they held their food between the claws of their fore feet, and tore it with their teeth.

The master horse ordered a sorrel nag, one of his servants, to untie the largest of these animals, and take him into a yard. The beast and I were brought close together; and our countenances diligently compared, both by master and servant, who thereupon repeated several times the word "Yahoo." My horror and astonishment are not to be described, when I observed, in this abominable animal, a perfect human figure; the face of it, indeed, was flat and broad, the nose depressed, the lips large, and the mouth wide: but these differences are common to all savage nations, where the lineaments of the countenance are distorted by the natives suffering their infants to lie grovelling on the earth, or by carrying them on their backs, nuzzling with their face against the mother's shoulders. The forefeet of the Yahoo differed from my hands in nothing else, but the length of the nails, the coarseness and brownness of the palms, and the hairiness on the backs. There was the same resemblance between our feet, with the same differences, which I knew very well, although the horses did not, because of my shoes and stockings; the same in every part of our bodies, except as to hairiness and colour, which I have already described.

The great difficulty that seemed to stick with the two horses, was, to see the rest of my body so very different from that of a Yahoo, for which I was obliged to my cloaths, whereof they had no conception: the sorrel nag offered me a root, which he held (after their manner, as we shall describe in its proper place) between his hoof and pastern; I took it in my hand, and having smelt it, returned it to him again as civilly as I could. He brought out of the Yahoo's kennel a piece of ass's flesh, but it smelt so offensively that I turned from it with loathing; he then threw it to the Yahoo, by whom it was greedily devoured. He afterwards shewed me a wisp of hay, and a fettlock full of oats; but I shook my head, to signify, that neither of these were food for me. And indeed, I now apprehended, that I must absolutely starve, if I did not get to some of my own species: for as to those filthy Yahoos, although there were few greater lovers of mankind, at that time, than my self; yet I confess I never saw any sensitive being so detestable on all accounts; and the more I came near them, the more hateful they grew, while I stayed in that country. This the master horse observed by my behaviour, and therefore sent the Yahoo back to his kennel. He then put his forehoof to his mouth, at which I was much surprized, although he did it with ease, and with a motion that appeared perfectly natural; and made other signs to know what I would eat; but I could not return him such an answer as he was able to apprehend; and if he had understood me, I did not see how it was possible to contrive any way for finding my self nourishment. While we were thus engaged, I observed a cow passing by; whereupon I pointed to her, and expressed a desire to let me go and milk her. This had its effect; for he led me back into the house, and ordered a mare-servant to open a room, where a good store of milk lay in earthen and wooden vessels, after a very orderly and cleanly manner. She gave me a large bowl full, of which I drank very heartily, and found my self well refreshed.

About noon I saw coming towards the house a kind of vehicle, drawn like a sledge by four Yahoos. There was in it an old steed, who seemed to be of quality; he alighted with his hind-feet forward, having by accident got a hurt in his left fore-foot. He came to dine with our horse, who received him with great civility. They dined in the best room, and had oats boiled in milk for the second course; which the old horse eat warm, but the rest cold. Their mangers were placed circular in the middle of the room, and divided into several partitions, round which they sat on their haunches upon bosses of straw. In the middle was a large rack, with angles answering to every partition of the manger. So that each horse and mare eat their own hay, and their own mash of oats and milk, with much decency and regularity. The behaviour of the young colt and fole appeared very modest; and that of the master and mistress extremely chearful and complaisant to their guest. The grey ordered me to stand by him; and much discourse passed between him and his friend concerning me, as I found by the strangers often looking on me, and the frequent repetition of the word "Yahoo."

I happened to wear my gloves, which the master grey observing, seemed perplexed, discovering signs of wonder what I had done to my fore feet; he put his hoof three or four times to them, as if he would signify, that I should reduce them to their former shape, which I presently did, pulling off both my gloves, and putting them into my pocket. This occasioned further talk, and I saw the company was pleased with my behaviour, whereof I soon found the good effects. I was ordered to speak the few words I understood; and while they were at dinner, the master taught me the names for oats, milk, fire, water, and some others; which I could readily pronounce after him, having from my youth a great facility in learning languages.

When dinner was done, the master horse took me aside, and by signs and words made me understand the concern he was in, that I had nothing to eat. Oats in their tongue, are called "hlunnh." This word I pronounced two or three times: for although I had refused them at first, yet upon second thoughts, I considered that I could contrive to make of them a kind of bread, which might be sufficient with milk to keep me alive, until I could make my escape to some other country, and to creatures of my own species. The horse immediately ordered a white mare-servant of his family to bring me a good quantity of oats in a sort of wooden tray. These I heated before the fire as well as I could, and rubbed them until the husks came off, which I made a shift to winnow from the grain; I ground and beat them between two stones, then took water, and made them into a paste or cake, which I toasted at the fire, and eat warm with milk. It was at first a very insipid diet, although common enough in many parts of Europe, but grew tolerable by time; and having been often reduced to hard fare in my life, this was not the first experiment I had made how easily nature is satisfied. And I cannot but observe, that I never had one hour's sickness, while I stayed in this island. It is true, I sometimes made a shift to catch a rabbit, or a bird, by springes made of Yahoos hairs; and I often gathered wholesome herbs, which I boiled, or eat as salades with my bread; and now and then, for a rarity, I made a little butter, and drank the whey. I was at first at a great loss for salt; but custom soon reconciled the want of it; and I am confident, that the frequent use of salt among us, is an effect of luxury, and was first introduced only as a provocative to drink; except where it is necessary for preserving of flesh in long voyages, or in places remote from great markets. For we observe no animal to be fond of it but man: and as to my self, when I left this country, it was a great while before I could endure the taste of it in any thing that I eat.

This is enough to say upon the subject of my diet, wherewith other travellers fill their books, as if the readers were personally concerned, whether we fare well or ill. However, it was necessary to mention this matter, lest the world should think it impossible that I could find sustenance for three years in such a country, and among such inhabitants.

When it grew towards evening, the master horse ordered a place for me to lodge in; it was but six yards from the house, and separated from the stable of the Yahoos. Here I got some straw, and covering my self with my own cloaths, slept very sound. But I was in a short time better accommodated, as the reader shall know hereafter, when I come to treat more particularly about my way of living.

CHAPTER III

The author studies to learn the language, the Houyhnhnm his master assists in teaching him. The language described. Several Houyhnhnms of quality come out of curiosity to see the author. He gives his master a short account of his voyage.

My principal endeavour was to learn the language, which my master (for so I shall henceforth call him) and his children, and every servant of his house were desirous to teach me. For they looked upon it as a prodigy, that a brute animal should discover such marks of a rational creature. I pointed to every thing, and enquired the name of it, which I wrote down in my journal book when I was alone, and corrected my bad accent, by desiring those of the family to pronounce it often. In this employment, a sorrel nag, one of the under servants, was very ready to assist me.

In speaking, they pronounce through the nose and throat, and their language approacheth nearest to the High-Dutch or German, of any I know in Europe; but is much more graceful and significant. The Emperor Charles V. made almost the same observation, when he said, that if he were to speak to his horse, it should be in High-Dutch.

The curiosity and impatience of my master were so great, that he spent many hours of his leisure to instruct me. He was convinced (as he afterwards told me) that I must be a Yahoo, but my teachableness, civility and cleanliness, astonished him; which were qualities altogether so opposite to those animals. He was most perplexed about my cloaths, reasoning sometimes with himself, whether they were a part of my body; for I never pulled them off until the family were asleep, and got them on before they waked in the morning. My master was eager to learn from whence I came; how I acquired those appearances of reason, which I discovered in all my actions; and to know my story from my own mouth, which he hoped he should soon do by the great proficiency I made in learning and pronouncing their words and sentences. To help my memory, I formed all I learned into the English alphabet, and writ the words down with the translations. This last, after some time, I ventured to do in my master's presence. It cost me much trouble to explain to him what I was doing; for the inhabitants have not the least idea of books or literature.

In about ten weeks time I was able to understand most of his questions; and in three months could give him some tolerable answers. He was extremely curious to know from what part of the country I came, and how I was taught to imitate a rational creature; because the Yahoos, (whom he saw I exactly resembled in my head, hands and face, that were only visible,) with some appearance of cunning, and the strongest disposition to mischief, were observed to be the most unteachable of all brutes. I answered, that I came over the sea, from a far place, with many others of my own kind, in a great hollow vessel made of the bodies of trees: that, my companions forced me to land on this coast, and then left me to shift for my self. It was with

some difficulty, and by the help of many signs, that I brought him to understand me. He replyed, that I must needs be mistaken, or that I *said the
thing which was not.* (For they have no word in their language to express
lying or falshood.) He knew it was impossible that there could be a country beyond the sea, or that a parcel of brutes could move a wooden vessel
whither they pleased upon water. He was sure no Houyhnhnm alive could
make such a vessel, or would trust Yahoos to manage it.

The word "Houyhnhnm," in their tongue, signifies a horse; and its etymology, "the perfection of nature." I told my master, that I was at a loss for
expression, but would improve as fast as I could; and hoped in a short time
I should be able to tell him wonders: he was pleased to direct his own mare,
his colt and fole, and the servants of the family to take all opportunities of
instructing me; and every day for two or three hours, he was at the same
pains himself: several horses and mares of quality in the neighbourhood
came often to our house, upon the report spread of a wonderful Yahoo, that
could speak like a Houyhnhnm, and seemed in his words and actions to discover some glimmerings of reason. These delighted to converse with me;
they put many questions, and received such answers, as I was able to return.
By all which advantages, I made so great a progress, that in five months
from my arrival, I understood whatever was spoke, and could express my
self tolerably well.

The Houyhnhnms who came to visit my master, out of a design of seeing
and talking with me, could hardly believe me to be a right Yahoo, because
my body had a different covering from others of my kind. They were astonished to observe me without the usual hair or skin, except on my head, face
and hands: but I discovered that secret to my master, upon an accident,
which happened about a fortnight before.

I have already told the reader, that every night when the family were
gone to bed, it was my custom to strip and cover myself with my cloaths: it
happened one morning early, that my master sent for me, by the sorrel nag,
who was his valet; when he came, I was fast asleep, my cloaths fallen off on
one side, and my shirt above my waiste. I awaked at the noise he made,
and observed him to deliver his message in some disorder; after which he
went to my master, and in a great fright gave him a very confused account of
what he had seen: this I presently discovered; for going as soon as I was
dressed, to pay my attendance upon his honour, he asked me the meaning
of what his servant had reported; that I was not the same thing when I
slept as I appeared to be at other times; that his valet assured him, some
part of me was white, some yellow, at least not so white, and some brown.

I had hitherto concealed the secret of my dress, in order to distinguish
my self as much as possible, from that cursed race of Yahoos; but now I
found it in vain to do so any longer. Besides, I considered that my cloaths
and shoes would soon wear out, which already were in a declining condition,
and must be supplied by some contrivance from the hides of Yahoos, or
other brutes; whereby the whole secret would be known. I therefore told my
master, that in the country from whence I came, those of my kind always
covered their bodies with the hairs of certain animals prepared by art,
as well for decency, as to avoid inclemencies of air both hot and cold; of

which, as to my own person, I would give him immediate conviction, if he pleased to command me; only desiring his excuse, if I did not expose those parts that nature taught us to conceal. He said, my discourse was all very strange, but especially the last part; for he could not understand why nature should teach us to conceal what nature had given. That neither himself, nor family, were ashamed of any parts of their bodies; but however I might do as I pleased. Whereupon, I first unbottoned my coat, and pulled it off. I did the same with my waistecoat; I drew off my shoes, stockings, and breeches. I let my shirt down to my waiste, and drew up the bottom, fastening it like a girdle about my middle to hide my nakedness.

My master observed the whole performance with great signs of curiosity and admiration. He took up all my cloaths in his pastern, one piece after another, and examined them diligently; he then stroaked my body very gently, and looked round me several times; after which he said, it was plain I must be a perfect Yahoo; but that I differed very much from the rest of my species, in the whiteness, and smoothness of my skin, my want of hair in several parts of my body, the shape and shortness of my claws behind and before, and my affectation of walking continually on my two hinder feet. He desired to see no more; and gave me leave to put on my cloaths again, for I was shuddering with cold.

I expressed my uneasiness at his giving me so often the appellation of Yahoo, an odious animal, for which I had so utter an hatred and contempt. I begged he would forbear applying that word to me, and take the same order in his family, and among his friends whom he suffered to see me. I requested likewise, that the secret of my having a false covering to my body might be known to none but himself, at least as long as my present cloathing should last: for, as to what the sorrel nag, his valet, had observed, his honour might command him to conceal it.

All this my master very graciously consented to; and thus the secret was kept until my cloaths began to wear out, which I was forced to supply by several contrivances, that shall hereafter be mentioned. In the mean time, he desired I would go on with my utmost diligence to learn their language, because he was more astonished at my capacity for speech and reason, than at the figure of my body, whether it were covered or no; adding, that he waited with some impatience to hear the wonders which I promised to tell him.

From thenceforward he doubled the pains he had been at to instruct me; he brought me into all company, and made them treat me with civility, because, as he told them privately, this would put me into good humour, and make me more diverting.

Every day when I waited on him, beside the trouble he was at in teaching, he would ask me several questions concerning my self, which I answered as well as I could; and by those means he had already received some general ideas, although very imperfect. It would be tedious to relate the several steps by which I advanced to a more regular conversation: but the first account I gave of my self in any order and length, was to this purpose:

That, I came from a very far country, as I already had attempted to tell him, with about fifty more of my own species; that, we travelled upon the seas, in a great hollow vessel made of wood, and larger than his honour's house. I described the ship to him in the best terms I could; and explained by the help of my handkerchief displayed, how it was driven forward by the wind. That, upon a quarrel among us, I was set on shoar on this coast, where I walked forward without knowing whither, until he delivered me from the persecution of those execrable Yahoos. He asked me, who made the ship, and how it was possible that the Houyhnhnms of my country would leave it to the management of brutes? My answer was, that I durst proceed no farther in my relation, unless he would give me his word and honour that he would not be offended; and then I would tell him the wonders I had so often promised. He agreed; and I went on by assuring him, that the ship was made by creatures like my self, who in all the countries I had travelled, as well as in my own, were the only governing, rational animals; and that upon my arrival hither, I was as much astonished to see the Houyhnhnms act like rational beings, as he or his friends could be in finding some marks of reason in a creature he was pleased to call a Yahoo; to which I owned my resemblance in every part, but could not account for their degenerate and brutal nature. I said farther, that if good fortune ever restored me to my native country, to relate my travels hither, as I resolved to do, every body would believe that I *said the thing which was not;* that I invented the story out of my own head: and with all possible respect to himself, his family, and friends, and under his promise of not being offended, our countrymen would hardly think it probable, that a Houyhnhnm should be the presiding creature of a nation, and a Yahoo the brute.

CHAPTER IV

The Houyhnhnms notion of truth and falshood. The author's discourse disapproved by his master. The author gives a more particular account of himself, and the accidents of his voyage.

My master heard me with great appearances of uneasiness in his countenance; because *doubting* or *not believing,* are so little known in this country, that the inhabitants cannot tell how to behave themselves under such circumstances. And I remember in frequent discourses with my master concerning the nature of manhood, in other parts of the world, having occasion to talk of *lying* and *false representation,* it was with much difficulty that he comprehended what I meant; although he had otherwise a most acute judgment. For he argued thus; that the use of speech was to make us understand one another, and to receive information of facts; now if any one *said the thing which was not,* these ends were defeated; because I cannot properly be said to understand him; and I am so far from receiving information, that he leaves me worse than in ignorance; for I am led to believe a thing *black,* when it is *white;* and *short,* when it is *long.* And these were all the notions he had concerning that faculty of *lying,* so perfectly well understood, and so universally practised among human creatures.

To return from this digression; when I asserted that the Yahoos were the only governing animals in my country, which my master said was alto-

gether past his conception, he desired to know, whether we had Houyhnhnms among us, and what was their employment: I told him, we had great
numbers; that in summer they grazed in the fields, and in winter were kept
in houses, with hay and oats, where Yahoo-servants were employed to rub
their skins smooth, comb their manes, pick their feet, serve them with food,
and make their beds. "I understand you well." said my master; "it is now
very plain from all you have spoken, that whatever share of reason the
Yahoos pretend to, the Houyhnhnms are your masters; I heartily wish our
Yahoos would be so tractable." I begged his honour would please to excuse
me from proceeding any farther, because I was very certain that the account
he expected from me would be highly displeasing. But he insisted in commanding me to let him know the best and the worst: I told him he should
be obeyed. I owned, that the Houyhnhnms among us, whom we called
"horses," were the most generous and comely animal we had; that they excelled in strength and swiftness; and when they belonged to persons of
quality, employed in travelling, racing, and drawing chariots, they were
treated with much kindness and care, until they fell into diseases, or became foundered in the feet; but then they were sold, and used to all kind of
drudgery until they died; after which, their skins were stripped and sold for
what they were worth, and their bodies left to be devoured by dogs and
birds of prey. But the common race of horses had not so good fortune, being
kept by farmers and carriers, and other mean people, who put them to
greater labour, and fed them worse. I described as well as I could, our way
of riding; the shape and use of a bridle, a saddle, a spur, and a whip; of
harness and wheels. I added, that we fastned plates of a certain hard substance called iron at the bottom of their feet, to preserve their hoofs from
being broken by the stony ways on which we often travelled.

My master, after some expressions of great indignation, wondered how
we dared to venture upon a Houyhnhnm's back; for he was sure, that the
meanest servant in his house would be able to shake off the strongest
Yahoo; or by lying down, and rolling upon his back, squeeze the brute to
death. I answered, that our horses were trained up from three or four years
old to the several uses we intended them for; that, if any of them proved in-
tolerably vicious, they were employed for carriages; that, they were severely
beaten while they were young for any mischievous tricks: that, the males,
designed for the common use of riding or draught, were generally *castrated*
about two years after their birth, to take down their spirits, and make them
more tame and gentle: that, they were indeed sensible of rewards and pun-
ishments; but his honour would please to consider, that they had not the
least tincture of reason any more than the Yahoos in this country.

It put me to the pains of many circumlocutions to give my master a right
idea of what I spoke; for their language doth not abound in variety of words,
because their wants and passions are fewer than among us. But it is impossible to express his noble resentment at our savage treatment of the Houyhnhnm race; particularly after I had explained the manner and use of
castrating horses among us, to hinder them from propagating their kind,
and to render them more servile. He said, if it were possible there could be
any country where Yahoos alone were endued with reason, they certainly

must be the governing animal, because reason will in time always prevail against brutal strength. But, considering the frame of our bodies, and especially of mine, he thought no creature of equal bulk was so ill contrived, for employing that reason in the common offices of life; whereupon he desired to know whether those among whom I lived, resembled me or the Yahoos of his country. I assured him, that I was as well shaped as most of my age; but the younger and the females were much more soft and tender, and the skins of the latter generally as white as milk. He said, I differed indeed from other Yahoos, being much more cleanly, and not altogether so deformed; but in point of real advantage, he thought I differed for the worse: that my nails were of no use either to my fore or hinder feet: as to my fore feet, he could not properly call them by that name, for he never observed me to walk upon them; that, they were too soft to bear the ground; that, I generally went with them uncovered, neither was the covering I sometimes wore on them, of the same shape, or so strong as that on my feet behind: that I could not walk with any security; for if either of my hinder feet slipped, I must inevitably fall. He then began to find fault with other parts of my body; the flatness of my face, the prominence of my nose, mine eyes placed directly in front, so that I could not look on either side without turning my head: that I was not able to feed my self, without lifting one of my fore feet to my mouth: and therefore nature had placed those joints to answer that necessity. He knew not what could be the use of those several clefts and divisions in my feet behind; that these were too soft to bear the hardness and sharpness of stones without a covering made from the skin of some other brute; that, my whole body wanted a fence against heat and cold, which I was forced to put on and off every day with tediousness and trouble. And lastly, that he observed every animal in this country naturally to abhor the Yahoos, whom the weaker avoided, and the stronger drove from them. So that supposing us to have the gift of reason, he could not see how it were possible to cure that natural antipathy which every creature discovered against us; nor consequently, how we could tame and render them serviceable. However, he would (as he said) debate the matter no farther, because he was more desirous to know my own story, the country where I was born, and the several actions and events of my life before I came hither.

I assured him, how extreamly desirous I was that he should be satisfied in every point; but I doubted much, whether it would be possible for me to explain my self on several subjects whereof his honour could have no conception, because I saw nothing in his country to which I could resemble them. That however, I would do my best, and strive to express my self by similitudes, humbly desiring his assistance when I wanted proper words; which he was pleased to promise me.

I said, my birth was of honest parents, in an island called England, which was remote from this country, as many days journey as the strongest of his honour's servants could travel in the annual course of the sun. That, I was bred a surgeon, whose trade is to cure wounds and hurts in the body, got by accident or violence. That, my country was governed by a female man, whom we called "queen." That, I left it to get riches, whereby I might maintain my self and family when I should return. That, in my last voyage, I was commander of the ship, and had about fifty Yahoos under me, many of which died at sea, and I was forced to supply them by others picked out from several nations. That, our ship was twice in danger of being sunk; the first time by a great storm, and the second, by striking against a rock. Here my master interposed, by asking me, how I could persuade strangers out of different countries to venture with me, after the losses I had sustained, and the hazards I had run. I said, they were fellows of desperate fortunes, forced to fly from the places of their birth, on account of their poverty or their crimes. Some were undone by law suits; others spent all they had in drinking, whoring, and gaming; others fled for treason; many for murder, theft, poysoning, robbery, perjury, forgery, coining false money; for committing rapes or sodomy; for flying from their colours, or deserting the enemy; and most of them had broken prison. None of these durst return to their native countries for fear of being hanged, or of starving in a jail; and therefore were under a necessity of seeking a livelihood in other places.

During this discourse, my master was pleased often to interrupt me. I had made use of many circumlocutions, in describing to him the nature of the several crimes, for which most of our crew had been forced to fly their country. This labour took up several days conversation before he was able to comprehend me. He was wholly at a loss to know what could be the use or necessity of practising those vices. To clear up which, I endeavoured to give him some ideas of the desire of power and riches; of the terrible effects of lust, intemperance, malice, and envy. All this I was forced to define and describe by putting of cases, and making suppositions. After which, like one whose imagination was struck with something never seen or heard of before, he would lift up his eyes with amazement and indignation. Power, government, war, law, punishment, and a thousand other things, had no terms, wherein that language could express them; which made the difficulty almost insuperable to give my master any conception of what I meant; but being of an excellent understanding, much improved by contemplation and converse, he at last arrived at a competent knowledge of what human nature in our parts of the world is capable to perform; and desired I would give him some particular account of that land, which we call Europe, especially of my own country.

CHAPTER V

The author, at his master's commands, informs him of the state of England. The causes of war among the princes of Europe. The author begins to explain the English constitution.

THE reader may please to observe, that the following extract of many conversations I had with my master, contains a summary of the most material points, which were discoursed at several times for above two years; his honour often desiring fuller satisfaction, as I farther improved in the Houyhnhnm tongue. I laid before him, as well as I could, the whole state of Europe; I discoursed of trade and manufactures, of arts and sciences; and the answers I gave to all the questions he made, as they arose upon several subjects, were a fund of conversation not to be exhausted. But, I shall here only set down the substance of what passed between us concerning my own country, reducing it into order as well as I can, without any regard to time or other circumstances, while I strictly adhere to truth. My only concern is, that I shall hardly be able to do justice to my master's arguments and expressions, which must needs suffer by my want of capacity, as well as by a translation into our barbarous English.

In obedience therefore to his honour's commands, I related to him the *revolution* under the Prince of Orange; the long war with France entered into by the said prince, and renewed by his successor the present queen; wherein the greatest powers of Christendom were engaged, and which still continued: I computed at his request, that about a million of Yahoos might have been killed in the whole progress of it; and perhaps a hundred or more cities taken, and five times as many ships burnt or sunk.

He asked me what were the usual causes or motives, that made one country go to war with another. I answered they were innumerable; but I should only mention a few of the chief. Sometimes the ambition of princes, who never think they have land or people enough to govern: sometimes the corruption of ministers, who engage their master in a war, in order to stifle or divert the clamour of the subjects against their evil administration. Difference in opinions hath cost many millions of lives: for instance, whether *flesh* be *bread*, or *bread* be *flesh:* whether the juice of a certain *berry* be *blood* or *wine:* whether *whistling* be a vice or a virtue: whether it be better to *kiss a post*, or throw it into the fire: what is the best colour for a *coat*, whether *black, white, red*, or *grey*; and whether it should be *long* or *short, narrow* or *wide, dirty* or *clean*; with many more. Neither are any wars so furious and bloody, or of so long continuance, as those occasioned by difference in opinion, especially if it be in things indifferent.

Sometimes the quarrel between two princes is to decide which of them shall dispossess a third of his dominions, where neither of them pretend to any right. Sometimes one prince quarrelleth with another, for fear the other should quarrel with him. Sometimes a war is entered upon, because the enemy is too *strong*, and sometimes because he is too *weak*. Sometimes our neighbours *want* the *things* which we *have*, or *have* the things which we want; and we both fight, until they take ours, or give us theirs. It is a very justifiable cause of war, to invade a country after the people have been wasted by famine, destroyed by pestilence, or embroiled by factions amongst themselves. It is justifiable to enter into a war against our nearest ally, when one of his towns lie convenient for us, or a territory of land, that would render our dominions round and compact. If a prince send forces into a nation, where the people are poor and ignorant, he may lawfully put half of them to death, and make slaves of the rest, in order to civilize and reduce them from their barbarous way of living. It is a very kingly, honourable, and frequent practice, when one prince desires the assistance of another to secure him against an invasion, that the assistant, when he hath driven out the invader, should seize on the dominions himself, and kill, imprison, or banish the prince he came to relieve. Alliance by blood or marriage, is a sufficient cause of war between princes; and the nearer the kindred is, the greater is their disposition to quarrel: *poor* nations are *hungry*, and *rich* nations are *proud;* and pride and hunger will ever be at variance. For these reasons, the trade of a *soldier* is held the most honourable of all others: because a *soldier* is a Yahoo hired to kill in cold blood as many of his own species, who have never offended him, as possibly he can.

There are likewise another kind of princes in Europe, not able to make war by themselves, who hire out their troops to richer nations for so much a day to each man; of which they keep three fourths to themselves, and it is the best part of their maintenance; such are those in many northern parts of Europe.

"What you have told me" (said my master) "upon the subject of war, doth indeed discover most admirably the effects of that reason you pretend to: however, it is happy that the *shame* is greater than the *danger;* and that nature hath left you utterly uncapable of doing much mischief: for your mouths lying flat with your faces, you can hardly bite each other to any purpose, unless by consent. Then, as to the claws upon your feet before and behind, they are so short and tender, that one of our Yahoos would drive a dozen of yours before him. And therefore, in recounting the numbers of those who have been killed in battle, I cannot but think, that you have *said the thing which is not.*"

I could not forbear shaking my head and smiling a little at his ignorance. And, being no stranger to the art of war, I gave him a description of cannons, culverines, muskets, carabines, pistols, bullets, powder, swords, bayonets, sieges, retreats, attacks, undermines, countermines, bombardments, sea-fights; ships sunk with a thousand men; twenty thousand killed on each side; dying groans, limbs flying in the air: smoak, noise, confusion, trampling to death under horses feet: flight, pursuit, victory: fields strewed with carcases left for food to dogs, and wolves, and birds of prey; plundering, stripping, ravishing, burning and destroying. And, to set forth the valour of my own dear countrymen, I assured him, that I had seen them blow up a hundred enemies at once in a siege, and as many in a ship; and beheld the dead bodies drop down in pieces from the clouds, to the great diversion of all the spectators.

I was going on to more particulars, when my master commanded me silence. He said, whoever understood the nature of Yahoos might easily believe it possible for so vile an animal, to be capable of every action I had named, if their strength and cunning equalled their malice. But, as my discourse had increased the abhorrence of the whole species, so he found it gave him a disturbance in his mind, to which he was wholly a stranger before. He thought his ears being used to such abominable words, might by degrees admit them with less detestation. That, although he hated the Yahoos of this country, yet he no more blamed them for their odious qualities, than he did a *gnnayh* (a bird of prey) for its cruelty, or a sharp stone for cutting his hoof. But, when a creature pretending to reason, could be capable of such enormities, he dreaded lest the corruption of that faculty, might be worse than brutality itself. He seemed therefore confident, that instead of reason, we were only possessed of some quality fitted to increase our natural vices; as the reflection from a troubled stream, returns the image of an ill-shapen body, not only *large*, but more *distorted*.

He added, that he had heard too much upon the subject of war, both in this, and some former discourses. There was another point which a little perplexed him at present. I had said, that some of our crew left their country on account of being ruined by law: that, I had already explained the meaning of the word; but he was at a loss how it should come to pass, that the law which was intended for *every* man's preservation, should be any man's ruin. Therefore he desired to be farther satisfied what I meant by law, and the dispensers thereof, according to the present practice in my own country: because he thought, nature and reason were sufficient guides for a reasonable animal, as we pretended to be, in shewing us what we ought to do, and what to avoid.

I assured his honour, that law was a science wherein I had not much conversed, having little more knowledge of it than what I had obtained by employing advocates, in vain, upon some injustices that had been done me, and by conversing with some others who by the same method had first lost their substance and then left their own country under the mortification of such disappointments, however, I would give him all the satisfaction I was able.

I said that those who made profession of this science were exceedingly multiplied, being almost equal to the caterpillars in number; that they were of diverse degrees, distinctions, and denominations. The numerousness of those that dedicated themselves to this profession were such that the fair and justifiable advantage and income of the profession was not sufficient for the decent and handsome maintenance of multitudes of those who followed it. Hence it came to pass that it was found needful to supply that by artifice and cunning, which could not be procured by just and honest methods: the better to bring which about, very many men among us were bred up from their youth in the art of proving by words multiplied for the purpose that *white* is *black*, and *black* is *white*, according as they are paid. The greatness of these mens assurance and the boldness of their pretensions gained upon the opinion of the vulgar, whom in a manner they made slaves of, and got into their hands much the largest share of the practice of their profession. These practitioners were by men of discernment called *pettifoggers*, (that is, *confounders*, or rather, *destroyers of right*,) as it was my ill hap, as well as the misfortune of my suffering acquaintance to be engaged only with this species of the profession. I desired his honour to understand the description I had to give, and the ruin I had complained of to relate to these sectaries only, and how and by what means the misfortunes we met with were brought upon us by the management of these men, might be more easily conceived by explaining to him their method of proceeding, which could not be better done than by giving him an example.

My neighbour, said I, I will suppose, has a mind to my cow; he hires one of these advocates to prove that he ought to have my cow from me. I must then hire another of them to defend my right, it being against all rules of law that any man should be allowed to speak for himself. Now in this case, I who am the right owner lie under two great disadvantages. First, my advocate, being as I said before practised almost from his cradle in defending falshood, is quite out of his element when he would argue for right, which as an office unnatural he attempts with great awkwardness, if not with an ill-will. The second disadvantage is that my advocate must proceed with great caution; for, since the maintenance of so many depend on the keeping up of business, should he proceed too summarily, if he does not incur the displeasure of his superiors, he is sure to gain the ill-will and hatred of his brethren, as being by them esteemed one that would lessen the practice of the law. This being the case, I have but two methods to preserve my cow. The first is, to gain over my adversary's advocate with a double fee; from the manner and design of whose education before mentioned it is easy to expect he will be induced to drop his client and let the ballance fall on my side. The second way is for my advocate not to insist on the justice of my cause, by allowing the cow to belong to my adversary; and this if it be dexterously and skilfully done will go a great way towards obtaining a favourable verdict, it having been found, from a careful observation of issues and events, that the wrong side, under the management of such practitioners, has the fairer chance for success, and this more especially if it happens, as it did in mine and my friend's case, and may have done since, that the person appointed to decide all controversies of property as well as for the tryal of criminals, who should be taken out of the most knowing and wise of his profession, is by the recommendation of a great favourite, or court-mistress chosen out of the sect before mentioned, and so, having been under a strong byas all his life against equity and fair dealing, lies as it were under a fatal necessity of favouring, shifting, double dealing and oppression, and besides through age, infirmity, and distempers grown lazy, unactive, and inattentive, and thereby almost incapacitated from doing any thing becoming the nature of his imployment, and the duty of his office. In such cases, the decisions and determinations of men so bred, and so qualified, may with reason be expected on the wrong side of the cause, since those who can take harangue and noise, (if pursued with warmth, and drawn out into a length,) for reasoning, are not much to be wondered at, if they infer the weight of the argument from the heaviness of the pleading.

It is a maxim among these lawyers, that whatever hath been done before, may legally be done again: and therefore they take special care to record all the decisions formerly made against common justice, and the general reason of mankind. These, under the name of *precedents*, they produce as authorities to justify the most iniquitous opinions; and they are so lucky in this practice, that it rarely fails of decrees answerable to their intent and expectation.

In pleading, they studiously avoid entering into the *merits* of the cause; but are loud, violent and tedious in dwelling upon all *circumstances* which are not to the purpose. For instance, in the case already mentioned: they never desire to know what claim or title my adversary hath to my cow; but whether the said cow were red or black; her horns long or short; whether the field I graze her in be round or square; whether she were milked at home or abroad; what diseases she is subject to, and the like. After which, they consult *precedents*, adjourn the cause, from time to time, and in ten, twenty, or thirty years come to an issue.

It is likewise to be observed, that this society hath a peculiar cant and jargon of their own, that no other mortal can understand, and wherein all their laws are written, which they take special care to multiply; whereby they have wholly confounded the very essence of truth and falshood, of right and wrong; so that it will take thirty years to decide whether the field, left me by my ancestors for six generations, belong to me, or to a stranger three hundred miles off.

In the tryal of persons accused for crimes against the State, the method is much more short and commendable: for if those in power, who know well how to choose instruments fit for their purpose, take care to recommend and promote out of this clan a proper person, his method of education and practice makes it easy for him, when his patrons disposition is understood, without difficulty or study either to condemn and acquit the criminal, and at the same time strictly preserve all due forms of law.

Here my master interposing said it was a pity, that creatures endowed with such prodigious abilities of mind as these advocates by the description I gave of them must certainly be, were not rather encouraged to be instructors of others in wisdom and knowledge. In answer to which I assured his honour that the business and study of their own calling and profession so took up all their thoughts and engrossed all their time, that they minded nothing else, and that therefore, in all points out of their own trade, many of them were of so great ignorance and stupidity, that it was hard to pick out of any profession a generation of men more despicable in common conversation, or who were so much looked upon as avowed enemies to all knowledge and learning, being equally disposed to pervert the general reason of mankind in every other subject of discourse, as in that of their own calling.

CHAPTER VI

A continuation of the state of England, under Queen Anne. The character of a First Minister in the courts of Europe.

My master was yet wholly at a loss to understand what motives could incite this race of lawyers to perplex, disquiet, and weary themselves by engaging in a confederacy of injustice, merely for the sake of injuring their fellow-animals; neither could he comprehend what I meant in saying they did it for *hire*. Whereupon I was at much pains to describe to him the use of *money*, the materials it was made of, and the value of the metals: that, when a Yahoo had got a great store of this precious substance, he was able to purchase whatever he had a mind to; the finest cloathing, the noblest houses, great tracts of land, the most costly meats and drinks; and have his choice of the most beautiful females. Therefore since *money* alone, was able to perform all these feats, our Yahoos thought, they could never have enough of it to spend or to save, as they found themselves inclined from their natural bent either to profusion or avarice. That, the rich man enjoyed the fruit of the poor man's labour, and the latter were a thousand to one in proportion to the former. That, the bulk of our people was forced to live miserably, by labouring every day for small wages, to make a few live plentifully. I enlarged my self much on these and many other particulars to the same purpose: but his honour was still to seek: for he went upon a supposition, that all animals had a title to their share in the productions of the earth, and especially those who presided over the rest. Therefore he desired I would let him know what these costly meats were, and how any of us happened to want them. Whereupon I enumerated as many sorts as came into my head, with the various methods of dressing them, which could not be done without sending vessels by sea to every part of the world, as well for liquors to drink, as for sauces, and innumerable other conveniencies. I assured him, that this whole globe of earth must be at least three times gone round, before one of our better female Yahoos could get her breakfast, or a cup to put it in. He said, that must needs be a miserable country which cannot furnish food for its own inhabitants. But what he chiefly wondered at, was how such vast tracts of ground as I described, should be wholly without *freshwater*, and the people put to the necessity of sending over the sea for drink. I replied, that England (the dear place of my nativity) was computed to produce three times the quantity of food, more than its inhabitants are able to consume, as well as liquors extracted from grain, or pressed out of the fruit of certain trees, which made excellent drink; and the same proportion in every other convenience of life. But, in order to feed the luxury and intemperance of the males, and the vanity of the females, we sent away the greatest part of our necessary things to other countries, from whence in return we brought the materials of diseases, folly, and vice, to spend among our selves. Hence it follows of necessity, that vast numbers of our people are compelled to seek their livelihood by begging, robbing, stealing, cheating, pimping, forswearing, flattering, suborning, forging, gaming, lying, fawning, hectoring, voting, scribling, stargazing, poysoning, whoring, canting, libelling, freethinking, and the like occupations: every one of which terms, I was at much pains to make him understand.

That, *wine* was not imported among us from foreign countries, to supply the want of water or other drinks, but because it was a sort of liquid which made us merry, by putting us out of our senses; diverted all melancholy thoughts, begat wild extravagant imaginations in the brain, raised our hopes, and banished our fears; suspended every office of reason for a time, and deprived us of the use of our limbs, until we fell into a profound sleep; although it must be confessed, that we always awaked sick and dispirited; and that the use of this liquor filled us with diseases, which made our lives uncomfortable and short.

But beside all this, the bulk of our people supported themselves by furnishing the necessities or conveniencies of life to the rich, and to each other. For instance, when I am at home and dressed as I ought to be, I carry on my body the workmanship of an hundred tradesmen; the building and furniture of my house employ as many more; and five times the number to adorn my wife.

I was going on to tell him of another sort of people, who get their livelihood by attending the sick, having upon some occasions informed his honour that many of my crew had died of diseases: but here it was with the utmost difficulty that I brought him to apprehend what I meant. He could easily conceive, that a Houyhnhnm grew weak and heavy a few days before his death; or by some accident might hurt a limb. But that nature, who worketh all things to perfection, should suffer any pains to breed in our bodies, he thought impossible; and desired to know the reason of so unaccountable an evil. I told him, we fed on a thousand things which operated contrary to each other: that, we eat when we were not hungry, and drank without the provocation of thirst: that, we sat whole nights drinking strong liquors without eating a bit, which disposed us to sloth, enflamed our bodies, and precipitated or prevented digestion. That, prostitute female Yahoos acquired a certain malady, which bred rottenness in the bones of those, who fell into their embraces: that, this and many other diseases, were propagated from father to son; so that great numbers come into the world with complicated maladies upon them: that, it would be endless to give him a catalogue of all diseases incident to human bodies; for they could not be fewer than five or six hundred, spread over every limb, and joint: in short, every part, external and intestine, having diseases appropriated to each. To remedy which, there was a sort of people bred up among us, in the profession or pretence of curing the sick. And, because I had some skill in the faculty, I would in gratitude to his honour, let him know the whole mystery and method by which they proceed.

Their fundamental is, that all diseases arise from *repletion;* from whence they conclude, that a great *evacuation* of the body is necessary, either through the natural passage, or upwards at the mouth. Their next business is, from herbs, minerals, gums, oyls, shells, salts, juices, sea-weed, excrements, barks of trees, serpents, toads, frogs, spiders, dead mens flesh and bones, beasts and fishes, to form a composition for smell and taste the most abominable, nauseous and detestable, that they can possibly contrive, which the stomach immediately rejects with loathing: and this they call a *vomit.* Or else from the same store-house, with some other poysonous additions, they command us to take in at the orifice *above* or *below* (just as the physician then happens to be disposed) a medicine equally annoying and disgustful to the bowels; which relaxing the belly, drives down all before it: and this they call a *purge,* or a *glyster.* For nature (as the physicians alledge) having intended the superior anterior orifice only for the *intromission* of solids and liquids, and the inferior posterior for ejection, these artists ingeniously considering that in all diseases nature is forced out of her seat; therefore to replace her in it, the body must be treated in a manner directly contrary, by interchanging the use of each orifice; forcing solids and liquids in at the *anus,* and making evacuations at the mouth.

But, besides real diseases, we are subject to many that are only imaginary, for which the physicians have invented imaginary cures; these have their several names, and so have the drugs that are proper for them; and with these our female Yahoos are always infested.

One great excellency in this tribe is their skill at *prognosticks,* wherein they seldom fail; their predictions in real diseases, when they rise to any degree of malignity, generally portending *death,* which is always in their power, when recovery is not: and therefore, upon any unexpected signs of amendment, after they have pronounced their sentence, rather than be accused as false prophets, they know how to approve their sagacity to the world by a seasonable dose.

They are likewise of special use to husbands and wives, who are grown weary of their mates; to eldest sons, to great ministers of State, and often to princes.

I had formerly upon occasion discoursed with my master upon the nature of *government* in general, and particularly of our own *excellent constitution*, deservedly the wonder and envy of the whole world. But having here accidentally mentioned a *minister of State*, he commanded me some time after to inform him, what species of Yahoo I particularly meant by that appellation.

I told him, that our She Governor or Queen having no ambition to gratify, no inclination to satisfy of extending her power to the injury of her neighbours, or the prejudice of her own subjects, was therefore so far from needing a corrupt ministry to carry on or cover any sinister designs, that she not only directs her own actions to the good of her people, conducts them by the direction, and restrains them within the limitation of the laws of her own country; but submits the behaviour and acts of those she intrusts with the administration of her affairs to the examination of her great council, and subjects them to the penalties of the law; and therefore never puts any such confidence in any of her subjects as to entrust them with the whole and entire administration of her affairs: but I added, that in some former reigns here, and in many other courts of Europe now, where princes grew indolent and careless of their own affairs through a constant love and pursuit of pleasure, they made use of such an administrator, as I had mentioned, under the title of *First* or *Chief Minister of State*, the description of which, as far as it may be collected not only from their actions, but from the letters, memoirs, and writings published by themselves, the truth of which has not yet been disputed, may be allowed to be as follows: that he is a person wholly exempt from joy and grief, love and hatred, pity and anger; at least makes use of no other passions but a violent desire of wealth, power, and titles: that, he applies his words to all uses, except to the indication of his mind: that, he never tells a *truth*, but with an intent that you should take it for a *lye*; nor a *lye*, but with a design that you should take it for a *truth*; that those he speaks worst of behind their backs, are in the surest way to preferment; and whenever he begins to praise you to others or to your self, you are from that day forlorn. The worst mark you can receive is a *promise*, especially when it is confirmed with an oath; after which every wise man retires, and gives over all hopes.

There are three methods by which a man may rise to be Chief Minister: the first is, by knowing how with prudence to dispose of a wife, a daughter, or a sister: the second, by betraying or undermining his predecessor: and the third is, by a *furious zeal* in publick assemblies against the corruptions of the court. But a wise prince would rather chuse to employ those who practise the last of these methods; because such zealots prove always the most obsequious and subservient to the will and passions of their master. That, these *ministers* having all employments at their disposal, preserve themselves in power by bribing the majority of a Senate, or Great Council;

and at last by an expedient called an Act of Indemnity (whereof I described the nature to him) they secure themselves from after-reckonings, and retire from the publick, laden with the spoils of the nation.

The palace of a Chief Minister, is a seminary to breed up others in his own trade: the pages, lacquies, and porters, by imitating their master, become ministers of State in their several districts, and learn to excel in the three principal *ingredients*, of *insolence, lying*, and *bribery*. Accordingly, they have a *subaltern* court paid to them by persons of the best rank; and sometimes by the force of dexterity and impudence, arrive through several gradations to be successors to their lord.

He is usually governed by a decayed wench, or favourite footman, who are the tunnels through which all graces are conveyed, and may properly be called, *in the last resort*, the governors of the kingdom.

One day, my master, having heard me mention the *nobility* of my country, was pleased to make me a compliment which I could not pretend to deserve: that, he was sure, I must have been born of some noble family, because I far exceeded in shape, colour, and cleanliness, all the Yahoos of his nation, although I seemed to fail in strength, and agility, which must be imputed to my different way of living from those other brutes; and besides, I was not only endowed with the faculty of speech, but likewise with some rudiments of reason, to a degree, that with all his acquaintance I passed for a prodigy.

He made me observe, that among the Houyhnhnms, the White, the Sorrel, and the Iron-Grey, were not so exactly shaped as the Bay, the Dapple Grey, and the Black; nor born with equal talents of mind, or a capacity to improve them; and therefore continued always in the condition of servants, without ever aspiring to match out of their own race, which in that country would be reckoned monstrous and unnatural.

I made his honour my most humble acknowledgments for the good opinion he was pleased to conceive of me; but assured him at the same time, that my birth was of the lower sort, having been born of plain, honest parents, who were just able to give me a tolerable education: that, *nobility* among us was altogether a different thing from the idea he had of it: that, our young *noblemen* are bred from their childhood in idleness and luxury: that, as soon as years will permit, they consume their vigour, and contract odious diseases among lewd females; and when their fortunes are almost ruined, they marry some woman of mean birth, disagreeable person, and unsound constitution, merely for the sake of money, whom they hate and despise: that, the production of such marriages are generally scrophulous, rickety, or deformed children; by which means the family seldom continues above three generations, unless the wife take care to provide a healthy father among her neighbours, or domesticks, in order to improve and continue the breed: that, a weak diseased body, a meager countenance, and sallow complexion, are the true marks of *noble blood;* and a healthy robust appearance is so disgraceful in a man of quality, that the world concludes his real father to have been a groom or a coachman. The imperfections of his mind run parallel with those of his body; being a composition of spleen, dulness, ignorance, caprice, sensuality, and pride.

CHAPTER VII

The author's great love of his native country. His master's observations upon the constitution and administration of England, as described by the author, with parallel cases and comparisons. His master's observations upon human nature.

THE reader may be disposed to wonder how I could prevail on my self to give so free a representation of my own species, among a race of mortals who were already too apt to conceive the vilest opinion of human kind, from that entire congruity betwixt me and their Yahoos. But I must freely confess, that the many virtues of those excellent *quadrupeds* placed in opposite view to human corruptions, had so far opened mine eyes, and enlarged my understanding, that I began to view the actions and passions of man in a very different light, and to think the honour of my own kind not worth managing; which, besides, it was impossible for me to do before a person of so acute a judgment as my master, who daily convinced me of a thousand faults in my self, whereof I had not the least perception before, and which with us would never be numbered, even among human infirmities. I had likewise learned from his example an utter detestation of all falshood or disguise; and truth appeared so amiable to me, that I determined upon sacrificing every thing to it.

Let me deal so candidly with the reader, as to confess, that there was yet a much stronger motive for the freedom I took in my representation of things. I had not been a year in this country, before I contracted such a love and veneration for the inhabitants, that I entered on a firm resolution never to return to human kind, but to pass the rest of my life among these admirable Houyhnhnms in the contemplation and practice of every virtue; where I could have no example or incitement to vice. But it was decreed by fortune, my perpetual enemy, that so great a felicity should not fall to my share. However, it is now some comfort to reflect, that in what I said of my countrymen, I *extenuated* their faults as much as I durst before so strict an examiner; and upon every article, gave as *favourable* a turn as the matter would bear. For, indeed, who is there alive that will not be swayed by his byass and partiality to the place of his birth?

I have related the substance of several conversations I had with my master, during the greatest part of the time I had the honour to be in his service; but have indeed for brevity sake omitted much more than is here set down.

When I had answered all his questions, and his curiosity seemed to be fully satisfied; he sent for me one morning early, and commanding me to sit down at some distance (an honour which he had never before conferred upon me) he said, he had been very seriously considering my whole story, as far as it related both to my self and my country: that, he looked upon us as a sort of animals to whose share, by what accident he could not conjecture, some small pittance of *reason* had fallen, whereof we made no other use than by its assistance to aggravate our *natural* corruptions, and to acquire new ones which nature had not given us: that, we disarmed our selves of the few abilities she had bestowed; had been very successful in multiplying our original wants, and seemed to spend our whole lives in vain endeavours to supply them by our own inventions: that, as to my self, it was manifest I had neither the strength or agility of a common Yahoo: that, I walked infirmly on my hinder feet; had found out a contrivance to make my claws of no use or defence, and to remove the hair from my chin, which was intended as a shelter from the sun and the weather. Lastly, that I could neither run with speed, nor climb trees like my *brethren* (as he called them) the Yahoos in this country.

That, our institutions of government and law were plainly owing to our gross defects in *reason*, and by consequence, in *virtue;* because *reason* alone is sufficient to govern a *rational* creature; which was therefore a character we had no pretence to challenge, even from the account I had given of my own people; although he manifestly perceived, that in order to favour them, I had concealed many particulars, and often *said the thing which was not.*

He was the more confirmed in this opinion, because he observed, that as I agreed in every feature of my body with other Yahoos, except where it was to my real disadvantage in point of strength, speed and activity, the shortness of my claws, and some other particulars where nature had no part; so, from the representation I had given him of our lives, our manners, and our actions, he found as near a resemblance in the disposition of our minds. He said, the Yahoos were known to hate one another more than they did any different species of animals; and the reason usually assigned, was, the odiousness of their own shapes, which all could see in the rest, but not in themselves. He had therefore begun to think it not unwise in us to *cover* our bodies, and by that invention, conceal many of our deformities from each other, which would else be hardly supportable. But, he now found he had been mistaken; and that the dissentions of those brutes in his country were owing to the same cause with ours, as I had described them. For, if (said he) you throw among five Yahoos as much food as would be sufficient for fifty, they will, instead of eating peaceably, fall together by the ears, each single one impatient to *have all to itself;* and therefore a servant was usually employed to stand by while they were feeding abroad, and those kept at home were tied at a distance from each other: that, if a cow died of age or accident, before a Houyhnhnm could secure it for his own Yahoos, those in the neighbourhood would come in herds to seize it, and then would ensue such a battle as I had described, with terrible wounds made by their claws on both sides, although they seldom were able to kill one another, for want of such convenient instruments of death as we had invented. At other times the like battles have been fought between the Yahoos of several neighbourhoods without any visible cause: those of one district watching all opportunities to surprize the next before they are prepared. But, if they find their project hath miscarried, they return home, and for want of enemies, engage in what I call a *civil war* among themselves.

That, in some fields of his country, there are certain *shining stones* of several colours, whereof the Yahoos are violently fond; and when part of these *stones* are fixed in the earth, as it sometimes happeneth, they will dig with their claws for whole days to get them out, and carry them away, and hide them by heaps in their kennels; but still looking round with great caution, for fear their comrades should find out their treasure. My master said, he could never discover the reason of this unnatural appetite, or how these *stones* could be of any use to a Yahoo; but now he believed it might proceed from the same principle of *avarice*, which I had ascribed to mankind: that, he had once, by way of experiment, privately removed a heap of these *stones* from the place where one of his Yahoos had buried it: whereupon, the sordid animal missing his treasure, by his loud lamenting brought the whole herd to the place, there miserably howled, then fell to biting and tearing the rest; began to pine away, would neither eat nor sleep, nor work, until he ordered a servant privately to convey the *stones* into the same hole, and hide them as before; which when his Yahoo had found, he presently recovered his spirits and good humour; but took care to remove them to a better hiding place; and hath ever since been a very serviceable brute.

My master farther assured me, which I also observed my self, that in the fields where these *shining stones* abound, the fiercest and most frequent battles are fought, occasioned by perpetual inroads of the neighbouring Yahoos.

He said, it was common when two Yahoos discovered such a *stone* in a field, and were contending which of them should be the proprietor, a third would take the advantage, and carry it away from them both; which my master would needs contend to have some resemblance with our *suits at law;* wherein I thought it for our credit not to undeceive him; since the decision he mentioned was much more equitable than many decrees among us: because the plaintiff and defendant there lost nothing beside the *stone* they contended for; whereas our *courts of equity*, would never have dismissed the cause while either of them had any thing left.

My master continuing his discourse, said, there was nothing that rendered the Yahoos more odious, than their undistinguished appetite to devour every thing that came in their way, whether herbs, roots, berries, corrupted flesh of animals; or all mingled together: and, it was peculiar in their temper, that they were fonder of what they could get by rapine or stealth at a greater distance, than much better food provided for them at home: if their prey held out, they would eat until they were ready to burst, after which nature had pointed out to them a certain *root* that gave them a general evacuation.

There was also another kind of *root* very *juicy*, but something rare and difficult to be found; which the Yahoos fought for with much eagerness, and would suck it with great delight: it produced the same effects that wine hath upon us. It would make them sometimes hug, and sometimes tear one another; they would howl and grin, and chatter, and tumble, and then fall asleep in the dirt.

I did indeed observe, that the Yahoos were the only animals in this country subject to any diseases; which, however, were much fewer than horses have among us, and contracted not by any ill treatment they meet with, but by the nastiness and greediness of that sordid brute. Neither has their language any more than a general appellation for those maladies; which is borrowed from the name of the beast, and called "Hnea Yahoo," or the Yahoo's-evil; and the cure prescribed is a mixture of *their own dung* and *urine*, forcibly put down the Yahoo's throat. This I have since often known to have been taken with success: and do here freely recommend it to my countrymen, for the publick good, as an admirable specifick against all diseases produced by repletion.

As to learning, government, arts, manufactures, and the like, my master confessed he could find little or no resemblance between the Yahoos of that country, and those in ours. For, he only meant to observe what parity there was in our natures. He had heard indeed some curious Houyhnhnms observe, that in most herds there was a sort of ruling Yahoo, (as among us there is generally some leading or principal stag in a park) who was always more *deformed* in body, and *mischievous in disposition*, than any of the rest. That, this *leader* had usually a favourite as *like himself* as he could get, whose employment was to *lick his master's feet and posteriors, and drive the female Yahoos to his kennel;* for which he was now and then rewarded with a piece of ass's flesh. This *favourite* is hated by the whole herd; and therefore to protect himself, keeps always *near the person of his leader*. He usually continues in office until a worse can be found; but the very moment he is discarded, his successor, at the head of all the Yahoos in that district, young and old, male and female, come in a body, and discharge their excrements upon him from head to foot. But how far this might be applicable to our *courts* and *favourites*, and *ministers of State*, my master said I could best determine.

I durst make no return to this malicious insinuation, which debased human understanding below the sagacity of a common *hound*, who hath judgment enough to distinguish and follow the cry of the *ablest dog in the pack*, without being ever mistaken.

My master told me, there were some qualities remarkable in the Yahoos, which he had not observed me to mention, or at least very slightly, in the accounts I had given him of human kind. He said, those animals, like other brutes, had their females in common; but in this they differed, that the she-Yahoo would admit the male, while she was pregnant; and that the hees would quarrel and fight with the females as fiercely as with each other. Both which practices were such degrees of infamous brutality, that no other sensitive creature ever arrived at.

Another thing he wondered at in the Yahoos, was their strange disposition to nastiness and dirt; whereas there appears to be a natural love of cleanliness in all other animals. As to the two former accusations, I was glad to let them pass without any reply, because I had not a word to offer upon them in defence of my species, which otherwise I certainly had done from my own inclinations. But I could have easily vindicated human kind from the imputation of singularity upon the last article, if there had been any *swine* in that country, (as unluckily for me there were not) which although it may be a *sweeter quadruped* than a Yahoo, cannot I humbly conceive in justice pretend to more cleanliness; and so his honour himself must have owned, if he had seen their filthy way of feeding, and their custom of wallowing and sleeping in the mud.

My master likewise mentioned another quality, which his servants had discovered in several Yahoos, and to him was wholly unaccountable. He said, a fancy would sometimes take a Yahoo, to retire into a corner, to lie down and howl, and groan, and spurn away all that came near him, although he were young and fat, and wanted neither food nor water; nor did the servants imagine what could possibly ail him. And the only remedy they found, was to set him to hard work, after which he would infallibly come to himself. To this I was silent out of partiality to my own kind; yet here I could plainly discover the true seeds of *spleen*, which only seizeth on the *lazy*, the *luxurious*, and the *rich*; who, if they were forced to undergo the *same regimen*, I would undertake for the cure.

His honour had farther observed, that a female-Yahoo would often stand behind a bank or a bush, to gaze on the young males passing by, and then appear, and hide, using many antick gestures and grimaces; at which time it was observed, that she had a most *offensive smell*; and when any of the males advanced, would slowly retire, looking often back, and with a counterfeit shew of fear, run off into some convenient place where she knew the male would follow her.

At other times, if a female stranger came among them, three or four of her own sex would get about her, and stare and chatter, and grin, and smell her all over; and then turn off with gestures that seemed to express contempt and disdain.

Perhaps my master might refine a little in these speculations, which he had drawn from what he observed himself, or had been told him by others: however, I could not reflect without some amazement, and much sorrow, that the rudiments of *lewdness*, *coquetry*, *censure*, and *scandal*, should have place by instinct in womankind.

I expected every moment, that my master would accuse the Yahoos of those unnatural appetites in both sexes, so common among us. But nature it seems hath not been so expert a school-mistress; and these politer pleasures are entirely the productions of art and reason, on our side of the globe.

CHAPTER VIII

The author relateth several particulars of the Yahoos. The great virtues of the Houyhnhnms. The education and exercise of their youth. Their general assembly.

As I ought to have understood human nature much better than I supposed it possible for my master to do, so it was easy to apply the character he gave of the Yahoos to myself and my countrymen; and I believed I could yet make farther discoveries from my own observation. I therefore often begged his honour to let me go among the herds of Yahoos in the neighbourhood; to which he always very graciously consented, being perfectly convinced that the hatred I bore those brutes would never suffer me to be corrupted by them; and his honour ordered one of his servants, a strong sorrel nag, very honest and good-natured, to be my guard; without whose protection

I durst not undertake such adventures. For I have already told the reader how much I was pestered by those odious animals upon my first arrival. I afterwards failed very narrowly three or four times of falling into their clutches, when I happened to stray at any distance without my hanger. And I have reason to believe, they had some imagination that I was of their own species, which I often assisted myself, by stripping up my sleeves, and shewing my naked arms and breast in their sight, when my protector was with me: at which times they would approach as near as they durst, and imitate my actions after the manner of monkeys, but ever with great signs of hatred; as a tame *jack daw* with cap and stockings, is always persecuted by the wild ones, when he happens to be got among them.

They are prodigiously nimble from their infancy; however, I once caught a young male of three years old, and endeavoured by all marks of tenderness to make it quiet; but the little imp fell a squalling, and scratching, and biting with such violence, that I was forced to let it go; and it was high time, for a whole troop of old ones came about us at the noise; but finding the cub was safe, (for away it ran) and my sorrel nag being by, they durst not venture near us. I observed the young animal's flesh to smell very rank, and the stink was somewhat between a *weasel* and a *fox*, but much more disagreeable. I forgot another circumstance, (and perhaps I might have the readers pardon, if it were wholly omitted) that while I held the odious vermin in my hands, it voided its filthy excrements of a yellow liquid substance, all over my cloaths; but by good fortune there was a small brook hard by, where I washed myself as clean as I could; although I durst not come into my master's presence, until I were sufficiently aired.

By what I could discover, the Yahoos appear to be the most unteachable of all animals, their capacities never reaching higher than to draw or carry burthens. Yet I am of opinion, this defect ariseth chiefly from a perverse, restive disposition. For they are cunning, malicious, treacherous and revengeful. They are strong and hardy, but of a cowardly spirit, and by consequence insolent, abject, and cruel. It is observed, that the *red-haired* of both sexes are more libidinous and mischievous than the rest, whom yet they much exceed in strength and activity.

The Houyhnhnms keep the Yahoos for present use in huts not far from the house; but the rest are sent abroad to certain fields, where they dig up roots, eat several kinds of herbs, and search about for carrion, or sometimes catch *weasels* and *luhimuhs* (a sort of *wild rat*) which they greedily devour. Nature hath taught them to dig deep holes with their nails on the side of a rising ground, wherein they lie by themselves; only the kennels of the females are larger, sufficient to hold two or three cubs.

They swim from their infancy like frogs, and are able to continue long under water, where they often take fish, which the females carry home to their young. And upon this occasion, I hope the reader will pardon my relating an odd adventure.

Being one day abroad with my protector the sorrel nag, and the weather exceeding hot, I entreated him to let me bathe in a river that was near. He consented, and I immediately stripped myself stark naked, and went down softly into the stream. It happened that a young female Yahoo standing behind a bank, saw the whole proceeding; and inflamed by desire, as the nag and I conjectured, came running with all speed, and leaped into the water within five yards of the place where I bathed. I was never in my life so terribly frighted; the nag was grazing at some distance, not suspecting any harm; she embraced me after a most fulsome manner; I roared as loud as I could, and the nag came galloping towards me, whereupon she quitted her grasp, with the utmost reluctancy, and leaped upon the opposite bank, where she stood gazing and howling all the time I was putting on my cloaths.

This was matter of diversion to my master and his family, as well as of mortification to my self. For now I could no longer deny, that I was a real Yahoo, in every limb and feature, since the females had a natural propensity to me as one of their own species: neither was the hair of this brute of a red colour (which might have been some excuse for an appetite a little irregular) but black as sloe, and her countenance did not make an appearance altogether so hideous as the rest of the kind; for, I think, she could not be above eleven years old.

Having lived three years in this country, the reader I suppose will expect, that I should, like other travellers, give him some account of the manners and customs of its inhabitants, which it was indeed my principal study to learn.

As these noble Houyhnhnms are endowed by nature with a general disposition to all virtues, and have no conceptions or ideas of what is evil in a rational creature, so their grand maxim is, to cultivate *reason*, and to be wholly governed by it. Neither is *reason* among them a point problematical as with us, where men can argue with plausibility on both sides of the question; but strikes you with immediate conviction; as it must needs do where it is not mingled, obscured, or discoloured by passion and interest. I remember it was with extreme difficulty that I could bring my master to understand the meaning of the word *opinion*, or how a point could be disputable; because *reason* taught us to affirm or deny, only where we are certain; and beyond our knowledge, we cannot do either. So that controversies, wranglings, disputes, and positiveness in false or dubious propositions, are evils unknown among the Houyhnhnms. In the like manner, when I used to explain to him our several systems of *natural philosophy*, he would laugh that a creature pretending to *reason*, should value it self upon the knowledge of other peoples conjectures, and in things, where that knowledge, if it were certain, could be of no use. Wherein he agreed entirely with the sentiments of Socrates, as Plato delivers them; which I mention as the highest honour I can do that prince of philosophers. I have often since reflected what destruction such a doctrine would make in the libraries of Europe; and how many paths to fame would be then shut up in the learned world.

Friendship and *benevolence* are the two principal virtues among the Houyhnhnms; and these not confined to particular objects, but universal to the whole race, for, a stranger from the remotest part, is equally treated with the nearest neighbour, and wherever he goes, looks upon himself as at home. They preserve *decency* and *civility* in the highest degrees, but are altogether ignorant of *ceremony*. They have no fondness for their colts or foles; but the care they take in educating them proceedeth entirely from the dictates of *reason*. And, I observed my master to shew the same affection to his neighbour's issue, that he had for his own. They will have it that *nature* teaches them to love the whole species, and it is *reason* only that maketh a distinction of persons, where there is a superior degree of virtue.

When the matron Houyhnhnms have produced one of each sex, they no longer accompany with their consorts, except they lose one of their issue by some casualty, which very seldom happens: but in such a case they meet again; or when the like accident befalls a person, whose wife is past bearing, some other couple bestows on him one of their own colts, and then go together a second time, until the mother be pregnant. This caution is necessary to prevent the country from being overburthened with numbers. But the race of inferior Houyhnhnms bred up to be servants, is not so strictly limited upon this article; these are allowed to produce three of each sex, to be domesticks in the noble families.

In their marriages, they are exactly careful to chuse such colours as will not make any disagreeable mixture in the breed. *Strength* is chiefly valued in the male, and *comeliness* in the female; not upon the account of *love*, but to preserve the race from degenerating: for, where a female happens to excel in *strength*, a consort is chosen with regard to *comeliness*. Courtship, love, presents, joyntures, settlements, have no place in their thoughts; or terms whereby to express them in their language. The young couple meet and are joined, merely because it is the determination of their parents and friends: it is what they see done every day; and they look upon it as one of the necessary actions in a reasonable being. But, the violation of marriage, or any other unchastity, was never heard of: and the married pair pass their lives with the same friendship, and mutual benevolence that they bear to all others of the same species, who come in their way; without jealousy, fondness, quarrelling, or discontent.

In educating the youth of both sexes, their method is admirable, and highly deserveth our imitation. These are not suffered to taste a grain of *oats*, except upon certain days, until eighteen years old; nor *milk*, but very rarely; and in summer, they graze two hours in the morning, and as many in the evening, which their parents likewise observe; but the servants are not allowed above half that time; and a great part of the grass is brought home, which they eat at the most convenient hours, when they can be best spared from work.

Temperance, *industry*, *exercise*, and *cleanliness*, are the lessons equally enjoyned to the young ones of both sexes; and my master thought it monstrous in us to give the females a different kind of education from the males, except in some articles of domestick management; whereby, as he truly observed, one half of our natives were good for nothing but bringing children into the world: and to trust the care of their children to such useless animals, he said was yet a greater instance of brutality.

But, the Houyhnhnms train up their youth to strength, speed, and hardiness, by exercising them in running races up and down steep hills, or over hard stony grounds; and when they are all in a sweat, they are ordered to leap over head and ears into a pond or river. Four times a year the youth of certain districts meet to shew their proficiency in running, and leaping, and other feats of strength or agility; where the victor is rewarded with a song, made in his or her praise. On this festival, the servants drive a herd of Yahoos into the field, laden with hay, and oats, and milk for a repast to the Houyhnhnms; after which, these brutes are immediately driven back again, for fear of being noisome to the assembly.

Every fourth year, at the *vernal equinox*, there is a representative council of the whole nation, which meets in a plain about twenty miles from our house, and continueth about five or six days. Here they inquire into the state and condition of the several districts; whether they abound, or be deficient in hay, or oats, or cows, or Yahoos? And wherever there is any want (which is but seldom) it is immediately supplied by unanimous consent and contribution. Here likewise the regulation of children is settled: as for instance, if a Houyhnhnm hath two males, he changeth one of them with another who hath two females: and when a child hath been lost by any casualty, where the mother is past breeding, it is determined what family shall breed another to supply the loss.

CHAPTER IX

A grand debate at the general assembly of the Houyhnhnms; and how it was determined. The learning of the Houyhnhnms. Their buildings. Their manner of burials. The defectiveness of their language.

ONE of these grand assemblies was held in my time, about three months before my departure, whither my master went as the representative of our district. In this council was resumed their old debate, and indeed, the only debate that ever happened in their country; whereof my master, after his return, gave me a very particular account.

The question to be debated was, whether the Yahoos should be exterminated from the face of the earth. One of the *members* for the affirmative offered several arguments of great strength and weight; alledging, that, as the Yahoos were the most filthy, noisome, and deformed animal which nature ever produced, so they were the most restive and indocible, mischievous and malicious: they would privately suck the teats of the Houyhnhnms cows; kill and devour their cats, trample down their oats and grass, if they were not continually watched; and commit a thousand other extravagancies. He took notice of a general tradition, that Yahoos had not been always in their country: but, that many ages ago, two of these brutes appeared together upon a mountain; whether produced by the heat of the sun upon corrupted mud and slime, or from the ooze and froth of the sea, was never known. That, these Yahoos engendered, and their brood in a short time grew so numerous, as to overrun and infest the whole nation. That, the Houyhnhnms, to get rid of this evil, made a general hunting, and at last inclosed the whole herd; and destroying the older, every Houyhnhnm kept two young ones in a kennel, and brought them to such a degree of tameness, as an animal so savage by nature, can be capable of acquiring; using them for draught and carriage. That, there seemed to be much truth in this tradition, and that those creatures could not be *ylnhniamshy* (or *aborigines* of the land) because of the violent hatred the Houyhnhnms, as well as all other animals bore them; which although their evil disposition sufficiently deserved, could never have arrived at so high a degree, if they had been *aborigines*, or else they would have long since been rooted out. That, the inhabitants taking a fancy to use the service of the Yahoos, had very imprudently neglected to cultivate the breed of *asses*, which were a comely animal, easily kept, more tame and orderly, without any offensive smell, strong enough for labour, although they yield to the other in agility of body; and if their braying be no agreeable sound, it is far preferable to the horrible howlings of the Yahoos.

Several others declared their sentiments to the same purpose, when my master proposed an expedient to the assembly, whereof he had indeed borrowed the hint from me. He approved of the tradition mentioned by the *honourable member*, who spoke before; and affirmed, that the two Yahoos said to be first seen among them, had been driven thither over the sea: that, coming to land, and being forsaken by their companions, they retired to the mountains, and degenerating by degrees, became in process of time, much more savage than those of their own species in the country from whence these two originals came. The reason of his assertion was, that he had now in his possession, a certain wonderful Yahoo (meaning my self) which most of them had heard of, and many of them had seen. He then related to them, how he first found me: that, my body was all covered with an artificial composure of the skins and hairs of other animals: that, I spoke in a language of my own, and had thoroughly learned theirs: that, I had related to him the accidents which brought me thither: that, when he saw me without my covering, I was an exact Yahoo in every part, only of a whiter colour, less hairy, and with shorter claws. He added, how I had endeavoured to persuade him, that in my own and other countries, the Yahoos acted as the governing, rational animal, and held the Houyhnhnms in servitude: that, he observed in me, all the qualities of a Yahoo, only a little more civilized by some tincture of reason; which however, was in a degree as far inferior to the Houyhnhnm race, as the Yahoos of their country were to me: that, among other things, I mentioned a custom we had of *castrating* Houyhnhnms when they were young, in order to render them tame; that the operation was easy and safe: that, it was no shame to learn wisdom from brutes, as industry is taught by the ant, and building by the swallow: (for so I translate the word "lyhannh," although it be a much larger fowl) that, this invention might be practised upon the younger Yahoos here, which, besides rendering them tractable and fitter for use, would in an age, put an end to the whole species, without destroying life: that, in the mean time, the Houyhnhnms should be *exhorted* to cultivate the breed of asses, which, as they are in all respects more valuable brutes, so they have this advantage, to be fit for service at five years old, which the others are not until twelve.

This was all my master thought fit to tell me at that time, of what passed in the Grand Council. But he was pleased to conceal one particular, which related personally to my self, whereof I soon felt the unhappy effect, as the reader will know in its proper place, and from whence I date all the succeeding misfortunes of my life.

The Houyhnhnms have no letters, and consequently, their knowledge is all traditional. But, there happening few events of any moment among a people so well united, naturally disposed to every virtue, wholly governed by reason, and cut off from all commerce with other nations, the historical part is easily preserved without burthening their memories. I have already observed, that they are subject to no diseases, and therefore can have no need of physicians. However, they have excellent medicines composed of herbs, to cure accidental bruises and cuts in the pastern or frog of the foot by sharp stones, as well as other maims and hurts in the several parts of the body.

They calculate the year by the revolution of the sun and the moon, but use no subdivisions into weeks. They are well enough acquainted with the motions of those two luminaries, and understand the nature of *eclipses*; and this is the utmost progress of their *astronomy*.

In *poetry*, they must be allowed to excel all other mortals; wherein the justness of their similes, and the minuteness, as well as exactness of their descriptions, are indeed, inimitable. Their verses abound very much in both of these; and usually contain either some exalted notions of friendship and benevolence, or the praises of those who were victors in races, and other bodily exercises. Their buildings, although very rude and simple, are not inconvenient, but well contrived to defend them from all injuries of cold and heat. They have a kind of tree, which at forty years old loosens in the root, and falls with the first storm; it grows very strait, and being pointed like stakes with a sharp stone, (for the Houyhnhnms know not the use of iron) they stick them erect in the ground about ten inches asunder, and then weave in oat straw, or sometimes wattles betwixt them. The roof is made after the same manner, and so are the doors.

The Houyhnhnms use the hollow part between the pastern and the hoof of their fore-feet, as we do our hands, and this with greater dexterity, than I could at first imagine. I have seen a white mare of our family thread a needle (which I lent her on purpose) with that joynt. They milk their cows, reap their oats, and do all the work which requires hands, in the same manner. They have a kind of hard flints, which by grinding against other stones, they form into instruments, that serve instead of wedges, axes, and hammers. With tools made of these flints, they likewise cut their hay, and reap their oats, which there groweth naturally in several fields: the Yahoos draw home the sheaves in carriages, and the servants tread them in certain covered hutts, to get out the grain, which is kept in stores. They make a rude kind of earthen and wooden vessels, and bake the former in the suu.

If they can avoid casualties, they die only of old age, and are buried in the obscurest places that can be found, their friends and relations expressing neither joy nor grief at their departure; nor does the dying person discover the least regret that he is leaving the world, any more than if he were upon returning home from a visit to one of his neighbours. I remember, my master having once made an appointment with a friend and his family to come to his house upon some affair of importance, on the day fixed, the mistress and her two children came very late; she made two excuses, first for her husband, who, as she said happened that very morning to *lhduwhn*. The word is strongly expressed in their language, but not easily rendered into English; it signifies, *to retire to his first mother*. Her excuse for not coming sooner, was, that her husband dying late in the morning, she was a good while consulting her servants about a convenient place where his body should be laid; and I observed, she behaved her self at our house, as chearfully as the rest: she died about three months after.

They live generally to seventy or seventy-five years, very seldom to fourscore: some weeks before their death, they feel a gradual decay, but without pain. During this time, they are much visited by their friends, because they cannot go abroad with their usual ease and satisfaction. However, about ten days before their death, which they seldom fail in computing, they return the visits that have been made them by those who are nearest in the neighbourhood, being carried in a convenient sledge drawn by Yahoos; which vehicle they use, not only upon this occasion, but when they grow old, upon long journies, or when they are lamed by any accident. And therefore, when the dying Houyhnhnms return those visits, they take a solemn leave of their friends, as if they were going to some remote part of the country, where they designed to pass the rest of their lives.

I know not whether it may be worth observing, that the Houyhnhnms have no word in their language to express any thing that is *evil*, except what they borrow from the deformities or ill-qualities of the Yahoos. Thus they denote the folly of a servant, an omission of a child, a stone that cuts their feet, a continuance of foul or unseasonable weather, and the like, by adding to each, the epithet of Yahoo. For instance, *hhnum Yahoo, whnaholm Yahoo, ynlhmnawihlma Yahoo*, and an ill contrived house, *ynholmhnmrohlnw Yahoo*.

I could with great pleasure enlarge farther upon the manners and virtues of this excellent people; but intending in a short time to publish a volume by it self expressly upon that subject, I refer the reader thither. And in the mean time, proceed to relate my own sad catastrophe.

CHAPTER X

The author's œconomy and happy life among the Houyhnhnms. His great improvement in virtue, by conversing with them. Their conversations. The author hath notice given him by his master, that he must depart from the country. He falls into a swoon for grief, but submits. He contrives and finishes a canoo, by the help of a fellow-servant; and puts to sea at a venture.

I HAD settled my little œconomy to my own heart's content. My master had ordered a room to be made for me after their manner, about six yards from the house; the sides and floors of which I plaistered with clay, and covered with rush-mats of my own contriving. I had beaten hemp, which there grows wild, and made of it a sort of ticking: this I filled with the feathers of several birds I had taken with springes made of Yahoos' hairs, and were

excellent food. I had worked two chairs with my knife, the sorrel nag helping me in the grosser and more laborious part. When my cloaths were worn
to rags, I made my self others with the skins of rabbets, and of a certain
beautiful animal about the same size, called *nnuhnoh*, the skin of which is
covered with a fine down. Of these I likewise made very tolerable stockings.
I soaled my shoes with wood, which I cut from a tree, and fitted to the upper leather, and when this was worn out, I supplied it with the skins of
Yahoos, dried in the sun. I often got honey out of hollow trees, which I
mingled with water, or eat it with my bread. No man could more verify the
truth of these two maxims: *that nature is very easily satisfied;* and, *that
necessity is the mother of invention.* I enjoyed perfect health of body, and
tranquillity of mind; I did not feel the treachery or inconstancy of a friend,
nor the injuries of a secret or open enemy. I had no occasion of bribing,
flattering or pimping, to procure the favour of any great man, or of his
minion. I wanted no fence against fraud or oppression: here was neither
physician to destroy my body, nor lawyer to ruin my fortune: no informer
to watch my words and actions, or forge accusations against me for hire:
here were no gibers, censurers, backbiters, pickpockets, highwaymen,
house-breakers, attorneys, bawds, buffoons, gamesters, politicians, wits,
spleneticks, tedious talkers, controvertists, ravishers, murderers, robbers,
virtuosoes; no leaders or followers of party and faction; no encouragers to
vice, by seducement or examples: no dungeon, axes, gibbets, whipping-
posts, or pillories: no cheating shop-keepers or mechanicks: no pride, vanity
or affectation: no fops, bullies, drunkards, strolling whores, or poxes: no
ranting, lewd expensive wives: no stupid, proud pedants: no importunate,
over-bearing, quarrelsome, noisy, roaring, empty, conceited, swearing companions: no scoundrels raised from the dust upon the merit of their vices;
or nobility thrown into it, on account of their virtues: no lords, fiddlers,
judges, or dancing-masters.

I had the favour of being admitted to several Houyhnhnms, who came to
visit or dine with my master, where his honour graciously suffered me to
wait in the room, and listen to their discourse. Both he and his company
would often condescend to ask me questions, and receive my answers. I had
also sometimes the honour of attending my master in his visits to others. I
never presumed to speak, except in answer to a question; and then I did it
with inward regret, because it was a loss of so much time for improving my
self: but, I was infinitely delighted with the station of an humble auditor in
such conversations, where nothing passed but what was useful, expressed
in the fewest and most significant words: where (as I have already said)
the greatest *decency* was observed, without the least degree of ceremony;
where no person spoke without being pleased himself, and pleasing his
companions: where there was no interruption, tediousness, heat, or difference of sentiments. They have a notion, that when people are met together,
a short silence doth much improve conversation: this I found to be true; for
during those little intermissions of talk, new ideas would arise in their
minds, which very much enlivened the discourse. Their subjects are generally on friendship and benevolence; on order and œconomy; sometimes
upon the visible operations of nature, or ancient traditions; upon the

bounds and limits of virtue; upon the unerring rules of reason; or upon some determinations, to be taken at the next great assembly; and often upon the various excellencies of *poetry*. I may add, without vanity, that my presence often gave them sufficient matter for discourse, because it afforded my master an occasion of letting his friends into the history of me and my country, upon which they were all pleased to descant in a manner not very advantageous to human kind; and for that reason, I shall not repeat what they said: only I may be allowed to observe, that his honour, to my great admiration, appeared to understand the nature of Yahoos much better than my self. He went through all our vices and follies, and discovered many which I had never mentioned to him, by only supposing what qualities a Yahoo of their country, with a small proportion of reason, might be capable of exerting: and concluded, with too much probability, how vile as well as miserable such a creature must be.

I freely confess, that all the little knowledge I have of any value, was acquired by the lectures I received from my master, and from hearing the discourses of him and his friends; to which I should be prouder to listen, than to dictate to the greatest and wisest assembly in Europe. I admired the strength, comeliness and speed of the inhabitants; and such a constellation of virtues in such amiable persons, produced in me the highest veneration. At first, indeed, I did not feel that natural awe, which the Yahoos and all other animals, bear towards them; but it grew upon me by degrees, much sooner than I imagined, and was mingled with a respectful love and gratitude, that they would condescend to distinguish me from the rest of my species.

When I thought of my family, my friends, my countrymen, or human race in general, I considered them as they really were, Yahoos in shape and disposition, perhaps a little more civilized, and qualified with the gift of speech; but making no other use of reason, than to improve and multiply those vices, whereof their brethren in this country, had only the share that nature allotted them. When I happened to behold the reflection of my own form in a lake or fountain, I turned away my face in horror and detestation of my self; and could better endure the sight of a common Yahoo, than of my own person. By conversing with the Houyhnhnms, and looking upon them with delight, I fell to imitate their gait and gesture, which is now grown into a habit; and my friends often tell me in a blunt way, that *I trot like a horse*; which, however, I take for a great compliment: neither shall I disown, that in speaking I am apt to fall into the voice and manner of the Houyhnhnms, and hear my self ridiculed on that account without the least mortification.

In the midst of this happiness, when I looked upon my self to be fully settled for life, my master sent for me one morning a little earlier than his usual hour. I observed by his countenance, that he was in some perplexity, and at a loss how to begin what he had to speak. After a short silence, he told me, he did not know how I would take what he was going to say: that, in the last general assembly, when the affair of the Yahoos was entered upon, the representatives had taken offence at his keeping a Yahoo (meaning my self) in his family more like a Houyhnhnm than a brute animal:

that, he was known frequently to converse with me, as if he could receive some advantage or pleasure in my company: that, such a practice was not agreeable to reason or nature, or a thing ever heard of before among them. The assembly did therefore *exhort* him, either to employ me like the rest of my species, or command me to swim back to the place from whence I came: that, the first of these expedients was utterly rejected by all the Houyhnhnms, who had ever seen me at his house or their own: for, they alledged, that because I had some rudiments of reason, added to the natural pravity of those animals, it was to be feared, I might be able to seduce them into the woody and mountainous parts of the country, and bring them in troops by night to destroy the Houyhnhnms cattle, as being naturally of the ravenous kind, and averse from labour.

My master added, that he was daily pressed by the Houyhnhnms of the neighbourhood to have the assembly's *exhortation* executed, which he could not put off much longer. He doubted, it would be impossible for me to swim to another country; and therefore wished I would contrive some sort of vehicle resembling those I had described to him, that might carry me on the sea; in which work I should have the assistance of his own servants, as well as those of his neighbours. He concluded, that for his own part he could have been content to keep me in his service as long as I lived; because he found I had cured myself of some bad habits and dispositions, by endeavouring, as far as my inferior nature was capable, to imitate the Houyhnhnms.

I should here observe to the reader, that a decree of the general assembly in this country, is expressed by the word "hnhloayn," which signifies an *exhortation;* as near as I can render it: for they have no conception how a rational creature can be *compelled,* but only advised, or *exhorted;* because no person can disobey reason, without giving up his claim to be a rational creature.

I was struck with the utmost grief and despair at my master's discourse; and being unable to support the agonies I was under, I fell into a swoon at his feet: when I came to my self, he told me, that he concluded I had been dead. (For these people are subject to no such imbecillities of nature.) I answered, in a faint voice, that death would have been too great a happiness: that, although I could not blame the assembly's *exhortation,* or the urgency of his friends; yet in my weak and corrupt judgment, I thought it might consist with reason to have been less rigorous: that, I could not swim a league, and probably the nearest land to theirs might be distant above an hundred: that, many materials, necessary for making a small vessel to carry me off, were wholly wanting in this country; which, however, I would attempt in obedience and gratitude to his honour, although I concluded the thing to be impossible, and therefore looked on my self as already devoted to destruction: that, the certain prospect of an unnatural death, was the least of my evils: for, supposing I should escape with life by some strange adventure, how could I think with temper, of passing my days among Yahoos, and relapsing into my old corruptions, for want of examples to lead and keep me within the paths of virtue: that, I knew too well upon what solid reasons all the determinations of the wise Houyhnhnms were founded, not to be shaken by arguments of mine, a miserable Yahoo; and therefore, after presenting him with my humble thanks for the offer of his servants assistance in making a vessel, and desiring a reasonable time for so difficult a work, I told him, I would endeavour to preserve a wretched being; and, if ever I returned to England, was not without hopes of being useful to my own species, by celebrating the praises of the renowned Houy-hnhnms, and proposing their virtues to the imitation of mankind.

My master in a few words made me a very gracious reply, allowed me the space of two *months* to finish my boat; and ordered the sorrel nag, my fellow-servant, (for so at this distance I may presume to call him) to follow my instructions, because I told my master, that his help would be sufficient, and I knew he had a tenderness for me.

In his company my first business was to go to that part of the coast, where my rebellious crew had ordered me to be set on shore. I got upon a height, and looking on every side into the sea, fancied I saw a small island, towards the north-east: I took out my pocket-glass, and could then clearly distinguish it about five leagues off, as I computed; but it appeared to the sorrel nag to be only a blue cloud: for, as he had no conception of any coun-try beside his own, so he could not be as expert in distinguishing remote objects at sea, as we who so much converse in that element.

After I had discovered this island, I considered no farther; but resolved, it should, if possible, be the first place of my banishment, leaving the con-sequence to fortune.

I returned home, and consulting with the sorrel nag, we went into a copse at some distance, where I with my knife, and he with a sharp flint fastened very artificially, after their manner, to a wooden handle, cut down several oak wattles about the thickness of a walking staff, and some larger pieces. But I shall not trouble the reader with a particular description of my own mechanicks: let it suffice to say, that in six weeks time, with the help of the sorrel nag, who performed the parts that required most labour, I finished a sort of Indian canoo, but much larger, covering it with the skins of Yahoos well stitched together, with hempen threads of my own making. My sail was likewise composed of the skins of the same animal; but I made use of the youngest I could get, the older being too tough and thick; and I likewise provided my self with four paddles. I laid in a stock of boiled flesh, of rabbets and fowls; and took with me two vessels, one filled with milk, and the other with water.

I tried my canoo in a large pond near my master's house, and then cor-rected in it what was amiss; stopping all the chinks with Yahoos tallow, until I found it stanch, and able to bear me, and my freight. And when it was as compleat as I could possibly make it, I had it drawn on a carriage very gently by Yahoos, to the sea-side, under the conduct of the sorrel nag, and another servant.

When all was ready, and the day came for my departure, I took leave of my master and lady, and the whole family, mine eyes flowing with tears, and my heart quite sunk with grief. But his honour, out of curiosity, and perhaps (if I may speak it without vanity) partly out of kindness, was de-termined to see me in my canoo; and got several of his neighbouring friends to accompany him. I was forced to wait above an hour for the tide, and then observing the wind very fortunately bearing towards the island, to which I intended to steer my course, I took a second leave of my master: but, as I was going to prostrate my self to kiss his hoof, he did me the honour to raise it gently to my mouth. I am not ignorant how much I have been censured for mentioning this last particular. Detractors are pleased to think it improbable, that so illustrious a person should descend to give so great a mark of distinction to a creature so inferior as I. Neither have I forgot, how apt some travellers are to boast of extraordinary favours they have received. But, if these censurers were better acquainted with the noble and courteous disposition of the Houyhnhnms, they would soon change their opinion.

I paid my respects to the rest of the Houyhnhnms in his honour's company; then getting into my canoo, I pushed off from shoar.

CHAPTER XI

The author's dangerous voyage. He arrives at New-Holland, hoping to settle there. Is wounded with an arrow by one of the natives. Is seized and carried by force into a Portugueze ship. The great civilities of the captain. The author arrives at England.

I BEGAN this desperate voyage on February 15, 1714/5, at nine o'clock in the morning. The wind was very favourable; however, I made use at first only of my paddles; but considering I should soon be weary, and that the wind might probably chop about, I ventured to set up my little sail; and thus, with the help of the tide, I went at the rate of a league and a half an hour, as near as I could guess. My master and his friends continued on the shoar, until I was almost out of sight; and I often heard the sorrel nag (who always loved me) crying out, "Hnuy illa nyha maiah Yahoo" (Take care of thy self, gentle Yahoo).

My design was, if possible, to discover some small island uninhabited, yet sufficient by my labour to furnish me with necessaries of life, which I would have thought a greater happiness than to be first minister in the politest court of Europe; so horrible was the idea I conceived of returning to live in the society and under the government of Yahoos. For, in such a solitude as I desired, I could at least enjoy my own thoughts, and reflect with delight on the virtues of those inimitable Houyhnhnms, without any opportunity of degenerating into the vices and corruptions of my own species.

The reader may remember what I related when my crew conspired against me, and confined me to my cabbin. How I continued there several weeks, without knowing what course we took; and when I was put ashoar in the long-boat, how the sailors told me with oaths, whether true or false, that they knew not in what part of the world we were. However, I did then believe us to be about ten degrees southward of the Cape of Good Hope, or about 45 degrees southern latitude, as I gathered from some general words I overheard among them, being I supposed to the south-east in their intended voyage to Madagascar. And although this were but little better than conjecture, yet I resolved to steer my course eastward, hoping to reach the south-west coast of New-Holland, and perhaps some such island as I desired, lying westward of it. The wind was full west, and by six in the evening I computed I had gone eastward at least eighteen leagues, when I spied a very small island about half a league off, which I soon reached. It was nothing but a rock with one creek, naturally arched by the force of tempests. Here I put in my canoo, and climbing a part of the rock, I could plainly discover land to the east, extending from south to north. I lay all night in my canoo; and repeating my voyage early in the morning, I arrived in seven hours to the south-east point of New-Holland. This confirmed me in the opinion I have long entertained, that the *maps* and *charts* place this country at least three degrees more to the east than it really is; which thought I communicated many years ago to my worthy friend Mr. Herman Moll, and gave him my reasons for it, although he hath rather chosen to follow other authors.

I saw no inhabitants in the place where I landed; and being unarmed, I was afraid of venturing far into the country. I found some shell-fish on the shoar, and eat them raw, not daring to kindle a fire, for fear of being discovered by the natives. I continued three days feeding on oysters and limpits, to save my own provisions; and I fortunately found a brook of excellent water, which gave me great relief.

On the fourth day, venturing out early a little too far, I saw twenty or thirty natives upon a height, not above five hundred yards from me. They were stark naked, men, women, and children, round a fire, as I could discover by the smoke. One of them spied me, and gave notice to the rest; five of them advanced towards me, leaving the women and children at the fire. I made what haste I could to the shoar, and getting into my canoo, shoved off: the savages observing me retreat, ran after me; and before I could get far enough into the sea, discharged an arrow, which wounded me deeply on the inside of my left knee (I shall carry the mark to my grave.) I apprehended the arrow might be poisoned; and paddling out of the reach of their darts (being a calm day) I made a shift to suck the wound, and dress it as well as I could.

I was at a loss what to do, for I durst not return to the same landing-place, but stood to the north, and was forced to paddle; for the wind, although very gentle, was against me, blowing north-west. As I was looking about for a secure landing place, I saw a sail to the north north-east, which appearing every minute more visible, I was in some doubt, whether I should wait for them or no; but at last my detestation of the Yahoo race prevailed; and turning my canoo, I sailed and paddled together to the south, and got into the same creek from whence I set out in the morning; choosing rather to trust my self among these *barbarians*, than live with European Yahoos. I drew up my canoo as close as I could to the shoar, and hid my self behind a stone by the little brook, which, as I have already said, was excellent water.

The ship came within half a league of this creek, and sent out her long-boat with vessels to take in fresh water (for the place it seems was very well known) but I did not observe it until the boat was almost on shoar; and it was too late to seek another hiding-place. The seamen at their landing observed my canoo, and rummaging it all over, easily conjectured that the owner could not be far off. Four of them well armed, searched every cranny and lurking-hole, until at last they found me flat on my face behind the stone. They gazed a while in admiration at my strange uncouth dress; my coat made of skins, my wooden-soaled shoes, and my furred stockings; from whence, however, they concluded I was not a native of the place, who all go naked. One of the seamen in Portugueze bid me rise, and asked who I was. I understood that language very well, and getting upon my feet, said I was a poor Yahoo, banished from the Houyhnhnms, and desired they would please to let me depart. They admired to hear me answer them in their own tongue, and saw by my complexion I must be an European; but were at a loss to know what I meant by Yahoos and Houyhnhnms; and at the same time fell a laughing at my strange tone in speaking, which resembled the neighing of a horse. I trembled all the while betwixt fear and hatred: I again desired leave to depart, and was gently moving to my canoo; but they laid hold on me, desiring to know what country I was of? Whence I came? With many other questions. I told them I was born in England, from whence I came about five years ago, and then their country and ours was at peace. I therefore hoped they would not treat me as an enemy, since I meant them no harm, but was a poor Yahoo, seeking some desolate place where to pass the remainder of my unfortunate life.

When they began to talk, I thought I never heard or saw any thing so unnatural; for it appeared to me as monstrous as if a dog or a cow should speak in England, or a Yahoo in Houyhnhnm-land. The honest Portugueze were equally amazed at my strange dress, and the odd manner of delivering my words, which however they understood very well. They spoke to me with great humanity, and said they were sure their captain would carry me *gratis* to Lisbon, from whence I might return to my own country: that, two of the seamen would go back to the ship, to inform the captain of what they had seen, and receive his orders; in the mean time, unless I would give my solemn oath not to fly, they would secure me by force. I thought it best to comply with their proposal. They were very curious to know my story, but I gave them very little satisfaction; and they all conjectured, that my misfortunes had impaired my reason. In two hours the boat, which went loaden with vessels of water, returned with the captain's commands to fetch me on board. I fell on my knees to preserve my liberty; but all was in vain, and the men having tied me with cords, heaved me into the boat, from whence I was taken into the ship, and from thence into the captain's cabbin.

His name was Pedro de Mendez; he was a very courteous and generous person; he entreated me to give some account of my self, and desired to know what I would eat or drink; said, I should be used as well as himself, and spoke so many obliging things, that I wondered to find such civilities from a Yahoo. However, I remained silent and sullen; I was ready to faint at the very smell of him and his men. At last I desired something to eat out of my own canoo; but he ordered me a chicken and some excellent wine, and then directed that I should be put to bed in a very clean cabbin. I would not undress my self, but lay on the bed-cloaths; and in half an hour stole out, when I thought the crew was at dinner; and getting to the side of the ship, was going to leap into the sea, and swim for my life, rather than continue among Yahoos: but one of the seamen prevented me, and having informed the captain, I was chained to my cabbin.

After dinner Don Pedro came to me, and desired to know my reason for so desperate an attempt; assured me he only meant to do me all the service he was able; and spoke so very movingly, that at last I descended to treat him like an animal which had some little portion of reason. I gave him a very short relation of my voyage; of the conspiracy against me by my own men; of the country where they set me on shoar; and of my five years residence there. All which he looked upon as if it were a dream or a vision, whereat I took great offence: for I had quite forgot the faculty of lying, so peculiar to Yahoos in all countries where they preside, and consequently the disposition of suspecting truth in others of their own species. I asked him, whether it were the custom of his country to *say the thing that was not?* I assured him I had almost forgot what he meant by falshood; and if I had lived a thousand years in Houyhnhnmland, I should never have heard a lie from the meanest servant: that, I was altogether indifferent whether he believed me or no; but however, in return for his favours, I would give so much allowance to the corruption of his nature, as to answer any objection he would please to make; and then he might easily discover the truth.

The captain, a wise man, after many endeavours to catch me tripping in some part of my story, at last began to have a better opinion of my veracity, and the rather, because he confessed, he met with a Dutch skipper, who pretended to have landed with five others of his crew upon a certain island or continent south of New Holland, where they went for fresh water, and observed a horse driving before him several animals exactly resembling those I described under the name of Yahoos, with some other particulars, which the captain said he had forgot; because he then concluded them all to be lies. But he added, that since I professed so inviolable an attachment to truth, I must give him my word of honour to bear him company in this voyage without attempting any thing against my life; or else he would continue me a prisoner until we arrived at Lisbon. I gave him the promise he required; but at the same time protested, that I would suffer the greatest hardships rather than return to live among Yahoos.

Our voyage passed without any considerable accident. In gratitude to the captain I sometimes sat with him at his earnest request, and strove to conceal my antipathy against human kind, although it often broke out, which he suffered to pass without observation. But the greatest part of the day, I confined my self to my cabbin, to avoid seeing any of the crew. The captain had often intreated me to strip myself of my savage dress, and offered to lend me the best suit of cloaths he had. This I would not be prevailed on to accept, abhorring to cover myself with any thing that had been on the back of a Yahoo. I only desired he would lend me two clean shirts, which having been washed since he wore them, I believed would not so much defile me. These I changed every second day, and washed them my self.

We arrived at Lisbon, Nov. 5, 1715. At our landing, the captain forced me to cover my self with his cloak, to prevent the rabble from crouding about me. I was conveyed to his own house; and at my earnest request, he led me up to the highest room backwards. I conjured him to conceal from all persons what I had told him of the Houyhnhnms, because the least hint of such a story would not only draw numbers of people to see me, but probably put me in danger of being imprisoned, or burnt by the *Inquisition*. The captain persuaded me to accept a suit of cloaths newly made; but I would not suffer the taylor to take my measure; however, Don Pedro being almost of my size, they fitted me well enough. He accoutred me with other necessaries all new, which I aired for twenty four hours before I would use them.

The captain had no wife, nor above three servants, none of which were suffered to attend at meals; and his whole deportment was so obliging, added to very good *human* understanding, that I really began to tolerate his company. He gained so far upon me, that I ventured to look out of the back window. By degrees I was brought into another room, from whence I peeped into the street, but drew my head back in a fright. In a week's time he seduced me down to the door. I found my terror gradually lessened, but my hatred and contempt seemed to increase. I was at last bold enough to walk the street in his company, but kept my nose well stopped with rue, or sometimes with tobacco.

In ten days, Don Pedro, to whom I had given some account of my domestick affairs, put it upon me as a point of honour and conscience, that I ought to return to my native country, and live at home with my wife and children. He told me, there was an English ship in the port just ready to sail, and he would furnish me with all things necessary. It would be tedious to repeat his arguments, and my contradictions. He said, it was altogether impossible to find such a solitary island as I had desired to live in; but I might command in my own house, and pass my time in a manner as recluse as I pleased.

I complied at last, finding I could not do better. I left Lisbon the 24th day of November, in an English merchantman, but who was the master I never inquired. Don Pedro accompanied me to the ship, and lent me twenty pounds. He took kind leave of me, and embraced me at parting, which I bore as well as I could. During this last voyage I had no commerce with the master, or any of his men; but pretending I was sick kept close in my cabbin. On the fifth of December, 1715, we cast anchor in the Downs about nine in the morning, and at three in the afternoon I got safe to my house at Redriff.

My wife and family received me with great surprize and joy, because they concluded me certainly dead; but I must freely confess, the sight of them filled me only with hatred, disgust and contempt; and the more, by reflecting on the near alliance I had to them. For, although since my unfortunate exile from the Houyhnhnm country, I had compelled my self to tolerate the sight of Yahoos, and to converse with Don Pedro de Mendez; yet my memory and imaginations were perpetually filled with the virtues and ideas of those exalted Houyhnhnms. And when I began to consider, that by copulating with one of the Yahoo-species, I had become a parent of more, it struck me with the utmost shame, confusion, and horror.

As soon as I entered the house, my wife took me in her arms, and kissed me; at which, having not been used to the touch of that odious animal for so many years, I fell in a swoon for almost an hour. At the time I am writing, it is five years since my last return to England: during the first year I could not endure my wife or children in my presence, the very smell of them was intolerable; much less could I suffer them to eat in the same room. To this hour they dare not presume to touch my bread, or drink out of the same cup; neither was I ever able to let one of them take me by the hand. The first money I laid out was to buy two young stone-horses, which I keep in a good stable, and next to them the groom is my greatest favourite; for I feel my spirits revived by the smell he contracts in the stable. My horses understand me tolerably well; I converse with them at least four hours every day. They are strangers to bridle or saddle; they live in great amity with me, and friendship to each other.

CHAPTER XII

The author's veracity. His design in publishing this work. His censure of those travellers who swerve from the truth. The author clears himself from any sinister ends in writing. An objection answered. The method of planting colonies. His native country commended. The right of the Crown to those countries described by the author, is justified. The difficulty of conquering them. The author taketh his last leave of the reader; proposeth his manner of living for the future; gives good advice, and concludeth.

THUS, gentle reader, I have given thee a faithful history of my travels for sixteen years and above seven months; wherein I have not been so studious of ornament as of truth. I could perhaps, like others, have astonished thee with strange improbable tales; but, I rather chose to relate plain matter of fact in the simplest manner and style; because my principal design was to inform, and not to amuse thee.

It is easy for us who travel into remote countries, which are seldom visited by Englishmen or other Europeans, to form descriptions of wonderful animals both at sea and land. Whereas, a traveller's chief aim should be to make men wiser and better, and to improve their minds by the bad, as well as good example of what they deliver concerning foreign places.

I could heartily wish a law were enacted, that every traveller, before he were permitted to publish his voyages, should be obliged to make oath before the Lord High Chancellor, that all he intended to print was absolutely true to the best of his knowledge; for, then the world would no longer be deceived as it usually is, while some writers, to make their works pass the better upon the publick, impose the grossest falsities on the unwary reader. I have perused several books of travels with great delight in my younger days; but having since gone over most parts of the globe, and been able to contradict many fabulous accounts from my own observation, it hath given me a great disgust against this part of reading, and some indignation to see the credulity of mankind so impudently abused. Therefore, since my acquaintance were pleased to think my poor endeavours might not be unacceptable to my country, I imposed on my self as a maxim, never to be swerved from, that I would *strictly adhere to truth;* neither indeed, can I be ever under the least temptation to vary from it, while I retain in my mind the lectures and example of my noble master, and the other illustrious Houyhnhnms, of whom I had so long the honour to be an humble hearer.

Nec si miserum Fortuna Sinonem
Finxit, vanum etiam, mendacemque improba finget.

I know very well, how little reputation is to be got by writings which require neither genius nor learning, nor indeed any other talent, except a good memory, or an exact *journal*. I know likewise, that writers of travels, like dictionary-makers, are sunk into oblivion by the weight and bulk of those who come last, and therefore lie uppermost. And, it is highly probable, that such travellers who shall hereafter visit the countries described in this work of mine, may by detecting my errors, (if there be any) and adding many new discoveries of their own, jostle me out of vogue, and stand in my place; making the world forget that ever I was an author. This indeed would be too great a mortification if I wrote for fame: but, as my sole intention was the PUBLICK GOOD, I cannot be altogether disappointed. For, who can read the virtues I have mentioned in the glorious Houyhnhnms, without being ashamed of his own vices, when he considers himself as the reasoning, governing animal of his country? I shall say nothing of those remote nations where Yahoos preside, amongst which the least corrupted are the Brobdingnagians, whose wise maxims in morality and government, it would be our happiness to observe. But I forbear descanting further, and rather leave the judicious reader to his own remarks and applications.

I am not a little pleased that this work of mine can possibly meet with no censurers: for what objections can be made against a writer who relates only plain facts that happened in such distant countries, where we have not the least interest with respect either to trade or negociations? I have carefully avoided every fault with which common writers of travels are often too justly charged. Besides, I meddle not the least with any *party*, but write without passion, prejudice, or ill-will against any man or number of men whatsoever. I write for the noblest end, to inform and instruct mankind, over whom I may, without breach of modesty, pretend to some superiority, from the advantages I received by conversing so long among the most accomplished Houyhnhnms. I write without any view towards profit or praise. I never suffer a word to pass that may look like reflection, or possibly give the least offence even to those who are most ready to take it. So that, I hope, I may with justice pronounce my self an author perfectly blameless, against whom the tribes of answerers, considerers, observers, reflecters, detecters, remarkers, will never be able to find matter for exercising their talents.

I confess, it was whispered to me, that I was bound in duty as a subject of England, to have given in a memorial to a Secretary of State, at my first coming over; because, whatever lands are discovered by a subject, belong to the Crown. But I doubt whether our conquests in the countries I treat of, would be as easy as those of Ferdinando Cortez, over the naked Americans. The Lilliputians I think, are hardly worth the charge of a fleet and army to reduce them; and I question whether it might be prudent or safe to attempt the Brobdingnagians: or, whether an English army would be much at their ease with the flying island over their heads. The Houy-hnhnms, indeed, appear not to be so well prepared for war, a science to which they are perfect strangers, and especially against missive weapons. However, supposing my self to be a Minister of State, I could never give my advice for invading them. Their prudence, unanimity, unacquaintedness with fear, and their love of their country, would amply supply all defects in the military art. Imagine twenty thousand of them breaking into the midst of an European army, confounding the ranks, overturning the carriages, battering the warriors faces into mummy, by terrible yerks from their hinder hoofs: for they would well deserve the character given to Augustus; "Recalcitrat undique tutus." But instead of proposals for conquering that magnanimous nation, I rather wish they were in a capacity or disposition to send a sufficient number of their inhabitants for civilizing Europe; by teaching us the first principles of honour, justice, truth, temperance, pub-lick spirit, fortitude, chastity, friendship, benevolence, and fidelity. The *names* of all which virtues are still retained among us in most languages, and are to be met with in modern as well as ancient authors; which I am able to assert from my own small reading.

But, I had another reason which made me less forward to enlarge his Majesty's dominions by my discoveries: to say the truth, I had conceived a few scruples with relation to the distributive justice of princes upon those occasions. For instance, a crew of pyrates are driven by a storm they know not whither; at length a boy discovers land from the top-mast; they go on shoar to rob and plunder; they see an harmless people, are entertained with kindness, they give the country a new name, they take formal possession of it for the king, they set up a rotten plank or a stone for a memorial, they murder two or three dozen of the natives, bring away a couple more by force for a sample, return home, and get their pardon. Here commenceth a new dominion acquired with a title by *divine right*. Ships are sent with the first opportunity; the natives driven out or destroyed, their princes tortured to discover their gold; a free licence given to all acts of inhumanity and lust, the earth reeking with the blood of its inhabitants: and this execrable crew of butchers employed in so pious an expedition, is a *modern colony* sent to convert and civilize an idolatrous and barbarous people.

But this description, I confess, doth by no means affect the British nation, who may be an example to the whole world for their wisdom, care, and jus-tice in planting colonies; the liberal endowments for the advancement of religion and learning; their choice of devout and able pastors to propagate Christianity; their caution in stocking their provinces with people of sober lives and conversations from this the mother kingdom; their strict regard to the distribution of justice, in supplying the civil administration through all their colonies with officers of the greatest abilities, utter strangers to corruption: and to crown all, by sending the most vigilant and virtuous governors, who have no other views than the happiness of the people over whom they preside, and the honour of the king their master.

But, as those countries which I have described do not appear to have a desire of being conquered, and enslaved, murdered or driven out by colonies; nor abound either in gold, silver, sugar or tobacco; I did humbly conceive they were by no means proper objects of our zeal, our valour, or our interest. However, if those whom it may concern, think fit to be of another opinion, I am ready to depose, when I shall be lawfully called, that no European did ever visit these countries before me. I mean, if the inhabitants ought to be believed; unless a dispute may arise about the two Yahoos, said to have been seen many ages ago on a mountain in Houyhnhnmland, from whence the opinion is, that the race of those brutes hath descended; and these, for any thing I know, may have been English, which indeed I was apt to suspect from the lineaments of their posterity's countenances, although very much defaced. But, how far that will go to make out a title, I leave to the learned in colony-law.

But, as to the formality of taking possession in my sovereign's name, it never came once into my thoughts; and if it had, yet as my affairs then stood, I should perhaps in point of prudence and self-preservation, have put it off to a better opportunity.

Having thus answered the *only* objection that can be raised against me as a traveller, I here take a final leave of my courteous readers, and return to enjoy my own speculations in my little garden at Redriff; to apply those excellent lessons of virtue which I learned among the Houyhnhnms; to instruct the Yahoos of my own family as far as I shall find them docible animals; to behold my figure often in a glass, and thus, if possible, habituate my self, by time, to tolerate the sight of a human creature; to lament the brutality of Houyhnhnms in my own country, but always treat their persons with respect, for the sake of my noble master, his family, his friends, and the whole Houyhnhnm race, whom these of ours have the honour to resemble in all their lineaments, however their intellectuals came to degenerate.

I began last week to permit my wife to sit at dinner with me, at the farthest end of a long table; and to answer (but with the utmost brevity) the few questions I asked her. Yet the smell of a Yahoo continuing very offensive, I always keep my nose well stopped with rue, lavender, or tobacco-leaves. And although it be hard for a man late in life to remove old habits, I am not altogether out of hopes in some time to suffer a neighbour Yahoo in my company, without the apprehensions I am yet under of his teeth or his claws.

My reconcilement to the Yahoo-kind in general might not be so difficult, if they would be content with those vices and follies only which nature hath entitled them to. I am not in the least provoked at the sight of a lawyer, a pickpocket, a colonel, a fool, a lord, a gamester, a politician, a whoremonger, a physician, an evidence, a suborner, an attorney, a traytor, or the like: this is all according to the due course of things: but, when I behold a lump of deformity, and diseases both in body and mind, smitten with *pride*, it immediately breaks all the measures of my patience; neither shall I be ever able to comprehend how such an animal and such a vice could tally together. The wise and virtuous Houyhnhnms, who abound in all excellencies that can adorn a rational creature, have no name for this vice in their language, which hath no terms to express any thing that is evil, except those whereby they describe the detestable qualities of their Yahoos; among which they were not able to distinguish this of pride, for want of thoroughly understanding human nature, as it sheweth it self in other countries, where that animal presides. But I, who had more experience, could plainly observe some rudiments of it among the wild Yahoos.

But the Houyhnhnms, who live under the government of reason, are no more proud of the good qualities they possess, than I should be for not wanting a leg or an arm, which no man in his wits would boast of, although he must be miserable without them. I dwell the longer upon this subject from the desire I have to make the society of an English Yahoo by any means not insupportable; and therefore, I here intreat those who have any tincture of this absurd vice, that they will not presume to appear in my sight.

FINIS

TRISTRAM SHANDY

BIOGRAPHICAL NOTE

LAURENCE STERNE, 1713–1768

THE Treaty of Utrecht having been concluded, Roger Sterne with his British regiment landed in Clonmel, Ireland, where his wife joined him. A few days later, on November 24, 1713, their son, Laurence, was born. "My birthday," Laurence Sterne records in the short autobiographical sketch written for his daughter, "was ominous to my poor father, who was the day after our arrival, with many other brave officers, broke and sent adrift into the wide world with a wife and two children."

Until Roger Sterne's death in 1731, the Sterne family "decamped bag and baggage" every time new orders were issued to his regiment. Children were born and died, one on an expedition from Bristol to Hampshire, another in the barracks at Dublin, two others at Carrickfergus. "My father's children were not made to last long," Sterne comments. At the siege of Gibraltar, Roger Sterne was run through the body in a duel "about a goose." Although he survived, it impaired his constitution; he contracted the "country fever, which made a child of him" and one day "he sat down in an armchair and breathed his last."

Sterne's memoir is permeated with a tender regard for the "little smart man" who was his father; for his patience in the face of fatigue and disappointments "of which it pleased God to give him full measure;" and for the innocence of his intentions, which caused him to suspect no one, "so that you might have cheated him ten times in a day, if nine had not been sufficient for your purpose." Sterne appears to have had little affection for his mother and implies that his father married her because he was in debt to her stepfather. She seems to have been perpetually in need of money after her husband's death, and Sterne found irksome the continual demands she made upon him.

"By God's care of me, my cousin Sterne became a father to me and sent me to the University." This was in 1732. At Jesus College, Cambridge, where his great-grandfather, the Cavalier Archbishop of York, had once been

Master, Sterne took both A.B. and A.M. degrees, as well as holy orders. Through the good offices of his uncle, a clergyman with strong Whig tendencies, he obtained the parish of Sutton-in-the-Forest immediately after his ordination and other preferments later. Eventually, uncle and nephew quarreled; Sterne refused to "write paragraphs in the newspapers" furthering the Whig cause, which he considered "dirty work."

In 1741 he married Elizabeth Lumley, wooing her in a series of elaborate love letters, overflowing with "sensibility." After their marriage, Sterne resided at Sutton and for the next twenty years was occupied with the fairly light duties of an eighteenth century English cleric. He made frequent jaunts to Skelton Castle to visit the Rabelaisian friend of his Cambridge days, John Hall-Stevenson, the "Eugenius" of *Tristram Shandy* and the author of *Crazy Tales* and other perverse fables and verse. Sterne ranged with enjoyment in Hall-Stevenson's extraordinary library of obscure learning and his name came to be associated with the "Demoniacs" of Skelton Castle, a society founded by its "ingenious" master.

Sterne was forty-six before his metamorphosis into a writer, and by the time he was fifty-five he was dead. Before 1759 his literary efforts had been sparse: a few political pamphlets for his uncle, two sermons, and other random pieces. In writing a political allegory on a local ecclesiastical intrigue, Sterne seems to have discovered his talent as a humorist.

In 1759, Sterne began work on *Tristram Shandy*. He described it as a "picture of himself" and wrote at it with feverish exuberance so that the first two volumes were ready for publication by January 1760. They enjoyed an immediate and sensational reception, and in March 1760 Sterne went to London. Reporting the progress of his triumph, he wrote: "My rooms are filling every hour with great people of first rank who strive who shall most honor me." His literary renown resulted in his being presented with the curacy of Coxwold, which Sterne described as "a sweet retirement" and named Shandy Hall.

In the next two years he produced four more volumes of *Tristram*, completing them rapidly in a few months and going up to London to be entertained and fêted. But the strain caused a flare-up of a chronic lung condition, and it was decided he should avoid the rigours of the English winter by a sojourn in the South of France.

Tired and ill upon his arrival, he was warned by the French doctors that he had not long to live, but soon after he was up and about with "a fortnight of dinners and suppers on my hands. . . . I Shandy it more than ever," he wrote to a friend, "and verily believe that by mere Shandyism . . . I fence as much against infirmities, as I do by the benefits of air and climate." In the summer of 1762 his wife and daughter joined him and, somewhat against his will, he spent the next two years in Toulouse and elsewhere in the South, returning alone to England in 1764. By January of the following year the seventh and eighth volumes of *Tristram* were finished.

In 1761 a volume of Sterne's sermons had appeared as *The Sermons of Mr. Yorick*, rather ordinary in themselves but remarkable in their contrast to the author's other writings. In 1766 a second and more unorthodox series of Mr. Yorick's sermons appeared, which sought to "avoid all commonplace cant" and to add a fillip of Shandyism to the interpretation of the parables.

It was in the winter of 1767 when he brought the ninth volume of *Tristram* to London that he met Mrs. Draper, a young and attractive Anglo-Indian matron with a pathetic history. So violent and widely publicized was the "sentimental" relationship that developed that Mrs. Sterne heard of it in France, and Mr. Draper ordered his wife back to India immediately. From the 13th of April until the 4th of August, Sterne kept his *Journal to Eliza* in which he recorded his sufferings separated from his "Bramine."

Out of a second trip to the continent in 1765 was spun the *Sentimental Journey through France and Italy*. It was finished by February of 1768, but Yorick had "worn out both his spirits and his body with the *Sentimental Journey*," as he wrote a friend. "'Tis true that an author must feel himself, or his reader will not—but I have torn my whole frame into pieces by my feelings." In what proved to be his last letter to his daughter, he speaks of "this vile influenza" which soon turned to pleurisy. He was bled and blistered, to no avail. On March 18th, in the course of a dinner party at which a number of Sterne's friends were present, a footman was dispatched to inquire after his health. It is in the words of this man that the writer's last moments are recorded: "I went into the room, and he was just a-dying. I waited ten minutes; but in five he said, '*Now it is come.*' He put up his hand, as if to stop a blow, and died in a minute."

CONTENTS

To the Right Honourable

Mr PITT

Sir,

Never poor Wight of a Dedicator had less hopes from his Dedication, than I have from this of mine; for it is written in a bye corner of the kingdom, and in a retired thatched house, where I live in a constant endeavour to fence against the infirmities of ill health, and other evils of life, by mirth; being firmly persuaded that every time a man smiles,—but much more so, when he laughs, it adds something to this Fragment of Life.

I humbly beg, Sir, that you will honour this book, by taking it—(not under your Protection,—it must protect itself, but)—into the country with you; where, if I am ever told, it has made you smile; or can conceive it has beguiled you of one moment's pain—I shall think myself as happy as a minister of state;—perhaps much happier than any one (one only excepted) that I have read or heard of.

I am, great sir,
(*and what is more to your Honour*)
I am, good sir,
Your Well-wisher, and
most humble Fellow-subject,

The Author

The
LIFE and OPINIONS
of
TRISTRAM SHANDY, Gent.

BOOK I

CHAPTER I

I WISH either my father or my mother, or indeed both of them, as they
were in duty both equally bound to it, had minded what they were
about when they begot me; had they duly considered how much depended upon what they were then doing;—that not only the production of
a rational Being was concerned in it, but that possibly the happy formation
and temperature of his body, perhaps his genius and the very cast of his
mind;—and, for aught they knew to the contrary, even the fortunes of his
whole house might take their turn from the humours and dispositions which
were then uppermost;—Had they duly weighed and considered all this, and
proceeded accordingly,—I am verily persuaded I should have made a quite
different figure in the world, from that in which the reader is likely to see
me.—Believe me, good folks, this is not so inconsiderable a thing as many
of you may think it;—you have all, I dare say, heard of the animal spirits,
as how they are transfused from father to son etc. etc.—and a great deal to
that purpose:—Well, you may take my word, that nine parts in ten of a
man's sense or his nonsense, his successes and miscarriages in this world depend upon their motions and activity, and the different tracts and trains
you put them into, so that when they are once set a-going, whether right or
wrong, 'tis not a halfpenny matter,—away they go cluttering like hey-go
mad; and by treading the same steps over and over again, they presently
make a road of it, as plain and as smooth as a garden-walk, which, when they
are once used to, the Devil himself sometimes shall not be able to drive them
off it.

"Pray, my Dear," quoth my mother, "have you not forgot to wind up the clock?"——"Good G—!" cried my father, making an exclamation, but taking care to moderate his voice at the same time,—"Did ever woman, since the creation of the world, interrupt a man with such a silly question?" Pray, what was your father saying?—Nothing.

CHAPTER 2

——THEN, positively, there is nothing in the question that I can see, either good or bad.—Then, let me tell you, Sir, it was a very unseasonable question at least,—because it scattered and dispersed the animal spirits, whose business it was to have escorted and gone hand in hand with the HOMUN-CULUS, and conducted him safe to the place destined for his reception.

The Homunculus, Sir, in however low and ludicrous a light he may appear, in this age of levity, to the eye of folly or prejudice;—to the eye of reason in scientific research, he stands confessed—a Being guarded and circumscribed with rights.—The minutest philosophers, who, by the bye, have the most enlarged understandings, (their souls being inversely as their enquiries) shew us incontestably, that the Homunculus is created by the same hand,—engendered in the same course of nature,—endowed with the same locomotive powers and faculties with us:—That he consists as we do, of skin, hair, fat, flesh, veins, arteries, ligaments, nerves, cartilages, bones, marrow, brains, glands, genitals, humours, and articulations;—is a Being of as much activity,—and, in all senses of the word, as much and as truly our fellow-creature as my Lord Chancellor of England.——He may be benefited,—he may be injured,—he may obtain redress;—in a word, he has all the claims and rights of humanity, which Tully, Puffendorf, or the best ethic writers allow to arise out of that state and relation.

Now, dear Sir, what if any accident had befallen him in his way alone!— or that, through terror of it, natural to so young a traveller, my little Gentleman had got to his journey's end miserably spent;—his muscular strength and virility worn down to a thread;—his own animal spirits ruffled beyond description,—and that in this sad disordered state of nerves, he had lain down a prey to sudden starts, or a series of melancholy dreams and fancies, for nine long, long months together.——I tremble to think what a foundation had been laid for a thousand weaknesses both of body and mind, which no skill of the physician or the philosopher could ever afterwards have set thoroughly to rights.

CHAPTER 3

To my uncle Mr. Toby Shandy do I stand indebted for the preceding anecdote, to whom my father, who was an excellent natural philosopher, and much given to close reasoning upon the smallest matters, had oft, and heavily complained of the injury; but once more particularly, as my uncle Toby well remembered, upon his observing a most unaccountable obliquity, (as he called it) in my manner of setting up my top, and justifying the principles upon which I had done it,—the old gentleman shook his head, and in a tone more expressive by half of sorrow than reproach,—he said his heart all along foreboded, and he saw it verified in this, and from a thousand other observations he had made upon me, That I should neither think nor act like any other man's child:—"But alas!" continued he, shaking his head a second time, and wiping away a tear which was trickling down his cheeks, "My Tristram's misfortunes began nine months before ever he came into the world."

——My mother, who was sitting by, looked up,—but she knew no more than her backside what my father meant,—but my uncle, Mr. Toby Shandy, who had been often informed of the affair,—understood him very well.

Chapter 4

I know there are readers in the world, as well as many other good people in it, who are no readers at all,—who find themselves ill at ease, unless they are let into the whole secret from first to last, of everything which concerns you.

It is in pure compliance with this humour of theirs, and from a backwardness in my nature to disappoint any one soul living, that I have been so very particular already. As my life and opinions are likely to make some noise in the world, and, if I conjecture right, will take in all ranks, professions, and denominations of men whatever,—be no less read than the *Pilgrim's Progress* itself—and in the end, prove the very thing which Montaigne dreaded his Essays should turn out, that is, a book for a parlour-window;—I find it necessary to consult every one a little in his turn; and therefore must beg pardon for going on a little further in the same way: For which cause, right glad I am, that I have begun the history of myself in the way I have done; and that I am able to go on, tracing every thing in it, as Horace says, *ab Ovo*.

Horace, I know does not recommend this fashion altogether: But that gentleman is speaking only of an epic poem or a tragedy;—(I forget which,) —besides, if it was not so, I should beg Mr. Horace's pardon;—for in writing what I have set about, I shall confine myself neither to his rules, nor to any man's rules that ever lived.

To such, however, as do not choose to go so far back into these things, I can give no better advice, than that they skip over the remaining part of this chapter; for I declare before-hand, 'tis wrote only for the curious and inquisitive.

————————————————— Shut the door —————————————————

I was begot in the night, betwixt the first Sunday and the first Monday in the month of March, in the year of our Lord one thousand seven hundred and eighteen. I am positive I was,—But how I came to be so very particular in my account of a thing which happened before I was born, is owing to another small anecdote known only in our own family, but now made public for the better clearing up this point.

My father, you must know, who was originally a Turkey merchant, but had left off business for some years, in order to retire to, and die upon, his paternal estate in the county of ——, was, I believe, one of the most regular men in everything he did, whether 'twas matter of business, or matter of amusement, that ever lived. As a small specimen of this extreme ex-

actness of his, to which he was in truth a slave,—he had made it a rule for
many years of his life,—on the first Sunday-night of every month throughout the whole year,—as certain as ever the Sunday-night came,—to wind
up a large house-clock, which we had standing on the backstairs head, with
his own hands:—And being somewhere between fifty and sixty years of age
at the time I have been speaking of,—he had likewise gradually brought some
other little family concernments to the same period, in order, as he would
often say to my uncle Toby, to get them all out of the way at one time,
and be no more plagued and pestered with them the rest of the month.

It was attended with but one misfortune, which, in a great measure, fell
upon myself, and the effects of which I fear I shall carry with me to my
grave; namely, that from an unhappy association of ideas, which have no
connection in nature, it so fell out at length, that my poor mother could
never hear the said clock wound up,—but the thoughts of some other things
unavoidably popped into her head—and *vice versa:*—Which strange combination of ideas, the sagacious Locke, who certainly understood the nature
of these things better than most men, affirms to have produced more wry
actions than all other sources of prejudice whatsoever.

But this by the bye.

Now it appears by a memorandum in my father's pocket-book, which
now lies upon the table, "That on Lady-day, which was on the 25th of
the same month in which I date my geniture,—my father set out upon
his journey to London, with my eldest brother Bobby, to fix him at
Westminster school"; and, as it appears from the same authority, "That
he did not get down to his wife and family till the second week in May
following,"—it brings the thing almost to a certainty. However, what follows in the beginning of the next chapter, puts it beyond all possibility
of doubt.

——But pray, Sir, What was your father doing all December,—January,
and February?——Why, Madam,—he was all that time afflicted with a
Sciatica.

CHAPTER 5

On the fifth day of November, 1718, which to the era fixed on, was as near
nine calendar months as any husband could in reason have expected,—was
I Tristram Shandy, Gentleman, brought forth into this scurvy and disastrous world of ours.——I wish I had been born in the Moon, or in any of the
planets, (except Jupiter or Saturn, because I never could bear cold weather)
for it could not well have fared worse with me in any of them (though I will
not answer for Venus) than it has in this vile, dirty planet of ours,—which,
o' my conscience, with reverence be it spoken, I take to be made up of the
shreds and clippings of the rest;—not but the planet is well enough, provided a man could be born in it to a great title or to a great estate; or could
any how contrive to be called up to public charges, and employments of
dignity or power;—but that is not my case;—and therefore every man will
speak of the fair as his own market has gone in it;—for which cause I affirm
it over again to be one of the vilest worlds that ever was made;—for I can
truly say, that from the first hour I drew my breath in it, to this, that I can

now scarce draw it at all, for an asthma I got in skating against the wind in Flanders;—I have been the continual sport of what the world calls Fortune; and though I will not wrong her by saying, She has ever made me feel the weight of any great or signal evil;—yet with all the good temper in the world, I affirm it of her, that in every stage of my life, and at every turn and corner where she could get fairly at me, the ungracious duchess has pelted me with a set of as pitiful misadventures and cross accidents as ever small Hero sustained.

Chapter 6

In the beginning of the last chapter, I informed you exactly when I was born; but I did not inform you how. No, that particular was reserved entirely for a chapter by itself;—besides, Sir, as you and I are in a manner perfect strangers to each other, it would not have been proper to have let you into too many circumstances relating to myself all at once.——You must have a little patience. I have undertaken, you see, to write not only my life, but my opinions also; hoping and expecting that your knowledge of my character, and of what kind of a mortal I am, by the one, would give you a better relish for the other: As you proceed farther with me, the slight acquaintance, which is now beginning betwixt us, will grow into familiarity; and that, unless one of us is in fault, will terminate in friendship.——*O diem praeclarum!*—then nothing which has touched me will be thought trifling in its nature, or tedious in its telling. Therefore, my dear friend and companion, if you should think me somewhat sparing of my narrative on my first setting out—bear with me,—and let me go on, and tell my story my own way:—Or, if I should seem now and then to trifle upon the road,—or should sometimes put on a fool's cap with a bell to it, for a moment or two as we pass along,—don't fly off,—but rather courteously give me credit for a little more wisdom than appears upon my outside;—and as we jog on, either laugh with me, or at me, or in short do any thing,—only keep your temper.

Chapter 7

In the same village where my father and my mother dwelt, dwelt also a thin, upright, motherly, notable, good old body of a midwife, who with the help of a little plain good sense, and some years' full employment in her business, in which she had all along trusted little to her own efforts, and a great deal to those of dame Nature,—had acquired, in her way, no small degree of reputation in the world:—by which word *world*, need I in this place inform your worship, that I would be understood to mean no more of it, than a small circle described upon the circle of the great world, of four English miles diameter, or thereabouts, of which the cottage where the good old woman lived, is supposed to be the centre?—She had been left, it seems, a widow in great distress, with three or four small children, in her forty-seventh year; and as she was at that time a person of decent carriage,—grave deportment,—a woman moreover of few words, and withal an object of compassion, whose distress, and silence under it, called out the louder for a friendly lift: the wife of the parson of the parish was touched with pity;

and having often lamented an inconvenience, to which her husband's flock had for many years been exposed, inasmuch as there was no such thing as a midwife, of any kind or degree, to be got at, let the case have been never so urgent, within less than six or seven long miles riding; which said seven long miles in dark nights and dismal roads, the country thereabouts being nothing but a deep clay, was almost equal to fourteen; and that in effect was sometimes next to having no midwife at all; it came into her head, that it would be doing as seasonable a kindness to the whole parish, as to the poor creature herself, to get her a little instructed in some of the plain principles of the business, in order to set her up in it. As no woman thereabouts was better qualified to execute the plan she had formed than herself, the gentlewoman very charitably undertook it; and having great influence over the female part of the parish, she found no difficulty in effecting it to the utmost of her wishes. In truth, the parson joined his interest with his wife's in the whole affair; and in order to do things as they should be, and give the poor soul as good a title by law to practice, as his wife had given by institution,—he cheerfully paid the fees for the ordinary's licence himself, amounting in the whole, to the sum of eighteen shillings and fourpence; so that betwixt them both, the good woman was fully invested in the real and corporal possession of her office, together with all its rights, members, and appurtenances whatsoever.

These last words, you must know, were not according to the old form in which such licences, faculties, and powers usually ran, which in like cases had heretofore been granted to the sisterhood. But it was according to a neat Formula of Didius his own devising, who having a particular turn for taking to pieces, and new framing over again, all kinds of instruments in that way, not only hit upon this dainty amendment, but coaxed many of the old licensed matrons in the neighbourhood, to open their faculties afresh, in order to have this wham-wham of his inserted.

I own I never could envy Didius in these kinds of fancies of his:—But every man to his own taste.——Did not Dr. Kunastrokius, that great man, at his leisure hours, take the greatest delight imaginable in combing of asses' tails, and plucking the dead hairs out with his teeth, though he had tweezers always in his pocket? Nay, if you come to that, Sir, have not the wisest of men in all ages, not excepting Solomon himself,—have they not had their Hobby-Horses;—their running horses,—their coins and their cockle-shells, their drums and their trumpets, their fiddles, their pallets,—their maggots and their butterflies?—and so long as a man rides his Hobby-Horse peaceably and quietly along the King's highway, and neither compels you or me to get up behind him,—pray, Sir, what have either you or I to do with it?

CHAPTER 8

——*De gustibus non est disputandum;*—that is, there is no disputing against Hobby-Horses; and for my part, I seldom do; nor could I with any sort of grace, had I been an enemy to them at the bottom; for happening, at certain intervals and changes of the moon, to be both fiddler and painter, according as the fly stings:—Be it known to you, that I keep a couple of pads myself, upon which, in their turns (nor do I care who knows it) I frequently ride out and take the air;—though sometimes, to my shame be it spoken, I take somewhat longer journeys than what a wise man would think altogether right.——But the truth is,—I am not a wise man;—and besides am a mortal of so little consequence in the world, it is not much matter what I do: so I seldom fret or fume at all about it: Nor does it much disturb my rest, when I see such great Lords and tall Personages as hereafter follow;—such, for instance, as my Lord A, B, C, D, E, F, G, H, I, K, L, M, N, O, P, Q, and so on, all of a row, mounted upon their several horses, some with large stirrups, getting on in a more grave and sober pace;—others on the contrary, tucked up to their very chins, with whips across their mouths, scouring and scampering it away like so many little party-coloured devils astride a mortgage,—and as if some of them were resolved to break their necks.—— So much the better—say I to myself;—for in case the worst should happen, the world will make a shift to do excellently well without them: and for the rest,—why—God speed them—e'en let them ride on without opposition from me; for were their lordships unhorsed this very night—'tis ten to one but that many of them would be worse mounted by one half before tomorrow morning.

Not one of these instances therefore can be said to break in upon my rest. —But there is an instance, which I own puts me off my guard, and that is, when I see one born for great actions, and what is still more for his honour, whose nature ever inclines him to good ones;—when I behold such a one, my Lord, like yourself, whose principles and conduct are as generous and noble as his blood, and whom, for that reason, a corrupt world cannot spare one moment;—when I see such a one, my Lord, mounted, though it is but for a minute beyond the time which my love to my country has prescribed to him, and my zeal for his glory wishes,—then, my Lord, I cease to be a philosopher, and in the first transport of an honest impatience, I wish the Hobby-Horse, with all his fraternity, at the Devil.

"My Lord,

"I maintain this to be a dedication, notwithstanding its singularity in the three great essentials of matter, form, and place: I beg, therefore, you will accept it as such, and that you will permit me to lay it, with the most respectful humility, at your Lordship's feet,—when you are upon them— which you can be when you please;—and that is, my Lord, whenever there is occasion for it, and I will add, to the best purposes too. I have the honour to be,

"*My Lord,*
Your Lordship's most obedient,
and most devoted,
and most humble servant,
Tristram Shandy."

CHAPTER 9

I SOLEMNLY declare to all mankind, that the above dedication was made for no one Prince, Prelate, Pope, or Potentate,—Duke, Marquis, Earl, Viscount, or Baron, of this, or any other Realm in Christendom;—nor has it yet been hawked about, or offered publicly or privately, directly or indirectly, to any one person or personage, great or small; but is honestly a true Virgin-Dedication untried on, upon any soul living.

I labour this point so particularly, merely to remove any offence or objection which might arise against it from the manner in which I propose to make the most of it;—which is the putting it up fairly to public sale; which I now do.

——Every author has a way of his own in bringing his points to bear;—for my own part, as I hate chaffering and higgling for a few guineas in a dark entry;—I resolved within myself, from the very beginning, to deal squarely and openly with your Great Folks in this affair, and try whether I should not come off the better by it.

If therefore there is any one Duke, Marquis, Earl, Viscount, or Baron, in these his Majesty's dominions, who stands in need of a tight, genteel dedication, and whom the above will suit (for by the bye, unless it suits in some degree I will not part with it)—it is much at his service for fifty guineas;—which I am positive is twenty guineas less than it ought to be afforded for, by any man of genius.

My Lord, if you examine it over again, it is far from being a gross piece of daubing, as some dedications are. The design, your Lordship sees, is good,—the colouring transparent,—the drawing not amiss;—or to speak more like a man of science,—and measure my piece in the painter's scale, divided into 20,—I believe, my Lord, the outlines will turn out as 12,—the composition as 9,—the colouring as 6,—the expression 13 and a half,—and the design,—if I may be allowed, my Lord, to understand my own design, and supposing absolute perfection in designing, to be as 20,—I think it cannot well fall short of 19. Besides all this,—there is keeping in it, and the dark strokes in the Hobby-Horse, (which is a secondary figure, and a kind of back-ground to the whole) give great force to the principal lights in your own figure, and make it come off wonderfully;—and besides, there is an air of originality in the *tout ensemble*.

Be pleased, my good Lord, to order the sum to be paid into the hands of Mr. Dodsley, for the benefit of the author, and in the next edition care shall be taken that this chapter be expunged, and your Lordship's titles, distinctions, arms, and good actions, be placed at the front of the preceding chapter: All which, from the words, *De gustibus non est disputandum*, and whatever else in this book relates to Hobby-Horses, but no more, shall stand dedicated to your Lordship.—The rest I dedicate to the Moon, who, by the bye, of all the Patrons or Matrons I can think of, has most power to set my book agoing, and make the world run mad after it.

Bright Goddess,
If thou art not too busy with Candid and Miss Cunegund's affairs,—take Tristram Shandy's under thy protection also.

Chapter 10

WHATEVER degree of small merit the act of benignity in favour of the midwife might justly claim, or in whom that claim truly rested,—at first sight
seems not very material to this history;—certain however it was that the
gentlewoman, the parson's wife, did run away at that time with the whole
of it: And yet, for my life, I cannot help thinking but that the parson himself, though he had not the good fortune to hit upon the design first,—yet,
as he heartily concurred in it the moment it was laid before him, and as
heartily parted with his money to carry it into execution, had a claim to
some share of it,—if not to a full half of whatever honour was due to it.

The world at that time was pleased to determine the matter otherwise.

Lay down the book, and I will allow you half a day to give a probable
guess at the grounds of this procedure.

Be it known then, that, for about five years before the date of the midwife's licence, of which you have had so circumstantial an account,—the
parson we have to do with had made himself a country-talk by a breach of
all decorum, which he had committed against himself, his station, and his
office;—and that was in never appearing better, or otherwise mounted, than
upon a lean, sorry, jack-ass of a horse, value about one pound fifteen shillings; who, to shorten all description of him, was full brother to Rosinante,
as far as similitude congenial could make him; for he answered his description to a hairbreadth in every thing,—except that I do not remember 'tis
any where said, that Rosinante was broken-winded; and that, moreover,
Rosinante, as is the happiness of most Spanish horses, fat or lean,—was
undoubtedly a horse at all points.

I know very well that the Hero's horse was a horse of chaste deportment,
which may have given grounds for the contrary opinion; But it is as certain
at the same time, that Rosinante's continency (as may be demonstrated
from the adventure of the Yanguesian carriers) proceeded from no bodily
defect or cause whatsoever, but from the temperance and orderly current of
his blood.——And let me tell you, Madam, there is a great deal of very good
chastity in the world, in behalf of which you could not say more for your life.

Let that be as it may, as my purpose is to do exact justice to every creature brought upon the stage of this dramatic work,—I could not stifle this
distinction in favour of Don Quixote's horse;—in all other points, the parson's horse, I say, was just such another,—for he was as lean, and as lank,
and as sorry a jade, as Humility herself could have bestrided.

In the estimation of here and there a man of weak judgment, it was greatly in the parson's power to have helped the figure of this horse of his,—for
he was master of a very handsome demi-peaked saddle, quilted on the seat
with green plush, garnished with a double row of silver-headed studs, and a
noble pair of shining brass stirrups, with a housing altogether suitable, of
grey superfine cloth, with an edging of black lace, terminating in a deep,
black, silk fringe, *poudré d'or,*—all which he had purchased in the pride and
prime of his life, together with a grand embossed bridle, ornamented at all
points as it should be.——But not caring to banter his beast, he had hung

all these up behind his study door:—and, in lieu of them, had seriously be-
fitted him with just such a bridle and such a saddle, as the figure and value
of such a steed might well and truly deserve.

In the several sallies about his parish, and in the neighbouring visits to
the gentry who lived around him,—you will easily comprehend, that the
parson, so appointed, would both hear and see enough to keep his philosophy
from rusting. To speak the truth, he never could enter a village, but he
caught the attention of both old and young.——Labour stood still as he
passed—the bucket hung suspended in the middle of the well,—the spin-
ning-wheel forgot its round,—even chuck-farthing and shuffle-cap themselves stood gaping till he had got out of sight; and as his movement was
not of the quickest, he had generally time enough upon his hands to make
his observations,—to hear the groans of the serious,—and the laughter of
the light-hearted;—all which he bore with excellent tranquillity.——His
character was,—he loved a jest in his heart—and as he saw himself in the
true point of ridicule, he would say he could not be angry with others for
seeing him in a light, in which he so strongly saw himself: So that to his
friends, who knew his foible was not the love of money, and who therefore
made the less scruple in bantering the extravagance of his humour,—instead of giving the true cause,—he chose rather to join in the laugh against
himself; and as he never carried one single ounce of flesh upon his own
bones, being altogether as spare a figure as his beast,—he would sometimes
insist upon it, that the horse was as good as the rider deserved;—that they
were, centaur-like,—both of a piece. At other times, and in other moods,
when his spirits were above the temptation of false wit,—he would say, he
found himself going off fast in a consumption; and, with great gravity,
would pretend, he could not bear the sight of a fat horse, without a dejec-
tion of heart, and a sensible alteration in his pulse; and that he had made
choice of the lean one he rode upon, not only to keep himself in countenance, but in spirits.

At different times he would give fifty humorous and apposite reasons for
riding a meek-spirited jade of a broken-winded horse, preferably to one of
mettle;—for on such a one he could sit mechanically, and meditate as delightfully *de vanitate mundi et fugâ sæculi*, as with the advantage of a
death's-head before him;—that, in all other exercitations, he could spend
his time, as he rode slowly along,—to as much account as in his study; that
he could draw up an argument in his sermon,—or a hole in his breeches, as
steadily on the one as in the other;—that brisk trotting and slow argumentation, like wit and judgment, were two incompatible movements.——But
that upon his steed—he could unite and reconcile every thing,—he could
compose his sermon,—he could compose his cough,—and, in case nature
gave a call that way, he could likewise compose himself to sleep.——In
short, the parson upon such encounters would assign any cause but the true
cause,—and he withheld the true one, only out of a nicety of temper,
because he thought it did honour to him.

But the truth of the story was as follows: In the first years of this gentleman's life, and about the time when the superb saddle and bridle were
purchased by him, it had been his manner, or vanity, or call it what you

will,—to run into the opposite extreme.—In the language of the county
where he dwelt, he was said to have loved a good horse, and generally had
one of the best in the whole parish standing in his stable always ready for
saddling; and as the nearest midwife, as I told you, did not live nearer to
the village than seven miles, and in a vile country,—it so fell out that the
poor gentleman was scarce a whole week together without some piteous application for his beast; and as he was not an unkindhearted man, and every
case was more pressing and more distressful than the last,—as much as he
loved his beast, he had never a heart to refuse him; the upshot of which was
generally this, that his horse was either clapped, or spavined, or greazed;—
or he was twitter-boned, or broken-winded, or something, in short, or other
had befallen him, which would let him carry no flesh;—so that he had every
nine or ten months a bad horse to get rid of,—and a good horse to purchase
in his stead.

What the loss in such a balance might amount to, *communibus annis*, I
would leave to a special jury of sufferers in the same traffic, to determine;—
but let it be what it would, the honest gentleman bore it for many years
without a murmur, till at length, by repeated ill accidents of the kind, he
found it necessary to take the thing under consideration; and upon weigh-
ing the whole, and summing it up in his mind, he found it not only dispro-
portioned to his other expenses, but withal so heavy an article in itself, as to
disable him from any other act of generosity in his parish: Besides this, he
considered that with half the sum thus galloped away, he could do ten times
as much good;—and what still weighed more with him than all other considerations put together, was this, that it confined all his charity into one
particular channel, and where, as he fancied, it was the least wanted,
namely to the child-bearing and child-getting part of his parish; reserving
nothing for the impotent,—nothing for the aged,—nothing for the many
comfortless scenes he was hourly called forth to visit, where poverty, and
sickness, and affliction dwelt together.

For these reasons he resolved to discontinue the expense; and there
appeared but two possible ways to extricate him clearly out of it;—and
these were, either to make it an irrevocable law never more to lend his steed
upon any application whatever,—or else be content to ride the last poor
devil, such as they had made him, with all his aches and infirmities, to the
very end of the chapter.

As he dreaded his own constancy in the first—he very cheerfully betook
himself to the second; and though he could very well have explained it, as I
said, to his honour,—yet, for that very reason, he had a spirit above it;
choosing rather to bear the contempt of his enemies, and the laughter of his
friends, than undergo the pain of telling a story, which might seem a panegyric upon himself.

I have the highest idea of the spiritual and refined sentiments of this reverend gentleman, from this single stroke in his character, which I think
comes up to any of the honest refinements of the peerless knight of La
Mancha, whom, by the bye, with all his follies, I love more, and would
actually have gone farther to have paid a visit to, than the greatest hero of
antiquity.

But this is not the moral of my story: The thing I had in view was to shew the temper of the world in the whole of this affair.—For you must know, that so long as this explanation would have done the parson credit, the devil a soul could find it out,—I suppose his enemies would not, and that his friends could not.——But no sooner did he bestir himself in behalf of the midwife, and pay the expenses of the ordinary's licence to set her up, —but the whole secret came out; every horse he had lost, and two horses more than ever he had lost, with all the circumstances of their destruction, were known and distinctly remembered.——The story ran like wild-fire— "The parson had a returning fit of pride which had just seized him; and he was going to be well mounted once again in his life; and if it was so, 'twas plain as the sun at noon-day, he would pocket the expense of the licence, ten times told, the very first year:—So that every body was left to judge what were his views in this act of charity."

What were his views in this, and in every other action of his life,—or rather what were the opinions which floated in the brains of other people concerning it, was a thought which too much floated in his own, and too often broke in upon his rest, when he should have been sound asleep.

About ten years ago this gentleman had the good fortune to be made entirely easy upon that score,—it being just so long since he left his parish, —and the whole world at the same time behind him,—and stands accountable to a Judge of whom he will have no cause to complain.

But there is a fatality attends the actions of some men: Order them as they will, they pass thro' a certain medium, which so twists and refracts them from their true directions—that, with all the titles to praise which a rectitude of heart can give, the doers of them are nevertheless forced to live and die without it.

Of the truth of which, this gentleman was a painful example.——But to know by what means this came to pass,—and to make that knowledge of use to you, I insist upon it that you read the two following chapters, which contain such a sketch of his life and conversation, as will carry its moral along with it.—When this is done, if nothing stops us in our way, we will go on with the midwife.

CHAPTER II

YORICK was this parson's name, and, what is very remarkable in it, (as appears from a most ancient account of the family, wrote upon strong vellum, and now in perfect preservation) it had been exactly so spelt for near,—I was within an ace of saying nine hundred years;—but I would not shake my credit in telling an improbable truth, however indisputable in itself;—and therefore I shall content myself with only saying—It had been exactly so spelt, without the least variation or transposition of a single letter, for I do not know how long; which is more than I would venture to say of one half of the best surnames in the kingdom; which, in a course of years, have generally undergone as many chops and changes as their owners.—Has this been owing to the pride, or to the shame of the respective proprietors?——In honest truth, I think sometimes to the one, and sometimes to the other, just as the temptation has wrought. But a villainous affair it is, and will one day so blend and confound us altogether, that no one shall be able to stand up and swear, "That his own great grandfather was the man who did either this or that."

This evil had been sufficiently fenced against by the prudent care of the Yorick's family, and their religious preservation of these records I quote, which do farther inform us, That the family was originally of Danish extraction, and had been transplanted into England as early as in the reign of Horwendillus, king of Denmark, in whose court, it seems, an ancestor of this Mr. Yorick's, and from whom he was lineally descended, held a considerable post to the day of his death. Of what nature this considerable post was, this record saith not;—It only adds, That, for near two centuries, it had been totally abolished, as altogether unnecessary, not only in that court, but in every other court of the Christian world.

It has often come into my head, that this post could be no other than that of the king's chief Jester;—and that Hamlet's Yorick, in our Shakespeare, many of whose plays, you know, are founded upon authenticated facts, was certainly the very man.

I have not the time to look into Saxo-Grammaticus's Danish history to know the certainty of this;—but if you have leisure, and can easily get at the book, you may do it full as well yourself.

I had just time, in my travels through Denmark with Mr. Noddy's eldest son, whom, in the year 1741, I accompanied as governor, riding along with him at a prodigious rate thro' most parts of Europe, and of which original journey performed by us two, a most delectable narrative will be given in the progress of this work; I had just time, I say, and that was all, to prove the truth of an observation made by a long sojourner in that country;—namely, "That nature was neither very lavish, nor was she very stingy in her gifts of genius and capacity to its inhabitants;—but, like a discreet parent, was moderately kind to them all; observing such an equal tenor in the distribution of her favours, as to bring them, in those points, pretty near to a level with each other; so that you will meet with few instances in that kingdom of refined parts; but a great deal of good plain household understanding amongst all ranks of people, of which every body has a share"; which is, I think, very right.

With us, you see, the case is quite different:—we are all ups and downs in this matter;—you are a great genius; or 'tis fifty to one, Sir, you are a great dunce and a blockhead;—not that there is a total want of intermediate steps,—no,—we are not so irregular as that comes to;—but the two extremes are more common, and in a greater degree in this unsettled island, where nature, in her gifts and dispositions of this kind, is most whimsical and capricious; fortune herself not being more so in the bequest of her goods and chattels than she.

This is all that ever staggered my faith in regard to Yorick's extraction, who, by what I can remember of him, and by all the accounts I could ever get of him, seemed not to have had one single drop of Danish blood in his whole crasis; in nine hundred years, it might possibly have all run out:—I will not philosophize one moment with you about it; for happen how it would, the fact was this:—That instead of that cold phlegm and exact regularity of sense and humours, you would have looked for, in one so extracted;—he was, on the contrary, as mercurial and sublimated a composition,—as heteroclite a creature in all his declensions;—with as much life and whim, and *gaité de cœur* about him, as the kindliest climate could have engendered and put together. With all this sail, poor Yorick carried not one ounce of ballast; he was utterly unpractised in the world: and, at the age of twenty-six, knew just about as well how to steer his course in it, as a romping, unsuspicious girl of thirteen: So that upon his first setting out, the brisk gale of his spirits, as you will imagine, ran him foul ten times in a day of somebody's tackling; and as the grave and more slow-paced were oftenest in his way,—you may likewise imagine, 'twas with such he had generally the ill luck to get the most entangled. For aught I know there might be some mixture of unlucky wit at the bottom of such Fracas:—For, to speak the truth, Yorick had an invincible dislike and opposition in his nature to gravity;—not to gravity as such;—for where gravity was wanted, he would be the most grave or serious of mortal men for days and weeks together;—but he was an enemy to the affectation of it, and declared open war against it, only as it appeared a cloak for ignorance, or for folly: and then, whenever it fell in his way, however sheltered and protected, he seldom gave it much quarter.

Sometimes, in his wild way of talking, he would say, that Gravity was an errant scoundrel, and he would add,—of the most dangerous kind too,—because a sly one; and that he verily believed, more honest, well-meaning people were bubbled out of their goods and money by it in one twelve-month, than by pocket-picking and shop-lifting in seven. In the naked temper which a merry heart discovered, he would say there was no danger, —but to itself:—whereas the very essence of gravity was design, and consequently deceit;—'twas a taught trick to gain credit of the world for more sense and knowledge than a man was worth; and that, with all its pretensions,—it was no better, but often worse, than what a French wit had long ago defined it,—viz. "A mysterious carriage of the body to cover the defects of the mind";—which definition of gravity, Yorick, with great imprudence, would say, deserved to be wrote in letters of gold.

But, in plain truth, he was a man unhackneyed and unpractised in the world, and was altogether as indiscreet and foolish on every other subject of discourse where policy is wont to impress restraint. Yorick had no impression but one, and that was what arose from the nature of the deed spoken of; which impression he would usually translate into plain English without any periphrasis;—and too oft without much distinction of either person, time, or place;—so that when mention was made of a pitiful or an ungenerous proceeding—he never gave himself a moment's time to reflect who was the hero of the piece,—what his station,—or how far he had power to hurt him hereafter;—but if it was a dirty action,—without more ado,— The man was a dirty fellow,—and so on.——And as his comments had usually the ill fate to be terminated either in a *bon mot*, or to be enlivened throughout with some drollery or humour of expression, it gave wings to Yorick's indiscretion. In a word, tho' he never sought, yet, at the same time, as he seldom shunned occasions of saying what came uppermost, and without much ceremony:—he had but too many temptations in life, of scattering his wit and his humour,—his gibes and his jests about him.——They were not lost for want of gathering.

What were the consequences, and what was Yorick's catastrophe thereupon, you will read in the next chapter.

CHAPTER 12

THE Mortgager and Mortgagee differ the one from the other, not more in length of purse, than the Jester and Jestée do, in that of memory. But in this the comparison between them runs, as the scholiasts call it, upon all-four; which, by the bye, is upon one or two legs more than some of the best of Homer's can pretend to;—namely, That the one raises a sum, and the other a laugh at your expense, and thinks no more about it. Interest, however, still runs on in both cases;—the periodical or accidental payments of it, just serving to keep the memory of the affair alive; till, at length, in some evil hour,—pop comes the creditor upon each, and by demanding principal upon the spot, together with full interest to the very day, makes them both feel the full extent of their obligations.

As the reader (for I hate your *ifs*) has a thorough knowledge of human nature, I need not say more to satisfy him, that my Hero could not go on at this rate without some slight experience of these incidental mementos. To speak the truth, he had wantonly involved himself in a multitude of small book-debts of this stamp, which, notwithstanding Eugenius's frequent advice, he too much disregarded; thinking, that as not one of them was contracted thro' any malignancy;—but, on the contrary, from an honesty of mind, and a mere jocundity of humour, they would all of them be crossed out in course.

Eugenius would never admit this; and would often tell him, that one day or other he would certainly be reckoned with; and he would often add, in an accent of sorrowful apprehension,—to the uttermost mite. To which Yorick, with his usual carelessness of heart, would as often answer with a pshaw!—and if the subject was started in the fields,—with a hop, skip, and a jump at the end of it; but if close pent up in the social chimney-corner, where the culprit was barricadoed in, with a table and a couple of arm-chairs, and could not so readily fly off in a tangent,—Eugenius would then go on with his lecture upon discretion in words to this purpose, though somewhat better put together.

Trust me, dear Yorick, this unwary pleasantry of thine will sooner or later bring thee into scrapes and difficulties, which no after-wit can extricate thee out of.——In these sallies, too oft, I see, it happens, that a person laughed at, considers himself in the light of a person injured, with all the rights of such a situation belonging to him; and when thou viewest him in that light too, and reckons up his friends, his family, his kindred and allies, —and musters up with them the many recruits which will list under him from a sense of common danger;—'tis no extravagant arithmetic to say, that for every ten jokes,—thou hast got an hundred enemies; and till thou hast gone on, and raised a swarm of wasps about thine ears, and art half stung to death by them, thou wilt never be convinced it is so.

I cannot suspect it in the man whom I esteem, that there is the least spur from spleen or malevolence of intent in these sallies—I believe and know them to be truly honest and sportive:—But consider, my dear lad, that fools cannot distinguish this,—and that knaves will not: and thou knowest not what it is, either to provoke the one, or to make merry with the other:—whenever they associate for mutual defence, depend upon it, they will carry on the war in such a manner against thee, my dear friend, as to make thee heartily sick of it, and of thy life too.

Revenge from some baneful corner shall level a tale of dishonour at thee, which no innocence of heart or integrity of conduct shall set right.——The fortunes of thy house shall totter,—thy character, which led the way to them, shall bleed on every side of it,—thy faith questioned,—thy works belied,—thy wit forgotten,—thy learning trampled on. To wind up the last scene of thy tragedy, Cruelty and Cowardice, twin ruffians, hired and set on by Malice in the dark, shall strike together at all thy infirmities and mistakes:——The best of us, my dear lad, lie open there,——and trust me,—trust me, Yorick, when to gratify a private appetite, it is once resolved upon, that an innocent and an helpless creature shall be sacrificed, 'tis an easy matter to pick up sticks enough from any thicket where it has strayed, to make a fire to offer it up with.

Yorick scarce ever heard this sad vaticination of his destiny read over to him, but with a tear stealing from his eye, and a promissory look attending it, that he was resolved, for the time to come, to ride his tit with more sobriety.——But, alas, too late!—a grand confederacy, with ***** and ***** at the head of it, was formed before the first prediction of it.—The whole plan of the attack, just as Eugenius had foreboded, was put in execution all at once,—with so little mercy on the side of the allies,—and so little suspicion in Yorick, of what was carrying on against him,—that when he thought, good easy man! full surely preferment was o' ripening,—they had smote his root, and then he fell, as many a worthy man had fallen before him.

Yorick, however, fought it out with all imaginable gallantry for some time; till, overpowered by numbers, and worn out at length by the calamities of the war,—but more so, by the ungenerous manner in which it was carried on,—he threw down the sword; and though he kept up his spirits in appearance to the last, he died, nevertheless, as was generally thought, quite broken-hearted.

What inclined Eugenius to the same opinion was as follows:

A few hours before Yorick breathed his last, Eugenius stept in with an intent to take his last sight and last farewell of him. Upon his drawing Yorick's curtain, and asking how he felt himself, Yorick looking up in his face took hold of his hand,—and after thanking him for the many tokens of his friendship to him, for which, he said, if it was their fate to meet hereafter,—he would thank him again and again,—he told him, he was within a few hours of giving his enemies the slip for ever.——I hope not, answered Eugenius, with tears trickling down his cheeks, and with the tenderest tone that ever man spoke.——I hope not, Yorick, said he.——Yorick replied, with a look up, and a gentle squeeze of Eugenius's hand, and that was all,—but it cut Eugenius to his heart.——Come,—come, Yorick, quoth Eugenius, wiping his eyes, and summoning up the man within him,—my dear lad, be comforted,—let not all thy spirits and fortitude forsake thee at this crisis when thou most wants them;—who knows what resources are in store, and what the power of God may yet do for thee?——Yorick laid his hand upon his heart, and gently shook his head;—For my part, continued Eugenius, crying bitterly as he uttered the words,—I declare I know not, Yorick, how to part with thee, and would gladly flatter my hopes, added Eugenius, cheering up his voice, that there is still enough left of thee to make a bishop, and that I may live to see it.——I beseech thee, Eugenius, quoth Yorick, taking off his night-cap as well as he could with his left hand, —his right being still grasped close in that of Eugenius,—I beseech thee to take a view of my head.—I see nothing that ails it, replied Eugenius. Then, alas! my friend, said Yorick, let me tell you, that 'tis so bruised and mis-shapened with the blows which ***** and *****, and some others have so unhandsomely given me in the dark, that I might say with Sancho Pança, that should I recover, and "Mitres thereupon be suffered to rain down from heaven as thick as hail, not one of them would fit it."——Yorick's last breath was hanging upon his trembling lips ready to depart as he uttered this:—yet still it was uttered with something of a Cervantick tone; —and as he spoke it, Eugenius could perceive a stream of lambent fire lighted up for a moment in his eyes;—faint picture of those flashes of his spirit, which (as Shakespeare said of his ancestor) were wont to set the table in a roar!

Eugenius was convinced from this, that the heart of his friend was broke: he squeezed his hand,—and then walked softly out of the room, weeping as he walked. Yorick followed Eugenius with his eyes to the door, —he then closed them,—and never opened them more.

He lies buried in the corner of his church-yard, in the parish of —, under a plain marble slab, which his friend Eugenius, by leave of his executors, laid upon his grave, with no more than these three words of inscription, serving both for his epitaph and elegy,

Alas, poor YORICK!

Ten times a day has Yorick's ghost the consolation to hear his monumental inscription read over with such a variety of plaintive tones, as denote a general pity and esteem for him;—a foot-way crossing the churchyard close by the side of his grave,—not a passenger goes by without stopping to cast a look upon it,—and sighing as he walks on,

Alas, poor YORICK!

CHAPTER 13

IT is so long since the reader of this rhapsodical work has been parted from the midwife, that it is high time to mention her again to him, merely to put him in mind that there is such a body still in the world, and whom, upon the best judgment I can form upon my own plan at present,—I am going to introduce to him for good and all: But as fresh matter may be started, and much unexpected business fall out betwixt the reader and myself, which may require immediate dispatch;—'twas right to take care that the poor woman should not be lost in the meantime;—because when she is wanted we can no way do without her.

I think I told you that this good woman was a person of no small note and consequence throughout our whole village and township;—that her fame had spread itself to the very out-edge and circumference of that circle of importance, of which kind every soul living, whether he has a shirt to his back or no,—has one surrounding him;—which said circle, by the way, whenever 'tis said that such a one is of great weight and importance in the world,—I desire may be enlarged or contracted in your worship's fancy, in a compound ratio of the station, profession, knowledge, abilities, height and depth (measuring both ways) of the personage brought before you.

In the present case, if I remember, I fixed it about four or five miles, which not only comprehended the whole parish, but extended itself to two or three of the adjacent hamlets in the skirts of the next parish; which made a considerable thing of it. I must add, That she was, moreover, very well looked on at one large grange-house, and some other odd houses and farms within two or three miles, as I said, from the smoke of her own chimney:
——But I must here, once for all, inform you, that all this will be more exactly delineated and explained in a map, now in the hands of the engraver, which with many other pieces and developements of this work, will be added to the end of the twentieth volume,—not to swell the work,—I detest the thought of such a thing;—but by way of commentary, scholium, illustration, and key to such passages, incidents, or innuendos as shall be thought to be either of private interpretation, or of dark or doubtful meaning, after my life and my opinions shall have been read over (now don't forget the meaning of the word) by all the world;—which, betwixt you and me, and in spite of all the gentlemen-reviewers in Great Britain, and of all that their worships shall undertake to write or say to the contrary,—I am determined shall be the case.——I need not tell your worship, that all this is spoke in confidence.

CHAPTER 14

UPON looking into my mother's marriage-settlement, in order to satisfy myself and reader in a point necessary to be cleared up, before we could proceed any farther in this history;—I had the good fortune to pop upon the very thing I wanted before I had read a day and a half straight forwards,—it might have taken me up a month;—which shews plainly that when a man sits down to write a history,—tho' it be but the history of **Jack Hickathrift** or Tom Thumb, he knows no more than his heels what lets and confounded hindrances he is to meet with in his way,—or what a dance he may be led, by one excursion or another, before all is over. Could a historiographer drive on his history, as a muleteer drives on his mule,—straight forward;—for instance, from Rome all the way to Loretto, without ever once turning his head aside either to the right hand or to the left,—he might venture to foretell you to an hour when he should get to his journey's end: ———but the thing is, morally speaking, impossible: For, if he is a man of the least spirit he will have fifty deviations from a straight line to make with this or that party as he goes along, which he can no ways avoid. He will have views and prospects to himself perpetually soliciting his eye, which he can no more help standing still to look at than he can fly; he will moreover have various

   Accounts to reconcile:
   Anecdotes to pick up:
   Inscriptions to make out:
   Stories to weave in:
   Traditions to sift:
   Personages to call upon:
   Panegyrics to paste up at this door;

Pasquinades at that:—All which both the man and his mule are quite exempt from. To sum up all; there are archives at every stage to be looked into, and rolls, records, documents, and endless genealogies, which justice ever and anon calls him back to stay the reading of:—In short, there is no end of it;—for my own part, I declare I have been at it these six weeks, making all the speed I possibly could,—and am not yet born:—I have just been able, and that's all, to tell you *when* it happened, but not *how;*—so that you see the thing is yet far from being accomplished.

These unforeseen stoppages, which I own I had no conception of when I first set out;—but which, I am convinced now, will rather increase than diminish as I advance,—have struck out a hint which I am resolved to follow;—and that is,—not to be in a hurry; but to go on leisurely, writing and publishing two volumes of my life every year;—which, if I am suffered to go on quietly, and can make a tolerable bargain with my bookseller, I shall continue to do as long as I live.

CHAPTER 15

THE article in my mother's marriage-settlement, which I told the reader I was at the pains to search for, and which, now that I have found it, I think proper to lay before him,—is so much more fully expressed in the deed itself, than ever I can pretend to do it, that it would be barbarity to take it out of the lawyer's hand:—It is as follows.

"**And this Indenture further witnesseth,** That the said Walter Shandy, merchant, in consideration of the said intended marriage to be had, and, by God's blessing, to be well and truly solemnized and consummated between the said Walter Shandy and Elizabeth Mollineux aforesaid, and divers other good and valuable causes and considerations him thereunto specially moving,—doth grant, covenant, condescend, consent, conclude, bargain, and fully agree to and with John Dixon, and James Turner, Esqrs., the above-named Trustees, &c. &c.—**to wit,**—That in case it should hereafter so fall out, chance, happen, or otherwise come to pass,—That the said Walter Shandy, merchant, shall have left off business before the time or times, that the said Elizabeth Mollineux shall, according to the course of nature or otherwise, have left off bearing and bringing forth children;— and that, in consequence of the said Walter Shandy having so left off business, he shall in despite, and against the free-will, consent, and good-liking of the said Elizabeth Mollineux,—make a departure from the city of London, in order to retire to, and dwell upon, his estate at Shandy Hall, in the county of——, or at any other country-seat, castle, hall, mansion-house, messuage or grange-house, now purchased, or hereafter to be purchased, or upon any part or parcel thereof:—That then, and as often as the said Elizabeth Mollineux shall happen to be enceint with child or children severally and lawfully begot, or to be begotten, upon the body of the said Elizabeth Mollineux, during her said coverture,—he the said Walter Shandy shall, at his own proper cost and charges, and out of his own proper monies, upon good and reasonable notice, which is hereby agreed to be within six weeks of her the said Elizabeth Mollineux's full reckoning, or time of supposed and computed delivery,—pay, or cause to be paid, the sum of one hundred and twenty pounds of good and lawful money, to John Dixon, and James Turner, Esqrs. or assigns,—upon TRUST and confidence, and for and unto the use and uses, intent, end, and purpose following:—**That is to say,** —That the said sum of one hundred and twenty pounds shall be paid into the hands of the said Elizabeth Mollineux, or to be otherwise applied by them the said Trustees, for the well and truly hiring of one coach, with able and sufficient horses, to carry and convey the body of the said Elizabeth Mollineux, and the child or children which she shall be then and there enceint and pregnant with,—unto the city of London; and for the further paying and defraying of all other incidental costs, charges, and expenses whatsoever,—in and about, and for, and relating to, her said intended delivery and lying-in, in the said city or suburbs thereof. And that the said Elizabeth Mollineux shall and may, from time to time, and at all such time and times as are here covenanted and agreed upon,—peaceably and quietly hire the said coach and horses, and have free ingress, egress, and regress throughout her journey, in and from the said coach, according to the tenor, true intent, and meaning of these presents, without any let, suit, trouble, disturbance, molestation, discharge, hindrance, forfeiture, eviction, vexation, interruption, or incumbrance whatsoever.——And that it shall moreover be lawful to and for the said Elizabeth Mollineux, from time to time, and as oft or often as she shall well and truly be advanced in her said pregnancy, to the time heretofore stipulated and agreed upon,—to live and reside in such place or places, and in such family or families, and with such relations, friends, and other persons within the said city of London, as she at her own will and pleasure, notwithstanding her present coverture, and as if she was a *femme sole* and unmarried,—shall think fit.——**And this**

Indenture further witnesseth, That for the more effectually carrying of the said covenant into execution, the said Walter Shandy, merchant, doth hereby grant, bargain, sell, release, and confirm unto the said John Dixon, and James Turner, Esqrs. their heirs, executors, and assigns, in their actual possession now being, by virtue of an indenture of bargain and sale for a year to them the said John Dixon, and James Turner, Esqrs. by him the said Walter Shandy, merchant, thereof made; which said bargain and sale for a year, bears date the day next before the date of these presents, and by force and virtue of the statute for transferring of uses into possession,—**All** that the manor and lordship of Shandy, in the county of ——, with all the rights, members, and appurtenances thereof; and all and every the messuages, houses, buildings, barns, stables, orchards, gardens, backsides, tofts, crofts, garths, cottages, lands, meadows, feedings, pastures, marshes, commons, woods, underwoods, drains, fisheries, waters, and water-courses;—together with all rents, reversions, services, annuities, fee-farms, knights' fees, views of frankpledge, escheats, reliefs, mines, quarries, goods and chattels of felons and fugitives, felons of themselves, and put in exigent, deodands, free warrens, and all other royalties and seigniories, rights and jurisdictions, privileges and hereditaments whatsoever. ——**And also** the advowson, donation, presentation, and free disposition of the rectory or parsonage of Shandy aforesaid, and all and every the tenths, tithes, glebe-lands."——In three words,—"My mother was to lay in, (if she chose it) in London."

But in order to put a stop to the practice of any unfair play on the part of my mother, which a marriage-article of this nature too manifestly opened a door to, and which indeed had never been thought of at all, but for my uncle Toby Shandy;—a clause was added in security of my father, which was this:—"That in case my mother hereafter should, at any time, put my father to the trouble and expense of a London journey, upon false cries and tokens;—that for every such instance, she should forfeit all the right and title which the covenant gave her to the next turn;—but to no more,—and so on, *toties quoties*, in as effectual a manner, as if such a covenant betwixt them had not been made."——This, by the way, was no more than what was reasonable;—and yet, as reasonable as it was, I have ever thought it hard that the whole weight of the article should have fallen entirely, as it did, upon myself.

But I was begot and born to misfortunes:—for my poor mother, whether it was wind or water—or a compound of both,—or neither;—or whether it was simply the mere swell of imagination and fancy in her;—or how far a strong wish and desire to have it so, might mislead her judgment:—in short, whether she was deceived or deceiving in this matter, it no way becomes me to decide. The fact was this, That in the latter end of September 1717, which was the year before I was born, my mother having carried my father up to town much against the grain,—he peremptorily insisted upon the clause;—so that I was doomed, by marriage-articles, to have my nose squeezed as flat to my face, as if the destinies had actually spun me without one.

How this event came about,—and what a train of vexatious disappointments, in one stage or other of my life, have pursued me from the mere loss, or rather compression, of this one single member,—shall be laid before the reader all in due time.

CHAPTER 16

My father, as any body may naturally imagine, came down with my mother into the country, in but a pettish kind of a humour. The first twenty or five-and-twenty miles he did nothing in the world but fret and teaze himself, and indeed my mother too, about the cursed expense, which he said might every shilling of it have been saved;—then what vexed him more than every thing else was, the provoking time of the year,—which, as I told you, was towards the end of September, when his wall-fruit and green gages especially, in which he was very curious, were just ready for pulling:— "Had he been whistled up to London, upon a Tom Fool's errand, in any other month of the whole year, he should not have said three words about it."

For the next two whole stages, no subject would go down, but the heavy blow he had sustained from the loss of a son, whom it seems he had fully reckoned upon in his mind, and registered down in his pocket-book, as a second staff for his old age, in case Bobby should fail him. The disappointment of this, he said, was ten times more to a wise man, than all the money which the journey, etc., had cost him, put together,—rot the hundred and twenty pounds,—he did not mind it a rush.

From Stilton, all the way to Grantham, nothing in the whole affair provoked him so much as the condolences of his friends, and the foolish figure they should both make at church, the first Sunday;—of which, in the satirical vehemence of his wit, now sharpened a little by vexation, he would give so many humorous and provoking descriptions,—and place his rib and self in so many tormenting lights and attitudes in the face of the whole congregation;—that my mother declared, these two stages were so truly tragicomical, that she did nothing but laugh and cry in a breath, from one end to the other of them all the way.

From Grantham, till they had crossed the Trent, my father was out of all kind of patience at the vile trick and imposition which he fancied my mother had put upon him in this affair—"Certainly," he would say to himself, over and over again, "the woman could not be deceived herself—if she could,—what weakness!"——tormenting word!—which led his imagination a thorny dance, and before all was over, played the deuce and all with him; —for sure as ever the word weakness was uttered, and struck full upon his brain—so sure it set him upon running divisions upon how many kinds of weaknesses there were;—that there was such a thing as weakness of the body,—as well as weakness of the mind,—and then he would do nothing but syllogize within himself for a stage or two together, How far the cause of all these vexations might, or might not, have arisen out of himself.

In short, he had so many little subjects of disquietude springing out of this one affair, all fretting successively in his mind as they rose up in it, that my mother, whatever was her journey up, had but an uneasy journey of it down.——In a word, as she complained to my uncle Toby, he would have tired out the patience of any flesh alive.

Chapter 17

THOUGH my father travelled homewards, as I told you, in none of the best of moods,—pshawing and pishing all the way down,—yet he had the complaisance to keep the worst part of the story still to himself;—which was the resolution he had taken of doing himself the justice, which my uncle Toby's clause in the marriage-settlement empowered him; nor was it till the very night in which I was begot, which was thirteen months after, that she had the least intimation of his design: when my father, happening, as you remember, to be a little chagrined and out of temper,—took occasion as they lay chatting gravely in bed afterwards, talking over what was to come, —to let her know that she must accommodate herself as well as she could to the bargain made between them in their marriage-deeds; which was to lie-in of her next child in the country, to balance the last year's journey.

My father was a gentleman of many virtues,—but he had a strong spice of that in his temper, which might, or might not, add to the number.—— 'Tis known by the name of perseverance in a good cause,—and of obstinacy in a bad one: Of this my mother had so much knowledge, that she knew 'twas to no purpose to make any remonstrance,—so she e'en resolved to sit down quietly, and make the most of it.

Chapter 18

As the point was that night agreed, or rather determined, that my mother should lie-in of me in the country, she took her measures accordingly; for which purpose, when she was three days, or thereabouts, gone with child, she began to cast her eyes upon the midwife, whom you have so often heard me mention; and before the week was well got round, as the famous Dr. Manningham was not to be had, she had to come to a final determination in her mind,—notwithstanding there was a scientific operator within so near a call as eight miles of us, and who, moreover, had expressly wrote a five shillings book upon the subject of midwifery, in which he had exposed, not only the blunders of the sisterhood itself,—but had likewise super-added many curious improvements for the quicker extraction of the foetus in cross births, and some other cases of danger, which belay us in getting into the world; notwithstanding all this, my mother, I say, was absolutely determined to trust her life, and mine with it, into no soul's hand but this old woman's only.——Now this I like;—when we cannot get at the very thing we wish—never to take up with the next best in degree to it:—no; that's pitiful beyond description;—it is no more than a week from this very day, in which I am now writing this book for the edification of the world;— which is March 9, 1759,—that my dear, dear Jenny, observing I looked a little grave, as she stood cheapening a silk of five-and-twenty shillings a yard,—told the mercer, she was sorry she had given him so much trouble;— and immediately went and bought herself a yard-wide stuff of ten-pence a yard.——'Tis the duplication of one and the same greatness of soul; only what lessened the honour of it, somewhat, in my mother's case, was that she could not heroine it into so violent and hazardous an extreme, as one in her situation might have wished, because the old midwife had really some little claim to be depended upon,—as much, at least, as success could give her; having, in the course of her practice of near twenty years in the parish, brought every mother's son of them into the world without any one slip or accident which could fairly be laid to her account.

These facts, tho' they had their weight, yet did not altogether satisfy some few scruples and uneasiness which hung upon my father's spirits in relation to this choice.—To say nothing of the natural workings of humanity and justice—or of the yearnings of parental and connubial love, all which prompted him to leave as little to hazard as possible in a case of this kind;—he felt himself concerned in a particular manner, that all should go right in the present case;—from the accumulated sorrow he lay open to, should any evil betide his wife and child in lying-in at Shandy Hall.—He knew the world judged by events, and would add to his afflictions in such a misfortune, by loading him with the whole blame of it.——"Alas o' day;—had Mrs. Shandy, poor gentlewoman! had but her wish in going up to town just to lie-in and come down again;—which, they say, she begged and prayed for upon her bare knees,—and which, in my opinion, considering the fortune which Mr. Shandy got with her,—was no such mighty matter to have complied with, the lady and her babe might both of 'em have been alive at this hour."

This exclamation, my father knew, was unanswerable;—and yet, it was not merely to shelter himself,—nor was it altogether for the care of his offspring and wife that he seemed so extremely anxious about this point;—my father had extensive views of things,—and stood moreover, as he thought, deeply concerned in it for the public good, from the dread he entertained of the bad uses an ill-fated instance might be put to.

He was very sensible that all political writers upon the subject had unanimously agreed and lamented, from the beginning of Queen Elizabeth's reign down to his own time, that the current of men and money towards the metropolis, upon one frivolous errand or another,—set in so strong,—as to become dangerous to our civil rights,—though, by the bye,—a current was not the image he took most delight in,—a distemper was here his favourite metaphor, and he would run it down into a perfect allegory, by maintaining it was identically the same in the body national as in the body natural, where the blood and spirits were driven up into the head faster than they could find their ways down;—a stoppage of circulation must ensue, which was death in both cases.

There was little danger, he would say, of losing our liberties by French politics or French invasions;—nor was he so much in pain of a consumption from the mass of corrupted matter and ulcerated humours in our constitution, which he hoped was not so bad as it was imagined;—but he verily feared, that in some violent push, we should go off, all at once, in a state-apoplexy;—and then he would say, "The Lord have mercy upon us all."

My father was never able to give the history of this distemper,—without the remedy along with it.

"Was I an absolute prince," he would say, pulling up his breeches with both his hands, as he rose from his armchair, "I would appoint able judges at every avenue of my metropolis, who should take cognizance of every fool's business who came there;—and if, upon a fair and candid hearing, it appeared not of weight sufficient to leave his own home, and come up, bag and baggage, with his wife and children, farmer's sons, etc. etc., at his back-side, they should be all sent back, from constable to constable, like vagrants as they were, to the place of their legal settlements. By this means I shall take care, that my metropolis tottered not thro' its own weight;—that the head be no longer too big for the body;—that the extremes, now wasted and pinned in, be restored to their due share of nourishment, and regain with it their natural strength and beauty:—I would effectually provide, That the meadows and corn-fields of my dominions, should laugh and sing; —that good cheer and hospitality flourish once more;—and that such weight and influence be put thereby into the hands of the Squirality of my kingdom, as should counterpoise what I perceive my Nobility are now taking from them.

"Why are there so few palaces and gentlemen's seats," he would ask, with some emotion, as he walked across the room, "throughout so many delicious provinces in France? Whence is it that the few remaining Cha-teaus amongst them are so dismantled,—so unfurnished, and in so ruinous and desolate a condition?——Because, Sir," (he would say) "in that king-dom no man has any country-interest to support;—the little interest of any kind which any man has anywhere in it, is concentrated in the court, and the looks of the Grand Monarch: by the sunshine of whose countenance, or the clouds which pass across it, every French man lives or dies."

Another political reason which prompted my father so strongly to guard against the least evil accident in my mother's lying-in in the country,—was, That any such instance would infallibly throw a balance of power, too great already, into the weaker vessels of the gentry, in his own, or higher stations;—which, with the many other usurped rights which that part of the constitution was hourly establishing,—would, in the end, prove fatal to the monarchical system of domestic government established in the first creation of things by God.

In this point he was entirely of Sir Robert Filmer's opinion, That the plans and institutions of the greatest monarchies in the eastern parts of the world, were, originally, all stolen from that admirable pattern and proto-type of this household and paternal power;—which, for a century, he said, and more, had gradually been degenerating away into a mixed government; —the form of which, however desirable in great combinations of the species, —was very troublesome in small ones,—and seldom produced any thing, that he saw, but sorrow and confusion.

For all these reasons, private and public, put together,—my father was for having the man-midwife by all means,—my mother by no means. My father begged and intreated, she would for once recede from her prerogative in this matter, and suffer him to choose for her;—my mother, on the con-trary, insisted upon her privilege in this matter, to choose for herself,—and have no mortal's help but the old woman's.—What could my father do? He was almost at his wits' end;—talked it over with her in all moods;—placed

his arguments in all lights;—argued the matter with her like a christian,—like a heathen,—like a husband,—like a father,—like a patriot,—like a man:—My mother answered every thing only like a woman; which was a little hard upon her;—for as she could not assume and fight it out behind such a variety of characters,—'twas no fair match:—'twas seven to one.
——What could my mother do?——She had the advantage (otherwise she had been certainly overpowered) of a small reinforcement of chagrin personal at the bottom, which bore her up, and enabled her to dispute the affair with my father with so equal an advantage,—that both sides sung *Te Deum.* In a word, my mother was to have the old woman,—and the operator was to have licence to drink a bottle of wine with my father and my uncle Toby Shandy in the back parlour,—for which he was to be paid five guineas.

I must beg leave, before I finish this chapter, to enter a caveat in the breast of my fair reader;—and it is this,—Not to take it absolutely for granted, from an unguarded word or two which I have dropped in it,—"That I am a married man."—I own, the tender appellation of my dear, dear Jenny,—with some other strokes of conjugal knowledge, interspersed here and there, might, naturally enough, have misled the most candid judge in the world into such a determination against me.—All I plead for, in this case, Madam, is strict justice, and that you do so much of it, to me as well as to yourself,—as not to prejudge, or receive such an impression of me, till you have better evidence than, I am positive, at present can be produced against me.—Not that I can be so vain or unreasonable, Madam, as to desire you should therefore think, that my dear, dear Jenny is my kept mistress;—no,—that would be flattering my character in the other extreme, and giving it an air of freedom, which, perhaps, it has no kind of right to. All I contend for, is the utter impossibility, for some volumes, that you, or the most penetrating spirit upon earth, should know how this matter really stands.—It is not impossible, but that my dear, dear Jenny! tender as the appellation is, may be my child.——Consider,—I was born in the year eighteen.—Nor is there anything unnatural or extravagant in the supposition, that my dear Jenny may be my friend.——Friend!——My friend.——Surely, Madam, a friendship between the two sexes may subsist, and be supported without—Fy! Mr. Shandy:—Without any thing, Madam, but that tender and delicious sentiment, which ever mixes in friendship, where there is a difference of sex. Let me intreat you to study the pure and sentimental parts of the best French Romances;—it will really, Madam, astonish you to see with what a variety of chaste expressions this delicious sentiment, which I have the honour to speak of, is dressed out.

CHAPTER 19

I WOULD sooner undertake to explain the hardest problem in geometry, than pretend to account for it, that a gentleman of my father's great good sense,—knowing, as the reader must have observed him, and curious too in philosophy,—wise also in political reasoning,—and in polemical (as he will find) no way ignorant,—could be capable of entertaining a notion in his head, so out of the common track,—that I fear the reader, when I come to mention it to him, if he is the least of a choleric temper, will immediately throw the book by; if mercurial, he will laugh most heartily at it;—and if he is of a grave and saturnine cast, he will, at first sight, absolutely condemn as fanciful and extravagant; and that was in respect to the choice and imposition of christian names, on which he thought a great deal more depended than what superficial minds were capable of conceiving.

His opinion, in this matter, was, That there was a strange kind of magic bias, which good or bad names, as he called them, irresistibly impressed upon our characters and conduct.

The hero of Cervantes argued not the point with more seriousness,—nor had he more faith,—or more to say on the powers of necromancy in dishonouring his deeds,—or on Dulcinea's name, in shedding lustre upon them, than my father had on those of Trismegistus or Archimedes, on the one hand—or of Nyky and Simkin on the other. How many Caesars and Pompeys, he would say, by mere inspiration of the names, have been rendered worthy of them? And how many, he would add, are there, who might have done exceeding well in the world, had not their characters and spirits been totally depressed and Nicodemused into nothing?

I see plainly, Sir, by your looks, (or as the case happened) my father would say—that you do not heartily subscribe to this opinion of mine,—which, to those, he would add, who have not carefully sifted it to the bottom,—I own has an air more of fancy than of solid reasoning in it;—and yet, my dear Sir, if I may presume to know your character, I am morally assured, I should hazard little in stating a case to you,—not as a party in the dispute,—but as a judge, and trusting my appeal upon it to your own good sense and candid disquisition in this matter;—you are a person free from any narrow prejudices of education as most men;—and, if I may presume to penetrate farther into you,—of a liberality of genius above bearing down an opinion, merely because it wants friends. Your son,—your dear son,—from whose sweet and open temper you have so much to expect.—Your Billy, Sir!—would you, for the world, have called him Judas?—Would you, my dear Sir, he would say, laying his hand upon your breast, with the genteelest address,—and in that soft and irresistible piano of voice, which the nature of the *argumentum ad hominem* absolutely requires,—Would you, Sir, if a Jew of a godfather had proposed the name for your child, and offered you his purse along with it, would you have consented to such a desecration of him?——O my God! he would say, looking up, if I know your temper right, Sir—you are incapable of it;—you would have trampled upon the offer; you would have thrown the temptation at the tempter's head with abhorrence.

Your greatness of mind in this action, which I admire, with that generous contempt of money, which you shew me in the whole transaction, is really noble;—and what renders it more so, is the principle of it;—the workings of a parent's love upon the truth and conviction of this very hypothesis, namely, That was your son called Judas,—the sordid and treacherous idea, so inseparable from the name, would have accompanied him through life like his shadow, and, in the end, made a miser and a rascal of him, in spite, Sir, of your example.

I never knew a man able to answer this argument.——But, indeed, to speak of my father as he was;—he was certainly irresistible; both in his orations and disputations;—he was born an orator;—Θεοδίδακτος.——Persuasion hung upon his lips, and the elements of Logic and Rhetoric were so blended up in him,—and, withal, he had so shrewd a guess at the weaknesses and passions of his respondent,—that Nature might have stood up and said,—"This man is eloquent."—In short, whether he was on the weak or the strong side of the question, 'twas hazardous in either case to attack him.—And yet, 'tis strange he had never read Cicero, nor Quintilian *de Oratore*, nor Isocrates, nor Aristotle, nor Longinus amongst the ancients;—nor Vossius, nor Scioppius, nor Ramus, nor Farnaby amongst the moderns;—and what is more astonishing, he had never in his whole life the least light or spark of subtlety struck into his mind, by one single lecture upon Crackenthorp or Burgersdicius, or any Dutch logician or commentator;—he knew not so much as in what the difference of an argument *ad ignorantiam* and an argument *ad hominem* consisted; so that I well remember, when he went up along with me to enter my name at Jesus College in ****,—it was a matter of just wonder with my worthy tutor, and two or three fellows of that learned society,—that a man who knew not so much as the names of his tools, should be able to work after that fashion with them.

To work with them in the best manner he could, was what my father was, however, perpetually forced upon;—for he had a thousand little sceptical notions of the comic kind to defend—most of which notions, I verily believe, at first entered upon the footing of mere whims, and of a *vive la Bagatelle;* and as such he would make merry with them for half an hour or so, and having sharpened his wit upon them, dismiss them till another day.

I mention this, not only as matter of hypothesis or conjecture upon the progress and establishment of my father's many odd opinions,—but as a warning to the learned reader against the indiscreet reception of such guests, who, after a free and undisturbed entrance, for some years, into our brains,—at length claim a kind of settlement there,—working sometimes like yeast;—but more generally after the manner of the gentle passion, beginning in jest,—but ending in downright earnest.

Whether this was the case of the singularity of my father's notions—or that his judgment, at length, became the dupe of his wit;—or how far, in many of his notions, he might, though odd, be absolutely right;—the reader, as he comes at them, shall decide. All that I maintain here, is, that in this one, of the influence of christian names, however it gained footing, he was serious;—he was all uniformity;—he was systematical, and, like all systematic reasoners, he would move both heaven and earth, and twist and torture every thing in nature, to support his hypothesis. In a word, I repeat it over again;—he was serious; and, in consequence of it, he would lose all kind of patience whenever he saw people, especially of condition, who should have known better,—as careless and as indifferent about the name they imposed upon their child,—or more so, than in the choice of Ponto or Cupid for their puppy-dog.

This, he would say, looked ill;—and had, moreover, this particular aggravation in it, viz., That when once a vile name was wrongfully or injudiciously given, 'twas not like the case of a man's character, which, when wronged, might hereafter be cleared;—and, possibly, some time or other, if not in the man's life, at least after his death,—be, somehow or other, set to rights with the world: But the injury of this, he would say, could never be undone;—nay, he doubted even whether an act of parliament could reach it:—He knew as well as you, that the legislature assumed a power over sur-names;—but for very strong reasons, which he could give, it had never yet adventured, he would say, to go a step farther.

It was observable, that tho' my father, in consequence of this opinion, had, as I have told you, the strongest likings and dislikings towards certain names;—that there were still numbers of names which hung so equally in the balance before him, that they were absolutely indifferent to him. Jack, Dick, and Tom were of this class: These my father called neutral names;—affirming of them, without a satire, That there had been as many knaves and fools, at least, as wise and good men, since the world began, who had indifferently borne them;—so that, like equal forces acting against each other in contrary directions, he thought they mutually destroyed each other's effects; for which reason, he would often declare, He would not give a cherry-stone to choose amongst them. Bob, which was my brother's name, was another of these neutral kinds of christian names, which operated very little either way; and as my father happened to be at Epsom, when it was given him,—he would ofttimes thank Heaven it was no worse. Andrew was something like a negative quantity in Algebra with him;—'twas worse, he said, than nothing.—William stood pretty high:—Numps again was low with him:—and Nick, he said, was the Devil.

But, of all the names in the universe, he had the most unconquerable aversion for Tristram;—he had the lowest and most contemptible opinion of it of any thing in the world,—thinking it could possibly produce nothing in *rerum naturâ*, but what was extremely mean and pitiful: So that in the midst of a dispute on the subject, in which, by the bye, he was frequently involved,—he would sometimes break off in a sudden and spirited Epipho-nema, or rather Erotesis, raised a third, and sometimes a full fifth above the key of the discourse,—and demand it categorically of his antagonist, Whether he would take upon him to say, he had ever remembered,—whether he had ever read,—or even whether he had ever heard tell of a man, called Tristram, performing any thing great or worth recording?——No,—he would say,—Tristram!——The thing is impossible.

What could be wanting in my father but to have wrote a book to publish this notion of his to the world? Little boots it to the subtle speculatist to stand single in his opinions,—unless he gives them proper vent:—It was the identical thing which my father did:—for in the year sixteen, which was two years before I was born, he was at the pains of writing an express Dis-sertation simply upon the word Tristram,—shewing the world, with great candour and modesty, the grounds of his great abhorrence to the name.

When this story is compared with the title-page,—Will not the gentle reader pity my father from his soul?—to see an orderly and well-disposed gentleman, who tho' singular,—yet inoffensive in his notions,—so played upon in them by cross purposes;—to look down upon the stage, and see him baffled and overthrown in all his little systems and wishes; to behold a train of events perpetually falling out against him, and in so critical and cruel a way, as if they had purposedly been planned and pointed against him, merely to insult his speculations.——In a word, to behold such a one, in his old age, ill-fitted for troubles, ten times in a day suffering sorrow;—ten times in a day calling the child of his prayers Tristram!——Melancholy dissyllable of sound! which, to his ears, was unison to Nincompoop, and every name vituperative under heaven.——By his ashes! I swear it,—if ever malignant spirit took pleasure, or busied itself in traversing the purposes of mortal man,—it must have been here;—and if it was not necessary I should be born before I was christened, I would this moment give the reader an account of it.

CHAPTER 20

——How could you, Madam, be so inattentive in reading the last chapter? I told you in it, That my mother was not a Papist.——Papist! You told me no such thing, Sir.—Madam, I beg leave to repeat it over again, that I told you as plain, at least, as words, by direct inference, could tell you such a thing.—Then, Sir, I must have missed a page.—No, Madam,—you have not missed a word.——Then I was asleep, Sir.—My pride, Madam, cannot allow you that refuge.——Then, I declare, I know nothing at all about the matter.—That, Madam, is the very fault I lay to your charge; and as a punishment for it, I do insist upon it, that you immediately turn back, that is, as soon as you get to the next full stop, and read the whole chapter over again. I have imposed this penance upon the lady, neither out of wantonness nor cruelty; but from the best of motives; and therefore shall make her no apology for it when she returns back:—'Tis to rebuke a vicious taste, which has crept into thousands besides herself,—of reading straight forwards, more in quest of the adventures, than of the deep erudition and knowledge which a book of this cast, if read over as it should be, would infallibly impart with them——The mind should be accustomed to make wise reflections, and draw curious conclusions as it goes along; the habitude of which made Pliny the younger affirm, "That he never read a book so bad, but he drew some profit from it." The stories of Greece and Rome, run over without this turn and application,—do less service, I affirm it, than the history of Parismus and Parismenus, or of the Seven Champions of England, read with it.

——But here comes my fair lady. Have you read over again the chapter, Madam, as I desired you?——You have: And did you not observe the passage, upon the second reading, which admits the inference?——Not a word like it! Then, Madam, be pleased to ponder well the last line but one of the chapter, where I take upon me to say, "It was necessary I should be born before I was christened." Had my mother, Madam, been a Papist, that consequence did not follow.

It is a terrible misfortune for this same book of mine, but more so to the Republic of letters;—so that my own is quite swallowed up in the consideration of it,—that this self-same vile pruriency for fresh adventures in all things, has got so strongly into our habit and humour,—and so wholly intent are we upon satisfying the impatience of our concupiscence that way,—that nothing but the gross and more carnal parts of a composition will go down:—The subtle hints and sly communications of science fly off, like spirits upwards,—the heavy moral escapes downwards; and both the one and the other are as much lost to the world, as if they were still left in the bottom of the ink-horn.

I wish the male-reader has not passed by many a one, as quaint and curious as this one, in which the female-reader has been detected. I wish it may have its effects;—and that all good people, both male and female, from her example, may be taught to think as well as read.[1]

Mémoire présenté à Messieurs les Docteurs de Sorbonne[2]

Un Chirurgien Accoucheur représente à Messieurs les Docteurs de Sorbonne, qu'il y a des cas, quoique très rares, où une mere ne sçauroit accoucher, & même où l'enfant est tellement renfermé dans le sein da sa mère, qu'il ne fait parôître aucune partie de son corps, ce qui seroit un cas, suivant les Rituels, de lui conférer, du moins sous condition, le baptême. Le Chirurgien, qui consulte, prétend, par le moyen d'une petite canulle, de pouvoir baptiser immédiatement l'enfant, sans faire aucun tort à la mère.——Il demand si ce moyen, qu'il vient de proposer, est permis & légitimé, & s'il peut s'en servir dans les cas qu'il vient d'exposer.

Réponse

Le Conseil estime, que la question proposée souffre de grandes difficultés. Les Théologiens posent d'un côté pour principe, que le baptême, qui est une naissance spirituelle, suppose une première naissance; il faut être né dans le monde, pour renaître en Jésus-Christ, comme ils l'enseignent. S. Thomas, 3 part. quaest. 68, artic. 11, suit cette doctrine comme une vérité constante; l'on ne peut, dit ce S. Docteur, baptiser les enfans qui sont renfermés dans le sein de leurs mères, & S. Thomas est fondé sur ce, que les enfans ne sont point nés, & ne peuvent être comptés parmi les autres hommes; d'où il conclud, qu'ils ne peuvent être l'objet d'une action extérieure, pour recevoir par leur ministère, les sacremens nécessaires au salut: *Pueri in maternis uteris existentes nondum prodierunt in lucem ut cum aliis hominibus*

---

[1] The Romish Rituals direct the baptizing of the child, in cases of danger, before it is born;—but upon this proviso, That some part or other of the child's body be seen by the baptizer:——But the Doctors of the Sorbonne, by a deliberation held amongst them, April 10, 1733,—have enlarged the powers of the midwives, by determining, That though no part of the child's body should appear,—that baptism shall, nevertheless, be administered to it by injection—*par le moyen d'une petite canulle*,—Anglicé *a squirt*.——'Tis very strange that St. Thomas Aquinas, who had so good a mechanical head, both for tying and untying the knots of school-divinity,—should, after so much pains bestowed upon this,—give up the point at last, as a second *La chose impossible*,—"Infantes in maternis uteris existentes (quoth St. Thomas!) baptizari possunt *nullo modo*."——O Thomas! Thomas!

If the reader has the curiosity to see the question upon baptism by injection, as presented to the Doctors of the Sorbonne, with their consultation thereupon, it is as follows.

[2] Vide Deventer, Paris edit. 4to, 1734, p. 366.

vitam ducant; unde non possunt subjici actioni humanae, ut per eorum mini-
sterium sacramenta recipiant ad salutem. Les rituels ordonnent dans la pratique ce que les théologiens ont établi sur les mêmes matières, & ils def-
fendent tous d'une manière uniforme, de baptiser les enfans qui sont renfermés dans le sein de leurs mères, s'ils ne font paroître quelque partie de
leurs corps. Le concours des théologiens, & des rituels, qui sont les règles
des diocèses, paroît former une autorité qui termine la question présente;
cependant le conseil de conscience considérant d'un côté, que le raisonne-
ment des théologiens est uniquement fondé sur une raison de convenance,
& que la deffense des rituels suppose que l'on ne peut baptiser immédiatement les enfans ainsi renfermés dans le sein de leurs mères, ce qui est contre
la supposition présente; & d'un autre côté, considérant que les mêmes
théologiens enseignent, que l'on peut risquer les sacremens que Jésus-Christ
a établis comme des moyens faciles, mais nécessaires pour sanctifier les
hommes; & d'ailleurs estimant, que les enfans renfermés dans le sein de
leurs mères, pourroient être capables de salut, parcequ'ils sont capables de
damnation;—pour ces considérations, & en egard à l'exposé, suivant lequel
on assure avoir trouvé un moyen certain de baptiser ces enfans ainsi renfermés, sans faire aucun tort à la mère, le Conseil estime que l'on pourroit
se servir du moyen proposé, dans la confiance qu'il a, que Dieu n'a point
laissé ces sortes d'enfans sans aucuns secours, & supposant, comme il est
exposé, que le moyen dont il s'agit est propre à leur procurer le baptême;
cependant comme il s'agiroit, en autorisant la pratique proposée, de
changer une règle universellement établie, le Conseil croît que celui qui
consulte doit s'addresser à son évêque, & à qui il appartient de juger de
l'utilité, & du danger du moyen proposé, & comme, sous le bon plaisir de
l'évêque, le Conseil estime qu'il faudroit recourir au Pape, qui a le droit
d'expliquer les règles de l'église, & d'y déroger dans le cas, où la loi ne
sçauroit obliger, quelque sage & quelque utile que paroisse la manière de
baptiser dont il s'agit, le Conseil ne pourroit l'approuver sans le concours de
ces deux autorités. On conseile au moins à celui qui consulte, de s'addresser
à son évêque, & de lui faire part de la présente décision, afin que, si le prélat
entre dans les raisons sur lesquelles les docteurs soussignés s'appuyent, il
puisse être autorisé dans le cas de nécessité, ou il risqueroit trop d'attendre
que la permission fût demandée & accordée d'employer le moyen qu'il
propose si avantageux au salut de l'enfant. Au reste, le Conseil, en estimant
que l'on pourroit s'en servir, croît cependant, que si les enfans dont il s'agit,
venoient au monde, contre l'espérance de ceux qui se seroient servis du
même moyen, il seroit nécessaire de les baptiser sous condition; & en cela le
Conseil se conforme à tous les rituels, qui en autorisant le baptême d'un
enfant qui fait paroître quelque partie de son corps, enjoignent néantmoins,
& ordonnent de le baptiser sous condition, s'il vient heureusement au
monde.

Déliberé en Sorbonne, le 10 Avril, 1733.

A. Le Moyne.
L. De Romigny.
De Marcilly.

Mr. Tristram Shandy's compliments to Messrs. Le Moyne, De Romigny, and De Marcilly; hopes they all rested well the night after so tiresome a consultation.——He begs to know, whether after the ceremony of marriage, and before that of consummation, the baptizing all the Homunculi at once, slapdash, by injection, would not be a shorter and safer cut still; on condition, as above, That if the Homunculi do well, and come safe into the world after this, that each and every of them shall be baptized again (*sous condition*)—And provided, in the second place, That the thing can be done, which Mr. Shandy apprehends it may, *par le moyen d'une petite canulle*, and *sans faire aucun tort au père*.

CHAPTER 21

——I WONDER what's all that noise, and running backwards and forwards for, above stairs, quoth my father, addressing himself, after an hour and a half's silence, to my uncle Toby,—who, you must know, was sitting on the opposite side of the fire, smoking his social pipe all the time, in mute contemplation of a new pair of black plush breeches which he had got on:— What can they be doing, brother?—quoth my father,—we can scarce hear ourselves talk.

I think, replied my uncle Toby, taking his pipe from his mouth, and striking the head of it two or three times upon the nail of his left thumb, as he began his sentence,—I think, says he:—But to enter rightly into my uncle Toby's sentiments upon this matter, you must be made to enter first a little into his character, the outlines of which I shall just give you, and then the dialogue between him and my father will go on as well again.

Pray what was that man's name,—for I write in such a hurry, I have no time to recollect or look for it,—who first made the observation, "That there was great inconsistency in our air and climate"? Whoever he was, 'twas a just and good observation in him.——But the corollary drawn from it, namely, "That it is this which has furnished us with such a variety of odd and whimsical characters";—that was not his;—it was found out by another man, at least a century and a half after him: Then again,—that this copious storehouse of original materials, is the true and natural cause that our Comedies are so much better than those of France, or any others that either have, or can be wrote upon the Continent:—that discovery was not fully made till about the middle of King William's reign,—when the great Dryden, in writing one of his long prefaces, (if I mistake not) most fortunately hit upon it. Indeed toward the latter end of Queen Anne, the great Addison began to patronize the notion, and more fully explained it to the world in one or two of his *Spectators*;—but the discovery was not his.— Then, fourthly and lastly, that this strange irregularity in our climate, producing so strange an irregularity in our characters,—doth thereby, in some sort, make us amends, by giving us somewhat to make us merry with when the weather will not suffer us to go out of doors,—that observation is my own;—and was struck out by me this very rainy day, March 26, 1759, and betwixt the hours of nine and ten in the morning.

Thus—thus, my fellow-labourers and associates in this great harvest of our learning, now ripening before our eyes; thus it is, by slow steps of casual increase, that our knowledge physical, metaphysical, physiological, polemical, nautical, mathematical, enigmatical, technical, biographical, romantical, chemical, and obstetrical, with fifty other branches of it, (most of 'em ending as these do, in *ical*) have for these two centuries and more, gradually been creeping upwards towards that ἀκμή of their perfections, from which, if we may form a conjecture from the advances of these last seven years, we cannot possibly be far off.

When that happens, it is to be hoped, it will put an end to all kind of writings whatsoever;—the want of all kind of writing will put an end to all kind of reading;—and that in time, As war begets poverty; poverty peace, —must, in course, put an end to all kind of knowledge,—and then—we shall have all to begin over again; or, in other words, be exactly where we started.

——Happy! thrice happy times! I only wish that the era of my begetting, as well as the mode and manner of it, had been a little altered,—or that it could have been put off, with any convenience to my father or mother, for some twenty or five-and-twenty years longer, when a man in the literary world might have stood some chance.——

But I forget my uncle Toby, whom all this while we have left knocking the ashes out of his tobacco-pipe.

His humour was of that particular species, which does honour to our atmosphere; and I should have made no scruple of ranking him amongst one of the first-rate productions of it, had not there appeared too many strong lines in it of a family-likeness, which shewed that he derived the singularity of his temper more from blood, than either wind or water, or any modifications or combinations of them whatever: And I have, therefore, oft times wondered, that my father, tho' I believe he had his reasons for it, upon his observing some tokens of eccentricity, in my course, when I was a boy,—should never once endeavour to account for them in this way: for all the Shandy Family were of an original character throughout:—I mean the males,—the females had no character at all,—except, indeed, my great aunt Dinah, who, about sixty years ago, was married and got with child by the coachman, for which my father, according to his hypothesis of christian names, would often say, She might thank her godfathers and godmothers.

It will seem very strange,—and I would as soon think of dropping a riddle in the reader's way, which is not my interest to do, as set him upon guessing how it could come to pass, that an event of this kind, so many years after it had happened, should be reserved for the interruption of the peace and unity, which otherwise so cordially subsisted, between my father and my uncle Toby. One would have thought, that the whole force of the misfortune should have spent and wasted itself in the family at first,—as is generally the case.—But nothing ever wrought with our family after the ordinary way. Possibly at the very time this happened, it might have something else to afflict it; and as afflictions are sent down for our good, and that as this had never done the Shandy Family any good at all, it might lie waiting till apt times and circumstances should give it an opportunity to discharge its office.——Observe, I determine nothing upon this.——My way is ever to point out to the curious, different tracts of investigation, to come at the first springs of the events I tell;—not with a pedantic Fescue,—or in the decisive manner of Tacitus, who outwits himself and his reader;—but with the officious humility of a heart devoted to the assistance merely of the inquisitive;—to them I write,—and by them I shall be read,—if any such reading as this could be supposed to hold out so long,—to the very end of the world.

Why this cause of sorrow, therefore, was thus reserved for my father and uncle, is undetermined by me. But how and in what direction it exerted itself so as to become the cause of dissatisfaction between them, after it began to operate, is what I am able to explain with great exactness, and is as follows:

My uncle Toby Shandy, Madam, was a gentleman, who, with the virtues which usually constitute the character of a man of honour and rectitude,— possessed one in a very eminent degree, which is seldom or never put into the catalogue; and that was a most extreme and unparalleled modesty of nature;—though I correct the word nature, for this reason, that I may not prejudge a point which must shortly come to a hearing, and that is, Whether this modesty of his was natural or acquired.——Whichever way my uncle Toby came by it, 'twas nevertheless modesty in the truest sense of it; and that is, Madam, not in regard to words, for he was so unhappy as to have very little choice in them—but to things;—and this kind of modesty so possessed him, and it arose to such a height in him, as almost to equal, if such a thing could be, even the modesty of a woman: That female nicety, Madam, and inward cleanliness of mind and fancy, in your sex, which makes you so much the awe of ours.

You will imagine, Madam, that my uncle Toby had contracted all this from this very source;—that he had spent a great part of his time in converse with your sex; and that from a thorough knowledge of you, and the force of imitation which such fair examples render irresistible, he had acquired this amiable turn of mind.

I wish I could say so,—for unless it was with his sister-in-law, my father's wife and my mother—my uncle Toby scarce exchanged three words with the sex in as many years;—no, he got it, Madam, by a blow.——A blow! —Yes, Madam, it was owing to a blow from a stone, broke off by a ball from the parapet of a horn-work at the siege of Namur, which struck full upon my uncle Toby's groin.—Which way could that affect it? The story of that, Madam, is long and interesting;—but it would be running my history all upon heaps to give it you here.——'Tis for an episode hereafter; and every circumstance relating to it, in its proper place, shall be faithfully laid before you:—'Till then, it is not in my power to give farther light into this matter, or say more than what I have said already,—That my uncle Toby was a gentleman of unparalleled modesty, which happening to be somewhat subtilized and rarefied by the constant heat of a little family pride—they both so wrought together within him, that he could never bear to hear the affair of my aunt Dinah touched upon, but with the greatest emotion.—— The least hint of it was enough to make the blood fly into his face;—but when my father enlarged upon the story in mixed companies, which the illustration of his hypothesis frequently obliged him to do,—the unfortunate blight of one of the fairest branches of the family would set my uncle Toby's honour and modesty o'bleeding; and he would often take my father aside, in the greatest concern imaginable, to expostulate and tell him, he would give him any thing in the world, only to let the story rest.

My father, I believe, had the truest love and tenderness for my uncle Toby, that ever one brother bore towards another, and would have done anything in nature, which one brother in reason could have desired of another, to have made my uncle Toby's heart easy in this, or any other point. But this lay out of his power.

——My father, as I told you, was a philosopher in grain,—speculative,— systematical;—and my aunt Dinah's affair was a matter of as much conse- quence to him, as the retrogradation of the planets to Copernicus:——The backslidings of Venus in her orbit fortified the Copernican system, called so after his name; and the backslidings of my aunt Dinah in her orbit, did the same service in establishing my father's system, which, I trust, will for ever hereafter be called the Shandean System, after his.

In any other family dishonour, my father, I believe, had as nice a sense of shame as any man whatever;—and neither he, nor, I dare say, Copernicus, would have divulged the affair in either case, or have taken the least notice of it to the world, but for the obligations they owed, as they thought, to truth.——*Amicus Plato*, my father would say, construing the words to my uncle Toby, as he went along, *Amicus Plato; that is, Dinah was my aunt;— sed magis amica veritas*—but Truth is my sister.

This contrariety of humours betwixt my father and my uncle, was the source of many a fraternal squabble. The one could not bear to hear the tale of family disgrace recorded,—and the other would scarce ever let a day pass to an end without some hint at it.

For God's sake, my uncle Toby would cry,—and for my sake, and for all our sakes, my dear brother Shandy,—do let this story of our aunt's and her ashes sleep in peace;——how can you,—how can you have so little feeling and compassion for the character of our family?——What is the character of a family to an hypothesis? my father would reply.——Nay, if you come to that—what is the life of a family?——The life of a family!——my uncle Toby would say, throwing himself back in his arm chair, and lifting up his hands, his eyes, and one leg.——Yes, the life,—my father would say, main- taining his point. How many thousands of 'em are there every year that come cast away, (in all civilized countries at least)—and considered as nothing but common air, in competition of an hypothesis. In my plain sense of things, my uncle Toby would answer,—every such instance is downright Murder, let who will commit it.—There lies your mistake, my father would reply;—for, *in Foro Scientiæ* there is no such thing as Murder, —'tis only Death, brother.

My uncle Toby would never offer to answer this by any other kind of argument, than that of whistling half a dozen bars of *Lillabullero*.——You must know it was the usual channel thro' which his passions got vent, when any thing shocked or surprised him:—but especially when any thing, which he deemed very absurd, was offered.

As not one of our logical writers, nor any of the commentators upon them, that I remember, have thought proper to give a name to this particular species of argument,—I here take the liberty to do it myself, for two reasons. First, That, in order to prevent all confusion in disputes, it may stand as much distinguished for ever, from every other species of argument —as the *Argumentum ad Verecundiam, ex Absurdo, ex Fortiori*, or any other argument whatsoever:—And, secondly, That it may be said by my children's children, when my head is laid to rest,—that their learned grandfather's head had been busied to as much purpose once, as other people's; ——That he had invented a name,—and generously thrown it into the Treasury of the *Ars Logica*, for one of the most unanswerable arguments in the whole science. And, if the end of disputation is more to silence than convince,—they may add, if they please, to one of the best arguments too.

I do therefore, by these presents, strictly order and command, That it be known and distinguished by the name and title of the *Argumentum Fistulatorium*, and no other;—and that it rank hereafter with the *Argumentum Baculinum* and the *Argumentum ad Crumenam*, and for ever hereafter be treated of in the same chapter.

As for the *Argumentum Tripodium*, which is never used but by the woman against the man;—and the *Argumentum ad Rem*, which, contrarywise, is made use of by the man only against the woman;—As these two are enough in conscience for one lecture;—and, moreover, as the one is the best answer to the other,—let them likewise be kept apart, and be treated of in a place by themselves.

CHAPTER 22

THE learned Bishop Hall, I mean the famous Dr. Joseph Hall, who was Bishop of Exeter in King James the First's reign, tells us in one of his *Decads*, at the end of his divine art of meditation, imprinted at London, in the year 1610, by John Beal, dwelling in Aldersgate-street, "That it is an abominable thing for a man to commend himself";—and I really think it is so.

And yet, on the other hand, when a thing is executed in a masterly kind of a fashion, which thing is not likely to be found out;—I think it is full as abominable, that a man should lose the honour of it, and go out of the world with the conceit of it rotting in his head.

This is precisely my situation.

For in this long digression which I was accidentally led into, as in all my digressions (one only excepted) there is a master-stroke of digressive skill, the merit of which has all along, I fear, been overlooked by my reader,— not for want of penetration in him,—but because 'tis an excellence seldom looked for, or expected indeed, in a digression;—and it is this: That tho' my digressions are all fair, as you observe,—and that I fly off from what I am about, as far, and as often too, as any writer in Great Britain; yet I constantly take care to order affairs so that my main business does not stand still in my absence.

I was just going, for example, to have given you the great outlines of my uncle Toby's most whimsical character;—when my aunt Dinah and the coachman came across us, and led us a vagary some millions of miles into the very heart of the planetary system: Notwithstanding all this, you perceive that the drawing of my uncle Toby's character went on gently all the time;—not the great contours of it,—that was impossible,—but some familiar strokes and faint designations of it, were here and there touched on, as we went along, so that you are much better acquainted with my uncle Toby now than you was before.

By this contrivance the machinery of my work is of a species by itself; two contrary motions are introduced into it, and reconciled, which were thought to be at variance with each other. In a word, my work is digressive, and it is progressive too,—and at the same time.

This, Sir, is a very different story from that of the earth's moving round her axis, in her diurnal rotation, with her progress in her elliptic orbit which brings about the year, and constitutes that variety and vicissitude of seasons we enjoy;—though I own it suggested the thought,—as I believe the greatest of our boasted improvements and discoveries have come from such trifling hints.

Digressions, incontestably, are the sunshine;—they are the life, the soul of reading!—take them out of this book, for instance,—you might as well take the book along with them;—one cold eternal winter would reign in every page of it; restore them to the writer;—he steps forth like a bridegroom,—bids All-hail; brings in variety, and forbids the appetite to fail.

All the dexterity is in the good cookery and management of them, so as to be not only for the advantage of the reader, but also of the author, whose distress, in this matter, is truly pitiable: For, if he begins a digression,— from that moment, I observe, his whole work stands stock still;—and if he goes on with his main work,—then there is an end of his digression.

——This is vile work.—For which reason, from the beginning of this, you see, I have constructed the main work and the adventitious parts of it with such intersections, and have so complicated and involved the digressive and progressive movements, one wheel within another, that the whole machine, in general, has been kept a-going;—and, what's more, it shall be kept a-going these forty years, if it pleases the fountain of health to bless me so long with life and good spirits.

CHAPTER 23

I HAVE a strong propensity in me to begin this chapter very nonsensically, and I will not baulk my fancy.——Accordingly I set off thus:

If the fixture of Momus's glass in the human breast, according to the proposed emendation of that arch-critic, had taken place,—first, This foolish consequence would certainly have followed,—That the very wisest and very gravest of us all, in one coin or other, must have paid window-money every day of our lives.

And, secondly, That had the said glass been there set up, nothing more would have been wanting, in order to have taken a man's character, but to have taken a chair and gone softly, as you would to a dioptrical bee-hive, and looked in,—viewed the soul stark naked;—observed all her motions,— her machinations;—traced all her maggots from their first engendering to their crawling forth;—watched her loose in her frisks, her gambols, her capricios; and after some notice of her more solemn deportment, consequent upon such frisks, etc.,—then taken your pen and ink and set down nothing but what you had seen, and could have sworn to:—But this is an advantage not to be had by the biographer in this planet;—in the planet Mercury (belike) it may be so, if not better still for him;——for there the intense heat of the country, which is proved by computators, from its vicinity to the sun, to be more than equal to that of red-hot iron,—must, I think, long ago have vitrified the bodies of the inhabitants, (as the efficient cause) to suit them for the climate (which is the final cause;) so that betwixt them both, all the tenements of their souls, from top to bottom, may be nothing else, for aught the soundest philosophy can shew to the contrary, but one fine transparent body of clear glass (bating the umbilical knot)—so that, till the inhabitants grow old and tolerably wrinkled, whereby the rays of light, in passing through them, become so monstrously refracted,—or return reflected from their surfaces in such transverse lines to the eye, that a man cannot be seen through;—his soul might as well, unless for mere ceremony, or the trifling advantage which the umbilical point gave her,— might, upon all other accounts, I say, as well play the fool out o' doors as in her own house.

But this, as I said above, is not the case of the inhabitants of this earth;— our minds shine not through the body, but are wrapt up here in a dark covering of uncrystallized flesh and blood; so that, if we would come to the specific characters of them, we must go some other way to work.

Many, in good truth, are the ways, which human wit has been forced to take, to do this thing with exactness.

Some, for instance, draw all their characters with wind-instruments.—— Virgil takes notice of that way in the affair of Dido and Aeneas;—but it is as fallacious as the breath of fame;—and, moreover, bespeaks a narrow genius. I am not ignorant that the Italians pretend to a mathematical exactness in their designations of one particular sort of character among them, from the *forte* or *piano* of a certain wind-instrument they use,— which they say is infallible.——I dare not mention the name of the instrument in this place;—'tis sufficient we have it amongst us,—but never think of making a drawing by it;—this is enigmatical, and intended to be so, at least *ad populum*:—And therefore, I beg, Madam, when you come here, that you read on as fast as you can, and never stop to make any inquiry about it.

There are others again, who will draw a man's character from no other helps in the world, but merely from his evacuations;—but this often gives a very incorrect outline,—unless, indeed, you take a sketch of his repletions too; and by correcting one drawing from the other, compound one good figure out of them both.

I should have no objection to this method, but that I think it must smell too strong of the lamp—and be rendered still more operose, by forcing you to have an eye to the rest of his Non-naturals.——Why the most natural actions of a man's life should be called his Non-naturals,—is another question.

There are others, fourthly, who disdain every one of these expedients;— not from any fertility of their own, but from the various ways of doing it, which they have borrowed from the honourable devices which the Pentagraphic Brethren[1] of the brush have shewn in taking copies.—These, you must know, are your great historians.

One of these you will see drawing a full-length character against the light;—that's illiberal,—dishonest,—and hard upon the character of the man who sits.

Others, to mend the matter, will make a drawing of you in the Camera;—that is most unfair of all,—because, there you are sure to be represented in some of your most ridiculous attitudes.

To avoid all and every one of these errors in giving you my uncle Toby's character, I am determined to draw it by no mechanical help whatever;—nor shall my pencil be guided by any one wind-instrument which ever was blown upon, either on this, or on the other side of the Alps;—nor will I consider either his repletions or his discharges,—or touch upon his Non-naturals;—but, in a word, I will draw my uncle Toby's character from his Hobby-Horse.

CHAPTER 24

IF I was not morally sure that the reader must be out of all patience for my uncle Toby's character,——I would here previously have convinced him that there is no instrument so fit to draw such a thing with, as that which I have pitched upon.

A man and his Hobby-Horse, tho' I cannot say that they act and re-act exactly after the same manner in which the soul and body do upon each other: Yet doubtless there is a communication between them of some kind; and my opinion rather is, that there is something in it more of the manner of electrified bodies,—and that, by means of the heated parts of the rider, which come immediately into contact with the back of the Hobby-Horse,—by long journeys and much friction, it so happens, that the body of the rider is at length filled as full of Hobby-Horsical matter as it can hold;—so that if you are able to give but a clear description of the nature of the one, you may form a pretty exact notion of the genius and character of the other.

Now the Hobby-Horse which my uncle Toby always rode upon, was in my opinion an Hobby-Horse well worth giving a description of, if it was only upon the score of his great singularity;—for you might have travelled from York to Dover,—from Dover to Penzance in Cornwall, and from Penzance to York back again, and not have seen such another upon the road; or if you had seen such a one, whatever haste you had been in, you must infallibly have stopped to have taken a view of him. Indeed, the gait and figure of him was so strange, and so utterly unlike was he, from his head to his tail, to any one of the whole species, that it was now and then made a matter of dispute,—whether he was really a Hobby-Horse or no: but as the Philosopher would use no other argument to the Sceptic, who disputed with him against the reality of motion, save that of rising up upon his legs, and walking across the room;—so would my uncle Toby use no other argument to prove his Hobby-Horse was a Hobby-Horse indeed, but by getting upon his back and riding him about;—leaving the world, after that, to determine the point as it thought fit.

[1]Pentagraph, an instrument to copy prints and pictures mechanically, and in any proportion.

In good truth, my uncle Toby mounted him with so much pleasure, and he carried my Uncle Toby so well,—that he troubled his head very little with what the world either said or thought about it.

It is now high time, however, that I give you a description of him:—But to go on regularly, I only beg you will give me leave to acquaint you first, how my uncle Toby came by him.

CHAPTER 25

THE wound in my uncle Toby's groin, which he received at the siege of Namur, rendering him unfit for the service, it was thought expedient he should return to England, in order, if possible, to be set to rights.

He was four years totally confined,—part of it to his bed, and all of it to his room: and in the course of his cure, which was all that time in hand, suffered unspeakable miseries,—owing to a succession of exfoliations from the *os pubis*, and the outward edge of that part of the *coxendix* called the *os illium*,—both which bones were dismally crushed, as much by the irregularity of the stone, which I told you was broke off the parapet,—as by its size,—(tho' it was pretty large) which inclined the surgeon all along to think, that the great injury which it had done my uncle Toby's groin, was more owing to the gravity of the stone itself, than to the projectile force of it,—which he would often tell him was a great happiness.

My father at that time was just beginning business in London, and had taken a house;—and as the truest friendship and cordiality subsisted between the two brothers,—and that my father thought my uncle Toby could no where be so well nursed and taken care of as in his own house,—he assigned him the very best apartment in it.—And what was a much more sincere mark of his affection still, he would never suffer a friend or an acquaintance to step into the house on any occasion, but he would take him by the hand, and lead him upstairs to see his brother Toby, and chat an hour by his bedside.

The history of a soldier's wound beguiles the pain of it;—my uncle's visitors at least thought so, and in their daily calls upon him, from the courtesy arising out of that belief, they would frequently turn the discourse to that subject,—and from that subject the discourse would generally roll on to the siege itself.

These conversations were infinitely kind; and my uncle Toby received great relief from them, and would have received much more, but that they brought him into some unforeseen perplexities, which, for three months together, retarded his cure greatly; and if he had not hit upon an expedient to extricate himself out of them, I verily believe they would have laid him in his grave.

What these perplexities of my uncle Toby were,—'tis impossible for you to guess;—If you could,—I should blush; not as a relation,—not as a man,—nor even as a woman,—but I should blush as an author; inasmuch as I set no small store by myself upon this very account, that my reader has never yet been able to guess at any thing. And in this, Sir, I am of so nice and singular a humour, that if I thought you was able to form the least judgment or probable conjecture to yourself, of what was to come in the next page,—I would tear it out of my book.

BOOK II

CHAPTER I

I HAVE begun a new book, on purpose that I might have room enough to explain the nature of the perplexities in which my uncle Toby was involved, from the many discourses and interrogations about the siege of Namur, where he received his wound.

I must remind the reader, in case he has read the history of King William's wars,—but if he has not,—I then inform him, that one of the most memorable attacks in that siege, was that which was made by the English and Dutch upon the point of the advanced counterscarp, between the gate of St. Nicolas, which inclosed the great sluice or water-stop, where the English were terribly exposed to the shot of the counter-guard and demi-bastion of St. Roch: The issue of which hot dispute, in three words, was this; That the Dutch lodged themselves upon the counter-guard,—and that the English made themselves masters of the covered-way before St. Nicolas-gate, notwithstanding the gallantry of the French officers, who exposed themselves upon the glacis sword in hand.

As this was the principal attack of which my uncle Toby was an eye witness at Namur,—the army of the besiegers being cut off, by the confluence of the Maes and Sambre, from seeing much of each other's operations,—my uncle Toby was generally more eloquent and particular in his account of it; and the many perplexities he was in, arose out of the almost insurmountable difficulties he found in telling his story intelligibly, and giving such clear ideas of the differences and distinctions between the scarp and counterscarp,—the glacis and covered-way,—the half-moon and ravelin,—as to make his company fully comprehend where and what he was about.

Writers themselves are too apt to confound these terms; so that you will the less wonder, if in his endeavours to explain them, and in opposition to many misconceptions, that my uncle Toby did oft-times puzzle his visitors, and sometimes himself too.

To speak the truth, unless the company my father led up stairs were tolerably clear-headed, or my uncle Toby was in one of his explanatory moods, 'twas a difficult thing, do what he could, to keep the discourse free from obscurity.

What rendered the account of this affair the more intricate to my uncle Toby, was this,—that in the attack of the counterscarp, before the gate of St. Nicolas, extending itself from the bank of the Maes, quite up to the

233

great water-stop,—the ground was cut and cross cut with such a multitude of dykes, drains, rivulets, and sluices, on all sides,—and he would get so sadly bewildered, and set fast amongst them, that frequently he could neither get backwards or forwards to save his life; and was oft-times obliged to give up the attack upon that very account only.

These perplexing rebuffs gave my uncle Toby Shandy more perturbations than you would imagine: and as my father's kindness to him was continually dragging up fresh friends and fresh enquirers,—he had but a very uneasy task of it.

No doubt my uncle Toby had great command of himself,—and could guard appearances, I believe, as well as most men;—yet any one may imagine, that when he could not retreat out of the ravelin without getting into the half-moon, or get out of the covered-way without falling down the counterscarp, nor cross the dyke without danger of slipping into the ditch, but that he must have fretted and fumed inwardly:—He did so;—and the little and hourly vexations, which may seem trifling and of no account to the man who has not read Hippocrates, yet, whoever has read Hippocrates, or Dr. James Mackenzie, and has considered well the effects which the passions and affections of the mind have upon the digestion—(Why not of a wound as well as of a dinner?)—may easily conceive what sharp paroxysms and exacerbations of his wound my uncle Toby must have undergone upon that score only.

——My uncle Toby could not philosophize upon it;—'twas enough he felt it was so,—and having sustained the pain and sorrows of it for three months together, he was resolved some way or other to extricate himself.

He was one morning lying upon his back in his bed, the anguish and nature of the wound upon his groin suffering him to lie in no other position, when a thought came into his head, that if he could purchase such a thing, and have it pasted down upon a board, as a large map of the fortification of the town and citadel of Namur, with its environs, it might be a means of giving him ease.——I take notice of his desire to have the environs along with the town and citadel, for this reason,—because my uncle Toby's wound was got in one of the traverses, about thirty toises from the returning angle of the trench, opposite to the salient angle of the demi-bastion of St. Roch:—so that he was pretty confident he could stick a pin upon the identical spot of ground where he was standing on when the stone struck him.

All this succeeded to his wishes, and not only freed him from a world of sad explanations, but, in the end, it proved the happy means, as you will read, of procuring my uncle Toby his Hobby-Horse.

CHAPTER 2

THERE is nothing so foolish, when you are at the expense of making an entertainment of this kind, as to order things so badly, as to let your critics and gentry of refined taste run it down: Nor is there any thing so likely to make them do it, as that of leaving them out of the party, or, what is full as offensive, of bestowing your attention upon the rest of your guests in so particular a way, as if there was no such thing as a critic (by occupation) at table.

——I guard against both; for, in the first place, I have left half a dozen places purposely open for them;—and in the next place, I pay them all court.——Gentlemen, I kiss your hands, I protest no company could give me half the pleasure,—by my soul I am glad to see you—I beg only you will make no strangers of yourselves, but sit down without any ceremony, and fall on heartily.

I said I had left six places, and I was upon the point of carrying my complaisance so far, as to have left a seventh open for them,—and in this very spot I stand on; but being told by a Critic, (tho' not by occupation, —but by nature) that I had acquitted myself well enough, I shall fill it up directly, hoping, in the mean time, that I shall be able to make a great deal of more room next year.

——How, in the name of wonder! could your uncle Toby, who, it seems was a military man, and whom you have represented as no fool,—be at the same time such a confused, pudding-headed, muddle-headed fellow, as—Go look.

So, Sir Critic, I could have replied; but I scorn it.——'Tis language un-urbane,—and only befitting the man who cannot give clear and satisfactory accounts of things, or dive deep enough into the first causes of human ignorance and confusion. It is moreover the reply valiant—and therefore I reject it: for tho' it might have suited my uncle Toby's character as a soldier excellently well,—and had he not accustomed himself, in such at-tacks, to whistle the *Lillabullero*, as he wanted no courage, 'tis the very answer he would have given; yet it would by no means have done for me. You see as plain as can be, that I write as a man of erudition; that even my similes, my allusions, my illustrations, my metaphors, are erudite,—and that I must sustain my character properly, and contrast it properly too, —else what would become of me? Why, Sir, I should be undone:—at this very moment that I am going here to fill up one place against a critic,—I should have made an opening for a couple.

——Therefore I answer thus:

Pray, Sir, in all the reading which you have ever read, did you ever read such a book as Locke's Essay upon the Human Understanding?——Don't answer me rashly—because many, I know, quote the book, who have not read it—and many have read it who understand it not:—If either of these is your case, as I write to instruct, I will tell you in three words what the book is.—It is a history.——A history! of who? what? where? when? Don't hurry yourself—It is a history-book, Sir, (which may possibly recommend it to the world) of what passes in a man's own mind; and if you will say so much of the book, and no more, believe me, you will cut no contemptible figure in a metaphysic circle.

But this by the way.

Now if you will venture to go along with me, and look down into the bottom of this matter, it will be found that the cause of obscurity and con-fusion, in the mind of a man, is threefold.

Dull organs, dear Sir, in the first place. Secondly, slight and transient impressions made by the objects, when the said organs are not dull. And thirdly, a memory like unto a sieve, not able to retain what it has received. ——Call down Dolly your chamber-maid, and I will give you my cap and bell along with it, if I make not this matter so plain that Dolly herself should understand it as well as Malebranch.——When Dolly has indited her epistle to Robin, and has thrust her arm into the bottom of her pocket hanging by her right side;—take that opportunity to recollect that the organs and faculties of perception can, by nothing in this world be so aptly typified and explained as by that one thing which Dolly's hand is in search of.——Your organs are not so dull that I should inform you—'tis an inch, Sir, of red seal-wax.

When this is melted and dropped upon the letter, if Dolly fumbles too long for her thimble, till the wax is over hardened, it will not receive the mark of her thimble from the usual impulse which was wont to imprint it. Very well. If Dolly's wax, for want of better, is beeswax, or of a temper too soft—tho' it may receive,—it will not hold the impression, how hard soever Dolly thrusts against it; and last of all, supposing the wax good, and eke the thimble, but applied thereto in careless haste, as her Mistress rings the bell;—in any one of these three cases the print left by the thimble will be as unlike the prototype as a brass-jack.

Now you must understand that not one of these was the true cause of the confusion in my uncle Toby's discourse; and it is for that very reason I enlarge upon them so long, after the manner of great physiologists—to shew the world, what it did *not* arise from.

What it did arise from, I have hinted above, and a fertile source of obscurity it is,—and ever will be,—and that is the unsteady uses of words, which have perplexed the clearest and most exalted understandings.

It is ten to one (at Arthur's) whether you have ever read the literary histories of past ages;—if you have, what terrible battles, 'yclept logomachies, have they occasioned and perpetuated with so much gall and ink-shed,—that a good-natured man cannot read the accounts of them without tears in his eyes.

Gentle critic! when thou hast weighed all this, and considered within thyself how much of thy own knowledge, discourse, and conversation has been pestered and disordered, at one time or other, by this, and this only:—What a pudder and racket in Councils about οὐσία and ὑπόστασις; and in the Schools of the learned about power and about spirit;—about essences, and about quintessences;—about substances and about space.——What confusion in greater Theatres from words of little meaning, and as indeterminate a sense! when thou considerest this, thou wilt not wonder at my uncle Toby's perplexities,—thou wilt drop a tear of pity upon his scarp and his counterscarp;—his glacis and his covered way;—his ravelin and his half-moon: 'Twas not by ideas,—by Heaven; his life was put in jeopardy by words.

CHAPTER 3

When my uncle Toby got his map of Namur to his mind, he began immediately to apply himself, and with the utmost diligence, to the study of it; for nothing being of more importance to him than his recovery, and his recovery depending, as you have read, upon the passions and affections of his mind, it behoved him to take the nicest care to make himself so far master of his subject, as to be able to talk upon it without emotion.

In a fortnight's close and painful application, which, by the bye, did my uncle Toby's wound, upon his groin, no good,—he was enabled, by the help of some marginal documents at the feet of the elephant, together with Gobesius's military architecture and pyroballogy, translated from the Flemish, to form his discourse with passable perspicuity; and before he was two full months gone,—he was right eloquent upon it, and could make not only the attack of the advanced counterscarp with great order;—but having, by that time, gone much deeper into the art, than what his first motive made necessary, my uncle Toby was able to cross the Maes and Sambre; make diversions as far as Vauban's line, the abbey of Salsines, etc., and give his visitors as distinct a history of each of their attacks, as of that of the gate of St. Nicolas, where he had the honour to receive his wound.

But desire of knowledge, like the thirst of riches, increases ever with the acquisition of it. The more my uncle Toby pored over his map, the more he took a liking to it!—by the same process and electrical assimilation, as I told you, through which I ween the souls of connoisseurs themselves, by long friction and incumbition, have the happiness, at length, to get all be-virtued—be-pictured,—be-butterflied, and be-fiddled.

The more my uncle Toby drank of this sweet fountain of science, the greater was the heat and impatience of his thirst, so that before the first year of his confinement had well gone round, there was scarce a fortified town in Italy or Flanders, of which, by one means or other, he had not procured a plan, reading over as he got them, and carefully collating therewith the histories of their sieges, their demolitions, their improvements, and new works, all which he would read with that intense application and delight, that he would forget himself, his wound, his confinement, his dinner.

In the second year my uncle Toby purchased Ramelli and Cataneo, translated from the Italian;—likewise Stevinus, Moralis, the Chevalier de Ville, Lorini, Cochorn, Sheeter, the Count de Pagan, the Marshal Vauban, Mons. Blondel, with almost as many more books of military architecture, as Don Quixote was found to have of chivalry, when the curate and barber invaded his library.

Towards the beginning of the third year, which was in August, ninety-nine, my uncle Toby found it necessary to understand a little of projectiles:—and having judged it best to draw his knowledge from the fountainhead, he began with N. Tartaglia, who it seems was the first man who detected the imposition of a cannon-ball's doing all that mischief under the notion of a right line—This N. Tartaglia proved to my uncle Toby to be an impossible thing.

——Endless is the search of Truth.

No sooner was my uncle Toby satisfied which road the cannon-ball did not go, but he was insensibly led on, and resolved in his mind to enquire and find out which road the ball did go: For which purpose he was obliged to set off afresh with old Maltus, and studied him devoutly.—He proceeded next to Galileo and Torricellius, wherein, by certain Geometrical rules, infallibly laid down, he found the precise part to be a Parabola—or else an Hyperbola,—and that the parameter, or *latus rectum*, of the conic section of the said path, was to the quantity and amplitude in a direct ratio, as the whole line to the sine of double the angle of incidence, formed by the breech upon an horizontal plane;—and that the semi-parameter,—stop! my dear uncle Toby—stop!—go not one foot farther into this thorny and bewildered track,—intricate are the steps! intricate are the mazes of this labyrinth! intricate are the troubles which the pursuit of this bewitching phantom Knowledge will bring upon thee.——O my uncle;—fly—fly, fly from it as from a serpent.——Is it fit—good-natured man! thou should'st sit up, with the wound upon thy groin, whole nights baking thy blood with hectic watchings?——Alas! 'twill exasperate thy symptoms,—check thy perspirations—evaporate thy spirits—waste thy animal strength,—dry up thy radical moisture, bring thee into a costive habit of body,—impair thy health,—and hasten all the infirmities of thy old age.——O my uncle! my uncle Toby.

Chapter 4

I would not give a groat for that man's knowledge in pen-craft, who does not understand this,—That the best plain narrative in the world, tacked very close to the last spirited apostrophe to my uncle Toby—would have felt both cold and vapid upon the reader's palate;—therefore I forthwith put an end to the chapter, though I was in the middle of my story.

——Writers of my stamp have one principle in common with painters. Where an exact copying makes our pictures less striking, we choose the less evil; deeming it even more pardonable to trespass against truth, than beauty. This is to be understood *cum grano salis;* but be it as it will,—as the parallel is made more for the sake of letting the apostrophe cool, than any thing else,—'tis not very material whether upon any other score the reader approves of it or not.

In the latter end of the third year, my uncle Toby perceiving that the parameter and the semi-parameter of the conic section angered his wound, he left off the study of projectiles in a kind of a huff, and betook himself to the practical part of fortification only; the pleasure of which, like a spring held back, returned upon him with redoubled force.

It was in this year that my uncle began to break in upon the daily regularity of a clean shirt,—to dismiss his barber unshaven,—and to allow his surgeon scarce time sufficient to dress his wound, concerning himself so little about it, as not to ask him once in seven times dressing, how it went on: when, lo!—all of a sudden, for the change was quick as lightning, he began to sigh heavily for his recovery,—complained to my father, grew impatient with the surgeon:—and one morning, as he heard his foot coming up stairs, he shut up his books, and thrust aside his instruments, in order to expostulate with him upon the protraction of the cure, which, he told him, might surely have been accomplished at least by that time:—He dwelt long

upon the miseries he had undergone, and the sorrows of his four years'
melancholy imprisonment;—adding, that had it not been for the kind
looks and fraternal cheerings of the best of brothers,—he had long since
sunk under his misfortunes.——My father was by: My uncle Toby's eloquence brought tears into his eyes;—'twas unexpected:—My uncle Toby,
by nature was not eloquent;—it had the greater effect:——The surgeon
was confounded;—not that there wanted grounds for such, or greater
marks of impatience,—but 'twas unexpected too; in the four years he had
attended him, he had never seen any thing like it in my uncle Toby's
carriage; he had never once dropped one fretful or discontented word;—he
had been all patience,—all submission.

——We lose the right of complaining sometimes by forbearing it;—but
we often treble the force:—The surgeon was astonished; but much more
so, when he heard my uncle Toby go on, and peremptorily insist upon his
healing up the wound directly,—or sending for Monsieur Ronjat, the
king's serjeant-surgeon, to do it for him.

The desire of life and health is implanted in man's nature;—the love of
liberty and enlargement is a sister-passion to it: These my uncle Toby had
in common with his species;—and either of them had been sufficient to
account for his earnest desire to get well and out of doors;—but I have told
you before, that nothing wrought with our family after the common way;—
and from the time and manner in which this eager desire shewed itself in
the present case, the penetrating reader will suspect there was some other
cause or crotchet for it in my uncle Toby's head:—There was so, and 'tis
the subject of the next chapter to set forth what that cause and crotchet
was. I own, when that's done, 'twill be time to return back to the parlour
fire-side, where we left my uncle Toby in the middle of his sentence.

Chapter 5

When a man gives himself up to the government of a ruling passion,—or,
in other words, when his Hobby-Horse grows headstrong,—farewell cool
reason and fair discretion!

My uncle Toby's wound was near well, and as soon as the surgeon recovered his surprise, and could get leave to say as much——he told him,
'twas just beginning to incarnate; and that if no fresh exfoliation happened,
which there was no sign of,—it would be dried up in five or six weeks. The
sound of as many Olympiads, twelve hours before, would have conveyed
an idea of shorter duration to my uncle Toby's mind.—The succession of
his ideas was now rapid,—he broiled with impatience to put his design in
execution;—and so, without consulting farther with any soul living,—
which, by the bye, I think is right, when you are predetermined to take no
one soul's advice,—he privately ordered Trim, his man, to pack up a
bundle of lint and dressings, and hire a chariot-and-four to be at the door
exactly by twelve o'clock that day, when he knew my father would be upon
'Change.——So leaving a bank-note upon the table for the surgeon's care
of him, and a letter of tender thanks for his brother's—he packed up his
maps, his books of fortification, his instruments, etc., and by the help of a

crutch on one side, and Trim on the other,—my uncle Toby embarked for Shandy Hall.

The reason, or rather the rise of this sudden demigration was as follows:

The table in my uncle Toby's room, and at which, the night before this change happened, he was sitting with his maps, etc., about him—being somewhat of the smallest, for that infinity of great and small instruments of knowledge which usually lay crowded upon it—he had the accident, in reaching over for his tobacco-box, to throw down his compasses, and in stooping to take the compasses up, with his sleeve he threw down his case of instruments and snuffers;—and as the dice took a run against him, in his endeavouring to catch the snuffers in falling—he thrust Monsieur Blondel off the table, and Count de Pagan o' top of him.

'Twas to no purpose for a man, lame as my uncle Toby was, to think of redressing these evils by himself,—he rung his bell for his man Trim;—Trim, quoth my uncle Toby, prithee see what confusion I have here been making—I must have some better contrivance, Trim,—Can'st not thou take my rule, and measure the length and breadth of this table, and then go and bespeak me one as big again?——Yes, an' please your Honour, replied Trim, making a bow; but I hope your Honour will be soon well enough to get down to your country-seat, where,—as your Honour takes so much pleasure in fortification, we could manage this matter to a T.

I must here inform you, that this servant of my uncle Toby's, who went by the name of Trim, had been a corporal in my uncle's own company,—his real name was James Butler,—but having got the nick-name of Trim in the regiment, my uncle Toby, unless when he happened to be very angry with him, would never call him by any other name.

The poor fellow had been disabled for the service, by a wound on his left knee by a musket-bullet, at the battle of Landen, which was two years before the affair of Namur;—and as the fellow was well-beloved in the regiment, and a handy fellow into the bargain, my uncle Toby took him for his servant; and of an excellent use was he, attending my uncle Toby in the camp and in his quarters as a valet, groom, barber, cook, sempster, and nurse; and indeed, from first to last, waited upon him and served him with great fidelity and affection.

My uncle Toby loved the man in return, and what attached him more to him still, was the similitude of their knowledge.——For Corporal Trim, (for so, for the future, I shall call him) by four years' occasional attention to his Master's discourse upon fortified towns, and the advantage of prying and peeping continually into his Master's plans, etc., exclusive and besides what he gained Hobby-Horsically, as a body-servant, *Non Hobby Horsical per se;*—had become no mean proficient in the science; and was thought, by the cook and chamber-maid, to know as much of the nature of strong-holds as my uncle Toby himself.

I have but one more stroke to give to finish Corporal Trim's character,—and it is the only dark line in it.—The fellow loved to advise,—or rather to hear himself talk; his carriage, however, was so perfectly respectful, 'twas easy to keep him silent when you had him so; but set his tongue a-going,—you had no hold of him—he was voluble—the eternal interlardings of "your Honour," with the respectfulness of Corporal Trim's manner, interceding so strong in behalf of his elocution, that though you might have been incommoded,—you could not well be angry. My uncle Toby was seldom either the one or the other with him—or, at least, this fault, in Trim, broke no squares with them. My uncle Toby, as I said, loved the man;—and besides, as he ever looked upon a faithful servant,—but as an humble friend,—he could not bear to stop his mouth.——Such was Corporal Trim.

If I durst presume, continued Trim, to give your Honour my advice, and speak my opinion in this matter.——Thou art welcome, Trim, quoth my uncle Toby—speak,—speak what thou thinkest upon the subject, man, without fear. Why then, replied Trim, (not hanging his ears and scratching his head like a country-lout, but) stroking his hair back from his forehead, and standing erect as before his division,—I think, quoth Trim, advancing his left, which was his lame leg, a little forwards,—and pointing with his right hand open towards a map of Dunkirk, which was pinned against the hangings,—I think, quoth Corporal Trim, with humble submission to your Honour's better judgment,—that these ravelins, bastions, curtins, and hornworks, make but a poor, contemptible, fiddle-faddle piece of work of it here upon paper, compared to what your Honour and I could make of it were we in the country by ourselves, and had but a rood, or a rood and a half of ground to do what we pleased with: As summer is coming on, continued Trim, your Honour might sit out of doors, and give me the nography —(Call it ichnography, quoth my uncle),—of the town or citadel, your Honour was pleased to sit down before,—and I will be shot by your Honour upon the glacis of it, if I did not fortify it to your Honour's mind—I dare say thou would'st, Trim, quoth my uncle.——For if your Honour, continued the Corporal, could but mark me the polygon, with its exact lines and angles—That I could do very well, quoth my uncle.——I would begin with the fossé, and if your Honour could tell me the proper depth and breadth— I can to a hair's breadth, Trim, replied my uncle.——I would throw out the earth upon this hand towards the town for the scarp,—and on that hand towards the campaign for the counterscarp.——Very right, Trim, quoth my uncle Toby:—And when I had sloped them to your mind,—an' please your Honour, I would face the glacis, as the finest fortifications are done in Flanders, with sods,—and as your Honour knows they should be,— and I would make the walls and parapets with sods too.——The best engineers call them gazons, Trim, said my uncle Toby.——Whether they are gazons or sods, is not much matter, replied Trim; your Honour knows they are ten times beyond a facing either of brick or stone.——I know they are, Trim, in some respects,—quoth my uncle Toby, nodding his head;— for a cannon-ball enters into the gazon right onwards, without bringing any rubbish down with it, which might fill the fossé (as was the case at St. Nicolas's gate) and facilitate the passage over it.

Your Honour understands these matters, replied Corporal Trim, better than any officer in his Majesty's service;—but would your Honour please to let the bespeaking of the table alone, and let us but go into the country, I would work under your Honour's directions like a horse, and make fortifications for you something like a tansy, with all their batteries, saps, ditches, and palisadoes, that it should be worth all the world's riding twenty miles to go and see it.

My uncle Toby blushed as red as scarlet as Trim went on;—but it was not a blush of guilt,—of modesty,—or of anger,—it was a blush of joy;—he was fired with Corporal Trim's project and description.——Trim! said my uncle Toby, thou hast said enough.——We might begin the campaign, continued Trim, on the very day that his Majesty and the Allies take the field, and demolish them town by town as fast as—Trim, quoth my uncle Toby, say no more. Your Honour, continued Trim, might sit in your arm-chair (pointing to it) this fine weather, giving me your orders, and I would —Say no more, Trim, quoth my uncle Toby—Besides, your Honour would get not only pleasure and good pastime,—but good air, and good exercise, and good health,—and your Honour's wound would be well in a month. Thou hast said enough, Trim,—quoth my uncle Toby (putting his hand into his breeches-pocket)—I like thy project mightily.——And if your Honour pleases, I'll this moment go and buy a pioneer's spade to take down with us, and I'll bespeak a shovel and a pick-axe, and a couple of—Say no more, Trim, quoth my uncle Toby, leaping up upon one leg, quite overcome with rapture,—and thrusting a guinea into Trim's hand,—Trim, said my uncle Toby, say no more;—but go down, Trim, this moment, my lad, and bring up my supper this instant.

Trim ran down and brought up his master's supper,—to no purpose:— Trim's plan of operation ran so in my uncle Toby's head, he could not taste it.——Trim, quoth my uncle Toby, get me to bed.——'Twas all one. ——Corporal Trim's description had fired his imagination,—my uncle Toby could not shut his eyes.—The more he considered it, the more be-witching the scene appeared to him;—so that, two full hours before day-light, he had come to a final determination, and had concerted the whole plan of his and Corporal Trim's decampment.

My uncle Toby had a little neat country-house of his own, in the village where my father's estate lay at Shandy, which had been left him by an old uncle, with a small estate of about one hundred pounds a-year. Behind this house, and contiguous to it, was a kitchen-garden of about half an acre; and at the bottom of the garden, and cut off from it by a tall yew hedge, was a bowling-green, containing just about as much ground as Corporal Trim wished for;—so that as Trim uttered the words, "A rood and a half of ground to do what they would with,"—this identical bowling-green instantly presented itself, and became curiously painted all at once, upon the retina of my uncle Toby's fancy;—which was the physical cause of making him change colour, or at least of heightening his blush, to that immoderate degree I spoke of.

Never did lover post down to a beloved mistress with more heat and expectation, than my uncle Toby did, to enjoy this self-same thing in private;—I say in private;—for it was sheltered from the house, as I told you, by a tall yew hedge, and was covered on the other three sides, from mortal sight, by rough holly and thick-set flowering shrubs:—so that the idea of not being seen, did not a little contribute to the idea of pleasure preconceived in my uncle Toby's mind.—Vain thought! however thick it was planted about,—or private soever it might seem,—to think, dear uncle Toby, of enjoying a thing which took up a whole rood and a half of ground, —and not have it known!

How my uncle Toby and Corporal Trim managed this matter,—with the history of their campaigns, which were no way barren of events,—may make no uninteresting under-plot in the epitasis and working-up of this drama.—At present the scene must drop,—and change for the parlour fire-side.

CHAPTER 6

——WHAT can they be doing, brother? said my father.—I think, replied my uncle Toby,—taking, as I told you, his pipe from his mouth, and striking the ashes out of it as he began his sentence;—I think, replied he, — it would not be amiss, brother, if we rung the bell.

Pray, what's all that racket over our heads, Obadiah?—quoth my father; —my brother and I can scarce hear ourselves speak.

Sir, answered Obadiah, making a bow towards his left shoulder,—my Mistress is taken very badly.——And where's Susannah running down the garden there, as if they were going to ravish her?——Sir, she is running the shortest cut into the town, replied Obadiah, to fetch the old midwife.—— Then saddle a horse, quoth my father, and do you go directly for Dr. Slop, the man-midwife, with all our services,—and let him know your mistress is fallen into labour—and that I desire he will return with you with all speed.

It is very strange, says my father, addressing himself to my uncle Toby, as Obadiah shut the door,—as there is so expert an operator as Dr. Slop so near,—that my wife should persist to the very last in this obstinate humour of hers, in trusting the life of my child, who has had one misfortune already, to the ignorance of an old woman;—and not only the life of my child, brother,—but her own life, and with it the lives of all the children I might, peradventure, have begot out of her hereafter.

Mayhap, brother, replied my uncle Toby, my sister does it to save the expense:—A pudding's end,—replied my father,—the Doctor must be paid the same for inaction as action,—if not better,—to keep him in temper.

——Then it can be out of nothing in the whole world, quoth my uncle Toby, in the simplicity of his heart,—but Modesty.——My sister, I dare say, added he, does not care to let a man come so near her****. I will not say whether my uncle Toby had completed the sentence or not;—'tis for his advantage to suppose he had,—as, I think, he could have added no One Word which would have improved it.

If, on the contrary, my uncle Toby had not fully arrived at the period's end,—then the world stands indebted to the sudden snapping of my father's tobacco-pipe for one of the neatest examples of that ornamental figure in oratory, which Rhetoricians style the Aposiopesis—Just Heaven! how does the *Poco piu* and the *Poco meno* of the Italian artists;—the insensible more or less, determine the precise line of beauty in the sentence, as well as in the statue! How do the slight touches of the chisel, the pencil, the pen, the fiddle-stick, *et caetera*,—give the true swell, which gives the true pleasure!——O my countrymen;—be nice;—be cautious of your language;—and never, O! never let it be forgotten upon what small particles your eloquence and your fame depend.

——"My sister, mayhap," quoth my uncle Toby, "does not choose to let a man come so near her****." Make this dash,—'tis an Aposiopesis.——Take the dash away, and write Backside,—'tis Bawdy.——Scratch Backside out, and put Covered way in, 'tis a Metaphor; and, I dare say, as fortification ran so much in my uncle Toby's head, that if he had been left to have added one word to the sentence,—that word was it.

But whether that was the case or not the case;—or whether the snapping of my father's tobacco-pipe, so critically, happened through accident or anger, will be seen in due time.

Chapter 7

Tho' my father was a good natural philosopher,—yet he was something of a moral philosopher too; for which reason, when his tobacco-pipe snapped short in the middle,—he had nothing to do, as such, but to have taken hold of the two pieces, and thrown them gently upon the back of the fire.——He did no such thing;—he threw them with all the violence in the world;—and, to give the action still more emphasis,—he started upon both his legs to do it.

This looked something like heat;—and the manner of his reply to what my uncle Toby was saying, proved it was so.

——"Not choose," quoth my father, (repeating my uncle Toby's words), "to let a man come so near her!"——By Heaven, brother Toby! you would try the patience of Job;—and I think I have the plagues of one already without it.——Why?——Where?——Wherein?——Wherefore?——Upon what account? replied my uncle Toby, in the utmost astonishment.——To think, said my father, of a man living to your age, brother, and knowing so little about women!——I know nothing at all about them,—replied my uncle Toby: And I think, continued he, that the shock I received the year after the demolition of Dunkirk, in my affair with widow Wadman;—which shock you know I should not have received, but from my total ignorance of the sex,—has given me just cause to say, That I neither know nor do pretend to know any thing about 'em or their concerns either.——Methinks, brother, replied my father, you might, at least, know so much as the right end of a woman from the wrong.

It is said in Aristotle's Master Piece, "That when a man doth think of any thing which is past,—he looketh down upon the ground;—but that when he thinketh of something that is to come, he looketh up towards the heavens."

My uncle Toby, I suppose, thought of neither, for he looked horizontally.——Right end! quoth my uncle Toby, muttering the two words low to himself, and fixing his two eyes insensibly as he muttered them, upon a small crevice, formed by a bad joint in the chimney-piece—Right end of a woman!——I declare, quoth my uncle, I know no more which it is than the man in the moon;—and if I was to think, continued my uncle Toby (keeping his eye still fixed upon the bad joint) this month together, I am sure I should not be able to find it out.

Then, brother Toby, replied my father, I will tell you.

Every thing in this world, continued my father (filling a fresh pipe)—every thing in this world, my dear brother Toby, has two handles.——Not always, quoth my uncle Toby.——At least, replied my father, every one has two hands,—which comes to the same thing.——Now, if a man was to sit down coolly, and consider within himself the make, the shape, the construction, come-at-ability, and convenience of all the parts which constitute the whole of that animal, called Woman, and compare them analogically—I never understood rightly the meaning of that word,—quoth my uncle Toby.——

Analogy, replied my father, is the certain relation and agreement which different—Here a devil of a rap at the door snapped my father's definition (like his tobacco-pipe) in two,—and, at the same time, crushed the head of as notable and curious a dissertation as ever was engendered in the womb of speculation;—it was some months before my father could get an opportunity to be safely delivered of it:—And, at this hour, it is a thing full as problematical as the subject of the dissertation itself,—(considering the confusion and distresses of our domestic misadventures, which are now coming thick one upon the back of another) whether I shall be able to find a place for it in the third volume or not.

CHAPTER 8

IT is about an hour and a half's tolerable good reading since my uncle Toby rung the bell, when Obadiah was ordered to saddle a horse, and go for Dr. Slop, the man-midwife;—so that no one can say, with reason, that I have not allowed Obadiah time enough, poetically speaking, and considering the emergency too, both to go and come;—though, morally and truly speaking, the man perhaps has scarce had time to get on his boots.

If the hypercritic will go upon this; and is resolved after all to take a pendulum, and measure the true distance betwixt the ringing of the bell, and the rap at the door;—and, after finding it to be no more than two minutes, thirteen seconds, and three fifths,—should take upon him to insult over me for such a breach in the unity, or rather probability of time;—I would remind him, that the idea of duration, and of its simple modes, is got merely from the train and succession of our ideas,—and is the true scholastic pendulum,—and by which, as a scholar, I will be tried in this matter,—abjuring and detesting the jurisdiction of all other pendulums whatever.

I would therefore desire him to consider that it is but poor eight miles from Shandy Hall to Dr. Slop, the man-midwife's house;—and that whilst Obadiah has been going those said miles and back, I have brought my uncle Toby from Namur, quite across all Flanders, into England:—That I have had him ill upon my hands near four years;—and have since travelled him and Corporal Trim in a chariot-and-four, a journey of near two hundred miles down into Yorkshire,—all which put together, must have prepared the reader's imagination for the entrance of Dr. Slop upon the stage,—as much, at least (I hope) as a dance, a song, or a concerto between the acts.

If my hypercritic is intractable, alledging, that two minutes and thirteen seconds are no more than two minutes and thirteen seconds,—when I have said all I can about them; and that this plea, though it might save me dramatically, will damn me biographically, rendering my book from this very moment, a professed Romance, which, before, was a book apocryphal:—If I am thus pressed—I then put an end to the whole objection and controversy about it all at once,—by acquainting him, that Obadiah had not got above three-score yards from the stable-yard before he met with Dr. Slop;—and indeed he gave a dirty proof that he had met with him, and was within an ace of giving a tragical one too.

Imagine to yourself;—but this had better begin a new chapter.

Chapter 9

Imagine to yourself a little squat, uncourtly figure of a Doctor Slop, of about four feet and a half perpendicular height, with a breadth of back, and a sesquipedality of belly, which might have done honour to a serjeant in the horse-guards.

Such were the outlines of Dr. Slop's figure, which,—if you have read Hogarth's analysis of beauty, and if you have not, I wish you would;—you must know, may as certainly be caricatured, and conveyed to the mind by three strokes as three hundred.

Imagine such a one,—for such, I say, were the outlines of Dr. Slop's figure, coming slowly along, foot by foot, waddling thro' the dirt upon the vertebræ of a little diminutive pony, of a pretty colour—but of strength,—alack!—scarce able to have made an amble of it, under such a fardel, had the roads been in an ambling condition.——They were not.——Imagine to yourself, Obadiah mounted upon a strong monster of a coach-horse, pricked into a full gallop, and making all practicable speed the adverse way.

Pray, Sir, let me interest you a moment in this description.

Had Dr. Slop beheld Obadiah a mile off, posting in a narrow lane directly towards him, at that monstrous rate,—splashing and plunging like a devil thro' thick and thin, as he approached, would not such a phenomenon, with such a vortex of mud and water moving along with it, round its axis,—have been a subject of juster apprehension to Dr. Slop in his situation, than the worst of Whiston's comets?—To say nothing of the Nucleus: that is, of Obadiah and the coach-horse.—In my idea, the vortex alone of 'em was enough to have involved and carried, if not the doctor, at least the doctor's pony, quite away with it. What then do you think must the terror and hydrophobia of Dr. Slop have been, when you read (which you are just going to do) that he was advancing thus warily along towards Shandy Hall, and had approached to within sixty yards of it, and within five yards of a sudden turn, made by an acute angle of the garden-wall,—and in the dirtiest part of a dirty lane,—when Obadiah and his coach-horse turned the corner, rapid, furious,—pop,—full upon him!——Nothing, I think, in nature, can be supposed more terrible than such a rencounter,—so im- prompt! so ill prepared to stand the shock of it as Dr. Slop was.

What could Dr. Slop do?—he crossed himself+——Pugh!—but the doc- tor, Sir, was a Papist.——No matter; he had better have kept hold of the pummel.——He had so;—nay, as it happened, he had better have done noth- ing at all; for in crossing himself he let go his whip,—and in attempting to save his whip betwixt his knee and his saddle's skirt, as it slipped, he lost his stirrup,—in losing which he lost his seat;—and in the multitude of all these losses (which, by the bye, shews what little advantage there is in crossing) the unfortunate doctor lost his presence of mind. So that without waiting for Obadiah's onset, he left his pony to its destiny, tumbling off it diagon- ally, something in the style and manner of a pack of wool, and without any other consequence from the fall, save that of being left (as it would have been) with the broadest part of him sunk about twelve inches deep in the mire.

Obadiah pulled off his cap twice to Dr. Slop;—once as he was falling,— and then again when he saw him seated.——Ill-timed complaisance;—had not the fellow better have stopped his horse, and got off and helped him?— Sir, he did all that his situation would allow; but the Momentum of the coach-horse was so great, that Obadiah could not do it all at once; he rode in a circle three times round Dr. Slop, before he could fully accomplish it any how;—and at the last, when he did stop his beast, 'twas done with such an explosion of mud, that Obadiah had better been a league off. In short, never was a Dr. Slop so beluted, and so transubstantiated, since that affair came into fashion.

CHAPTER 10

WHEN Dr. Slop entered the back parlour, where my father and my uncle Toby were discoursing upon the nature of women,—it was hard to deter- mine whether Dr. Slop's figure, or Dr. Slop's presence, occasioned more surprise to them; for as the accident happened so near the house, as not to make it worth while for Obadiah to remount him,—Obadiah had led him in as he was, unwiped, unappointed, unannealed, with all his stains and blotches on him.—He stood like Hamlet's ghost, motionless and speechless, for a full minute and a half at the parlour-door (Obadiah still holding his hand) with all the majesty of mud. His hinder parts, upon which he had received his fall, totally besmeared,—and in every other part of him, blotched over in such a manner with Obadiah's explosion, that you would have sworn (without mental reservation) that every grain of it had taken effect.

Here was a fair opportunity for my uncle Toby to have triumphed over my father in his turn;—for no mortal, who had beheld Dr. Slop in that pickle, could have dissented from so much, at least, of my uncle Toby's opinion, "That mayhap his sister might not care to let such a Dr. Slop come so near her****." But it was the *Argumentum ad hominem;* and if my uncle Toby was not very expert at it, you may think, he might not care to use it.——No; the reason was,—'twas not his nature to insult.

Dr. Slop's presence at that time, was no less problematical than the mode of it; tho' it is certain, one moment's reflexion in my father might have solved it; for he had apprized Dr. Slop but the week before, that my mother was at her full reckoning; and as the doctor had heard nothing since, 'twas natural and very political too in him, to have taken a ride to Shandy Hall, as he did, merely to see how matters went on.

But my father's mind took unfortunately a wrong turn in the investigation; running, like the hypercritic's, altogether upon the ringing of the bell and the rap upon the door,—measuring their distance, and keeping his mind so intent upon the operation, as to have power to think of nothing else,—commonplace infirmity of the greatest mathematicians! working with might and main at the demonstration, and so wasting all their strength upon it, that they have none left in them to draw the corollary, to do good with.

The ringing of the bell, and the rap upon the door, struck likewise strong upon the sensorium of my uncle Toby,—but it excited a very different train of thoughts;—the two irreconcileable pulsations instantly brought Stevinus, the great engineer, along with them, into my uncle Toby's mind. What business Stevinus had in this affair,—is the greatest problem of all: —It shall be solved,—but not in the next chapter.

CHAPTER 11

WRITING, when properly managed (as you may be sure I think mine is) is but a different name for conversation. As no one, who knows what he is about in good company, would venture to talk all;—so no author, who understands the just boundaries of decorum and good-breeding, would presume to think all: The truest respect which you can pay to the reader's understanding, is to halve this matter amicably, and leave him something to imagine, in his turn, as well as yourself.

For my own part, I am eternally paying him compliments of this kind, and do all that lies in my power to keep his imagination as busy as my own.

'Tis his turn now;—I have given an ample description of Dr. Slop's sad overthrow, and of his sad appearance in the back parlour;—his imagination must now go on with it for a while.

Let the reader imagine then, that Dr. Slop has told his tale—and in what words, and with what aggravations, his fancy chooses;—Let him suppose, that Obadiah has told his tale also, and with such rueful looks of affected concern, as he thinks best will contrast the two figures as they stand by each other.——Let him imagine, that my father has stepped upstairs to see my mother.—And, to conclude this work of imagination,—let him imagine the doctor washed,—rubbed down, and condoled,—felicitated,— got into a pair of Obadiah's pumps, stepping forwards towards the door, upon the very point of entering upon action.

Truce!—truce, good Dr. Slop!—stay thy obstetric hand;—return it safe into thy bosom to keep it warm;—little dost thou know what obstacles, —little dost thou think what hidden causes, retard its operation!—Hast thou, Dr. Slop,—hast thou been intrusted with the secret articles of the solemn treaty, which has brought thee into this place?—Art thou aware that at this instant, a daughter of Lucina is put obstetrically over thy head? Alas! —'tis too true.—Besides, great son of Pilumnus! what canst thou do?—

Thou hast come forth unarmed;—thou hast left thy *tire-tête*,—thy new-invented forceps,—thy crotchet,—thy squirt, and all thy instruments of salvation and deliverance, behind thee,—By Heaven! at this moment they are hanging up in a green bays bag, betwixt thy two pistols, at the bed's head!—Ring;—call;—send Obadiah back upon the coach-horse to bring them with all speed.

——Make great haste, Obadiah, quoth my father, and I'll give thee a crown!—and quoth my uncle Toby, I'll give him another.

CHAPTER 12

YOUR sudden and unexpected arrival, quoth my uncle Toby, addressing himself to Dr. Slop, (all three of them sitting down to the fire together, as my uncle Toby began to speak)—instantly brought the great Stevinus into my head, who, you must know, is a favourite author with me.——Then, added my father, making use of the argument *Ad Crumenam*,—I will lay twenty guineas to a single crown-piece, (which will serve to give away to Obadiah when he gets back) that this same Stevinus was some engineer or other,—or has wrote something or other, either directly or indirectly, upon the science of fortification.

He has so,—replied my uncle Toby.——I knew it, said my father, though, for the soul of me, I cannot see what kind of connection there can be betwixt Dr. Slop's sudden coming, and a discourse upon fortification;—yet I feared it.——Talk of what we will, brother,—or let the occasion be never so foreign or unfit for the subject,—you are sure to bring it in. I would not, brother Toby, continued my father,—I declare I would not have my head so full of curtins and hornworks.——That I dare say you would not, quoth Dr. Slop, interrupting him, and laughing most immoderately at his pun.

Dennis the critic could not detest and abhor a pun, or the insinuation of a pun, more cordially than my father;—he would grow testy upon it at any time:—but to be broke in upon by one, in a serious discourse, was as bad, he would say, as a fillip upon the nose;—he saw no difference.

Sir, quoth my uncle Toby, addressing himself to Dr. Slop,—the curtins my brother Shandy mentions here, have nothing to do with bedsteads; tho', I know Du Cange says, "That bed-curtains, in all probability, have taken their name from them";—nor have the hornworks he speaks of, any thing in the world to do with the hornworks of cuckoldom; but the Curtin, Sir, is the word we use in fortification, for that part of the wall or rampart which lies between the two bastions and joins them—Besiegers seldom offer to carry on their attack directly against the curtin, for this reason, because they are so well flanked. ('Tis the case of other curtains, quoth Dr. Slop, laughing.) However, continued my uncle Toby, to make them sure, we generally choose to place ravelins before them, taking care only to extend them beyond the fossé or ditch:—The common men, who know very little of fortification, confound the ravelin and the half-moon together,—tho' they are very different things; not in their figure or construction, for we make them exactly alike in all points;—for they always consist of two faces, making a salient angle, with the gorges not straight, but in form of a crescent:—Where then lies the difference? (quoth my father, a little testily.) ——In their situations, answered my uncle Toby:—For when a ravelin, brother, stands before the curtin, it is a ravelin; and when a ravelin stands before a bastion, then the ravelin is not a ravelin;—it is a half-moon;—a half-moon likewise is a half-moon, and no more, so long as it stands before its bastion;—but was it to change place, and get before the curtin,—'twould be no longer a half-moon; a half-moon, in that case, is not a half-moon;— 'tis no more than a ravelin.——I think, quoth my father, that the noble science of defence has its weak sides—as well as others.

——As for the hornwork (high! ho! sighed my father) which, continued my uncle Toby, my brother was speaking of, they are a very considerable part of an outwork;—they are called by the French engineers, *Ouvrage à corne*, and we generally make them to cover such places as we suspect to be weaker than the rest;—'tis formed by two epaulments or demi-bastions— they are very pretty,—and if you will take a walk, I'll engage to shew you one well worth your trouble.——I own, continued my uncle Toby, when we crown them,—they are much stronger, but then they are very expensive, and take up a great deal of ground, so that, in my opinion, they are most of use to cover or defend the head of a camp; otherwise the double tenaille— By the mother who bore us!—brother Toby, quoth my father, not able to hold out any longer,—you would provoke a saint;—here have you got us, I know not how, not only souse into the middle of the old subject again:— But so full is your head of these confounded works, that though my wife is this moment in the pains of labour, and you hear her cry out, yet nothing will serve you but to carry off the man-midwife.——*Accoucheur*,—if you please, quoth Dr. Slop.——With all my heart, replied my father, I don't care what they call you,—but I wish the whole science of fortification, with all its inventors, at the devil;—it has been the death of thousands,—and it will be mine in the end.—I would not, I would not, brother Toby, have my brains so full of saps, mines, blinds, gabions, pallisadoes, ravelins, half-moons, and such trumpery, to be proprietor of Namur, and of all the towns in Flanders with it.

My uncle Toby was a man patient of injuries;—not from want of courage,—I have told you in a former chapter, "that he was a man of courage": —And will add here, that where just occasions presented, or called it forth, —I know no man under whose arm I would have sooner taken shelter;— nor did this arise from any insensibility or obtuseness of his intellectual parts;—for he felt this insult of my father's as feelingly as a man could do; —but he was of a peaceful, placid nature,—no jarring element in it,—all was mixed up so kindly within him; my uncle Toby had scarce a heart to retaliate upon a fly.

——Go—says he, one day at dinner, to an over-grown one which had buzzed about his nose, and tormented him cruelly all dinner-time,—and which after infinite attempts, he had caught at last, as it flew by him;—I'll not hurt thee, says my uncle Toby, rising from his chair, and going across the room, with the fly in his hand,—I'll not hurt a hair of thy head:—Go, says he, lifting up the sash, and opening his hand as he spoke, to let it escape;—go, poor devil, get thee gone, why should I hurt thee?——This world surely is wide enough to hold both thee and me.

I was but ten years old when this happened: but whether it was, that the action itself was more in unison to my nerves at that age of pity, which instantly set my whole frame into one vibration of most pleasurable sensation;—or how far the manner and expression of it might go towards it;—or in what degree, or by what secret magic,—a tone of voice and harmony of movement, attuned by mercy, might find a passage to my heart, I know not;—this I know, that the lesson of universal good-will then taught and imprinted by my uncle Toby, has never since been worn out of my mind: And tho' I would not depreciate what the study of the *Literae humaniores*, at the university, have done for me in that respect, or discredit the other helps of an expensive education bestowed upon me, both at home and abroad since;—yet I often think that I owe one half of my philanthropy to that one accidental impression.

☞ This is to serve for parents and governors instead of a whole volume upon the subject.

I could not give the reader this stroke in my uncle Toby's picture, by the instrument with which I drew the other parts of it,—that taking in no more than the mere Hobby-Horsical likeness:—this is a part of his moral character. My father, in this patient endurance of wrongs, which I mention, was very different, as the reader must long ago have noted; he had a much more acute and quick sensibility of nature, attended with a little soreness of temper; tho' this never transported him to any thing which looked like malignancy:—yet in the little rubs and vexations of life, 'twas apt to shew itself in a drollish and witty kind of peevishness:—He was, however, frank and generous in his nature;—at all times open to conviction; and in the little ebullitions of this subacid humour towards others, but particularly towards my uncle Toby, whom he truly loved:—he would feel more pain, ten times told (except in the affair of my aunt Dinah, or where an hypothesis was concerned) than what he ever gave.

The characters of the two brothers, in this view of them, reflected light upon each other, and appeared with great advantage in this affair which arose about Stevinus.

I need not tell the reader, if he keeps a Hobby-Horse,—that a man's Hobby-Horse is as tender a part as he has about him; and that these unprovoked strokes at my uncle Toby's could not be unfelt by him.—No:—as I said above, my uncle Toby did feel them, and very sensibly too.

Pray, Sir, what said he?——How did he behave?——O, Sir!—it was great: For as soon as my father had done insulting his Hobby-Horse,—he turned his head without the least emotion, from Dr. Slop, to whom he was addressing his discourse, and looking up into my father's face, with a countenance spread over with so much good-nature;—so placid;—so fraternal;—so inexpressibly tender towards him:—it penetrated my father to his heart: He rose up hastily from his chair, and seizing hold of both my uncle Toby's hands as he spoke:—Brother Toby, said he—I beg thy pardon;—forgive, I pray thee, this rash humour which my mother gave me. ——My dear, dear brother, answered my uncle Toby, rising up by my father's help, say no more about it;—you are heartily welcome, had it been ten times as much, brother. But 'tis ungenerous, replied my father, to hurt any man;—a brother worse;—but to hurt a brother of such gentle manners, —so unprovoking,—and so unresenting;—'tis base:—By Heaven, 'tis cowardly.——You are heartily welcome, brother, quoth my uncle Toby,— had it been fifty times as much.——Besides, what have I to do, my dear Toby, cried my father, either with your amusements or your pleasures, unless it was in my power (which it is not) to increase their measure?

——Brother Shandy, answered my uncle Toby, looking wistfully in his face,—you are much mistaken in this point:—for you do increase my pleasure very much, in begetting children for the Shandy family at your time of life.——But, by that, Sir, quoth Dr. Slop, Mr. Shandy increases his own.——Not a jot, quoth my father.

Chapter 13

My brother does it, quoth my uncle Toby, out of principle.——In a family way, I suppose, quoth Dr. Slop.——Pshaw!—said my father,—'tis not worth talking of.

Chapter 14

At the end of the last chapter, my father and my uncle Toby were left both standing, like Brutus and Cassius, at the close of the scene, making up their accounts.

As my father spoke the three last words,—he sat down;—my uncle Toby exactly followed his example, only, that before he took his chair, he rung the bell, to order Corporal Trim, who was in waiting, to step home for Stevinus:—my uncle Toby's house being no farther off than the opposite side of the way.

Some men would have dropped the subject of Stevinus;—but my uncle Toby had no resentment in his heart, and he went on with the subject, to shew my father that he had none.

Your sudden appearance, Dr. Slop, quoth my uncle, resuming his discourse, instantly brought Stevinus into my head. (My father, you may be sure, did not offer to lay any more wagers upon Stevinus's head.)—Because, continued my uncle Toby, the celebrated sailing chariot, which belonged to Prince Maurice, and was of such wonderful contrivance and velocity, as to carry half a dozen people thirty German miles, in I don't know how few minutes,—was invented by Stevinus, that great mathematician and engineer.

You might have spared your servant the trouble, quoth Dr. Slop (as the fellow is lame), of going for Stevinus's account of it, because in my return from Leyden thro' the Hague, I walked as far as Schevling, which is two long miles, on purpose to take a view of it.

That's nothing, replied my uncle Toby, to what the learned Peireskius did, who walked a matter of five hundred miles, reckoning from Paris to Schevling, and from Schevling to Paris back again, in order to see it,—and nothing else.

Some men cannot bear to be out-gone.

The more fool Peireskius, replied Dr. Slop. But mark, 'twas out of no contempt of Peireskius at all;—but that Peireskius's indefatigable labour in trudging so far on foot, out of love for the sciences, reduced the exploit of Dr. Slop, in that affair, to nothing:—the more fool Peireskius, said he again.—Why so?—replied my father, taking his brother's part, not only to make reparation as fast as he could for the insult he had given him, which sat still upon my father's mind;—but partly, that my father began really to interest himself in the discourse.——Why so?—said he. Why is Peireskius, or any man else, to be abused for an appetite for that, or any other morsel of sound knowledge: For notwithstanding I know nothing of the chariot in question, continued he, the inventor of it must have had a very mechanical head; and tho' I cannot guess upon what principles of philosophy he has achieved it;—yet certainly his machine has been constructed upon solid ones, be they what they will, or it could not have answered at the rate my brother mentions.

It answered, replied my uncle Toby, as well, if not better; for, as Peireskius elegantly expresses it, speaking of the velocity of its motion, *Tam citus erat, quam erat ventus;* which, unless I have forgot my Latin, is, that it was as swift as the wind itself.

But pray, Dr. Slop, quoth my father, interrupting my uncle (tho' not without begging pardon for it at the same time) upon what principles was this self-same chariot set a-going?——Upon very pretty principles to be sure, replied Dr. Slop:—And I have often wondered, continued he, evading the question, why none of our gentry, who live upon large plains like this of ours,—(especially they whose wives are not past child-bearing) attempt nothing of this kind; for it would not only be infinitely expeditious upon sudden calls, to which the sex is subject,—if the wind only served,—but would be excellent good husbandry to make use of the winds, which cost nothing, and which eat nothing, rather than horses, which (the devil take 'em) both cost and eat a great deal.

For that very reason, replied my father, "Because they cost nothing, and because they eat nothing,"—the scheme is bad;—it is the consumption of our products, as well as the manufactures of them, which gives bread to the hungry, circulates trade,—brings in money, and supports the value of our lands;—and tho', I own, if I was a Prince, I would generously recompense the scientific head which brought forth such contrivances;—yet I would as peremptorily suppress the use of them.

My father here had got into his element,—and was going on as prosperously with his dissertation upon trade, as my uncle Toby had before, upon his of fortification;—but to the loss of much sound knowledge, the destinies in the morning had decreed that no dissertation of any kind should be spun by my father that day,—for as he opened his mouth to begin the next sentence,

CHAPTER 15

IN popped Corporal Trim with Stevinus:—But 'twas too late,—all the discourse had been exhausted without him, and was running into a new channel.

——You may take the book home again, Trim, said my uncle Toby, nodding to him.

But prithee, Corporal, quoth my father, drolling,—look first into it, and see if thou canst spy aught of a sailing chariot in it.

Corporal Trim, by being in the service, had learned to obey,—and not to remonstrate;—so taking the book to a side-table, and running over the leaves; An' please your Honour, said Trim, I can see no such thing;—however, continued the Corporal, drolling a little in his turn, I'll make sure work of it, an' please your Honour;—so taking hold of the two covers of the book, one in each hand, and letting the leaves fall down, as he bent the covers back, he gave the book a good sound shake.

There is something falling out, however, said Trim, an' please your Honour;—but it is not a chariot, or any thing like one:—Prithee, Corporal, said my father, smiling, what is it then?—I think, answered Trim, stooping to take it up,—'tis more like a sermon,—for it begins with a text of scripture, and the chapter and verse;—and then goes on, not as a chariot, but like a sermon directly.

The company smiled.

I cannot conceive how it is possible, quoth my uncle Toby, for such a thing as a sermon to have got into my Stevinus.

I think 'tis a sermon, replied Trim;—but if it please your Honours, as it is a fair hand, I will read you a page;—for Trim, you must know, loved to hear himself read almost as well as talk.

I have ever a strong propensity, said my father, to look into things which cross my way, by such strange fatalities as these;—and as we have nothing better to do, at least till Obadiah gets back, I shall be obliged to you, brother, if Dr. Slop has no objection to it, to order the Corporal to give us a page or two of it,—if he is as able to do it, as he seems willing. An' please your Honour, quoth Trim, I officiated two whole campaigns, in Flanders, as clerk to the chaplain of the regiment.——He can read it, quoth my uncle Toby, as well as I can.——Trim, I assure you, was the best scholar in my company, and should have had the next halberd, but for the poor fellow's misfortune. Corporal Trim laid his hand upon his heart, and made an humble bow to his master;—then laying down his hat upon the floor, and taking up the sermon in his left hand, in order to have his right at liberty,—he advanced, nothing doubting, into the middle of the room, where he could best see, and be best seen by his audience.

Chapter 16

——If you have any objection,—said my father, addressing himself to Dr. Slop. Not in the least, replied Dr. Slop;—for it does not appear on which side of the question it is wrote;—it may be a composition of a divine of our church, as well as yours,—so that we run equal risks.——'Tis wrote upon neither side, quoth Trim, for 'tis only upon Conscience, an' please your Honours.

Trim's reason put his audience into good humour,—all but Dr. Slop, who turning his head about towards Trim, looked a little angry.

Begin, Trim,—and read distinctly, quoth my father.——I will, an' please your Honour, replied the Corporal, making a bow, and bespeaking attention with a slight movement of his right hand.

Chapter 17

——But before the Corporal begins, I must first give you a description of his attitude;—otherwise he will naturally stand represented, by your imagination, in an uneasy posture,—stiff,—perpendicular,—dividing the weight of his body equally upon both legs;—his eye fixed, as if on duty;—his look determined,—clenching the sermon in his left hand, like his fire-lock.——In a word, you would be apt to paint Trim, as if he was standing in his platoon ready for action.——His attitude was as unlike all this as you can conceive.

He stood before them with his body swayed, and bent forwards just so far, as to make an angle of 85 degrees and a half upon the plain of the horizon;—which sound orators, to whom I address this, know very well to be the true persuasive angle of incidence;—in any other angle you may talk and preach;—'tis certain;—and it is done every day;—but with what effect,—I leave the world to judge!

The necessity of this precise angle of 85 degrees and a half to a mathematical exactness,—does it not shew us, by the way, how the arts and sciences mutually befriend each other?

How the deuce Corporal Trim, who knew not so much as an acute angle from an obtuse one, came to hit it so exactly;—or whether it was chance or nature, or good sense or imitation, etc., shall be commented upon in that part of the cyclopædia of arts and sciences, where the instrumental parts of the eloquence of the senate, the pulpit, and the bar, the coffee-house, the bed-chamber, and fire-side, fall under consideration.

He stood,—for I repeat it, to take the picture of him in at one view, with his body swayed, and somewhat bent forwards,—his right leg from under him, sustaining seven-eighths of his whole weight,—the foot of his left leg, the defect of which was no disadvantage to his attitude, advanced a little,—not laterally, nor forwards, but in a line betwixt them;—his knee bent, but that not violently,—but so as to fall within the limits of the line of beauty;—and I add, of the line of science too;—for consider, it had one-eighth part of his body to bear up;—so that in this case the position of the leg is determined,—because the foot could be no further advanced, or the knee more bent, than what would allow him mechanically to receive an eighth part of his whole weight under it, and to carry it too.

☞This I recommend to painters:—need I add,—to orators!—I think not; for unless they practise it,—they must fall upon their noses.

So much for Corporal Trim's body and legs.——He held the sermon loosely, not carelessly, in his left hand, raised something above his stomach, and detached a little from his breast;—his right arm falling negligently by his side, as nature and the laws of gravity ordered it,—but with the palm of it open and turned towards his audience, ready to aid the sentiment in case it stood in need.

Corporal Trim's eyes and the muscles of his face were in full harmony with the other parts of him;—he looked frank,—unconstrained,—something assured,—but not bordering upon assurance.

Let not the critic ask how Corporal Trim could come by all this.——I've told him it should be explained;—but so he stood before my father, my uncle Toby, and Dr. Slop,—so swayed his body, so contrasted his limbs, and with such an oratorical sweep throughout the whole figure,—a statuary might have modelled from it;—nay, I doubt whether the oldest Fellow of a College,—or the Hebrew Professor himself, could have much mended it.

Trim made a bow, and read as follows:

The SERMON
HEBREWS xiii. 18

—For we trust *we have a good Conscience.—*

"TRUST!——Trust we have a good conscience!"

[Certainly, Trim, quoth my father, interrupting him, you give that sentence a very improper accent; for you curl up your nose, man, and read it with such a sneering tone, as if the Parson was going to abuse the Apostle.

He is, an' please your Honour, replied Trim. Pugh! said my father, smiling.

Sir, quoth Dr. Slop, Trim is certainly in the right; for the writer (who I perceive is a Protestant) by the snappish manner in which he takes up the apostle, is certainly going to abuse him:—if this treatment of him has not done it already. But from whence, replied my father, have you concluded so soon, Dr. Slop, that the writer is of our church?—for aught I can see yet,—he may be of any church.——Because, answered Dr. Slop, if he was of ours, —he durst no more take such a licence,—than a bear by his beard:—If, in our communion, Sir, a man was to insult an apostle,—a saint,—or even the paring of a saint's nail,—he would have his eyes scratched out.——What, by the saint? quoth my uncle Toby. No, replied Dr. Slop, he would have an old house over his head. Pray is the Inquisition an ancient building, answered my uncle Toby, or is it a modern one?——I know nothing of architecture, replied Dr. Slop.——An' please your Honours, quoth Trim, the Inquisition is the vilest—Prithee spare thy description, Trim, I hate the very name of it, said my father.——No matter for that, answered Dr. Slop, —it has its uses; for tho' I'm no great advocate for it, yet, in such a case as this, he would soon be taught better manners; and I can tell him, if he went on at that rate, would be flung into the Inquisition for his pains. God help him then, quoth my uncle Toby. Amen, added Trim; for Heaven above knows, I have a poor brother who has been fourteen years a captive in it. ——I never heard one word of it before, said my uncle Toby, hastily:—— How came he there, Trim?——O, Sir! the story will make your heart bleed, —as it has made mine a thousand times;—but it is too long to be told now; —your Honour shall hear it from first to last some day when I am working beside you in our fortifications;—but the short of the story is this;—That my brother Tom went over a servant to Lisbon,—and then married a Jew's widow, who kept a small shop, and sold sausages, which somehow or other, was the cause of his being taken in the middle of the night out of his bed, where he was lying with his wife and two small children, and carried directly to the Inquisition, where, God help him, continued Trim, fetching a sigh from the bottom of his heart,—the poor honest lad lies confined at this hour; he was as honest a soul, added Trim, (pulling out his handkerchief) as ever blood warmed.——

——The tears trickled down Trim's cheeks faster than he could well wipe them away.——A dead silence in the room ensued for some minutes. ——Certain proof of pity!

Come, Trim, quoth my father, after he saw the poor fellow's grief had got a little vent,—read on,—and put this melancholy story out of thy head: —I grieve that I interrupted thee; but prithee begin the sermon again;— for if the first sentence in it is matter of abuse, as thou sayest, I have a great desire to know what kind of provocation the apostle has given.

Corporal Trim wiped his face, and returned his handkerchief into his pocket, and, making a bow as he did it,—he began again.]

The SERMON

Hebrews xiii. 18

—For we trust we have a good Conscience.—

"Trust! trust we have a good conscience! Surely if there is any thing in this life which a man may depend upon, and to the knowledge of which he is capable of arriving upon the most indisputable evidence, it must be this very thing,—whether he has a good conscience or no."

[I am positive I am right, quoth Dr. Slop.]

"If a man thinks at all, he cannot well be a stranger to the true state of this account;—he must be privy to his own thoughts and desires;—he must remember his past pursuits, and know certainly the true springs and motives, which, in general, have governed the actions of his life."

[I defy him, without an assistant, quoth Dr. Slop.]

"In other matters we may be deceived by false appearances; and, as the wise man complains, 'hardly do we guess aright at the things that are upon the earth, and with labour do we find the things that are before us.' But here the mind has all the evidence and facts within herself;—is conscious of the web she has wove;—knows its texture and fineness, and the exact share which every passion has had in working upon the several designs which virtue or vice has planned before her."

[The language is good, and I declare Trim reads very well, quoth my father.]

"Now,—as conscience is nothing else but the knowledge which the mind has within herself of this; and the judgment, either of approbation or censure, which it unavoidably makes upon the successive actions of our lives; 'tis plain you will say, from the very terms of the proposition,—whenever this inward testimony goes against a man, and he stands self-accused, that he must necessarily be a guilty man.——And, on the contrary, when the report is favourable on his side, and his heart condemns him not:—that it is not a matter of trust, as the apostle intimates, but a matter of certainty and fact, that the conscience is good, and that the man must be good also."

[Then the apostle is altogether in the wrong, I suppose, quoth Dr. Slop, and the Protestant divine is in the right. Sir, have patience, replied my father, for I think it will presently appear that St. Paul and the Protestant divine are both of an opinion.——As nearly so, quoth Dr. Slop, as east is to west;—but this, continued he, lifting both hands, comes from the liberty of the press.

It is no more, at the worst, replied my uncle Toby, than the liberty of the pulpit; for it does not appear that the sermon is printed, or ever likely to be.

Go on, Trim, quoth my father.]

"At first sight this may seem to be a true state of the case: and I make no doubt but the knowledge of right and wrong is so truly impressed upon the mind of man,—that did no such thing ever happen, as that the conscience of a man, by long habits of sin, might (as the scripture assures it may) insensibly become hard;—and, like some tender parts of his body, by much stress and continual hard usage, lose by degrees that nice sense and perception with which God and nature endowed it:—Did this never happen; or was it certain that self-love would never hang the least bias upon the judgment;—or that the little interests below could rise up and perplex the faculties of our upper regions, and encompass them about with clouds and thick darkness:—Could no such thing as favour and affection enter this sacred Court:—Did Wit disdain to take a bribe in it;—or was ashamed to shew its face as an advocate for an unwarrantable enjoyment: Or, lastly, were we assured that Interest stood always unconcerned whilst the cause was hearing—and that Passion never got into the judgment-seat, and pronounced sentence in the stead of Reason, which is supposed always to preside and determine upon the case:—Was this truly so, as the objection must suppose;—no doubt then the religious and moral state of a man would be exactly what he himself esteemed it:—and the guilt or innocence of every man's life could be known, in general, by no better measure, than the degrees of his own approbation and censure.

"I own, in one case, whenever a man's conscience does accuse him (as it seldom errs on that side) that he is guilty; and unless in melancholy and hypocondriac cases, we may safely pronounce upon it, that there is always sufficient grounds for the accusation.

"But the converse of the proposition will not hold true;—namely, that whenever there is guilt, the conscience must accuse; and if it does not, that a man is therefore innocent.——This is not fact—So that the common consolation which some good christian or other is hourly administering to himself,—that he thanks God his mind does not misgive him; and that, consequently, he has a good conscience, because he hath a quiet one,—is fallacious;—and as current as the inference is, and as infallible as the rule appears at first sight, yet when you look nearer to it, and try the truth of this rule upon plain facts,—you see it liable to so much error from a false application;—the principle upon which it goes so often perverted;—the whole force of it lost, and sometimes so vilely cast away, that it is painful to produce the common examples from human life, which confirm the account.

"A man shall be vicious and utterly debauched in his principles;—exceptionable in his conduct to the world; shall live shameless, in the open commission of a sin which no reason or pretence can justify,—a sin by which, contrary to all the workings of humanity, he shall ruin for ever the deluded partner of his guilt;—rob her of her best dowry; and not only cover her own head with dishonour;—but involve a whole virtuous family in shame and sorrow for her sake. Surely, you will think conscience must lead such a man a troublesome life; he can have no rest night or day from its reproaches.

"Alas! Conscience had something else to do all this time, than break in upon him; as Elijah reproached the god Baal,—this domestic god 'was either talking, or pursuing, or was in a journey, or peradventure he slept and could not be awoke.'

"Perhaps He was gone out in company with Honour to fight a duel: to pay off some debt at play;—or dirty annuity, the bargain of his lust; Perhaps Conscience all this time was engaged at home, talking aloud against petty larceny, and executing vengeance upon some such puny crimes as his fortune and rank of life secured him against all temptation of committing; so that he lives as merrily"—[If he was of our church, tho', quoth Dr. Slop, he could not]—"sleeps as soundly in his bed;—and at last meets death as unconcernedly;—perhaps much more so, than a much better man."

[All this is impossible with us, quoth Dr. Slop, turning to my father,— the case could not happen in our church.—It happens in ours, however, replied my father, but too often.——I own, quoth Dr. Slop, (struck a little with my father's frank acknowledgment)—that a man in the Romish church may live as badly;—but then he cannot easily die so.——'Tis little matter, replied my father, with an air of indifference,—how a rascal dies.— I mean, answered Dr. Slop, he would be denied the benefits of the last sacraments.——Pray how many have you in all, said my uncle Toby,—for I always forget?——Seven, answered Dr. Slop.——Humph!—said my uncle Toby; tho' not accented as a note of acquiescence,—but as an interjection of that particular species of surprise, when a man in looking into a drawer, finds more of a thing than he expected.—Humph! replied my uncle Toby. Dr. Slop, who had an ear, understood my uncle Toby as well as if he had wrote a whole volume against the seven sacraments.——Humph! replied Dr. Slop, (stating my uncle Toby's argument over again to him)— Why, Sir, are there not seven cardinal virtues?—Seven mortal sins?— Seven golden candlesticks?—Seven heavens?—'Tis more than I know, replied my uncle Toby.——Are there not seven wonders of the world?—— Seven days of the creation?——Seven planets?——Seven plagues?——That there are, quoth my father with a most affected gravity. But prithee, continued he, go on with the rest of thy characters, Trim.]

"Another is sordid, unmerciful," (here Trim waved his right hand) "a strait-hearted, selfish wretch, incapable either of private friendship or public spirit. Take notice how he passes by the widow and orphan in their distress, and sees all the miseries incident to human life without a sigh or a prayer." [An' please your honours, cried Trim, I think this a viler man than the other.]

"Shall not conscience rise up and sting him on such occasions?——No; thank God there is no occasion, 'I pay every man his own;—I have no fornication to answer to my conscience;—no faithless vows or promises to make up;—I have debauched no man's wife or child; thank God, I am not as other men, adulterers, unjust, or even as this libertine, who stands before me.'

"A third is crafty and designing in his nature. View his whole life;—'tis nothing but a cunning contexture of dark arts and unequitable subterfuges, basely to defeat the true intent of all laws,—plain-dealing and the safe en-joyment of our several properties.——You will see such a one working out a frame of little designs upon the ignorance and perplexities of the poor and needy man;—shall raise a fortune upon the inexperience of a youth, or the unsuspecting temper of his friend, who would have trusted him with his life.

"When old age comes on, and repentance calls him to look back upon his black account, and state it over again with his conscience—Conscience looks into the Statutes at Large;—finds no express law broken by what he has done;—perceives no penalty or forfeiture of goods and chattels in-curred;—sees no scourge waving over his head, or prison opening his gates upon him:—What is there to affright his conscience?—Conscience has got safely entrenched behind the Letter of the Law; sits there invulnerable, fortified with **Cases** and **Reports** so strongly on all sides;—that it is not preaching can dispossess it of its hold."

[Here Corporal Trim and my uncle Toby exchanged looks with each other.——Aye, aye, Trim! quoth my uncle Toby, shaking his head,—these are but sorry fortifications, Trim.——O! very poor work, answered Trim, to what your Honour and I make of it.——The character of this last man, said Dr. Slop, interrupting Trim, is more detestable than all the rest; and seems to have been taken from some pettifogging Lawyer amongst you:—Amongst us, a man's conscience could not possibly continue so long blinded,—three times in a year, at least, he must go to confession. Will that restore it to sight? quoth my uncle Toby.——Go on, Trim, quoth my father, or Obadiah will have got back before thou hast got to the end of thy sermon.——'Tis a very short one, replied Trim.——I wish it was longer, quoth my uncle Toby, for I like it hugely.——Trim went on.]

"A fourth man shall want even this refuge;—shall break through all their ceremony of slow chicane;—scorns the doubtful workings of secret plots and cautious trains to bring about his purpose;—See the barefaced villain, how he cheats, lies, perjures, robs, murders!——Horrid!——But indeed much better was not to be expected, in the present case—the poor man was in the dark!—his priest had got the keeping of his conscience;—and all he would let him know of it, was, That he must believe in the Pope;—go to Mass;—cross himself;—tell his beads;—be a good Catholic, and that this, in all conscience, was enough to carry him to heaven. What;—if he perjures!——Why;—he had a mental reservation in it.—But if he is so wicked and abandoned a wretch as you represent him;—if he robs,—if he stabs, will not conscience, on every such act, receive a wound itself?——Aye,—but the man has carried it to confession;—the wound digests there, and will do well enough, and in a short time be quite healed up by absolu-tion. O Popery! what hast thou to answer for?—when, not content with the too many natural and fatal ways, thro' which the heart of man is every day thus treacherous to itself above all things;—thou hast wilfully set open the wide gate of deceit before the face of this unwary traveller, too apt, God knows, to go astray of himself; and confidently speak peace to himself, when there is no peace.

"Of this the common instances which I have drawn out of life, are too notorious to require much evidence. If any man doubts the reality of them, or thinks it impossible for a man to be such a bubble to himself,—I must refer him a moment to his own reflections, and will then venture to trust my appeal with his own heart.

"Let him consider in how different a degree of detestation, numbers of wicked actions stand there, tho' equally bad and vicious in their own natures;—he will soon find, that such of them as strong inclination and custom have prompted him to commit, are generally dressed out and painted with all the false beauties which a soft and a flattering hand can give them;—and that the others, to which he feels no propensity, appear, at once, naked and deformed, surrounded with all the true circumstances of folly and dishonour.

"When David surprised Saul sleeping in the cave, and cut off the skirt of his robe—we read his heart smote him for what he had done:—But in the matter of Uriah, where a faithful and gallant servant, whom he ought to have loved and honoured, fell to make way for his lust,—where conscience had so much greater reason to take the alarm, his heart smote him not. A whole year had almost passed from the first commission of that crime, to the time Nathan was sent to reprove him; and we read not once of the least sorrow or compunction of heart which he testified, during all that time, for what he had done.

"Thus conscience, this once able monitor,—placed on high as a judge within us, and intended by our Maker as a just and equitable one too,—by an unhappy train of causes and impediments, takes often such imperfect cognizance of what passes,—does its office so negligently,—sometimes so corruptly,—that it is not to be trusted alone; and therefore we find there is a necessity, an absolute necessity, of joining another principle with it, to aid, if not govern, its determinations.

"So that if you would form a just judgment of what is of infinite importance to you not to be misled in,—namely, in what degree of real merit you stand either as an honest man, an useful citizen, a faithful subject to your king, or a good servant to your God,—call in religion and morality.—— Look, What is written in the law of God?——How readest thou?——Consult calm reason and the unchangeable obligations of justice and truth;— what say they?

"Let Conscience determine the matter upon these reports;—and then if thy heart condemns thee not, which is the case the apostle supposes,—the rule will be infallible";—[Here Dr. Slop fell asleep]—"thou wilt have confidence towards God;—that is, have just grounds to believe the judgment thou hast passed upon thyself, is the judgment of God; and nothing else but an anticipation of that righteous sentence which will be pronounced upon thee hereafter by that Being, to whom thou art finally to give an account of thy actions.

" 'Blessed is the man,' indeed, then, as the author of the book of Ecclesiasticus expresses it, 'who is not pricked with the multitude of his sins: Blessed is the man whose heart hath not condemned him; whether he be rich, or whether he be poor, if he have a good heart' (a heart thus guided and informed) 'he shall at all times rejoice in a cheerful countenance; his mind shall tell him more than seven watch-men that sit above upon a tower on high.' "——[A tower has no strength, quoth my uncle Toby, unless 'tis flanked.]——"In the darkest doubts it shall conduct him safer than a thousand casuists, and give the state he lives in, a better security for his behaviour than all the causes and restrictions put together, which lawmakers are forced to multiply:—'Forced,' I say, as things stand; human laws not being a matter of original choice, but of pure necessity, brought in to fence against the mischievous effects of those consciences which are no law unto themselves; well intending, by the many provisions made,—that in all such corrupt and misguided cases, where principles and the checks of conscience will not make us upright,—to supply their force, and, by the terrors of gaols and halters, oblige us to it."

[I see plainly, said my father, that this sermon has been composed to be preached at the Temple,—or at some Assize.——I like the reasoning,—and am sorry that Dr. Slop has fallen asleep before the time of his conviction:—for it is now clear, that the Parson, as I thought at first, never insulted St. Paul in the least;—nor has there been, brother, the least difference between them.——A great matter, if they had differed, replied my uncle Toby,—the best friends in the world may differ sometimes.——True,—brother Toby, quoth my father, shaking hands with him—we'll fill our pipes, brother, and then Trim shall go on.

Well,—what dost thou think of it? said my father, speaking to Corporal Trim, as he reached his tobacco-box.

I think, answered the Corporal, that the seven watchmen upon the tower, who, I suppose, are all sentinels there,—are more, an' please your Honour, than were necessary;—and, to go on at that rate, would harass a regiment all to pieces, which a commanding officer, who loves his men, will never do, if he can help it, because two sentinels, added the Corporal, are as good as twenty.——I have been a commanding officer myself in the *Corps de Garde* a hundred times, continued Trim, rising an inch higher in his figure, as he spoke,—and all the time I had the honour to serve his Majesty King William, in relieving the most considerable ports, I never left more than two in my life.——Very right, Trim, quoth my uncle Toby,—but you do not consider, Trim, that the towers, in Solomon's days, were not such things as our bastions, flanked and defended by other works;—this, Trim, was an invention since Solomon's death; nor had they hornworks, or ravelins before the curtin, in his time;—or such a fossé as we make with a curvette in the middle of it, and with covered ways and counterscarps pallisadoed along it, to guard against a *Coup de main:*—So that the seven men upon the tower were a party, I dare say, from the *Corps de Garde*, set there, not only to look out, but to defend it.—They could be no more, an' please your Honour, than a Corporal's Guard.——My father smiled inwardly, but not outwardly;—the subject being rather too serious, considering what had happened, to make a jest of.——So putting his pipe into his mouth, which he had just lighted,—he contented himself with ordering Trim to read on. He read on as follows:]

"To have the fear of God before our eyes, and, in our mutual dealings with each other, to govern our actions by the eternal measures of right and wrong:—The first of these will comprehend the duties of religion;—the second, those of morality, which are so inseparably connected together, that you cannot divide these two tables, even in imagination, (tho' the attempt is often made in practice) without breaking and mutually destroying them both.

"I said the attempt is often made; and so it is;—there being nothing more common than to see a man who has no sense at all of religion, and indeed has so much honesty as to pretend to none, who would take it as the bitterest affront, should you but hint at a suspicion of his moral character, —or imagine he was not conscientiously just and scrupulous to the uttermost mite.

"When there is some appearance that it is so,—tho' one is unwilling even to suspect the appearance of so amiable a virtue as moral honesty, yet were we to look into the grounds of it, in the present case, I am persuaded we should find little reason to envy such a one the honour of his motive.

"Let him declaim as pompously as he chooses upon the subject, it will be found to rest upon no better foundation than either his interest, his pride, his ease, or some such little and changeable passion as will give us but small dependence upon his actions in matters of great distress.

"I will illustrate this by an example.

"I know the banker I deal with, or the physician I usually call in," [There is no need, cried Dr. Slop, (waking) to call in any physician in this case] "to be neither of them men of much religion: I hear them make a jest of it every day, and treat all its sanctions with so much scorn, as to put the matter past doubt. Well;—notwithstanding this, I put my fortune into the hands of the one:—and what is dearer still to me, I trust my life to the honest skill of the other.

"Now let me examine what is my reason for this great confidence. Why, in the first place, I believe there is no probability that either of them will employ the power I put into their hands to my disadvantage;—I consider that honesty serves the purposes of this life:—I know their success in the world depends upon the fairness of their characters.—In a word, I'm persuaded that they cannot hurt me without hurting themselves more.

"But put it otherwise, namely, that interest lay, for once, on the other side; that a case should happen, wherein the one, without stain to his reputation, could secrete my fortune, and leave me naked in the world;— or that the other could send me out of it, and enjoy an estate by my death, without dishonour to himself or his art:—In this case, what hold have I of either of them?—Religion, the strongest of all motives, is out of the question;—Interest, the next most powerful motive in the world, is strongly against me:—What have I left to cast into the opposite scale to balance this temptation?—Alas! I have nothing,—nothing but what is lighter than a bubble—I must lie at the mercy of Honour, or some such capricious principle—Strait security for two of the most valuable blessings!—my property and myself.

"As, therefore, we can have no dependence upon morality without religion;—so, on the other hand, there is nothing better to be expected from religion without morality; nevertheless, 'tis no prodigy to see a man whose real moral character stands very low, who yet entertains the highest notion of himself in the light of a religious man.

"He shall not only be covetous, revengeful, implacable,—but even wanting in points of common honesty; yet inasmuch as he talks aloud against the infidelity of the age,—is zealous for some points of religion,—goes twice a day to church,—attends the sacraments,—and amuses himself with a few instrumental parts of religion,—shall cheat his conscience into a judgment, that, for this, he is a religious man, and has discharged truly his duty to God: And you will find that such a man, through force of this delusion, generally looks down with spiritual pride upon every other man who has less affectation of piety,—though, perhaps, ten times more real honesty than himself.

" 'This likewise is a sore evil under the sun'; and I believe, there is no one mistaken principle, which, for its time, has wrought more serious mischiefs.——For a general proof of this,—examine the history of the Romish church";—[Well, what can you make of that? cried Dr. Slop]—"see what scenes of cruelty, murder, rapine, bloodshed,"—[They may thank their own obstinacy, cried Dr. Slop.]—"have all been sanctified by a religion not strictly governed by morality.

"In how many kingdoms of the world"—[Here Trim kept waving his right hand from the sermon to the extent of his arm, returning it backwards and forwards to the conclusion of the paragraph.]

"In how many kingdoms of the world has the crusading sword of this misguided saint-errant, spared neither age nor merit, or sex, or condition?—and, as he fought under the banners of a religion which set him loose from justice and humanity, he shewed none; mercilessly trampled upon both,—heard neither the cries of the unfortunate, nor pitied their distresses."

[I have been in many a battle, an' please your Honour, quoth Trim, sighing, but never in so melancholy a one as this,—I would not have drawn a trigger in it against these poor souls,—to have been made a general officer.——Why? what do you understand of the affair? said Dr. Slop, looking towards Trim, with something more of contempt than the Corporal's honest heart deserved.——What do you know, friend, about this battle you talk of?——I know, replied Trim, that I never refused quarter in my life to any man who cried out for it;—but to a woman or a child, continued Trim, before I would level my musket at them, I would lose my life a thousand times.——Here's a crown for thee, Trim, to drink with Obadiah to-night, quoth my uncle Toby, and I'll give Obadiah another too.—God bless your Honour, replied Trim,—I had rather these poor women and children had it.——Thou art an honest fellow, quoth my uncle Toby.——My father nodded his head,—as much as to say,—and so he is.——

But prithee, Trim, said my father, make an end,—for I see thou hast but a leaf or two left.

Corporal Trim read on.]

"If the testimony of past centuries in this matter is not sufficient,—consider at this instant, how the votaries of that religion are every day thinking to do service and honour to God, by actions which are a dishonour and scandal to themselves.

"To be convinced of this, go with me for a moment into the prisons of the Inquisition."——[God help my poor brother Tom.]——"Behold Religion, with Mercy and Justice chained down under her feet,——there sitting ghastly upon a black tribunal, propped up with racks and instruments of torment. Hark!—hark! what a piteous groan!"——[Here Trim's face turned as pale as ashes.]——"See the melancholy wretch who uttered it" —[Here the tears began to trickle down.]——"just brought forth to undergo the anguish of a mock trial, and endure the utmost pains that a studied system of cruelty has been able to invent."——[D—n them all, quoth Trim, his colour returning into his face as red as blood.]——"Behold this helpless victim delivered up to his tormentors,—his body so wasted with sorrow and confinement."——[Oh! 'tis my brother, cried poor Trim in a most passionate exclamation, dropping the sermon upon the ground, and clapping his hands together—I fear 'tis poor Tom. My father's and my uncle Toby's heart yearned with sympathy for the poor fellow's distress; even Slop himself acknowledged pity for him.——Why, Trim, said my father, this is not a history,—'tis a sermon thou art reading; prithee begin the sentence again.]——"Behold this helpless victim delivered up to his tormentors,—his body so wasted with sorrow and confinement, you will see every nerve and muscle as it suffers.

"Observe the last movement of that horrid engine!"——[I would rather face a cannon, quoth Trim, stamping.]——"See what convulsions it has thrown him into!——Consider the nature of the posture in which he now lies stretched,—what exquisite tortures he endures by it!"——[I hope 'tis not in Portugal.]——"'Tis all nature can bear! Good God! see how it keeps his weary soul hanging upon his trembling lips!" [I would not read another line of it, quoth Trim, for all this world;—I fear, an' please your Honours, all this is in Portugal, where my poor brother Tom is. I tell thee, Trim, again, quoth my father, 'tis not an historical account,—'tis a description. ——'Tis only a description, honest man, quoth Slop, there's not a word of truth in it.——That's another story, replied my father.—However as Trim reads it with so much concern,—'tis cruelty to force him to go on with it.—Give me hold of the sermon, Trim,—I'll finish it for thee, and thou may'st go. I must stay and hear it too, replied Trim, if your Honour will allow me;—tho' I would not read it myself for a Colonel's pay.——Poor Trim! quoth my uncle Toby. My father went on.]—

"——Consider the nature of the posture in which he now lies stretched, —what exquisite torture he endures by it!—'Tis all nature can bear! Good God! See how it keeps his weary soul hanging upon his trembling lips,— willing to take its leave,——but not suffered to depart!——Behold the unhappy wretch led back to his cell!"——[Then, thank God, however, quoth Trim, they have not killed him.]——"See him dragged out of it again to meet the flames, and the insults in his last agonies, which this principle,—this principle, that there can be religion without mercy, has prepared for him."——[Then, thank God,—he is dead, quoth Trim,—he is out of his pain,—and they have done their worst at him.——O Sirs!—— Hold your peace, Trim, said my father, going on with the sermon, lest Trim should incense Dr. Slop,—we shall never have done at this rate.]

"The surest way to try the merit of any disputed notion is, to trace down the consequences such a notion has produced, and compare them with the spirit of Christianity;—'tis the short and decisive rule which our Saviour hath left us, for these and such like cases, and it is worth a thousand arguments—'By their fruits ye shall know them.'

"I will add no further to the length of this sermon, than by two or three short and independent rules deducible from it.

"First, Whenever a man talks loudly against religion, always suspect that it is not his reason, but his passions, which have got the better of his creed. A bad life and a good belief are disagreeable and troublesome neighbours, and where they separate, depend upon it, 'tis for no other cause but quietness' sake.

"Secondly, When a man, thus represented, tells you in any particular instance,—That such a thing goes against his conscience,—always believe he means exactly the same thing, as when he tells you such a thing goes against his stomach;—a present want of appetite being generally the true cause of both.

"In a word,—trust that man in nothing, who has not a Conscience in every thing.

"And, in your own case, remember this plain distinction, a mistake in which has ruined thousands,—that your conscience is not a law:—No, God and reason made the law, and have placed conscience within you to determine;— not, like an Asiatic Cadi, according to the ebbs and flows of his own passions, —but like a British judge in this land of liberty and good sense, who makes no new law, but faithfully declares that law which he knows already written."

FINIS

Thou hast read the sermon extremely well, Trim, quoth my father.—— If he had spared his comments, replied Dr. Slop,—he would have read it much better. I should have read it ten times better, Sir, answered Trim, but that my heart was so full.—That was the very reason, Trim, replied my father, which has made thee read the sermon as well as thou hast done; and if the clergy of our church, continued my father, addressing himself to Dr. Slop, would take part in what they deliver as deeply as this poor fellow has done,—as their compositions are fine;—[I deny it, quoth Dr. Slop]—I maintain it,—that the eloquence of our pulpits, with such subjects to enflame it, would be a model for the whole world:—But alas! continued my father, and I own it, Sir, with sorrow, that, like French politicians in this respect, what they gain in the cabinet they lose in the field.——'Twere a pity, quoth my uncle, that this should be lost. I like the sermon well, replied my father,—'tis dramatic,—and there is something in that way of writing, when skilfully managed, which catches the attention.——We preach much in that way with us, said Dr. Slop.—I know that very well, said my father, —but in a tone and manner which disgusted Dr. Slop, full as much as his assent, simply, could have pleased him.——But in this, added Dr. Slop, a little piqued,—our sermons have greatly the advantage, that we never introduce any character into them below a patriarch or a patriarch's wife, or a martyr or a saint.——There are some very bad characters in this, however, said my father, and I do not think the sermon a jot the worse for 'em.——But pray, quoth my uncle Toby,—who's can this be?—How could it get into my Stevinus? A man must be as great a conjurer as Stevinus, said my father, to resolve the second question:—The first, I think, is not so difficult;—for unless my judgment greatly deceives me,—I know the author, for 'tis wrote, certainly, by the parson of the parish.

The similitude of the style and manner of it, with those my father constantly had heard preached in his parish-church, was the ground of his conjecture,—proving it as strongly, as an argument *à priori* could prove such a thing to a philosophic mind, That it was Yorick's and no one's else: —It was proved to be so, *à posteriori*, the day after, when Yorick sent a servant to my uncle Toby's house to enquire after it.

It seems that Yorick, who was inquisitive after all kinds of knowledge, had borrowed Stevinus of my uncle Toby, and had carelessly popped his sermon, as soon as he had made it, into the middle of Stevinus; and by an act of forgetfulness, to which he was ever subject, he had sent Stevinus home, and his sermon to keep him company.

Ill-fated sermon! Thou wast lost, after this recovery of thee, a second time, dropped thro' an unsuspected fissure in thy master's pocket, down into a treacherous and a tattered lining,—trod deep into the dirt by the left hind-foot of his Rosinante inhumanly stepping upon thee as thou falledst;—buried ten days in the mire,—raised up out of it by a beggar,— sold for a halfpenny to a parish-clerk,—transferred to his parson,—lost for ever to thy own, the remainder of his days,—nor restored to his restless Manes till this very moment, that I tell the world the story.

Can the reader believe, that this sermon of Yorick's was preached at an assize, in the cathedral of York, before a thousand witnesses, ready to give oath to it, by a certain prebendary of that church, and actually printed by him when he had done,—and within so short a space as two years and three months after Yorick's death?——Yorick indeed was never better served in his life;—but it was a little hard to maltreat him after, and plunder him after he was laid in his grave.

However, as the gentleman who did it was in perfect charity with Yorick,—and, in conscious justice, printed but a few copies to give away;— and that I am told he could moreover have made as good a one himself, had he thought fit,—I declare I would not have published this anecdote to the world;—nor do I publish it with an intent to hurt his character and advancement in the church;—I leave that to others;—but I find myself impelled by two reasons, which I cannot withstand.

The first is, That in doing justice, I may give rest to Yorick's ghost;— which—as the country-people, and some others, believe,—still walks.

The second reason is, That, by laying open this story to the world, I gain an opportunity of informing it,—That in case the character of parson Yorick, and this sample of his sermons, is liked,—there are now in the possession of the Shandy family, as many as will make a handsome volume, at the world's service,—and much good may they do it.

Chapter 18

Obadiah gained the two crowns without dispute; for he came in jingling, with all the instruments in the green bays bag we spoke of, slung across his body, just as Corporal Trim went out of the room.

It is now proper, I think, quoth Dr. Slop, (clearing up his looks) as we are in a condition to be of some service to Mrs. Shandy, to send up stairs to know how she goes on.

I have ordered, answered my father, the old midwife to come down to us upon the least difficulty;—for you must know, Dr. Slop, continued my father, with a perplexed kind of a smile upon his countenance, that by express treaty, solemnly ratified between me and my wife, you are no more than an auxiliary in this affair,—and not so much as that,—unless the lean old mother of a midwife above stairs cannot do without you.—Women have their particular fancies, and in points of this nature, continued my father, where they bear the whole burden, and suffer so much acute pain for the advantage of our families, and the good of the species,—they claim a right of deciding, *en Souveraines*, in whose hands, and in what fashion, they choose to undergo it.

They are in the right of it,—quoth my uncle Toby. But, Sir, replied Dr. Slop, not taking notice of my uncle Toby's opinion, but turning to my father,—they had better govern in other points;—and a father of a family, who wishes its perpetuity, in my opinion, had better exchange this prerogative with them, and give up some other rights in lieu of it.—I know not, quoth my father, answering a little too testily, to be quite dispassionate in what he said,—I know not, quoth he, what we have left to give up, in lieu of who shall bring our children into the world, unless that,—of who shall beget them.——One would almost give up any thing, replied Dr. Slop.—— I beg your pardon,—answered my uncle Toby.——Sir, replied Dr. Slop, it would astonish you to know what improvements we have made of late years in all branches of obstetrical knowledge, but particularly in that one single point of the safe and expeditious extraction of the foetus,—which has received such lights, that, for my part (holding up his hands) I declare I wonder how the world has—I wish, quoth my uncle Toby, you had seen what prodigious armies we had in Flanders.

Chapter 19

I have dropped the curtain over this scene for a minute,—to remind you of one thing,—and to inform you of another.

What I have to inform you, comes, I own, a little out of its due course; for it should have been told a hundred and fifty pages ago, but that I foresaw then 'twould come in pat hereafter, and be of more advantage here than elsewhere.——Writers had need look before them, to keep up the spirit and connection of what they have in hand.

When these two things are done,—the curtain shall be drawn up again, and my uncle Toby, my father, and Dr. Slop, shall go on with their discourse, without any more interruption.

First, then, the matter which I have to remind you of, is this;—that from the specimens of singularity in my father's notions in the point of Christian-names, and that other previous point thereto,—you was led, I think, into an opinion, (and I am sure I said as much) that my father was a gentleman altogether as odd and whimsical in fifty other opinions. In truth, there was not a stage in the life of man, from the very first act of his begetting,—down to the lean and slippered pantaloon in his second childishness, but he had some favourite notion to himself, springing out of it, as sceptical, and as far out of the high-way of thinking, as these two which have been explained.

——Mr. Shandy, my father, Sir, would see nothing in the light in which others placed it;—he placed things in his own light;—he would weigh nothing in common scales;—no, he was too refined a researcher to lie open to so gross an imposition.—To come at the exact weight of things in the scientific steel-yard, the fulcrum, he would say, should be almost invisible, to avoid all friction from popular tenets;—without this the minutiae of philosophy, which would always turn the balance, will have no weight at all. Knowledge, like matter, he would affirm, was divisible *in infinitum;*—that the grains and scruples were as much a part of it, as the gravitation of the whole world.——In a word, he would say, error was error,—no matter where it fell,—whether in a fraction,—or a pound,—'twas alike fatal to truth, and she was kept down at the bottom of her well, as inevitably by a mistake in the dust of a butterfly's wing,—as in the disk of the sun, the moon, and all the stars of heaven put together.

He would often lament that it was for want of considering this properly, and of applying it skilfully to civil matters, as well as to speculative truths, that so many things in this world were out of joint;—that the political arch was giving way;—and that the very foundations of our excellent constitution, in church and state, were so sapped as estimators had reported.

You cry out, he would say, we are a ruined, undone people. Why? he would ask, making use of the sorites or syllogism of Zeno and Chrysippus, without knowing it belonged to them.——Why? why are we a ruined people?——Because we are corrupted.——Whence is it, dear Sir, that we are corrupted?——Because we are needy;—our poverty, and not our wills, consent.——And wherefore, he would add, are we needy?——From the neglect, he would answer, of our pence and our halfpence:—Our bank notes, Sir, our guineas,—nay our shillings take care of themselves.

'Tis the same, he would say, throughout the whole circle of the sciences;—the great, the established points of them, are not to be broken in upon.——The laws of nature will defend themselves;—but error—(he would add, looking earnestly at my mother)—error, Sir, creeps in thro' the minute holes and small crevices which human nature leaves unguarded.

This turn of thinking in my father, is what I had to remind you of:—The point you are to be informed of, and which I have reserved for this place, is as follows.

Amongst the many and excellent reasons, with which my father had urged my mother to accept of Dr. Slop's assistance preferably to that of the old woman,—there was one of a very singular nature; which, when he had done arguing the matter with her as a Christian, and came to argue it over again with her as a philosopher, he had put his whole strength to, depending indeed upon it as his sheet-anchor.——It failed him; tho' from no defect in the argument itself; but that, do what he could, he was not able for his soul to make her comprehend the drift of it.——Cursed luck!——said he to himself, one afternoon, as he walked out of the room, after he had been stating it for an hour and a half to her, to no manner of purpose;—cursed luck! said he, biting his lip as he shut the door,—for a man to be master of one of the finest chains of reasoning in nature,—and have a wife at the same time with such a head-piece, that he cannot hang up a single inference within side of it, to save his soul from destruction.

This argument, though it was entirely lost upon my mother,—had more weight with him, than all his other arguments joined together:—I will therefore endeavour to do it justice,—and set it forth with all the perspicuity I am master of.

My father set out upon the strength of these two following axioms:

First, That an ounce of a man's own wit, was worth a ton of other people's; and,

Secondly, (Which by the bye, was the ground-work of the first axiom,—tho' it comes last) That every man's wit must come from every man's own soul,—and no other body's.

Now, as it was plain to my father that all souls were by nature equal,—and that the great difference between the most acute and the most obtuse understanding—was from no original sharpness or bluntness of one thinking substance above or below another,—but arose merely from the lucky or unlucky organization of the body, in that part where the soul principally took up her residence,—he had made it the subject of his enquiry to find out the identical place.

Now, from the best accounts he had been able to get of this matter, he was satisfied it could not be where Des Cartes had fixed it, upon the top of the pineal gland of the brain; which, as he philosophized, formed a cushion for her about the size of a marrow pea; tho', to speak the truth, as so many nerves did terminate all in that one place,—'twas no bad conjecture;—and my father had certainly fallen with that great philosopher plumb into the centre of the mistake, had it not been for my uncle Toby, who rescued him out of it, by a story he told him of a Walloon officer at the battle of Landen, who had one part of his brain shot away by a musket-ball,—and another part of it taken out after by a French surgeon; and after all, recovered, and did his duty very well without it.

If death, said my father, reasoning with himself, is nothing but the separation of the soul from the body; and if it is true that people can walk about and do their business without brains,—then certes the soul does not inhabit there. Q.E.D.

As for that certain, very thin, subtle and very fragrant juice which Coglionissimo Borri, the great Milanese physician affirms, in a letter to Bartholine, to have discovered in the cellulae of the occipital parts of the cerebellum, and which he likewise affirms to be the principal seat of the reasonable soul, (for, you must know, in these latter and more enlightened ages, there are two souls in every man living,—the one, according to the great Metheglingius, being called the *Animus*, the other, the *Anima;*)—as for the opinion, I say, of Borri,—my father could never subscribe to it by any means; the very idea of so noble, so refined, so immaterial, and so exalted a being as the *Anima*, or even the *Animus*, taking up her residence, and sitting dabbling, like a tadpole all day long, both summer and winter, in a puddle,—or in a liquid of any kind, how thick or thin soever, he would say, shocked his imagination; he would scarce give the doctrine a hearing.

What, therefore, seemed the least liable to objections of any, was that the chief sensorium, or headquarters of the soul, and to which place all intelligences were referred, and from whence all her mandates were issued,— was in, or near, the cerebellum,—or rather somewhere about the medulla oblongata, wherein it was generally agreed by Dutch anatomists, that all the minute nerves from all the organs of the seven senses concentered, like streets and winding alleys, into a square.

So far there was nothing singular in my father's opinion,—he had the best of philosophers, of all ages and climates, to go along with him.——But here he took a road of his own, setting up another Shandean hypothesis upon these corner-stones they had laid for him;—and which said hypothesis equally stood its ground; whether the subtlety and fineness of the soul depended upon the temperature and clearness of the said liquor, or of the finer net-work and texture in the cerebellum itself; which opinion he favoured.

He maintained, that next to the due care to be taken in the act of propagation of each individual, which required all the thought in the world, as it laid the foundation of this incomprehensible contexture, in which wit, memory, fancy, eloquence, and what is usually meant by the name of good natural parts, do consist;—that next to this and his Christian-name, which were the two original and most efficacious causes of all;—that the third cause, or rather what logicians call the *Causa sine quâ non*, and without which all that was done was of no manner of significance,—was the preservation of this delicate and fine-spun web, from the havoc which was generally made in it by the violent compression and crush which the head was made to undergo, by the nonsensical method of bringing us into the world by that foremost.

——This requires explanation.

My father, who dipped into all kinds of books, upon looking into *Lithopaedus Senonesis de Partu difficili,*[1] published by Adrianus Smelvgot, had

[1]The author is here twice mistaken;—for Lithopaedus should be wrote thus, *Lithopaedii Senonensis Icon.* The second mistake is, that this Lithopaedus is not an author, but a drawing of a petrified child. The account of this, published by Athosius 1580, may be seen at the end of Cordaeus's works in Spachius. Mr. Tristram Shandy has been led into this error, either from seeing Lithopaedus's name of late in a catalogue of learned writers in Dr.—, or by mistaking Lithopaedus for Trinecavellius,—from the too great similitude of the names.

found out, that the lax and pliable state of a child's head in parturition, the bones of the cranium having no sutures at that time, was such,—that by force of the woman's efforts, which, in strong labour-pains, was equal, upon an average, to the weight of 470 pounds avoirdupois acting perpendicularly upon it;—it so happened, that in 49 instances out of 50, the said head was compressed and moulded into the shape of an oblong conical piece of dough, such as a pastry-cook generally rolls up in order to make a pie of.——Good God! cried my father, what havoc and destruction must this make in the infinitely fine and tender texture of the cerebellum!—Or if there is such a juice as Borri pretends,—is it not enough to make the clearest liquid in the world both feculent and mothery?

But how great was his apprehension, when he farther understood, that this force acting upon the very vertex of the head, not only injured the brain itself, or cerebrum,—but that it necessarily squeezed and propelled the cerebrum towards the cerebellum, which was the immediate seat of the understanding!——Angels and ministers of grace defend us! cried my father,—can any soul withstand this shock?—No wonder the intellectual web is so rent and tattered as we see it; and that so many of our best heads are no better than a puzzled skein of silk,—all perplexity,—all confusion within-side.

But when my father read on, and was let into the secret, that when a child was turned topsy-turvy, which was easy for an operator to do, and was extracted by the feet;—that instead of the cerebrum being propelled towards the cerebellum, the cerebellum, on the contrary, was propelled simply towards the cerebrum, where it could do no manner of hurt:—By heavens! cried he, the world is in conspiracy to drive out what little wit God has given us,—and the professors of the obstetric art are lifted into the same conspiracy.——What is it to me which end of my son comes foremost into the world, provided all goes right after, and his cerebellum escapes uncrushed?

It is the nature of an hypothesis, when once a man has conceived it, that it assimilates every thing to itself, as proper nourishment; and, from the first moment of your begetting it, it generally grows the stronger by every thing you see, hear, read, or understand. This is of great use.

When my father was gone with this about a month, there was scarce a phenomenon of stupidity or of genius, which he could not readily solve by it;—it accounted for the eldest son being the greatest blockhead in the family.—Poor devil, he would say,—he made way for the capacity of his younger brothers.—It unriddled the observations of drivellers and monstrous heads,—shewing *à priori*, it could not be otherwise,—unless * * * * I don't know what. It wonderfully explained and accounted for the acumen of the Asiatic genius, and that spritelier turn, and a more penetrating intuition of minds, in warmer climates; not from the loose and commonplace solution of a clearer sky, and a more perpetual sunshine, etc.—which for aught we knew, might as well rarefy and dilute the faculties of the soul into nothing, by one extreme,—as they are condensed in colder climates by the other;—but he traced the affair up to its spring-head;—shewed that, in warmer climates, nature had laid a lighter tax upon the fairest parts of the

creation;—their pleasures more;—the necessity of their pains less, insomuch that the pressure and resistance upon the vertex was so slight, that
the whole organization of the cerebellum was preserved;—nay, he did not
believe, in natural births, that so much as a single thread of the network
was broke or displaced,—so that the soul might just act as she liked.

When my father had got so far,—what a blaze of light did the accounts
of the Caesarean section, and of the towering geniuses who had come safe
into the world by it, cast upon this hypothesis? Here you see, he would say,
there was no injury done to the sensorium;—no pressure of the head against
the pelvis;—no propulsion of the cerebrum towards the cerebellum, either
by the *os pubis* on this side, or the *os coxygis* on that;—and pray, what were
the happy consequences? Why, Sir, your Julius Caesar, who gave the
operation a name;—and your Hermes Trismegistus, who was born so before ever the operation had a name;—your Scipio Africanus; your Manlius
Torquatus; our Edward the Sixth,—who, had he lived, would have done
the same honour to the hypothesis:—These, and many more who figured
high in the annals of fame,—all came side-way, Sir, into the world.

The incision of the abdomen and uterus ran for six weeks together in my
father's head;—he had read, and was satisfied, that wounds in the epi-
gastrium, and those in the matrix, were not mortal;—so that the belly of the
mother might be opened extremely well to give a passage to the child.——
He mentioned the thing one afternoon to my mother,—merely as a matter
of fact; but seeing her turn as pale as ashes at the very mention of it, as
much as the operation flattered his hopes,—he thought it as well to say no
more of it,—contenting himself with admiring,—what he thought was to no
purpose to propose.

This was my father Mr. Shandy's hypothesis; concerning which I have
only to add, that my brother Bobby did as great honour to it (whatever he
did to the family) as any one of the great heroes we spoke of: For happening not only to be christened, as I told you, but to be born too, when my
father was at Epsom,—being moreover my mother's first child,—coming
into the world with his head foremost,—and turning out afterwards a lad
of wonderful slow parts,—my father spelt all these together into his opinion: and as he had failed at one end,—he was determined to try the other.

This was not to be expected from one of the sisterhood, who are not
easily to be put out of their way,—and was therefore one of my father's
great reasons in favour of a man of science, whom he could better deal with.

Of all men in the world, Dr. Slop was the fittest for my father's purpose;
—for though this new invented forceps was the armour he had proved, and
what he maintained to be the safest instrument of deliverance, yet, it
seems, he had scattered a word or two in his book, in favour of the very
thing which ran in my father's fancy;—tho' not with a view to the soul's
good in extracting by the feet, as was my father's system,—but for reasons
merely obstetrical.

This will account for the coalition betwixt my father and Dr. Slop, in the
ensuing discourse, which went a little hard against my uncle Toby.——In
what manner a plain man, with nothing but common sense, could bear up
against two such allies in science,—is hard to conceive.——You may con-

jecture upon it, if you please,—and whilst your imagination is in motion, you may encourage it to go on, and discover by what causes and effects in nature it could come to pass, that my uncle Toby got his modesty by the wound he received upon his groin.——You may raise a system to account for the loss of my nose by marriage-articles,—and shew the world how it could happen, that I should have the misfortune to be called Tristram, in opposition to my father's hypothesis, and the wish of the whole family, Godfathers and Godmothers not excepted.—These, with fifty other points left yet unravelled, you may endeavour to solve if you have time;—but I tell you beforehand it will be in vain, for not the sage Alquife, the magician in *Don Belianis of Greece*, nor the no less famous Urganda, the sorceress, his wife, (were they alive) could pretend to come within a league of the truth.

The reader will be content to wait for a full explanation of these matters till the next year,—when a series of things will be laid open which he little expects.

BOOK III

Multitudinis imperitae non formido judicia; meis tamen, rogo, parcant opusculis—
in quibus fuit propositi semper, a jocis ad seria, a seriis vicissim ad jocos transire.
——Joan. Saresberiensis, *Episcopus Lugdun.*

CHAPTER I

"I wish, Dr. Slop," quoth my uncle Toby, (repeating his wish for Dr. Slop a second time, and with a degree of more zeal and earnestness in his manner of wishing, than he had wished at first)—"I wish, Dr. Slop," quoth my uncle Toby, "you had seen what prodigious armies we had in Flanders."

My uncle Toby's wish did Dr. Slop a disservice which his heart never intended any man,—Sir, it confounded him—and thereby putting his ideas first into confusion, and then to flight, he could not rally them again for the soul of him.

In all disputes,—male or female,—whether for honour, for profit, or for love,—it makes no difference in the case;—nothing is more dangerous, Madam, than a wish coming sideways in this unexpected manner upon a man: the safest way in general to take off the force of the wish, is for the party wished at, instantly to get upon his legs—and wish the wisher something in return, of pretty near the same value,—so balancing the account upon the spot, you stand as you were—nay sometimes gain the advantage of the attack by it.

This will be fully illustrated to the world in my chapter of wishes.——

Dr. Slop did not understand the nature of this defence;—he was puzzled with it, and it put an entire stop to the dispute for four minutes and a half;—five had been fatal to it:—my father saw the danger—the dispute was one of the most interesting disputes in the world, "Whether the child of his prayers and endeavours should be born without a head or with one":—he waited to the last moment, to allow Dr. Slop, in whose behalf the wish was made, his right of returning it; but perceiving, I say, that he was confounded, and continued looking with that perplexed vacuity of eye which puzzled souls generally stare with—first in my uncle Toby's face—then in his—then up—then down—then east—east and by east, and so on,—coasting it along by the plinth of the wainscot till he had got to the opposite point of the compass,—and that he had actually begun to count the brass nails upon the arm of his chair,—my father thought there was no time to be lost with my uncle Toby, so took up the discourse as follows.

275

CHAPTER 2

"——WHAT prodigious armies you had in Flanders!——Brother Toby," replied my father, taking his wig from off his head with his right hand, and with his left pulling out a striped India handkerchief from his right coat pocket, in order to rub his head, as he argued the point with my uncle Toby.——

——Now, in this I think my father was much to blame; and I will give you my reasons for it.

Matters of no more seeming consequence in themselves than, "Whether my father should have taken off his wig with his right hand or with his left," —have divided the greatest kingdoms, and made the crowns of the monarchs who governed them, to totter upon their heads.——But need I tell you, Sir, that the circumstances with which every thing in this world is begirt, give every thing in this world its size and shape!—and by tightening it, or relaxing it, this way or that, make the thing to be, what it is—great— little—good—bad—indifferent or not indifferent, just as the case happens?

As my father's India handkerchief was in his right coat pocket, he should by no means have suffered his right hand to have got engaged: on the contrary, instead of taking off his wig with it, as he did, he ought to have committed that entirely to the left; and then, when the natural exigency my father was under of rubbing his head, called out for his handkerchief, he would have had nothing in the world to have done, but to have put his right hand into his right coat pocket and taken it out;—which he might have done without any violence, or the least ungraceful twist in any one tendon or muscle of his whole body.

In this case, (unless, indeed, my father had been resolved to make a fool of himself by holding the wig stiff in his left hand—or by making some nonsensical angle or other at his elbow-joint, or arm-pit)—his whole attitude had been easy—natural—unforced: Reynolds himself, as great and gracefully as he paints, might have painted him as he sat.

Now as my father managed this matter,—consider what a devil of a figure my father made of himself.

In the latter end of Queen Anne's reign, and in the beginning of the reign of King George the First—"Coat pockets were cut very low down in the skirt."——I need say no more—the father of mischief, had he been hammering at it a month, could not have contrived a worse fashion for one in my father's situation.

CHAPTER 3

IT was not an easy matter in any king's reign (unless you were as lean a subject as myself) to have forced your hand diagonally, quite across your whole body, so as to gain the bottom of your opposite coat pocket.—In the year one thousand seven hundred and eighteen, when this happened, it was extremely difficult; so that when my uncle Toby discovered the transverse zig-zaggery of my father's approaches towards it, it instantly brought into his mind those he had done duty in, before the gate of St. Nicolas;—the idea of which drew off his attention so entirely from the subject in debate, that he had got his right hand to the bell to ring up Trim to go and fetch his map of Namur, and his compasses and sector along with it, to measure the returning angles of the traverses of that attack,—but particularly of that one, where he received his wound upon his groin.

My father knit his brows, and as he knit them, all the blood in his body seemed to rush up into his face—my uncle Toby dismounted immediately.

——I did not apprehend your uncle Toby was o' horseback.——

CHAPTER 4

A man's body and his mind, with the utmost reverence to both I speak it, are exactly like a jerkin, and a jerkin's lining;—rumple the one,—you rumple the other. There is one certain exception however in this case, and that is, when you are so fortunate a fellow, as to have had your jerkin made of gum-taffeta, and the body-lining to it of a sarcenet, or thin persian.

Zeno, Cleanthes, Diogenes Babylonius, Dionysius Heracleotes, Antipater, Panaetius, and Posidonius amongst the Greeks;—Cato and Varro and Seneca amongst the Romans;—Pantaenus and Clemens Alexandrinus and Montaigne amongst the Christians; and a score and a half of good, honest, unthinking Shandean people as ever lived, whose names I can't recollect,—all pretended that their jerkins were made after this fashion,— you might have rumpled and crumpled, and doubled and creased, and fretted and fridged the outside of them all to pieces;—in short, you might have played the very devil with them, and at the same time, not one of the insides of them would have been one button the worse, for all you had done to them.

I believe in my conscience that mine is made up somewhat after this sort: —for never poor jerkin has been tickled off at such a rate as it has been these last nine months together,—and yet I declare, the lining to it,—as far as I am a judge of the matter, it is not a three-penny piece the worse;— pell-mell, helter-skelter, ding-dong, cut and thrust, back stroke and fore stroke, side way and long way, have they been trimming it for me:—had there been the least gumminess in my lining,—by heaven! it had all of it long ago been frayed and fretted to a thread.

——You Messrs. the Monthly reviewers!—how could you cut and slash my jerkin as you did?—how did you know but you would cut my lining too?

Heartily and from my soul, to the protection of that Being who will injure none of us, do I recommend you and your affairs,—so God bless you; —only next month, if any one of you should gnash his teeth, and storm and rage at me, as some of you did last May (in which I remember the weather was very hot)—don't be exasperated, if I pass it by again with good temper, —being determined as long as I live or write (which in my case means the same thing) never to give the honest gentleman a worse word or a worse wish than my uncle Toby gave the fly which buzzed about his nose all dinner-time,——"Go,—go, poor devil," quoth he,—"get thee gone,—why should I hurt thee? This world is surely wide enough to hold both thee and me."

CHAPTER 5

ANY man, Madam, reasoning upwards, and observing the prodigious suffusion of blood in my father's countenance,—by means of which (as all the blood in his body seemed to rush into his face, as I told you) he must have reddened, pictorically and scientifically speaking, six whole tints and a half, if not a full octave above his natural colour:—any man, Madam, but my uncle Toby, who had observed this, together with the violent knitting of my father's brows, and the extravagant contortion of his body during the whole affair,—would have concluded my father in a rage; and taking that for granted,—had he been a lover of such kind of concord as arises from two such instruments being put in exact tune,—he would instantly have screwed up his, to the same pitch;—and then the devil and all had broke loose—the whole piece, Madam, must have been played off like the sixth of Avison Scarlatti—*con furia,*—like mad.——Grant me patience!——What has *con furia,*—*con strepito,*—or any other hurly burly whatever to do with harmony?

Any man, I say, Madam, but my uncle Toby, the benignity of whose heart interpreted every motion of the body in the kindest sense the motion would admit of, would have concluded my father angry, and blamed him too. My uncle Toby blamed nothing but the tailor who cut the pocket hole; —so sitting still till my father had got his handkerchief out of it, and looking all the time up in his face with inexpressible good-will—my father, at length, went on as follows.

CHAPTER 6

"WHAT prodigious armies you had in Flanders!"——Brother Toby, quoth my father, I do believe thee to be as honest a man, and with as good and as upright a heart as ever God created;—nor is it thy fault, if all the children which have been, may, can, shall, will, or ought to be begotten, come with their heads foremost into the world:—but believe me, dear Toby, the accidents which unavoidably way-lay them, not only in the article of our begetting 'em—though these, in my opinion, are well worth considering,— but the dangers and difficulties our children are beset with, after they are got forth into the world, are enow—little need is there to expose them to unnecessary ones in their passage to it.——Are these dangers, quoth my uncle Toby, laying his hand upon my father's knee, and looking up seriously in his face for an answer,—are these dangers greater now o' days, brother, than in times past? Brother Toby, answered my father, if a child was but fairly begot, and born alive, and healthy, and the mother did well after it,—our forefathers never looked farther.——My uncle Toby instantly withdrew his hand from off my father's knee, reclined his body gently back in his chair, raised his head till he could just see the cornice of the room, and then directing the buccinatory muscles along his cheeks, and the orbicular muscles around his lips to do their duty—he whistled *Lillabullero.*

CHAPTER 7

WHILST my uncle Toby was whistling *Lillabullero* to my father,—Dr. Slop was stamping, and cursing and damning at Obadiah at a most dreadful rate, —it would have done your heart good, and cured you, Sir, for ever of the vile sin of swearing, to have heard him; I am determined therefore to relate the whole affair to you.

When Dr. Slop's maid delivered the green baize bag with her master's instruments in it, to Obadiah, she very sensibly exhorted him to put his head and one arm through the strings, and ride with it slung across his body: so undoing the bow-knot, to lengthen the strings for him, without any more ado, she helped him on with it. However, as this, in some measure, unguarded the mouth of the bag, lest any thing should bolt out in galloping back, at the speed Obadiah threatened, they consulted to take it off again; and in the great care and caution of their hearts, they had taken the two strings and tied them close (pursing up the mouth of the bag first) with half a dozen hard knots, each of which Obadiah, to make all safe, had twitched and drawn together with all the strength of his body.

This answered all that Obadiah and the maid intended; but was no remedy against some evils which neither he nor she foresaw. The instruments, it seems, as tight as the bag was tied above, had so much room to play in it, towards the bottom (the shape of the bag being conical) that Obadiah could not make a trot of it, but with such a terrible jingle, what with the *tire-tête*, forceps, and squirt, as would have been enough, had Hymen been taking a jaunt that way, to have frightened him out of the country; but when Obadiah accelerated his motion, and from a plain trot assayed to prick his coach-horse into a full gallop—by Heaven! Sir, the jingle was incredible.

As Obadiah had a wife and three children—the turpitude of fornication, and the many other political ill consequences of this jingling, never once entered his brain,—he had however his objection, which came home to himself, and weighed with him, as it has oft-times done with the greatest patriots.——"The poor fellow, Sir, was not able to hear himself whistle."

CHAPTER 8

As Obadiah loved wind-music preferably to all the instrumental music he carried with him,—he very considerately set his imagination to work, to contrive and to invent by what means he should put himself in a condition of enjoying it.

In all distresses (except musical) where small cords are wanted, nothing is so apt to enter a man's head as his hat-band:—the philosophy of this is so near the surface—I scorn to enter into it.

As Obadiah's was a mixed case—mark, Sirs,—I say, a mixed case; for it was obstetrical,—scriptical, squirtical, papistical—and as far as the coach horse was concerned in it,—caball-istical—and only partly musical;— Obadiah made no scruple of availing himself of the first expedient which offered;—so taking hold of the bag and instruments, and griping them hard together with one hand, and with the finger and thumb of the other putting the end of the hat-band betwixt his teeth, and then slipping his hand down to the middle of it,—he tied and cross-tied them all fast together from one end to the other (as you would cord a trunk) with such a multiplicity of roundabouts and intricate cross turns, with a hard knot at every inter-section or point where the strings met,—that Dr. Slop must have had three fifths of Job's patience at least to have unloosed them.—I think in my conscience, that had Nature been in one of her nimble moods, and in humour for such a contest—and she and Dr. Slop both fairly started to-gether—there is no man living who had seen the bag with all that Obadiah had done to it,—and known likewise the great speed the Goddess can make when she thinks proper, who would have had the least doubt remaining in his mind—which of the two would have carried off the prize. My mother, Madam, had been delivered sooner than the green bag infallibly—at least by twenty *knots*.——Sport of small accidents, Tristram Shandy! that thou art, and ever will be! had that trial been for thee, and it was fifty to one but it had,—thy affairs had not been so depressed—(at least by the depression of thy nose) as they have been; nor had the fortunes of thy house and the occasions of making them, which have so often presented themselves in the course of thy life, to thee, been so often, so vexatiously, so tamely, so irre-coverably abandoned—as thou hast been forced to leave them;—but 'tis over,—all but the account of 'em, which cannot be given to the curious till I am got out into the world.

CHAPTER 9

GREAT wits jump: for the moment Dr. Slop cast his eyes upon his bag (which he had not done till the dispute with my uncle Toby about mid-wifery put him in mind of it)—the very same thought occurred.—'Tis God's mercy, quoth he (to himself) that Mrs. Shandy has had so bad a time of it,—else she might have been brought to bed seven times told, before one half of these knots could have got untied.——But here you must distinguish—the thought floated only in Dr. Slop's mind, without sail or ballast to it, as a simple proposition; millions of which, as your worship knows, are every day swimming quietly in the middle of the thin juice of a man's understanding, without being carried backwards or forwards, till some little gusts of passion or interest drive them to one side.

A sudden trampling in the room above, near my mother's bed, did the pro-position the very service I am speaking of. By all that's unfortunate, quoth Dr. Slop, unless I make haste, the thing will actually befall me as it is.

CHAPTER 10

IN the case of knots,—by which, in the first place, I would not be under-stood to mean slip-knots—because in the course of my life and opinions—my opinions concerning them will come in more properly when I mention the catastrophe of my great uncle Mr. Hammond Shandy,—a little man,—but of high fancy:—he rushed into the duke of Monmouth's affair:—nor, secondly, in this place, do I mean that particular species of knots called bow-knots;—there is so little address, or skill, or patience required in the unloosing them, that they are below my giving any opinion at all about them.—But by the knots I am speaking of, may it please your reverences to believe, that I mean good, honest, devilish tight, hard knots, made *bona fide*, as Obadiah made his;—in which there is no quibbling provision made by the duplication and return of the two ends of the strings thro' the annulus or noose made by the second implication of them—to get them slipped and undone by.——I hope you apprehend me.

In the case of these knots then, and of the several obstructions, which, may it please your reverences, such knots cast in our way in getting through life—every hasty man can whip out his penknife and cut through them.——'Tis wrong. Believe me, Sirs, the most virtuous way, and which both reason and conscience dictate—is to take our teeth or our fingers to them.—Dr. Slop had lost his teeth—his favourite instrument, by extracting in a wrong direction, or by some misapplication of it, unfortunately slipping, he had formerly, in a hard labour, knocked out three of the best of them with the handle of it:—he tried his fingers—alas; the nails of his fingers and thumbs were cut close.——The deuce take it! I can make nothing of it either way, cried Dr. Slop.——The trampling over head near my mother's bed-side increased.—Pox take the fellow! I shall never get the knots untied as long as I live.——My mother gave a groan.——Lend me your penknife—I must e'en cut the knots at last—pugh!—psha!——Lord! I have cut my thumb quite across to the very bone—curse the fellow—if there was not another man-midwife within fifty miles—I am undone for this bout—I wish the scoundrel hanged—I wish he was shot—I wish all the devils in hell had him for a blockhead!——

My father had a great respect for Obadiah, and could not bear to hear him disposed of in such a manner—he had moreover some little respect for himself—and could as ill bear with the indignity offered to himself in it.

Had Dr. Slop cut any part about him, but his thumb—my father had passed it by—his prudence had triumphed: as it was, he was determined to have his revenge.

Small curses, Dr. Slop, upon great occasions, quoth my father (condoling with him first upon the accident) are but so much waste of our strength and soul's health to no manner of purpose.—I own it, replied Dr. Slop.—They are like sparrow-shot, quoth my uncle Toby (suspending his whistling) fired against a bastion.——They serve, continued my father, to stir the humours—but carry off none of their acrimony:—for my own part, I seldom swear or curse at all—I hold it bad—but if I fall into it by surprise, I generally retain so much presence of mind (right, quoth my uncle Toby) as to make it answer my purpose—that is, I swear on till I find myself easy. A wise and a just man however would always endeavour to proportion the vent given to these humours, not only to the degree of them stirring within himself—but to the size and ill intent of the offence upon which they are to fall.——"Injuries come only from the heart,"—quoth my uncle Toby. For this reason, continued my father, with the most Cervantic gravity, I have the greatest veneration in the world for that gentleman, who, in distrust of his own discretion in this point, sat down and composed (that is at his

leisure) fit forms of swearing suitable to all cases, from the lowest to the
highest provocation which could possibly happen to him—which forms
being well considered by him, and such moreover as he could stand to, he
kept them ever by him on the chimney-piece, within his reach, ready for
use.——I never apprehended, replied Dr. Slop, that such a thing was ever
thought of—much less executed. I beg your pardon, answered my father;
I was reading, though not using, one of them to my brother Toby this

Textus de Ecclesiâ Roffensi, per Ernulfum Episcopum.

CAP. XI

EXCOMMUNICATIO

Ex auctoritate Dei omnipotentis, Patris, et Filij, et Spiritus Sancti, et sanctorum canonum, sanctaeque et intemeratae Virginis Dei genetricis Mariae,—

——Atque omnium coelestium virtutum, angelorum, archangelorum,
thronorum, dominationum, potestatum, cherubin ac seraphin, & sanctorum
patriarcharum, prophetarum, & omnium apostolorum & evangelistarum,
& sanctorum innocentum, qui in conspectu Agni soli digni inventi sunt
canticum cantare novum, et sanctorum martyrum et sanctorum confessorum, et sanctarum virginum, atque omnium simul sanctorum et elec-
torum Dei,—Excommunicamus, et anathematizamus hunc furem, vel hunc
malefactorem, N. N. et a liminibus sanctae Dei ecclesiae sequestramus, et
aeternis suppliciis excruciandus, mancipetur, cum Dathan et Abiram, et
cum his qui dixerunt Domino Deo, Recede à nobis, scientiam viarum
tuarum nolumus: et sicut aquâ ignis extinguitur, sic extinguatur lucerna
ejus in secula seculorum nisi resipuerit, et ad satisfactionem venerit. Amen.

As the genuineness of the consultation of the Sorbonne upon the question of
baptism, was doubted by some, and denied by others——'twas thought proper to
print the original of this excommunication; for the copy of which Mr. Shandy returns thanks to the chapter clerk of the dean and chapter of Rochester.

morning, whilst he poured out the tea—'tis here upon the shelf over my head;—but if I remember right, 'tis too violent for a cut of the thumb.—— Not at all, quoth Dr. Slop—the devil take the fellow.——Then, answered my father, 'Tis much at your service, Dr. Slop—on condition you will read it aloud;—so rising up and reaching down a form of excommunication of the church of Rome, a copy of which, my father (who was curious in his collections) had procured out of the leger-book of the church of Rochester, writ by Ernulphus the bishop—with a most affected seriousness of look and voice, which might have cajoled Ernulphus himself—he put it into Dr. Slop's hands.—Dr. Slop wrapt his thumb up in the corner of his handkerchief, and with a wry face, though without any suspicion, read aloud, as follows—my uncle Toby whistling *Lillabullero* as loud as he could all the time.

CHAPTER II

"By the authority of God Almighty, the Father, Son, and Holy Ghost, and of the holy canons, and of the undefiled Virgin Mary, mother and patroness of our Saviour." I think there is no necessity, quoth Dr. Slop, dropping the paper down to his knee, and addressing himself to my father—as you have read it over, Sir, so lately, to read it aloud—and as Captain Shandy seems to have no great inclination to hear it—I may as well read it to myself. That's contrary to treaty, replied my father:—besides, there is something so whimsical, especially in the latter part of it, I should grieve to lose the pleasure of a second reading. Dr. Slop did not altogether like it,—but my uncle Toby offering at that instant to give over whistling, and read it himself to them;—Dr. Slop thought he might as well read it under the cover of my uncle Toby's whistling—as suffer my uncle Toby to read it alone;—so raising up the paper to his face, and holding it quite parallel to it, in order to hide his chagrin—he read it aloud as follows—my uncle Toby whistling *Lillabullero*, though not quite so loud as before.

"By the authority of God Almighty, the Father, Son, and Holy Ghost, and of the undefiled Virgin Mary, mother and patroness of our Saviour, and of all the celestial virtues, angels, archangels, thrones, dominions, powers, cherubins and seraphins, and of all the holy patriarchs, prophets, and of all the apostles and evangelists, and of the holy innocents, who in the sight of the Holy Lamb, are found worthy to sing the new song of the holy martyrs and holy confessors, and of the holy virgins, and of all the saints, together with the holy and elect of God,—May he" (Obadiah) "be damned" (for tying these knots)—"We excommunicate, and anathematize him, and from the thresholds of the holy church of God Almighty we sequester him, that he may be tormented, disposed, and delivered over with Dathan and Abiram, and with those who say unto the Lord God, Depart from us, we desire none of thy ways. And as fire is quenched with water, so let the light of him be put out for evermore, unless it shall repent him" (Obadiah, of the knots which he has tied) "and make satisfaction" (for them) "Amen."

Maledicat illum Deus Pater qui hominem creavit. Maledicat illum Dei Filius qui pro homine passus est. Maledicat illum Spiritus Sanctus qui in baptismo effusus est. Maledicat illum sancta crux, quam Christus pro nostrâ salute hostem triumphans ascendit.

Maledicat illum sancta Dei genetrix et perpetua Virgo Maria. Maledicat illum sanctus Michael, animarum susceptor sacrarum. Maledicant illum omnes angeli et archangeli, principatus et potestates, omnisque militia coelestis.

Maledicat illum patriarcharum et prophetarum laudabilis numerus. Maledicat illum sanctus Johannes Praecursor et Baptista Christi, et sanctus Petrus, et sanctus Paulus, atque sanctus Andreas, omnesque Christi apostoli, simul et caeteri discipuli, quatuor quoque evangelistae, qui sua praedicatione mundum universum converterunt. Maledicat illum cuneus martyrum et confessorum mirificus, qui Deo bonis operibus placitus inventus est.

Maledicant illum sacrarum virginum chori, quae mundi vana causa honoris Christi respuenda contempserunt. Maledicant illum omnes sancti qui ab initio mundi usque in finem seculi Deo dilecti inveniuntur.

Maledicant illum coeli et terra, et omnia sancta in eis manentia.

Maledictus sit ubicunque fuerit, sive in domo, sive in agro, sive in viâ, sive in semitâ, sive in silvâ, sive in aquâ, sive in ecclesiâ.

Maledictus sit vivendo, moriendo, —————— ———— ——— ———— ————— ——————— ——— —————— ——— ——— ————— ——————— ———— —————————— ———— ——————— ———— ——— manducando, bibendo, esuriendo, sitiendo, jejunando, dormitando, dormiendo, vigilando, ambulando, stando, sedendo, jacendo, operando, quiescendo, mingendo, cacando, flebotomando.

Maledictus sit in totis viribus corporis,

Maledictus sit intus et exterius.

Maledictus sit in capillis; maledictus sit in cerebro.

Maledictus sit in vertice, in temporibus, in fronte, in auriculis, in superciliis, in oculis, in genis, in maxillis, in naribus, in dentibus, mordacibus, sive molaribus, in labiis, in guttere, in humeris, in harnis, in brachiis, in manubus, in digitis, in pectore, in corde, et in omnibus interioribus stomacho tenus, in renibus, in inguinibus, in femore, in genitalibus, in coxis, in genubus, in cruribus, in pedibus, et in inguibus.

"May the Father who created man, curse him.——May the Son who suffered for us, curse him.——May the Holy Ghost, who was given to us in baptism, curse him (Obadiah)—May the holy cross which Christ, for our salvation triumphing over his enemies, ascended, curse him.

"May the holy and eternal Virgin Mary, mother of God, curse him.—— May St. Michael, the advocate of holy souls, curse him.——May all the angels and archangels, principalities and powers, and all the heavenly armies, curse him." [Our armies swore terribly in Flanders, cried my uncle Toby,—but nothing to this.—For my own part I could not have a heart to curse my dog so.]

"May St. John, the Praecursor, and St. John the Baptist, and St. Peter and St. Paul, and St. Andrew, and all other Christ's apostles, together curse him. And may the rest of his disciples and four evangelists, who by their preaching converted the universal world, and may the holy and wonderful company of martyrs and confessors who by their holy works are found pleasing to God Almighty, curse him" (Obadiah).

"May the holy choir of the holy virgins, who for the honour of Christ have despised the things of the world, damn him—May all the saints, who from the beginning of the world to everlasting ages are found to be beloved of God, damn him——

"May the heavens and earth, and all the holy things remaining therein, damn him," (Obadiah) "or her," (or who ever else had a hand in tying these knots).

"May he (Obadiah) be damned wherever he be—whether in the house or the stables, the garden or the field, or the highway, or in the path, or in the

wood, or in the water, or in the church.——May he be cursed in living, in dying." [Here my uncle Toby, taking the advantage of a minim in the second bar of his tune, kept whistling one continued note to the end of the sentence.——Dr. Slop, with his division of curses moving under him, like a running bass all the way.] "May he be cursed in eating and drinking, in being hungry, in being thirsty, in fasting, in sleeping, in slumbering, in walking, in standing, in sitting, in lying, in working, in resting, in pissing, in shitting, and in blood-letting!"

"May he" (Obadiah) "be cursed in all the faculties of his body!

"May he be cursed inwardly and outwardly!——May he be cursed in

the hair of his head!——May he be cursed in his brains, and in his vertex," (that is a sad curse, quoth my father) "in his temples, in his forehead, in his ears, in his eye-brows, in his cheeks, in his jaw-bones, in his nostrils, in his fore-teeth and grinders, in his lips, in his throat, in his shoulders, in his wrists, in his arms, in his hand, in his fingers!

Maledictus sit in totis compagibus membrorum, a vertice capitis, usque ad plantam pedis—non sit in eo sanitas.

Maledicat illum Christus Filius Dei vivi toto suae majestatis imperio.—

——et insurgat adversus illum coelum cum omnibus virtutibus quae in eo moventur ad *damnandum* eum, nisi penituerit et ad satisfactionem venerit. Amen. Fiat. fiat. Amen.

"May he be damned in his mouth, in his breast, in his heart and purtenance, down to the very stomach!

"May he be cursed in his reins, and in his groin," (God in heaven forbid! quoth my uncle Toby) "in his thighs, in his genitals," (my father shook his head) "and in his hips, and in his knees, his legs, and feet, and toenails!

"May he be cursed in all the joints and articulations of his members, from the top of his head to the sole of his foot! May there be no soundness in him!

"May the Son of the living God, with all the glory of his Majesty"—[Here my uncle Toby, throwing back his head, gave a monstrous, long, loud Whew—w—w—something betwixt the interjectional whistle of Heyday! and the word itself.——

——By the golden beard of Jupiter—and of Juno (if her majesty wore one) and by the beards of the rest of your heathen worships, which by the bye was no small number, since what with the beards of your celestial gods, and gods aerial and aquatic—to say nothing of the beards of town-gods and country-gods, or of the celestial goddesses your wives, or of the infernal goddesses your whores and concubines (that is in case they wore 'em)—all which beards, as Varro tells me, upon his word and honour, when mustered up together, made no less than thirty thousand effective beards upon the pagan establishment;—every beard of which claimed the rights and privileges of being stroken and sworn by—by all these beards together then—I vow and protest, that of the two bad cassocks I am worth in the world, I would have given the better of them, as freely as ever Cid Hamet offered his—to have stood by, and heard my uncle Toby's accompaniment.]

——"Curse him!" continued Dr. Slop,—"and may heaven, with all the powers which move therein, rise up against him, curse and damn him" (Obadiah) "unless he repent and make satisfaction! Amen. So be it,—so be it. Amen."

I declare, quoth my uncle Toby, my heart would not let me curse the devil himself with so much bitterness.——He is the father of curses, replied Dr. Slop.——So am not I, replied my uncle.——But he is cursed and damned already, to all eternity, replied Dr. Slop.

I am sorry for it, quoth my uncle Toby.

Dr. Slop drew up his mouth, and was just beginning to return my uncle Toby the compliment of his Whu—u—u—or interjectional whistle—when the door hastily opening in the next chapter but one—put an end to the affair.

CHAPTER 12

Now don't let us give ourselves a parcel of airs, and pretend that the oaths we make free with in this land of liberty of ours are our own; and because we have the spirit to swear them,—imagine that we have had the wit to invent them too.

I'll undertake this moment to prove it to any man in the world, except to a connoisseur:—though I declare I object only to a connoisseur in swearing, —as I would do to a connoisseur in painting, etc., etc., the whole set of 'em are so hung round and befetished with the bobs and trinkets of criticism,— or to drop my metaphor, which by the bye is a pity,—for I have fetched it as far as from the coast of Guiney;—their heads, Sir, are stuck so full of rules and compasses, and have that eternal propensity to apply them upon all occasions, that a work of genius had better go to the devil at once, than stand to be pricked and tortured to death by 'em.

——And how did Garrick speak the soliloquy last night?——Oh, against all rule, my Lord,—most ungrammatically! betwixt the substantive and the adjective, which should agree together in number, case, and gender, he made a breach thus,—stopping, as if the point wanted settling;—and betwixt the nominative case, which your lordship knows should govern the verb, he suspended his voice in the epilogue a dozen times three seconds and three fifths by a stop-watch, my Lord, each time.——Admirable grammarian!——But in suspending his voice—was the sense suspended likewise? Did no expression of attitude or countenance fill up the chasm?—Was the eye silent? Did you narrowly look?——I looked only at the stop-watch, my Lord.——Excellent observer!

And what of this new book the whole world makes such a rout about?——Oh! 'tis out of all plumb, my Lord,——quite an irregular thing!—not one of the angles at the four corners was a right angle.——I had my rule and compasses, etc., my Lord, in my pocket.——Excellent critic!

——And for the epic poem your lordship bid me look at—upon taking the length, breadth, height, and depth of it, and trying them at home upon an exact scale of Bossu's—'tis out, my Lord, in every one of its dimensions.——Admirable connoisseur!

——And did you step in, to take a look at the grand picture in your way back?——'Tis a melancholy daub! my Lord; not one principle of the pyramid in any one group!—and what a price!—for there is nothing of the colouring of Titian—the expression of Rubens—the grace of Raphael—the purity of Dominichino—the corregiescity of Correggio—the learning of Poussin—the airs of Guido—the taste of the Carrachis—or the grand contour of Angelo.——Grant me patience, just Heaven!——Of all the cants which are canted in this canting world—though the cant of hypocrites may be the worst—the cant of criticism is the most tormenting!

I would go fifty miles on foot, for I have not a horse worth riding on, to kiss the hand of that man whose generous heart will give up the reins of his imagination into his author's hands—be pleased he knows not why, and cares not wherefore.

Great Apollo! if thou art in a giving humour—give me—I ask no more, but one stroke of native humour, with a single spark of thy own fire along with it—and send Mercury, with the rules and compasses, if he can be spared, with my compliments to—no matter.

Now to any one else I will undertake to prove, that all the oaths and imprecations which we have been puffing off upon the world for these two hundred and fifty years last past as originals—except St. Paul's thumb—God's flesh and God's fish, which were oaths monarchical, and, considering who made them, not much amiss; and as kings' oaths, 'tis not much matter whether they were fish or flesh;—else I say, there is not an oath, or at least a curse amongst them, which has not been copied over and over again out of Ernulphus a thousand times; but, like all other copies, how infinitely short

of the force and spirit of the original!——It is thought to be no bad oath—
and by itself passes very well—"G—d damn you."——Set it beside Ernulphus's—"God Almighty the Father damn you—God the Son damn you—
God the Holy Ghost damn you"—you see 'tis nothing.——There is an
orientality in his, we cannot rise up to: besides, he is more copious in his
invention—possessed more of the excellencies of a swearer—had such a
thorough knowledge of the human frame, its membranes, nerves, ligaments,
knittings of the joints, and articulations,—that when Ernulphus cursed—
no part escaped him.——'Tis true there is something of a hardness in his
manner—and, as in Michael Angelo, a want of grace—but then there is
such a greatness of gusto!

My father, who generally looked upon every thing in a light very different from all mankind, would, after all, never allow this to be an original.
—He considered rather Ernulphus's anathema as an institute of swearing,
in which, as he suspected, upon the decline of swearing in some milder
pontificate, Ernulphus, by order of the succeeding pope, had with great
learning and diligence collected together all the laws of it;—for the same
reason that Justinian, in the decline of the empire, had ordered his chancellor Tribonian to collect the Roman or civil laws all together into one code
or digest—lest, through the rust of time—and the fatality of all things
committed to oral tradition—they should be lost to the world for ever.

For this reason my father would oft-times affirm, there was not an oath,
from the great and tremendous oath of William the Conqueror (By the
splendour of God) down to the lowest oath of a scavenger (Damn your
eyes) which was not to be found in Ernulphus.——In short, he would add—
I defy a man to swear *out* of it.

The hypothesis is, like most of my father's, singular and ingenious too;—
nor have I any objection to it, but that it overturns my own.

Chapter 13

——Bless my soul!—my poor mistress is ready to faint—and her pains
are gone—and the drops are done—and the bottle of julap is broke—and
the nurse has cut her arm—(and I, my thumb, cried Dr. Slop,) and the
child is where it was, continued Susannah,—and the midwife has fallen
backwards upon the edge of the fender, and bruised her hip as black as your
hat.——I'll look at it, quoth Dr. Slop.——There is no need of that, replied
Susannah,—you had better look at my mistress—but the midwife would
gladly first give you an account how things are, so desires you would go up
stairs and speak to her this moment.

Human nature is the same in all professions.

The midwife had just before been put over Dr. Slop's head—He had not
digested it.——No, replied Dr. Slop, 'twould be full as proper, if the midwife came down to me.—I like subordination, quoth my uncle Toby,—and
but for it, after the reduction of Lisle, I know not what might have become
of the garrison of Ghent, in the mutiny for bread, in the year Ten.——Nor,
replied Dr. Slop, (parodying my uncle Toby's hobby-horsical reflection;
though full as hobby-horsical himself)—do I know, Captain Shandy, what

might have become of the garrison above stairs, in the mutiny and confusion I find all things are in at present, but for the subordination of fingers and thumbs to ******—the application of which, Sir, under this accident of mine, comes in so *à propos*, that without it, the cut upon my thumb might have been felt by the Shandy family, as long as the Shandy family had a name.

CHAPTER 14

LET us go back to the ******—in the last chapter. It is a singular stroke of eloquence (at least it was so, when eloquence flourished at Athens and Rome, and would be so now, did orators wear mantles) not to mention the name of a thing, when you had the thing about you *in petto*, ready to produce, pop, in the place you want it. A scar, an axe, a sword, a pinked doublet, a rusty helmet, a pound and a half of pot-ashes in an urn, or a three-halfpenny pickle pot—but above all, a tender infant royally accoutred.——Tho' if it was too young, and the oration as long as Tully's second Philippic—it must certainly have beshit the orator's mantle.—— And then again, if too old,—it must have been unwieldy and incommodious to his action—so as to make him lose by his child almost as much as he could gain by it.——Otherwise, when a state orator has hit the precise age to a minute—hid his BAMBINO in his mantle so cunningly that no mortal could smell it—and produced so critically, that no soul could say, it came in by head and shoulders—Oh Sirs! it has done wonders—It has opened the sluices, and turned the brains, and shook the principles, and unhinged the politics of half a nation.

These feats however are not to be done, except in those states and times, I say, where orators wore mantles—and pretty large ones too, my brethren, with some twenty or five-and-twenty yards of good purple, super-fine, marketable cloth in them—with large flowing folds and doubles, and in a great style of design.——All which plainly shews, may it please your worships, that the decay of eloquence, and the little good service it does at present, both within and without doors, is owing to nothing else in the world, but short coats, and the disuse of trunk-hose.——We can conceal nothing under ours, Madam, worth shewing.

CHAPTER 15

DR. SLOP was within an ace of being an exception to all this argumentation: for happening to have his green baize bag upon his knees, when he began to parody my uncle Toby—'twas as good as the best mantle in the world to him: for which purpose, when he foresaw the sentence would end in his new-invented forceps, he thrust his hand into the bag in order to have them ready to clap in, where your reverences took so much notice of the ***, which had he managed—my uncle Toby had certainly been overthrown: the sentence and the argument in that case jumping closely in one point, so like the two lines which form the salient angle of a ravelin,—Dr. Slop would never have given them up; and my uncle Toby would as soon have thought of flying, as taking them by force: but Dr. Slop fumbled so vilely in pulling them out, it took off the whole effect, and what was a ten times worse evil (for they seldom come alone in this life) in pulling out his forceps, his forceps unfortunately drew out the squirt along with it.

When a proposition can be taken in two senses—'tis a law in disputation, That the respondent may reply to which of the two he pleases, or finds most convenient for him.——This threw the advantage of the argument quite on my uncle Toby's side.——"Good God!" cried my uncle Toby, "are children brought into the world with a squirt?"

CHAPTER 16

——Upon my honour, Sir, you have tore every bit of skin quite off the back of both my hands with your forceps, cried my uncle Toby—and you have crushed all my knuckles into the bargain with them to a jelly. 'Tis your own fault, said Dr. Slop—you should have clinched your two fists together into the form of a child's head as I told you, and sat firm.——I did so, answered my uncle Toby.——Then the points of my forceps have not been sufficiently armed, or the rivet wants closing—or else the cut on my thumb has made me a little awkward—or possibly—'Tis well, quoth my father, interrupting the detail of possibilities—that the experiment was not first made upon my child's head-piece.——It would not have been a cherry-stone the worse, answered Dr. Slop.——I maintain it, said my uncle Toby, it would have broke the cerebellum (unless indeed the skull had been as hard as a granado) and turned it all into a perfect posset.——Pshaw! replied Dr. Slop, a child's head is naturally as soft as the pap of an apple;—the sutures give way—and besides, I could have extracted by the feet after.——Not you, said she.——I rather wish you would begin that way, quoth my father.

Pray do, added my uncle Toby.

CHAPTER 17

——And pray, good woman, after all, will you take upon you to say, it may not be the child's hip, as well as the child's head?——'Tis most certainly the head, replied the midwife. Because, continued Dr. Slop (turning to my father) as positive as these old ladies generally are—'tis a point very difficult to know—and yet of the greatest consequence to be known;—because, Sir, if the hip is mistaken for the head—there is a possibility (if it is a boy) that the forceps **************

——What the possibility was, Dr. Slop whispered very low to my father, and then to my uncle Toby.——There is no such danger, continued he, with the head.——No, in truth, quoth my father—but when your possibility has taken place at the hip—you may as well take off the head too.

——It is morally impossible the reader should understand this—'tis enough Dr. Slop understood it:—so taking the green baize bag in his hand, with the help of Obadiah's pumps, he tripped pretty nimbly, for a man of his size, across the room to the door—and from the door was shewn the way, by the good old midwife, to my mother's apartment.

CHAPTER 18

IT is two hours, and ten minutes—and no more—cried my father, looking at his watch, since Dr. Slop and Obadiah arrived—and I know not how it happens, brother Toby—but to my imagination it seems almost an age.

——Here—pray, Sir, take hold of my cap—nay, take the bell along with it, and my pantoufles too.

Now, Sir, they are all at your service; and I freely make you a present of 'em, on condition you give me all your attention to this chapter.

Though my father said, "he knew not how it happened,"—yet he knew very well how it happened;—and at the instant he spoke it, was pre-determined in his mind to give my uncle Toby a clear account of the matter by a metaphysical dissertation upon the subject of duration and its simple modes, in order to show my uncle Toby by what mechanism and mensurations in the brain it came to pass, that the rapid succession of their ideas, and the eternal scampering of the discourse from one thing to another, since Dr. Slop had come into the room, had lengthened out so short a period to so inconceivable an extent.

——"I know not how it happens—cried my father,—but it seems an age."

——'Tis owing entirely, quoth my uncle Toby, to the succession of our ideas.

My father, who had an itch, in common with all philosophers, of reasoning upon every thing which happened, and accounting for it too—proposed infinite pleasure to himself in this, of the succession of ideas, and had not the least apprehension of having it snatched out of his hands by my uncle Toby, who (honest man!) generally took every thing as it happened;—and who, of all things in the world, troubled his brain the least with abstruse thinking;—the ideas of time and space—or how we came by those ideas—or of what stuff they were made—or whether they were born with us—or we picked them up afterwards as we went along—or whether we did it in frocks—or not till we had got into breeches—with a thousand other inquiries and disputes about Infinity, Prescience, Liberty, Necessity, and so forth, upon whose desperate and unconquerable theories so many fine heads have been turned and cracked—never did my uncle Toby's the least injury at all; my father knew it—and was no less surprised than he was disappointed, with my uncle's fortuitous solution.

Do you understand the theory of that affair? replied my father.

Not I, quoth my uncle.

——But you have some ideas, said my father, of what you talk about?——

No more than my horse, replied my uncle Toby.

Gracious heaven! cried my father, looking upwards, and clasping his two hands together—there is a worth in thy honest ignorance, brother Toby— 'twere almost a pity to exchange it for a knowledge.——But I'll tell thee.——

To understand what time is aright, without which we never can comprehend infinity, insomuch as one is a portion of the other—we ought seriously to sit down and consider what idea it is we have of duration, so as to give a satisfactory account how we came by it.——What is that to any body? quoth my uncle Toby.[1] For if you will turn your eyes inwards upon your

[1] *Vide* Locke.

mind, continued my father, and observe attentively, you will perceive, brother, that whilst you and I are talking together, and thinking, and smoking our pipes, or whilst we receive successively ideas in our minds, we know that we do exist, and so we estimate the existence, or the continuation of the existence of ourselves, or any thing else, commensurate to the succession of any ideas in our minds, the duration of ourselves, or any such other thing co-existing with our thinking—and so according to that preconceived—You puzzle me to death, cried my uncle Toby.

——'Tis owing to this, replied my father, that in our computations of time, we are so used to minutes, hours, weeks, and months—and of clocks (I wish there was not a clock in the kingdom) to measure out their several portions to us, and to those who belong to us—that 'twill be well, if in time to come, the succession of our ideas be of any use or service to us at all.

Now, whether we observe it or no, continued my father, in every sound man's head, there is a regular succession of ideas of one sort or other, which follow each other in train just like—A train of artillery? said my uncle Toby—A train of a fiddle-stick!—quoth my father—which follow and succeed one another in our minds at certain distances, just like the images in the inside of a lanthorn turned round by the heat of a candle.—I declare, quoth my uncle Toby, mine are more like a smoke-jack.——Then, brother Toby, I have nothing more to say to you upon the subject, said my father.

Chapter 19

——What a conjuncture was here lost!——My father in one of his best explanatory moods—in eager pursuit of a metaphysical point into the very regions, where clouds and thick darkness would soon have encompassed it about;—my uncle Toby in one of the finest dispositions for it in the world; his head like a smoke-jack;—the funnel unswept, and the ideas whirling round and round about in it, all obfuscated and darkened over with fuliginous matter!——By the tombstone of Lucian—if it is in being—if not, why then by his ashes! by the ashes of my dear Rabelais, and dearer Cervantes!——my father and my uncle Toby's discourse upon Time and Eternity—was a discourse devoutly to be wished for! and the petulancy of my father's humour, in putting a stop to it as he did, was a robbery of the Ontologic Treasury of such a jewel, as no coalition of great occasions and great men are ever likely to restore to it again.

Chapter 20

Tho' my father persisted in not going on with the discourse—yet he could not get my uncle Toby's smoke-jack out of his head—piqued as he was at first with it;—there was something in the comparison at the bottom, which hit his fancy; for which purpose, resting his elbow upon the table, and reclining the right side of his head upon the palm of his hand—but looking first stedfastly in the fire—he began to commune with himself, and philosophize about it: but his spirits being wore out with the fatigues of investigating new tracts, and the constant exertion of his faculties upon that variety of subjects which had taken their turn in the discourse—the idea of the smoke-jack soon turned all his ideas upside down—so that he fell asleep almost before he knew what he was about.

As for my uncle Toby, his smoke-jack had not made a dozen revolutions, before he fell asleep also.——Peace be with them both!——Dr. Slop is engaged with the midwife and my mother above stairs.——Trim is busy in turning an old pair of jack-boots into a couple of mortars, to be employed in the siege of Messina next summer—and is this instant boring the touch-holes with the point of a hot poker.——All my heroes are off my hands;—'tis the first time I have had a moment to spare—and I'll make use of it, and write my preface.

The Author's PREFACE

No, I'll not say a word about it—here it is;—in publishing it—I have appealed to the world—and to the world I leave it;—it must speak for itself.

All I know of the matter is—when I sat down, my intent was to write a good book; and so far as the tenuity of my understanding would hold out—a wise, aye, and a discreet—taking care only, as I went along, to put into it all the wit and the judgment, (be it more or less) which the great Author and Bestower of them had thought fit originally to give me—so that, as your worships see—'tis just as God pleases.

Now, Agelastes (speaking dispraisingly) sayeth, That there may be some wit in it, for aught he knows—but no judgment at all. And Triptolemus and Phutatorius agreeing thereto, ask, How is it possible there should? for that wit and judgment in this world never go together; inasmuch as they are two operations differing from each other as wide as east from west——So, says Locke—so are farting and hiccuping, say I. But in answer to this, Didius the great church lawyer, in his code *de fartendi et illustrandi fallaciis*, doth maintain and make fully appear, That an illustration is no argument—nor do I maintain the wiping of a looking-glass clean to be a syllogism;—but you all, may it please your worships, see the better for it——so that the main good these things do is only to clarify the understanding, previous to the application of the argument itself, in order to free it from any little motes, or specks of opacular matter, which, if left swimming therein, might hinder a conception and spoil all.

Now, my dear Anti-Shandeans, and thrice able critics, and fellow-labourers (for to you I write this Preface)—and to you, most subtle statesmen and discreet doctors (do—pull off your beards) renowned for gravity and wisdom;—Monopolus, my politician—Didius, my counsel; Kysarcius, my friend;—Phutatorius, my guide;—Gastripheres, the preserver of my life; Somnolentius, the balm and repose of it—not forgetting all others, as well sleeping as waking, ecclesiastical as civil, whom for brevity, but out of no resentment to you, I lump all together.——Believe me, right worthy.

My most zealous wish and fervent prayer in your behalf, and in my own too, in case the thing is not done already for us—is, that the great gifts and endowments both of wit and judgment, with every thing which usually goes along with them—such as memory, fancy, genius, eloquence, quick parts, and what not, may this precious moment, without stint or measure, let or hindrance, be poured down warm as each of us could bear it—scum and sediment and all (for I would not have a drop lost) into the several receptacles, cells, cellules, domiciles, dormitories, refectories, and spare places of our brains—in such sort, that they might continue to be injected and tunned into, according to the true intent and meaning of my wish, until every vessel of them both great and small, be so replenished, saturated, and filled up therewith, that no more, would it save a man's life, could possibly be got either in or out.

Bless us!—what noble work we should make!—how should I tickle it off!—and what spirits should I find myself in, to be writing away for such readers!—and you—just heaven!—with what raptures would you sit and read—but oh!—'tis too much—I am sick—I faint away deliciously at the thoughts of it—'tis more than nature can bear!—lay hold of me—I am giddy—I am stone blind—I'm dying—I am gone.——Help! Help! Help!——But hold—I grow something better again, for I am beginning to foresee, when this is over, that as we shall all of us continue to be great wits—we should never agree amongst ourselves, one day to an end:—there would be so much satire and sarcasm—scoffing and flouting, with rallying and reparteeing of it—thrusting and parrying in one corner or another—there would be nothing but mischief among us—Chaste stars! what biting and scratching, and what a racket and a clatter we should make, what with breaking of heads, rapping of knuckles, and hitting of sore places—there would be no such thing as living for us.

But then again, as we should all of us be men of great judgment, we should make up matters as fast as ever they went wrong; and though we should abominate each other ten times worse than so many devils or devilesses, we should nevertheless, my dear creatures, be all courtesy and kindness, milk and honey—'twould be a second land of promise—a paradise upon earth, if there was such a thing to be had—so that upon the whole we should have done well enough.

All I fret and fume at, and what most distresses my invention at present, is how to bring the point itself to bear; for as your worships well know, that of these heavenly emanations of wit and judgment, which I have so bountifully wished both for your worships and myself—there is but a certain *quantum* stored up for us all for the use and behoof of the whole race of mankind; and such small modicums of 'em are only sent forth into this wide world, circulating here and there in one bye corner or another—and in such narrow streams, and at such prodigious intervals from each other, that one would wonder how it holds out, or could be sufficient for the wants and emergencies of so many great estates, and populous empires.

Indeed there is one thing to be considered, that in Nova Zembla, North Lapland, and in all those cold and dreary tracts of the globe, which lie more directly under the arctic and antarctic circles, where the whole province of man's concernments lies for near nine months together within the narrow compass of his cave—where the spirits are compressed almost to nothing—and where the passions of a man, with every thing which belongs to them, are as frigid as the zone itself—there the least quantity of judgment imaginable does the business—and of wit—there is a total and an absolute saving—for as not one spark is wanted—so not one spark is given. Angels and ministers of grace defend us! what a dismal thing would it have been to have governed a kingdom, to have fought a battle, or made a treaty, or run a match, or wrote a book, or got a child, or held a provincial chapter there, with so plentiful a lack of wit and judgment about us! For mercy's sake, let us think no more about it but travel on as fast as we can southwards into Norway—crossing over Swedeland, if you please, through the small triangular province of Angermania to the lake of Bothnia; coasting along it through east and west Bothnia, down to Carelia, and so on, through all those states and provinces which border upon the far side of the Gulf of Finland, and the north-east of the Baltic, up to Petersbourg, and just stepping into Ingria;—then stretching over directly from thence through the north parts of the Russian empire—leaving Siberia a little upon the left hand, till we got into the very heart of Russian and Asiatic Tartary.

Now throughout this long tour which I have led you, you observe the good people are better off by far, than in the polar countries which we have just left:—for if you hold your hand over your eyes, and look very attentively, you may perceive some small glimmerings (as it were) of wit, with a comfortable provision of good plain household judgment, which, taking the quality and quantity of it together, they make a very good shift with—and had they more of either the one or the other, it would destroy the proper balance betwixt them, and I am satisfied they moreover would want occasions to put them to use.

Now, Sir, if I conduct you home again into this warmer and more luxuriant island, where you perceive the springtide of our blood and humours runs high—where we have more ambition, and pride, and envy, and lechery, and other whoreson passions upon our hands to govern and subject to reason —the height of our wit, and the depth of our judgment, you see, are exactly proportioned to the length and breadth of our necessities—and accordingly we have them sent down amongst us in such a flowing kind of descent and creditable plenty, that no one thinks he has any cause to complain.

It must however be confessed on this head, that, as our air blows hot and cold—wet and dry, ten times in a day, we have them in no regular and settled way;—so that sometimes for near half a century together, there shall be very little wit or judgment either to be seen or heard of amongst us:—the small channels of them shall seem quite dried up—then all of a sudden the sluices shall break out, and take a fit of running again like fury —you would think they would never stop:—and then it is, that in writing, and fighting, and twenty other gallant things, we drive all the world before us.

It is by these observations, and a wary reasoning by analogy in that kind of argumentative process, which Suidas calls dialectic induction—that I draw and set up this position as most true and veritable;

That of these two luminaries so much of their irradiations are suffered from time to time to shine down upon us, as he, whose infinite wisdom which dispenses every thing in exact weight and measure, knows will just serve to light us on our way in this night of our obscurity; so that your reverences and worships now find out, nor is it a moment longer in my power to conceal it from you, That the fervent wish in your behalf with which I set out, was no more than the first insinuating How d'ye of a caressing prefacer, stifling his reader, as a lover sometimes does a coy mistress, into silence. For alas! could this effusion of light have been as easily procured, as the exordium wished it—I tremble to think how many thousands for it, of benighted travellers (in the learned sciences at least) must have groped and blundered on in the dark, all the nights of their lives—running their heads against posts, and knocking out their brains without ever getting to their journies' end;—some falling with their noses perpendicularly into sinks—others horizontally with their tails into kennels. Here one half of a learned profession tilting full butt against the other half of it, and then tumbling and rolling one over the other in the dirt like hogs.—Here the brethren of another profession, who should have run in opposition to each other, flying on contrary like a flock of wild geese, all in a row the same way.—What confusion!—what mistakes!—fiddlers and painters judging by their eyes and ears—admirable!—trusting to the passions excited—in an air sung, or a story painted to the heart—instead of measuring them by a quadrant.

In the fore-ground of this picture, a statesman turning the political wheel, like a brute, the wrong way round—against the stream of corruption—by Heaven!—instead of with it.

In this corner, a son of the divine Esculapius, writing a book against predestination; perhaps worse—feeling his patient's pulse, instead of his apothecary's—a brother of the faculty in the back-ground upon his knees in tears—drawing the curtains of a mangled victim to beg his forgiveness;—offering a fee—instead of taking one.

In that spacious Hall, a coalition of the gown, from all the bars of it, driving a damned, dirty, vexatious cause before them, with all their might and main, the wrong way!—kicking it *out* of the great doors, instead of, *in*—and with such fury in their looks, and such a degree of inveteracy in their manner of kicking it, as if the laws had been originally made for the peace and preservation of mankind;——perhaps a more enormous mistake committed by them still—a litigated point fairly hung up;—for instance, Whether John o'Nokes his nose could stand in Tom o'Stiles his face, without a trespass, or not—rashly determined by them in five-and-twenty minutes, which, with the cautious pros and cons required in so intricate a proceeding, might have taken up as many months—and if carried on upon a military plan, as your honours know an Action should be, with all the stratagems practicable therein,—such as feints,—forced marches,—surprises—ambuscades—mask-batteries, and a thousand other strokes of generalship, which consist in catching at all advantages on both sides—might reasonably have lasted them as many years, finding food and raiment all that term for a centumvirate of the profession.

As for the clergy—No—if I say a word against them, I'll be shot.—I have no desire;—and besides, if I had—I durst not for my soul touch upon the subject—with such weak nerves and spirits, and in the condition I am in at present, 'twould be as much as my life was worth, to deject and contrist myself with so bad and melancholy an account—and therefore 'tis safer to draw a curtain across, and hasten from it, as fast as I can, to the main and principal point I have undertaken to clear up—and that is, How it comes to pass, that your men of least wit are reported to be men of most judgment.—

But mark—I say, reported to be—for it is no more, my dear sirs, than a report, and which, like twenty others taken up every day upon trust, I maintain to be a vile and a malicious report into the bargain.

This by the help of the observation already premised, and I hope already weighed and perpended by your reverences and worships, I shall forthwith make appear.

I hate set dissertations—and above all things in the world, 'tis one of the silliest things in one of them, to darken your hypothesis by placing a number of tall, opaque words, one before another, in a right line, betwixt your own and your reader's conception—when in all likelihood, if you had looked about, you might have seen something standing, or hanging up, which would have cleared the point at once—"for what hindrance, hurt, or harm doth the laudable desire of knowledge bring to any man, if even from a sot, a pot, a fool, a stool, a winter-mitten, a truckle for a pully, the lid of a goldsmith's crucible, an oil bottle, an old slipper, or a cane chair?"——I am this moment sitting upon one. Will you give me leave to illustrate this affair of wit and judgment, by the two knobs on the top of the back of it? —they are fastened on, you see, with two pegs stuck slightly into two gimlet-holes, and will place what I have to say in so clear a light, as to let you see through the drift and meaning of my whole preface, as plainly as if every point and particle of it was made up of sun-beams.

I now enter directly upon the point.

——Here stands Wit—and there stands Judgment, close beside it, just like the two knobs I'm speaking of, upon the back of this self-same chair on which I am sitting.

——You see they are the highest and most ornamental parts of its frame —as wit and judgment are of ours—and like them too, indubitably both made and fitted to go together, in order, as we say in all such cases of duplicated embellishments—to answer one another.

Now for the sake of an experiment, and for the clearer illustrating this matter—let us for a moment take off one of these two curious ornaments (I care not which) from the point or pinnacle of the chair it now stands on— nay, don't laugh at it,—but did you ever see, in the whole course of your lives, such a ridiculous business as this has made of it?——Why, 'tis as miserable a sight as a sow with one ear; and there is just as much sense and symmetry in the one as in the other:—do—pray, get off your seats only to take a view of it.——Now would any man who valued his character a straw, have turned a piece of work out of his hand in such a condition?— nay, lay your hands upon your hearts, and answer this plain question, Whether this one single knob, which now stands here like a blockhead by itself, can serve any purpose upon earth, but to put one in mind of the want of the other?—and let me further ask, in case the chair was your own, if you would not in your conscience think, rather than be as it is, that it would be ten times better without any knob at all.

Now these two knobs—or top ornaments of the mind of man, which crown the whole entablature—being, as I said, wit and judgment, which of all others, as I have proved it, are the most needful—the most prized—the most calamitous to be without, and consequently the hardest to come at—

for all these reasons put together, there is not a mortal among us, so destitute of a love of good fame or feeding—or so ignorant of what will do him good therein—who does not wish and stedfastly resolve in his own mind, to be, or to be thought at least, master of the one or the other, and indeed of both of them, if the thing seems any way feasible, or likely to be brought to pass.

Now your graver gentry having little or no kind of chance in aiming at the one—unless they laid hold of the other,—pray what do you think would become of them?——Why, Sirs, in spite of all their gravities, they must e'en have been contented to have gone with their insides naked—this was not to be borne, but by an effort of philosophy not to be supposed in the case we are upon—so that no one could well have been angry with them, had they been satisfied with what little they could have snatched up and secreted under their cloaks and great perriwigs, had they not raised a hue and cry at the same time against the lawful owners.

I need not tell your worships, that this was done with so much cunning and artifice—that the great Locke, who was seldom outwitted by false sounds—was nevertheless bubbled here. The cry, it seems, was so deep and solemn a one, and what with the help of great wigs, grave faces, and other implements of deceit, was rendered so general a one against the poor wits in this matter, that the philosopher himself was deceived by it—it was his glory to free the world from the lumber of a thousand vulgar errors;—but this was not of the number; so that instead of sitting down coolly, as such a philosopher should have done, to have examined the matter of fact before he philosophized upon it—on the contrary he took the fact for granted, and so joined in with the cry, and hallooed it as boisterously as the rest.

This has been made the *Magna Charta* of stupidity ever since—but your reverences plainly see, it has been obtained in such a manner, that the title to it is not worth a groat:—which by the bye is one of the many and vile impositions which gravity and grave folks have to answer for hereafter.

As for great wigs, upon which I may be thought to have spoken my mind too freely—I beg leave to qualify whatever has been unguardedly said to their dispraise or prejudice, by one general declaration—That I have no abhorrence whatever, nor do I detest and abjure either great wigs or long beards, any farther than when I see they are bespoke and let grow on purpose to carry on this self-same imposture—for any purpose—peace be with them!——☞ mark only—I write not for them.

CHAPTER 21

EVERY day for at least ten years together did my father resolve to have it mended—'tis not mended yet;—no family but ours would have borne with it an hour—and what is most astonishing, there was not a subject in the world upon which my father was so eloquent, as upon that of door-hinges. ——And yet at the same time, he was certainly one of the greatest bubbles to them, I think, that history can produce: his rhetoric and conduct were at perpetual handy-cuffs.——Never did the parlour-door open—but his philosophy or his principles fell a victim to it;—three drops of oil with a feather, and a smart stroke of a hammer, had saved his honour for ever.

———Inconsistent soul that man is!—languishing under wounds, which he has the power to heal!—his whole life a contradiction to his knowledge!— his reason, that precious gift of God to him—(instead of pouring in oil) serving but to sharpen his sensibilities—to multiply his pains, and render him more melancholy and uneasy under them!——Poor unhappy creature, that he should do so!——Are not the necessary causes of misery in this life enow, but he must add voluntary ones to his stock of sorrow;—struggle against evils which cannot be avoided, and submit to others, which a tenth part of the trouble they create him would remove from his heart for ever?

By all that is good and virtuous, if there are three drops of oil to be got, and a hammer to be found within ten miles of Shandy Hall—the parlour door hinge shall be mended this reign.

CHAPTER 22

WHEN Corporal Trim had brought his two mortars to bear, he was delighted with his handy-work beyond measure; and knowing what a pleasure it would be to his master to see them, he was not able to resist the desire he had of carrying them directly into his parlour.

Now next to the moral lesson I had in view in mentioning the affair of hinges, I had a speculative consideration arising out of it, and it is this.

Had the parlour door opened and turned upon its hinges, as a door should do——

Or for example, as cleverly as our government has been turning upon its hinges—(that is, in case things have all along gone well with your worship,— otherwise I give up my simile)—in this case, I say, there had been no danger either to master or man, in Corporal Trim's peeping in: the moment he had beheld my father and my uncle Toby fast asleep—the respectfulness of his carriage was such, he would have retired as silent as death, and left them both in their arm-chairs, dreaming as happy as he had found them: but the thing was, morally speaking, so very impracticable, that for the many years in which this hinge was suffered to be out of order, and amongst the hourly grievances my father submitted to upon its account—this was one; that he never folded his arms to take his nap after dinner, but the thoughts of being unavoidably awakened by the first person who should open the door, was always uppermost in his imagination, and so incessantly stepped in betwixt him and the first balmy presage of his repose, as to rob him, as he often declared, of the whole sweets of it.

"When things move upon bad hinges, an' please your lordships, how can it be otherwise?"

Pray what's the matter? Who is there? cried my father, waking, the moment the door began to creak.——I wish the smith would give a peep at that confounded hinge.——'Tis nothing, an' please your honour, said Trim, but two mortars I am bringing in.——They shan't make a clatter with them here, cried my father hastily.——If Dr. Slop has any drugs to pound, let him do it in the kitchen.——May it please your honour, cried Trim, they are two mortar-pieces for a siege next summer, which I have been making out of a pair of jack-boots, which Obadiah told me your honour had left off wearing.——By Heaven! cried my father, springing out of his chair, as he swore—I have not one appointment belonging to me, which I set so much store by as I do by these jack-boots—they were our great grandfather's, brother Toby—they were hereditary. Then I fear, quoth my uncle Toby, Trim has cut off the entail.——I have only cut off the tops, an' please your honour, cried Trim—I hate perpetuities as much as any man alive, cried my father—but these jack-boots, continued he (smiling, though very angry at the same time) have been in the family, brother, ever since the civil wars;—Sir Roger Shandy wore them at the battle of Marston-Moor.——I declare I would not have taken ten pounds for them.—— I'll pay you the money, brother Shandy, quoth my uncle Toby, looking at the two mortars with infinite pleasure, and putting his hand into his breeches pocket as he viewed them—I'll pay you the ten pounds this moment with all my heart and soul.——

Brother Toby, replied my father, altering his tone, you care not what money you dissipate and throw away, provided, continued he, 'tis but upon a siege.——Have I not one hundred and twenty pounds a year, besides my half pay? cried my uncle Toby.——What is that—replied my father hastily —to ten pounds for a pair of jack-boots?—twelve guineas for your pontoons?—half as much for your Dutch draw-bridge?—to say nothing of the train of little brass artillery you bespoke last week, with twenty other preparations for the siege of Messina: believe me, dear brother Toby, continued my father, taking him kindly by the hand—these military operations of yours are above your strength;—you mean well, brother—but they carry you into greater expenses than you were first aware of;—and take my word, dear Toby, they will in the end quite ruin your fortune, and make a beggar of you.——What signifies it if they do, brother, replied my uncle Toby, so long as we know 'tis for the good of the nation?——

My father could not help smiling for his soul—his anger at the worst was never more than a spark;—and the zeal and simplicity of Trim—and the generous (though hobby-horsical) gallantry of my uncle Toby, brought him into perfect good-humour with them in an instant.

Generous souls!——God prosper you both, and your mortar-pieces too! quoth my father to himself.

CHAPTER 23

ALL is quiet and hush, cried my father, at least above stairs—I hear not one foot stirring.——Prithee, Trim, who's in the kitchen? There is no one soul in the kitchen, answered Trim, making a low bow as he spoke, except Dr. Slop.—Confusion! cried my father (getting up upon his legs a second time) —not one single thing has gone right this day! had I faith in astrology, brother, (which, by the bye, my father had) I would have sworn some retrograde planet was hanging over this unfortunate house of mine,—and turning every individual thing in it out of its place.——Why, I thought Dr. Slop had been above stairs with my wife, and so said you.——What can the fellow be puzzling about in the kitchen?——He is busy, an' please your honour, replied Trim, in making a bridge.——'Tis very obliging in him, quoth my uncle Toby:—pray, give my humble service to Dr. Slop, Trim, and tell him I thank him heartily.

You must know, my uncle Toby mistook the bridge—as widely as my father mistook the mortars;—but to understand how my uncle Toby could mistake the bridge—I fear I must give you an exact account of the road which led to it;—or to drop my metaphor (for there is nothing more dishonest in an historian than the use of one)—in order to conceive the probability of this error in my uncle Toby aright, I must give you some account of an adventure of Trim's, though much against my will, I say much against my will, only because the story, in one sense, is certainly out of its place here; for by right it should come in, either amongst the anecdotes of my uncle Toby's amours with widow Wadman, in which Corporal Trim was no mean actor—or else in the middle of his and my uncle Toby's campaigns on the bowling-green—for it will do very well in either place;—but then if I reserve it for either of those parts of my story—I ruin the story I'm upon; —and if I tell it here—I anticipate matters, and ruin it there.

——What would your worships have me do in this case?

——Tell it, Mr. Shandy, by all means.——You are a fool, Tristram, if you do.

O ye Powers! (for powers ye are, and great ones too)—which enable mortal man to tell a story worth the hearing—that kindly shew him, where he is to begin it—and where he is to end it—what he is to put into it—and what he is to leave out—how much of it he is to cast into a shade—and whereabouts he is to throw his light!——Ye, who preside over this vast empire of biographical freebooters, and see how many scrapes and plunges your subjects hourly fall into;—will you do one thing?

I beg and beseech you (in case you will do nothing better for us) that wherever in any part of your dominions it so falls out, that three several roads meet in one point, as they have done just here—that at least you set up a guide-post in the centre of them, in mere charity, to direct an uncertain devil which of the three he is to take.

Chapter 24

Tho' the shock my uncle Toby received the year after the demolition of Dunkirk, in his affair with widow Wadman, had fixed him in a resolution never more to think of the sex—or of aught which belonged to it;—yet Corporal Trim had made no such bargain with himself. Indeed in my uncle Toby's case there was a strange and unaccountable concurrence of circumstances, which insensibly drew him in, to lay siege to that fair and strong citadel.——In Trim's case there was a concurrence of nothing in the world, but of him and Bridget in the kitchen;—though in truth, the love and veneration he bore his master was such, and so fond was he of imitating him in all he did, that had my uncle Toby employed his time and genius in tagging of points—I am persuaded the honest corporal would have laid down his arms, and followed his example with pleasure. When therefore my uncle Toby sat down before the mistress—Corporal Trim incontinently took ground before the maid.

Now, my dear friend Garrick, whom I have so much cause to esteem and honour—(why, or wherefore, 'tis no matter)—can it escape your penetration—I defy it—that so many play-wrights, and opificers of chit-chat have ever since been working upon Trim's and my uncle Toby's pattern.—I care not what Aristotle, or Pacuvius, or Bossu, or Ricaboni say—(though I never read one of them)—there is not a greater difference between a single-horse chair and madam Pompadour's *vis-à-vis;* than betwixt a single amour, and an amour thus nobly doubled, and going upon all four, prancing throughout a grand drama—Sir, a simple, single, silly affair of that kind—is quite lost in five acts;—but that is neither here nor there.

After a series of attacks and repulses in a course of nine months on my uncle Toby's quarter, a most minute account of every particular of which shall be given in its proper place, my uncle Toby, honest man! found it necessary to draw off his forces and raise the siege somewhat indignantly.

Corporal Trim, as I said, had made no such bargain either with himself—or with any one else—the fidelity however of his heart not suffering him to go into a house which his master had forsaken with disgust—he contented himself with turning his part of the siege into a blockade;—that is, he kept others off;—for though he never after went to the house, yet he never met Bridget in the village, but he would either nod or wink, or smile, or look kindly at her—or (as circumstances directed) he would shake her by the hand—or ask her lovingly how she did—or would give her a ribbon—and now-and-then, though never but when it could be done with decorum, would give Bridget a——

Precisely in this situation, did these things stand for five years; that is, from the demolition of Dunkirk in the year 13, to the latter end of my uncle Toby's campaign in the year 18, which was about six or seven weeks before the time I'm speaking of.—When Trim, as his custom was, after he had put my uncle Toby to bed, going down one moonshiny night to see that every thing was right at his fortifications—in the lane separated from the bowling-green with flowering shrubs and holly—he espied his Bridget.

As the Corporal thought there was nothing in the world so well worth shewing as the glorious works which he and my uncle Toby had made, Trim courteously and gallantly took her by the hand, and led her in: this was not done so privately, but that the foul-mouthed trumpet of Fame carried it from ear to ear, till at length it reached my father's, with this untoward circumstance along with it, that my uncle Toby's curious drawbridge, constructed and painted after the Dutch fashion, and which went quite across the ditch—was broke down, and somehow or other crushed all to pieces that very night.

My father, as you have observed, had no great esteem for my uncle Toby's hobby-horse, he thought it the most ridiculous horse that ever gentleman mounted; and indeed unless my uncle Toby vexed him about it, could never think of it once, without smiling at it—so that it could never get lame or happen any mischance, but it tickled my father's imagination beyond measure; for this being an accident much more to his humour than any one which had yet befallen it, it proved an inexhaustible fund of entertainment to him.——Well—but, dear Toby! my father would say, do tell me seriously how this affair of the bridge happened.——How can you tease me so much about it? my uncle Toby would reply—I have told it you twenty times, word for word as Trim told it me.——Prithee, how was it then, Corporal? my father would cry, turning to Trim.——It was a mere misfortune, an' please your honour;—I was shewing Mrs. Bridget our fortifications, and in going too near the edge of the fossé, I unfortunately slipped in—Very well, Trim! my father would cry—(smiling mysteriously, and giving a nod—but without interrupting him)—and being linked fast, an' please your honour, arm in arm with Mrs. Bridget, I dragged her after me, by means of which she fell backwards soss against the bridge—and Trim's foot (my uncle Toby would cry, taking the story out of his mouth) getting into the curvette, he tumbled full against the bridge too.——It was a thousand to one, my uncle Toby would add, that the poor fellow did not break his leg.——Ay truly, my father would say—a limb is soon broke, brother Toby, in such encounters.——And so, an' please your honour, the bridge, which your honour knows was a very slight one, was broke down betwixt us, and splintered all to pieces.

At other times, but especially when my uncle Toby was so unfortunate as to say a syllable about cannons, bombs, or petards—my father would exhaust all the stores of his eloquence (which indeed were very great) in a panegyric upon the battering-rams of the ancients—the vinea which Alexander made use of at the siege of Troy.——He would tell my uncle Toby of the catapultae of the Syrians, which threw such monstrous stones so many hundred feet, and shook the strongest bulwarks from their very foundation:—he would go on and describe the wonderful mechanism of the ballista which Marcellinus makes so much rout about!—the terrible effects of the pyroboli, which cast fire;—the danger of the terebra and scorpio, which cast javelins.——But what are these, would he say, to the destructive machinery of Corporal Trim? ——Believe me, brother Toby, no bridge, or bastion, or sally-port, that ever was constructed in this world, can hold out against such artillery.

My uncle Toby would never attempt any defence against the force of this ridicule, but that of redoubling the vehemence of smoking his pipe; in doing which, he raised so dense a vapour one night after supper, that it set my father, who was a little phthisical, into a suffocating fit of violent coughing: my uncle Toby leaped up without feeling the pain upon his groin— and, with infinite pity, stood beside his brother's chair, tapping his back with one hand, and holding his head with the other, and from time to time wiping his eyes with a clean cambric handkerchief, which he pulled out of his pocket.——The affectionate and endearing manner in which my uncle Toby did these little offices cut my father thro' his reins, for the pain he had just been giving him.——May my brains be knocked out with a battering-ram or a catapulta, I care not which, quoth my father to himself—if ever I insult this worthy soul more!

CHAPTER 25

THE draw-bridge being held irreparable, Trim was ordered directly to set about another—but not upon the same model: for cardinal Alberoni's intrigues at that time being discovered, and my uncle Toby rightly foreseeing that a flame would inevitably break out betwixt Spain and the Empire, and that the operations of the ensuing campaign must in all likelihood be either in Naples or Sicily—he determined upon an Italian bridge—(my uncle Toby, by the bye, was not far out of his conjectures)—but my father, who was infinitely the better politician, and took the lead as far of my uncle Toby in the cabinet, as my uncle Toby took it of him in the field—convinced him, that if the king of Spain and the Emperor went together by the ears, England and France and Holland must, by force of their pre-engagements, all enter the lists too;—and if so, he would say, the combatants, brother Toby, as sure as we are alive, will fall to it again, pell-mell, upon the old prize-fighting stage of Flanders;—then what will you do with your Italian bridge?

——We will go on with it then upon the old model, cried my uncle Toby.

When Corporal Trim had about half finished it in that style—my uncle Toby found out a capital defect in it, which he had never thoroughly considered before. It turned, it seems, upon hinges at both ends of it, opening in the middle, one half of which turning to one side of the fossé, and the other to the other; the advantage of which was this, that by dividing the weight of the bridge into two equal portions, it empowered my uncle Toby to raise it up or let it down with the end of his crutch, and with one hand, which, as his garrison was weak, was as much as he could well spare—but the disadvantages of such a construction were insurmountable;—for by this means, he would say, I leave one half of my bridge in my enemy's possession—and pray of what use is the other?

The natural remedy for this was, no doubt, to have his bridge fast only at one end with hinges, so that the whole might be lifted up together, and stand bolt upright—but that was rejected for the reason given above.

For a whole week after he was determined in his mind to have one of that particular construction which is made to draw back horizontally, to hinder a passage; and to thrust forwards again to gain a passage—of which sorts your worship might have seen three famous ones at Spires before its destruction—and one now at Brisac, if I mistake not;—but my father advising my uncle Toby, with great earnestness, to have nothing more to do with thrusting bridges—and my uncle foreseeing moreover that it would but perpetuate the memory of the Corporal's misfortune—he changed his mind for that of the marquis d'Hôpital's invention, which the younger Bernouilli has so well and learnedly described, as your worships may see—*Act. Erud. Lips.* an. 1695—to these a lead weight is an eternal balance, and keeps watch as well as a couple of sentinels, inasmuch as the construction of them was a curve line approximating to a cycloid—if not a cycloid itself.

My uncle Toby understood the nature of a parabola as well as any man in England—but was not quite such a master of the cycloid;—he talked however about it every day—the bridge went not forwards.——We'll ask somebody about it, cried my uncle Toby to Trim.

CHAPTER 26

WHEN Trim came in and told my father, that Dr. Slop was in the kitchen, and busy in making a bridge—my uncle Toby—the affair of the jack-boots having just then raised a train of military ideas in his brain—took it instantly for granted that Dr. Slop was making a model of the marquis d'Hôpital's bridge.——'Tis very obliging in him, quoth my uncle Toby;—pray give my humble service to Dr. Slop, Trim, and tell him I thank him heartily.

Had my uncle Toby's head been a Savoyard's box, and my father peeping in all the time at one end of it—it could not have given him a more distinct conception of the operations of my uncle Toby's imagination, than what he had; so, notwithstanding the catapulta and battering-ram, and his bitter imprecation about them, he was just beginning to triumph——

When Trim's answer, in an instant, tore the laurel from his brows, and twisted it to pieces.

CHAPTER 27

——This unfortunate draw-bridge of yours, quoth my father—God bless your honour, cried Trim, 'tis a bridge for master's nose.——In bringing him into the world with his vile instruments, he has crushed his nose, Susannah says, as flat as a pancake to his face, and he is making a false bridge with a piece of cotton and a thin piece of whalebone out of Susannah's stays, to raise it up.

——Lead me, brother Toby, cried my father, to my room this instant.

CHAPTER 28

FROM the first moment I sat down to write my life for the amusement of the world, and my opinions for its instruction, has a cloud insensibly been gathering over my father.——A tide of little evils and distresses has been setting in against him.——Not one thing, as he observed himself, has gone right: and now is the storm thickened and going to break, and pour down full upon his head.

I enter upon this part of my story in the most pensive and melancholy frame of mind that ever sympathetic breast was touched with.——My nerves relax as I tell it.——Every line I write, I feel an abatement of the quickness of my pulse, and of that careless alacrity with it, which every day of my life prompts me to say and write a thousand things I should not—And this moment that I last dipped my pen into my ink, I could not help taking notice what a cautious air of sad composure and solemnity there appeared in my manner of doing it.—Lord! how different from the rash jerks and hair-brained squirts thou art wont, Tristram, to transact it with in other humours—dropping thy pen—spurting thy ink about thy table and thy books—as if thy pen and thy ink, thy books and furniture cost thee nothing.

CHAPTER 29

I WON'T go about to argue the point with you—'tis so—and I am persuaded of it, madam, as much as can be, "That both man and woman bear pain or sorrow (and, for aught I know, pleasure too) best in a horizontal position."

The moment my father got up into his chamber, he threw himself prostrate across his bed in the wildest disorder imaginable, but at the same time in the most lamentable attitude of a man borne down with sorrows, that ever the eye of pity dropped a tear for.——The palm of his right hand, as he fell upon the bed, receiving his forehead, and covering the greatest part of both his eyes, gently sunk down with his head (his elbow giving way backwards) till his nose touched the quilt;—his left arm hung insensible over the side of the bed, his knuckles reclining upon the handle of the chamber-pot, which peeped out beyond the valance—his right leg (his left being drawn up towards his body) hung half over the side of the bed, the edge of it pressing upon his shin-bone—He felt it not. A fixed, inflexible sorrow took possession of every line of his face.——He sighed once—heaved his breast often—but uttered not a word.

An old set-stitched chair, valanced and fringed around with party-coloured worsted bobs, stood at the bed's head, opposite to the side where my father's head reclined.——My uncle Toby sat him down in it.

Before an affliction is digested—consolation ever comes too soon;—and after it is digested—it comes too late: so that you see, madam, there is but a mark between these two, as fine almost as a hair, for a comforter to take aim at: my uncle Toby was always either on this side, or on that of it, and would often say, he believed in his heart he could as soon hit the longitude; for this reason, when he sat down in the chair, he drew the curtain a little forwards, and having a tear at every one's service—he pulled out a cambric handkerchief—gave a low sigh—but held his peace.

CHAPTER 30

——"ALL is not gain that is got into the purse."——So that notwithstanding my father had the happiness of reading the oldest books in the universe, and had moreover, in himself, the oddest way of thinking that ever man in it was blessed with, yet it had this drawback upon him after all—that it laid him open to some of the oddest and most whimsical distresses; of which this particular one, which he sunk under at present, is as strong an example as can be given.

No doubt, the breaking down of the bridge of a child's nose, by the edge of a pair of forceps—however scientifically applied—would vex any man in the world, who was at so much pains in begetting a child, as my father was —yet it will not account for the extravagance of his affliction, nor will it justify the unchristian manner he abandoned and surrendered himself up to.

To explain this, I must leave him upon the bed for half an hour—and my uncle Toby in his old fringed chair sitting beside him.

CHAPTER 31

——I THINK it a very unreasonable demand—cried my great-grandfather, twisting up the paper, and throwing it upon the table.——By this account, madam, you have but two thousand pounds fortune, and not a shilling more—and you insist upon having three hundred pounds a year jointure for it.——

——"Because," replied my great-grandmother, "you have little or no nose, Sir."——

Now before I venture to make use of the word Nose a second time—to avoid all confusion in what will be said upon it, in this interesting part of my story, it may not be amiss to explain my own meaning, and define, with all possible exactness and precision, what I would willingly be understood to mean by the term: being of opinion, that 'tis owing to the negligence and perverseness of writers in despising this precaution, and to nothing else— that all the polemical writings in divinity are not as clear and demonstrative as those upon a Will o' the Wisp, or any other sound part of philosophy, and natural pursuit; in order to which, what have you to do, before you set out, unless you intend to go puzzling on to the day of judgment—but to give the world a good definition, and stand to it, of the main word you have most occasion for—changing it, Sir, as you would a guinea, into small coin? —which done—let the father of confusion puzzle you, if he can; or put a different idea either into your head, or your reader's head, if he knows how.

In books of strict morality and close reasoning, such as this I am engaged in—the neglect is inexcusable; and Heaven is witness, how the world has revenged itself upon me for leaving so many openings to equivocal strictures—and for depending so much as I have done, all along, upon the cleanliness of my readers' imaginations.

——Here are two senses, cried Eugenius, as we walked along, pointing with the fore finger of his right hand to the word Crevice, in the one hundred and seventy-eighth page of the first volume of this book of books;— here are two senses—quoth he—And here are two roads, replied I, turning short upon him—a dirty and a clean one—which shall we take?——The clean, by all means, replied Eugenius. Eugenius, said I, stepping before him, and laying my hand upon his breast—to define—is to distrust.—Thus I triumphed over Eugenius; but I triumphed over him as I always do, like a fool.——'Tis my comfort, however, I am not an obstinate one: therefore

I define a nose as follows—intreating only beforehand, and beseeching my readers, both male and female, of what age, complexion, and condition soever, for the love of God and their own souls, to guard against the temptations and suggestions of the devil, and suffer him by no art or wile to put any other ideas into their minds, than what I put into my definition—For by the word Nose, throughout all this long chapter of noses, and in every other part of my work, where the word Nose occurs—I declare, by that word I mean a nose, and nothing more, or less.

Chapter 32

——"Because," quoth my great-grandmother, repeating the words again —"you have little or no nose, Sir."——

'Sdeath! cried my great-grandfather, clapping his hand upon his nose,— 'tis not so small as that comes to;—'tis a full inch longer than my father's.

——Now, my great-grandfather's nose was for all the world like unto the noses of all the men, women, and children, whom Pantagruel found dwelling upon the island of Ennasin.——By the way, if you would know the strange way of getting a-kin amongst so flat-nosed a people—you must read the book;—find it out yourself, you never can.——

——'Twas shaped, Sir, like an ace of clubs.

——'Tis a full inch, continued my grandfather, pressing up the ridge of his nose with his finger and thumb; and repeating his assertion—'tis a full inch longer, madam, than my father's—You must mean your uncle's, replied my great-grandmother.

——My great-grandfather was convinced.—He untwisted the paper, and signed the article.

CHAPTER 33

——WHAT an unconscionable jointure, my dear, do we pay out of this small estate of ours, quoth my grandmother to my grandfather.

My father, replied my grandfather, had no more nose, my dear, saving the mark, than there is upon the back of my hand.

——Now, you must know, that my great-grandmother outlived my grandfather twelve years; so that my father had the jointure to pay, a hundred and fifty pounds half-yearly—(on Michaelmas and Lady-day,)—during all that time.

No man discharged pecuniary obligations with a better grace than my father.——And as far as a hundred pounds went, he would fling it upon the table, guinea by guinea, with that spirited jerk of an honest welcome, which generous souls, and generous souls only, are able to fling down money: but as soon as ever he entered upon the odd fifty—he generally gave a loud Hem! rubbed the side of his nose leisurely with the flat part of his fore finger—inserted his hand cautiously betwixt his head and the caul of his wig—looked at both sides of every guinea as he parted with it—and seldom could get to the end of the fifty pounds, without pulling out his handkerchief, and wiping his temples.

Defend me, gracious Heaven! from those persecuting spirits who make no allowances for these workings within us.——Never—O never may I lay down in their tents, who cannot relax the engine, and feel pity for the force of education, and the prevalence of opinions long derived from ancestors!

For three generations at least this tenet in favour of long noses had gradually been taking root in our family.——Tradition was all along on its side, and Interest was every half-year stepping in to strengthen it; so that the whimsicality of my father's brain was far from having the whole honour of this, as it had of almost all his other strange notions.—For in a great measure he might be said to have sucked this in with his mother's milk. He did his part however.——If education planted the mistake (in case it was one) my father watered it, and ripened it to perfection.

He would often declare, in speaking his thoughts upon the subject, that he did not conceive how the greatest family in England could stand it out against an uninterrupted succession of six or seven short noses.——And for the contrary reason, he would generally add, That it must be one of the greatest problems in civil life, where the same number of long and jolly noses, following one another in a direct line, did not raise and hoist it up into the best vacancies in the kingdom.——He would often boast that the Shandy family ranked very high in King Harry the VIIIth's time, but owed its rise to no state engine—he would say—but to that only;—but that, like other families, he would add—it had felt the turn of the wheel, and had never recovered the blow of my great-grandfather's nose.—It was an ace of clubs indeed, he would cry, shaking his head—and as vile a one for an unfortunate family as ever turned up trumps.

——Fair and softly, gentle reader!—where is thy fancy carrying thee?—If there is truth in man, by my great-grandfather's nose, I mean the external organ of smelling, or that part of man which stands prominent in his face—and which painters say, in good jolly noses and well-proportioned faces, should comprehend a full third—that is, measured downwards from the setting on of the hair.——

——What a life of it has an author, at this pass!

Chapter 34

It is a singular blessing, that nature has formed the mind of man with the same happy backwardness and renitency against conviction, which is observed in old dogs—"of not learning new tricks."

What a shuttlecock of a fellow would the greatest philosopher that ever existed be whisked into at once, did he read such books, and observe such facts, and think such thoughts, as would eternally be making him change sides!

Now, my father, as I told you last year, detested all this—He picked up an opinion, Sir, as a man in a state of nature picks up an apple.——It becomes his own—and if he is a man of spirit, he would lose his life rather than give it up.

I am aware that Didius, the great civilian, will contest this point; and cry out against me, Whence comes this man's right to this apple? *ex confesso*, he will say—things were in a state of nature—The apple, as much Frank's apple as John's. Pray, Mr. Shandy, what patent has he to shew for it? and how did it begin to be his? was it, when he set his heart upon it? or when he gathered it? or when he chewed it? or when he roasted it? or when he peeled, or when he brought it home? or when he digested?—or when he —?—for 'tis plain, Sir, if the first picking up of the apple, made it not his—that no subsequent act could.

Brother Didius, Tribonius will answer—(now Tribonius the civilian and church lawyer's beard being three inches and a half and three eighths longer than Didius his beard—I'm glad he takes up the cudgels for me, so I give myself no farther trouble about the answer).——Brother Didius, Tribonius will say, it is a decreed case, as you may find it in the fragments of Gregorius and Hermogenes's codes, and in all the codes from Justinian's down to the codes of Louis and Des Eaux—That the sweat of a man's brows, and the exsudations of a man's brains, are as much a man's own property as the breeches upon his backside;—which said exsudations, etc., being dropped upon the said apple by the labour of finding it, and picking it up; and being moreover indissolubly wasted, and as indissolubly annexed, by the picker up, to the thing picked up, carried home, roasted, peeled, eaten, digested, and so on;—'tis evident that the gatherer of the apple, in so doing, has mixed up something which was his own, with the apple which was not his own, by which means he has acquired a property;—or, in other words, the apple is John's apple.

By the same learned chain of reasoning my father stood up for all his opinions; he had spared no pains in picking them up, and the more they lay out of the common way, the better still was his title.——No mortal claimed them; they had cost him moreover as much labour in cooking and digesting as in the case above, so that they might well and truly be said to be of his own goods and chattels.——Accordingly he held fast by 'em, both by teeth and claws—would fly to whatever he could lay his hands on—and, in a word, would intrench and fortify them round with as many circumvallations and breast-works, as my uncle Toby would a citadel.

There was one plaguy rub in the way of this—the scarcity of materials to make any thing of a defence with, in case of a smart attack; inasmuch as few men of great genius had exercised their parts in writing books upon the subject of great noses: by the trotting of my lean horse, the thing is incredible! and I am quite lost in my understanding, when I am considering what a treasure of precious time and talents together has been wasted upon worse subjects—and how many millions of books in all languages, and in all possible types and bindings, have been fabricated upon points not half so much tending to the unity and peace-making of the world. What was to be had, however, he set the greater store by; and though my father would ofttimes sport with my uncle Toby's library—which, by the bye, was ridiculous enough—yet at the very same time he did it, he collected every book and treatise which had been systematically wrote upon noses, with as much care as my honest uncle Toby had done those upon military architecture. ——'Tis true, a much less table would have held them—but that was not thy transgression, my dear uncle.——

Here—but why here—rather than in any other part of my story—I am not able to tell:—but here it is—my heart stops me to pay to thee, my dear uncle Toby, once for all, the tribute I owe thy goodness.——Here let me thrust my chair aside, and kneel down upon the ground, whilst I am pouring forth the warmest sentiment of love for thee, and veneration for the excellency of thy character, that ever virtue and nature kindled in a nephew's bosom.—Peace and comfort rest for evermore upon thy head!— Thou enviedst no man's comforts—insultedst no man's opinions—Thou blackenedst no man's character—devouredst no man's bread: gently, with faithful Trim behind thee, didst thou amble round the little circle of thy pleasures, jostling no creature in thy way:—for each one's sorrows, thou hadst a tear,—for each man's need, thou hadst a shilling.

Whilst I am worth one, to pay a weeder—thy path from thy door to thy bowling-green shall never be grown up.—Whilst there is a rood and a half of land in the Shandy family, thy fortifications, my dear uncle Toby, shall never be demolished.

CHAPTER 35

MY father's collection was not great, but to make amends, it was curious; and consequently he was some time in making it; he had the great good fortune however, to set off well, in getting Bruscambille's prologue upon long noses, almost for nothing—for he gave no more for Bruscambille than three half-crowns; owing indeed to the strong fancy which the stall-man saw my father had for the book the moment he laid his hands upon it.—— There are not three Bruscambilles in Christendom—said the stall-man, except what are chained up in the libraries of the curious. My father flung down the money as quick as lightning—took Bruscambille into his bosom— hied home from Piccadilly to Coleman Street with it, as he would have hied home with a treasure, without taking his hand once off from Bruscambille all the way.

To those who do not yet know of which gender Bruscambille is—inasmuch as a prologue upon long noses might easily be done by either—'twill be no objection against the simile—to say, That when my father got home, he solaced himself with Bruscambille after the manner in which, 'tis ten to one, your worship solaced yourself with your first mistress—that is, from morning even unto night: which, by the bye, how delightful soever it may prove to the inamorato—is of little or no entertainment at all to by-standers.——Take notice, I go no farther with the simile—my father's eye was greater than his appetite—his zeal greater than his knowledge—he cooled—his affections became divided—he got hold of Prignitz—purchased Scroderus, Andrea Paraeus, Bouchet's Evening Conferences, and above all, the great and learned Hafen Slawkenbergius; of which, as I shall have much to say by and bye—I will say nothing now.

Chapter 36

Of all the tracts my father was at the pains to procure and study in support of his hypothesis, there was not any one wherein he felt a more cruel disappointment at first, than in the celebrated dialogue between Pamphagus and Cocles, written by the chaste pen of the great and venerable Erasmus, upon the various uses and seasonable applications of long noses.——Now don't let Satan, my dear girl, in this chapter, take advantage of any one spot of rising ground to get astride of your imagination, if you can any ways help it; or if he is so nimble as to slip on—let me beg of you, like an unbacked filly, to frisk it, to squirt it, to jump it, to rear it, to bound it—and to kick it, with long kicks and short kicks, till, like Tickletoby's mare, you break a strap or a crupper, and throw his worship into the dirt.——You need not kill him.——

——And pray who was Tickletoby's mare?—'tis just as discreditable and unscholarlike a question, Sir, as to have asked what year (*ab urb. con.*) the second Punic war broke out.——Who was Tickletoby's mare?—— Read, read, read, read, my unlearned reader! read—or by the knowledge of the great saint Paraleipomenon—I tell you before-hand, you had better throw down the book at once; for without much reading, by which your reverence knows I mean much knowledge, you will no more be able to penetrate the moral of the next marbled page (motley emblem of my work!) than the world with all its sagacity has been able to unravel the many opinions, transactions, and truths which still lie mystically hid under the dark veil of the black one.

Chapter 37

"*Nihil me paenitet hujus nasi,*" quoth Pamphagus;—that is—"My nose has been the making of me."——"*Nec est cur paeniteat,*" replies Cocles; that is, "How the deuce should such a nose fail?"

The doctrine, you see, was laid down by Erasmus, as my father wished it, with the utmost plainness; but my father's disappointment was, in finding nothing more from so able a pen, but the bare fact itself; without any of that speculative subtlety or ambidexterity of argumentation upon it, which Heaven had bestowed upon man on purpose to investigate truth, and fight for her on all sides.——My father pished and pughed at first most terribly —'tis worth something to have a good name. As the dialogue was of Erasmus, my father soon came to himself, and read it over and over again with great application, studying every word and every syllable of it thro' and thro' in its most strict and literal interpretation—he could still make nothing of it, that way. Mayhap there is more meant, than is said in it, quoth my father.——Learned men, brother Toby, don't write dialogues upon long noses for nothing.——I'll study the mystic and the allegoric sense—here is some room to turn a man's self in, brother.

My father read on.——

Now I find it needful to inform your reverences and worships, that besides the many nautical uses of long noses enumerated by Erasmus, the dialogist affirmeth that a long nose is not without its domestic conveniences also; for that in a case of distress—and for want of a pair of bellows, it will do excellently well, *ad excitandum focum* (to stir up the fire).

Nature had been prodigal in her gifts to my father beyond measure, and had sown the seeds of verbal criticism as deep within him as she had done the seeds of all other knowledge—so that he got out his pen-knife, and was trying experiments upon the sentence, to see if he could not scratch some better sense into it.——I've got within a single letter, brother Toby, cried my father, of Erasmus his mystic meaning.——You are near enough, brother, replied my uncle, in all conscience.——Pshaw! cried my father, scratching on—I might as well be seven miles off.——I've done it—said my father, snapping his fingers—See, my dear brother Toby, how I have mended the sense.——But you have marred a word, replied my uncle Toby.——My father put on his spectacles—bit his lip—and tore out the leaf in a passion.

Chapter 38

O SLAWKENBERGIUS! thou faithful analyzer of my Disgrazias—thou sad foreteller of so many of the whips and short turns which in one stage or other of my life have come slap upon me from the shortness of my nose, and no other cause that I am conscious of.—Tell me, Slawkenbergius! what secret impulse was it? what intonation of voice? whence came it? how did it sound in thy ears?—art thou sure thou heard'st it?—which first cried out to thee—go—go, Slawkenbergius! dedicate the labours of thy life—neglect thy pastimes—call forth all the powers and faculties of thy nature—macerate thyself in the service of mankind, and write a grand Folio for them, upon the subject of their noses.

How the communication was conveyed into Slawkenbergius's sensorium —so that Slawkenbergius should know whose finger touched the key—and whose hand it was that blew the bellows—as Hafen Slawkenbergius has been dead and laid in his grave above fourscore and ten years—we can only raise conjectures.

Slawkenbergius was played upon, for aught I know, like one of White-field's disciples—that is, with such a distinct intelligence, Sir, of which of the two masters it was that had been practising upon his instrument—as to make all reasoning upon it needless.

——For in the account which Hafen Slawkenbergius gives the world of his motives and occasions for writing, and spending so many years of his life upon this one work—towards the end of his prolegomena, which by the bye should have come first—but the bookbinder has most injudiciously placed it betwixt the analytical contents of the book, and the book itself— he informs his reader, that ever since he had arrived at the age of discern-ment, and was able to sit down coolly, and consider within himself the true state and condition of man, and distinguish the main end and design of his being;—or—to shorten my translation, for Slawkenbergius's book is in Latin, and not a little prolix in this passage—ever since I understood, quoth Slawkenbergius, any thing—or rather what was what—and could per-ceive that the point of long noses had been too loosely handled by all who had gone before;—have I, Slawkenbergius, felt a strong impulse, with a mighty and unresistible call within me, to gird up myself to this undertaking.

And to do justice to Slawkenbergius, he has entered the list with a stronger lance, and taken a much larger career in it than any one man who had ever entered it before him—and indeed, in many respects, deserves to be en-niched as a prototype for all writers, of voluminous works at least, to model their books by—for he has taken in, Sir, the whole subject—exam-ined every part of it dialectically—then brought it into full day; dilucidat-ing it with all the light which either the collision of his own natural parts could strike—or the profoundest knowledge of the sciences had impowered him to cast upon it—collating, collecting, and compiling—begging, bor-rowing, and stealing, as he went along, all that had been wrote or wrangled thereupon in the schools and porticos of the learned: so that Slawken-bergius his book may properly be considered, not only as a model—but as a thorough-stitched digest and regular institute of noses, comprehending in it all that is or can be needful to be known about them.

For this cause it is that I forbear to speak of so many (otherwise) valu-able books and treatises of my father's collecting, wrote either, plump upon noses—or collaterally touching them;—such for instance as Prignitz, now lying upon the table before me, who with infinite learning, and from the most candid and scholar-like examination of above four thousand different skulls, in upwards of twenty charnel-houses in Silesia, which he had rum-maged—has informed us, that the mensuration and configuration of the osseous or bony parts of human noses, in any given tract of country, except Crim Tartary, where they are all crushed down by the thumb, so that no

judgment can be formed upon them—are much nearer alike, than the
world imagines;—the difference amongst them being, he says, a mere trifle,
not worth taking notice of;—but that the size and jollity of every individual nose, and by which one nose ranks above another, and bears a
higher price, is owing to the cartilaginous and muscular parts of it, into
whose ducts and sinuses the blood and animal spirits being impelled and
driven by the warmth and force of the imagination, which is but a step from
it (bating the case of idiots whom Prignitz, who had lived many years in
Turky, supposes under the more immediate tutelage of Heaven)—it so
happens, and ever must, says Prignitz, that the excellency of the nose is in
a direct arithmetical proportion to the excellency of the wearer's fancy.

It is for the same reason, that is, because 'tis all comprehended in Slawkenbergius, that I say nothing likewise of Scroderus (Andrea) who, all the
world knows, set himself to oppugn Prignitz with great violence—proving
it in his own way, first logically, and then by a series of stubborn facts,
"That so far was Prignitz from the truth, in affirming that the fancy begat
the nose, that on the contrary—the nose begat the fancy."

——The learned suspected Scroderus of an indecent sophism in this—
and Prignitz cried out aloud in the dispute, that Scroderus had shifted the
idea upon him—but Scroderus went on, maintaining his thesis.

My father was just balancing within himself, which of the two sides he
should take in this affair; when Ambrose Paraeus decided it in a moment,
and by overthrowing the systems, both of Prignitz and Scroderus, drove my
father out of both sides of the controversy at once.

Be witness——

I don't acquaint the learned reader—in saying it, I mention it only to
shew the learned, I know the fact myself——

That this Ambrose Paraeus was chief surgeon and nose-mender to
Francis the Ninth of France, and in high credit with him and the two preceding, or succeeding kings (I know not which)—and that, except in the
slip he made in his story of Taliacotius's noses, and his manner of setting
them on—he was esteemed by the whole college of physicians at that time,
as more knowing in matters of noses, than any one who had ever taken them
in hand.

Now Ambrose Paraeus convinced my father, that the true and efficient
cause of what had engaged so much the attention of the world, and upon
which Prignitz and Scroderus had wasted so much learning and fine parts—
was neither this nor that—but that the length and goodness of the nose was
owing simply to the softness and flaccidity in the nurse's breast—as the
flatness and shortness of puisne noses was to the firmness and elastic re-
pulsion of the same organ of nutrition in the hale and lively—which, tho'
happy for the woman, was the undoing of the child, inasmuch as his nose
was so snubbed, so rebuffed, so rebated, and so refrigerated thereby, as
never to arrive *ad mensuram suam legitimam;*—but that in case of the
flaccidity and softness of the nurse or mother's breast—by sinking into it,
quoth Paraeus, as into so much butter, the nose was comforted, nourished,
plumped up, refreshed, refocillated, and set a-growing for ever.

I have but two things to observe of Paraeus; first, That he proves and explains all this with the utmost chastity and decorum of expression:—for which may his soul for ever rest in peace!

And, secondly, that besides the systems of Prignitz and Scroderus, which Ambrose Paraeus his hypothesis effectually overthrew—it overthrew at the same time the system of peace and harmony of our family; and for three days together, not only embroiled matters between my father and my mother, but turned likewise the whole house and every thing in it, except my uncle Toby, quite upside down.

Such a ridiculous tale of a dispute between a man and his wife, never surely in any age or country got vent through the key-hole of a street-door.

My mother, you must know—but I have fifty things more necessary to let you know first—I have a hundred difficulties which I have promised to clear up, and a thousand distresses and domestic misadventures crowding in upon me thick and threefold, one upon the neck of another. A cow broke in (to-morrow morning) to my uncle Toby's fortifications, and eat up two rations and a half of dried grass, tearing up the sods with it, which faced his horn-work and covered-way.——Trim insists upon being tried by a court-martial—the cow to be shot—Slop to be crucified—myself to be tristramed and at my very baptism made a martyr of;—poor unhappy devils that we all are!——I want swaddling—but there is no time to be lost in exclamations—I have left my father lying across his bed, and my uncle Toby in his old fringed chair, sitting beside him, and promised I would go back to them in half an hour; and five-and-thirty minutes are lapsed already.——Of all the perplexities a mortal author was ever seen in—this certainly is the greatest, for I have Hafen Slawkenbergius's folio, Sir, to finish—a dialogue between my father and my uncle Toby, upon the solution of Prignitz, Scroderus, Ambrose Paraeus, Ponocrates, and Grangousier to relate—a tale out of Slawkenbergius to translate, and all this in five minutes less than no time at all;—such a head!—would to Heaven my enemies only saw the inside of it!

CHAPTER 39

THERE was not any one scene more entertaining in our family—and to do it justice in this point;—and I here put off my cap and lay it upon the table close beside my ink-horn, on purpose to make my declaration to the world concerning this one article the more solemn—that I believe in my soul (unless my love and partiality to my understanding blinds me) the hand of the supreme Maker and first Designer of all things never made or put a family together (in that period at least of it which I have sat down to write the story of)—where the characters of it were cast or contrasted with so dramatic a felicity as ours was, for this end; or in which the capacities of affording such exquisite scenes, and the powers of shifting them perpetually from morning to night, were lodged and intrusted with so unlimited a con-fidence, as in the Shandy Family.

Not any one of these was more diverting, I say, in this whimsical theatre of ours—than what frequently arose out of this self-same chapter of long noses—especially when my father's imagination was heated with the en-quiry, and nothing would serve him but to heat my uncle Toby's too.

My uncle Toby would give my father all possible fair play in this attempt; and with infinite patience would sit smoking his pipe for whole hours together, whilst my father was practising upon his head, and trying every accessible avenue to drive Prignitz and Scroderus's solutions into it.

Whether they were above my uncle Toby's reason—or contrary to it—or that his brain was like damp timber, and no spark could possibly take hold —or that it was so full of saps, mines, blinds, curtins, and such military disqualifications to his seeing clearly into Prignitz and Scroderus's doctrines— I say not—let schoolmen—scullions, anatomists, and engineers, fight for it among themselves——

'Twas some misfortune, I make no doubt, in this affair, that my father had every word of it to translate for the benefit of my uncle Toby, and render out of Slawkenbergius's Latin, of which, as he was no great master, his translation was not always of the purest—and generally least so where 'twas most wanted.——This naturally opened a door to a second misfortune;—that in the warmer paroxysms of his zeal to open my uncle Toby's eyes—my father's ideas ran on as much faster than the translation, as the translation outmoved my uncle Toby's—neither the one nor the other added much to the perspicuity of my father's lecture.

CHAPTER 40

THE gift of ratiocination and making syllogisms—I mean in man—for in superior classes of beings, such as angels and spirits—'tis all done, may it please your worships, as they tell me, by Intuition;—and beings inferior, as your worships all know—syllogize by their noses: though there is an island swimming in the sea (though not altogether at its ease) whose inhabitants, if my intelligence deceives me not, are so wonderfully gifted, as to syllogize after the same fashion, and oft-times to make very well out too:——but that's neither here nor there——

The gift of doing it as it should be, amongst us, or—the great and principal act of ratiocination in man, as logicians tell us, is the finding out the agreement or disagreement of two ideas one with another, by the intervention of a third (called the *medius terminus*); just as a man, as Locke well observes, by a yard, finds two men's ninepin-alleys to be of the same length, which could not be brought together, to measure their equality, by juxtaposition.

Had the same great reasoner looked on, as my father illustrated his systems of noses, and observed my uncle Toby's deportment—what great attention he gave to every word—and as oft as he took his pipe from his mouth, with what wonderful seriousness he contemplated the length of it— surveying it transversely as he held it betwixt his finger and his thumb— then foreright—then this way, and then that, in all its possible directions and foreshortenings—he would have concluded my uncle Toby had got hold of the *medius terminus*, and was syllogizing and measuring with it the truth of each hypothesis of long noses, in order, as my father laid them before him. This, by the bye, was more than my father wanted—his aim in all the pains he was at in these philosophic lectures—was to enable my uncle Toby not to discuss—but comprehend—to hold the grains and scruples of learning—not to weigh them.——My uncle Toby, as you will read in the next chapter, did neither the one nor the other.

Chapter 41

'Tis a pity, cried my father one winter's night, after a three hours' painful translation of Slawkenbergius—'tis a pity, cried my father, putting my mother's thread-paper into the book for a mark, as he spoke—that truth, brother Toby, should shut herself up in such impregnable fastnesses, and be so obstinate as not to surrender herself sometimes upon the closest siege.——

Now it happened then, as indeed it had often done before, that my uncle Toby's fancy, during the time of my father's explanation of Prignitz to him—having nothing to stay it there, had taken a short flight to the bowling-green;—his body might as well have taken a turn there too—so that with all the semblance of a deep school-man intent upon the *medius terminus*—my uncle Toby was in fact as ignorant of the whole lecture, and all its pros and cons, as if my father had been translating Hafen Slawkenbergius from the Latin tongue into the Cherokee. But the word "siege," like a talismanic power, in my father's metaphor, wafting back my uncle Toby's fancy, quick as a note could follow the touch—he opened his ears—and my father observing that he took his pipe out of his mouth, and shuffled his chair nearer the table, as with a desire to profit—my father with great pleasure began his sentence again—changing only the plan, and dropping the metaphor of the siege of it, to keep clear of some dangers my father apprehended from it.

'Tis a pity, said my father, that truth can only be on one side, brother Toby—considering what ingenuity these learned men have all shewn in their solutions of noses.—Can noses be dissolved? replied my uncle Toby.

——My father thrust back his chair—rose up—put on his hat—took four long strides to the door—jerked it open—thrust his head half way out—shut the door again—took no notice of the bad hinge—returned to the table—plucked my mother's thread-paper out of Slawkenbergius's book—went hastily to his bureau—walked slowly back—twisted my mother's thread-paper about his thumb—unbuttoned his waistcoat—threw my mother's thread-paper into the fire—bit her satin pincushion in two, filled his mouth with bran—confounded it;—but mark!—the oath of confusion was levelled at my uncle Toby's brain—which was e'en confused enough already—the curse came charged only with the bran—the bran, may it please your honours, was no more than powder to the ball.

'Twas well my father's passions lasted not long; for so long as they did last, they led him a busy life on't; and it is one of the most unaccountable problems that ever I met with in my observations of human nature, that nothing should prove my father's mettle so much, or make his passions go off so like gunpowder, as the unexpected strokes his science met with from the quaint simplicity of my uncle Toby's questions.——Had ten dozen of hornets stung him behind in so many different places all at one time—he could not have exerted more mechanical functions in fewer seconds—or started half so much, as with one single *quaere* of three words unseasonably popping in full upon him in his hobby-horsical career.

'Twas all one to my uncle Toby—he smoked his pipe on with unvaried composure—his heart never intended offence to his brother—and as his head could seldom find out where the sting of it lay—he always gave my father the credit of cooling by himself.——He was five minutes and thirty-five seconds about it in the present case.

By all that's good! said my father, swearing, as he came to himself, and taking the oath out of Ernulphus's digest of curses—(though to do my father justice it was a fault (as he told Dr. Slop in the affair of Ernulphus) which he as seldom committed as any man upon earth)—By all that's good and great! brother Toby, said my father, if it was not for the aids of philosophy, which befriend one so much as they do—you would put a man beside all temper.——Why, by the solutions of noses, of which I was telling you, I meant, as you might have known, had you favoured me with one grain of attention, the various accounts which learned men of different kinds of knowledge have given the world of the causes of the short and long noses. ——There is no cause but one, replied my uncle Toby—why one man's nose is longer than another's, but because that God pleases to have it so.—— That is Grangousier's solution, said my father.——'Tis he, continued my uncle Toby, looking up, and not regarding my father's interruption, who makes us all, and frames and puts us together in such forms and proportions, and for such ends, as is agreeable to his infinite wisdom.——'Tis a pious account, cried my father, but not philosophical—there is more religion in it than sound science. 'Twas no inconsistent part of my uncle Toby's character—that he feared God, and reverenced religion.——So the moment my father finished his remark—my uncle Toby fell a-whistling *Lillabullero* with more zeal (though more out of tune) than usual.——

What is become of my wife's thread-paper?

CHAPTER 42

No matter—as an appendage to seamstressy, the thread-paper might be of some consequence to my mother—of none to my father, as a mark in Slawkenbergius. Slawkenbergius in every page of him was a rich treasure of inexhaustible knowledge to my father—he could not open him amiss; and he would often say in closing the book, that if all the arts and sciences in the world, with the books which treated of them, were lost—should the wisdom and policies of governments, he would say, through disuse, ever happen to be forgot, and all that statesmen had wrote or caused to be written, upon the strong or the weak sides of courts and kingdoms, should they be forgot also—and Slawkenbergius only left—there would be enough in him in all conscience, he would say, to set the world a-going again. A treasure therefore was he indeed! an institute of all that was necessary to be known of noses, and every thing else—at matin, noon, and vespers was Hafen Slawkenbergius his recreation and delight: 'twas for ever in his hands—you would have sworn, Sir, it had been a canon's prayer-book—so worn, so glazed, so contrited and attrited was it with fingers and with thumbs in all its parts, from one end even unto the other.

I am not such a bigot to Slawkenbergius as my father;—there is a fund in him, no doubt: but in my opinion, the best, I don't say the most profitable, but the most amusing part of Hafen Slawkenbergius, is his tales—and, considering he was a German, many of them told not without fancy:—these take up his second book, containing nearly one half of his folio, and are comprehended in ten decads, each decad containing ten tales—Philosophy is not built upon tales; and therefore 'twas certainly wrong in Slawkenbergius to send them into the world by that name!—there are a few of them in his eighth, ninth, and tenth decads, which I own seem rather playful and sportive, than speculative—but in general they are to be looked upon by the learned as a detail of so many independent facts, all of them turning round somehow or other upon the main hinges of his subject, and collected by him with great fidelity, and added to his work as so many illustrations upon the doctrines of noses.

As we have leisure enough upon our hands—if you give me leave, madam, I'll tell you the ninth tale of his tenth decad.

BOOK IV

SLAWKENBERGII
Fabella[1]

VESPERA quâdam frigidulâ, posteriori in parte mensis Augusti, *peregrinus, mulo fusco colore insidens, manticâ a tergo, paucis indusiis, binis calceis, braccisque sericis coccineis repleta,* Argentoratum *ingressus est.*

Militi eum percontanti, quum portas intraret, dixit, se apud Nasorum promontorium fuisse, Francofurtum proficisci, et Argentoratum, transitu ad fines Sarmatiae mensis intervallo, reversurum.

Miles peregrini in faciem suspexit—Dî boni, nova forma nasi!

At multum mihi profuit, inquit peregrinus, carpum amento extrahens, e quo pependit acinaces: Loculo manum inseruit, et magnâ cum urbanitate, pilei parte anteriore tactâ manu sinistrâ, ut extendit dextram, militi florinum dedit et processit.

Dolet mihi, ait miles, tympanistam nanum et valgum alloquens, virum adeo urbanum vaginam perdidisse: itinerari haud poterit nudâ acinaci; neque vaginam toto Argentorato habilem inveniet.—Nullam unquam habui, respondit peregrinus respiciens—seque comiter inclinans—hoc more gesto, nudam acinacem elevans, mulo lentò progrediente, ut nasum tueri possim.

Non immerito, benigne peregrine, respondit miles.
Nihili aestimo, ait ille tympanista, e pergamenâ factitius est.

Prout christianus sum, inquit miles, nasus ille, ni sexties major sit, meo esset conformis.
Crepitare audivi ait tympanista.
Mehercule! sanguinem emisit, respondit miles.
Miseret me, inquit tympanista, qui non ambo tetigimus!
Eodem temporis puncto, quo haec res argumentata fuit inter militem et

[1]As Hafen Slawkenbergius *de Nasis* is extremely scarce, it may not be unacceptable to the learned reader to see the specimen of a few pages of his original; I will make no reflection upon it, but that his story-telling Latin is much more concise than his philosophic—and, I think, has more of Latinity in it.

322

BOOK IV

SLAWKENBERGIUS's

TALE

It was one cool refreshing evening, at the close of a very sultry day, in the latter end of the month of August, when a stranger, mounted upon a dark mule, with a small cloak-bag behind him, containing a few shirts, a pair of shoes, and a crimson-satin pair of breeches, entered the town of Strasburg.

He told the sentinel, who questioned him as he entered the gates, that he had been at the Promontory of Noses—was going on to Frankfort—and should be back again at Strasburg that day month, in his way to the borders of Grim Tartary.

The sentinel looked up into the stranger's face—he never saw such a Nose in his life!

——I have made a very good venture of it, quoth the stranger—so slipping his wrist out of the loop of a black ribbon, to which a short scimetar was hung, he put his hand into his pocket, and with great courtesy touching the fore part of his cap with his left hand, as he extended his right—he put a florin into the sentinel's hand, and passed on.

It grieves me, said the sentinel, speaking to a little dwarfish bandy-legged drummer, that so courteous a soul should have lost his scabbard—he cannot travel without one to his scimetar, and will not be able to get a scabbard to fit it in all Strasburg.——I never had one, replied the stranger, looking back to the sentinel, and putting his hand up to his cap as he spoke—I carry it, continued he, thus—holding up his naked scimetar, his mule moving on slowly all the time—on purpose to defend my nose.

It is well worth it, gentle stranger, replied the sentinel.

——'Tis not worth a single stiver, said the bandy-legged drummer—'tis a nose of parchment.

As I am a true catholic—except that it is six times as big—'tis a nose, said the sentinel, like my own.

——I heard it crackle, said the drummer.

By dunder, said the sentinel, I saw it bleed.

What a pity, cried the bandy-legged drummer, we did not both touch it!

At the very time that this dispute was maintaining by the sentinel and

323

tympanistam, disceptabatur ibidem tubicine et uxore suâ qui tunc accesserunt, et peregrino praetereunte, restiterunt.

Quantus nasus! aeque longus est, ait tubicina, ac tuba.

Et ex eodem metallo, ait tubicen, velut sternutamento audias.
Tantum abest, respondit illa, quod fistulam dulcedine vincit.
Aeneus est, ait tubicen.
Nequaquam, respondit uxor.
Rursum affirmo, ait tubicen, quod aeneus est.
Rem penitus explorabo; prius enim digito tangam, ait uxor, quam dormivero.

Mulus peregrini gradu lento progressus est, ut unumquodque verbum controversiae, non tantum inter militem et tympanistam, verum etiam inter tubicinem et uxorem ejus, audiret.
Nequaquam, ait ille, in muli collum fraena demittens, et manibus ambabus in pectus positis, (mulo lentè progrediente) nequaquam, ait ille respiciens, non necesse est ut res isthaec dilucidata foret. Minime gentium! meus nasus nunquam tangetur, dum spiritus hos reget artus—Ad quid agendum? ait uxor burgomagistri.

Peregrinus illi non respondit. Votum faciebat tunc temporis sancto Nicolao; quo facto, in sinum dextrum inserens, e quâ negligenter pependit acinaces, lento gradu processit per plateam Argentorati latam quae ad diversorium templo ex adversum ducit.

Pereginus mulo descendens stabulo includi, et manticam inferri jussit: quâ apertâ et coccineis sericis femoralibus extractis cum argenteo laciniato Περιζώμαντὲ, his sese induit, statimque, acinaci in manu, ad forum deambulavit.

Quod ubi peregrinus esset ingressus, uxorem tubicinis obviam euntem aspicit; illico cursum flectit, metuens ne nasus suus exploraretur, atque ad diversorium regressus est—exuit se vestibus; braccas coccineas sericas manticae imposuit mulumque educi jussit.

Francofurtum proficiscor, ait ille, et Argentoratum quatuor abhinc hebdomadis revertar.
Bene curasti hoc jumentum? (ait) muli faciem manu demulcens—me, manticamque meam, plus sexcentis mille passibus portavit.

Longa via est! respondet hospes, nisi plurimum esset negoti.—Enimvero, ait peregrinus, a Nasorum promontorio redii, et nasum speciosissimum, egregiosissimumque quem unquam quisquam sortitus est, acquisivi.

the drummer—was the same point debating betwixt a trumpeter and a trumpeter's wife, who were just then coming up, and had stopped to see the stranger pass by.

Benedicity!——What a nose! 'tis as long, said the trumpeter's wife, as a trumpet.

And of the same metal, said the trumpeter, as you hear by its sneezing.

'Tis as soft as a flute, said she.

——'Tis brass, said the trumpeter.

——'Tis a pudding's end, said his wife.

I tell thee again, said the trumpeter, 'tis a brazen nose.

I'll know the bottom of it, said the trumpeter's wife, for I will touch it with my finger before I sleep.

The stranger's mule moved on at so slow a rate, that he heard every word of the dispute, not only betwixt the sentinel and the drummer, but betwixt the trumpeter and trumpeter's wife.

No! said he, dropping his reins upon his mule's neck, and laying both his hands upon his breast, the one over the other, in a saint-like position (his mule going on easily all the time)——No! said he, looking up—I am not such a debtor to the world—slandered and disappointed as I have been—as to give it that conviction—no! said he, my nose shall never be touched whilst Heaven gives me strength—To do what? said a burgomaster's wife.

The stranger took no notice of the burgomaster's wife—he was making a vow to Saint Nicolas; which done, having uncrossed his arms with the same solemnity with which he crossed them, he took up the reins of his bridle with his left hand, and putting his right hand into his bosom, with his scimetar hanging loosely to the wrist of it, he rode on, as slowly as one foot of the mule could follow another, through the principal streets of Strasburg, till chance brought him to the great inn in the market-place over-against the church.

The moment the stranger alighted, he ordered his mule to be led into the stable, and his cloak-bag to be brought in; then opening, and taking out of it his crimson-satin breeches, with a silver-fringed—(appendage to them, which I dare not translate)—he put his breeches, with his fringed codpiece on, and forthwith, with his short scimetar in his hand, walked out to the grand parade.

The stranger had just taken three turns upon the parade, when he perceived the trumpeter's wife at the opposite side of it—so turning short, in pain lest his nose should be attempted, he instantly went back to his inn—undressed himself, packed up his crimson-satin breeches, etc., in his cloak-bag, and called for his mule.

I am going forwards, said the stranger, for Frankfort—and shall be back at Strasburg this day month.

I hope, continued the stranger, stroking down the face of his mule with his left hand as he was going to mount it, that you have been kind to this faithful slave of mine—it has carried me and my cloak-bag, continued he, tapping the mule's back, above six hundred leagues.

——'Tis a long journey, Sir, replied the master of the inn—unless a man has great business.——Tut! tut! said the stranger, I have been at the Promontory of Noses; and have got me one of the goodliest, thank Heaven, that ever fell to a single man's lot.

Dum peregrinus hanc miram rationem de seipso reddit, hospes et uxor ejus, oculis intentis, peregrini nasum contemplantur—Per sanctos sanctasque omnes, ait hospitis uxor, nasis duodecim maximis in toto Argentorato major est!—estne, ait illa mariti in aurem insusurrans, nonne est nasus praegrandis?

Dolus inest, anime mî, ait hospes—nasus est falsus.
Verus est, respondit uxor—
Ex abiete factus est, ait ille, terebinthinum olet——
Carbunculus inest, ait uxor.
Mortuus est nasus, respondit hospes.
Vivus est, ait illa,—et si ipsa vivam tangam.

Votum feci sancto Nicolao, ait peregrinus, nasum meum intactum fore usque ad—Quodnam tempus? illico respondit illa.

Minimo tangetur, inquit ille (manibus in pectus compositis) usque ad illam horam—Quam horam? ait illa—Nullam, respondit peregrinus, donec pervenio ad—Quem locum,—obsecro? ait illa—Peregrinus nil respondens mulo conscenso discessit.

Whilst the stranger was giving this odd account of himself, the master of the inn and his wife kept both their eyes fixed full upon the stranger's nose —By Saint Radagunda, said the inn-keeper's wife to herself, there is more of it than in any dozen of the largest noses put together in all Strasburg! is it not, said she, whispering her husband in his ear, is it not a noble nose?

'Tis an imposture, my dear, said the master of the inn—'tis a false nose.

'Tis a true nose, said his wife.

'Tis made of fir-tree, said he, I smell the turpentine.—

There's a pimple on it, said she.

'Tis a dead nose, replied the inn-keeper.

'Tis a live nose, and if I am alive myself, said the inn-keeper's wife, I will touch it.

I have made a vow to Saint Nicolas this day, said the stranger, that my nose shall not be touched till—Here the stranger, suspending his voice, looked up.——Till when? said she hastily.

It never shall be touched, said he, clasping his hands and bringing them close to his breast, till that hour—What hour? cried the inn-keeper's wife.—— Never!——never! said the stranger, never till I am got—For Heaven's sake, into what place? said she—The stranger rode away without saying a word.

The stranger had not got half a league on his way towards Frankfort before all the city of Strasburg was in an uproar about his nose. The Compline bells were just ringing to call the Strasburgers to their devotions, and shut up the duties of the day in prayer:—no soul in all Strasburg heard 'em—the city was like a swarm of bees—men, women, and children (the Compline bells tinkling all the time) flying here and there—in at one door, out at another—this way and that way—long ways and cross ways—up one street, down another street—in at this alley, out of that—did you see it? did you see it? did you see it? O! did you see it?—who saw it? who did see it? for mercy's sake, who saw it?

Alack o' day! I was at vespers!——I was washing, I was starching, I was scouring, I was quilting—God help me! I never saw it—I never touched it! —would I had been a sentinel, a bandy-legged drummer, a trumpeter, a trumpeter's wife, was the general cry and lamentation in every street and corner of Strasburg.

Whilst all this confusion and disorder triumphed throughout the great city of Strasburg, was the courteous stranger going on as gently upon his mule in his way to Frankfort, as if he had no concern at all in the affair— talking all the way he rode in broken sentences sometimes to his mule— sometimes to himself—sometimes to his Julia.

O Julia, my lovely Julia!—nay I cannot stop to let thee bite that thistle —that ever the suspected tongue of a rival should have robbed me of enjoyment when I was upon the point of tasting it.——

——Pugh!—'tis nothing but a thistle—never mind it—thou shalt have a better supper at night.

——Banished from my country—my friends—from thee.——

Poor devil, thou'rt sadly tired with thy journey!—come—get on a little faster—there's nothing in my cloak-bag but two shirts—a crimson-satin pair of breeches, and a fringed—Dear Julia!

——But why to Frankfort?—is it that there is a hand unfelt, which secretly is conducting me through these meanders and unsuspected tracts?

——Stumbling! by Saint Nicolas! every step—why, at this rate we shall be all night in getting in——

——To happiness—or am I to be the sport of fortune and slander—destined to be driven forth unconvicted—unheard—untouched—if so, why did I not stay at Strasburg, where justice—but I had sworn! Come, thou shalt drink—to Saint Nicolas—O Julia!——What dost thou prick up thy ears at?—'tis nothing but a man, etc.

The stranger rode on communing in this manner with his mule and Julia—till he arrived at his inn, where, as soon as he arrived, he alighted—saw his mule, as he had promised it, taken good care of—took off his cloak-bag, with his crimson-satin breeches, etc., in it—called for an omelet to his supper, went to his bed about twelve o'clock and in five minutes fell fast asleep.

It was about the same hour when the tumult in Strasburg being abated for that night,—the Strasburgers had all got quietly into their beds—but not like the stranger, for the rest either of their minds or bodies; Queen Mab, like an elf as she was, had taken the stranger's nose, and without reduction of its bulk, had that night been at the pains of slitting and dividing it into as many noses of different cuts and fashions, as there were heads in Strasburg to hold them. The abbess of Quedlinburg, who with the four great dignitaries of her chapter, the prioress, the deaness, the sub-chantress, and senior canoness, had that week come to Strasburg to consult the university upon a case of conscience relating to their placket-holes—was ill all the night.

The courteous stranger's nose had got perched upon the top of the pineal gland of her brain, and made such rousing work in the fancies of the four great dignitaries of her chapter, they could not get a wink of sleep the whole night thro' for it—there was no keeping a limb still amongst them—in short, they got up like so many ghosts.

The penitentiaries of the third order of Saint Francis—the nuns of mount Calvary—the Praemonstratenses—the Clunienses[1]—the Carthusians, and all the severer orders of nuns who lay that night in blankets or haircloth, were still in a worse condition than the abbess of Quedlinburg—by tumbling and tossing, and tossing and tumbling from one side of their beds to the other the whole night long—the several sisterhoods had scratched and mauled themselves all to death—they got out of their beds almost flayed alive—every body thought Saint Antony had visited them for probation with his fire—they had never once, in short, shut their eyes the whole night long from vespers to matins.

The nuns of Saint Ursula acted the wisest—they never attempted to go to bed at all.

The dean of Strasburg, the prebendaries, the capitulars and domiciliars (capitularly assembled in the morning to consider the case of buttered buns) all wished they had followed the nuns of Saint Ursula's example.——

[1]Hafen Slawkenbergius means the Benedictine nuns of Cluny, founded in the year 940, by Odo, abbé de Cluny.

In the hurry and confusion every thing had been in the night before, the bakers had all forgot to lay their leaven—there were no buttered buns to be had for breakfast in all Strasburg—the whole close of the cathedral was in one eternal commotion—such a cause of restlessness and disquietude, and such a zealous inquiry into the cause of that restlessness, had never happened in Strasburg, since Martin Luther, with his doctrines, had turned the city upside down.

If the stranger's nose took this liberty of thrusting himself thus into the dishes[1] of religious orders, etc., what a carnival did his nose make of it, in those of the laity!—'tis more than my pen, worn to the stump as it is, has power to describe; tho' I acknowledge, (cries Slawkenbergius, with more gaiety of thought than I could have expected from him) that there is many a good simile now subsisting in the world which might give my countrymen some idea of it; but at the close of such a folio as this, wrote for their sakes, and in which I have spent the greatest part of my life—tho' I own to them the simile is in being, yet would it not be unreasonable in them to expect I should have either time or inclination to search for it? Let it suffice to say, that the riot and disorder it occasioned in the Strasburgers' fantasies was so general—such an overpowering mastership had it got of all the faculties of the Strasburgers' minds—so many strange things, with equal confidence on all sides, and with equal eloquence in all places, were spoken and sworn to concerning it, that turned the whole stream of all discourse and wonder towards it—every soul, good and bad—rich and poor—learned and unlearned—doctor and student—mistress and maid—gentle and simple—nun's flesh and woman's flesh, in Strasburg spent their time in hearing tidings about it—every eye in Strasburg languished to see it—every finger—every thumb in Strasburg burned to touch it.

Now what might add, if any thing may be thought necessary to add, to so vehement a desire—was this, that the sentinel, the bandy-legged drummer, the trumpeter, the trumpeter's wife, the burgomaster's widow, the master of the inn, and the master of the inn's wife, how widely soever they all differed every one from another in their testimonies and description of the stranger's nose—they all agreed together in two points—namely, that he was gone to Frankfort, and would not return to Strasburg till that day month; and secondly, whether his nose was true or false, that the stranger himself was one of the most perfect paragons of beauty—the finest-made man—the most genteel!—the most generous of his purse—the most courteous in his carriage, that had ever entered the gates of Strasburg—that as he rode, with scimetar slung loosely to his wrist, thro' the streets—and walked with his crimson-satin breeches across the parade—'twas with so sweet an air of careless modesty, and so manly withal—as would have put the heart in jeopardy (had his nose not stood in his way) of every virgin who had cast her eyes upon him.

I call not upon that heart which is a stranger to the throbs and yearnings of curiosity, so excited, to justify the abbess of Quedlinburg, the prioress,

---

[1] Mr. Shandy's compliments to orators—is very sensible that Slawkenbergius has here changed his metaphor—which he is very guilty of:—that as a translator, Mr. Shandy has all along done what he could to make him stick to it—but that here 'twas impossible.

the deaness, and sub-chantress, for sending at noon-day for the trumpeter's wife: she went through the streets of Strasburg with her husband's trumpet in her hand,—the best apparatus the straitness of the time would allow her, for the illustration of her theory—she staid no longer than three days.

The sentinel and bandy-legged drummer!—nothing on this side of old Athens could equal them! they read their lectures under the city-gates to comers and goers, with all the pomp of a Chrysippus and a Crantor in their porticos.

The master of the inn, with his ostler on his left-hand, read his also in the same style—under the portico or gateway of his stable-yard—his wife, hers more privately in a back room: all flocked to their lectures; not promiscuously—but to this or that, as is ever the way, as faith and credulity marshalled them—in a word, each Strasburger came crowding for intelligence—and every Strasburger had the intelligence he wanted.

'Tis worth remarking, for the benefit of all demonstrators in natural philosophy, etc., that as soon as the trumpeter's wife had finished the abbess of Quedlinburg's private lecture, and had begun to read in public, which she did upon a stool in the middle of the great parade,—she incommoded the other demonstrators mainly, by gaining incontinently the most fashionable part of the city of Strasburg for her auditory—But when a demonstrator in philosophy (cries Slawkenbergius) has a trumpet for an apparatus, pray what rival in science can pretend to be heard besides him?

Whilst the unlearned, thro' these conduits of intelligence, were all busied in getting down to the bottom of the well, where Truth keeps her little court—were the learned in their way as busy in pumping her up thro' the conduits of dialect induction—they concerned themselves not with facts—they reasoned——

Not one profession had thrown more light upon this subject than the Faculty—had not all their disputes about it run into the affair of Wens and oedematous swellings, they could not keep clear of them for their bloods and souls—the stranger's nose had nothing to do either with wens or oedematous swellings.

It was demonstrated however very satisfactorily, that such a ponderous mass of heterogeneous matter could not be congested and conglomerated to the nose, whilst the infant was *in Utero*, without destroying the statical balance of the foetus, and throwing it plump upon its head nine months before the time.——

——The opponents granted the theory—they denied the consequences.

And if a suitable provision of veins, arteries, etc., said they, was not laid in, for the due nourishment of such a nose, in the very first stamina and rudiments of its formation, before it came into the world (bating the case of Wens) it could not regularly grow and be sustained afterwards.

This was all answered by a dissertation upon nutriment, and the effect which nutriment had in extending the vessels, and in the increase and prolongation of the muscular parts to the greatest growth and expansion imaginable—In the triumph of which theory, they went so far as to affirm, that there was no cause in nature, why a nose might not grow to the size of the man himself.

The respondents satisfied the world this event could never happen to them so long as a man had but one stomach and one pair of lungs—For the stomach, said they, being the only organ destined for the reception of food, and turning it into chyle—and the lungs the only engine of sanguification— it could possibly work off no more, than what the appetite brought it: or admitting the possibility of a man's overloading his stomach, nature had set bounds however to his lungs—the engine was of a determined size and strength, and could elaborate but a certain quantity in a given time—that is, it could produce just as much blood as was sufficient for one single man, and no more; so that, if there was as much nose as man—they proved a mortification must necessarily ensue; and forasmuch as there could not be a support for both, that the nose must either fall off from the man, or the man inevitably fall off from his nose.

Nature accommodates herself to these emergencies, cried the opponents —else what do you say to the case of a whole stomach—a whole pair of lungs, and but half a man, when both his legs have been unfortunately shot off.

He dies of a plethora, said they—or must spit blood, and in a fortnight or three weeks go off in a consumption.——

——It happens otherwise—replied the opponents.——

It ought not, said they.

The more curious and intimate inquirers after Nature and her doings, though they went hand in hand a good way together, yet they all divided about the nose at last, almost as much as the Faculty itself.

They amicably laid it down, that there was a just and geometrical ar-rangement and proportion of the several parts of the human frame to its several destinations, offices, and functions, which could not be transgressed but within certain limits—that nature, though she sported—she sported within a certain circle;—and they could not agree about the diameter of it.

The logicians stuck much closer to the point before them than any of the classes of the literati;—they began and ended with the word Nose; and had it not been for a *petitio principii*, which one of the ablest of them ran his head against in the beginning of the combat, the whole controversy had been settled at once.

A nose, argued the logician, cannot bleed without blood—and not only blood—but blood circulating in it to supply the phenomenon with a suc-cession of drops—(a stream being but a quicker succession of drops, that is included, said he).——Now death, continued the logician, being nothing but the stagnation of the blood——

I deny the definition—Death is the separation of the soul from the body, said his antagonist—Then we don't agree about our weapons, said the logician—Then there is an end of the dispute, replied the antagonist.

The civilians were still more concise: what they offered being more in the nature of a decree—than a dispute.

Such a monstrous nose, said they, had it been a true nose, could not possibly have been suffered in civil society—and if false—to impose upon society with such false signs and tokens, was a still greater violation of its rights, and must have had still less mercy shown it.

The only objection to this was, that if it proved any thing, it proved the stranger's nose was neither true nor false.

This left room for the controversy to go on. It was maintained by the advocates of the ecclesiastic court, that there was nothing to inhibit a decree, since the stranger *ex mero motu* had confessed he had been at the Promontory of Noses, and had got one of the goodliest, etc. etc.——To this it was answered, it was impossible there should be such a place as the Promontory of Noses, and the learned be ignorant where it lay. The commissary of the bishop of Strasburg undertook the advocates, explained this matter in a treatise upon proverbial phrases, showing them, that the Promontory of Noses was a mere allegoric expression, importing no more than that nature had given him a long nose: in proof of which, with great learning, he cited the underwritten authorities,[1] which had decided the point incontestably, had it not appeared that a dispute about some franchises of dean and chapter-lands had been determined by it nineteen years before.

It happened—I must not say unluckily for Truth, because they were giving her a lift another way in so doing; that the two universities of Strasburg—the Lutheran, founded in the year 1538 by Jacobus Surmis, counsellor of the senate,—and the Popish, founded by Leopold, archduke of Austria, were, during all this time, employing the whole depth of their knowledge (except just what the affair of the abbess of Quedlinburg's placket-holes required)—in determining the point of Martin Luther's damnation.

The Popish doctors had undertaken to demonstrate *à priori*, that from the necessary influence of the planets on the twenty-second day of October 1483—when the moon was in the twelfth house, Jupiter, Mars, and Venus in the third, the Sun, Saturn, and Mercury, all got together in the fourth—that he must in course, and unavoidably, be a damned man—and that his doctrines, by a direct corollary, must be damned doctrines too.

By inspection into his horoscope, where five planets were in coition all at once with Scorpio[2] (in reading this my father would always shake his head) in the ninth house, which the Arabians allotted to religion—it appeared

---

[1]Nonnulli ex nostratibus eadem loquendi formulâ utun. Quinimo & Logistae & Canonistae— Vid. Parce Barne Jas in d. L. Provincial. Constitut. de conjec. vid. Vol. Lib. 4. Titul. 1. n. 7. quâ etiam in re conspir. Om de Promontorio Nas. Tichmak. ff. d. tit. 3. fol. 189. passim. Vid. Glos. de contrahend. empt. &c. necnon J. Scrudr. in cap. § refut. per totum. Cum his cons. Rever. J. Tubal, Sentent. & Prov. cap. 9. ff. 11, 12. obiter. V. & Librum, cui Tit. de Terris & Phras. Belg. ad finem, cum comment. N. Bardy Belg. Vid. Scrip. Argentotarens. de Antiq. Ecc. in Episc. Archiv. fid. coll. per Von Jacobum Koinshoven Folio Argent. 1583. praecip. ad finem. Quibus add. Rebuff in L. obvenire de Signif. Nom. ff. fol. & de jure Gent. & Civil. de protib. aliena feud. per federa, test. Joha. Luxius in prolegom. quem velim videas, de Analy. Cap. 1, 2, 3. Vid. Idea.

[2]Haec mira, satisque horrenda Planetarum coitio sub Scorpio Asterismo in nona coeli statione, quam Arabes religioni deputabant, efficit Martinum Lutherum sacrilegum hereticum, Christianae religionis hostem acerrimum atque prophanum, ex horoscopi directione ad Martis coitum, religiosissimus obiit, ejus Anima scelestissima ad infernos navigavit—ab Alecto, Tisiphone & Megara flagellis igneis cruciata perenniter.

——Lucas Gauricus in Tractatu astrologico de praeteritis multorum hominum accidentibus per genituras examinatis.

that Martin Luther did not care one stiver about the matter—and that from the horoscope directed to the conjunction of Mars—they made it plain likewise he must die cursing and blaspheming—with the blast of which his soul (being steeped in guilt) sailed before the wind, in the lake of hell-fire.

The little objection of the Lutheran doctors to this, was, that it must certainly be the soul of another man, born Oct. 22, '83, which was forced to sail down before the wind in that manner—inasmuch as it appeared from the register of Eisleben in the county of Mansfelt, that Luther was not born in the year 1483, but in '84; and not on the 22nd day of October, but on the 10th of November, the eve of Martinmas day, from whence he had the name of Martin.

[——I must break off my translation for a moment; for if I did not, I know I should no more be able to shut my eyes in bed, than the abbess of Quedlinburg—It is to tell the reader, that my father never read this passage of Slawkenbergius to my uncle Toby, but with triumph—not over my uncle Toby, for he never opposed him in it—but over the whole world.

——Now you see, brother Toby, he would say, looking up, "that christian names are not such indifferent things";—had Luther here been called by any other name but Martin, he would have been damned to all eternity —Not that I look upon Martin, he would add, as a good name—far from it—'tis something better than a neutral, and but a little—yet little as it is, you see it was of some service to him.

My father knew the weakness of this prop to his hypothesis, as well as the best logician could shew him—yet so strange is the weakness of man at the same time, as it fell in his way, he could not for his life but make use of it; and it was certainly for this reason, that though there are many stories in Hafen Slawkenbergius's Decads full as entertaining as this I am translating, yet there is not one amongst them which my father read over with half the delight—it flattered two of his strangest hypotheses together—his Names and his Noses.——I will be bold to say, he might have read all the books in the Alexandrian Library, had not fate taken other care of them, and not have met with a book or passage in one, which hit two such nails as these upon the head at one stroke.]

The two universities of Strasburg were hard tugging at this affair of Luther's navigation. The Protestant doctors had demonstrated, that he had not sailed right before the wind, as the Popish doctors had pretended; and as every one knew there was no sailing full in the teeth of it—they were going to settle, in case he had sailed, how many points he was off; whether Martin had doubled the cape, or had fallen upon a lee-shore; and no doubt, as it was an enquiry of much edification, at least to those who understood this sort of Navigation, they had gone on with it in spite of the size of the stranger's nose, had not the size of the stranger's nose drawn off the attention of the world from what they were about—it was their business to follow.

The abbess of Quedlinburg and her four dignitaries was no stop; for the enormity of the stranger's nose running full as much in their fancies as their case of conscience—the affair of their placket-holes kept cold—in a word, the printers were ordered to distribute their types—all controversies dropped.

'Twas a square cap with a silver tassel upon the crown of it—to a nut-shell—to have guessed on which side of the nose the two universities would split.

'Tis above reason, cried the doctors on one side.

'Tis below reason, cried the others.

'Tis faith, one cried.

'Tis a fiddle-stick, said the other.

'Tis possible, cried the one.

'Tis impossible, said the other.

God's power is infinite, cried the Nosarians, he can do any thing.

He can do nothing, replied the Antinosarians, which implies contradictions.

He can make matter think, said the Nosarians.

As certainly as you can make a velvet cap out of a sow's ear, replied the Antinosarians.

He cannot make two and two five, replied the Popish doctors.—'Tis false, said their other opponents.—

Infinite power is infinite power, said the doctors who maintained the reality of the nose.——It extends only to all possible things, replied the Lutherans.

By God in heaven, cried the Popish doctors, he can make a nose, if he thinks fit, as big as the steeple of Strasburg.

Now the steeple of Strasburg being the biggest and the tallest church-steeple to be seen in the whole world, the Antinosarians denied that a nose of 575 geometrical feet in length could be worn, at least by a middle-sized man—The Popish doctors swore it could—The Lutheran doctors said No; —it could not.

This at once started a new dispute, which they pursued a great way, upon the extent and limitation of the moral and natural attributes of God—That controversy led them naturally into Thomas Aquinas, and Thomas Aquinas to the devil.

The stranger's nose was no more heard of in the dispute—it just served as a frigate to launch them into the gulf of school-divinity—and then they all sailed before the wind.

Heat is in proportion to the want of true knowledge.

The controversy about the attributes, etc., instead of cooling, on the contrary had inflamed the Strasburgers' imaginations to a most inordinate degree—The less they understood of the matter, the greater was their wonder about it—they were left in all the distresses of desire unsatisfied— saw their doctors, the Parchmentarians, the Brassarians, the Turpentarians, on one side—the Popish doctors on the other, like Pantagruel and his companions in quest of the oracle of the bottle, all embarked out of sight.

——The poor Strasburgers left upon the beach!

——What was to be done?——No delay—the uproar increased—every one in disorder—the city gates set open.——

Unfortunate Strasburgers! was there in the storehouse of nature—was there in the lumber-rooms of learning—was there in the great arsenal of chance, one single engine left undrawn forth to torture your curiosities, and stretch your desires, which was not pointed by the hand of Fate to play upon your hearts!—I dip not my pen into my ink to excuse the surrender of yourselves—'tis to write your panegyric. Shew me a city so macerated with expectation—who neither eat, or drank, or slept, or prayed, or hearkened to the calls either of religion or nature for seven-and-twenty days together, who could have held out one day longer.

On the twenty-eighth the courteous stranger had promised to return to Strasburg.

Seven thousand coaches (Slawkenbergius must certainly have made some mistake in his numeral characters); 7,000 coaches—15,000 single-horse chairs—20,000 waggons, crowded as full as they could all hold with senators, counsellors, syndics—beguines, widows, wives, virgins, canons, concubines, all in their coaches—The abbess of Quedlinburg, with the prioress, the deaness and sub-chantress, leading the procession in one coach, and the dean of Strasburg, with the four great dignitaries of his chapter, on her left-hand—the rest following higglety-pigglety as they could; some on horseback—some on foot—some led—some driven—some down the Rhine—some this way—some that—all set out at sun-rise to meet the courteous stranger on the road.

Haste we now towards the catastrophe of my tale—I say Catastrophe (cries Slawkenbergius) inasmuch as a tale, with parts rightly disposed, not only rejoiceth (*gaudet*) in the Catastrophe and Peripetia of a Drama, but rejoiceth moreover in all the essential and integrant parts of it—it has its Protasis, Epitasis, Catastasis, its Catastrophe or Peripetia growing one out of the other in it, in the order Aristotle first planted them—without which a tale had better never been told at all, says Slawkenbergius, but be kept to a man's self.

In all my ten tales, in all my ten decads, have I Slawkenbergius tied down every tale of them as tightly to this rule, as I have done this of the stranger and his nose.

——From his first parley with the sentinel, to his leaving the city of Strasburg, after pulling off his crimson-satin pair of breeches, is the Protasis or first entrance—where the characters of the *Personae Dramatis* are just touched in, and the subject slightly begun.

The Epitasis, wherein the action is more fully entered upon and heightened, till it arrives at its state or height called the Catastasis, and which usually takes up the 2nd and 3rd act, is included within that busy period of my tale, betwixt the first night's uproar about the nose, to the conclusion of the trumpeter's wife's lectures upon it in the middle of the grand parade: and from the first embarking of the learned in the dispute—to the doctors finally sailing away, and leaving the Strasburgers upon the beach in distress, is the Catastasis or the ripening of the incidents and passions for their bursting forth in the fifth act.

This commences with the setting out of the Strasburgers in the Frank-fort road, and terminates in unwinding the labyrinth and bringing the hero out of a state of agitation (as Aristotle calls it) to a state of rest and quietness.

This, says Hafen Slawkenbergius, constitutes the Catastrophe or Peripetia of my tale—and that is the part of it I am going to relate.

We left the stranger behind the curtain asleep—he enters now upon the stage.

——What dost thou prick up thy ears at?—'tis nothing but a man upon a horse—was the last word the stranger uttered to his mule. It was not proper then to tell the reader, that the mule took his master's word for it; and without any more *ifs* or *ands*, let the traveller and his horse pass by.

The traveller was hastening with all diligence to get to Strasburg that night. What a fool am I, said the traveller to himself, when he had rode about a league farther, to think of getting into Strasburg this night.—— Strasburg!——the great Strasburg!——Strasburg, the capital of all Alsatia! Strasburg, an imperial city! Strasburg, a sovereign state! Strasburg, garrisoned with five thousand of the best troops in all the world!——Alas! if I was at the gates of Strasburg this moment, I could not gain admittance into it for a ducat—nay a ducat and half—'tis too much—better go back to the last inn I have passed—than lie I know not where—or give I know not what. The traveller, as he made these reflections in his mind, turned his horse's head about, and three minutes after the stranger had been conducted into his chamber, he arrived at the same inn.

——We have bacon in the house, said the host, and bread—and till eleven o'clock this night had three eggs in it—but a stranger, who arrived an hour ago, has had them dressed into an omelet, and we have nothing.——

Alas! said the traveller, harassed as I am, I want nothing but a bed.—— I have one as soft as is in Alsatia, said the host.

——The stranger, continued he, should have slept in it, for 'tis my best bed, but upon the score of his nose.——He has got a defluxion, said the traveller.——Not that I know, cried the host.—But 'tis a camp-bed, and Jacinta, said he, looking towards the maid, imagined there was not room in it to turn his nose in.——Why so? cried the traveller, starting back.—It is so long a nose, replied the host.——The traveller fixed his eyes upon Jacinta, then upon the ground—kneeled upon his right knee—had just got his hand laid upon his breast—Trifle not with my anxiety, said he, rising up again.——'Tis no trifle, said Jacinta, 'tis the most glorious nose!—— The traveller fell upon his knee again—laid his hand upon his breast— then, said he, looking up to heaven, thou hast conducted me to the end of my pilgrimage—'Tis Diego.

The traveller was the brother of the Julia, so often invoked that night by the stranger as he rode from Strasburg upon his mule; and was come, on her part, in quest of him. He had accompanied his sister from Valladolid across the Pyrenean mountains through France, and had many an entangled skein to wind off in pursuit of him through the many meanders and abrupt turnings of a lover's thorny tracks.

——Julia had sunk under it—and had not been able to go a step farther than to Lyons, where, with the many disquietudes of a tender heart, which all talk of—but few feel—she sickened, but had just strength to write a letter to Diego; and having conjured her brother never to see her face till he had found him out, and put the letter into his hands, Julia took to her bed.

Fernandez (for that was her brother's name)—tho' the camp-bed was as soft as any one in Alsace, yet he could not shut his eyes in it.——As soon as it was day he rose, and hearing Diego was risen too, he entered his chamber, and discharged his sister's commission.

The letter was as follows:

"Seig. DIEGO,

"Whether my suspicions of your nose were justly excited or not—'tis not now to inquire—it is enough I have not had firmness to put them to farther trial.

"How could I know so little of myself, when I sent my Duenna to forbid your coming more under my lattice? or how could I know so little of you, Diego, as to imagine you would not have stayed one day in Valladolid to have given ease to my doubts?——Was I to be abandoned, Diego, because I was deceived? or was it kind to take me at my word, whether my suspicions were just or no, and leave me, as you did, a prey to much uncertainty and sorrow?

"In what manner Julia has resented this—my brother, when he puts this letter into your hands, will tell you; He will tell you in how few moments she repented of the rash message she had sent you—in what frantic haste she flew to her lattice, and how many days and nights together she leaned immoveably upon her elbow, looking through it towards the way which Diego was wont to come.

"He will tell you, when she heard of your departure—how her spirits deserted her—how her heart sickened—how piteously she mourned—how low she hung her head. O Diego! how many weary steps has my brother's pity led me by the hand languishing to trace out yours; how far has desire carried me beyond strength—and how oft have I fainted by the way, and sunk into his arms, with only power to cry out—O my Diego!

"If the gentleness of your carriage has not belied your heart, you will fly to me, almost as fast as you fled from me—haste as you will—you will arrive but to see me expire.——'Tis a bitter draught, Diego, but oh! 'tis embittered still more by dying un——"

She could proceed no farther.

Slawkenbergius supposes the word intended was "unconvinced," but her strength would not enable her to finish her letter. The heart of the courteous Diego overflowed as he read the letter—he ordered his mule forthwith and Fernandez's horse to be saddled; and as no vent in prose is equal to that of poetry in such conflicts—chance, which as often directs us to remedies as to diseases, having thrown a piece of charcoal into the window—Diego availed himself of it, and whilst the hostler was getting ready his mule, he eased his mind against the wall as follows.

ODE

Harsh and untuneful are the notes of love,
Unless my Julia strikes the key,
Her hand alone can touch the part,
Whose dulcet move-
ment charms the heart,
And governs all the man with sympathetic sway.
2nd.
O Julia!

The lines were very natural—for they were nothing at all to the purpose, says Slawkenbergius, and 'tis a pity there were no more of them; but whether it was that Seig. Diego was slow in composing verses—or the hostler quick in saddling mules—is not averred; certain it was, that Diego's mule and Fernandez's horse were ready at the door of the inn, before Diego was ready for his second stanza; so without staying to finish his ode, they both mounted, sallied forth, passed the Rhine, traversed Alsace, shaped their course towards Lyons, and before the Strasburgers and the abbess of Quedlinburg had set out on their cavalcade, had Fernandez, Diego, and his Julia crossed the Pyrenean mountains, and got safe to Valladolid.

'Tis needless to inform the geographical reader, that when Diego was in Spain, it was not possible to meet the courteous stranger in the Frankfort road; it is enough to say, that of all restless desires, curiosity being the strongest—the Strasburgers felt the full force of it; and that for three days and nights they were tossed to and fro in the Frankfort road, with the tempestuous fury of this passion, before they could submit to return home. ——When alas! an event was prepared for them, of all other, the most grievous that could befall a free people.

As this revolution of the Strasburgers' affairs is often spoken of, and little understood, I will, in ten words, says Slawkenbergius, give the world an explanation of it, and with it put an end to my tale.

Every body knows of the grand system of Universal Monarchy, wrote by order of Mons. Colbert, and put in manuscript into the hands of Lewis the fourteenth, in the year 1664.

'Tis as well known, that one branch out of many of that system, was the getting possession of Strasburg, to favour an entrance at all times into Suabia, in order to disturb the quiet of Germany—and that in consequence of this plan, Strasburg unhappily fell at length into their hands.

It is the lot of a few to trace out the true springs of this and such like revolutions—The vulgar look too high for them—Statesmen look too low— Truth (for once) lies in the middle.

What a fatal thing is the popular pride of a free city! cries one historian— The Strasburgers deemed it a diminution of their freedom to receive an imperial garrison—so fell a prey to a French one.

The fate, says another, of the Strasburgers, may be a warning to all free people to save their money.——They anticipated their revenues—brought themselves under taxes, exhausted their strength, and in the end became so weak a people, they had not strength to keep their gates shut, and so the French pushed them open.

Alas! alas! cries Slawkenbergius, 'twas not the French,—'twas curiosity pushed them open—The French indeed, who are ever upon the catch, when they saw the Strasburgers, men, women, and children, all marched out to follow the stranger's nose—each man followed his own, and marched in.

Trade and manufactures have decayed and gradually grown down ever since—but not from any cause which commercial heads have assigned; for it is owing to this only, that noses have ever so run in their heads, that the Strasburgers could not follow their business.

Alas! alas! cries Slawkenbergius, making an exclamation—it is not the first—and I fear will not be the last fortress that has been either won—or lost by noses.

The End of Slawkenbergius's Tale.

CHAPTER I

WITH all this learning upon noses running perpetually in my father's fancy —with so many family prejudices—and ten decads of such tales running on for ever along with them—how was it possible with such exquisite—was it a true nose?—That a man with such exquisite feelings as my father had, could bear the shock at all below stairs—or indeed above stairs, in any other posture, but the very posture I have described?

——Throw yourself down upon the bed, a dozen times—taking care only to place a looking-glass first in a chair on one side of it, before you do it— But was the stranger's nose a true nose, or was it a false one?

To tell that before-hand, madam, would be to do injury to one of the best tales in the Christian-world; and that is the tenth of the tenth decad, which immediately follows this.

This tale, cried Slawkenbergius, somewhat exultingly, has been reserved by me for the concluding tale of my whole work; knowing right well, that when I shall have told it, and my reader shall have read it thro'—'twould be even high time for both of us to shut up the book; inasmuch, continues Slawkenbergius, as I know of no tale which could possibly ever go down after it.

——'Tis a tale indeed!

This sets out with the first interview in the inn at Lyons, when Fernandez left the courteous stranger and his sister Julia alone in her chamber, and is over-written

The INTRICACIES OF *Diego* and *Julia*.

Heavens! thou art a strange creature, Slawkenbergius! what a whimsical view of the involutions of the heart of woman hast thou opened! how this can ever be translated, and yet if this specimen of Slawkenbergius's tales, and the exquisitiveness of his moral, should please the world—translated shall a couple of volumes be.——Else, how this can ever be translated into good English, I have no sort of conception—There seems in some passages to want a sixth sense to do it rightly.——What can he mean by the lambent

pupilability of slow, low, dry chat, five notes below the natural tone—
which you know, madam, is little more than a whisper? The moment I pronounced the words, I could perceive an attempt towards a vibration in the
strings, about the region of the heart.——The brain made no acknowledgment.——There's often no good understanding betwixt 'em—I felt as if I
understood it.——I had no ideas.——The movement could not be without
cause.——I'm lost. I can make nothing of it—unless, may it please your
worships, the voice, in that case being little more than a whisper, unavoidably forces the eyes to approach not only within six inches of each other—
but to look into the pupils—is not that dangerous?—But it can't be avoided
—for to look up to the ceiling, in that case the two chins unavoidably meet
—and to look down into each other's lap, the foreheads come to immediate
contact, which at once puts an end to the conference—I mean to the sentimental part of it.——What is left, madam, is not worth stooping for.

Chapter 2

My father lay stretched across the bed as still as if the hand of death had
pushed him down, for a full hour and a half before he began to play upon
the floor with the toe of that foot which hung over the bed-side; my uncle
Toby's heart was a pound lighter for it.——In a few moments, his left-
hand, the knuckles of which had all the time reclined upon the handle of
the chamber-pot, came to its feeling—he thrust it a little more within the
valance—drew up his hand, when he had done, into his bosom—gave a
hem! My good uncle Toby, with infinite pleasure, answered it; and full
gladly would have ingrafted a sentence of consolation upon the opening it
afforded: but having no talents, as I said, that way, and fearing moreover
that he might set out with something which might make a bad matter
worse, he contented himself with resting his chin placidly upon the cross of
his crutch.

Now whether the compression shortened my uncle Toby's face into a
more pleasurable oval—or that the philanthropy of his heart, in seeing his
brother beginning to emerge out of the sea of his afflictions, had braced up
his muscles—so that the compression upon his chin only doubled the benignity which was there before, is not hard to decide.——My father, in
turning his eyes, was struck with such a gleam of sunshine in his face, as
melted down the sullenness of his grief in a moment.

He broke silence as follows.

Chapter 3

Did ever man, brother Toby, cried my father, raising himself upon his elbow, and turning himself round to the opposite side of the bed, where my
uncle Toby was sitting in his old fringed chair, with his chin resting upon
his crutch—did ever a poor unfortunate man, brother Toby, cried my
father, receive so many lashes?——The most I ever saw given, quoth my
uncle Toby (ringing the bell at the bed's head for Trim) was to a grenadier,
I think in Mackay's regiment.

——Had my uncle Toby shot a bullet through my father's heart, he could not have fallen down with his nose upon the quilt more suddenly.

Bless me! said my uncle Toby.

CHAPTER 4

Was it Mackay's regiment, quoth my uncle Toby, where the poor grenadier was so unmercifully whipped at Bruges about the ducats?——O Christ! he was innocent! cried Trim, with a deep sigh.—And he was whipped, may it please your honour, almost to death's door.——They had better have shot him outright, as he begged, and he had gone directly to heaven, for he was as innocent as your honour.——I thank thee, Trim, quoth my uncle Toby. ——I never think of his, continued Trim, and my poor brother Tom's misfortunes, for we were all three school-fellows, but I cry like a coward. ——Tears are no proof of cowardice, Trim.——I drop them oft-times myself, cried my uncle Toby.——I know your honour does, replied Trim, and so am not ashamed of it myself.—But to think, may it please your honour, continued Trim, a tear stealing into the corner of his eye as he spoke—to think of two virtuous lads with hearts as warm in their bodies, and as honest as God could make them—the children of honest people, going forth with gallant spirits to seek their fortunes in the world—and fall into such evils!—poor Tom! to be tortured upon a rack for nothing—but marrying a Jew's widow who sold sausages—honest Dick Johnson's soul to be scourged out of his body, for the ducats another man put into his knapsack!——O!— these are misfortunes, cried Trim,—pulling out his handkerchief—these are misfortunes, may it please your honour, worth lying down and crying over.

——My father could not help blushing.

'Twould be a pity, Trim, quoth my uncle Toby, thou shouldst ever feel sorrow of thy own—thou feelest it so tenderly for others.——Alack-o-day, replied the Corporal, brightening up his face—your honour knows I have neither wife or child—I can have no sorrows in this world.—My father could not help smiling.—As few as any man, Trim, replied my uncle Toby; nor can I see how a fellow of thy light heart can suffer, but from the distress of poverty in thy old age—when thou art passed all services, Trim—and hast outlived thy friends.——An' please your honour, never fear, replied Trim, cheerily.——But I would have thee never fear, Trim, replied my uncle Toby, and therefore, continued my uncle Toby, throwing down his crutch, and getting up upon his legs as he uttered the word "therefore"— in recompense, Trim, of thy long fidelity to me, and that goodness of thy heart I have had such proofs of—whilst thy master is worth a shilling—thou shalt never ask elsewhere, Trim, for a penny. Trim attempted to thank my uncle Toby—but had not power—tears trickled down his cheeks faster than he could wipe them off—He laid his hands upon his breast—made a bow to the ground, and shut the door.

——I have left Trim my bowling-green, cried my uncle Toby.——My father smiled.——I have left him moreover a pension, continued my uncle Toby.——My father looked grave.

Chapter 5

Is this a fit time, said my father to himself, to talk of Pensions and Grenadiers?

Chapter 6

WHEN my uncle Toby first mentioned the grenadier, my father, I said, fell down with his nose flat to the quilt, and as suddenly as if my uncle Toby had shot him; but it was not added that every other limb and member of my father instantly relapsed with his nose into the same precise attitude in which he lay first described; so that when Corporal Trim left the room, and my father found himself disposed to rise off the bed—he had all the little preparatory movements to run over again, before he could do it. Attitudes are nothing, madam—'tis the transition from one attitude to another—like the preparation and resolution of the discord into harmony, which is all in all.

For which reason my father played the same jig over again with his toe upon the floor—pushed the chamber-pot still a little further within the valance—gave a hem—raised himself up upon his elbow—and was just beginning to address himself to my uncle Toby—when recollecting the unsuccessfulness of his first effort in that attitude—he got upon his legs, and in making the third turn across the room, he stopped short before my uncle Toby; and laying the three first fingers of his right-hand in the palm of his left, and stooping a little, he addressed himself to my uncle Toby as follows:

Chapter 7

WHEN I reflect, brother Toby, upon Man; and take a view of that dark side of him which represents his life as open to so many causes of trouble—when I consider, brother Toby, how oft we eat the bread of affliction, and that we are born to it, as to the portion of our inheritance—I was born to nothing, quoth my uncle Toby, interrupting my father—but my commission. Zooks! said my father, did not my uncle leave you a hundred and twenty pounds a year?——What could I have done without it? replied my uncle Toby—— That's another concern, said my father testily—But I say, Toby, when one runs over the catalogue of all the cross-reckonings and sorrowful Items with which the heart of man is overcharged, 'tis wonderful by what hidden resources the mind is enabled to stand out, and bear itself up, as it does, against the impositions laid upon our nature.——'Tis by the assistance of Almighty God, cried my uncle Toby, looking up, and pressing the palms of his hands close together—'tis not from our own strength, brother Shandy— a sentinel in a wooden sentry-box might as well pretend to stand it out against a detachment of fifty men.——We are upheld by the grace and the assistance of the best of Beings.

——That is cutting the knot, said my father, instead of untying it—— But give me leave to lead you, brother Toby, a little deeper into the mystery.

With all my heart, replied my uncle Toby.

My father instantly exchanged the attitude he was in, for that in which Socrates is so finely painted by Raffael in his school of Athens; which your connoisseurship knows is so exquisitely imagined, that even the particular manner of the reasoning of Socrates is expressed by it—for he holds the fore-finger of his left-hand between the fore-finger and the thumb of his right, and seems as if he was saying to the libertine he is reclaiming—"You grant me this—and this: and this, and this, I don't ask of you—they follow of themselves in course."

So stood my father, holding fast his fore-finger betwixt his finger and his thumb, and reasoning with my uncle Toby as he sat in his old fringed chair, valanced around with party-coloured worsted bobs—O Garrick!—what a rich scene of this would thy exquisite powers make! and how gladly would I write such another to avail myself of thy immortality, and secure my own behind it.

CHAPTER 8

THOUGH man is of all others the most curious vehicle, said my father, yet at the same time 'tis of so slight a frame, and so totteringly put together, that the sudden jerks and hard jostlings it unavoidably meets with in this rugged journey, would overset and tear it to pieces a dozen times a day— was it not, brother Toby, that there is a secret spring within us.——Which spring, said my uncle Toby, I take to be Religion.——Will that set my child's nose on? cried my father, letting go his finger, and striking one hand against the other.——It makes every thing straight for us, answered my uncle Toby.——Figuratively speaking, dear Toby, it may, for aught I know, said my father; but the spring I am speaking of, is that great and elastic power within us of counterbalancing evil, which, like a secret spring in a well-ordered machine, though it can't prevent the shock—at least it imposes upon our sense of it.

Now, my dear brother, said my father, replacing his fore-finger, as he was coming closer to the point—had my child arrived safe into the world, un- martyred in that precious part of him—fanciful and extravagant as I may appear to the world in my opinion of christian names, and of that magic bias which good or bad names irresistibly impress upon our characters and conducts—Heaven is witness! that in the warmest transports of my wishes for the prosperity of my child, I never once wished to crown his head with more glory and honour than what George or Edward would have spread around it.

But alas! continued my father, as the greatest evil has befallen him—I must counteract and undo it with the greatest good.

He shall be christened Trismegistus, brother.

I wish it may answer—replied my uncle Toby, rising up.

CHAPTER 9

WHAT a chapter of chances, said my father, turning himself about upon the first landing, as he and my uncle Toby were going downstairs—what a long chapter of chances do the events of this world lay open to us! Take pen and ink in hand, brother Toby, and calculate it fairly—I know no more of calculation than this balluster, said my uncle Toby (striking short of it with his crutch, and hitting my father a desperate blow souse upon his shinbone)—'Twas a hundred to one—cried my uncle Toby—I thought, quoth my father, (rubbing his shin) you had known nothing of calculations, brother Toby. 'Tis a mere chance, said my uncle Toby.——Then it adds one to the chapter—replied my father.

The double success of my father's repartees tickled off the pain of his shin at once—it was well it so fell out—(chance! again)—or the world to this day had never known the subject of my father's calculation—to guess it—there was no chance—What a lucky chapter of chances has this turned out! for it has saved me the trouble of writing one express, and in truth I have enough already upon my hands without it.——Have not I promised the world a chapter of knots? two chapters upon the right and the wrong end of a woman? a chapter upon whiskers? a chapter upon wishes?—a chapter of noses?——No, I have done that—a chapter upon my uncle Toby's modesty? to say nothing of a chapter upon chapters, which I will finish before I sleep—by my great-grandfather's whiskers, I shall never get half of 'em through this year.

Take pen and ink in hand, and calculate it fairly, brother Toby, said my father, and it will turn out a million to one, that of all the parts of the body, the edge of the forceps should have the ill luck just to fall upon and break down that one part, which should break down the fortunes of our house with it.

It might have been worse, replied my uncle Toby.——I don't comprehend, said my father.——Suppose the hip had presented, replied my uncle Toby, as Dr. Slop foreboded.

My father reflected half a minute—looked down—touched the middle of his forehead slightly with his finger——

——True, said he.

CHAPTER 10

Is it not a shame to make two chapters of what passed in going down one pair of stairs? for we are got no farther yet than to the first landing, and there are fifteen more steps down to the bottom; and for aught I know, as my father and my uncle Toby are in a talking humour, there may be as many chapters as steps:—let that be as it will, Sir. I can no more help it than my destiny:—A sudden impulse comes across me—drop the curtain, Shandy—I drop it—Strike a line here across the paper, Tristram—I strike it—and hey for a new chapter.

The deuce of any other rule have I to govern myself by in this affair—and if I had one—as I do all things out of all rule—I would twist it and tear it to pieces, and throw it into the fire when I had done—Am I warm? I am, and the cause demands it—a pretty story! is a man to follow rules—or rules to follow him?

Now this, you must know, being my chapter upon chapters, which I promised to write before I went to sleep, I thought it meet to ease my conscience entirely before I laid down, by telling the world all I knew about

the matter at once: Is not this ten times better than to set out dogmatically
with a sententious parade of wisdom, and telling the world a story of a
roasted horse—that chapters relieve the mind—that they assist—or impose
upon the imagination—and that in a work of this dramatic cast they are as
necessary as the shifting of scenes—with fifty other cold conceits, enough to
extinguish the fire which roasted him?——O! but to understand this, which
is a puff at the fire of Diana's temple—you must read Longinus—read away
—if you are not a jot the wiser by reading him the first time over—never
fear—read him again—Avicenna and Licetus read Aristotle's metaphysics
forty times through a-piece, and never understood a single word.——But
mark the consequence—Avicenna turned out a desperate writer at all
kinds of writing—for he wrote books *de omni scribili;* and for Licetus
(Fortunio) though all the world knows he was born a foetus,[1] of no more
than five and a half inches in length, yet he grew to that astonishing height
in literature, as to write a book with a title as long as himself—the learned
know I mean his Gonopsychanthropologia, upon the origin of the human
soul.

So much for my chapter upon chapters, which I hold to be the best
chapter in my whole work; and take my word, whoever reads it, is full as
well employed, as in picking straws.

CHAPTER 11

WE shall bring all things to rights, said my father, setting his foot upon the
first step from the landing.——This Trismegistus, continued my father,
drawing his leg back and turning to my uncle Toby—was the greatest
(Toby) of all earthly beings—he was the greatest king—the greatest law-
giver—the greatest philosopher—and the greatest priest—and engineer—
said my uncle Toby.

——In course, said my father.

[1]Ce Foetus n'étoit pas plus grand que la paume de la main; mais son père l'ayant examiné
en qualité de Médecin, & ayant trouvé que c'étoit quelque chose de plus qu'un Embryon, le fit
transporter tout vivant à Raqallo, où il le fit voir à Jérôme Bardi & à d'autres Médecins du lieu.
On trouva qu'il ne lui manquoit rien d'essentiel à la vie; & son père pour faire voir un essai de
son expérience, entreprit d'achever l'ouvrage de la Nature, & de travailler à la formation de
l'Enfant avec le même artifice que celui dont on se sert pour faire éclore les Poulets en Egypte.
Il instruisit une Nourrice de tout ce qu'elle avoit à faire, & ayant fait mettre son fils dans un
four proprement accommodé, il réussit à l'élever & à lui faire prendre ses accroissemens nécessaires, par l'uniformité d'une chaleur étrangère mesurée exactement sur les dégrés d'un
Thermomètre, ou d'un autre instrument équivalent. (Vide Mich. Giustinian negli Scritt. Li-
guri à Cart. 223. 488.)

On auroit toujours été très satisfait de l'industrie d'un père si expérimenté dans l'Art de la
Génération, quand il n'auroit pu prolonger la vie à sons fils que pour quelques mois, ou pour
peu d'années.

Mais quand on se représente que l'Enfant a vecu près de quatre-vingts ans, & qu'il a com-
posé quatre-vingts Ouvrages différents tous fruits d'une longue lecture—il faut convenir que
tout ce qui est incroyable n'est pas toujours faux, & que la Vraisemblance n'est pas toujours
du côté de la Vérité.

Il n'avoit que dix neuf ans lorsqu'il composa Gonopsychanthropologia de Origine Animae
humanae.

(*Les Enfans célèbres*, revu & corrigé par M. de la Monnoye de l'Académie Françoise.)

Chapter 12

——And how does your mistress? cried my father, taking the same step over again from the landing, and calling to Susannah, whom he saw passing by the foot of the stairs with a huge pincushion in her hand——how does your mistress? As well, said Susannah, tripping by, but without looking up, as can be expected.——What a fool am I! said my father, drawing his leg back again——let things be as they will, brother Toby, 'tis ever the precise answer ——And how is the child, pray?——No answer. And where is Dr. Slop? added my father, raising his voice aloud, and looking over the ballusters—— Susannah was out of hearing.

Of all the riddles of a married life, said my father, crossing the landing in order to set his back against the wall, whilst he propounded it to my uncle Toby——of all the puzzling riddles, said he, in a marriage state,——of which you may trust me, brother Toby, there are more asses' loads than all Job's stock of asses could have carried——there is not one that has more intricacies in it than this——that from the very moment the mistress of the house is brought to bed, every female in it, from my lady's gentlewoman down to the cinder-wench, becomes an inch taller for it; and give themselves more airs upon that single inch, than all the other inches put together.

I think rather, replied my uncle Toby, that 'tis we who sink an inch lower.——If I meet but a woman with child——I do it.——'Tis a heavy tax upon that half of our fellow-creatures, brother Shandy, said my uncle Toby —'Tis a piteous burden upon 'em, continued he, shaking his head——Yes, yes, 'tis a painful thing——said my father, shaking his head too——but certainly since shaking of heads came into fashion, never did two heads shake together, in concert, from two such different springs.

God bless {'em all——said my uncle Toby and my
Deuce take {father, each to himself.

Chapter 13

Holla!——you, chairman!——here's sixpence——do step into that bookseller's shop, and call me a day-tall critic. I am very willing to give any one of 'em a crown to help me with his tackling, to get my father and my uncle Toby off the stairs, and to put them to bed.

——'Tis even high time; for except a short nap, which they both got whilst Trim was boring the jack-boots——and which, by the bye, did my father no sort of good, upon the score of the bad hinge——they have not else shut their eyes, since nine hours before the time that Dr. Slop was led into the back parlour in that dirty pickle by Obadiah.

Was every day of my life to be as busy a day as this——and to take up—— Truce.

I will not finish that sentence till I have made an observation upon the strange state of affairs between the reader and myself, just as things stand at present——an observation never applicable before to any one biographical writer since the creation of the world, but to myself——and I believe, will never hold good to any other, until its final destruction—and therefore, for the very novelty of it alone, it must be worth your worships attending to.

I am this month one whole year older than I was this time twelve-month; and having got, as you perceive, almost into the middle of my fourth volume[1]—and no farther than to my first day's life—'tis demonstrative that I have three hundred and sixty-four days more life to write just now, than when I first set out; so that instead of advancing, as a common writer, in my work with what I have been doing at it—on the contrary, I am just thrown so many volumes back—was every day of my life to be as busy a day as this—And why not?—and the transactions and opinions of it to take up as much description—And for what reason should they be cut short? as at this rate I should just live 364 times faster than I should write—It must follow, an' please your worships, that the more I write, the more I shall have to write—and consequently, the more your worships will have to read.

Will this be good for your worships' eyes?

It will do well for mine; and, was it not that my Opinions will be the death of me, I perceive I shall lead a fine life of it out of this self-same life of mine; or, in other words, shall lead a couple of fine lives together.

As for the proposal of twelve volumes a year, or a volume a month, it no way alters my prospect—write as I will, and rush as I may into the middle of things, as Horace advises—I shall never overtake myself whipped and driven to the last pinch; at the worst I shall have one day the start of my pen—and one day is enough for two volumes—and two volumes will be enough for one year.——

Heaven prosper the manufacturers of paper under this propitious reign, which is now opened to us—as I trust its providence will prosper every thing else in it that is taken in hand.——

As for the propagation of Geese—I give myself no concern—Nature is all bountiful—I shall never want tools to work with.

——So then, friend! you have got my father and my uncle Toby off the stairs, and seen them to bed?——And how did you manage it?——You dropped a curtain at the stair-foot—I thought you had no other way for it —Here's a crown for your trouble.

Chapter 14

——Then reach me my breeches off the chair, said my father to Susannah. ——There is not a moment's time to dress you, Sir, cried Susannah—the child is as black in the face as my—As your what? said my father, for like all orators, he was a dear searcher into comparisons.——Bless me, Sir, said Susannah, the child's in a fit.——And where's Mr. Yorick?——Never where he should be, said Susannah, but his curate's in the dressing-room, with the child upon his arm, waiting for the name—and my mistress bid me run as fast as I could to know, as Captain Shandy is the godfather, whether it should not be called after him.

[1 *i.e.* According to the original editions.]

Were one sure, said my father to himself, scratching his eye-brow, that the child was expiring, one might as well compliment my brother Toby as not—and it would be a pity, in such a case, to throw away so great a name as Trismegistus upon him—but he may recover.

No, no,—said my father to Susannah, I'll get up—There is no time, cried Susannah, the child's as black as my shoe. Trismegistus, said my father—— But stay—thou art a leaky vessel, Susannah, added my father; canst thou carry Trismegistus in thy head, the length of the gallery without scattering? ——Can I? cried Susannah, shutting the door in a huff.——If she can, I'll be shot, said my father, bouncing out of bed in the dark, and groping for his breeches.

Susannah ran with all speed along the gallery.

My father made all possible speed to find his breeches.

Susannah got the start, and kept it.——'Tis Tris—something, cried Susannah—There is no christian-name in the world, said the curate, beginning with Tris—but Tristram. Then 'tis Tristram-gistus, quoth Susannah.

——There is no gistus to it, noddle!—'tis my own name, replied the curate, dipping his hand, as he spoke, into the bason—Tristram! said he, etc. etc. etc. etc., so Tristram was I called, and Tristram shall I be to the day of my death.

My father followed Susannah, with his night-gown across his arm, with nothing more than his breeches on, fastened through haste with but a single button, and that buttom through haste thrust only half into the button-hole.

——She has not forgot the name? cried my father, half opening the door. ——No, no, said the curate, with a tone of intelligence.—And the child is better, cried Susannah.——And how does your mistress? As well, said Susannah, as can be expected.——Pish! said my father, the button of his breeches slipping out of the button-hole—So that whether the interjection was levelled at Susannah, or the button-hole—whether Pish was an interjection of contempt or an interjection of modesty, is a doubt, and must be a doubt till I shall have time to write the three following favourite chapters, that is, my chapter of chamber-maids, my chapter of pishes, and my chapter of button-holes.

All the light I am able to give the reader at present is this, that the moment my father cried Pish! he whisked himself about—and with his breeches held up by one hand, and his night-gown thrown across the arm of the other, he turned along the gallery to bed, something slower than he came.

CHAPTER 15

I wish I could write a chapter upon sleep.

A fitter occasion could never have presented itself, than what this moment offers, when all the curtains of the family are drawn—the candles put out—and no creature's eyes are open but a single one, for the other has been shut these twenty years, of my mother's nurse.

It is a fine subject!

And yet, as fine as it is, I would undertake to write a dozen chapters upon button-holes, both quicker and with more fame, than a single chapter upon this.

Button-holes! there is something lively in the very idea of 'em—and trust me, when I get amongst 'em—You gentry with great beards—look as grave as you will——I'll make merry work with my button-holes—I shall have 'em all to myself—'tis a maiden subject—I shall run foul of no man's wisdom or fine sayings in it.

But for sleep—I know I shall make nothing of it before I begin—I am no dab at your fine sayings in the first place—and in the next, I cannot for my soul set a grave face upon a bad matter, and tell the world—'tis the refuge of the unfortunate—the enfranchisement of the prisoner—the downy lap of the hopeless, the weary, and the broken-hearted; nor could I set out with a lie in my mouth, by affirming, that of all the soft and delicious functions of our nature, by which the great Author of it, in his bounty, has been pleased to recompense the sufferings wherewith his justice and his good pleasure has wearied us—that this is the chiefest (I know pleasures worth ten of it); or what a happiness it is to man, when the anxieties and passions of the day are over, and he lies down upon his back, that his soul shall be so seated within him, that whichever way she turns her eyes, the heavens shall look calm and sweet above her—no desire—or fear—or doubt that troubles the air, nor any difficulty past, present, or to come, that the imagination may not pass over without offence, in that sweet secession.

"God's blessing," said Sancho Pança, "be upon the man who first invented this self-same thing called sleep—it covers a man all over like a cloak." Now there is more to me in this, and it speaks warmer to my heart and affections, than all the dissertations squeezed out of the heads of the learned together upon the subject.

——Not that I altogether disapprove of what Montaigne advances upon it—'tis admirable in its way—(I quote by memory).

The world enjoys other pleasures, says he, as they do that of sleep, without tasting or feeling it as it slips and passes by.——We should study and ruminate upon it, in order to render proper thanks to him who grants it to us.——For this end I cause myself to be disturbed in my sleep, that I may the better and more sensibly relish it.——And yet I see few, says he again, who live with less sleep, when need requires; my body is capable of a firm, but not of a violent and sudden agitation—I evade of late all violent exercises—I am never weary with walking—but from my youth I never liked to ride upon pavements. I love to lie hard and alone, and even without my wife—This last word may stagger the faith of the world—but remember, "La Vraisemblance (as Bayle says in the affair of Liceti) n'est pas toujours du Côté de la Vérité." And so much for sleep.

Chapter 16

If my wife will but venture him—brother Toby, Trismegistus shall be dressed and brought down to us, whilst you and I are getting our breakfasts together.

——Go, tell Susannah, Obadiah, to step here.

She is run up stairs, answered Obadiah, this very instant, sobbing and crying, and wringing her hands as if her heart would break.

We shall have a rare month of it, said my father, turning his head from Obadiah, and looking wistfully in my uncle Toby's face for some time—we shall have a devilish month of it, brother Toby, said my father, setting his arms a-kimbo, and shaking his head; fire, water, women, wind—brother Toby!——'Tis some misfortune, quoth my uncle Toby.——That it is, cried my father—to have so many jarring elements breaking loose, and riding triumph in every corner of a gentleman's house—Little boots it to the peace of a family, brother Toby, that you and I possess ourselves, and sit here silent and unmoved—whilst such a storm is whistling over our heads.——

And what's the matter, Susannah? They have called the child Tristram— and my mistress is just got out of an hysteric fit about it—No!—'tis not my fault, said Susannah—I told him it was Tristram-gistus.

——Make tea for yourself, brother Toby, said my father, taking down his hat—but how different from the sallies and agitations of voice and members which a common reader would imagine!

——For he spake in the sweetest modulation—and took down his hat with the genteelest movement of limbs, that ever affliction harmonized and attuned together.

——Go to the bowling-green for Corporal Trim, said my uncle Toby, speaking to Obadiah, as soon as my father left the room.

Chapter 17

WHEN the misfortune of my nose fell so heavily upon my father's head;— the reader remembers that he walked instantly up stairs, and cast himself down upon his bed; and from hence, unless he has a great insight into human nature, he will be apt to expect a rotation of the same ascending and descending movements from him, upon this misfortune of my name;—no.

The different weight, dear Sir—nay even the different package of two vexations of the same weight—makes a very wide difference in our manner of bearing and getting through with them.—It is not half an hour ago, when (in the great hurry and precipitation of a poor devil's writing for daily bread) I threw a fair sheet, which I had just finished, and carefully wrote out, slap into the fire, instead of the foul one.

Instantly I snatched off my wig, and threw it perpendicularly, with all imaginable violence, up to the top of the room—indeed I caught it as it fell —but there was an end of the matter; nor do I think any thing else in Nature would have given such immediate ease: She, dear Goddess, by an instantaneous impulse, in all provoking cases, determines us to a sally of this or that member—or else she thrusts us into this or that place, or posture of body, we know not why—But mark, madam, we live amongst riddles and mysteries—the most obvious things, which come in our way, have dark sides, which the quickest sight cannot penetrate into; and even the clearest and most exalted understandings amongst us find ourselves puzzled and at a loss in almost every cranny of nature's works: so that this, like a thousand other things, falls out for us in a way, which tho' we cannot reason upon it—yet we find the good of it, may it please your reverences and your worships—and that's enough for us.

Now, my father could not lie down with this affliction for his life—nor could he carry it up stairs like the other—he walked composedly out with it to the fish-pond.

Had my father leaned his head upon his hand, and reasoned an hour which way to have gone—reason, with all her force, could not have directed him to any thing like it: there is something, Sir, in fish-ponds—but what it is, I leave to system-builders and fish-pond-diggers betwixt 'em to find out—but there is something, under the first disorderly transport of the humours, so unaccountably becalming in an orderly and a sober walk towards one of them, that I have often wondered that neither Pythagoras, nor Plato, nor Solon, nor Lycurgus, nor Mahomet, nor any one of your noted lawgivers, ever gave order about them.

CHAPTER 18

YOUR honour, said Trim, shutting the parlour-door before he began to speak, has heard, I imagine, of this unlucky accident—O yes, Trim, said my uncle Toby, and it gives me great concern.——I am heartily concerned too, but I hope your honour, replied Trim, will do me the justice to believe, that it was not in the least owing to me.——To thee—Trim?—cried my uncle Toby, looking kindly in his face—'twas Susannah's and the curate's folly betwixt them.——What business could they have together, an' please your honour, in the garden?——In the gallery thou meanest, replied my uncle Toby.

Trim found he was upon a wrong scent, and stopped short with a low bow—Two misfortunes, quoth the corporal to himself, are twice as many at least as are needful to be talked over at one time;—the mischief the cow has done in breaking into the fortifications, may be told his honour hereafter.——Trim's casuistry and address, under the cover of his low bow, prevented all suspicion in my uncle Toby, so he went on with what he had to say to Trim as follows:

——For my own part, Trim, though I can see little or no difference betwixt my nephew's being called Tristram or Trismegistus—yet as the thing sits so near my brother's heart, Trim—I would freely have given a hundred pounds rather than it should have happened.——A hundred pounds, an' please your honour! replied Trim,—I would not give a cherry-stone to boot.——Nor would I, Trim, upon my own account, quoth my uncle Toby—but my brother, whom there is no arguing with in this case—maintains that a great deal more depends, Trim, upon christian-names, than what ignorant people imagine—for he says there never was a great or heroic action performed since the world began by one called Tristram—nay, he will have it, Trim, that a man can neither be learned, or wise, or brave.— 'Tis all fancy, an' please your honour—I fought just as well, replied the corporal, when the regiment called me Trim, as when they called me James

Butler.—And for my own part, said my uncle Toby, though I should blush to boast of myself, Trim—yet had my name been Alexander, I could have done no more at Namur than my duty.——Bless your honour! cried Trim, advancing three steps as he spoke, does a man think of his christian-name when he goes upon the attack?——Or when he stands in the trench, Trim? cried my uncle Toby, looking firm.——Or when he enters a breach? said Trim, pushing in between two chairs.——Or forces the lines? cried my uncle, rising up, and pushing his crutch like a pike.——Or facing a platoon? cried Trim, presenting his stick like a firelock.——Or when he marches up the glacis? cried my uncle Toby, looking warm and setting his foot upon his stool.——

CHAPTER 19

My father was returned from his walk to the fish-pond—and opened the parlour-door in the very height of the attack, just as my uncle Toby was marching up the glacis—Trim recovered his arms—never was my uncle Toby caught in riding at such a desperate rate in his life! Alas! my uncle Toby! had not a weightier matter called forth all the ready eloquence of my father—how hadst thou then and thy poor Hobby-Horse too been insulted!

My father hung up his hat with the same air he took it down; and after giving a slight look at the disorder of the room, he took hold of one of the chairs which had formed the corporal's breach, and placing it over-against my uncle Toby, he sat down in it, and as soon as the tea-things were taken away, and the door shut, he broke out in a lamentation as follows.

MY FATHER'S LAMENTATION

IT is vain longer, said my father, addressing himself as much to Ernulphus's curse, which was laid upon the corner of the chimney-piece—as to my uncle Toby, who sat under it—it is in vain longer, said my father, in the most querulous monotony imaginable, to struggle as I have done against this most uncomfortable of human persuasions—I see it plainly, that either for my own sins, brother Toby, or the sins and follies of the Shandy family, Heaven has thought fit to draw forth the heaviest of its artillery against me; and that the prosperity of my child is the point upon which the whole force of it is directed to play.——Such a thing would batter the whole universe about our ears, brother Shandy, said my uncle Toby—if it was so— Unhappy Tristram! child of wrath! child of decrepitude! interruption! mistake! and discontent! What one misfortune or disaster in the book of embryotic evils, that could unmechanize thy frame, or entangle thy filaments! which has not fallen upon thy head, or ever thou camest into the world— what evils in thy passage into it!—what evils since!—produced into being, in the decline of thy father's days—when the powers of his imagination and of his body were waxing feeble—when radical heat and radical moisture, the elements which should have tempered thine, were drying up; and nothing left to found thy stamina in, but negations—'tis pitiful—brother Toby, at the best, and called out for all the little helps that care and attention on both sides could give it. But how were we defeated! You know the event, brother Toby—'tis too melancholy a one to be repeated now—when the few animal spirits I was worth in the world, and with which memory, fancy, and quick parts should have been conveyed—were all dispersed, confused, confounded, scattered, and sent to the devil.——

Here then was the time to have put a stop to this persecution against him; —and tried an experiment at least—whether calmness and serenity of mind in your sister, with a due attention, brother Toby, to her evacuations and repletions—and the rest of her non-naturals, might not, in a course of nine months' gestation, have set all things to rights.——My child was bereft of these!——What a teazing life did she lead herself, and consequently her foetus too, with that nonsensical anxiety of hers about lying-in in town! I thought my sister submitted with the greatest patience, replied my uncle Toby—I never heard her utter one fretful word about it.——She fumed inwardly, cried my father; and that, let me tell you, brother, was ten times worse for the child—and then! what battles did she fight with me, and what perpetual storms about the midwife.——There she gave vent, said my uncle Toby.——Vent! cried my father, looking up.

But what was all this, my dear Toby, to the injuries done us by my child's coming head foremost into the world, when all I wished, in this general wreck of his frame, was to have saved this little casket unbroke, unrifled.——

With all my precautions, how was my system turned topside-turvy in the womb with my child! his head exposed to the hand of violence, and a pressure of 470 pounds avoirdupois weight acting so perpendicularly upon its apex—that at this hour 'tis ninety per cent. insurance, that the fine network of the intellectual web be not rent and torn to a thousand tatters.

——Still we could have done.—Fool, coxcomb, puppy—give him but a Nose—Cripple, Dwarf, Driveller, Goosecap—(shape him as you will) the door of fortune stands open—O Licetus! Licetus! had I been blest with a foetus five inches long and a half, like thee—Fate might have done her worst.

Still, brother Toby, there was one cast of the die left for our child after all—O Tristram! Tristram! Tristram!

We will send for Mr. Yorick, said my uncle Toby.

——You may send for whom you will, replied my father.

Chapter 20

WHAT a rate have I gone on at, curveting and frisking it away, two up and two down for four volumes[1] together, without looking once behind, or even on one side of me, to see whom I trod upon!——I'll tread upon no one— quoth I to myself when I mounted—I'll take a good rattling gallop; but I'll not hurt the poorest jackass upon the road.——So off I set—up one lane—down another, through this turnpike—over that, as if the arch-jockey of jockeys had got behind me.

Now ride at this rate with what good intention and resolution you may— 'tis a million to one you'll do some one a mischief, if not yourself—He's flung—he's off—he's lost his hat—he's down—he'll break his neck—see!— if he has not galloped full among the scaffolding of the undertaking critics! —he'll knock his brains out against some of their posts—he's bounced out!

[1 *i.e.* According to the original editions.]

—look—he's now riding like a mad-cap full tilt through a whole crowd of painters, fiddlers, poets, biographers, physicians, lawyers, logicians, players, schoolmen, churchmen, statesmen, soldiers, casuists, connoisseurs, prelates, popes, and engineers—Don't fear, said I—I'll not hurt the poorest jack-ass upon the king's highway.——But your horse throws dirt; see you've splashed a bishop—I hope in God, 'twas only Ernulphus, said I.—— But you have squirted full in the faces of Mess. Le Moyne, De Romigny, and De Marcilly, doctors of the Sorbonne.——That was last year, replied I.——But you have trod this moment upon a king.—Kings have bad times on't, said I, to be trod upon by such people as me.

You have done it, replied my accuser.

I deny it, quoth I, and so have got off, and here am I standing with my bridle in one hand, and with my cap in the other, to tell my story.——And what is it? You shall hear in the next chapter.

Chapter 21

As Francis the First of France was one winterly night warming himself over the embers of a wood fire, and talking with his first minister of sundry things for the good of the state[1]—It would not be amiss, said the king, stirring up the embers with his cane, if this good understanding betwixt ourselves and Switzerland was a little strengthened.——There is no end, Sire, replied the minister, in giving money to these people—they would swallow up the treasury of France.——Poo! poo! answered the king—there are more ways, Mons. le Premier, of bribing states, besides that of giving money—I'll pay Switzerland the honour of standing godfather for my next child.——Your majesty, said the minister, in so doing, would have all the grammarians in Europe upon your back;—Switzerland, as a republic, being a female, can in no construction be godfather.—She may be godmother, replied Francis hastily—so announce my intentions by a courier to-morrow morning.

I am astonished, said Francis the First, (that day fortnight) speaking to his minister as he entered the closet, that we have had no answer from Switzerland.——Sire, I wait upon you this moment, said Mons. le Premier, to lay before you my dispatches upon that business.——They take it kindly, said the king.——They do, Sire, replied the minister, and have the highest sense of the honour your majesty has done them—but the republic, as godmother, claims her right, in this case, of naming the child.

In all reason, quoth the king—she will christen him Francis, or Henry, or Lewis, or some name that she knows will be agreeable to us. Your majesty is deceived, replied the minister—I have this hour received a dispatch from our resident, with the determination of the republic on that point also. —And what name has the republic fixed upon for the Dauphin?—Shadrach, Meshech, Abed-nego, replied the minister.—By Saint Peter's girdle, I will have nothing to do with the Swiss, cried Francis the First, pulling up his breeches and walking hastily across the floor.

Your majesty, replied the minister calmly, cannot bring yourself off.

We'll pay them in money—said the king.

[1] *Vide* Menagiana, vol. i.

Sire, there are not sixty thousand crowns in the treasury, answered the minister.—I'll pawn the best jewel in my crown, quoth Francis the First.

Your honour stands pawned already in this matter, answered Monsieur le Premier.

Then, Mons. le Premier, said the king, by—we'll go to war with 'em.

CHAPTER 22

ALBEIT, gentle reader, I have lusted earnestly, and endeavoured carefully (according to the measure of such a slender skill as God has vouchsafed me, and as convenient leisure from other occasions of needful profit and health-ful pastime have permitted) that these little books which I here put into thy hands, might stand instead of many bigger books—yet have I carried myself towards thee in such fanciful guise of careless disport, that right sore am I ashamed now to intreat thy lenity seriously—in beseeching thee to believe it of me, that in the story of my father and his christian-names— I have no thoughts of treading upon Francis the First—nor in the affair of the nose—upon Francis the Ninth—nor in the character of my uncle Toby —of characterizing the militiating spirits of my country—the wound upon his groin, is a wound to every comparison of that kind—nor by Trim—that I meant the Duke of Ormond—or that my book is wrote against predestina-tion, or free-will, or taxes—If 'tis wrote against any thing,—'tis wrote, an' please your worships, against the spleen! in order, by a more frequent and a more convulsive elevation and depression of the diaphragm, and the suc-cussations of the intercostal and abdominal muscles in laughter, to drive the gall and other bitter juices from the gall-bladder, liver, and sweet-bread of his majesty's subjects, with all the inimicitious passions which be-long to them, down into their duodenums.

CHAPTER 23

——BUT can the thing be undone, Yorick? said my father—for in my opinion, continued he, it cannot. I am a vile canonist, replied Yorick—but of all evils, holding suspense to be the most tormenting, we shall at least know the worst of this matter. I hate these great dinners—said my father— The size of the dinner is not the point, answered Yorick—we want, Mr. Shandy, to dive into the bottom of this doubt, whether the name can be changed or not—and as the beards of so many commissaries, officials, ad-vocates, proctors, registers, and of the most eminent of our school-divines, and others, are all to meet in the middle of one table, and Didius has so pressingly invited you—who in your distress would miss such an occasion? All that is requisite, continued Yorick, is to apprise Didius, and let him manage a conversation after dinner so as to introduce the subject.——Then my brother Toby, cried my father, clapping his two hands together, shall go with us.

——Let my old tie-wig, quoth my uncle Toby, and my laced regimentals, be hung to the fire all night, Trim.

Chapter 25

——No doubt, Sir,—there is a whole chapter wanting here—and a chasm of ten pages made in the book by it—but the book-binder is neither a fool, or a knave, or a puppy—nor is the book a jot more imperfect (at least upon that score)—but, on the contrary, the book is more perfect and complete by wanting the chapter, than having it, as I shall demonstrate to your reverences in this manner.——I question first, by the bye, whether the same experiment might not be made as successfully upon sundry other chapters— but there is no end, an' please your reverences, in trying experiments upon chapters—we have had enough of it—So there's an end of that matter.

But before I begin my demonstration, let me only tell you, that the chapter which I have torn out, and which otherwise you would all have been reading just now, instead of this—was the description of my father's, my uncle Toby's, Trim's, and Obadiah's setting out and journeying to the visitation at ****.

We'll go in the coach, said my father—Prithee, have the arms been altered, Obadiah?—It would have made my story much better to have begun with telling you, that at the time my mother's arms were added to the Shandys', when the coach was re-painted upon my father's marriage, it had so fallen out, that the coach-painter, whether by performing all his works with the left-hand, like Turpilius the Roman, or Hans Holbein of Basil— or whether 'twas more from the blunder of his head than hand—or whether, lastly, it was from the sinister turn which every thing relating to our family was apt to take—it so fell out, however, to our reproach, that instead of the bend-dexter, which since Harry the Eighth's reign was honestly our due—a bend-sinister, by some of these fatalities, had been drawn quite across the field of the Shandy arms. 'Tis scarce credible that the mind of so wise a man as my father was, could be so much incommoded with so small a matter. The word coach—let it be whose it would—or coach-man, or coach-horse, or coach-hire, could never be named in the family, but he constantly complained of carrying this vile mark of illegitimacy upon the door of his own; he never once was able to step into the coach, or out of it, without turning round to take a view of the arms, and making a vow at the same time, that it was the last time he would ever set his foot in it again, till the bend-sinister was taken out—but like the affair of the hinge, it was one of the many things which the Destinies had set down in their books ever to be grumbled at (and in wiser families than ours)—but never to be mended.

——Has the bend-sinister been brushed out, I say? said my father.— There has been nothing brushed out, Sir, answered Obadiah, but the lining. We'll go o' horseback, said my father, turning to Yorick.——Of all things in the world, except politics, the clergy know the least of heraldry, said Yorick.——No matter for that, cried my father—I should be sorry to appear with a blot in my escutcheon before them.——Never mind the bend-sinister, said my uncle Toby, putting on his tie-wig.——No, indeed, said my father—you may go with my aunt Dinah to a visitation with a bend-sinister, if you think fit—My poor uncle Toby blushed. My father was vexed at himself.——No—my dear brother Toby, said my father, changing his tone—but the damp of the coach-lining about my loins, may give me the sciatica again, as it did December, January, and February last winter—so if you please you shall ride my wife's pad—and as you are to preach, Yorick, you had better make the best of your way before—and leave me to take care of my brother Toby, and to follow at our own rates.

Now the chapter I was obliged to tear out, was the description of this cavalcade, in which Corporal Trim and Obadiah, upon two coach-horses a-breast, led the way as slow as a patrole—whilst my uncle Toby, in his laced regimentals and tie-wig, kept his rank with my father, in deep roads and dissertations alternately upon the advantage of learning and arms, as each could get the start.

——But the painting of this journey, upon reviewing it, appears to be so much above the style and manner of any thing else I have been able to paint in this book, that it could not have remained in it, without depreciating every other scene; and destroying at the same time that necessary equipoise and balance, (whether of good or bad) betwixt chapter and chapter, from whence the just proportions and harmony of the whole work results. For my own part, I am but just set up in the business, so know little about it—but, in my opinion, to write a book is for all the world like humming a song—be but in tune with yourself, madam, 'tis no matter how high or how low you take it.

——This is the reason, may it please your reverences, that some of the lowest and flattest compositions pass off very well—(as Yorick told my uncle Toby one night)—by siege.——My uncle Toby looked brisk at the sound of the word siege, but could make neither head or tail of it.

I'm to preach at court next Sunday, said Homenas—run over my notes—so I hummed over doctor Homenas's notes—the modulation's very well—'twill do, Homenas, if it holds on at this rate—so on I hummed—and a tolerable tune I thought it was; and to this hour, may it please your reverences, had never found out how low, how flat, how spiritless and jejune it was, but that all of a sudden, up started an air in the middle of it, so fine, so rich, so heavenly,—it carried my soul up with it into the other world; now had I (as Montaigne complained in a parallel accident)—had I found the declivity easy, or the ascent accessible—certes I had been outwitted.——Your notes, Homenas, I should have said, are good notes;—but it was so perpendicular a precipice—so wholly cut off from the rest of the work, that by the first note I hummed I found myself flying into the other world, and from thence discovered the vale from whence I came, so deep, so low, and dismal, that I shall never have the heart to descend into it again. A dwarf who brings a standard along with him to measure his own size —take my word, is a dwarf in more articles than one.——And so much for tearing out of chapters.

CHAPTER 26

——SEE if he is not cutting it into slips, and giving them about him to light their pipes!——'Tis abominable, answered Didius; it should not go unnoticed, said doctor Kysarcius— he was of the Kysarcii of the Low Countries.

Methinks, said Didius, half rising from his chair, in order to remove a bottle and a tall decanter, which stood in a direct line betwixt him and Yorick—you might have spared this sarcastic stroke, and have hit upon a more proper place, Mr. Yorick—or at least upon a more proper occasion to have shewn your contempt of what we have been about: If the sermon is of no better worth than to light pipes with—'twas certainly, Sir, not good enough to be preached before so learned a body; and if 'twas good enough to be preached before so learned a body—'twas certainly, Sir, too good to light their pipes with afterwards.

——I have got him fast hung up, quoth Didius to himself, upon one of the two horns of my dilemma—let him get off as he can.

I have undergone such unspeakable torments, in bringing forth this sermon, quoth Yorick, upon this occasion—that I declare, Didius, I would suffer martyrdom—and if it was possible my horse with me, a thousand times over, before I would sit down and make such another: I was delivered of it at the wrong end of me—it came from my head instead of my heart—and it is for the pain it gave me, both in the writing and the preaching of it, that I revenge myself of it, in this manner—To preach, to shew the extent of our reading, or the subtleties of our wit—to parade in the eyes of the vulgar with the beggarly accounts of a little learning, tinselled over with a few words which glitter, but convey little light and less warmth—is a dishonest use of the poor single half hour in a week which is put into our hands—'Tis not preaching the gospel—but ourselves—For my own part, continued Yorick, I had rather direct five words point-blank to the heart.——

As Yorick pronounced the word point-blank, my uncle Toby rose up to say something upon projectiles—when a single word and no more uttered from the opposite side of the table drew every one's ears towards it—a word of all others in the dictionary the last in that place to be expected—a word I am ashamed to write—yet must be written—must be read—illegal—uncanonical—guess ten thousand guesses, multiplied into themselves—rack—torture your invention for ever, you're where you was—In short, I'll tell it in the next chapter.

CHAPTER 27

ZOUNDS!——————————————————————— Z——ds! cried Phutatorius, partly to himself—and yet high enough to be heard—and what seemed odd, 'twas uttered in a construction of look, and in a tone of voice, somewhat between that of a man in amazement and one in bodily pain.

One or two who had very nice ears, and could distinguish the expression and mixture of the two tones as plainly as a third or a fifth, or any other chord in music—were the most puzzled and perplexed with it—the concord was good in itself—but then 'twas quite out of the key, and no way applicable to the subject started;—so that with all their knowledge, they could not tell what in the world to make of it.

Others who knew nothing of musical expression, and merely lent their ears to the plain import of the word, imagined that Phutatorius, who was somewhat of a choleric spirit, was just going to snatch the cudgels out of

Didius's hands, in order to bemaul Yorick to some purpose—and that the desperate monosyllable Z——ds was the exordium to an oration, which, as they judged from the sample, presaged but a rough kind of handling of him; so that my uncle Toby's good-nature felt a pang for what Yorick was about to undergo. But seeing Phutatorius stop short, without any attempt or desire to go on—a third party began to suppose, that it was no more than an involuntary respiration, casually forming itself into the shape of a twelve-penny oath—without the sin or substance of one.

Others, and especially one or two who sat next him, looked upon it on the contrary as a real and substantial oath, propensely formed against Yorick, to whom he was known to bear no good liking—which said oath, as my father philosophized upon it, actually lay fretting and fuming at that very time in the upper regions of Phutatorius's purtenance; and so was naturally, and according to the due course of things, first squeezed out by the sudden influx of blood which was driven into the right ventricle of Phutatorius's heart, by the stroke of surprise which so strange a theory of preaching had excited.

How finely we argue upon mistaken facts!

There was not a soul busied in all these various reasonings upon the monosyllable which Phutatorius uttered—who did not take this for granted, proceeding upon it as from an axiom, namely, that Phutatorius's mind was intent upon the subject of debate which was arising between Didius and Yorick; and indeed as he looked first towards the one and then towards the other, with the air of a man listening to what was going for-wards—who would not have thought the same? But the truth was, that Phutatorius knew not one word or one syllable of what was passing—but his whole thoughts and attention were taken up with a transaction which was going forwards at that very instant within the precincts of his own Galligaskins, and in a part of them, where of all others he stood most inter-ested to watch accidents: So that notwithstanding he looked with all the attention in the world, and had gradually screwed up every nerve and muscle in his face, to the utmost pitch the instrument would bear, in order, as it was thought, to give a sharp reply to Yorick, who sat over-against him—yet, I say, was Yorick never once in any one domicile of Phutatorius's brain—but the true cause of his exclamation lay at least a yard below.

This I will endeavour to explain to you with all imaginable decency.

You must be informed then, that Gastripheres, who had taken a turn into the kitchen a little before dinner, to see how things went on—observing a wicker-basket of fine chestnuts standing upon the dresser, had ordered that a hundred or two of them might be roasted and sent in, as soon as dinner was over—Gastripheres inforcing his orders about them, that Di-dius, but Phutatorius especially, were particularly fond of 'em.

About two minutes before the time that my uncle Toby interrupted Yorick's harangue—Gastripheres's chestnuts were brought in—and as Phutatorius's fondness for 'em was uppermost in the waiter's head, he laid them directly before Phutatorius, wrapt up hot in a clean damask napkin.

Now whether it was physically impossible, with half a dozen hands all thrust into the napkin at a time—but that some one chestnut, of more life and rotundity than the rest, must be put in motion—it so fell out, however, that one was actually sent rolling off the table; and as Phutatorius sat straddling under—it fell perpendicularly into that particular aperture of Phutatorius's breeches, for which, to the shame and indelicacy of our language be it spoke, there is no chaste word throughout all Johnson's dictionary—let it suffice to say—it was that particular aperture which, in all good societies, the laws of decorum do strictly require, like the temple of Janus (in peace at least) to be universally shut up.

The neglect of this punctilio in Phutatorius (which by the bye should be a warning to all mankind) had opened a door to this accident.——

Accident I call it, in compliance to a received mode of speaking——but in no opposition to the opinion either of Acrites or Mythogeras in this matter; I know they were both prepossessed and fully persuaded of it—and are so to this hour, That there was nothing of accident in the whole event—but that the chestnut's taking that particular course, and in a manner of its own accord—and then falling with all its heat directly into that one particular place, and no other—was a real judgment upon Phutatorius, for that filthy and obscene treatise *de Concubinis retinendis*, which Phutatorius had published about twenty years ago—and was that identical week going to give the world a second edition of.

It is not my business to dip my pen in this controversy—much undoubtedly may be wrote on both sides of the question—all that concerns me as a historian, is to represent the matter of fact, and render it credible to the reader, that the hiatus in Phutatorius's breeches was sufficiently wide to receive the chestnut;—and that the chestnut, somehow or other, did fall perpendicularly and piping hot into it, without Phutatorius's perceiving it, or any one else at that time.

The genial warmth which the chestnut imparted, was not undelectable for the first twenty or five-and-twenty seconds—and did no more than gently solicit Phutatorius's attention towards the part:—But the heat gradually increasing, and in a few seconds more getting beyond the point of all sober pleasure, and then advancing with all speed into the regions of pain, the soul of Phutatorius, together with all his ideas, his thoughts, his attention, his imagination, judgment, resolution, deliberation, ratiocination, memory, fancy, with ten battalions of animal spirits, all tumultuously crowded down, through different defiles and circuits, to the place of danger, leaving all his upper regions, as you may imagine, as empty as my purse.

With the best intelligence which all these messengers could bring him back, Phutatorius was not able to dive into the secret of what was going forwards below, nor could he make any kind of conjecture, what the devil was the matter with it: However, as he knew not what the true cause might turn out, he deemed it most prudent, in the situation he was in at present, to bear it, if possible, like a Stoic; which, with the help of some wry faces and compursions of the mouth, he had certainly accomplished, had his imagination continued neuter;—but the sallies of the imagination are ungovernable in things of this kind—a thought instantly darted into his mind, that tho' the anguish had the sensation of glowing heat—it might, notwithstanding that, be a bite as well as a burn; and if so, that possibly a newt or an asker, or some such detested reptile, had crept up, and was fastening his teeth—the horrid idea of which, with a fresh glow of pain arising that instant from the chestnut, seized Phutatorius with a sudden panic, and in the first terrifying disorder of the passion, it threw him, as it has done the best generals upon earth, quite off his guard:—the effect of which was this, that he leapt incontinently up, uttering as he rose that interjection of surprise so much descanted upon, with the aposiopestic break after it, marked thus, Z——ds—which, though not strictly canonical, was still as little as any man could have said upon the occasion;—and which, by the bye, whether canonical or not, Phutatorius could no more help than he could the cause of it.

Though this has taken up some time in the narrative, it took up little more time in the transaction, than just to allow time for Phutatorius to draw forth the chestnut, and throw it down with violence upon the floor—and for Yorick to rise from his chair, and pick the chestnut up.

It is curious to observe the triumph of slight incidents over the mind:—What incredible weight they have in forming and governing our opinions, both of men and things—that trifles, light as air, shall waft a belief into the soul, and plant it so immoveably within it—that Euclid's demonstrations, could they be brought to batter it in breach, should not all have power to overthrow it.

Yorick, I said, picked up the chestnut which Phutatorius's wrath had flung down—the action was trifling—I am ashamed to account for it—he did it, for no reason, but that he thought the chestnut not a jot worse for the adventure—and that he held a good chestnut worth stooping for.—— But this incident, trifling as it was, wrought differently in Phutatorius's head: He considered this act of Yorick's in getting off his chair and picking up the chestnut, as a plain acknowledgment in him, that the chestnut was originally his—and in course, that it must have been the owner of the chestnut, and no one else, who could have played him such a prank with it: What greatly confirmed him in this opinion, was this, that the table being parallelogramical and very narrow, it afforded a fair opportunity for Yorick, who sat directly over against Phutatorius, of slipping the chestnut in—and consequently that he did it. The look of something more than suspicion, which Phutatorius cast full upon Yorick as these thoughts arose, too evidently spoke his opinion—and as Phutatorius was naturally supposed to know more of the matter than any person besides, his opinion at once became the general one;—and for a reason very different from any which have been yet given—in a little time it was put out of all manner of dispute.

When great or unexpected events fall out upon the stage of this sublunary world—the mind of man, which is an inquisitive kind of a substance, naturally takes a flight behind the scenes to see what is the cause and first spring of them.——The search was not long in this instance.

It was well known that Yorick had never a good opinion of the treatise which Phutatorius had wrote *de Concubinis retinendis*, as a thing which he feared had done hurt in the world—and 'twas easily found out, that there was a mystical meaning in Yorick's prank—and that his chucking the chestnut hot into Phutatorius's ***—*****, was a sarcastical fling at his book—the doctrines of which, they said, had enflamed many an honest man in the same place.

This conceit awakened Somnolentus—made Agelastes smile—and if you can recollect the precise look and air of a man's face intent in finding out a riddle—it threw Gastripheres's into that form—and in short was thought by many to be a master-stroke of arch-wit.

This, as the reader has seen from one end to the other, was as groundless as the dreams of philosophy: Yorick, no doubt, as Shakespeare said of his ancestor—"was a man of jest," but it was tempered with something which withheld him from that, and many other ungracious pranks, of which he as undeservedly bore the blame;—but it was his misfortune all his life long to bear the imputation of saying and doing a thousand things, of which (unless my esteem blinds me) his nature was incapable. All I blame him for— or rather, all I blame and alternately like him for, was that singularity of his temper, which would never suffer him to take pains to set a story right with the world, however in his power. In every ill usage of that sort, he acted precisely as in the affair of his lean horse—he could have explained it to his honour, but his spirit was above it; and besides, he ever looked upon the inventor, the propagator and believer of an illiberal report alike so injurious to him—he could not stoop to tell his story to them—and so trusted to time and truth to do it for him.

This heroic cast produced him inconveniences in many respects—in the present it was followed by the fixed resentment of Phutatorius, who, as Yorick had just made an end of his chestnut, rose up from his chair a second time, to let him know it—which indeed he did with a smile; saying only— that he would endeavour not to forget the obligation.

But you must mark and carefully separate and distinguish these two things in your mind.

——The smile was for the company.

——The threat was for Yorick.

CHAPTER 28

——Can you tell me, quoth Phutatorius, speaking to Gastripheres who sat next to him—for one would not apply to a surgeon in so foolish an affair— can you tell me, Gastripheres, what is best to take out the fire?——Ask Eugenius, said Gastripheres.——That greatly depends, said Eugenius, pretending ignorance of the adventure, upon the nature of the part—If it is a tender part, and a part which can conveniently be wrapt up—It is both the one and the other, replied Phutatorius, laying his hand as he spoke, with an emphatical nod of his head, upon the part in question, and lifting up his right leg at the same time to ease and ventilate it.——If that is the case, said Eugenius, I would advise you, Phutatorius, not to tamper with it by any means; but if you will send to the next printer, and trust your cure to such a simple thing as a soft sheet of paper just come off the press—you need do nothing more than twist it round.——The damp paper, quoth Yorick (who sat next to his friend Eugenius) though I know it has a re-

freshing coolness in it—yet I presume is no more than the vehicle—and that
the oil and lamp-black with which the paper is so strongly impregnated,
does the business.——Right, said Eugenius, and is, of any outward application I would venture to recommend, the most anodyne and safe.

Was it my case, said Gastripheres, as the main thing is the oil and lamp-
black, I should spread them thick upon a rag, and clap it on directly.——
That would make a very devil of it, replied Yorick.——And besides, added
Eugenius, it would not answer the intention, which is the extreme neatness
and elegance of the prescription, which the Faculty hold to be half in half;
—for consider, if the type is a very small one (which it should be) the sana-
tive particles, which come into contact in this form, have the advantage of
being spread so infinitely thin, and with such a mathematical equality
(fresh paragraphs and large capitals excepted) as no art or management of
the spatula can come up to.——It falls out very luckily, replied Phutatorius, that the second edition of my treatise *de Concubinis retinendis* is at
this instant in the press.——You may take any leaf of it, said Eugenius—
no matter which.——Provided, quoth Yorick, there is no bawdry in it.——

They are just now, replied Phutatorius, printing off the ninth chapter—
which is the last chapter but one in the book.——Pray what is the title of
that chapter? said Yorick; making a respectful bow to Phutatorius as he
spoke.——I think, answered Phutatorius, 'tis that *de re concubinariâ.*

For Heaven's sake keep out of that chapter, quoth Yorick.

——By all means—added Eugenius.

CHAPTER 29

——Now, quoth Didius, rising up, and laying his right hand with his fingers
spread upon his breast—had such a blunder about a christian-name happened before the Reformation—[It happened the day before yesterday,
quoth my uncle Toby to himself] and when baptism was administered in
Latin—['Twas all in English, said my uncle]—many things might have
coincided with it, and upon the authority of sundry decreed cases, to have
pronounced the baptism null, with a power of giving the child a new name
—Had a priest, for instance, which was no uncommon thing, through ignorance of the Latin tongue, baptized a child of Tom o' Stiles, *in nomine
patriae & filia & spiritum sanctos*—the baptism was held null.—I beg your
pardon, replied Kysarcius—in that case, as the mistake was only the
terminations, the baptism was valid—and to have rendered it null, the
blunder of the priest should have fallen upon the first syllable of each noun
—and not, as in your case, upon the last.

My father delighted in subtleties of this kind, and listened with infinite
attention.

Gastripheres, for example, continued Kysarcius, baptizes a child of John
Stradling's in *Gomine* gatris, etc. etc., instead of *in Nomine* patris, etc.—is
this a baptism? No—say the ablest canonists; inasmuch as the radix of each
word is hereby torn up, and the sense and meaning of them removed and
changed quite to another object; for *Gomine* does not signify a name, nor
gatris a father.——What do they signify? said my uncle Toby.—Nothing

at all—quoth Yorick.——Ergo, such a baptism is null, said Kysarcius.——

In course, answered Yorick, in a tone two parts jest and one part earnest.——

But in the case cited, continued Kysarcius, where *patriae* is put for *patris*, *filia* for *filii*, and so on—as it is a fault only in the declension, and the roots of the words continue untouched, the inflections of their branches either this way or that, does not in any sort hinder the baptism, inasmuch as the same sense continues in the words as before.——But then, said Didius, the intention of the priest's pronouncing them grammatically must have been proved to have gone along with it.——Right, answered Kysarcius; and of this, brother Didius, we have an instance in a decree of the decretals of Pope Leo the IIId.——But my brother's child, cried my uncle Toby, has nothing to do with the Pope—'tis the plain child of a Protestant gentleman, christened Tristram against the wills and wishes both of his father and mother, and all who are a-kin to it.——

If the wills and wishes, said Kysarcius, interrupting my uncle Toby, of those only who stand related to Mr. Shandy's child, were to have weight in this matter, Mrs. Shandy, of all people, has the least to do in it.——My uncle Toby laid down his pipe, and my father drew his chair still closer to the table, to hear the conclusion of so strange an introduction.

——It has not only been a question, Captain Shandy, amongst the[1] best lawyers and civilians in this land, continued Kysarcius, "Whether the mother be of kin to her child,"—but, after much dispassionate enquiry and jactitation of the arguments on all sides—it has been adjudged for the negative—namely, "That the mother is not of kin to her child."[2] My father instantly clapped his hand upon my uncle Toby's mouth, under colour of whispering in his ear;—the truth was, he was alarmed for *Lillabullero*—and having a great desire to hear more of so curious an argument—he begged my uncle Toby, for Heaven's sake, not to disappoint him in it.—My uncle Toby gave a nod—resumed his pipe, and contenting himself with whistling *Lillabullero* inwardly—Kysarcius, Didius, and Triptolemus went on with the discourse as follows.

This determination, continued Kysarcius, how contrary soever it may seem to run to the stream of vulgar ideas, yet had reason strongly on its side; and has been put out of all manner of dispute from the famous case, known commonly by the name of the Duke of Suffolk's case.——It is cited in Brook, said Triptolemus—And taken notice of by Lord Coke, added Didius.——And you may find it in Swinburn on Testaments, said Kysarcius.

The case, Mr. Shandy, was this.

In the reign of Edward the Sixth, Charles duke of Suffolk having issue a son by one venter, and a daughter by another venter, made his last will, wherein he devised goods to his son, and died; after whose death the son died also—but without will, without wife, and without child—his mother and his sister by the father's side (for she was born of the former venter) then living. The mother took the administration of her son's goods, according to

[1] *Vide* Swinburn on Testaments, Part 7, § 8.
[2] *Vide* Brook, Abridg. Tit Administr. N. 47.

the statute of the 21st of Harry the Eighth, whereby it is enacted, That in case any person die intestate, the administration of his goods shall be committed to the next of kin.

The administration being thus (surreptitiously) granted to the mother, the sister by the father's side commenced a suit before the Ecclesiastical Judge, alleging, 1st, That she herself was next of kin; and 2ndly, That the mother was not of kin at all to the party deceased; and therefore prayed the court, that the administration granted to the mother might be revoked, and be committed unto her, as next of kin to the deceased, by force of the said statute.

Hereupon, as it was a great cause, and much depending upon its issue—and many causes of great property likely to be decided in times to come, by the precedent to be then made—the most learned, as well in the laws of this realm, as in the civil law, were consulted together, whether the mother was of kin to her son, or no.——Whereunto not only the temporal lawyers—but the church lawyers—the juris-consulti—the juris-prudents—the civilians—the advocates—the commissaries—the judges of the consistory and prerogative courts of Canterbury and York, with the master of the faculties, were all unanimously of opinion, That the mother was not of[1] kin to her child.——

And what said the duchess of Suffolk to it? said my uncle Toby.

The unexpectedness of my uncle Toby's question, confounded Kysarcius more than the ablest advocate—He stopped a full minute, looking in my uncle Toby's face without replying—and in that single minute Triptolemus put by him, and took the lead as follows.

'Tis a ground and principle in the law, said Triptolemus, that things do not ascend, but descend in it; and I make no doubt 'tis for this cause, that however true it is, that the child may be of the blood and seed of its parents —that the parents, nevertheless, are not of the blood and seed of it; inasmuch as the parents are not begot by the child, but the child by the parents —For so they write, *Liberi sunt de sanguine patris & matris, sed pater & mater non sunt de sanguine liberorum.*

——But this, Triptolemus, cried Didius, proves too much—for from this authority cited it would follow, not only what indeed is granted on all sides, that the mother is not of kin to her child—but the father likewise.—It is held, said Triptolemus, the better opinion; because the father, the mother, and the child, though they be three persons, yet are they but (*una caro*[2]) one flesh; and consequently no degree of kindred—or any method of acquiring one in nature.——There you push the argument again too far, cried Didius —for there is no prohibition in nature, though there is in the Levitical law— but that a man may beget a child upon his grandmother—in which case, supposing the issue a daughter, she would stand in relation both of—But who ever thought, cried Kysarcius, of lying with his grandmother?——The young gentleman, replied Yorick, whom Selden speaks of—who not only thought of it, but justified his intention to his father by the argument drawn from the law of retaliation.——"You lay, Sir, with my mother,"

[1]Mater non numeratur inter consanguineos, Bald. in ult. C. de Verb. signific.
[2]*Vide* Brook, Abridg. Tit. Administr. N. 47.

said the lad—"why may not I lie with yours?"——'Tis the *Argumentum commune*, added Yorick.—'Tis as good, replied Eugenius, taking down his hat, as they deserve.

The company broke up.

CHAPTER 30

——And pray, said my uncle Toby, leaning upon Yorick, as he and my father were helping him leisurely down the stairs—don't be terrified, madam, this stair-case conversation is not so long as the last—And pray, Yorick, said my uncle Toby, which way is this said affair of Tristram at length settled by these learned men? Very satisfactorily, replied Yorick; no mortal, Sir, has any concern with it—for Mrs. Shandy the mother is nothing at all a-kin to him—and as the mother's is the surest side—Mr. Shandy, in course, is still less than nothing—In short, he is not as much a-kin to him, Sir, as I am.——

——That may well be, said my father, shaking his head.

——Let the learned say what they will, there must certainly, quoth my uncle Toby, have been some sort of consanguinity betwixt the duchess of Suffolk and her son.

The vulgar are of the same opinion, quoth Yorick, to this hour.

CHAPTER 31

THOUGH my father was hugely tickled with the subtleties of these learned discourses—'twas still but like the anointing of a broken bone—The moment he got home, the weight of his afflictions returned upon him but so much the heavier, as is ever the case when the staff we lean on slips from under us.——He became pensive—walked frequently forth to the fish-pond —let down one loop of his hat—sighed often—forbore to snap—and, as the hasty sparks of temper, which occasion snapping, so much assist perspiration and digestion, as Hippocrates tells us—he had certainly fallen ill with the extinction of them, had not his thoughts been critically drawn off, and his health rescued by a fresh train of disquietudes left him, with a legacy of a thousand pounds, by my aunt Dinah.

My father had scarce read the letter, when taking the thing by the right end, he instantly began to plague and puzzle his head how to lay it out mostly to the honour of his family.——A hundred-and-fifty odd projects took possession of his brains by turns—he would do this, and that, and t'other—He would go to Rome—he would go to law—he would buy stock— he would buy John Hobson's farm—he would new forefront his house, and add a new wing to make it even—There was a fine water-mill on this side, and he would build a wind-mill on the other side of the river in full view to answer it—But above all things in the world, he would enclose the great Ox-moor, and send out my brother Bobby immediately upon his travels.

But as the sum was finite, and consequently could not do every thing— and in truth very few of these to any purpose—of all the projects which offered themselves upon this occasion, the two last seemed to make the deepest impression; and he would infallibly have determined upon both at once, but for the small inconvenience hinted at above, which absolutely put him under a necessity of deciding in favour either of the one or the other.

This was not altogether so easy to be done; for though 'tis certain my father had long before set his heart upon this necessary part of my brother's education, and like a prudent man had actually determined to carry it into execution, with the first money that returned from the second creation of actions in the Mississippi-scheme, in which he was an adventurer—yet the Ox-moor, which was a fine, large, whinny, undrained, unimproved common, belonging to the Shandy-estate, had almost as old a claim upon him: he had long and affectionately set his heart upon turning it likewise to some account.

But having never hitherto been pressed with such a conjuncture of things, as made it necessary to settle either the priority or justice of their claims—like a wise man he had refrained entering into any nice or critical examination about them: so that upon the dismission of every other project at this crisis—the two old projects, the Ox-moor and my Brother, divided him again; and so equal a match were they for each other, as to become the occasion of no small contest in the old gentleman's mind—which of the two should be set o'going first.

——People may laugh as they will—but the case was this.

It had ever been the custom of the family, and by length of time was almost become a matter of common right, that the eldest son of it should have free ingress, egress, and regress into foreign parts before marriage—not only for the sake of bettering his own private parts, by the benefit of exercise and change of so much air—but simply for the mere delectation of his fancy, by the feather put into his cap, of having been abroad—*tantum valet*, my father would say, *quantum sonat*.

Now as this was a reasonable, and in course a most christian indulgence—to deprive him of it, without why or wherefore—and thereby make an example of him, as the first Shandy unwhirled about Europe in a post-chaise, and only because he was a heavy lad—would be using him ten times worse than a Turk.

On the other hand, the case of the Ox-moor was full as hard.

Exclusive of the original purchase-money, which was eight hundred pounds—it had cost the family eight hundred pounds more in a law-suit about fifteen years before—besides the Lord knows what trouble and vexation.

It had been moreover in possession of the Shandy-family ever since the middle of the last century; and though it lay full in view before the house, bounded on one extremity by the water-mill, and on the other by the projected wind-mill spoken of above—and for all these reasons seemed to have the fairest title of any part of the estate to the care and protection of the family—yet by an unaccountable fatality, common to men, as well as the ground they tread on—it had all along most shamefully been overlooked; and to speak the truth of it, had suffered so much by it, that it would have made any man's heart have bled (Obadiah said) who understood the value of the land, to have rode over it, and only seen the condition it was in.

However, as neither the purchasing this tract of ground—nor indeed the placing of it where it lay, were either of them, properly speaking, of my father's doing—he had never thought himself any way concerned in the affair——till the fifteen years before, when the breaking out of that cursed law-suit mentioned above (and which had arose about its boundaries)—which being altogether my father's own act and deed, it naturally awakened every other argument in its favour, and upon summing them all up together, he saw, not merely in interest, but in honour, he was bound to do something for it—and that now or never was the time.

I think there must certainly have been a mixture of ill-luck in it, that the reasons on both sides should happen to be so equally balanced by each other; for though my father weighed them in all humours and conditions—spent many an anxious hour in the most profound and abstracted meditation upon what was best to be done—reading books of farming one day—books of travels another—laying aside all passion whatever—viewing the arguments on both sides in all their lights and circumstances—communing every day with my uncle Toby—arguing with Yorick, and talking over the whole affair of the Ox-moor with Obadiah—yet nothing in all that time appeared so strongly in behalf of the one, which was not either strictly applicable to the other, or at least so far counterbalanced by some consideration of equal weight, as to keep the scales even.

For to be sure, with proper helps, and in the hands of some people, tho' the Ox-moor would undoubtedly have made a different appearance in the world from what it did, or ever could do in the condition it lay—yet every tittle of this was true, with regard to my brother Bobby—let Obadiah say what he would.——

In point of interest—the contest, I own, at first sight, did not appear so undecisive betwixt them; for whenever my father took pen and ink in hand, and set about calculating the simple expense of paring and burning, and fencing in the Ox-moor, etc. etc.—with the certain profit it would bring him in return—the latter turned out so prodigiously in his way of working the account, that you would have sworn the Ox-moor would have carried all before it. For it was plain he should reap a hundred lasts of rape, at twenty pounds a last, the very first year—besides an excellent crop of wheat the year following—and the year after that, to speak within bounds, a hundred —but in all likelihood, a hundred and fifty—if not two hundred quarters of pease and beans—besides potatoes without end.—But then, to think he was all this while breeding up my brother, like a hog to eat them—knocked all on the head again, and generally left the old gentleman in such a state of suspense—that, as he often declared to my uncle Toby—he knew no more than his heels what to do.

No body, but he who has felt it, can conceive what a plaguing thing it is to have a man's mind torn asunder by two projects of equal strength, both obstinately pulling in a contrary direction at the same time: for to say nothing of the havoc, which by a certain consequence is unavoidably made by it all over the finer system of the nerves, which you know convey the animal spirits and more subtle juices from the heart to the head, and so on—it is not to be told in what a degree such a wayward kind of friction works upon the more gross and solid parts, wasting the fat and impairing the strength of a man every time as it goes backwards and forwards.

My father had certainly sunk under this evil, as certainly as he had done under that of my Christian name—had he not been rescued out of it, as he was out of that, by a fresh evil—the misfortune of my brother Bobby's death.

What is the life of man! Is it not to shift from side to side?—from sorrow to sorrow?—to button up one cause of vexation—and unbutton another?

CHAPTER 32

FROM this moment I am to be considered as heir-apparent to the Shandy family—and it is from this point properly, that the story of my Life and my Opinions sets out. With all my hurry and precipitation, I have but been clearing the ground to raise the building—and such a building do I foresee it will turn out, as never was planned, and as never was executed since Adam. In less than five minutes I shall have thrown my pen into the fire, and the little drop of thick ink which is left remaining at the bottom of my ink-horn, after it—I have but half a score things to do in the time—I have a thing to name—a thing to lament—a thing to hope—a thing to promise, and a thing to threaten—I have a thing to suppose—a thing to declare—a thing to conceal—a thing to choose, and a thing to pray for—This chapter, therefore, I name the chapter of Things—and my next chapter to it, that is, the first chapter of my next volume, if I live, shall be my chapter upon Whiskers, in order to keep up some sort of connection in my works.

The thing I lament is, that things have crowded in so thick upon me, that I have not been able to get into that part of my work, towards which I have all the way looked forwards, with so much earnest desire; and that is the Campaigns, but especially the amours of my uncle Toby, the events of which are of so singular a nature, and so Cervantic a cast, that if I can so manage it, as to convey but the same impressions to every other brain, which the occurrences themselves excite in my own—I will answer for it the book shall make its way in the world, much better than its master has done before it.—Oh Tristram! Tristram! can this but be once brought about— the credit, which will attend thee as an author, shall counterbalance the many evils which have befallen thee as a man—thou wilt feast upon the one —when thou hast lost all sense and remembrance of the other!——

No wonder I itch so much as I do, to get at these amours—They are the choicest morsel of my whole story! and when I do get at 'em—assure your-selves, good folks—(nor do I value whose squeamish stomach takes offence at it) I shall not be at all nice in the choice of my words!—and that's the thing I have to declare.——I shall never get all through in five minutes, that I fear—and the thing I hope is, that your worships and reverences are not offended—if you are, depend upon't I'll give you something, my good gentry, next year to be offended at—that's my dear Jenny's way—but who my Jenny is—and which is the right and which the wrong end of a woman, is the thing to be concealed—it shall be told you in the next chapter but one to my chapter of Button-holes—and not one chapter before.

And now that you have just got to the end of these four volumes[1]—the

[1]According to the original editions.

thing I have to ask is, how you feel your heads? my own aches dismally!—
as for your healths, I know, they are much better.——True Shandeism,
think what you will against it, opens the heart and lungs, and like all those
affections which partake of its nature, it forces the blood and other vital
fluids of the body to run freely through its channels, makes the wheel of life
run long and cheerfully round.

Was I left, like Sancho Pança, to choose my kingdom, it should not be
maritime—or a kingdom of blacks to make a penny of;—no, it should be a
kingdom of hearty laughing subjects: And as the bilious and more saturnine
passions, by creating disorders in the blood and humours, have as bad an
influence, I see, upon the body politic as body natural—and as nothing but
a habit of virtue can fully govern those passions, and subject them to reason
—I should add to my prayer—that God would give my subjects grace to be
as wise as they are merry; and then should I be the happiest monarch, and
they the happiest people under heaven.

And so, with this moral for the present, may it please your worships and
your reverences, I take my leave of you till this time twelve-month, when,
(unless this vile cough kills me in the mean time) I'll have another pluck at
your beards, and lay open a story to the world you little dream of.

To the Right Honorable

JOHN,

Lord Viscount SPENCER

MY LORD,

I HUMBLY beg leave to offer you these two Volumes;[1] they are the best my talents, with such bad health as I have, could produce:—had Providence granted me a larger stock of either, they had been a much more proper present to your Lordship.

I beg your Lordship will forgive me, if, at the same time I dedicate this work to you, I join Lady Spencer, in the liberty I take of inscribing the story of *Le Fever* to her name; for which I have no other motive, which my heart has informed me of, but that the story is a humane one.

I am, My Lord,

Your Lordship's most devoted

and most humble Servant,

LAUR. STERNE

[1] *i.e.* According to the original editions, Volumes V. and VI.

BOOK V

Dixero si quid fortè jocosius, hoc mihi juris
Cum venia dabis.——HOR.

——Si quis calumnietur levius esse quam decet theologum, aut mordacius quam
deceat Christianum—non Ego, sed Democritus dixit.——ERASMUS.

CHAPTER I

IF it had not been for those two mettlesome tits, and that madcap of a
postillion who drove them from Stilton to Stamford, the thought had
never entered my head. He flew like lightning—there was a slope of three
miles and a half—we scarce touched the ground—the motion was most
rapid—most impetuous—'twas communicated to my brain—my heart
partook of it—"By the great God of day," said I, looking towards the sun,
and thrusting my arm out of the fore-window of the chaise, as I made my
vow, "I will lock up my study-door the moment I get home, and throw the
key of it ninety feet below the surface of the earth, into the draw-well at
the back of my house."

The London waggon confirmed me in my resolution; it hung tottering
upon the hill, scarce progressive, dragged—dragged up by eight heavy
beasts—"by main strength!—quoth I, nodding—but your betters draw the
same way—and something of everybody's!——O rare!"

Tell me, ye learned, shall we for ever be adding so much to the bulk—so
little to the stock?

Shall we for ever make new books, as apothecaries make new mixtures,
by pouring only out of one vessel into another?

Are we for ever to be twisting, and untwisting the same rope? for ever in
the same track—for ever at the same pace?

Shall we be destined to the days of eternity, on holy-days, as well as
working-days, to be shewing the relics of learning, as monks do the relics
of their saints—without working one—one single miracle with them?

Who made Man, with powers which dart him from earth to heaven in a
moment—that great, that most excellent, and most noble creature of the
world—the miracle of nature, as Zoroaster in his book περὶ φύσεως called
him—the Skekinah of the divine presence, as Chrysostom—the image of
God, as Moses—the ray of divinity, as Plato—the marvel of marvels, as
Aristotle—to go sneaking on at this pitiful—pimping—pettifogging rate?

I scorn to be as abusive as Horace upon the occasion—but if there is no
catachresis in the wish, and no sin in it, I wish from my soul, that every
imitator in Great Britain, France, and Ireland, had the farcy for his pains;

383

and that there was a good farcical house, large enough to hold—aye—and sublimate them, shag rag and bobtail, male and female, all together: and this leads me to the affair of Whiskers—but, by what chain of ideas—I leave as a legacy in mort-main to Prudes and Tartufs, to enjoy and make the most of.

Upon Whiskers

I'm sorry I made it—'twas as inconsiderate a promise as ever entered a man's head—A chapter upon whiskers! alas! the world will not bear it—'tis a delicate world—but I knew not of what mettle it was made—nor had I ever seen the under-written fragment; otherwise, as surely as noses are noses, and whiskers are whiskers still (let the world say what it will to the contrary); so surely would I have steered clear of this dangerous chapter.

The Fragment

* * * * * * * * * * * * * * * * * * * *——You are half asleep, my good lady, said the old gentleman, taking hold of the old lady's hand, and giving it a gentle squeeze, as he pronounced the word Whiskers—shall we change the subject? By no means, replied the old lady —I like your account of those matters; so throwing a thin gauze handker-chief over her head, and leaning it back upon the chair with her face turned towards him, and advancing her two feet as she reclined herself—I desire, continued she, you will go on.

The old gentleman went on as follows:—Whiskers! cried the queen of Navarre, dropping her knotting ball, as La Fosseuse uttered the word— Whiskers, madam, said La Fosseuse, pinning the ball to the queen's apron, and making a courtesy as she repeated it.

La Fosseuse's voice was naturally soft and low, yet 'twas an articulate voice: and every letter of the word Whiskers fell distinctly upon the queen of Navarre's ear—Whiskers! cried the queen, laying a greater stress upon the word, and as if she had still distrusted her ears.—Whiskers! replied La Fosseuse, repeating the word a third time—There is not a cavalier, madam, of his age in Navarre, continued the maid of honour, pressing the page's interest upon the queen, that has so gallant a pair—Of what? cried Mar-garet, smiling—Of whiskers, said La Fosseuse, with infinite modesty.

The word Whiskers still stood its ground, and continued to be made use of in most of the best companies throughout the little kingdom of Navarre, notwithstanding the indiscreet use which La Fosseuse had made of it: the truth was, La Fosseuse had pronounced the word, not only before the queen, but upon sundry other occasions at court, with an accent which always im-plied something of a mystery—And as the court of Margaret, as all the world knows, was at that time a mixture of gallantry and devotion—and whiskers being as applicable to the one, as the other, the word naturally stood its ground—it gained full as much as it lost; that is, the clergy were for it—the laity were against it—and for the women,—they were divided.

The excellency of the figure and mien of the young Sieur De Croix, was at that time beginning to draw the attention of the maids of honour towards the terrace before the palace gate, where the guard was mounted. The lady

De Baussiere fell deeply in love with him,—La Battarelle did the same—it was the finest weather for it, that ever was remembered in Navarre—La Guyol, La Maronette, La Sabatiere, fell in love with the Sieur De Croix also—La Rebours and La Fosseuse knew better—De Croix had failed in an attempt to recommend himself to La Rebours; and La Rebours and La Fosseuse were inseparable.

The queen of Navarre was sitting with her ladies in the painted bow-window, facing the gate of the second court, as De Croix passed through it —He is handsome, said the Lady Baussiere.——He has a good mien, said La Battarelle—He is finely shaped, said La Guyol—I never saw an officer of the horse-guards in my life, said La Maronette, with two such legs—Or who stood so well upon them, said La Sabatiere—But he has no whiskers, cried La Fosseuse—Not a pile, said La Rebours.

The queen went directly to her oratory, musing all the way, as she walked through the gallery, upon the subject; turning it this way and that way in her fancy—*Ave Maria* †—what can La Fosseuse mean? said she, kneeling down upon the cushion.

La Guyol, La Battarelle, La Maronette, La Sabatiere, retired instantly to their chambers—Whiskers! said all four of them to themselves, as they bolted their doors on the inside.

The Lady Carnavallette was counting her beads with both hands, un-suspected, under her farthingal—from St. Anthony down to St. Ursula in-clusive, not a saint passed through her fingers without whiskers; St. Fran-cis, St. Dominic, St. Bennet, St. Basil, St. Bridget, had all whiskers.

The Lady Baussiere had got into a wilderness of conceits, with moral-izing too intricately upon La Fosseuse's text—She mounted her palfrey, her page followed her—the host passed by—The Lady Baussiere rode on.

One denier, cried the order of mercy—one single denier, in behalf of a thousand patient captives, whose eyes look towards heaven and you for their redemption.

——The Lady Baussiere rode on.

Pity the unhappy, said a devout, venerable, hoary-headed man, meekly holding up a box, begirt with iron, in his withered hands—I beg for the un-fortunate—good my Lady, 'tis for a prison—for an hospital—'tis for an old man—a poor man undone by shipwreck, by suretyship, by fire—I call God and all his angels to witness—'tis to clothe the naked—to feed the hungry— 'tis to comfort the sick and the broken-hearted.

The Lady Baussiere rode on.

A decayed kinsman bowed himself to the ground.

——The Lady Baussiere rode on.

He ran begging bare-headed on one side of her palfrey, conjuring her by the former bonds of friendship, alliance, consanguinity, etc.——Cousin, aunt, sister, mother,—for virtue's sake, for your own, for mine, for Christ's sake, remember me—pity me.

——The Lady Baussiere rode on.

Take hold of my whiskers, said the Lady Baussiere.——The page took hold of her palfrey. She dismounted at the end of the terrace.

There are some trains of certain ideas which leave prints of themselves about our eyes and eye-brows; and there is a consciousness of it, somewhere about the heart, which serves but to make these etchings the stronger—we see, spell, and put them together without a dictionary.

Ha, ha! he, hee! cried La Guyol and La Sabatiere, looking close at each other's prints—Ho, ho! cried La Battarelle and Maronette, doing the same: —Whist! cried one—st, st,—said a second—hush, quoth a third—poo, poo, replied a fourth—gramercy! cried the Lady Carnavallette;—'twas she who bewhiskered St. Bridget.

La Fosseuse drew her bodkin from the knot of her hair, and having traced the outline of a small whisker, with the blunt end of it, upon one side of her upper lip, put it into La Rebours' hand—La Rebours shook her head.

The Lady Baussiere coughed thrice into the inside of her muff—La Guyol smiled—Fy, said the Lady Baussiere. The queen of Navarre touched her eye with the tip of her fore-finger—as much as to say, I understand you all.

'Twas plain to the whole court the word was ruined: La Fosseuse had given it a wound, and it was not the better for passing through all these defiles—It made a faint stand, however, for a few months, by the expiration of which, the Sieur De Croix, finding it high time to leave Navarre for want of whiskers—the word in course became indecent, and (after a few efforts) absolutely unfit for use.

The best word, in the best language of the best world, must have suffered under such combinations.——The curate of d'Estella wrote a book against them, setting forth the dangers of accessory ideas, and warning the Navarois against them.

Does not all the world know, said the curate d'Estella at the conclusion of his work, that Noses ran the same fate some centuries ago in most parts of Europe, which Whiskers have now done in the kingdom of Navarre?— The evil indeed spread no farther then—but have not beds and bolsters, and nightcaps and chamber-pots stood upon the brink of destruction ever since? Are not trouse, and placket-holes, and pump-handles—and spigots and faucets, in danger still from the same association?——Chastity, by nature, the gentlest of all affections—give it but its head—'tis like a ramping and a roaring lion.

The drift of the curate d'Estella's argument was not understood.—They ran the scent the wrong way.——The world bridled his ass at the tail.—— And when the extremes of delicacy, and the beginnings of concupiscence, hold their next provincial chapter together, they may decree that bawdy also.

Chapter 2

WHEN my father received the letter which brought him the melancholy account of my brother Bobby's death, he was busy calculating the expense of his riding post from Calais to Paris, and so on to Lyons.

'Twas a most inauspicious journey; my father having had every foot of it to travel over again, and his calculation to begin afresh, when he had almost got to the end of it, by Obadiah's opening the door to acquaint him the family was out of yeast—and to ask whether he might not take the great coach-horse early in the morning and ride in search of some.——With all my heart, Obadiah, said my father (pursuing his journey)—take the coach-horse, and welcome.—But he wants a shoe, poor creature! said Obadiah.——Poor creature! said my uncle Toby, vibrating the note back again, like a string in unison. Then ride the Scotch horse, quoth my father hastily.——He cannot bear a saddle upon his back, quoth Obadiah, for the whole world.——The devil's in that horse; then take Patriot, cried my father, and shut the door.——Patriot is sold, said Obadiah. Here's for you! cried my father, making a pause, and looking in my uncle Toby's face, as if the thing had not been a matter of fact.—Your worship ordered me to sell him last April, said Obadiah.——Then go on foot for your pains, cried my father—I had much rather walk than ride, said Obadiah, shutting the door.

What plagues, cried my father, going on with his calculation.——But the waters are out, said Obadiah,—opening the door again.

Till that moment, my father, who had a map of Sanson's, and a book of the post-roads before him, had kept his hand upon the head of his compasses, with one foot of them fixed upon Nevers, the last stage he had paid for—purposing to go on from that point with his journey and calculation, as soon as Obadiah quitted the room: but this second attack of Obadiah's, in opening the door and laying the whole country under water, was too much.——He let go his compasses—or rather with a mixed motion between accident and anger, he threw them upon the table; and then there was nothing for him to do, but to return back to Calais (like many others) as wise as he had set out.

When the letter was brought into the parlour, which contained the news of my brother's death, my father had got forwards again upon his journey to within a stride of the compasses of the very same stage of Nevers.——By your leave, Mons. Sanson, cried my father, striking the point of his compasses through Nevers into the table—and nodding to my uncle Toby to see what was in the letter—twice of one night, is too much for an English gentleman and his son, Mons. Sanson, to be turned back from so lousy a town as Nevers—What think'st thou, Toby? added my father in a sprightly tone.——Unless it be a garrison town, said my uncle Toby—for then—I shall be a fool, said my father, smiling to himself, as long as I live.——So giving a second nod—and keeping his compasses still upon Nevers with one hand, and holding his book of the post-roads in the other—half calculating and half listening, he leaned forwards upon the table with both elbows, as my uncle Toby hummed over the letter.

———— —— —— ——— — ——— — — —— — — —— — — —

—— ——— — —— —he's gone! said my uncle Toby.—Where—Who? cried my father.——My nephew, said my uncle Toby.——What—without leave —without money—without governor? cried my father in amazement. No: —he is dead, my dear brother, quoth my uncle Toby.—Without being ill? cried my father again.——I dare say not, said my uncle Toby, in a low voice, and fetching a deep sigh from the bottom of his heart, he has been ill enough, poor lad! I'll answer for him—for he is dead.

When Agrippina was told of her son's death, Tacitus informs us, that, not being able to moderate the violence of her passions, she abruptly broke off her work.——My father stuck his compasses into Nevers, but so much the faster.——What contrarieties! his, indeed, was matter of calculation! ——Agrippina's must have been quite a different affair; who else could pretend to reason from history?

How my father went on, in my opinion, deserves a chapter to itself.——

CHAPTER 3

——AND a chapter it shall have, and a devil of a one too—so look to yourselves.

'Tis either Plato, or Plutarch, or Seneca, or Xenophon, or Epictetus, or Theophrastus, or Lucian—or some one perhaps of later date—either Cardan, or Budaeus, or Petrarch, or Stella—or possibly it may be some divine or father of the church, St. Austin, or St. Cyprian, or Bernard, who affirms that it is an irresistible and natural passion to weep for the loss of our friends or children—and Seneca (I'm positive) tells us somewhere, that such griefs evacuate themselves best by that particular channel—And accordingly we find, that David wept for his son Absalom—Adrian for his Antinous—Niobe for her children, and that Apollodorus and Crito both shed tears for Socrates before his death.

My father managed his affliction otherwise; and indeed differently from most men either ancient or modern; for he neither wept it away, as the Hebrews and the Romans—or slept it off, as the Laplanders—or hanged it, as the English, or drowned it, as the Germans—nor did he curse it, or damn it, or excommunicate it, or rhyme it, or lillabullero it.——

——He got rid of it, however.

Will your worships give me leave to squeeze in a story between these two pages?

When Tully was bereft of his dear daughter Tullia, at first he laid it to his heart,—he listened to the voice of nature, and modulated his own unto it. ——O my Tullia! my daughter! my child!—still, still, still,—'twas O my Tullia!—my Tullia! Methinks I see my Tullia, I hear my Tullia, I talk with my Tullia.—But as soon as he began to look into the stores of philosophy, and consider how many excellent things might be said upon the occasion— no body upon earth can conceive, says the great orator, how happy, how joyful it made me.

My father was as proud of his eloquence as Marcus Tullius Cicero could be for his life, and for aught I am convinced of to the contrary at present, with as much reason: it was indeed his strength—and his weakness too.— His strength—for he was by nature eloquent; and his weakness—for he was hourly a dupe to it; and, provided an occasion in life would but permit him to shew his talents, or say either a wise thing, a witty, or a shrewd one— (bating the case of a systematic misfortune)—he had all he wanted.—A blessing which tied up my father's tongue, and a misfortune which let it loose with a good grace, were pretty equal: sometimes, indeed, the misfortune was the better of the two; for instance, where the pleasure of the harangue was as ten, and the pain of the misfortune but as five—my father gained half in half, and consequently was as well again off, as if it had never befallen him.

This clue will unravel what otherwise would seem very inconsistent in my father's domestic character; and it is this, that, in the provocations arising from the neglects and blunders of servants, or other mishaps unavoidable in a family, his anger, or rather the duration of it, eternally ran counter to all conjecture.

My father had a favourite little mare, which he had consigned over to a most beautiful Arabian horse, in order to have a pad out of her for his own riding: he was sanguine in all his projects; so talked about his pad every day with as absolute a security, as if it had been reared, broke,—and bridled and saddled at his door ready for mounting. By some neglect or other in Obadiah, it so fell out, that my father's expectations were answered with nothing better than a mule, and as ugly a beast of the kind as ever was produced.

My mother and my uncle Toby expected my father would be the death of Obadiah—and that there never would be an end of the disaster.——See here! you rascal, cried my father, pointing to the mule, what you have done!——It was not me, said Obadiah.——How do I know that? replied my father.

Triumph swam in my father's eyes, at the repartee—the Attic salt brought water into them—and so Obadiah heard no more about it.

Now let us go back to my brother's death.

Philosophy has a fine saying for every thing.—For Death it has an entire set; the misery was, they all at once rushed into my father's head, that 'twas difficult to string them together, so as to make any thing of a consistent show out of them.——He took them as they came.

"'Tis an inevitable chance—the first statute in Magna Charta—it is an everlasting act of parliament, my dear brother,—All must die.

"If my son could not have died, it had been matter of wonder,—not that he is dead.

"Monarchs and princes dance in the same ring with us.

"——To die, is the great debt and tribute due unto nature: tombs and monuments, which should perpetuate our memories, pay it themselves; and the proudest pyramid of them all, which wealth and science have erected, has lost its apex, and stands obtruncated in the traveller's horizon." (My father found he got great ease, and went on)—"Kingdoms and provinces, and towns and cities, have they not their periods? and when those principles and powers, which at first cemented and put them together, have performed their several evolutions, they fall back."——Brother Shandy, said my uncle Toby, laying down his pipe at the word evolutions—Revolutions, I meant, quoth my father,—by heaven! I meant revolutions, brother Toby—evolutions is nonsense.——'Tis not nonsense—said my uncle Toby.——But is it not nonsense to break the thread of such a discourse upon such an occasion? cried my father—do not— dear Toby, continued he, taking him by the hand, do not—do not, I beseech thee, interrupt me at this crisis.—— My uncle Toby put his pipe into his mouth.

"Where is Troy and Mycenae, and Thebes and Delos, and Persepolis and Agrigentum?"—continued my father, taking up his book of post-roads, which he had laid down.——"What is become, brother Toby, of Nineveh and Babylon, of Cizicum and Mitylenae? The fairest towns that ever the sun rose upon, are now no more; the names only are left, and those (for many of them are wrong spelt) are falling themselves by piece-meals to decay, and in length of time will be forgotten, and involved with every thing in a perpetual night: the world itself, brother Toby, must—must come to an end.

"Returning out of Asia, when I sailed from Aegina towards Megara," (when can this have been? thought my uncle Toby) "I began to view the country round about. Aegina was behind me, Megara was before, Pyraeus on the right hand, Corinth on the left.——What flourishing towns now prostrate upon the earth! Alas! alas! said I to myself, that man should disturb his soul for the loss of a child, when so much as this lies awfully buried in his presence—Remember, said I to myself again—remember thou art a man."——

Now my uncle Toby knew not that this last paragraph was an extract of Servius Sulpicius's consolatory letter to Tully.—He had as little skill, honest man, in the fragments, as he had in the whole pieces of antiquity. ——And as my father, whilst he was concerned in the Turkey trade, had been three or four different times in the Levant, in one of which he had stayed a whole year and an half at Zant, my uncle Toby naturally concluded, that, in some one of these periods, he had taken a trip across the Archipelago into Asia; and that all this sailing affair with Aegina behind, and Megara before, and Pyraeus on the right hand, etc. etc., was nothing more than the true course of my father's voyage and reflections.——'Twas certainly in his manner, and many an undertaking critic would have built two stories higher upon worse foundations.——And pray, brother, quoth my uncle Toby, laying the end of his pipe upon my father's hand in a kindly way of interruption—but waiting till he finished the account—what year of our Lord was this?——'Twas no year of our Lord, replied my father.— That's impossible, cried my uncle Toby.—Simpleton! said my father,— 'twas forty years before Christ was born.

My uncle Toby had but two things for it; either to suppose his brother to be the wandering Jew, or that his misfortunes had disordered his brain. ——"May the Lord God of heaven and earth protect him and restore him," said my uncle Toby, praying silently for my father, and with tears in his eyes.

——My father placed the tears to a proper account, and went on with his harangue with great spirit.

"There is not such great odds, brother Toby, betwixt good and evil, as the world imagines"—(this way of setting off, by the bye, was not likely to cure my uncle Toby's suspicions)—"Labour, sorrow, grief, sickness, want, and woe, are the sauces of life."——Much good may it do them— said my uncle Toby to himself.——

"My son is dead!—so much the better;—'tis a shame in such a tempest to have but one anchor."

"But he is gone for ever from us!—be it so. He is got from under the hands of his barber before he was bald—he is but risen from a feast before he was surfeited—from a banquet before he had got drunken."

"The Thracians wept when a child was born"—(and we were very near it, quoth my uncle Toby)—"and feasted and made merry when a man went out of the world; and with reason.——Death opens the gate of fame, and shuts the gate of envy after it,—it unlooses the chain of the captive, and puts the bondsman's task into another man's hands."

"Shew me the man, who knows what life is, who dreads it, and I'll shew thee a prisoner who dreads his liberty."

Is it not better, my dear brother Toby, (for mark—our appetites are but diseases)—is it not better not to hunger at all, than to eat?—not to thirst, than to take physic to cure it?

Is it not better to be freed from cares and agues, from love and melancholy, and the other hot and cold fits of life, than, like a galled traveller, who comes weary to his inn, to be bound to begin his journey afresh?

There is no terror, brother Toby, in its looks, but what it borrows from groans and convulsions—and the blowing of noses and the wiping away of tears with the bottoms of curtains, in a dying man's room.——Strip it of these, what is it?——'Tis better in battle than in bed, said my uncle Toby. ——Take away its hearses, its mutes, and its mourning,—its plumes, scutcheons, and other mechanic aids—What is it?——Better in battle! continued my father, smiling, for he had absolutely forgot my brother Bobby—'tis terrible no way—for consider, brother Toby,—when we are— death is not;—and when death is—we are not. My uncle Toby laid down his pipe to consider the proposition; my father's eloquence was too rapid to stay for any man—away it went,—and hurried my uncle Toby's ideas along with it.——

For this reason, continued my father, 'tis worthy to recollect, how little alteration, in great men, the approaches of death have made.——Vespasian died in a jest upon his close-stool—Galba with a sentence—Septimus Severus in a dispatch—Tiberius in dissimulation, and Caesar Augustus in a compliment.—I hope 'twas a sincere one—quoth my uncle Toby.

——'Twas to his wife,—said my father.

CHAPTER 4

——And lastly—for all the choice anecdotes which history can produce of this matter, continued my father,—this, like the gilded dome which covers in the fabric—crowns all.——

'Tis of Cornelius Gallus, the praetor—which, I dare say, brother Toby, you have read,—I dare say I have not, replied my uncle.—He died, said my father, as ***************—And if it was with his wife, said my uncle Toby—there could be no hurt in it.——That's more than I know—replied my father.

CHAPTER 5

My mother was going very gingerly in the dark along the passage which led to the parlour, as my uncle Toby pronounced the word "wife."——'Tis a shrill penetrating sound of itself, and Obadiah had helped it by leaving the door a little a-jar, so that my mother heard enough of it to imagine herself the subject of the conversation; so laying the edge of her finger across her two lips—holding in her breath, and bending her head a little downwards, with a twist of her neck—(not towards the door, but from it, by which means her ear was brought to the chink)—she listened with all her powers: —the listening slave, with the Goddess of Silence at his back, could not have given a finer thought for an intaglio.

In this attitude I am determined to let her stand for five minutes: till I bring up the affairs of the kitchen (as Rapin does those of the church) to the same period.

Chapter 6

THOUGH in one sense, our family was certainly a simple machine, as it consisted of a few wheels; yet there was thus much to be said for it, that these wheels were set in motion by so many different springs, and acted one upon the other from such a variety of strange principles and impulses—that though it was a simple machine, it had all the honour and advantages of a complex one,—and a number of as odd movements within it, as ever were beheld in the inside of a Dutch silk-mill.

Amongst these there was one, I am going to speak of, in which, perhaps, it was not altogether so singular, as in many others; and it was this, that whatever motion, debate, harangue, dialogue, project, or dissertation, was going forwards in the parlour, there was generally another at the same time, and upon the same subject, running parallel along with it in the kitchen.

Now to bring this about, whenever an extraordinary message, or letter, was delivered in the parlour—or a discourse suspended till a servant went out—or the lines of discontent were observed to hang upon the brows of my father or mother—or, in short, when any thing was supposed to be upon the tapis worth knowing or listening to, 'twas the rule to leave the door, not absolutely shut, but somewhat a-jar—as it stands just now,—which, under covert of the bad hinge (and that possibly might be one of the many reasons why it was never mended), it was not difficult to manage; by which means, in all these cases, a passage was generally left, not indeed as wide as the Dardanelles, but wide enough, for all that, to carry on as much of this windward trade, as was sufficient to save my father the trouble of governing his house;—my mother at this moment stands profiting by it.——Obadiah did the same thing, as soon as he had left the letter upon the table which brought the news of my brother's death, so that before my father had well got over his surprise, and entered upon his harangue,—had Trim got upon his legs, to speak his sentiments upon the subject.

A curious observer of nature, had he been worth the inventory of all Job's stock—though by the bye, your curious observers are seldom worth a groat—would have given the half of it, to have heard Corporal Trim and my father, two orators so contrasted by nature and education, haranguing over the same bier.

My father—a man of deep reading—prompt memory—with Cato, and Seneca, and Epictetus, at his fingers' ends.——

The corporal—with nothing—to remember—of no deeper reading than his muster-roll—or greater names at his fingers' ends, than the contents of it.

The one proceeding from period to period, by metaphor and allusion, and striking the fancy as he went along (as men of wit and fancy do) with the entertainment and pleasantry of his pictures and images.

The other, without wit or antithesis, or point, or turn, this way or that; but leaving the images on one side, and the picture on the other, going straight forwards as nature could lead him, to the heart. O Trim! would to heaven thou had'st a better historian!—would thy historian had a better pair of breeches!—O ye critics! will nothing melt you?

CHAPTER 7

——My young master in London is dead! said Obadiah.——

——A green satin night-gown of my mother's, which had been twice scoured, was the first idea which Obadiah's exclamation brought into Susannah's head.——Well might Locke write a chapter upon the imperfections of words.——Then, quoth Susannah, we must all go into mourning. But note a second time: the word mourning, notwithstanding Susannah made use of it herself—failed also of doing its office; it excited not one single idea, tinged either with grey or black,—all was green.——The green satin night-gown hung there still.

——O! 'twill be the death of my poor mistress, cried Susannah.—My mother's whole wardrobe followed.——What a procession! her red damask, —her orange tawney,—her white and yellow lute-strings,—her brown taffata,—her bone-laced caps, her bed-gowns, and comfortable under-petti-coats.——Not a rag was left behind.——"No,—she will never look up again," said Susannah.

We had a fat, foolish scullion—my father, I think, kept her for her sim-plicity;—she had been all autumn struggling with a dropsy.—He is dead, said Obadiah,—he is certainly dead!——So am not I, said the foolish scullion.

——Here is sad news, Trim, cried Susannah, wiping her eyes as Trim stepped into the kitchen,—master Bobby is dead and buried—the funeral was an interpolation of Susannah's—we shall have all to go into mourning, said Susannah.

I hope not, said Trim.——You hope not! cried Susannah earnestly.— The mourning ran not in Trim's head, whatever it did in Susannah's.—I hope—said Trim, explaining himself, I hope in God the news is not true.—I heard the letter read with my own ears, answered Obadiah; and we shall have a terrible piece of work of it in stubbing the Ox-moor.——Oh! he's dead, said Susannah.—As sure, said the scullion, as I'm alive.

I lament for him from my heart and my soul, said Trim, fetching a sigh. ——Poor creature!—poor boy!—poor gentleman!

——He was alive last Whitsuntide! said the coachman.——Whitsuntide! alas! cried Trim, extending his right arm, and falling instantly into the same attitude in which he read the sermon,—What is Whitsuntide, Jonathan (for that was the coachman's name), or Shrovetide, or any tide or time past, to this? Are we not here now, continued the corporal (striking the end of his stick perpendicularly upon the floor, so as to give an idea of health and stability)—and are we not—(dropping his hat upon the ground) gone! in a moment!—'Twas infinitely striking! Susannah burst into a flood of tears. ——We are not stocks and stones.——Jonathan, Obadiah, the cook-maid, all melted.——The foolish fat scullion herself, who was scouring a fish-kettle upon her knees, was roused with it.——The whole kitchen crowded about the corporal.

Now, as I perceive plainly, that the preservation of our constitution in church and state,—and possibly the preservation of the whole world—or what is the same thing, the distribution and balance of its property and power, may in time to come depend greatly upon the right understanding of this stroke of the corporal's eloquence—I do demand your attention— your worships and reverences, for any ten pages together, take them where you will in any other part of the work, shall sleep for it at your ease.

I said, "we were not stocks and stones"—'tis very well. I should have added, nor are we angels, I wish we were,—but men clothed with bodies, and governed by our imaginations;—and what a junketing piece of work of it there is, betwixt these and our seven senses, especially some of them, for my own part, I own it, I am ashamed to confess. Let it suffice to affirm, that of all the senses, the eye (for I absolutely deny the touch, though most of your Barbati, I know, are for it) has the quickest commerce with the soul,— gives a smarter stroke, and leaves something more inexpressible upon the fancy, than words can either convey—or sometimes get rid of.

——I've gone a little about—no matter, 'tis for health—let us only carry it back in our mind to the mortality of Trim's hat.——"Are we not here now,—and gone in a moment?"——There was nothing in the sentence— 'twas one of your self-evident truths we have the advantage of hearing every day; and if Trim had not trusted more to his hat than his head—he had made nothing at all of it.

——"Are we not here now;" continued the corporal, "and are we not"— (dropping his hat plumb upon the ground—and pausing before he pronounced the word)—"gone! in a moment?" The descent of the hat was as if a heavy lump of clay had been kneaded into the crown of it.——Nothing could have expressed the sentiment of mortality, of which it was the type and forerunner, like it,—his hand seemed to vanish from under it,—it fell dead,—the corporal's eye fixed upon it, as upon a corpse, and Susannah burst into a flood of tears.

Now—Ten thousand, and ten thousand times ten thousand (for matter and motion are infinite) are the ways by which a hat may be dropped upon the ground, without any effect.——Had he flung it, or thrown it, or cast it, or skimmed it, or squirted it, or let it slip or fall in any possible direction under heaven,—or in the best direction that could be given to it,—had he dropped it like a goose—like a puppy—like an ass—or in doing it, or even after he had done, had he looked like a fool—like a ninny—like a nincompoop—it had failed, and the effect upon the heart had been lost.

Ye who govern this mighty world and its mighty concerns with the engines of eloquence,—who heat it, and cool it, and melt it, and mollify it,— and then harden it again to your purpose——

Ye who wind and turn the passions with this great windlass, and, having done it, lead the owners of them, whither ye think meet——

Ye, lastly, who drive—and why not, Ye also who are driven, like turkeys to market with a stick and a red clout—meditate—meditate, I beseech you, upon Trim's hat.

CHAPTER 8

STAY—I have a small account to settle with the reader before Trim can go on with his harangue.—It shall be done in two minutes.

Amongst many other book-debts, all of which I shall discharge in due time,—I own myself a debtor to the world for two items,—a chapter upon chamber-maids and button-holes, which, in the former part of my work, I promised and fully intended to pay off this year: but some of your worships and reverences telling me, that the two subjects, especially so connected together, might endanger the morals of the world,—I pray the chapter upon chamber-maids and button-holes may be forgiven me,—and that they will accept of the last chapter in lieu of it; which is nothing, an't please your reverences, but a chapter of chamber-maids, green gowns, and old hats.

Trim took his off the ground,—put it upon his head,—and then went on with his oration upon death, in manner and form following.

CHAPTER 9

——To us, Jonathan, who know not what want or care is—who live here in the service of two of the best of masters—(bating in my own case his majesty King William the Third, whom I had the honour to serve both in Ireland and Flanders)—I own it, that from Whitsuntide to within three weeks of Christmas,—'tis not long—'tis like nothing;—but to those, Jonathan, who know what death is, and what havoc and destruction he can make, before a man can well wheel about—'tis like a whole age.——O Jonathan! 'twould make a good-natured man's heart bleed, to consider, continued the corporal (standing perpendicularly), how low many a brave and upright fellow has been laid since that time!—And trust me, Susy, added the corporal, turning to Susannah, whose eyes were swimming in water,—before that time comes round again,—many a bright eye will be dim.——Susannah placed it to the right side of the page—she wept—but she court'sied too.——Are we not, continued Trim, looking still at Susannah—are we not like a flower of the field—a tear of pride stole in betwixt every two tears of humiliation—else no tongue could have described Susannah's affliction—is not all flesh grass?——'Tis clay,—'tis dirt.—— They all looked directly at the scullion,—the scullion had just been scouring a fish-kettle.——It was not fair.——

——What is the finest face that ever man looked at!——I could hear Trim talk so for ever, cried Susannah,—what is it! (Susannah laid her hand upon Trim's shoulder)—but corruption!——Susannah took it off.

Now I love you for this—and 'tis this delicious mixture within you which makes you dear creatures what you are—and he who hates you for it—all I can say of the matter is—That he has either a pumpkin for his head—or a pippin for his heart,—and whenever he is dissected 'twill be found so.

CHAPTER 10

WHETHER Susannah, by taking her hand too suddenly from off the corporal's shoulder (by the whisking about of her passions)—broke a little the chain of his reflections——

Or whether the corporal began to be suspicious, he had got into the doctor's quarters, and was talking more like the chaplain than himself——

Or whether- -
Or whether—for in all such cases a man of invention and parts may with pleasure fill a couple of pages with suppositions—which of all these was the cause, let the curious physiologist, or the curious any body determine—'tis certain, at least, the corporal went on thus with his harangue.

For my own part, I declare it, that out of doors, I value not death at all: —not this .. added the corporal, snapping his fingers,—but with an air which no one but the corporal could have given to the sentiment.—In battle, I value death not this . . . and let him not take me cowardly, like poor Joe Gibbins, in scouring his gun.——What is he? A pull of a trigger— a push of a bayonet an inch this way or that—makes the difference.—Look along the line—to the right—see! Jack's down! well,—'tis worth a regiment of horse to him.——No—'tis Dick. Then Jack's no worse.——Never mind which,—we pass on,—in hot pursuit the wound itself which brings him is not felt,—the best way is to stand up to him,—the man who flies, is in ten times more danger than the man who marches up into his jaws.——I've looked him, added the corporal, an hundred times in the face,—and know what he is.——He's nothing, Obadiah, at all in the field.——But he's very frightful in a house, quoth Obadiah.——I never mind it myself, said Jonathan, upon the coach-box.——It must, in my opinion, be most natural in bed, replied Susannah.——And could I escape him by creeping into the worst calf's skin that ever was made into a knapsack, I would do it there— said Trim—but that is nature.

——Nature is nature, said Jonathan.——And that is the reason, cried Susannah, I so much pity my mistress.——She will never get the better of it.——Now I pity the captain the most of any one in the family, answered Trim.——Madam will get ease of heart in weeping,—and the Squire in talking about it,—but my poor master will keep it all in silence to himself. ——I shall hear him sigh in his bed for a whole month together, as he did for lieutenant Le Fever.——An' please your honour, do not sigh so piteously, I would say to him as I laid beside him. I cannot help it, Trim, my master would say,—'tis so melancholy an accident—I cannot get it off my heart.——Your honour fears not death yourself.——I hope, Trim, I fear nothing, he would say, but the doing a wrong thing.——Well, he would add, whatever betides, I will take care of Le Fever's boy.——And with that, like a quieting draught, his honour would fall asleep.

I like to hear Trim's stories about the captain, said Susannah.——He is a kindly-hearted gentleman, said Obadiah, as ever lived.——Aye, and as brave a one too, said the corporal, as ever stept before a platoon.——There never was a better officer in the king's army,—or a better man in God's world; for he would march up to the mouth of a cannon, though he saw the lighted match at the very touch-hole,—and yet, for all that, he has a heart as soft as a child for other people.——He would not hurt a chicken.——I would sooner, quoth Jonathan, drive such a gentleman for seven pounds a year—than some for eight.——Thank thee, Jonathan! for thy twenty shillings,—as much, Jonathan, said the corporal, shaking him by the hand, as if thou hadst put the money into my own pocket.——I would serve him to the day of my death out of love. He is a friend and a brother to me,—and could I be sure my poor brother Tom was dead,—continued the corporal, taking out his handkerchief,—was I worth ten thousand pounds, I would leave every shilling of it to the captain.——Trim could not refrain from tears at this testamentary proof he gave of his affection to his master.—— The whole kitchen was affected.——Do tell us the story of the poor lieutenant, said Susannah.——With all my heart, answered the corporal.

Susannah, the cook, Jonathan, Obadiah, and Corporal Trim, formed a circle about the fire; and as soon as the scullion had shut the kitchen door, —the corporal begun.

CHAPTER 11

I AM a Turk if I had not as much forgot my mother, as if Nature had plaistered me up, and set me down naked upon the banks of the river Nile, without one.——Your most obedient servant, Madam—I've cost you a great deal of trouble,—I wish it may answer;—but you have left a crack in my back,—and here's a great piece fallen off here before,—and what must I do with this foot?——I shall never reach England with it.

For my own part, I never wonder at any thing;—and so often has my judgment deceived me in my life, that I always suspect it, right or wrong,— as least I am seldom hot upon cold subjects. For all this, I reverence truth as much as any body; and when it has slipped us, if a man will but take me by the hand, and go quietly and search for it, as for a thing we have both lost, and can neither of us do well without,—I'll go to the world's end with him:—But I hate disputes,—and therefore (bating religious points, or such as touch society) I would almost subscribe to any thing which does not choke me in the first passage, rather than be drawn into one—But I cannot bear suffocation,—and bad smells worst of all.—For which reasons, I resolved from the beginning, That if ever the army of martyrs was to be augmented,—or a new one raised,—I would have no hand in it, one way or t'other.

CHAPTER 12

——BUT to return to my mother.

My uncle Toby's opinion, Madam, "that there could be no harm in Cornelius Gallus, the Roman praetor's lying with his wife";—or rather the last word of that opinion,—(for it was all my mother heard of it) caught hold of her by the weak part of the whole sex:—You shall not mistake me,— I mean her curiosity,—she instantly concluded herself the subject of the conversation, and with that prepossession upon her fancy, you will readily conceive every word my father said, was accommodated either to herself, or her family concerns.

——Pray, Madam, in what street does the lady live, who would not have done the same?

From the strange mode of Cornelius's death, my father had made a transition to that of Socrates, and was giving my uncle Toby an abstract of his pleading before his judges;—'twas irresistible:—not the oration of Socrates,—but my father's temptation to it.——He had wrote the[1] *Life of Socrates* himself the year before he left off trade, which, I fear, was the means of hastening him out of it;—so that no one was able to set out with so full a sail, and in so swelling a tide of heroic loftiness upon the occasion, as my father was. Not a period in Socrates's oration, which closed with a shorter word than transmigration, or annihilation,—or a worse thought in the middle of it than to be—or not to be,—the entering upon a new and untried state of things,—or, upon a long, a profound and peaceful sleep, without dreams, without disturbance?—That we and our children were born to die,—but neither of us born to be slaves.——No—there I mistake; that was part of Eleazer's oration, as recorded by Josephus (*de Bell. Judaic.*)—Eleazer owns he had it from the philosophers of India; in all likelihood Alexander the Great, in his irruption into India, after he had over-run Persia, amongst the many things he stole,—stole that sentiment also; by which means it was carried, if not all the way by himself (for we all know he died at Babylon), at least by some of his marauders, into Greece,—from Greece it got to Rome,—from Rome to France,—and from France to England:—So things come round.——

By land carriage, I can conceive no other way.——

By water the sentiment might easily have come down the Ganges into the Sinus Gangeticus, or Bay of Bengal, and so into the Indian Sea; and following the course of trade (the way from India by the Cape of Good Hope being then unknown), might be carried with other drugs and spices up the Red Sea to Joddah, the port of Mekka, or else to Tor or Sues, towns at the bottom of the gulf; and from thence by karrawans to Coptos, but three days' journey distant, so down the Nile directly to Alexandria, where the sentiment would be landed at the very foot of the great stair-case of the Alexandrian library,—and from that store-house it would be fetched.—— Bless me! what a trade was driven by the learned in those days!

Chapter 13

——Now my father had a way, a little like that of Job's (in case there ever was such a man—if not, there's an end of the matter.——

Though, by the bye, because your learned men find some difficulty in fixing the precise era in which so great a man lived;—whether, for instance, before or after the patriarchs, etc.—to vote, therefore, that he never lived at all, is a little cruel,—'tis not doing as they would be done by,—happen that as it may)—My father, I say, had a way, when things went extremely

[1]This book my father would never consent to publish; 'tis in manuscript, with some other tracts of his, in the family, all, or most of which will be printed in due time.

wrong with him, especially upon the first sally of his impatience,—of wondering why he was begot,—wishing himself dead;—sometimes worse:——
And when the provocation ran high, and grief touched his lips with more
than ordinary powers—Sir, you scarce could have distinguished him from
Socrates himself.——Every word would breathe the sentiments of a soul
disdaining life, and careless about all its issues; for which reason, though my
mother was a woman of no deep reading, yet the abstract of Socrates's
oration, which my father was giving my uncle Toby, was not altogether
new to her.——She listened to it with composed intelligence, and would
have done so to the end of the chapter, had not my father plunged (which
he had no occasion to have done) into that part of the pleading where the
great philosopher reckons up his connections, his alliances, and children;
but renounces a security to be so won by working upon the passions of his
judges.——"I have friends—I have relations,—I have three desolate
children,"—says Socrates.——

——Then, cried my mother, opening the door,—you have one more, Mr.
Shandy, than I know of.

By heaven! I have one less,—said my father, getting up and walking out
of the room.

CHAPTER 14

——They are Socrates's children, said my uncle Toby. He has been dead a
hundred years ago, replied my mother.

My uncle Toby was no chronologer—so not caring to advance one step
but upon safe ground, he laid down his pipe deliberately upon the table, and
rising up, and taking my mother most kindly by the hand, without saying
another word, either good or bad, to her, he led her out after my father,
that he might finish the éclaircissement himself.

CHAPTER 15

Had this volume been a farce, which, unless every one's life and opinions
are to be looked upon as a farce as well as mine, I see no reason to suppose—
the last chapter, Sir, had finished the first act of it, and then this chapter
must have set off thus.

Ptr..r..r..ing—twing—twang—prut—trut—'tis a cursed bad fiddle.——
Do you know whether my fiddle's in tune or no?—trut..prut..—They should
be fifths.——'Tis wickedly strung—tr...a.e.i.o.u.-twang.——The bridge is
a mile too high, and the sound post absolutely down,—else—trut..prut—
hark! 'tis not so bad a tone.——Diddle diddle, diddle diddle, diddle diddle,
dum. There is nothing in playing before good judges,—but there's a man
there—no—not him with the bundle under his arm—the grave man in
black—'Sdeath! not the gentleman with the sword on.——Sir, I had rather
play a Capriccio to Calliope herself, than draw my bow across my fiddle
before that very man; and yet I'll stake my Cremona to a Jew's trump,
which is the greatest musical odds that ever were laid, that I will this
moment stop three hundred and fifty leagues out of tune upon my fiddle,
without punishing one single nerve that belongs to him—Twaddle diddle,

tweddle diddle,—twiddle diddle,—twoddle diddle,—twuddle diddle,—prut trut—krish—krash—krush.——I've undone you, Sir,—but you see he's no worse,—and was Apollo to take his fiddle after me, he can make him no better.

Diddle diddle, diddle diddle, diddle diddle—hum—dum—drum.

——Your worships and your reverences love music—and God has made you all with good ears—and some of you play delightfully yourselves— trut-prut,—prut-trut.

O! there is—whom I could sit and hear whole days,—whose talents lie in making what he fiddles to be felt,—who inspires me with his joys and hopes, and puts the most hidden springs of my heart into motion.——If you would borrow five guineas of me, Sir,—which is generally ten guineas more than I have to spare—or you Messrs. Apothecary and Tailor, want your bills paying,—that's your time.

CHAPTER 16

THE first thing which entered my father's head, after affairs were a little settled in the family and Susannah had got possession of my mother's green satin night-gown,—was to sit down coolly, after the example of Xenophon, and write a *Tristra-paedia*, or system of education for me; collecting first for that purpose his own scattered thoughts, counsels, and notions; and binding them together, so as to form an Institute for the government of my childhood and adolescence. I was my father's last stake—he had lost my brother Bobby entirely,—he had lost, by his own computation, full three-fourths of me—that is, he had been unfortunate in his three first great casts for me—my geniture, nose, and name,—there was but this one left; and accordingly my father gave himself up to it with as much devotion as ever my uncle Toby had done to his doctrine of projectiles.——The difference between them was, that my uncle Toby drew his whole knowledge of projectiles from Nicholas Tartaglia—My father spun his, every thread of it, out of his own brain,—or reeled and cross-twisted what all other spinners and spinsters had spun before him, that 'twas pretty near the same torture to him.

In about three years, or something more, my father had got advanced almost into the middle of his work.——Like all other writers, he met with disappointments.——He imagined he should be able to bring whatever he had to say, into so small a compass, that when it was finished and bound, it might be rolled up in my mother's hussive.——Matter grows under our hands.——Let no man say,—"Come—I'll write a duodecimo."

My father gave himself up to it, however, with the most painful diligence, proceeding step by step in every line, with the same kind of caution and circumspection (though I cannot say upon quite so religious a principle) as was used by John de la Casse, the lord archbishop of Benevento, in compassing his *Galatea;* in which his Grace of Benevento spent near forty years of his life; and when the thing came out, it was not of above half the size or the thickness of a Rider's Almanac.——How the holy man managed the affair, unless he spent the greatest part of his time in combing his whiskers, or playing at primero with his chaplain,—would pose any mortal not let into the true secret;—and therefore 'tis worth explaining to the world, was it only for the encouragement of those few in it, who write not so much to be fed—as to be famous.

I own had John de la Casse, the archbishop of Benevento, for whose memory (notwithstanding his *Galatea*) I retain the highest veneration,—had he been, Sir, a slender clerk—of dull wit—slow parts—costive head, and so forth,—he and his *Galatea* might have jogged on together to the age of Methuselah for me,—the phenomenon had not been worth a parenthesis.——

But the reverse of this was the truth: John de la Casse was a genius of fine parts and fertile fancy; and yet with all these great advantages of nature, which should have pricked him forwards with his *Galatea*, he lay under an impuissance at the same time of advancing above a line and a half in the compass of a whole summer's day: this disability in his Grace arose from an opinion he was afflicted with,—which opinion was this,—viz. that whenever a Christian was writing a book (not for his private amusement, but) where his intent and purpose was, *bonâ fide*, to print and publish it to the world, his first thoughts were always the temptations of the evil one.

——This was the state of ordinary writers: but when a personage of venerable character and high station, either in church or state, once turned author,—he maintained, that from the very moment he took pen in hand—all the devils in hell broke out of their holes to cajole him.——'Twas Termtime with them,—every thought, first and last, was captious;—how specious and good soever,—'twas all one;—in whatever form or colour it presented itself to the imagination,—'twas still a stroke of one or other of them levelled at him, and was to be fenced off.——So that the life of a writer, whatever he might fancy to the contrary, was not so much a state of composition, as a state of warfare; and his probation in it, precisely that of any other man militant upon earth,—both depending alike, not half so much upon the degrees of his wit—as his resistance.

My father was hugely pleased with this theory of John de la Casse, archbishop of Benevento; and (had it not cramped him a little in his creed) I believe would have given ten of the best acres in the Shandy estate, to have been the broacher of it.—How far my father actually believed in the devil, will be seen, when I come to speak of my father's religious notions, in the progress of this work: 'tis enough to say here, as he could not have the honour of it, in the literal sense of the doctrine—he took up with the allegory of it; and would often say, especially when his pen was a little retrograde, there was as much good meaning, truth, and knowledge, couched under the veil of John de la Casse's parabolical representation,—as was to be found in any one poetic fiction or mystic record of antiquity.——Prejudice of education, he would say, is the devil,—and the multitudes of them which we suck in with our mother's milk—are the devil and all.——We are haunted with them, brother Toby, in all our lucubrations and researches; and was a man fool enough to submit tamely to what they obtruded upon him,—what would his book be? Nothing,—he would add, throwing his pen away with a vengeance,—nothing but a farrago of the clack of nurses, and of the nonsense of the old women (of both sexes) throughout the kingdom.

This is the best account I am determined to give of the slow progress my father made in his *Tristra-paedia;* at which (as I said) he was three years, and something more, indefatigably at work, and, at last, had scarce completed, by his own reckoning, one half of his undertaking: the misfortune was, that I was all that time totally neglected and abandoned to my mother: and what was almost as bad, by the very delay, the first part of the work, upon which my father had spent the most of his pains, was rendered entirely useless,—every day a page or two became of no consequence.——

——Certainly it was ordained as a scourge upon the pride of human wisdom, That the wisest of us all should thus outwit ourselves, and eternally forego our purposes in the intemperate act of pursuing them.

In short, my father was so long in all his acts of resistance,—or in other words,—he advanced so very slow with his work, and I began to live and get forwards at such a rate, that if an event had not happened,—which, when we get to it, if it can be told with decency, shall not be concealed a moment from the reader—I verily believe, I had put by my father, and left him drawing a sun-dial, for no better purpose than to be buried under ground.

Chapter 17

——'Twas nothing,—I did not lose two drops of blood by it—'twas not worth calling in a surgeon, had he lived next door to us—thousands suffer by choice, what I did by accident—Doctor Slop made ten times more of it, than there was occasion:—some men rise, by the art of hanging great weights upon small wires,—and I am this day (August the 10th, 1761) paying part of the price of this man's reputation.——O 'twould provoke a stone, to see how things are carried on in this world!——The chamber-maid had left no ******* *** under the bed:—Cannot you contrive, master, quoth Susannah, lifting up the sash with one hand, as she spoke, and helping me up into the window-seat with the other,—cannot you manage, my dear, for a single time, to   **** *** ** *** *******?

I was five years old.——Susannah did not consider that nothing was well hung in our family,—so slap came the sash down like lightning upon us;—Nothing is left,—cried Susannah,—nothing is left—for me, but to run my country.——

My uncle Toby's house was a much kinder sanctuary; and so Susannah fled to it.

Chapter 18

When Susannah told the corporal the misadventure of the sash, with all the circumstances which attended the murder of me,—(as she called it)—the blood forsook his cheeks,—all accessaries in murders being principals,—Trim's conscience told him he was as much to blame as Susannah,—and if the doctrine had been true, my uncle Toby had as much of the bloodshed to answer for to heaven, as either of 'em;—so that neither reason or instinct, separate or together, could possibly have guided Susannah's steps to so proper an asylum. It is in vain to leave this to the Reader's imagination:—

to form any kind of hypothesis that will render these propositions feasible, he must cudgel his brains sore,—and to do it without,—he must have such brains as no reader ever had before him.——Why should I put them either to trial or to torture? 'Tis my own affair: I'll explain it myself.

CHAPTER 19

'Tis a pity, Trim, said my uncle Toby, resting with his hand upon the corporal's shoulder, as they both stood surveying their works,—that we have not a couple of field-pieces to mount in the gorge of that new redoubt;— 'twould secure the lines all along there, and make the attack on that side quite complete:—get me a couple cast, Trim.

Your honour shall have them, replied Trim, before to-morrow morning.

It was the joy of Trim's heart,—nor was his fertile head ever at a loss for expedients in doing it, to supply my uncle Toby in his campaigns, with whatever his fancy called for; had it been his last crown, he would have sate down and hammered it into a paderero, to have prevented a single wish in his Master. The corporal had already,—what with cutting off the ends of my uncle Toby's spouts—hacking and chiseling up the sides of his leaden gutters,—melting down his pewter shaving-basin,—and going at last, like Lewis the Fourteenth, on to the top of the church, for spare ends, etc.—he had that very campaign brought no less than eight new battering cannons, besides three demi-culverins, into the field; my uncle Toby's demand for two more pieces for the redoubt, had set the corporal at work again; and no better resource offering, he had taken the two leaden weights from the nursery window: and as the sash pullies, when the lead was gone, were of no kind of use, he had taken them away also, to make a couple of wheels for one of their carriages.

He had dismantled every sash-window in my uncle Toby's house long before, in the very same way,—though not always in the same order; for sometimes the pullies have been wanted, and not the lead,—so then he began with the pullies,—and the pullies being picked out, then the lead became useless,—and so the lead went to pot too.

——A great Moral might be picked handsomely out of this, but I have not time—'tis enough to say, wherever the demolition began, 'twas equally fatal to the sash-window.

CHAPTER 20

THE corporal had not taken his measure so badly in this stroke of artillery-ship, but that he might have kept the matter entirely to himself, and left Susannah to have sustained the whole weight of the attack, as she could;— true courage is not content with coming off so.——The corporal, whether as general or comptroller of the train,—'twas no matter,—had done that, without which, as he imagined, the misfortune could never have happened, —at least in Susannah's hands;—How would your honours have behaved? —He determined at once, not to take shelter behind Susannah,—but to give it; and with this resolution upon his mind, he marched upright into the parlour, to lay the whole manœuvre before my uncle Toby.

My uncle Toby had just then been giving Yorick an account of the Battle of Steenkirk, and of the strange conduct of count Solmes in ordering the foot to halt, and the horse to march where it could not act; which was directly contrary to the king's commands, and proved the loss of the day.

There are incidents in some families so pat to the purpose of what is going to follow,—they are scarce exceeded by the invention of a dramatic writer;—I mean of ancient days.——

Trim, by the help of his fore-finger, laid flat upon the table, and the edge of his hand striking across it at right angles, made a shift to tell his story so, that priests and virgins might have listened to it;—and the story being told,—the dialogue went on as follows.

CHAPTER 21

——I would be picquetted to death, cried the corporal, as he concluded Susannah's story, before I would suffer the woman to come to any harm,— 'twas my fault, an' please your honour,—not hers.

Corporal Trim, replied my uncle Toby, putting on his hat which lay upon the table,—if any thing can be said to be a fault, when the service absolutely requires it should be done,—'tis I certainly who deserve the blame,— you obeyed your orders.

Had count Solmes, Trim, done the same at the battle of Steenkirk, said Yorick, drolling a little upon the corporal, who had been run over by a dragoon in the retreat,—he had saved thee;—Saved! cried Trim, interrupting Yorick, and finishing the sentence after his own fashion,—he had saved five battalions, an' please your reverence, every soul of them:—there was Cutt's—continued the corporal, clapping the forefinger of his right hand upon the thumb of his left, and counting round his hand,—there was Cutts's,—Mackay's—Angus's—Graham's, and Leven's, all cut to pieces;—and so had the English life-guards too, had it not been for some regiments upon the right, who marched up boldly to their relief, and received the enemy's fire in their faces, before any one of their own platoons discharged a musket,—they'll go to heaven for it,—added Trim.——Trim is right, said my uncle Toby, nodding to Yorick,—he's perfectly right. What signified his marching the horse, continued the corporal, where the ground was so straight, that the French had such a nation of hedges, and copses, and ditches, and felled trees laid this way and that to cover them; (as they always have).——Count Solmes should have sent us,—we would have fired muzzle to muzzle with them for their lives.——There was nothing to be done for the horse:—he had his foot shot off however for his pains, continued the corporal, the very next campaign at Landen.——Poor Trim got his wound there, quoth my uncle Toby.——'Twas owing, an' please your honour, entirely to count Solmes,—had he drubbed them soundly at Steenkirk, they would not have fought us at Landen.——Possibly not,— Trim, said my uncle Toby;—though if they have the advantage of a wood, or you give them a moment's time to intrench themselves, they are a nation which will pop and pop for ever at you.——There is no way but to march coolly up to them,—receive their fire, and fall in upon them, pell-

mell—Ding dong, added Trim.——Horse and foot, said my uncle Toby.—
Helter skelter, said Trim.——Right and left, cried my uncle Toby.——
Blood an' ounds, shouted the corporal;—the battle raged.——Yorick drew
his chair a little to one side for safety, and after a moment's pause, my
uncle Toby sinking his voice a note,—resumed the discourse as follows.

CHAPTER 22

KING WILLIAM, said my uncle Toby, addressing himself to Yorick, was so
terribly provoked at count Solmes for disobeying his orders, that he would
not suffer him to come into his presence for many months after.——I fear,
answered Yorick, the squire will be as much provoked at the corporal, as
the King at the count.——But 'twould be singularly hard in this case, continued he, if Corporal Trim, who has behaved so diametrically opposite to
count Solmes, should have the fate to be rewarded with the same disgrace:
—too oft in this world, do things take that train ——I would spring a mine,
cried my uncle Toby, rising up,—and blow up my fortifications, and my
house with them, and we would perish under their ruins, ere I would stand by
and see it.—Trim directed a slight,—but a grateful bow towards his master,—
and so the chapter ends.

CHAPTER 23

——THEN, Yorick, replied my uncle Toby, you and I will lead the way
abreast,—and do you, corporal, follow a few paces behind us.—And Susannah, an' please your honour, said Trim, shall be put in the rear.——
'Twas an excellent disposition,—and in this order, without either drums
beating, or colours flying, they marched slowly from my uncle Toby's
house to Shandy-hall.

——I wish, said Trim, as they entered the door,—instead of the sash
weights, I had cut off the church spout, as I once thought to have done.
——You have cut off spouts enow, replied Yorick.——

CHAPTER 24

As many pictures as have been given of my father, how like him soever in
different airs and attitudes,—not one, or all of them, can ever help the
reader to any kind of preconception of how my father would think, speak,
or act, upon any untried occasion or occurrence of life.——There was that
infinitude of oddities in him, and of chances along with it, by which handle
he would take a thing,—it baffled, Sir, all calculations.——The truth was,
his road lay so very far on one side, from that wherein most men travelled,
—that every object before him presented a face and section of itself to his
eye, altogether different from the plan and elevation of it seen by the rest of
mankind.——In other words, 'twas a different object, and in course was
differently considered:

This is the true reason, that my dear Jenny and I, as well as all the world
besides us, have such eternal squabbles about nothing.——She looks at her
outside,—I, at her in—. How is it possible we should agree about her value?

CHAPTER 25

'Tis a point settled,—and I mention it for the comfort of Confucius,[1] who is apt to get entangled in telling a plain story—that provided he keeps along the line of his story,—he may go backwards and forwards as he will, —'tis still held to be no digression.

This being premised, I take the benefit of the act of going backwards myself.

CHAPTER 26

FIFTY thousand pannier loads of devils—(not of the Archbishop of Bene-vento's—I mean of Rabelais's devils) with their tails chopped off by their rumps, could not have made so diabolical a scream of it, as I did—when the accident befell me: it summoned up my mother instantly into the nursery, —so that Susannah had but just time to make her escape down the back stairs, as my mother came up the fore.

Now, though I was old enough to have told the story myself,—and young enough, I hope, to have done it without malignity; yet Susannah, in passing by the kitchen, for fear of accidents, had left it in shorthand with the cook —the cook had told it with a commentary to Jonathan, and Jonathan to Obadiah; so that by the time my father had rung the bell half a dozen times, to know what was the matter above,—was Obadiah enabled to give him a particular account of it, just as it had happened.—I thought as much, said my father, tucking up his night-gown;—and so walked up stairs.

One would imagine from this—(though for my own part I somewhat question it)—that my father, before that time, had actually wrote that re-markable chapter in the *Tristra-paedia*, which to me is the most original and entertaining one in the whole book;—and that is the chapter Upon Sash-Windows, with a bitter Philippic at the end of it, upon the forgetful-ness of chamber-maids.——I have but two reasons for thinking otherwise.

First, Had the matter been taken into consideration, before the event happened, my father certainly would have nailed up the sash-window for good an' all;—which, considering with what difficulty he composed books, —he might have done with ten times less trouble, than he could have wrote the chapter: this argument I foresee holds good against his writing a chap-ter, even after the event; but 'tis obviated under the second reason, which I have the honour to offer to the world in support of my opinion, that my father did not write the chapter Upon Sash-Windows and Chamber-Pots, at the time supposed,—and it is this.

——That in order to render the *Tristra-paedia* complete,—I wrote the chapter myself.

CHAPTER 27

MY father put on his spectacles—looked,—took them off,—put them into the case—all in less than a statutable minute; and without opening his lips,

[1] Mr. Shandy is supposed to mean ******** *** Esq.; member for ******,—and not the Chinese Legislator.

turned about and walked precipitately down stairs: my mother imagined he had stepped down for lint and basilicon; but seeing him return with a couple of folios under his arm, and Obadiah following him with a large reading-desk, she took it for granted 'twas an herbal, and so drew him a chair to the bedside, that he might consult upon the case at his ease.

——If it be but right done,—said my father, turning to the Section—*de sede vel subjecto circumcisionis*,—for he had brought up *Spenser de Legibus Hebraeorum Ritualibus*—and *Maimonides*, in order to confront and examine us altogether.——

——If it be but right done, quoth he:—only tell us, cried my mother, interrupting him, what herbs?—for that, replied my father, you must send for Dr. Slop.

My mother went down, and my father went on reading the section as follows,

* *
* * * * * * * * * * * *   ——Very well,—said my father,
* *
* * * * * * * * * *   ——nay, if it has that convenience—and so without stopping a moment to settle it first in his mind, whether the Jews had it from the Egyptians, or the Egyptians from the Jews,—he rose up, and rubbing his forehead two or three times across with the palm of his hand, in the manner we rub out the footsteps of care, when evil has trod lighter upon us than we foreboded,—he shut the book, and walked down stairs.——Nay, said he, mentioning the name of a different great nation upon every step as he set his foot upon it—if the Egyptians,—the Syrians,—the Phoenicians,—the Arabians,—the Cappadocians,—if the Colchi, and Troglodites did it—if Solon and Pythagoras submitted,—what is Tristram?——Who am I, that I should fret or fume one moment about the matter?

CHAPTER 28

DEAR Yorick, said my father, smiling (for Yorick had broke his rank with my uncle Toby in coming through the narrow entry, and so had stept first into the parlour)—this Tristram of ours, I find, comes very hardly by all his religious rites.——Never was the son of Jew, Christian, Turk, or Infidel initiated into them in so oblique and slovenly a manner.—But he is no worse, I trust, said Yorick.——There has been certainly, continued my father, the deuce and all to do in some part or other of the ecliptic, when this offspring of mine was formed.——That, you are a better judge of than I, replied Yorick.——Astrologers, quoth my father, know better than us both:—the trine and sextil aspects have jumped awry,—or the opposite of their ascendants have not hit it, as they should,—or the lords of the genitures (as they call them) have been at bo-peep,—or something has been wrong above, or below with us.

'Tis possible, answered Yorick.—But is the child, cried my uncle Toby, the worse?—The Troglodites say not, replied my father. And your theologists, Yorick, tell us—Theologically? said Yorick,—or speaking after the manner of [1]apothecaries?— [2]statesmen?—or [3]washerwomen?

—I'm not sure, replied my father,—but they tell us, brother Toby, he's the better for it.——Provided, said Yorick, you travel him into Egypt.—— Of that, answered my father, he will have the advantage when he sees the Pyramids.——

Now every word of this, quoth my uncle Toby, is Arabic to me.——I wish, said Yorick, 'twas so to half the world.

——[4]Ilus, continued my father, circumcised his whole army one morning. ——Not without a court martial? cried my uncle Toby.——Though the learned, continued he, taking no notice of my uncle Toby's remark, but turning to Yorick,—are greatly divided still who Ilus was;—some say Saturn;—some the Supreme being;—others, no more than a brigadier general under Pharaoh-neco.——Let him be who he will, said my uncle Toby, I know not by what article of war he could justify it.

The controvertists, answered my father, assign two-and-twenty different reasons for it:—others, indeed, who have drawn their pens on the opposite • side of the question, have shewn the world the futility of the greatest part of them.——But then again, our best polemic divines—I wish there was not a polemic divine, said Yorick, in the kingdom;—one ounce of practical divinity—is worth a painted ship-load of all their reverences have imported these fifty years.——Pray, Mr. Yorick, quoth my uncle Toby,—do tell me what a polemic divine is?——The best description, Captain Shandy, I have ever read, is of a couple of 'em, replied Yorick, in the account of the battle fought single hands betwixt Gymnast and Captain Tripet; which I have in my pocket.——I beg I may hear it, quoth my uncle Toby earnestly.—— You shall, said Yorick,—And as the corporal is waiting for me at the door, —and I know the description of a battle will do the poor fellow more good than his supper,—I beg, brother, you'll give him leave to come in.——With all my soul, said my father.——Trim came in, erect and happy as an emperor; and having shut the door, Yorick took a book from his right-hand coat-pocket, and read, or pretended to read, as follows.

CHAPTER 29

——"which words being heard by all the soldiers which were there, divers of them being inwardly terrified, did shrink back and make room for the assailant: all this did Gymnast very well remark and consider; and therefore, making as if he would have alighted from off his horse, as he was poising himself on the mounting side, he most nimbly (with his short sword by his thigh) shifting his feet in the stirrup and performing the stirrup-leather feat, whereby, after the inclining of his body downwards, he forthwith launched himself aloft into the air, and placed both his feet together upon the saddle, standing upright, with his back turned towards his horse's head,

---

[1]Χαλεπῆς νόσου καὶ δυσιάτου ἀπαλλαγὴ, ἣν ἄνθρακα καλοῦσιν.—PHILO.
[2]Τὰ τεμνόμενα τῶν ἐθνῶν πολυγονώτατα καὶ πολυανθρωπότατα εἶναι.
[3]Καθαριότητος εἵνεκεν.—BOCHART.
[4]Ὁ Ἴλος τὰ αἰδοῖα περιτέμνεται, ταυτὸ ποῖησαι καὶ τοὺς ἀμ' αὐτῷ συμμάχους καταναγκάσας. —SANCHUNIATHO.

—Now (said he) my case goes forward. Then suddenly in the same posture wherein he was, he fetched a gambol upon one foot, and turning to the left-hand, failed not to carry his body perfectly round, just into his former position, without missing one jot.——Ha! said Tripet, I will not do that at this time,—and not without cause. Well, said Gymnast, I have failed,—I will undo this leap; then with a marvellous strength and agility, turning towards the right-hand, he fetched another frisking gambol as before; which done, he set his right-hand thumb upon the bow of the saddle, raised himself up, and sprung into the air, poising and upholding his whole weight upon the muscle and nerve of the said thumb, and so turned and whirled himself about three times: at the fourth, reversing his body, and overturning it upside down, and fore-side back, without touching any thing, he brought himself betwixt the horse's two ears, and then giving himself a jerking swing, he seated himself upon the crupper—"

(This can't be fighting, said my uncle Toby.——The corporal shook his head at it.——Have patience, said Yorick.)

"Then (Tripet) passed his right leg over his saddle, and placed himself *en croup.*——But, said he, 'twere better for me to get into the saddle; then putting the thumbs of both hands upon the crupper before him, and thereupon leaning himself, as upon the only supporters of his body, he incontinently turned heels over head in the air, and straight found himself betwixt the bow of the saddle in a tolerable seat; then springing into the air with a summerset, he turned him about like a wind-mill, and made above a hundred frisks, turns, and demi-pommadas."——Good God! cried Trim, losing all patience,—one home thrust of a bayonet is worth it all.—I think so too, replied Yorick.——

I am of a contrary opinion, quoth my father.

CHAPTER 30

——No,—I think I have advanced nothing, replied my father, making answer to a question which Yorick had taken the liberty to put to him,—I have advanced nothing in the *Tristra-paedia*, but what is as clear as any one proposition in *Euclid.*——Reach me, Trim, that book from off the scrutoir:—it has oft-times been in my mind, continued my father, to have read it over both to you, Yorick, and to my brother Toby, and I think it a little unfriendly in myself, in not having done it long ago:—shall we have a short chapter or two now,—and a chapter or two hereafter, as occasions serve; and so on, till we get through the whole? My uncle Toby and Yorick made the obeisance which was proper; and the corporal, though he was not included in the compliment, laid his hand upon his breast, and made his bow at the same time.——The company smiled. Trim, quoth my father, has paid the full price for staying out the entertainment.——He did not seem to relish the play, replied Yorick.——'Twas a Tom-fool-battle, an' please your reverence, of Captain Tripet's and that other officer, making so many summersets, as they advanced;—the French come on capering now and then in that way,—but not quite so much.

My uncle Toby never felt the consciousness of his existence with more complacency than what the corporal's, and his own reflections, made him do at that moment;—he lighted his pipe,—Yorick drew his chair closer to the table—Trim snuffed the candle,—my father stirred up the fire,—took up the book,—coughed twice, and began.

CHAPTER 31

THE first thirty pages, said my father, turning over the leaves,—are a little dry; and as they are not closely connected with the subject,—for the present we'll pass them by: 'tis a prefatory introduction, continued my father, or an introductory preface (for I am not determined which name to give it) upon political or civil government; the foundation of which being laid in the first conjunction betwixt male and female, for procreation of the species —I was insensibly led into it.——'Twas natural, said Yorick.

The original of society, continued my father, I'm satisfied is, what Politian tells us, *i.e.*, merely conjugal; and nothing more than the getting together of one man and one woman;—to which (according to Hesiod) the philosopher adds a servant:—but supposing in the first beginning there were no men servants born—he lays the foundation of it, in a man,—a woman—and a bull.——I believe 'tis an ox, quoth Yorick, quoting the passage (οἶκον μὲν πρώτιστα, γυναῖκά τε, βοῦν τ' ἀροτῆρα).——A bull must have given more trouble than his head was worth.——But there is a better reason still, said my father (dipping his pen into his ink); for the ox being the most patient of animals, and the most useful withal in tilling the ground for their nourishment,—was the properest instrument, and emblem too, for the new joined couple, that the creation could have associated with them. ——And there is a stronger reason, added my uncle Toby, than them all for the ox.——My father had not power to take his pen out of his ink-horn, till he had heard my uncle Toby's reason.——For when the ground was tilled, said my uncle Toby, and made worth inclosing, then they began to secure it by walls and ditches, which was the origin of fortification.——True, true, dear Toby, cried my father, striking out the bull, and putting the ox in his place.

My father gave Trim a nod, to snuff the candle, and resumed his discourse.

——I enter upon this speculation, said my father carelessly, and half shutting the book, as he went on,—merely to shew the foundation of the natural relation between a father and his child; the right and jurisdiction over whom he acquires these several ways——

1st, by marriage.

2nd, by adoption.

3rd, by legitimation.

And 4th, by procreation; all which I consider in their order.

I lay a slight stress upon one of them, replied Yorick—the act, especially where it ends there, in my opinion lays as little obligation upon the child, as

it conveys power to the father.——You are wrong,—said my father, argutely, and for this plain reason * * * * * * * * * * * * * * *
* * * ——I own, added my father, that the offspring, upon this account, is not so under the power and jurisdiction of the mother.——But the reason, replied Yorick, equally holds good for her.——She is under authority herself, said my father:—and besides, continued my father, nodding his head, and laying his finger upon the side of his nose, as he assigned his reason,—she is not the principal agent, Yorick.——In what, quoth my uncle Toby? stopping his pipe.——Though by all means, added my father (not attending to my uncle Toby) "The son ought to pay her respect," as you may read, Yorick, at large in the first book of the *Institutes of Justinian*, at the eleventh title and the tenth section.——I can read it as well, replied Yorick, in the Catechism.

Chapter 32

Trim can repeat every word of it by heart, quoth my uncle Toby.——Pugh! said my father, not caring to be interrupted with Trim's saying his Catechism. He can, upon my honour, replied my uncle Toby.——Ask him, Mr. Yorick, any question you please.——

—The fifth Commandment, Trim—said Yorick, speaking mildly, and with a gentle nod, as to a modest Cathechumen. The corporal stood silent.
——You don't ask him right, said my uncle Toby, raising his voice, and giving it rapidly like the word of command:—The fifth—cried my uncle Toby.—I must begin with the first, an' please your honour, said the corporal.——

——Yorick could not forbear smiling.——Your reverence does not consider, said the corporal, shouldering his stick like a musket, and marching into the middle of the room, to illustrate his position,—that 'tis exactly the same thing, as doing one's exercise in the field.——

"Join your right-hand to your firelock," cried the corporal, giving the word of command, and performing the motion.——

"Poise your firelock," cried the corporal, doing the duty still both of adjutant and private man.

"Rest your firelock";—one motion, an' please your reverence, you see leads into another.——If his honour will begin but with the first—

The First—cried my uncle Toby, setting his hand upon his side— * *
* * * * * * * * * * * * *

The Second—cried my uncle Toby, waving his tobacco-pipe, as he would have done his sword at the head of a regiment.——The corporal went through his manual with exactness; and having honoured his father and mother, made a low bow, and fell back to the side of the room.

Every thing in this world, said my father, is big with jest,—and has wit in it, and instruction too,—if we can but find it out.

——Here is the scaffold work of Instruction, its true point of folly, without the building behind it.

——Here is the glass for pedagogues, preceptors, tutors, governors, gerund-grinders, and bear-leaders to view themselves in, in their true dimensions.—

Oh! there is a husk and shell, Yorick, which grows up with learning, which their unskilfulness knows not how to fling away!

——Sciences may be learned by rote, but Wisdom not.

Yorick thought my father inspired.——I will enter into obligations this moment, said my father, to lay out all my aunt Dinah's legacy in charitable uses (of which, by the bye, my father had no high opinion), if the corporal has any one determinate idea annexed to any one word he has repeated. ——Prythee, Trim, quoth my father, turning round to him,—What dost thou mean by "honouring thy father and mother"?

Allowing them, an' please your honour, three halfpence a day out of my pay, when they grew old.——And didst thou do that, Trim? said Yorick. ——He did indeed, replied my uncle Toby.——Then, Trim, said Yorick, springing out of his chair, and taking the corporal by the hand, thou art the best commentator upon that part of the Decalogue; and I honour thee more for it, Corporal Trim, than if thou hadst had a hand in the *Talmud* itself.

Chapter 33

O BLESSED health! cried my father, making an exclamation, as he turned over the leaves to the next chapter, thou art above all gold and treasure; 'tis thou who enlargest the soul,—and openest all its powers to receive instruction and to relish virtue. He that has thee, has little more to wish for; —and he that is so wretched as to want thee,—wants every thing with thee.

I have concentrated all that can be said upon this important head, said my father, into a very little room, therefore we'll read the chapter quite through.

My father read as follows:

"The whole secret of health depending upon the due contention for mastery betwixt the radical heat and the radical moisture"—You have proved that matter of fact, I suppose, above, said Yorick. Sufficiently, replied my father.

In saying this, my father shut the book,—not as if he resolved to read no more of it, for he kept his forefinger in the chapter:—nor pettishly,—for he shut the book slowly; his thumb resting, when he had done it, upon the upper-side of the cover, as his three fingers supported the lower side of it, without the least compressive violence.——

I have demonstrated the truth of that point, quoth my father, nodding to Yorick, most sufficiently in the preceding chapter.

Now could the man in the moon be told, that a man in the earth had wrote a chapter, sufficiently demonstrating, That the secret of all health depended upon the due contention for mastery betwixt the radical heat and the radical moisture,—and that he had managed the point so well, that there was not one single word wet or dry upon radical heat or radical moisture, throughout the whole chapter,—or a single syllable in it, *pro* or *con*, directly or indirectly, upon the contention betwixt these two powers in any part of the animal economy.——

"O thou eternal Maker of all beings!"—he would cry, striking his breast with his right hand (in case he had one)—"Thou whose power and goodness can enlarge the faculties of Thy creatures to this infinite degree of excellence and perfection,—What have we Moonites done!"

CHAPTER 34

WITH two strokes, the one at Hippocrates, the other at Lord Verulam, did my father achieve it.

The stroke at the prince of physicians, with which he began, was no more than a short insult upon his sorrowful complaint of the *Ars longa*,—and *Vita brevis*. Life short, cried my father, and the art of healing tedious! And who are we to thank for both the one and the other, but the ignorance of quacks themselves,—and the stage-loads of chemical nostrums, and peripatetic lumber, with which, in all ages, they have first flattered the world, and at last deceived it?

——O my lord Verulam! cried my father, turning from Hippocrates, and making his second stroke at him, as the principal of nostrum-mongers, and the fittest to be made an example of to the rest,—What shall I say to thee, my great lord Verulam? What shall I say to thy internal spirit,—thy opium, thy salt-petre,—thy greasy unctions,—thy daily purges,—thy nightly clysters, and succedaneums?

—My father was never at a loss what to say to any man, upon any subject; and had the least occasion for the exordium of any man breathing: how he dealt with his lordship's opinion,—you shall see;—but when—I know not:—we must first see what his lordship's opinion was.

CHAPTER 35

"THE two great causes, which conspire with each other to shorten life, says lord Verulam, are first—

"The internal spirit, which, like a gentle flame, wastes the body down to death:—And secondly, the external air, that parches the body up to ashes: —which two enemies attacking us on both sides of our bodies together, at length destroy our organs, and render them unfit to carry on the functions of life."

This being the state of the case, the road to Longevity was plain; nothing more being required, says his lordship, but to repair the waste committed by the internal spirit, by making the substance of it more thick and dense, by a regular course of opiates on one side, and by refrigerating the heat of it on the other, by three grains and a half of salt-petre every morning before you got up.——

Still this frame of ours was left exposed to the inimical assaults of the air without;—but this was fenced off again by a course of greasy unctions, which so fully saturated the pores of the skin, that no spicula could enter; —nor could any one get out.——This put a stop to all perspiration, sensible and insensible, which being the cause of so many scurvy distempers—a course of clysters was requisite to carry off redundant humours,—and render the system complete.

What my father had to say to my lord of Verulam's opiates, his salt-

petre, and greasy unctions and clysters, you shall read,—but not to-day—
or to-morrow: time presses upon me,—my reader is impatient—I must get
forwards.—You shall read the chapter at your leisure (if you choose it), as
soon as ever the *Tristra-paedia* is published.——

Sufficeth it at present, to say, my father levelled the hypothesis with the
ground, and in doing that, the learned know, he built up and established
his own.——

Chapter 36

The whole secret of health, said my father, beginning the sentence again,
depending evidently upon the due contention betwixt the radical heat and
radical moisture within us;—the least imaginable skill had been sufficient
to have maintained it, had not the schoolmen confounded the talk, merely
(as Van Helmont, the famous chemist, has proved) by all along mistaking
the radical moisture for the tallow and fat of animal bodies.

Now the radical moisture is not the tallow or fat of animals, but an oily
and balsamous substance; for the fat and tallow, as also the phlegm or
watery parts, are cold; whereas the oily and balsamous parts are of a lively
heat and spirit, which accounts for the observation of Aristotle, "*Quod
omne animal post coitum est triste.*"

Now it is certain, that the radical heat lives in the radical moisture, but
whether *vice versâ*, is a doubt: however, when the one decays, the other decays also; and then is produced, either an unnatural heat, which causes an
unnatural dryness—or an unnatural moisture, which causes dropsies.——
So that if a child, as he grows up, can but be taught to avoid running into
fire or water, as either of 'em threaten his destruction,—'twill be all that is
needful to be done upon that head.——

Chapter 37

The description of the siege of Jericho itself, could not have engaged the
attention of my uncle Toby more powerfully than the last chapter;—his
eyes were fixed upon my father throughout it;—he never mentioned radical
heat and radical moisture, but my uncle Toby took his pipe out of his
mouth, and shook his head; and as soon as the chapter was finished, he
beckoned to the corporal to come close to his chair, to ask him the following
question,—aside.—— * * * * * * * * * * * * * * * *. It was at
the siege of Limerick, an' please your honour, replied the corporal, making
a bow.

The poor fellow and I, quoth my uncle Toby, addressing himself to my
father, were scarce able to crawl out of our tents, at the time the siege of
Limerick was raised, upon the very account you mention.—Now what can
have got into that precious noddle of thine, my dear brother Toby? cried
my father, mentally.——By Heaven! continued he, communing still with
himself, it would puzzle an Oedipus to bring it in point.——

I believe, an' please your honour, quoth the corporal, that if it had not
been for the quantity of brandy we set fire to every night, and the claret
and cinnamon with which I plied your honour of;—And the geneva, Trim,

added my uncle Toby, which did us more good than all—I verily believe, continued the corporal, we had both, an' please your honour, left our lives in the trenches, and been buried in them too.——The noblest grave, corporal! cried my uncle Toby, his eyes sparkling as he spoke, that a soldier could wish to lie down in.——But a pitiful death for him! an' please your honour, replied the corporal.

All this was as much Arabic to my father, as the rites of the Colchi and Troglodites had been before to my uncle Toby; my father could not determine whether he was to frown or to smile.——

My uncle Toby, turning to Yorick, resumed the case at Limerick, more intelligibly than he had begun it,—and so settled the point for my father at once.

CHAPTER 38

IT was undoubtedly, said my uncle Toby, a great happiness for myself and the corporal, that we had all along a burning fever, attended with a most raging thirst, during the whole five-and-twenty days the flux was upon us in the camp; otherwise what my brother calls the radical moisture, must, as I conceive it, inevitably have got the better.——My father drew in his lungs top-full of air, and looking up, blew it forth again, as slowly as he possibly could.——

——It was Heaven's mercy to us, continued my uncle Toby, which put it into the corporal's head to maintain that due contention betwixt the radical heat and the radical moisture, by reinforcing the fever, as he did all along, with hot wine and spices: whereby the corporal kept up (as it were) a continual firing, so that the radical heat stood its ground from the beginning to the end, and was a fair match for the moisture, terrible as it was.

——Upon my honour, added my uncle Toby, you might have heard the contention within our bodies, brother Shandy, twenty toises.——If there was no firing, said Yorick.

Well—said my father, with a full aspiration, and pausing a while after the word—Was I a judge, and the laws of the country which made me one permitted it, I would condemn some of the worst malefactors, provided they had had their clergy—Yorick, foreseeing the sentence was likely to end with no sort of mercy, laid his hand upon my father's breast, and begged he would respite it for a few minutes, till he asked the corporal a question.——Prithee, Trim, said Yorick, without staying for my father's leave,—tell us honestly—what is thy opinion concerning this self-same radical heat and radical moisture?

With humble submission to his honour's better judgment, quoth the corporal, making a bow to my uncle Toby—Speak thy opinion freely, corporal, said my uncle Toby.——The poor fellow is my servant,—not my slave,—added my uncle Toby, turning to my father.——

The corporal put his hat under his left arm, and with his stick hanging upon the wrist of it, by a black thong split into a tassel about the knot, he marched up to the ground where he had performed his catechism; then touching his under-jaw with the thumb and fingers of his right-hand before he opened his mouth,—he delivered his notion thus.

Chapter 39

Just as the corporal was humming, to begin—in waddled Dr. Slop.——
'Tis not two-pence matter—the corporal shall go on in the next chapter, let
who will come in.——

Well, my good doctor, cried my father sportively, for the transitions of
his passions were unaccountably sudden,—and what has this whelp of mine
to say to the matter?

Had my father been asking after the amputation of the tail of a puppy-
dog—he could not have done it in a more careless air: the system which Dr.
Slop had laid down, to treat the accident by, no way allowed of such a mode
of enquiry.——He sat down.

Pray, Sir, quoth my uncle Toby, in a manner which could not go un-
answered,—in what condition is the boy?—'Twill end in a phimosis, replied
Dr. Slop.

I am no wiser than I was, quoth my uncle Toby—returning his pipe into
his mouth.—Then let the corporal go on, said my father, with his medical
lecture.——The corporal made a bow to his old friend, Dr. Slop, and then
delivered his opinion concerning radical heat and radical moisture, in the
following words.

Chapter 40

The city of Limerick, the siege of which was begun under his majesty King
William himself, the year after I went into the army—lies, an' please your
honours, in the middle of a devilish wet, swampy country.——'Tis quite
surrounded, said my uncle Toby, with the Shannon, and is, by its situation,
one of the strongest fortified places in Ireland.——

I think this is a new fashion, quoth Dr. Slop, of beginning a medical
lecture.——'Tis all true, answered Trim.——Then I wish the faculty would
follow the cut of it, said Yorick.——'Tis all cut through, an' please your
reverence, said the corporal, with drains and bogs; and besides, there was
such a quantity of rain fell during the siege, the whole country was like a
puddle,—'twas that, and nothing else, which brought on the flux, and
which had like to have killed both his honour and myself; now there was no
such thing, after the first ten days, continued the corporal, for a soldier to
lie dry in his tent, without cutting a ditch round it, to draw off the water;—
nor was that enough, for those who could afford it, as his honour could,
without setting fire every night to a pewter dish full of brandy, which took
off the damp of the air, and made the inside of the tent as warm as a
stove.——

And what conclusion dost thou draw, Corporal Trim, cried my father,
from all these premises?

I infer, an' please your worship, replied Trim, that the radical moisture
is nothing in the world but ditch-water—and that the radical heat, of those
who can go to the expense of it, is burnt brandy,—the radical heat and
moisture of a private man, an' please your honour, is nothing but ditch-
water—and a dram of geneva—and give us but enough of it, with a pipe of

tobacco, to give us spirits, and drive away the vapours—we know not what it is to fear death.

I am at a loss, Captain Shandy, quoth Dr. Slop, to determine in which branch of learning your servant shines most, whether in physiology or divinity.——Slop had not forgot Trim's comment upon the sermon.——

It is but an hour ago, replied Yorick, since the corporal was examined in the latter, and passed muster with great honour.——

The radical heat and moisture, quoth Dr. Slop, turning to my father, you must know, is the basis and foundation of our being—as the root of a tree is the source and principle of its vegetation.——It is inherent in the seeds of all animals, and may be preserved sundry ways, but principally in my opinion by consubstantials, impriments, and occludents.——Now this poor fellow, continued Dr. Slop, pointing to the corporal, has had the mis-fortune to have heard some superficial empiric discourse upon this nice point.——That he has,—said my father.—Very likely, said my uncle.—— I'm sure of it—quoth Yorick.——

CHAPTER 41

DOCTOR SLOP being called out to look at a cataplasm he had ordered, it gave my father an opportunity of going on with another chapter in the *Tristra-paedia.*——Come! cheer up, my lads; I'll shew you land—for when we have tugged through that chapter, the book shall not be opened again this twelvemonth.——Huzza!——

CHAPTER 42

——FIVE years with a bib under his chin;
   Four years in travelling from Christ-cross-row to Malachi;
   A year and a half in learning to write his own name;
   Seven long years and more τυπτω-ing it, at Greek and Latin;
   Four years at his probations and his negations—the fine statue still lying in the middle of the marble block,—and nothing done, but his tools sharp-ened to hew it out!——'Tis a piteous delay!——Was not the great Julius Scaliger within an ace of never getting his tools sharpened at all?—— Forty-four years old was he before he could manage his Greek;—and Peter Damianus, lord bishop of Ostia, as all the world knows, could not so much as read, when he was of man's estate.—And Baldus himself, as eminent as he turned out after, entered upon the law so late in life, that every body imagined he intended to be an advocate in the other world: no wonder, when Eudamidas, the son of Archidamas, heard Xenocrates at seventy-five disputing about wisdom, that he asked gravely,—If the old man be yet disputing and enquiring concerning wisdom,—what time will he have to make use of it?

Yorick listened to my father with great attention; there was a seasoning of wisdom unaccountably mixed up with his strangest whims, and he had sometimes such illuminations in the darkest of his eclipses, as almost atoned for them:—be wary, Sir, when you imitate him.

I am convinced, Yorick, continued my father, half reading and half discoursing, that there is a North-west passage to the intellectual world; and
that the soul of man has shorter ways of going to work, in furnishing itself
with knowledge and instruction, than we generally take with it.——But,
alack! all fields have not a river or a spring running beside them;—every
child, Yorick, has not a parent to point it out.

——The whole entirely depends, added my father, in a low voice, upon
the auxiliary verbs, Mr. Yorick.

Had Yorick trod upon Virgil's snake, he could not have looked more
surprised.——I am surprised too, cried my father, observing it,—and I
reckon it as one of the greatest calamities which ever befel the republic of
letters, That those who have been entrusted with the education of our
children, and whose business it was to open their minds, and stock them
early with ideas, in order to set the imagination loose upon them, have made
so little use of the auxiliary verbs in doing it, as they have done—So that,
except Raymond Lullius, and the elder Pelegrini, the last of which arrived
to such perfection in the use of 'em, with his topics, that, in a few lessons,
he could teach a young gentleman to discourse with plausibility upon any
subject, *pro* and *con*, and to say and write all that could be spoken or
written concerning it, without blotting a word, to the admiration of all who
beheld him.——I should be glad, said Yorick, interrupting my father, to be
made to comprehend this matter. You shall, said my father.

The highest stretch of improvement a single word is capable of, is a high
metaphor,—for which, in my opinion, the idea is generally the worse, and
not the better;—but be that as it may,—when the mind has done that with
it—there is an end,—the mind and the idea are at rest,—until a second idea
enters;—and so on.

Now the use of the Auxiliaries is, at once to set the soul a-going by herself
upon the materials as they are brought her; and by the versability of this
great engine, round which they are twisted, to open new tracts of enquiry
and make every idea engender millions.

You excite my curiosity greatly, said Yorick.

For my own part, quoth my uncle Toby, I have given it up.——The
Danes, an' please your honour, quoth the corporal, who were on the left at
the siege of Limerick, were all auxiliaries.——And very good ones, said my
uncle Toby.——But the auxiliaries, Trim, my brother is talking about,—
I conceive to be different things.——

——You do? said my father, rising up.

CHAPTER 43

MY father took a single turn across the room, then sat down, and finished
the chapter.

The verbs auxiliary we are concerned in here, continued my father, are,
am; was; have; had; do; did; make; made; suffer; shall; should; will; would;
can; could; owe; ought; used; or is wont.——And these varied with tenses,
present, past, future, and conjugated with the verb see,—or with these
questions added to them;—Is it? Was it? Will it be? Would it be? May it

be? Might it be? And these again put negatively, Is it not? Was it not? Ought it not?—Or affirmatively,—It is; It was; It ought to be. Or chronologically,—Has it been always? Lately? How long ago?—Or hypothetically,—If it was? If it was not? What would follow?—If the French should beat the English? If the Sun go out of the Zodiac?

Now, by the right use and application of these, continued my father, in which a child's memory should be exercised, there is no one idea can enter his brain, how barren soever, but a magazine of conceptions and conclusions may be drawn forth from it.——Didst thou ever see a white bear? cried my father, turning his head round to Trim, who stood at the back of his chair: —No, an' please your honour, replied the corporal.——But thou couldst discourse about one, Trim, said my father, in case of need?——How is it possible, brother, quoth my uncle Toby, if the corporal never saw one?—— 'Tis the fact I want, replied my father,—and the possibility of it is as follows.

A white bear! Very well. Have I ever seen one? Might I ever have seen one? Am I ever to see one? Ought I ever to have seen one? Or can I ever see one?

Would I had seen a white bear! (for how can I imagine it?)

If I should see a white bear, what should I say? If I should never see a white bear, what then?

If I never have, can, must, or shall see a white bear alive; have I ever seen the skin of one? Did I ever see one painted?—described? Have I never dreamed of one?

Did my father, mother, uncle, aunt, brothers or sisters, ever see a white bear? What would they give? How would they behave? How would the white bear have behaved? Is he wild? Tame? Terrible? Rough? Smooth?

——Is the white bear worth seeing?——

——Is there no sin in it?——

Is it better than a black one?

BOOK VI

Chapter 1

WE'LL not stop two moments, my dear Sir,—only, as we have got through these five volumes, (do, Sir, sit down upon a set—they are better than nothing) let us just look back upon the country we have passed through.——

——What a wilderness has it been! and what a mercy that we have not both of us been lost, or devoured by wild beasts in it!

Did you think the world itself, Sir, had contained such a number of Jack Asses?——How they viewed and reviewed us as we passed over the rivulet at the bottom of that little valley!—and when we climbed over that hill, and were just getting out of sight—good God! what a braying did they all set up together!

——Prithee, shepherd! who keeps all those Jack Asses? ***

——Heaven be their comforter—What! are they never curried?—Are they never taken in in winter?——Bray bray—bray. Bray on,—the world is deeply your debtor; louder still—that's nothing:—in good sooth, you are ill-used:—Was I a Jack Asse, I solemnly declare, I would bray in G-fol-re-ut from morning, even unto night.

Chapter 2

WHEN my father had danced his white bear backwards and forwards through half a dozen pages, he closed the book for good and all,—and in a kind of triumph re-delivered it into Trim's hand, with a nod to lay it upon the 'scrutoire, where he found it.——Tristram, said he, shall be made to conjugate every word in the dictionary, backwards and forwards the same way;—every word, Yorick, by this means, you see, is converted into a thesis or an hypothesis;—every thesis and hypothesis have an offspring of propositions;—and each proposition has its own consequences and conclusions; every one of which leads the mind on again, into fresh tracks of enquiries and doubtings.——The force of this engine, added my father, is incredible in opening a child's head.——'Tis enough, brother Shandy, cried my uncle Toby, to burst it into a thousand splinters.——

I presume, said Yorick, smiling,—it must be owing to this,—(for let logicians say what they will, it is not to be accounted for sufficiently from the bare use of the ten predicaments)—That the famous Vincent Quirino, amongst the many other astonishing feats of his childhood, of which the

421

Cardinal Bembo has given the world so exact a story,—should be able to paste up in the public schools at Rome, so early as in the eighth year of his age, no less than four thousand five hundred and fifty different theses, upon the most abstruse points of the most abstruse theology;—and to defend and maintain them in such sort, as to cramp and dumbfound his opponents.—— What is that, cried my father, to what is told us of Alphonsus Tostatus, who, almost in his nurse's arms, learned all the sciences and liberal arts without being taught any one of them?——What shall we say of the great Piereskius?——That's the very man, cried my uncle Toby, I once told you of, brother Shandy, who walked a matter of five hundred miles, reckoning from Paris to Shevling, and from Shevling back again, merely to see Stevinus's flying chariot.——He was a very great man! added my uncle Toby (meaning Stevinus)—He was so, brother Toby, said my father (meaning Piereskius)—and had multiplied his ideas so fast, and increased his knowledge to such a prodigious stock, that, if we may give credit to an anecdote concerning him, which we cannot withhold here, without shaking the authority of all anecdotes whatever—at seven years of age, his father committed entirely to his care the education of his younger brother, a boy of five years old,—with the sole management of all his concerns.——Was the father as wise as the son? quoth my uncle Toby:—I should think not, said Yorick:—But what are these, continued my father—(breaking out in a kind of enthusiasm)—what are these, to those prodigies of childhood in Grotius, Scioppius, Heinsius, Politian, Pascal, Joseph Scaliger, Ferdinand de Cordouè, and others—some of which left off their substantial forms at nine years old, or sooner, and went on reasoning without them;—others went through their classics at seven;—wrote tragedies at eight;—Ferdinand de Cordouè was so wise at nine,—'twas thought the Devil was in him;— and at Venice gave such proofs of his knowledge and goodness, that the monks imagined he was Antichrist, or nothing.——Others were masters of fourteen languages at ten,—finished the course of their rhetoric, poetry, logic, and ethics, at eleven,—put forth their commentaries upon Servius and Martianus Capella at twelve,—and at thirteen received their degrees in philosophy, laws, and divinity:—But you forget the great Lipsius, quoth Yorick, who composed a work[1] the day he was born:—They should have wiped it up, said my uncle Toby, and said no more about it.

Chapter 3

WHEN the cataplasm was ready, a scruple of decorum had unseasonably rose up in Susannah's conscience, about holding the candle, whilst Slop tied it on; Slop had not treated Susannah's distemper with anodynes,—and so a quarrel had ensued betwixt them.

——Oh! oh!—said Slop, casting a glance of undue freedom in Susannah's

[1] Nous aurions quelque interêt, says Baillet, de montrer qu'il n'a rien de ridicule s'il étoit véritable, au moins dans le sens énigmatique que Nicius Erythraeus a tâché de lui donner. Cet auteur dit que pour comprendre comme Lipse, il a pu composer un ouvrage le premier jour de sa vie, il faut s'imaginer, que ce premier jour n'est pas celui de sa naissance charnelle, mais celui au quel il a commencé d'user de la raison; il veut que ç'ait été à l'âge de neuf ans; et il nous veut persuader que ce fut en cet âge, que Lipse fit un poëme.—Le tour est ingénieux, etc., etc.

face, as she declined the office;—then, I think I know you, madam—You know me, Sir! cried Susannah fastidiously, and with a toss of her head, levelled evidently, not at his profession, but at the doctor himself,—you know me! cried Susannah again.——Doctor Slop clapped his finger and his thumb instantly upon his nostrils;—Susannah's spleen was ready to burst at it;—'Tis false, said Susannah.—Come, come, Mrs. Modesty, said Slop, not a little elated with the success of his last thrust,—If you won't hold the candle, and look—you may hold it and shut your eyes:—That's one of your Popish shifts, cried Susannah:—'Tis better, said Slop, with a nod, than no shift at all, young woman;—I defy you, Sir, cried Susannah, pulling her shift sleeve below her elbow.

It was almost impossible for two persons to assist each other in a surgical case with a more splenetic cordiality.

Slop snatched up the cataplasm,—Susannah snatched up the candle;—a little this way, said Slop; Susannah looking one way, and rowing another, instantly set fire to Slop's wig, which being somewhat bushy and unctuous withal, was burnt out before it was well kindled.——You impudent whore! cried Slop,—(for what is passion, but a wild beast?)—you impudent whore, cried Slop, getting upright, with the cataplasm in his hand;—I never was the destruction of any body's nose, said Susannah,—which is more than you can say:—Is it? cried Slop, throwing the cataplasm in her face;—Yes, it is, cried Susannah, returning the compliment with what was left in the pan.

Chapter 4

Doctor Slop and Susannah filed cross-bills against each other in the parlour; which done, as the cataplasm had failed, they retired into the kitchen to prepare a fomentation for me;—and whilst that was doing, my father determined the point as you will read.

Chapter 5

You see 'tis high time, said my father, addressing himself equally to my uncle Toby and Yorick, to take this young creature out of these women's hands, and put him into those of a private governor. Marcus Antoninus provided fourteen governors all at once to superintend his son Commodus's education,—and in six weeks he cashiered five of them;—I know very well, continued my father, that Commodus's mother was in love with a gladiator at the time of her conception, which accounts for a great many of Commodus's cruelties when he became emperor;—but still I am of opinion, that those five whom Antoninus dismissed, did Commodus's temper, in that short time, more hurt than the other nine were able to rectify all their lives long.

Now as I consider the person who is to be about my son, as the mirror in which he is to view himself from morning to night, and by which he is to adjust his looks, his carriage, and perhaps the inmost sentiments of his heart;—I would have one, Yorick, if possible, polished at all points, fit for my child to look into.——This is very good sense, quoth my uncle Toby to himself.

——There is, continued my father, a certain mien and motion of the body and all its parts, both in acting and speaking, which argues a man well within; and I am not at all surprised that Gregory of Nazianzum, upon observing the hasty and untoward gestures of Julian, should foretell he would one day become an apostate;—or that St. Ambrose should turn his Amanuensis out of doors, because of an indecent motion of his head, which went backwards and forwards like a flail;—or that Democritus should conceive Protagoras to be a scholar, from seeing him bind up a faggot, and thrusting, as he did it, the small twigs inwards.——There are a thousand unnoticed openings, continued my father, which let a penetrating eye at once into a man's soul; and I maintain it, added he, that a man of sense does not lay down his hat in coming into a room,—or take it up in going out of it, but something escapes, which discovers him.

It is for these reasons, continued my father, that the governor I make choice of shall neither[1] lisp, or squint, or wink, or talk loud, or look fierce, or foolish;—or bite his lips, or grind his teeth, or speak through his nose, or pick it, or blow it with his fingers.——

He shall neither walk fast,—or slow, or fold his arms,—for that is laziness;—or hang them down,—for that is folly; or hide them in his pocket, for that is nonsense.——

He shall neither strike, or pinch, or tickle,—or bite, or cut his nails, or hawk, or spit, or snift, or drum with his feet or fingers in company;—nor (according to Erasmus) shall he speak to any one in making water,—nor shall he point to carrion or excrement.——Now this is all nonsense again, quoth my uncle Toby to himself.——

I will have him, continued my father, cheerful, faceté, jovial; at the same time, prudent, attentive to business, vigilant, acute, argute, inventive, quick in resolving doubts and speculative questions;—he shall be wise, and judicious, and learned:—And why not humble, and moderate, and gentle-tempered, and good? said Yorick:—And why not, cried my uncle Toby, free, and generous, and bountiful, and brave?——He shall, my dear Toby, replied my father, getting up and shaking him by his hand.——Then, brother Shandy, answered my uncle Toby, raising himself off the chair, and laying down his pipe to take hold of my father's other hand,—I humbly beg I may recommend poor Le Fever's son to you;—a tear of joy of the first water sparkled in my uncle Toby's eye, and another, the fellow to it, in the corporal's, as the proposition was made;—you will see why when you read Le Fever's story:—fool that I was! nor can I recollect (nor perhaps you) without turning back to the place, what it was that hindered me from letting the corporal tell it in his own words;—but the occasion is lost,—I must tell it now in my own.

CHAPTER 6
The Story of Le Fever

IT was some time in the summer of that year in which Dendermond was taken by the allies,—which was about seven years before my father came into the country,—and about as many, after the time, that my uncle Toby

[1] *Vid.* Pellegrina.

and Trim had privately decamped from my father's house in town, in order to lay some of the finest sieges to some of the finest fortified cities in Europe —when my uncle Toby was one evening getting his supper, with Trim sitting behind him at a small sideboard,—I say, sitting—for in consideration of the corporal's lame knee (which sometimes gave him exquisite pain)— when my uncle Toby dined or supped alone, he would never suffer the corporal to stand; and the poor fellow's veneration for his master was such, that, with a proper artillery, my uncle Toby could have taken Dendermond itself, with less trouble than he was able to gain this point over him; for many a time when my uncle Toby supposed the corporal's leg was at rest, he would look back, and detect him standing behind him with the most dutiful respect: this bred more little squabbles betwixt them, than all other causes for five-and-twenty years together—But this is neither here nor there—why do I mention it?—Ask my pen,—it governs me,—I govern not it.

He was one evening sitting thus at his supper, when the landlord of a little inn in the village came into the parlour, with an empty phial in his hand, to beg a glass or two of sack; 'Tis for a poor gentleman,—I think, of the army, said the landlord, who has been taken ill at my house four days ago, and has never held up his head since, or had a desire to taste any thing, till just now, that he has a fancy for a glass of sack and a thin toast,—I think, says he, taking his hand from his forehead, it would comfort me.——

——If I could neither beg, borrow, or buy such a thing——added the landlord,—I would almost steal it for the poor gentleman, he is so ill.—I hope in God he will still mend, continued he,—we are all of us concerned for him.

Thou art a good-natured soul, I will answer for thee, cried my uncle Toby; and thou shalt drink the poor gentleman's health in a glass of sack thyself,—and take a couple of bottles with my service, and tell him he is heartily welcome to them, and to a dozen more if they will do him good.

Though I am persuaded, said my uncle Toby, as the landlord shut the door, he is a very compassionate fellow—Trim,—yet I cannot help entertaining a high opinion of his guest too; there must be something more than common in him, that in so short a time should win so much upon the affections of his host;—And of his whole family, added the corporal, for they are all concerned for him.——Step after him, said my uncle Toby,—do, Trim, —and ask if he knows his name.

——I have quite forgot it truly, said the landlord, coming back into the parlour with the corporal,—but I can ask his son again:—Has he a son with him then? said my uncle Toby.—A boy, replied the landlord, of about eleven or twelve years of age;—but the poor creature has tasted almost as little as his father; he does nothing but mourn and lament for him night and day:—He has not stirred from the bed-side these two days.

My uncle Toby laid down his knife and fork, and thrust his plate from before him, as the landlord gave him the account; and Trim, without being ordered, took away, without saying one word, and in a few minutes after brought him his pipe and tobacco.

——Stay in the room a little, said my uncle Toby.

Trim!—said my uncle Toby, after he lighted his pipe, and smoked about a dozen whiffs.—Trim came in front of his master, and made his bow;—my uncle Toby smoked on, and said no more.——Corporal! said my uncle Toby—the corporal made his bow.—My uncle Toby proceeded no farther, but finished his pipe.

Trim! said my uncle Toby, I have a project in my head, as it is a bad night, of wrapping myself up warm in my roquelaure, and paying a visit to this poor gentleman.——Your honour's roquelaure, replied the corporal, has not once been had on, since the night before your honour received your wound, when we mounted guard in the trenches before the gate of St. Nicolas;—and besides, it is so cold and rainy a night, that what with the roquelaure, and what with the weather, 'twill be enough to give your honour your death, and bring on your honour's torment in your groin. I fear so, replied my uncle Toby; but I am not at rest in my mind, Trim, since the account the landlord has given me.—I wish I had not known so much of this affair,—added my uncle Toby,—or that I had known more of it:—How shall we manage it? Leave it, an't please your honour, to me, quoth the corporal;—I'll take my hat and stick and go to the house and reconnoitre, and act accordingly; and I will bring your honour a full account in an hour.——Thou shalt go, Trim, said my uncle Toby, and here's a shilling for thee to drink with his servant.——I shall get it all out of him, said the corporal, shutting the door.

My uncle Toby filled his second pipe; and had it not been, that he now and then wandered from the point, with considering whether it was not full as well to have the curtain of the tenaille a straight line, as a crooked one,—he might be said to have thought of nothing else but poor Le Fever and his boy the whole time he smoked it.

CHAPTER 7
The Story of Le Fever Continued

IT was not till my uncle Toby had knocked the ashes out of his third pipe, that Corporal Trim returned from the inn, and gave him the following account.

I despaired, at first, said the corporal, of being able to bring back your honour any kind of intelligence concerning the poor sick lieutenant—Is he in the army, then? said my uncle Toby—He is, said the corporal—And in what regiment? said my uncle Toby—I'll tell your honour, replied the corporal, every thing straight forwards, as I learnt it.——Then, Trim, I'll fill another pipe, said my uncle Toby, and not interrupt thee till thou hast done; so sit down at thy ease, Trim, in the window-seat, and begin thy story again. The corporal made his old bow, which generally spoke as plain as a bow could speak it—Your honour is good:—And having done that, he sat down, as he was ordered,—and begun the story to my uncle Toby over again in pretty near the same words.

I despaired at first, said the corporal, of being able to bring back any intelligence to your honour, about the lieutenant and his son; for when I asked where his servant was, from whom I made myself sure of knowing every thing which was proper to be asked,—That's a right distinction, Trim, said my uncle Toby—I was answered, an' please your honour, that he had no servant with him;—that he had come to the inn with hired horses, which, upon finding himself unable to proceed (to join, I suppose, the regiment), he had dismissed the morning after he came.——If I get better, my dear, said he, as he gave his purse to his son to pay the man,—we can hire horses from hence.——But alas! the poor gentleman will never get from hence, said the landlady to me,—for I heard the death-watch all night long;—and when he dies, the youth, his son, will certainly die with him; for he is broken-hearted already.

I was hearing this account, continued the corporal, when the youth came into the kitchen, to order the thin toast the landlord spoke of;—but I will do it for my father myself, said the youth.——Pray let me save you the trouble, young gentleman, said I, taking up a fork for the purpose, and offering him my chair to sit down upon by the fire, whilst I did it.——I believe, Sir, said he, very modestly, I can please him best myself.——I am sure, said I, his honour will not like the toast the worse for being toasted by an old soldier.——The youth took hold of my hand, and instantly burst into tears.——Poor youth! said my uncle Toby,—he has been bred up from an infant in the army, and the name of a soldier, Trim, sounded in his ears like the name of a friend;—I wish I had him here.

——I never, in the longest march, said the corporal, had so great a mind to my dinner, as I had to cry with him for company:—What could be the matter with me, an' please your honour? Nothing in the world, Trim, said my uncle Toby, blowing his nose,—but that thou art a good-natured fellow.

When I gave him the toast, continued the corporal, I thought it was proper to tell him I was Captain Shandy's servant, and that your honour (though a stranger) was extremely concerned for his father;—and that if there was any thing in your house or cellar—(and thou might'st have added my purse too, said my uncle Toby)—he was heartily welcome to it:—He made a very low bow (which was meant to your honour), but no answer—for his heart was full—so he went up stairs with the toast;—I warrant you, my dear, said I, as I opened the kitchen-door, your father will be well again. —Mr. Yorick's curate was smoking a pipe by the kitchen fire,—but said not a word good or bad to comfort the youth.—I thought it wrong; added the corporal—I think so too, said my uncle Toby.

When the lieutenant had taken his glass of sack and toast, he felt himself a little revived, and sent down into the kitchen, to let me know, that in about ten minutes he should be glad if I would step up stairs.—I believe, said the landlord, he is going to say his prayers,—for there was a book laid upon the chair by his bed-side, and as I shut the door, I saw his son take up a cushion.——

I thought, said the curate, that you gentlemen of the army, Mr. Trim, never said your prayers at all.—I heard the poor gentleman say his prayers last night, said the landlady, very devoutly, and with my own ears, or I could not have believed it.——Are you sure of it? replied the curate.——A soldier, an' please your reverence, said I, prays as often (of his own accord) as a parson;—and when he is fighting for his king, and for his own life, and for his honour too, he has the most reason to pray to God of any one in the whole world—'Twas well said of thee, Trim, said my uncle Toby.——But when a soldier, said I, an' please your reverence, has been standing for twelve hours together in the trenches, up to his knees in cold water,—or engaged, said I, for months together in long and dangerous marches;—harassed, perhaps, in his rear to-day;—harassing others to-morrow;—detached here;—countermanded there;—resting this night out upon his arms;—beat up in his shirt the next;—benumbed in his joints;—perhaps without straw in his tent to kneel on;—must say his prayers how and when he can.——I believe, said I,—for I was piqued, quoth the corporal, for the reputation of the army,—I believe, an' please your reverence, said I, that when a soldier gets time to pray,—he prays as heartily as a parson,—though not with all his fuss and hypocrisy.—Thou shouldst not have said that, Trim, said my uncle Toby,—for God only knows who is a hypocrite, and who is not:—At the great and general review of us all, corporal, at the day of judgment (and not till then)—it will be seen who has done their duties in this world,—and who has not; and we shall be advanced, Trim, accordingly.——I hope we shall, said Trim.——It is in the Scripture, said my uncle Toby; and I will shew it thee to-morrow:—In the mean time we may depend upon it, Trim, for our comfort, said my uncle Toby, that God Almighty is so good and just a governor of the world, that if we have but done our duties in it,—it will never be enquired into, whether we have done them in a red coat or a black one:—I hope not, said the corporal—But go on, Trim, said my uncle Toby, with thy story.

When I went up, continued the corporal, into the lieutenant's room, which I did not do till the expiration of the ten minutes,—he was lying in his bed with his head raised upon his hand, with his elbow upon the pillow, and a clean white cambric handkerchief beside it:—The youth was just stooping down to take up the cushion, upon which I supposed he had been kneeling,—the book was laid upon the bed,—and, as he rose, in taking up the cushion with one hand, he reached out his other to take it away at the same time.——Let it remain there, my dear, said the lieutenant.

He did not offer to speak to me, till I had walked up close to his bed-side:—If you are Captain Shandy's servant, said he, you must present my thanks to your master, with my little boy's thanks along with them, for his courtesy to me;—if he was of Leven's—said the lieutentant.——I told him your honour was—Then, said he, I served three campaigns with him in Flanders, and remember him,—but 'tis most likely, as I had not the honour of any acquaintance with him, that he knows nothing of me.—You will tell him, however, that the person his good-nature has laid under obligations to him, is one Le Fever, a lieutenant in Angus's—but he knows me not,—said he, a second time, musing;—possibly he may my story—added he—pray tell the captain, I was the ensign at Breda, whose wife was most unfortunately killed with a musket-shot, as she lay in my arms in my tent.——I remember the story, an't please your honour, said I, very well.—Do you so? said he, wiping his eyes with his handkerchief,—then well may I.—In saying this, he drew a little ring out of his bosom, which seemed tied with a black ribband about his neck, and kissed it twice—Here, Billy, said he,—the boy flew across the room to the bed-side—and falling down upon his knee, took the ring in his hand, and kissed it too,—then kissed his father, and sat down upon the bed and wept.

I wish, said my uncle Toby, with a deep sigh,—I wish, Trim, I was asleep.

Your honour, replied the corporal, is too much concerned;—shall I pour your honour out a glass of sack to your pipe?——Do, Trim, said my uncle Toby.

I remember, said my uncle Toby, sighing again, the story of the ensign and his wife, with a circumstance his modesty omitted;—and particularly well that he, as well as she, upon some account or other (I forget what) was universally pitied by the whole regiment;—but finish the story thou art upon:—'Tis finished already, said the corporal,—for I could stay no longer, —so wished his honour a good night; young Le Fever rose from off the bed, and saw me to the bottom of the stairs; and as we went down together, told me they had come from Ireland, and were on their route to join the regiment in Flanders.——But alas! said the corporal,—the lieutenant's last day's march is over.——Then what is to become of his poor boy? cried my uncle Toby.

Chapter 8
The Story of Le Fever Continued

It was to my uncle Toby's eternal honour,—though I tell it only for the sake of those, who, when cooped in betwixt a natural and a positive law, know not, for their souls, which way in the world to turn themselves—That notwithstanding my uncle Toby was warmly engaged at that time in carrying on the siege of Dendermond, parallel with the allies, who pressed theirs on so vigorously, that they scarce allowed him time to get his dinner—that nevertheless he gave up Dendermond, though he had already made a lodgment upon the counterscarp;—and bent his whole thoughts towards the private distresses at the inn; and except that he ordered the garden gate to be bolted up, by which he might be said to have turned the siege of Dendermond into a blockade,—he left Dendermond to itself—to be relieved or not by the French king, as the French king thought good: and only considered how he himself should relieve the poor lieutenant and his son.

——That kind Being, who is a friend to the friendless, shall recompense thee for this.

Thou hast left this matter short, said my uncle Toby to the corporal, as he was putting him to bed,—and I will tell thee in what, Trim.——In the first place, when thou madest an offer of my services to Le Fever,—as sickness and travelling are both expensive, and thou knowest he was but a poor lieutenant, with a son to subsist as well as himself out of his pay,—that thou didst not make an offer to him of my purse; because, had he stood in need, thou knowest, Trim, he had been as welcome to it as myself.——Your honour knows, said the corporal, I had no orders;—True, quoth my uncle Toby,—thou didst very right, Trim, as a soldier,—but certainly very wrong as a man.

In the second place, for which, indeed, thou hast the same excuse, continued my uncle Toby,—when thou offeredst him whatever was in my house,—thou shouldst have offered him my house too:—A sick brother officer should have the best quarters, Trim, and if we had him with us,— we could tend and look to him:—Thou art an excellent nurse thyself,

Trim,—and what with thy care of him, and the old woman's, and his boy's, and mine together, we might recruit him again at once, and set him upon his legs.——

——In a fortnight or three weeks, added my uncle Toby smiling,—he might march.—He will never march, an' please your honour, in this world, said the corporal:—He will march, said my uncle Toby, rising up from the side of the bed, with one shoe off:—An' please your honour, said the corporal, he will never march but to his grave:—He shall march, cried my uncle Toby, marching the foot which had a shoe on, though without advancing an inch,—he shall march to his regiment.——He cannot stand it, said the corporal;—He shall be supported, said my uncle Toby;—He'll drop at last, said the corporal, and what will become of his boy?——He shall not drop, said my uncle Toby, firmly.——A-well-o'-day,—do what we can for him, said Trim, maintaining his point,—the poor soul will die:—He shall not die, by G—, cried my uncle Toby.

——The Accusing Spirit, which flew up to heaven's chancery with the oath, blushed as he gave it in;—and the Recording Angel, as he wrote it down, dropped a tear upon the word, and blotted it out for ever.

Chapter 9

——My uncle Toby went to his bureau,—put his purse into his breeches pocket, and having ordered the corporal to go early in the morning for a physician,—he went to bed, and fell asleep.

Chapter 10
The Story of Le Fever Continued

The sun looked bright the morning after, to every eye in the village but Le Fever's and his afflicted son's; the hand of death pressed heavy upon his eye-lids,—and hardly could the wheel at the cistern turn round its circle,—when my uncle Toby, who had rose up an hour before his wonted time, entered the lieutenant's room, and without preface or apology, sat himself down upon the chair by the bed-side, and, independently of all modes and customs, opened the curtain in the manner an old friend and brother officer would have done it, and asked him how he did,—how he had rested in the night,—what was his complaint,—where was his pain,—and what he could do to help him:—and without giving him time to answer any one of the enquiries, went on, and told him of the little plan which he had been concerting with the corporal the night before for him.——

——You shall go home directly, Le Fever, said my uncle Toby, to my house,—and we'll send for a doctor to see what's the matter,—and we'll have an apothecary,—and the corporal shall be your nurse;—and I'll be your servant, Le Fever.

There was a frankness in my uncle Toby,—not the effect of familiarity,—but the cause of it,—which let you at once into his soul, and shewed you the goodness of his nature; to this, there was something in his looks, and voice, and manner, superadded, which eternally beckoned to the unfortunate to come and take shelter under him; so that before my uncle Toby had half finished the kind offers he was making to the father, had the son insensibly pressed up close to his knees, and had taken hold of the breast of his coat, and was pulling it towards him.——The blood and spirits of Le Fever, which were waxing cold and slow within him, and were retreating to their last citadel, the heart—rallied back,—the film forsook his eyes for a moment,—he looked up wishfully in my uncle Toby's face,—then cast a look upon his boy,—and that ligament, fine as it was,—was never broken.—

Nature instantly ebbed again,—the film returned to its place,—the pulse fluttered—stopped—went on—throbbed—stopped again—moved—stopped —shall I go on?——No.

CHAPTER 11

I AM so impatient to return to my own story, that what remains of young Le Fever's, that is, from this turn of his fortune, to the time my uncle Toby recommended him for my preceptor, shall be told in a very few words in the next chapter.—All that is necessary to be added to this chapter is as follows.——

That my uncle Toby, with young Le Fever in his hand, attended the poor lieutenant, as chief mourners, to his grave.

That the governor of Dendermond paid his obsequies all military honours,—and that Yorick, not to be behindhand—paid him all ecclesiastic— for he buried him in his chancel:—And it appears likewise, he preached a funeral sermon over him—I say it appears,—for it was Yorick's custom, which I suppose a general one with those of his profession, on the first leaf of every sermon which he composed, to chronicle down the time, the place, and the occasion of its being preached: to this, he was ever wont to add some short comment or stricture upon the sermon itself, seldom, indeed, much to its credit:—For instance, This sermon upon the Jewish dispensation—I don't like it at all:—Though I own there is a world of water-landish knowledge in it,—but 'tis all tritical, and most tritically put together.—— This is but a flimsy kind of a composition; what was in my head when I made it?

——*N.B.* The excellency of this text is, that it will suit any sermon,— and of this sermon,—that it will suit any text.——

——For this sermon I shall be hanged,—for I have stolen the greatest part of it. Doctor Paidagunes found me out.☞ Set a thief to catch a thief.——

On the back of half a dozen I find written, *So, so,* and no more—and upon a couple *Moderato;* by which, as far as one may gather from Altieri's Italian dictionary,—but mostly from the authority of a piece of green whipcord, which seemed to have been the unravelling of Yorick's whip-lash, with which he has left us the two sermons marked *Moderato,* and the half dozen of *So, so,* tied fast together in one bundle by themselves,—one may safely suppose he meant pretty near the same thing.

There is but one difficulty in the way of this conjecture, which is this, that the *moderato's* are five times better than the *so, so's;*—shew ten times more knowledge of the human heart;—have seventy times more wit and spirit in them;—(and, to rise properly in my climax)—discovered a thousand times more genius;—and to crown all, are infinitely more entertaining than those tied up with them:—for which reason, whene'er Yorick's dramatic sermons are offered to the world, though I shall admit but one out of the whole number of the *so, so's*, I shall, nevertheless, adventure to print the two *moderato's* without any sort of scruple.

What Yorick could mean by the words *lentamente,—tenutè,—grave,*—and sometimes *adagio,*—as applied to theological compositions, and with which he has characterized some of these sermons, I dare not venture to guess.—I am more puzzled still upon finding *a l'octava alta!* upon one;—*Con strepito* upon the back of another;—*Siciliana* upon a third;—*Alla capella* upon a fourth;—*Con l'arco* upon this;—*Senza l'arco* upon that.—All I know is, that they are musical terms, and have a meaning;—and as he was a musical man, I will make no doubt, but that by some quaint application of such metaphors to the compositions in hand, they impressed very distinct ideas of their several characters upon his fancy,—whatever they may do upon that of others.

Amongst these, there is that particular sermon which has unaccountably led me into this digression—The funeral sermon upon poor Le Fever, wrote out very fairly, as if from a hasty copy.——I take notice of it the more, because it seems to have been his favourite composition—It is upon mortality; and is tied lengthways and crossways with a yarn thrum, and then rolled up and twisted round with a half-sheet of dirty blue paper, which seems to have been once the cast cover of a general review, which to this day smells horribly of horse drugs.——Whether these marks of humiliation were designed,—I something doubt;—because at the end of the sermon (and not at the beginning of it)—very different from his way of treating the rest, he had wrote——

Bravo!

——Though not very offensively,—for it is at two inches, at least, and a half's distance from, and below the concluding line of the sermon, at the very extremity of the page, and in that right-hand corner of it, which, you know, is generally covered with your thumb; and, to do it justice, it is wrote besides with a crow's quill so faintly in a small Italian hand, as scarce to solicit the eye towards the place, whether your thumb is there or not,— so that from the manner of it, it stands half excused; and being wrote moreover with very pale ink, diluted almost to nothing,—'tis more like a *ritratto* of the shadow of vanity, than of Vanity herself—of the two; resembling rather a faint thought of transient applause, secretly stirring up in the heart of the composer; than a gross mark of it, coarsely obtruded upon the world.

With all these extenuations, I am aware, that in publishing this, I do no service to Yorick's character as a modest man;—but all men have their failings! and what lessons this still farther, and almost wipes it away, is this; that the word was struck through some time afterwards (as appears from a different tint of the ink) with a line quite across it in this manner, BRAVO—as if he had retracted, or was ashamed of the opinion he had once entertained of it.

These short characters of his sermons were always written, excepting in this one instance, upon the first leaf of his sermon, which served as a cover to it; and usually upon the inside of it, which was turned towards the text; —but at the end of his discourse, where, perhaps, he had five or six pages, and sometimes, perhaps, a whole score to turn himself in,—he took a large circuit, and, indeed, a much more mettlesome one;—as if he had snatched the occasion of unlacing himself with a few more frolicsome strokes at vice, than the straitness of the pulpit allowed.——These, though hussar-like, they skirmish lightly and out of all order, are still auxiliaries on the side of virtue;—tell me then, Mynheer Vander Blonederdondergewdenstronke, why they should not be printed together?

Chapter 12

WHEN my uncle Toby had turned every thing into money, and settled all accounts betwixt the agent of the regiment and Le Fever, and betwixt Le Fever and all mankind,—there remained nothing more in my uncle Toby's hands, than an old regimental coat and a sword; so that my uncle Toby found little or no opposition from the world in taking administration. The coat my uncle Toby gave the corporal;—Wear it, Trim, said my uncle Toby, as long as it will hold together, for the sake of the poor lieutenant— And this,—said my uncle Toby, taking up the sword in his hand, and drawing it out of the scabbard as he spoke—and this, Le Fever, I'll save for thee, —'tis all the fortune, continued my uncle Toby, hanging it up upon a crook, and pointing to it,—'tis all the fortune, my dear Le Fever, which God has left thee; but if He has given thee a heart to fight thy way with it in the world,—and thou doest it like a man of honour,—'tis enough for us.

As soon as my uncle Toby had laid a foundation, and taught him to inscribe a regular polygon in a circle, he sent him to a public school, where, excepting Whitsuntide and Christmas, at which times the corporal was punctually dispatched for him,—he remained to the spring of the year, seventeen; when the stories of the emperor's sending his army into Hungary against the Turks, kindling a spark of fire in his bosom, he left his Greek and Latin without leave, and throwing himself upon his knees before my uncle Toby, begged his father's sword, and my uncle Toby's leave along with it, to go and try his fortune under Eugene.——Twice did my uncle Toby forget his wound and cry out, Le Fever! I will go with thee, and thou shalt fight beside me—And twice he laid his hand upon his groin, and hung down his head in sorrow and disconsolation.

My uncle Toby took down the sword from the crook, where it had hung untouched ever since the lieutenant's death, and delivered it to the corporal to brighten up;—and having detained Le Fever a single fortnight to equip him, and contract for his passage to Leghorn,—he put the sword into his hand.——If thou art brave, Le Fever, said my uncle Toby, this will not fail thee,—but Fortune, said he (musing a little),—Fortune may—And if she does,—added my uncle Toby, embracing him, come back again to me, Le Fever, and we will shape thee another course.

The greatest injury could not have oppressed the heart of Le Fever more than my uncle Toby's paternal kindness;—he parted from my uncle Toby, as the best of sons from the best of fathers—both dropped tears—and as my uncle Toby gave him his last kiss, he slipped sixty guineas, tied up in an old purse of his father's, in which was his mother's ring, into his hand,— and bid God bless him.

CHAPTER 13

LE FEVER got up to the Imperial army just time enough to try what metal his sword was made of, at the defeat of the Turks before Belgrade; but a series of unmerited mischances had pursued him from that moment, and trod close upon his heels for four years together after; he had withstood these buffetings to the last, till sickness overtook him at Marseilles, from whence he wrote my uncle Toby word, he had lost his time, his services, his health, and, in short, every thing but his sword;—and was waiting for the first ship to return back to him.

As this letter came to hand about six weeks before Susannah's accident, Le Fever was hourly expected; and was uppermost in my uncle Toby's mind all the time my father was giving him and Yorick a description of what kind of a person he would choose for a preceptor to me: but as my uncle Toby thought my father at first somewhat fanciful in the accomplishments he required, he forbore mentioning Le Fever's name,—till the character, by Yorick's interposition, ending unexpectedly, in one, who should be gentle-tempered, and generous, and good, it impressed the image of Le Fever, and his interest, upon my uncle Toby so forcibly, he rose instantly off his chair; and laying down his pipe, in order to take hold of both my father's hands—I beg, brother Shandy, said my uncle Toby, I may recommend poor Le Fever's son to you—I beseech you do, added Yorick— He has a good heart, said my uncle Toby—And a brave one too, an' please your honour, said the corporal.

——The best hearts, Trim, are ever the bravest, replied my uncle Toby.

——And the greatest cowards, an' please your honour, in our regiment, were the greatest rascals in it.——There was serjeant Kumber, and ensign——

——We'll talk of them, said my father, another time.

CHAPTER 14

WHAT a jovial and a merry world would this be, may it please your worships, but for that inextricable labyrinth of debts, cares, woes, want, grief, discontent, melancholy, large jointures, impositions, and lies!

Doctor Slop, like a son of a w——, as my father called him for it,—to exalt himself,—debased me to death,—and made ten thousand times more of Susannah's accident, than there was any grounds for; so that in a week's time, or less, it was in every body's mouth, That poor Master Shandy * * * * * * * * * * * * * * * * * * entirely.—And Fame, who loves to double every thing,—in three days more, had sworn, positively she saw it,—and all the world, as usual, gave credit to her evidence— "That the nursery window had not only * * * * * * * * * * * *

* * * * * * * * * * ;—but that * * * * * * * * * * *
* * * * * * 's also."

Could the world have been sued like a body-corporate,—my father had brought an action upon the case, and trounced it sufficiently; but to fall foul of individuals about it—as every soul who had mentioned the affair, did it with the greatest pity imaginable;—'twas like flying in the very face of his best friends:—And yet to acquiesce under the report, in silence—was to acknowledge it openly,—at least in the opinion of one half of the world; and to make a bustle again, in contradicting it,—was to confirm it as strongly in the opinion of the other half.——

——Was ever poor devil of a country gentleman so hampered? said my father.

I would shew him publicly, said my uncle Toby, at the market cross.

——'Twill have no effect, said my father.

CHAPTER 15

——I'll put him, however, into breeches, said my father,—let the world say what it will.

CHAPTER 16

There are a thousand resolutions, Sir, both in church and state, as well as in matters, Madam, of a more private concern;—which, though they have carried all the appearance in the world of being taken, and entered upon in a hasty, hare-brained, and unadvised manner, were, notwithstanding this (and could you or I have got into the cabinet, or stood behind the curtain, we should have found it was so), weighed, poised, and perpended—argued upon—canvassed through—entered into, and examined on all sides with so much coolness, that the goddess of coolness herself (I do not take upon me to prove her existence) could neither have wished it, or done it better.

Of the number of these was my father's resolution of putting me into breeches; which, though determined at once,—in a kind of huff, and a defiance of all mankind, had, nevertheless, been proed and conned, and judicially talked over betwixt him and my mother about a month before, in two several beds of justice, which my father had held for that purpose. I shall explain the nature of these beds of justice in my next chapter; and in the chapter following that, you shall step with me, Madam, behind the curtain, only to hear in what kind of manner my father and my mother debated between themselves, this affair of the breeches,—from which you may form an idea, how they debated all lesser matters.

CHAPTER 17

The ancient Goths of Germany, who (the learned Cluverius is positive) were first seated in the country between the Vistula and the Oder, and who afterwards incorporated the Herculi, the Bugians, and some other Vandallic clans to 'em—had all of them a wise custom of debating every thing of importance to their state, twice; that is,—once drunk, and once sober:—

Drunk—that their councils might not want vigour;—and sober—that they might not want discretion.

Now my father being entirely a water-drinker,—was a long time gravelled almost to death, in turning this as much to his advantage, as he did every other thing which the ancients did or said; and it was not till the seventh year of his marriage, after a thousand fruitless experiments and devices, that he hit upon an expedient which answered the purpose;—and that was, when any difficult and momentous point was to be settled in the family, which required great sobriety, and great spirit too, in its determination,—he fixed and set apart the first Sunday night in the month, and the Saturday night which immediately preceded it, to argue it over, in bed, with my mother: By which contrivance, if you consider, Sir, with yourself,

* *
* * * * * * * * * * * * * *

These my father, humorously enough, called his beds of justice;—for from the two different counsels taken in these two different humours, a middle one was generally found out which touched the point of wisdom as well, as if he had got drunk and sober a hundred times.

It must not be made a secret of to the world, that this answers full as well in literary discussions, as either in military or conjugal; but it is not every author that can try the experiment as the Goths and Vandals did it —or, if he can, may it be always for his body's health; and to do it, as my father did it,—am I sure it would be always for his soul's.

My way is this:——

In all nice and ticklish discussions—(of which, heaven knows, there are but too many in my book),—where I find I cannot take a step without the danger of having either their worships or their reverences upon my back— I write one-half full,—and t'other fasting; or write it all full,—and correct it fasting;—or write it fasting,—and correct it full, for they all come to the same thing:—So that with a less variation from my father's plan, than my father's from the Gothic—I feel myself upon a par with him in his first bed of justice,—and no way inferior to him in his second.——These different and almost irreconcileable effects, flow uniformly from the wise and wonderful mechanism of nature,—of which,—be her's the honour.——All that we can do, is to turn and work the machine to the improvement and better manufactory of the arts and sciences.——

Now, when I write full,—I write as if I was never to write fasting again as long as I live;—that is, I write free from the cares as well as the terrors of the world.—I count not the number of my scars,—nor does my fancy go forth into dark entries and bye-corners to antedate my stabs.——In a word, my pen takes its course; and I write on as much from the fulness of my heart, as my stomach.——

But when, an' please your honours, I indite fasting, 'tis a different history. ——I pay the world all possible attention and respect,—and have as great a share (whilst it lasts) of that under-strapping virtue of discretion as the best of you.——So that betwixt both, I write a careless kind of a civil, nonsensical, good-humoured Shandean book, which will do all your hearts good——

——And all your heads too,—provided you understand it.

Chapter 18

WE should begin, said my father, turning himself half round in bed, and shifting his pillow a little towards my mother's, as he opened the debate—We should begin to think, Mrs. Shandy, of putting this boy into breeches.—

We should so,—said my mother.——We defer it, my dear, quoth my father, shamefully.——

I think we do, Mr. Shandy,—said my mother.

——Not but the child looks extremely well, said my father, in his vests and tunics.——

——He does look very well in them,—replied my mother.——

——And for that reason it would be almost a sin, added my father, to take him out of 'em.——

——It would so,—said my mother:—But indeed he is growing a very tall lad,—rejoined my father.

——He is very tall for his age, indeed, said my mother.——

——I can not (making two syllables of it) imagine, quoth my father, who the deuce he takes after.——

I cannot conceive, for my life,—said my mother.——

Humph!—said my father.

(The dialogue ceased for a moment.)

——I am very short myself,—continued my father gravely.

You are very short, Mr. Shandy,—said my mother.

Humph! quoth my father to himself, a second time: in muttering which, he plucked his pillow a little further from my mother's,—and turning about again, there was an end of the debate for three minutes and a half.

——When he gets these breeches made, cried my father in a higher tone, he'll look like a beast in 'em.

He will be very awkward in them at first, replied my mother.——

——And 'twill be lucky, if that's the worst on't, added my father.

It will be very lucky, answered my mother.

I suppose, replied my father,—making some pause first,—he'll be exactly like other people's children.——

Exactly, said my mother.——

——Though I shall be sorry for that, added my father: and so the debate stopped again.

——They should be of leather, said my father, turning him about again.

They will last him, said my mother, the longest.

But he can have no linings to 'em, replied my father.——

He cannot, said my mother.

'Twere better to have them of fustian, quoth my father.

Nothing can be better, quoth my mother.——

——Except dimity,—replied my father:—'Tis best of all,—replied my mother.

——One must not give him his death, however,—interrupted my father.

By no means, said my mother:—and so the dialogue stood still again.

I am resolved, however, quoth my father, breaking silence the fourth time, he shall have no pockets in them.——

——There is no occasion for any, said my mother.——

I mean in his coat and waistcoat,—cried my father.

——I mean so too,—replied my mother.

——Though if he gets a gig or top—Poor souls! it is a crown and a sceptre to them,—they should have where to secure it.——

Order it as you please, Mr. Shandy, replied my mother.——

——But don't you think it right? added my father, pressing the point home to her.

Perfectly, said my mother, if it pleases you, Mr. Shandy.——

——There's for you! cried my father, losing temper—Pleases me!——You never will distinguish, Mrs. Shandy, nor shall I ever teach you to do it, betwixt a point of pleasure and a point of convenience.——This was on the Sunday night:—and further this chapter sayeth not.

CHAPTER 19

AFTER my father had debated the affair of the breeches with my mother,—he consulted Albertus Rubenius upon it; and Albertus Rubenius used my father ten times worse in the consultation (if possible) than even my father had used my mother: For as Rubenius had wrote a quarto express, *De re Vestiaria Veterum*,—it was Rubenius's business to have given my father some lights.——On the contrary, my father might as well have thought of extracting the seven cardinal virtues out of a long beard,—as of extracting a single word out of Rubenius upon the subject.

Upon every other article of ancient dress, Rubenius was very communicative to my father;—gave him a full and satisfactory account of

The Toga, or loose gown.
The Chlamys.
The Ephod.
The Tunica, or Jacket.
The Synthesis.
The Paenula.
The Lacema, with its Cucullus.
The Paludamentum.
The Praetexta.
The Sagum, or soldier's jerkin.
The Trabea: of which, according to Suetonius, there were three kinds.——

——But what are all these to the breeches? said my father.

Rubenius threw him down upon the counter all kinds of shoes which had been in fashion with the Romans.——

There was,

The open shoe.
The close shoe.

The slip shoe.
The wooden shoe.
The soc.
The buskin.
And The military shoe with hobnails in it, which Juvenal takes notice of.

There were, The clogs.
The pattins.
The pantoufles.
The brogues.
The sandals, with latchets to them.

There was, The felt shoe.
The linen shoe.
The laced shoe.
The braided shoe.
The calceus incisus.
And The calceus rostratus.

Rubenius shewed my father how well they all fitted,—in what manner they laced on,—with what points, straps, thongs, latchets, ribbands, jaggs, and ends.——

——But I want to be informed about the breeches, said my father.

Albertus Rubenius informed my father that the Romans manufactured stuffs of various fabrics,—some plain, some striped,—others diapered throughout the whole contexture of the wool, with silk and gold—That linen did not begin to be in common use till towards the declension of the empire, when the Egyptians, coming to settle amongst them, brought it into vogue.

——That persons of quality and fortune distinguished themselves by the fineness and whiteness of their clothes; which colour (next to purple, which was appropriated to the great offices) they most affected, and wore on their birth-days and public rejoicings.—That it appeared from the best historians of those times, that they frequently sent their clothes to the fuller, to be cleaned and whitened:—but that the inferior people, to avoid that expense, generally wore brown clothes, and of a something coarser texture,—till towards the beginning of Augustus's reign, when the slave dressed like his master, and almost every distinction of habiliment was lost, but the *Latus Clavus*.

And what was the *Latus Clavus?* said my father.

Rubenius told him, that the point was still litigating amongst the learned:—That Egnatius, Sigonius, Bossius Ticinensis, Bayfius, Budaeus, Salmasius, Lipsius, Lazius, Isaac Casaubon, and Joseph Scaliger, all differed from each other,—and he from them: That some took it to be the button,—some the coat itself,—others only the colour of it:—That the great Bayfius, in his *Wardrobe of the Ancients*, chap. 12—honestly said, he knew not what it was,—whether a tibula,—a stud,—a button,—a loop,—a buckle,—or clasps and keepers.——

——My father lost the horse, but not the saddle—They are hooks and eyes, said my father—and with hooks and eyes he ordered my breeches to be made.

CHAPTER 20

WE are now going to enter upon a new scene of events.——

——Leave we then the breeches in the tailor's hands, with my father standing over him with his cane, reading him as he sat at work a lecture upon the *latus clavus*, and pointing to the precise part of the waistband, where he was determined to have it sewed on.——

Leave we my mother—(truest of all the *Pococurantes* of her sex!)—careless about it, as about every thing else in the world which concerned her;—that is,—indifferent whether it was done this way or that,—provided it was but done at all.——

Leave we Slop likewise to the full profits of all my dishonours.——

Leave we poor Le Fever to recover, and get home from Marseilles as he can.—And last of all,—because the hardest of all——

Let us leave, if possible, myself:—But 'tis impossible,—I must go along with you to the end of the work.

CHAPTER 21

IF the reader has not a clear conception of the rood and the half of ground which lay at the bottom of my uncle Toby's kitchen-garden, and which was the scene of so many of his delicious hours,—the fault is not in me,—but in his imagination; for I am sure I gave him so minute a description, I was almost ashamed of it.

When Fate was looking forwards one afternoon, into the great transactions of future times,—and recollected for what purposes this little plot, by a decree fast bound down in iron, had been destined,—she gave a nod to Nature,—'twas enough—Nature threw half a spade full of her kindliest compost upon it, with just so much clay in it, as to retain the forms of angles and indentings,—and so little of it too, as not to cling to the spade, and render works of so much glory, nasty in foul weather.

My uncle Toby came down, as the reader has been informed, with plans along with him, of almost every fortified town in Italy and Flanders; so let the Duke of Marlborough, or the allies, have set down before what town they pleased, my uncle Toby was prepared for them.

His way, which was the simplest one in the world, was this; as soon as ever a town was invested—(but sooner when the design was known) to take the plan of it (let it be what town it would), and enlarge it upon a scale to the exact size of his bowling-green; upon the surface of which, by means of a large role of packthread, and a number of small piquets driven into the ground, at the several angles and redans, he transferred the lines from his paper; then taking the profile of the place, with its works, to determine the depths and slopes of the ditches,—the talus of the glacis, and the precise height of the several banquets, parapets, etc.—he set the corporal to work—and sweetly went it on:—The nature of the soil,—the nature of the work itself,—and above all, the good-nature of my uncle Toby sitting by from morning to night, and chatting kindly with the corporal upon past-done deeds,—left labour little else but the ceremony of the name.

When the place was finished in this manner, and put into a proper posture of defence,—it was invested,—and my uncle Toby and the corporal began to run their first parallel.—I beg I may not be interrupted in my story, by being told, That the first parallel should be at least three hundred toises distant from the main body of the place,—and that I have not left a single inch for it;——for my uncle Toby took the liberty of encroaching upon his kitchen-garden, for the sake of enlarging his works on the bowling-green, and for that reason generally ran his first and second parallels betwixt two rows of his cabbages and his cauliflowers; the conveniences and the inconveniences of which will be considered at large in the history of my uncle Toby's and the corporal's campaigns, of which, this I'm now writing is but a sketch, and will be finished, if I conjecture right, in three pages (but there is no guessing)—The campaigns themselves will take up as many books; and therefore I apprehend it would be hanging too great a weight of one kind of matter in so flimsy a performance as this, to rhapsodize them, as I once intended, into the body of the work—surely they had better be printed apart,—we'll consider the affair—so take the following sketch of them in the mean time.

CHAPTER 22

WHEN the town, with its works, was finished, my uncle Toby and the corporal began to run their first parallel—not at random, or any how—but from the same points and distances the allies had begun to run theirs; and regulating their approaches and attacks, by the accounts my uncle Toby received from the daily papers,—they went on, during the whole siege, step by step with the allies.

When the duke of Marlborough made a lodgment,—my uncle Toby made a lodgment too,—And when the face of a bastion was battered down, or a defence ruined,—the corporal took his mattock and did as much,—and so on;—gaining ground, and making themselves masters of the works one after another, till the town fell into their hands.

To one who took pleasure in the happy state of others,—there could not have been a greater sight in the world, than, on a post-morning, in which a practicable breach had been made by the duke of Marlborough, in the main body of the place,—to have stood behind the horn-beam hedge, and observed the spirit with which my uncle Toby, with Trim behind him, sallied forth;—the one with the *Gazette* in his hand,—the other with a spade on his shoulder to execute the contents.—What an honest triumph in my uncle Toby's looks as he marched up to the ramparts! What intense pleasure swimming in his eye as he stood over the corporal, reading the paragraph ten times over to him, as he was at work, lest, peradventure, he should make the breach an inch too wide,—or leave it an inch too narrow.——But when the *chamade* was beat, and the corporal helped my uncle up it, and followed with the colours in his hand, to fix them upon the ramparts—Heaven!

Earth! Sea!—but what avails apostrophes?—with all your elements, wet or dry, ye never compounded so intoxicating a draught.

In this track of happiness for many years, without one interruption to it, except now and then when the wind continued to blow due west for a week or ten days together, which detained the Flanders mail, and kept them so long in torture,—but still 'twas the torture of the happy—In this track, I say, did my uncle Toby and Trim move for many years, every year of which, and sometimes every month, from the invention of either the one or the other of them, adding some new conceit or quirk of improvement to their operations, which always opened fresh springs of delight in carrying them on.

The first year's campaign was carried on from beginning to end, in the plain and simple method I've related.

In the second year, in which my uncle Toby took Liege and Ruremond, he thought he might afford the expense of four handsome draw-bridges, of two of which I have given an exact description in the former part of my work.

At the latter end of the same year he added a couple of gates with port-cullises:—These last were converted afterwards into orgues, as the better thing; and during the winter of the same year, my uncle Toby, instead of a new suit of clothes, which he always had at Christmas, treated himself with a handsome sentry-box, to stand at the corner of the bowling-green, be-twixt which point and the foot of the glacis, there was left a little kind of an esplanade for him and the corporal to confer and hold councils of war upon.

——The sentry-box was in case of rain.

All these were painted white three times over the ensuing spring, which enabled my uncle Toby to take the field with great splendour.

My father would often say to Yorick, that if any mortal in the whole universe had done such a thing, except his brother Toby, it would have been looked upon by the world as one of the most refined satires upon the parade and prancing manner in which Lewis XIV. from the beginning of the war, but particularly that very year, had taken the field—But 'tis not my brother Toby's nature, kind soul! my father would add, to insult any one.

——But let us go on.

CHAPTER 23

I MUST observe, that although in the first year's campaign, the word town is often mentioned,—yet there was no town at that time within the poly-gon; that addition was not made till the summer following the spring in which the bridges and sentry-box were painted, which was the third year of my uncle Toby's campaigns,—when upon his taking Amberg, Bonn, and Rhinberg, and Huy and Limbourg, one after another, a thought came into the corporal's head, that to talk of taking so many towns, without one town to show for it,—was a very nonsensical way of going to work, and so pro-posed to my uncle Toby, that they should have a little model of a town built for them,—to be run up together of slit deals, and then painted, and clapped within the interior polygon to serve for all.

My uncle Toby felt the good of the project instantly, and instantly agreed to it, but with the addition of two singular improvements, of which he was almost as proud as if he had been the original inventor of the project itself.

The one was, to have the town built exactly in the style of those of which it was most likely to be the representative:—with grated windows, and the gable ends of the houses, facing the streets, etc. etc.—as those in Ghent and Bruges, and the rest of the towns in Brabant and Flanders.

The other was, not to have the houses run up together, as the corporal proposed, but to have every house independent, to hook on, or off, so as to form into the plan of whatever town they pleased. This was put directly into hand, and many and many a look of mutual congratulation was exchanged between my uncle Toby and the corporal, as the carpenter did the work.

——It answered prodigiously the next summer—the town was a perfect Proteus—It was Landen, and Trerebach, and Santvliet, and Drusen, and Hagenau,—and then it was Ostend and Menin, and Aeth and Dendermond.

——Surely never did any town act so many parts, since Sodom and Gomorrah, as my uncle Toby's town did.

In the fourth year, my uncle Toby thinking a town looked foolishly without a church, added a very fine one with a steeple.—Trim was for having bells in it;—my uncle Toby said, the metal had better be cast into cannon.

This led the way the next campaign for half a dozen brass field-pieces, to be planted three and three on each side of my uncle Toby's sentry-box; and in a short time, these led the way for a train of somewhat larger—and so on—(as must always be the case in hobby-horsical affairs) from pieces of half an inch bore, till it came at last to my father's jack boots.

The next year, which was that in which Lisle was besieged, and at the close of which both Ghent and Bruges fell into our hands,—my uncle Toby was sadly put to it for proper ammunition;—I say proper ammunition— because his great artillery would not bear powder; and 'twas well for the Shandy family they would not—For so full were the papers, from the beginning to the end of the siege, of the incessant firings kept up by the besiegers,—and so heated was my uncle Toby's imagination with the accounts of them, that he had infallibly shot away all his estate.

Something therefore was wanting as a succedaneum, especially in one or two of the more violent paroxysms of the siege, to keep up something like a continual firing in the imagination,—and this something, the corporal, whose principal strength lay in invention, supplied by an entire new system of battering of his own,—without which, this had been objected to by military critics, to the end of the world, as one of the great *desiderata* of my uncle Toby's apparatus.

This will not be explained the worse, for setting off, as I generally do, at a little distance from the subject.

CHAPTER 24

WITH two or three other trinkets, small in themselves, but of great regard, which poor Tom, the corporal's unfortunate brother, had sent him over, with the account of his marriage with the Jew's widow—there was

A Montero-cap and two Turkish tobacco-pipes.

The Montero-cap I shall describe by and bye.——The Turkish tobacco-pipes had nothing particular in them, they were fitted up and ornamented as usual, with flexible tubes of Morocco leather and gold wire, and mounted at their ends, the one of them with ivory,—the other with black ebony, tipped with silver.

My father, who saw all things in lights different from the rest of the world, would say to the corporal, that he ought to look upon these two presents more as tokens of his brother's nicety, than his affection.——Tom did not care, Trim, he would say, to put on the cap, or to smoke in the to-bacco-pipe of a Jew.——God bless your honour, the corporal would say, (giving a strong reason to the contrary)—how can that be?

The Montero-cap was scarlet, of a superfine Spanish cloth, dyed in grain, and mounted all round with fur, except about four inches in the front, which was faced with a light blue, slightly embroidered,—and seemed to have been the property of a Portuguese quartermaster, not of foot, but of horse, as the word denotes.

The corporal was not a little proud of it, as well for its own sake, as the sake of the giver, so seldom or never put it on but upon Gala-days; and yet never was a Montero-cap put to so many uses; for in all controverted points, whether military or culinary, provided the corporal was sure he was in the right,—it was either his oath,—his wager,—or his gift.

——'Twas his gift in the present case.

I'll be bound, said the corporal, speaking to himself, to give away my Montero-cap to the first beggar who comes to the door, if I do not manage this matter to his honour's satisfaction.

The completion was no further off, than the very next morning; which was that of the storm of the counterscarp betwixt the Lower Deule, to the right, and the gate St. Andrew,—and on the left, between St. Magdalen's and the river.

As this was the most memorable attack in the whole war,—the most gallant and obstinate on both sides,—and I must add the most bloody too, for it cost the allies themselves that morning above eleven hundred men,—my uncle Toby prepared himself for it with a more than ordinary solemnity.

The eve which preceded, as my uncle Toby went to bed, he ordered his ramallie wig, which had laid inside out for many years in the corner of an old campaigning trunk, which stood by his bedside, to be taken out and laid upon the lid of it, ready for the morning;—and the very first thing he did in his shirt, when he had stepped out of bed, my uncle Toby, after he had turned the rough side outwards,—put it on:—This done, he proceeded next to his breeches, and having buttoned the waistband, he forthwith buckled on his sword-belt, and had got his sword half way in,—when he considered he should want shaving, and that it would be very inconvenient doing it with his sword on,—so took it off:—In assaying to put on his regimental coat and waistcoat, my uncle Toby found the same objection in his wig,—so that went off too:—So that what with one thing and what with another, as always falls out when a man is in the most haste,—'twas ten o'clock, which was half an hour later than his usual time, before my uncle Toby sallied out.

CHAPTER 25

MY uncle Toby had scarce turned the corner of his yew hedge, which separated his kitchen-garden from his bowling-green, when he perceived the corporal had begun the attack without him.——

Let me stop and give you a picture of the corporal's apparatus; and of the corporal himself in the height of his attack, just as it struck my uncle Toby, as he turned towards the sentry-box, where the corporal was at work,—for in nature there is not such another,—nor can any combination of all that is grotesque and whimsical in her works produce its equal.

The corporal——

——Tread lightly on his ashes, ye men of genius,—for he was your kinsman: Weed his grave clean, ye men of goodness,—for he was your brother.—O corporal! had I thee, but now,—now, that I am able to give thee a dinner and protection,—how would I cherish thee! thou should'st wear thy Montero-cap every hour of the day, and every day of the week,—and when it was worn out, I would purchase thee a couple like it:—But alas! alas! alas! now that I can do this in spite of their reverences—the occasion is lost—for thou art gone;—thy genius fled up to the stars from whence it came;—and that warm heart of thine, with all its generous and open vessels, compressed into a clod of the valley!

——But what—what is this, to that future and dreaded page, where I look towards the velvet pall, decorated with the military ensigns of thy master—the first—the foremost of created beings;—where, I shall see thee, faithful servant! laying his sword and scabbard with a trembling hand across his coffin, and then returning pale as ashes to the door, to take his mourning horse by the bridle, to follow his hearse, as he directed thee;—where—all my father's systems shall be baffled by his sorrows; and, in spite of his philosophy, I shall behold him, as he inspects the lacquered plate, twice taking his spectacles from off his nose, to wipe away the dew which nature has shed upon them—When I see him cast in the rosemary with an air of disconsolation, which cries through my ears,—O Toby! in what corner of the world shall I seek thy fellow?

——Gracious powers! which erst have opened the lips of the dumb in his distress, and made the tongue of the stammerer speak plain—when I shall arrive at this dreaded page, deal not with me, then, with a stinted hand.

CHAPTER 26

THE corporal, who the night before had resolved in his mind to supply the grand *desideratum*, of keeping up something like an incessant firing upon the enemy during the heat of the attack,—had no further idea in his fancy at that time, than a contrivance of smoking tobacco against the town, out of one of my uncle Toby's six field-pieces, which were planted on each side of his sentry-box; the means of effecting which occurring to his fancy at the same time, though he had pledged his cap, he thought it in no danger from the miscarriage of his projects.

Upon turning it this way, and that, a little in his mind, he soon began to find out, that by means of his two Turkish tobacco-pipes, with the supplement of three smaller tubes of wash-leather at each of their lower ends, to be tagged by the same number of tin-pipes fitted to the touch-holes, and sealed with clay next the cannon, and then tied hermetically with waxed silk at their several insertions into the Morocco tube,—he should be able to fire the six field-pieces all together, and with the same ease as to fire one.——

——Let no man say from what tags and jags hints may not be cut out for the advancement of human knowledge. Let no man, who has read my father's first and second beds of justice, ever rise up and say again, from collision of what kinds of bodies light may or may not be struck out, to carry the arts and sciences up to perfection.—Heaven! thou knowest how I love them;—thou knowest the secrets of my heart, and that I would this moment give my shirt—Thou art a fool, Shandy, says Eugenius, for thou hast but a dozen in the world,—and 'twill break thy set.——

No matter for that, Eugenius; I would give the shirt off my back to be burned into tinder, were it only to satisfy one feverish enquirer, how many sparks at one good stroke, a good flint and steel could strike into the tail of it.——Think ye not that in striking these in,—he might, peradventure, strike something out? as sure as a gun.——

——But this project, by the bye.

The corporal sat up the best part of the night, in bringing his to perfection; and having made a sufficient proof of his cannon, with charging them to the top with tobacco,—he went with contentment to bed.

Chapter 27

The corporal had slipped out about ten minutes before my uncle Toby, in order to fix his apparatus, and just give the enemy a shot or two before my uncle Toby came.

He had drawn the six field-pieces for this end, all close up together in front of my uncle Toby's sentry-box, leaving only an interval of about a yard and a half betwixt the three, on the right and left, for the convenience of charging, etc.—and the sake possibly of two batteries, which he might think double the honour of one.

In the rear and facing this opening, with his back to the door of the sentry-box, for fear of being flanked, had the corporal wisely taken his post:— He held the ivory pipe, appertaining to the battery on the right, betwixt the finger and thumb of his right hand,—and the ebony pipe tipped with silver, which appertained to the battery on the left, betwixt the finger and thumb of the other—and with his right knee fixed firm upon the ground, as if in the front rank of his platoon, was the corporal, with his Montero-cap upon his head, furiously playing off his two cross batteries at the same time against the counter-guard, which faced the counterscarp, where the attack was to be made that morning. His first intention, as I said, was no more than giving the enemy a single puff or two;—but the pleasure of the puffs, as well as the puffing, had insensibly got hold of the corporal, and drawn him on

from puff to puff, into the very height of the attack, by the time my uncle
Toby joined him.

'Twas well for my father, that my uncle Toby had not his will to make
that day.

CHAPTER 28

MY uncle Toby took the ivory pipe out of the corporal's hand, looked at it
for half a minute, and returned it.

In less than two minutes, my uncle Toby took the pipe from the corporal
again, and raised it half way to his mouth—then hastily gave it back a
second time.

The corporal redoubled the attack,—my uncle Toby smiled,—then
looked grave,—then smiled for a moment,—then looked serious for a long
time;—Give me hold of the ivory pipe, Trim, said my uncle Toby—my
uncle Toby put it to his lips,—drew it back directly,—gave a peep over the
horn-beam hedge;—never did my uncle Toby's mouth water so much for a
pipe in his life.—My uncle Toby retired into the sentry-box with the pipe
in his hand.——

——Dear uncle Toby! don't go into the sentry-box with the pipe,—
there's no trusting a man's self with such a thing in such a corner.

CHAPTER 29

I BEG the reader will assist me here, to wheel off my uncle Toby's ordnance
behind the scenes,—to remove his sentry-box, and clear the theatre, if
possible, of horn-works and half moons, and get the rest of his military
apparatus out of the way;—that done, my dear friend Garrick, we'll snuff
the candles bright,—sweep the stage with a new broom,—draw up the curtain, and exhibit my uncle Toby dressed in a new character, throughout
which the world can have no idea how he will act: and yet, if pity be a-kin
to love,—and bravery no alien to it, you have seen enough of my uncle Toby
in these, to trace these family likenesses, betwixt the two passions (in case
there is one) to your heart's content.

Vain science! thou assistest us in no case of this kind——and thou puz-
zlest us in every one.

There was, Madam, in my uncle Toby, a singleness of heart which misled
him so far out of the little serpentine tracks in which things of this nature
usually go on; you can—you can have no conception of it: with this, there
was a plainness and simplicity of thinking, with such an unmistrusting
ignorance of the plies and foldings of the heart of woman;—and so naked
and defenceless did he stand before you, (when a siege was out of his head,)
that you might have stood behind any one of your serpentine walks, and
shot my uncle Toby ten times in a day, through his liver, if nine times in a
day, Madam, had not served your purpose.

With all this, Madam,—and what confounded every thing as much on
the other hand, my uncle Toby had that unparalleled modesty of nature I
once told you of, and which, by the bye, stood eternal sentry upon his feelings, that you might as soon—But where am I going? these reflections

crowd in upon me ten pages at least too soon, and take up that time, which I ought to bestow upon facts.

Chapter 30

Of the few legitimate sons of Adam whose breasts never felt what the sting of love was,—(maintaining first, all mysogynists to be bastards)—the greatest heroes of ancient and modern story have carried off amongst them nine parts in ten of the honour; and I wish for their sakes I had the key of my study, out of my draw-well, only for five minutes, to tell you their names—recollect them I cannot—so be content to accept of these, for the present, in their stead.——

There was the great king Aldrovandus, and Bosphorus, and Cappadocius, and Dardanus, and Pontus, and Asius,—to say nothing of the iron-hearted Charles the XIIth, whom the Countess of K ***** herself could make nothing of.——There was Babylonicus, and Mediterraneus, and Polixenes, and Persicus, and Prusicus, not one of whom (except Cappadocius and Pontus, who were both a little suspected) ever once bowed down his breast to the goddess—The truth is, they had all of them something else to do—and so had my uncle Toby—till Fate—till Fate I say, envying his name the glory of being handed down to posterity with Aldrovandus's and the rest,—she basely patched up the peace of Utrecht.

——Believe me, Sirs, 'twas the worst deed she did that year.

Chapter 31

Amongst the many ill consequences of the treaty of Utrecht, it was within a point of giving my uncle Toby a surfeit of sieges; and though he recovered his appetite afterwards, yet Calais itself left not a deeper scar in Mary's heart, than Utrecht upon my uncle Toby's. To the end of his life he never could hear Utrecht mentioned upon any account whatever,—or so much as read an article of news extracted out of the *Utrecht Gazette*, without fetching a sigh, as if his heart would break in twain.

My father, who was a great motive-monger, and consequently a very dangerous person for a man to sit by, either laughing or crying,—for he generally knew your motive for doing both, much better than you knew it yourself—would always console my uncle Toby upon these occasions, in a way, which shewed plainly, he imagined my uncle Toby grieved for nothing in the whole affair, so much as the loss of his hobby-horse.—Never mind, brother Toby, he would say,—by God's blessing we shall have another war break out again some of these days; and when it does,—the belligerent powers, if they would hang themselves, cannot keep us out of play.——I defy 'em, my dear Toby he would add, to take countries without taking towns,—or towns without sieges.

My uncle Toby never took this back-stroke of my father's at his hobby-horse kindly.—He thought the stroke ungenerous; and the more so, because in striking the horse he hit the rider too, and in the most dishonourable part a blow could fall; so that upon these occasions, he always laid down his pipe upon the table with more fire to defend himself than common.

I told the reader, this time two years, that my uncle Toby was not eloquent; and in the very same page gave an instance to the contrary:—I repeat the observation, and a fact which contradicts it again.—He was not eloquent,—it was not easy to my uncle Toby to make long harangues,—and he hated florid ones; but there were occasions where the stream overflowed the man, and ran so counter to its usual course, that in some parts my uncle Toby, for a time, was at least equal to Tertullus—but in others, in my own opinion, infinitely above him.

My father was so highly pleased with one of these apologetical orations of my uncle Toby's, which he had delivered one evening before him and Yorick, that he wrote it down before he went to bed.

I have had the good fortune to meet with it amongst my father's papers, with here and there an insertion of his own, betwixt two crooks, thus [   ], and is endorsed,

My Brother Toby's Justification of his own Principles and Conduct in wishing to Continue the War.

I may safely say, I have read over this apologetical oration of my uncle Toby's a hundred times, and think it so fine a model of defence,—and shews so sweet a temperament of gallantry and good principles in him, that I give it to the world, word for word (interlineations and all), as I find it.

CHAPTER 32
My Uncle Toby's Apologetical Oration

I AM not insensible, brother Shandy, that when a man whose profession is arms, wishes, as I have done, for war,—it has an ill aspect to the world;—and that, how just and right soever his motives and intentions may be,—he stands in an uneasy posture in vindicating himself from private views in doing it.

For this cause, if a soldier is a prudent man, which he may be without being a jot the less brave, he will be sure not to utter his wish in the hearing of an enemy; for say what he will, an enemy will not believe him.—He will be cautious of doing it even to a friend,—lest he may suffer in his esteem:—But if his heart is overcharged, and a secret sigh for arms must have its vent, he will reserve it for the ear of a brother, who knows his character to the bottom, and what his true notions, dispositions, and principles of honour are: What, I hope, I have been in all these, brother Shandy, would be unbecoming in me to say:—much worse, I know, have I been than I ought, —and something worse, perhaps, than I think: But such as I am, you, my dear brother Shandy, who have sucked the same breasts with me,—and with whom I have been brought up from my cradle,—and from whose knowledge, from the first hours of our boyish pastimes, down to this, I have concealed no one action of my life, and scarce a thought in it—Such as I am, brother, you must by this time know me, with all my vices, and with all my weaknesses too, whether of my age, my temper, my passions, or my understanding.

Tell me then, my dear brother Shandy, upon which of them it is, that when I condemned the peace of Utrecht, and grieved the war was not carried on with vigour a little longer, you should think your brother did it upon unworthy views; or that in wishing for war, he should be bad enough to wish more of his fellow-creatures slain,—more slaves made, and more families driven from their peaceful habitations, merely for his own pleasure: —Tell me, brother Shandy, upon what one deed of mine do you ground it? [The devil a deed do I know of, dear Toby, but one for a hundred pounds, which I lent thee to carry on these cursed sieges.]

If, when I was a school-boy, I could not hear a drum beat, but my heart beat with it—was it my fault?—Did I plant the propensity?——Did I sound the alarm within, or Nature?

When Guy, Earl of Warwick, and Parismus and Parismenus, and Valentine and Orson, and the Seven Champions of England, were handed around the school,—were they not all purchased with my own pocket-money? Was that selfish, brother Shandy? When we read over the siege of Troy, which lasted ten years and eight months,—though with such a train of artillery as we had at Namur, the town might have been carried in a week—was I not as much concerned for the destruction of the Greeks and Trojans as any boy of the whole school? Had I not three strokes of a ferula given me, two on my right hand, and one on my left, for calling Helena a bitch for it? Did any one of you shed more tears for Hector? And when king Priam came to the camp to beg his body, and returned weeping back to Troy without it,— you know, brother, I could not eat my dinner.——

——Did that bespeak me cruel? Or because, brother Shandy, my blood flew out into the camp, and my heart panted for war,—was it a proof it could not ache for the distresses of war too?

O brother! 'tis one thing for a soldier to gather laurels,—and 'tis another to scatter cypress.——[Who told thee, my dear Toby, that cypress was used by the ancients on mournful occasions?]

——'Tis one thing, brother Shandy, for a soldier to hazard his own life— to leap first down into the trench, where he is sure to be cut in pieces:—'Tis one thing, from public spirit and a thirst of glory, to enter the breach the first man,—To stand in the foremost rank, and march bravely on with drums and trumpets, and colours flying about his ears:—'Tis one thing, I say, brother Shandy, to do this,—and 'tis another thing to reflect on the miseries of war;—to view the desolations of whole countries, and consider the intolerable fatigues and hardships which the soldier himself, the instrument who works them, is forced (for sixpence a day, if he can get it), to undergo.

Need I be told, dear Yorick, as I was by you, in Le Fever's funeral sermon, That so soft and gentle a creature, born to love, to mercy, and kindness, as man is, was not shaped for this?—But why did you not add, Yorick, —if not by nature—that he is so by necessity?—For what is war? what is it, Yorick, when fought as ours has been, upon principles of liberty, and upon principles of honour—what is it, but the getting together of quiet and harmless people, with their swords in their hands, to keep the ambitious and the turbulent within bounds? And heaven is my witness, brother Shandy, that the pleasure I have taken in these things,—and that infinite delight, in particular, which has attended my sieges in my bowling-green, has arose within me, and I hope in the corporal too, from the consciousness we both had, that in carrying them on, we were answering the great ends of our creation.

CHAPTER 33

I TOLD the Christian reader—I say Christian—hoping he is one—and if he is not, I am sorry for it—and only beg he will consider the matter with himself, and not lay the blame entirely upon this book—

I told him, Sir—for in good truth, when a man is telling a story in the strange way I do mine, he is obliged continually to be going backwards and forwards to keep all tight together in the reader's fancy—which, for my own part, if I did not take heed to do more than at first, there is so much unfixed and equivocal matter starting up, with so many breaks and gaps in it, —and so little service do the stars afford, which, nevertheless, I hang up in some of the darkest passages, knowing that the world is apt to lose its way, with all the lights the sun itself at noon-day can give it—and now you see, I am lost myself!——

——But 'tis my father's fault; and whenever my brains come to be dissected, you will perceive, without spectacles, that he has left a large uneven thread, as you sometimes see in an unsaleable piece of cambric, running along the whole length of the web, and so untowardly, you cannot so much as cut out a * *, (here I hang up a couple of lights again)—or a fillet, or a thumb-stall, but it is seen or felt.——

Quanto id diligentius in liberis procreandis cavendum, sayeth Cardan. All which being considered, and that you see 'tis morally impracticable for me to wind this round to where I set out.——

I begin the chapter over again.

CHAPTER 34

I TOLD the Christian reader in the beginning of the chapter which preceded my uncle Toby's apologetical oration,—though in a different trope from what I should make use of now, That the peace of Utrecht was within an ace of creating the same shyness betwixt my uncle Toby and his hobbyhorse, as it did betwixt the queen and the rest of the confederating powers.

There is an indignant way in which a man sometimes dismounts his horse, which as good as says to him, "I'll go afoot, Sir, all the days of my life, before I would ride a single mile upon your back again." Now my uncle Toby could not be said to dismount his horse in this manner; for in strictness of language, he could not be said to dismount his horse at all—his horse rather flung him—and somewhat viciously, which made my uncle Toby take it ten times more unkindly. Let this matter be settled by statejockeys as they like.——It created, I say, a sort of shyness betwixt my uncle Toby and his hobby-horse.——He had no occasion for him from the month of March to November, which was the summer after the articles were signed, except it was now and then to take a short ride out, just to see that the fortifications and harbour of Dunkirk were demolished, according to stipulation.

The French were so backwards all that summer in setting about that affair, and Monsieur Tugghe, the Deputy from the magistrates of Dunkirk, presented so many affecting petitions to the queen,—beseeching her majesty to cause only her thunder-bolts to fall upon the martial works, which might have incurred her displeasure,—but to spare—to spare the mole, for the mole's sake; which, in its naked situation, could be no more than an object of pity—and the queen (who was but a woman) being of a pitiful disposition,—and her ministers also, they not wishing in their hearts to have the town dismantled, for these private reasons, * * * * * * * * * * * * * * * * * * *____

* ; so that the whole went heavily on with my uncle Toby; insomuch, that it was not within three full months, after he and the corporal had constructed the town, and put it in a condition to be destroyed, that the several commandants, commissaries, deputies, negotiators, and intendants, would permit him to set about it.——Fatal interval of inactivity!

The corporal was for beginning the demolition, by making a breach in the ramparts, or main fortifications of the town—No,—that will never do, corporal, said my uncle Toby, for in going that way to work with the town, the English garrison will not be safe in it an hour; because if the French are treacherous—They are as treacherous as devils, an' please your honour, said the corporal—It gives me concern always when I hear it, Trim, said my uncle Toby,—for they don't want personal bravery; and if a breach is made in the ramparts, they may enter it, and make themselves masters of the place when they please:—Let them enter it, said the corporal, lifting up his pioneer's spade in both his hands, as if he was going to lay about him with it,—let them enter, an' please your honour, if they dare.—In cases like this, corporal, said my uncle Toby, slipping his right hand down to the middle of his cane, and holding it afterwards truncheon-wise with his forefinger extended,—'tis no part of the consideration of a commandant, what the enemy dare,—or what they dare not do; he must act with prudence. We will begin with the outworks both towards the sea and the land, and particularly with fort Louis, the most distant of them all, and demolish it first,—and the rest, one by one, both on our right and left, as we retreat towards the town;—then we'll demolish the mole,—next fill up the harbour,—then retire into the citadel, and blow it up into the air: and having done that, corporal, we'll embark for England.——We are there, quoth the corporal, recollecting himself—Very true, said my uncle Toby—looking at the church.

CHAPTER 35

A DELUSIVE, delicious consultation or two of this kind, betwixt my uncle Toby and Trim, upon the demolition of Dunkirk,—for a moment rallied back the ideas of those pleasures, which were slipping from under him:—still—still all went on heavily—the magic left the mind the weaker—Stillness, with Silence at her back, entered the solitary parlour, and drew their gauzy mantle over my uncle Toby's head;—and Listlessness, with her lax fibre and undirected eye, sat quietly down beside him in his arm-chair.—No longer Amberg and Rhinberg, and Limbourg, and Huy, and Bonn, in one year,—and the prospect of Landen, and Trerebach, and Drusen, and Dendermond, the next,—hurried on the blood:—No longer did saps, and mines, and blinds, and gabions, and palisadoes, keep out this fair enemy of man's repose:—No more could my uncle Toby, after passing the French lines, as he eat his egg at supper, from thence break into the heart of France,—cross over the Oyes, and with all Picardie open behind him, march up to the gates of Paris, and fall asleep with nothing but ideas of glory:—No more was he to dream, he had fixed the royal standard upon the tower of the Bastile, and awake with it streaming in his head.

——Softer visions,—gentler vibrations stole sweetly in upon his slumbers;—the trumpet of war fell out of his hands,—he took up the lute, sweet instrument! of all others the most delicate! the most difficult!—how wilt thou touch it, my dear uncle Toby?

CHAPTER 36

Now, because I have once or twice said, in my inconsiderate way of talking, That I was confident the following memoirs of my uncle Toby's courtship of widow Wadman, whenever I got time to write them, would turn out one of the most complete systems, both of the elementary and practical part of love and love-making, that ever was addressed to the world—are you to imagine from thence, that I shall set out with a description of what love is? whether part God and part Devil, as Plotinus will have it——

——Or by a more critical equation, and supposing the whole of love to be as ten—to determine with Ficinus, "How many parts of it—the one,—and how many the other";—or whether it is all of it one great Devil, from head to tail, as Plato has taken upon him to pronounce; concerning which conceit of his, I shall not offer my opinion:—but my opinion of Plato is this; that he appears, from this instance, to have been a man of much the same temper and way of reasoning with doctor Baynyard, who being a great enemy to blisters, as imagining that half a dozen of 'em at once, would draw a man as surely to his grave, as a hearse and six—rashly concluded, that the Devil himself was nothing in the world, but one great bouncing Cantharidis.——

I have nothing to say to people who allow themselves this monstrous liberty in arguing, but what Nazianzen cried out (that is, polemically) to Philagrius——

"'Ευγε!" O rare! 'tis fine reasoning, Sir, indeed!——" ὅτι φιλοσοφεῖς ἐν Πάθεσι"—and most nobly do you aim at truth, when you philosophize about it in your moods and passions.

Nor is it to be imagined, for the same reason, I should stop to inquire, whether love is a disease,—or embroil myself with Rhasis and Dioscorides, whether the seat of it is in the brain or liver;—because this would lead me on, to an examination of the two very opposite manners in which patients have been treated—the one, of Aaetius, who always began with a cooling clyster of hempseed and bruised cucumbers;—and followed on with thin potations of water-lilies and purslane—to which he added a pinch of snuff, of the herb Hanea;—and where Aaetius durst venture it,—his topaz-ring.

——The other, that of Gordonius, who (in his cap. 15. *de Amore*) directs they should be thrashed, *"ad putorem usque,"*—till they stink again.

These are disquisitions, which my father, who had laid in a great stock of knowledge of this kind, will be very busy with in the progress of my uncle Toby's affairs: I must anticipate thus much, That from his theories of love, (with which, by the way, he contrived to crucify my uncle Toby's mind, al-most as much as his amours themselves)—he took a single step into prac-tice;—and by means of a camphorated cerecloth, which he found means to impose upon the tailor for buckram, whilst he was making my uncle Toby a new pair of breeches, he produced Gordonius's effect upon my uncle Toby without the disgrace.

What changes this produced, will be read in its proper place: all that is needful to be added to the anecdote, is this—That whatever effect it had upon my uncle Toby,—it had a vile effect upon the house;—and if my uncle Toby had not smoked it down as he did, it might have had a vile effect upon my father too.

CHAPTER 37

——'TWILL come out of itself by and bye.——All I contend for is, that I am not obliged to set out with a definition of what love is; and so long as I can go on with my story intelligibly, with the help of the word itself, with-out any other idea to it, than what I have in common with the rest of the world, why should I differ from it a moment before the time?——When I can get on no further,—and find myself entangled on all sides of this mystic labyrinth,—my Opinion will then come in, in course,—and lead me out.

At present, I hope I shall be sufficiently understood, in telling the reader, my uncle Toby fell in love:

——Not that the phrase is at all to my liking: for to say a man is fallen in love,—or that he is deeply in love,—or up to the ears in love,—and some-times even over head and ears in it,—carries an idiomatical kind of im-plication, that love is a thing below a man:—this is recurring again to Plato's opinion, which, with all his divinityship,—I hold to be damnable and heretical:—and so much for that.

Let love therefore be what it will,—my uncle Toby fell into it.

——And possibly, gentle reader, with such a temptation—so wouldst thou: For never did thy eyes behold, or thy concupiscence covet any thing in this world, more concupiscible than widow Wadman.

CHAPTER 38

To conceive this right,—call for pen and ink—here's paper ready to your hand.——Sit down, Sir, paint her to your own mind—as like your mistress as you can—as unlike your wife as your conscience will let you—'tis all one to me—please but your own fancy in it.

——Was ever anything in Nature so sweet!—so exquisite!

——Then, dear Sir, how could my uncle Toby resist it?

Thrice happy book! thou wilt have one page, at least, within thy covers, which Malice will not blacken, and which Ignorance cannot misrepresent.

CHAPTER 39

As Susannah was informed by an express from Mrs. Bridget, of my uncle Toby's falling in love with her mistress fifteen days before it happened,—the contents of which express, Susannah communicated to my mother the next day,—it has just given me an opportunity of entering upon my uncle Toby's amours a fortnight before their existence.

I have an article of news to tell you, Mr. Shandy, quoth my mother, which will surprise you greatly.——

Now my father was then holding one of his second beds of justice, and was musing within himself about the hardships of matrimony, as my mother broke silence.——

"——My brother Toby, quoth she, is going to be married to Mrs. Wadman."

——Then he will never, quoth my father, be able to lie diagonally in his bed again as long as he lives.

It was a consuming vexation to my father, that my mother never asked the meaning of a thing she did not understand.

——That she is not a woman of science, my father would say—is her misfortune—but she might ask a question.——

My mother never did.—In short, she went out of the world at last without knowing whether it turned round, or stood still.——My father had officiously told her above a thousand times which way it was,—but she always forgot.

For these reasons, a discourse seldom went on much further betwixt them, than a proposition,—a reply, and a rejoinder; at the end of which, it generally took breath for a few minutes (as in the affair of the breeches), and then went on again.

If he marries, 'twill be the worse for us,—quoth my mother.

Not a cherry-stone, said my father,—he may as well batter away his means upon that, as any thing else.

——To be sure, said my mother: so here ended the proposition,—the reply,—and the rejoinder, I told you of.

It will be some amusement to him, too,—said my father.

A very great one, answered my mother, if he should have children.——

——Lord have mercy upon me,—said my father to himself— * * *
* *
* * * * * * * * * * * * * * *

CHAPTER 40

I AM now beginning to get fairly into my work; and by the help of a vege-
table diet, with a few of the cold seeds, I make no doubt but I shall be
able to go on with my uncle Toby's story, and my own, in a tolerable
straight line. Now,

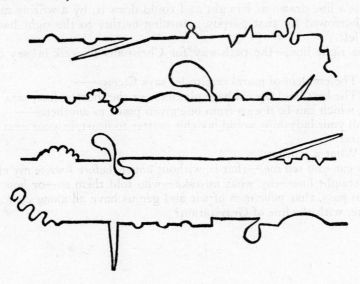

These were the four lines I moved in through my first, second, third
and fourth volumes.——In the fifth volume I have been very good,—the
precise line I have described in it being this:

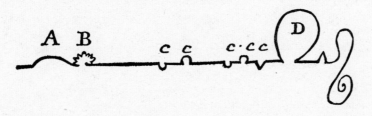

By which it appears, that except at the curve, marked A, where I took
a trip to Navarre,—and the indented curve B, which is the short airing
when I was there with the Lady Baussiere and her page,—I have not
taken the least frisk of a digression, till John de la Casse's devils led me
the round you see marked D.——for as for *c c c c* they are nothing but
parentheses, and the common ins and outs incident to the lives of the
greatest ministers of state; and when compared with what men have done,
—or with my own transgressions at the letters A B D—they vanish into
nothing.

In this last volume I have done better still—for from the end of Le Fever's episode, to the beginning of my uncle Toby's campaigns,—I have scarce stepped a yard out of my way.

If I mend at this rate, it is not impossible—by the good leave of his grace of Benevento's devils—but I may arrive hereafter at the excellency of going on even thus:

———————————————

which is a line drawn as straight as I could draw it, by a writing-master's ruler (borrowed for that purpose), turning neither to the right hand nor to the left.

This right line,—the path-way for Christians to walk in! say divines

——The emblem of moral rectitude! says Cicero——

——The best line! say cabbage planters—is the shortest line, says Archimedes, which can be drawn from one given point to another.——

I wish your ladyships would lay this matter to heart, in your next birth-day suits!

——What a journey!

Pray can you tell me,—that is, without anger, before I write my chapter upon straight lines—by what mistake—who told them so—or how it has come to pass, that your men of wit and genius have all along confounded this line, with the line of Gravitation?

BOOK VII

N<small>O</small>—I think, I said, I would write two volumes every year, provided the vile cough which then tormented me, and which to this hour I dread worse than the devil, would but give me leave—and in another place—(but where, I can't recollect now) speaking of my book as a machine, and laying my pen and ruler down cross-wise upon the table, in order to gain the greater credit to it—I swore it should be kept agoing at that rate these forty years, if it pleased but the fountain of life to bless me so long with health and good spirits.

Now as for my spirits, little have I to lay to their charge—nay so very little (unless the mounting me upon a long stick and playing the fool with me nineteen hours out of the twenty-four, be accusations) that on the contrary, I have much—much to thank 'em for: cheerily have ye made me tread the path of life with all the burthens of it (except its cares) upon my back; in no one moment of my existence, that I remember, have ye once deserted me, or tinged the objects which came in my way, either with sable, or with a sickly green; in dangers ye gilded my horizon with hope, and when Death himself knocked at my door—ye bad him come again; and in so gay a tone of careless indifference did ye do it, that he doubted of his commission——

"——There must certainly be some mistake in this matter," quoth he.

Now there is nothing in this world I abominate worse, than to be interrupted in a story—and I was that moment telling Eugenius a most tawdry one in my way, of a nun who fancied herself a shell-fish, and of a monk damned for eating a mussel, and was shewing him the grounds and justice of the procedure—

"——Did ever so grave a personage get into so vile a scrape?" quoth Death. Thou hast had a narrow escape, Tristram, said Eugenius, taking hold of my hand as I finished my story——

But there is no living, Eugenius, replied I, at this rate; for as this son of a whore has found out my lodgings——

——You call him rightly, said Eugenius,—for by sin, we are told, he entered the world—I care not which way he entered, quoth I, provided he be not in such a hurry to take me out with him—for I have forty volumes to write, and forty thousand things to say and do which no body in the world will say and do for me, except thyself; and as thou seest he has got me by the throat (for Eugenius could scarce hear me speak across the table), and that I am no match for him in the open field, had I not better, whilst these few scattered spirits remain, and these two spider legs of mine (holding one of them up to him) are able to support me—had I not better, Eugenius, fly for my life? 'Tis my advice, my dear Tristram, said Eugenius—Then by heaven! I will lead him a dance he little thinks of—for I will gallop, quoth I, without looking once behind me, to the banks of the Garonne; and if I hear him clattering at my heels—I'll scamper away to mount Vesuvius—from thence to Joppa, and from Joppa to the world's end; where, if he follows me, I pray God he may break his neck—

——He runs more risk, there, said Eugenius, than thou.

Eugenius's wit and affection brought blood into the cheek from whence it had been some months banished—'twas a vile moment to bid adieu in; he led me to my chaise—Allons! said I; the post-boy gave a crack with his whip—off I went like a cannon, and in half a dozen bounds got into Dover.

CHAPTER 2

Now hang it! quoth I, as I looked towards the French coast—a man should know something of his own country too, before he goes abroad—and I never gave a peep into Rochester church, or took notice of the dock of Chatham, or visited St. Thomas at Canterbury, though they all three laid in my way——

——But mine, indeed, is a particular case——

So without arguing the matter further with Thomas o' Becket, or any one else—I skipped into the boat, and in five minutes we got under sail, and scudded away like the wind.

Pray, captain, quoth I, as I was going down into the cabin, is a man never overtaken by Death in this passage?

Why, there is not time for a man to be sick in it, replied he—What a cursed liar! for I am sick as a horse, quoth I, already—what a brain! upside down!—hey-day! the cells are broke loose one into another, and the blood, and the lymph, and the nervous juices, with the fixed and volatile salts, are all jumbled into one mass—Good G—! every thing turns round in it like a thousand whirlpools—I'd give a shilling to know if I shan't write the clearer for it——

Sick! sick! sick! sick!——

——When shall we get to land? captain—they have hearts like stones—O I am deadly sick!—reach me that thing, boy—'tis the most discomfiting sickness—I wish I was at the bottom—Madam! how is it with you? Undone! undone! un—O! undone! sir—What the first time?—No, 'tis the second, third, sixth, tenth time, sir,—hey-day!—what a trampling over head!—hollo! cabin boy! what's the matter?——

The wind chopped about! s'death!—then I shall meet him full in the face.

What luck!—'tis chopped about again, master—O the devil chop it——

Captain, quoth she, for heaven's sake, let us get ashore.

CHAPTER 3

IT is a great inconvenience to a man in a haste, that there are three distinct roads between Calais and Paris, in behalf of which there is so much to be said by the several deputies from the towns which lie along them, that half a day is easily lost in settling which you'll take.

First, the road by Lisle and Arras, which is the most about—but most interesting, and instructing.

The second, that by Amiens, which you may go, if you would see Chantilly——

And that by Beauvais, which you may go, if you will.

For this reason a great many choose to go by Beauvais.

CHAPTER 4

"Now before I quit Calais," a travel-writer would say, "it would not be amiss to give some account of it."——Now I think it very much amiss— that a man cannot go quietly through a town and let it alone, when it does not meddle with him, but that he must be turning about and drawing his pen at every kennel he crosses over, merely o' my conscience for the sake of drawing it; because, if we may judge from what has been wrote of these things, by all who have wrote and galloped—or who have galloped and wrote, which is a different way still; or who, for more expedition than the rest, have wrote galloping, which is the way I do at present—from the great Addison, who did it with his satchel of school books hanging at his a—, and galling his beast's crupper at every stroke—there is not a galloper of us all who might not have gone on ambling quietly in his own ground (in case he had any), and have wrote all he had to write, dryshod, as well as not.

For my own part, as heaven is my judge, and to which I shall ever make my last appeal—I know no more of Calais (except the little my barber told me of it as he was whetting his razor), than I do this moment of Grand Cairo; for it was dusky in the evening when I landed, and dark as pitch in the morning when I set out, and yet by merely knowing what is what, and by drawing this from that in one part of the town, and by spelling and putting this and that together in another—I would lay any travelling odds, that I this moment write a chapter upon Calais as long as my arm; and with so distinct and satisfactory a detail in every item, which is worth a stranger's curiosity in the town—that you would take me for the town-clerk of Calais itself—and where, sir, would be the wonder? was not Democritus, who laughed ten times more than I—town-clerk of Abdera? and was not (I forget his name) who had more discretion than us both, town-clerk of Ephesus?—it should be penned moreover, sir, with so much knowledge and good sense, and truth, and precision——

——Nay—if you don't believe me, you may read the chapter for your pains.

CHAPTER 5

CALAIS, *Calatium, Calusium, Calesium.*

This town, if we may trust its archives, the authority of which I see no reason to call in question in this place—was once no more than a small village belonging to one of the first Counts de Guignes; and as it boasts at present of no less than fourteen thousand inhabitants, exclusive of four hundred and twenty distinct families in the *basse ville*, or suburbs—it must have grown up by little and little, I suppose, to its present size.

Though there are four convents, there is but one parochial church in the whole town; I had not an opportunity of taking its exact dimensions, but it is pretty easy to make a tolerable conjecture of 'em—for as there are fourteen thousand inhabitants in the town, if the church holds them all it must be considerably large—and if it will not—'tis a very great pity they have not another—it is built in form of a cross, and dedicated to the Virgin Mary; the steeple, which has a spire to it, is placed in the middle of the church, and stands upon four pillars elegant and light enough, but sufficiently strong at the same time—it is decorated with eleven altars, most of which are rather fine than beautiful. The great altar is a masterpiece in its kind; 'tis of white marble, and, as I was told, near sixty feet high—had it been much higher, it had been as high as mount Calvary itself—therefore, I suppose it must be high enough in all conscience.

There was nothing struck me more than the great Square; tho' I cannot say 'tis either well paved or well built; but 'tis in the heart of the town, and most of the streets, especially those in that quarter, all terminate in it; could there have been a fountain in all Calais, which it seems there cannot, as such an object would have been a great ornament, it is not to be doubted, but that the inhabitants would have had it in the very centre of this square, —not that it is properly a square,—because 'tis forty feet longer from east to west, than from north to south; so that the French in general have more reason on their side in calling them Places than Squares, which, strictly speaking, to be sure, they are not.

The town-house seems to be but a sorry building, and not to be kept in the best repair; otherwise it had been a second great ornament to this place; it answers however its destination, and serves very well for the reception of the magistrates, who assemble in it from time to time; so that 'tis presumable, justice is regularly distributed.

I have heard much of it, but there is nothing at all curious in the Courgain; 'tis a distinct quarter of the town, inhabited solely by sailors and fishermen; it consists of a number of small streets, neatly built and mostly of brick; 'tis extremely populous, but as that may be accounted for, from the principles of their diet,—there is nothing curious in that neither.——A traveller may see it to satisfy himself—he must not omit however taking notice of La Tour de Guet, upon any account; 'tis so called from its particular destination, because in war it serves to discover and give notice of the enemies which approach the place, either by sea or land;—but 'tis monstrous high, and catches the eye so continually, you cannot avoid taking notice of it if you would.

It was a singular disappointment to me, that I could not have permission to take an exact survey of the fortifications, which are the strongest in the world, and which, from first to last, that is, from the time they were set about by Philip of France, Count of Boulogne, to the present war, wherein many reparations were made, have cost (as I learned afterwards from an engineer in Gascony)—above a hundred millions of livres. It is very remarkable, that at the Tête de Gravelenes, and where the town is naturally the weakest, they have expended the most money; so that the outworks stretch a great way into the campaign, and consequently occupy a large

tract of ground—However, after all that is said and done, it must be acknowledged that Calais was never upon any account so considerable from
itself, as from its situation, and that easy entrance which it gave our ancestors, upon all occasions, into France: it was not without its inconveniences also; being no less troublesome to the English in those times, than
Dunkirk has been to us, in ours; so that it was deservedly looked upon as
the key to both kingdoms, which no doubt is the reason that there have
arisen so many contentions who should keep it: of these, the siege of Calais,
or rather the blockade (for it was shut up both by land and sea), was the
most memorable, as it withstood the efforts of Edward the Third a whole
year, and was not terminated at last but by famine and extreme misery; the
gallantry of Eustace de St. Pierre, who first offered himself a victim for his
fellow-citizens, has ranked his name with heroes. As it will not take up
above fifty pages, it would be injustice to the reader, not to give him a
minute account of that romantic transaction, as well as of the siege itself, in
Rapin's own words:

Chapter 6

——But courage! gentle reader!—I scorn it—'tis enough to have thee in
my power—but to make use of the advantage which the fortune of the pen
has now gained over thee, would be too much—No—! by that all-powerful
fire which warms the visionary brain, and lights the spirits through un-
worldly tracts! ere I would force a helpless creature upon this hard service,
and make thee pay, poor soul! for fifty pages, which I have no right to sell
thee,—naked as I am, I would browse upon the mountains, and smile that
the north wind brought me neither my tent or my supper.

——So put on, my brave boy! and make the best of thy way to Boulogne.

Chapter 7

——Boulogne!—hah!—so we are all got together—debtors and sinners
before heaven; a jolly set of us—but I can't stay and quaff it off with you—
I'm pursued myself like a hundred devils, and shall be overtaken, before I
can well change horses:—for heaven's sake, make haste—'Tis for high
treason, quoth a very little man, whispering as low as he could to a very tall
man, that stood next him—Or else for murder; quoth the tall man—Well
thrown, Size-ace! quoth I. No, quoth a third, the gentleman has been committing————.

Ah! ma chère fille! said I, as she tripped by from her matins—you look as
rosy as the morning (for the sun was rising, and it made the compliment the
more gracious)—No; it can't be that, quoth a fourth—(she made a curt'sy
to me—I kissed my hand) 'tis debt, continued he: 'Tis certainly for debt;
quoth a fifth; I would not pay that gentleman's debts, quoth Ace, for a
thousand pounds; nor would I, quoth Size, for six times the sum—Well
thrown, Size-ace, again! quoth I;—but I have no debt but the debt of
Nature, and I want but patience of her, and I will pay her every farthing I
owe her—How can you be so hard-hearted, Madam, to arrest a poor traveller going along without molestation to any one upon his lawful occasions?

do stop that death-looking, long-striding scoundrel of a scare-sinner, who is posting after me—he never would have followed me but for you—if it be but for a stage or two, just to give me start of him, I beseech you, madam—do, dear lady——

——Now, in troth, 'tis a great pity, quoth mine Irish host, that all this good courtship should be lost; for the young gentlewoman has been after going out of hearing of it all along.—

——Simpleton! quoth I.

——So you have nothing else in Boulogne worth seeing?

By Jasus! there is the finest Seminary for the Humanities——

——There cannot be a finer, quoth I.

Chapter 8

When the precipitancy of a man's wishes hurries on his ideas ninety times faster than the vehicle he rides in—woe be to truth! and woe be to the vehicle and its tackling (let 'em be made of what stuff you will) upon which he breathes forth the disappointment of his soul!

As I never give general characters either of men or things in choler, "the most haste the worst speed," was all the reflection I made upon the affair, the first time it happened;—the second, third, fourth, and fifth time, I confined it respectively to those times, and accordingly blamed only the second, third, fourth, and fifth post-boy for it, without carrying my reflections further; but the event continuing to befall me from the fifth, to the sixth, seventh, eighth, ninth, and tenth time, and without one exception, I then could not avoid making a national reflection of it, which I do in these words;

That something is always wrong in a French post-chaise, upon first setting out.

Or the proposition may stand thus:

A French postillion has always to alight before he has got three hundred yards out of town.

What's wrong now?—Diable!—a rope's broke!—a knot has slipt!—a staple's drawn!—a bolt's to whittle!—a tag, a rag, a jag, a strap, a buckle, or a buckle's tongue, want altering.

Now true as all this is, I never think myself impowered to excommunicate thereupon either the post-chaise, or its driver—nor do I take it into my head to swear by the living G—, I would rather go a-foot ten thousand times—or that I will be damned, if ever I get into another—but I take the matter coolly before me, and consider, that some tag, or rag, or jag, or bolt, or buckle, or buckle's tongue, will ever be awanting, or want altering, travel where I will—so I never chafe, but take the good and the bad as they fall in my road, and get on:—Do so, my lad! said I; he had lost five minutes already, in alighting in order to get a luncheon of black bread, which he had crammed into the chaise-pocket, and was remounted, and going leisurely on, to relish it the better—Get on, my lad, said I, briskly—but in the most persuasive tone imaginable, for I jingled a four-and-twenty sous piece against the glass, taking care to hold the flat side towards him, as he looked back: the dog grinned intelligence from his right ear to his left, and behind

his sooty muzzle discovered such a pearly row of teeth, that Sovereignty
would have pawned her jewels for them.——

Just heaven! { What masticators!——

{ What bread!——

and so as he finished the last mouthful of it, we entered the town of Montreuil.

CHAPTER 9

THERE is not a town in all France, which, in my opinion, looks better in the
map, than Montreuil;—I own, it does not look so well in the book of post-
roads; but when you come to see it—to be sure it looks most pitifully.

There is one thing, however, in it at present very handsome; and that is,
the inn-keeper's daughter: She has been eighteen months at Amiens, and
six at Paris, in going through her classes; so knits, and sews, and dances,
and does the little coquetries very well.——

——A slut! in running them over within these five minutes that I have
stood looking at her, she has let fall at least a dozen loops in a white thread
stocking—yes, yes—I see, you cunning gipsy!—'tis long and taper—you
need not pin it to your knee—and that 'tis your own—and fits you exactly.——

——That Nature should have told this creature a word about a statue's
thumb!

——But as this sample is worth all their thumbs—besides, I have
her thumbs and fingers in at the bargain, if they can be any guide to me,
—and as Janatone withal (for that is her name) stands so well for a
drawing—may I never draw more, or rather may I draw like a draught-
horse, by main strength all the days of my life,—if I do not draw her in all
her proportions, and with as determined a pencil, as if I had her in the
wettest drapery.——

——But your worships choose rather that I give you the length, breadth,
and perpendicular height of the great parish-church, or drawing of the
façade of the abbey of Saint Austreberte which has been transported from
Artois hither—every thing is just I suppose as the masons and carpenters
left them,—and if the belief in Christ continues so long, will be so these fifty
years to come—so your worships and reverences may all measure them at
your leisures—but he who measures thee, Janatone, must do it now—thou
carriest the principles of change within thy frame; and considering the
chances of a transitory life, I would not answer for thee a moment; ere
twice twelve months are passed and gone, thou mayest grow out like a
pumpkin, and lose thy shapes—or thou mayest go off like a flower, and lose
thy beauty—nay, thou mayest go off like a hussy—and lose thyself.—I
would not answer for my aunt Dinah, was she alive—'faith, scarce for her
picture—were it but painted by Reynolds—

But if I go on with my drawing, after naming that son of Apollo, I'll be
shot—

So you must e'en be content with the original; which, if the evening is
fine in passing thro' Montreuil, you will see at your chaise-door, as you
change horses: but unless you have as bad a reason for haste as I have—you

had better stop:—She has a little of the *dévote:* but that, sir, is a terce to a nine in your favour—

—L——help me! I could not count a single point: so had been piqued and repiqued, and capotted to the devil.

CHAPTER 10

ALL which being considered, and that Death moreover might be much nearer me than I imagined—I wish I was at Abbeville, quoth I, were it only to see how they card and spin—so off we set.

[1]*de Montreuil à Nampont - poste et demi*
de Nampont à Bernay - - - poste
de Bernay à Nouvion - - - poste
de Nouvion à Abbeville - - poste
—but the carders and spinners were all gone to bed.

CHAPTER 11

WHAT a vast advantage is travelling! only it heats one; but there is a remedy for that, which you will pick out of the next chapter.

CHAPTER 12

WAS I in a condition to stipulate with Death, as I am this moment with my apothecary, how and where I will take his clyster—I should certainly declare against submitting to it before my friends; and therefore I never seriously think upon the mode and manner of this great catastrophe, which generally takes up and torments my thoughts as much as the catastrophe itself; but I constantly draw the curtain across it with this wish, that the Disposer of all things may so order it, that it happen not to me in my own house—but rather in some decent inn—at home, I know it,—the concern of my friends, and the last services of wiping my brows, and smoothing my pillow, which the quivering hand of pale affection shall pay me, will so crucify my soul, that I shall die of a distemper which my physician is not aware of: but in an inn, the few cold offices I wanted, would be purchased with a few guineas, and paid me with an undisturbed, but punctual attention—but mark. This inn should not be the inn at Abbeville—if there was not another inn in the universe, I would strike that inn out of the capitulations: so

Let the horses be in the chaise exactly by four in the morning—Yes, by four, Sir,—or by Genevieve! I'll raise a clatter in the house shall wake the dead.

CHAPTER 13

"MAKE them like unto a wheel," is a bitter sarcasm, as all the learned know, against the grand tour, and that restless spirit for making it, which David prophetically foresaw would haunt the children of men in the latter days;

[1]*Vid.* Book of French post roads, page 36, edition of 1762.

and therefore, as thinketh the great bishop Hall, 'tis one of the severest imprecations which David ever uttered against the enemies of the Lord—and, as if he had said, "I wish them no worse luck than always to be rolling about"—So much motion, continues he (for he was very corpulent)—is so much unquietness; and so much of rest, by the same analogy, is so much of heaven.

Now, I (being very thin) think differently; and that so much of motion, is so much of life, and so much of joy—and that to stand still, or get on but slowly, is death and the devil——

Hollo! Ho!—the whole world's asleep!—bring out the horses—grease the wheels—tie on the mail—and drive a nail into that moulding—I'll not lose a moment—

Now the wheel we are talking of, and whereinto (but not whereonto, for that would make an Ixion's wheel of it) he curseth his enemies, according to the bishop's habit of body, should certainly be a post-chaise wheel, whether they were set up in Palestine at that time or not—and my wheel, for the contrary reasons, must as certainly be a cart-wheel groaning round its revolution once in an age; and of which sort, were I to turn commentator, I should make no scruple to affirm, they had great store in that hilly country.

I love the Pythagoreans (much more than ever I dare tell my dear Jenny) for their "χωρισμὸν ἀπὸ τοῦ Σώματος, εἰς τὸ καλῶς φιλοσοφεῖν"—[their] "getting out of the body, in order to think well." No man thinks right, whilst he is in it; blinded as he must be, with his congenial humours, and drawn differently aside, as the bishop and myself have been, with too lax or too tense a fibre—Reason is, half of it, Sense; and the measure of heaven itself is but the measure of our present appetites and concoctions——

——But which of the two, in the present case, do you think to be mostly in the wrong?

You, certainly: quoth she, to disturb a whole family so early.

CHAPTER 14

——But she did not know I was under a vow not to shave my beard till I got to Paris;—yet I hate to make mysteries of nothing;—'tis the cold cautiousness of one of those little souls from which Lessius (*lib.* 13, *de moribus divinis, cap.* 24) hath made his estimate, wherein he setteth forth, That one Dutch mile, cubically multiplied, will allow room enough, and to spare, for eight hundred thousand millions, which he supposes to be as great a number of souls (counting from the fall of Adam) as can possibly be damned to the end of the world.

From what he has made this second estimate—unless from the parental goodness of God—I don't know—I am much more at a loss what could be in Franciscus Ribbera's head, who pretends that no less a space than one of two hundred Italian miles multiplied into itself, will be sufficient to hold the like number—he certainly must have gone upon some of the old Roman souls, of which he had read, without reflecting how much, by a gradual and most tabid decline, in the course of eighteen hundred years, they must unavoidably have shrunk so as to have come, when he wrote, almost to nothing.

In Lessius's time, who seems the cooler man, they were as little as can be imagined——

——We find them less now——

And next winter we shall find them less again; so that if we go on from little to less, and from less to nothing, I hesitate not one moment to affirm, that in half a century, at this rate, we shall have no souls at all; which being the period beyond which I doubt likewise of the existence of the Christian faith, 'twill be one advantage that both of 'em will be exactly worn out together.

Blessed Jupiter! and blessed every other heathen god and goddess! for now ye will all come into play again, and with Priapus at your tails—what jovial times!—but where am I? and into what a delicious riot of things am I rushing? I—I who must be cut short in the midst of my days, and taste no more of 'em than what I borrow from my imagination—peace to thee, generous fool! and let me go on.

CHAPTER 15

——"So hating, I say, to make mysteries of nothing"—I intrusted it with the post-boy, as soon as ever I got off the stone; he gave a crack with his whip to balance the compliment; and with the thill-horse trotting, and a sort of an up and a down of the other, we danced it along to Ailly-au-clochers, famed in days of yore for the finest chimes in the world; but we danced through it without music—the chimes being greatly out of order—(as in truth they were through all France).

And so making all possible speed, from

Ailly-au-clochers, I got to Hixcourt,

from Hixcourt, I got to Pequignay, and

from Pequignay, I got to Amiens,

concerning which town I have nothing to inform you, but what I have informed you once before—and that was—that Janatone went there to school.

CHAPTER 16

IN the whole catalogue of those whiffling vexations which come puffing across a man's canvas, there is not one of a more teasing and tormenting nature, than this particular one which I am going to describe—and for which (unless you travel with an avance-courier, which numbers do in order to prevent it)—there is no help: and it is this.

That be you in never so kindly a propensity to sleep—tho' you are passing perhaps through the finest country—upon the best roads, and in the easiest carriage for doing it in the world—nay, was you sure you could sleep fifty miles straight forwards, without once opening your eyes—nay, what is more, was you as demonstratively satisfied as you can be of any truth in Euclid, that you should upon all accounts be full as well asleep as awake—nay, perhaps better—Yet the incessant returns of paying for the horses at every stage,—with the necessity thereupon of putting your hand into your pocket, and counting out from thence three livres fifteen sous

(sous by sous), puts an end to so much of the project, that you cannot execute above six miles of it (or supposing it is a post and a half, that is but nine)—were it to save your soul from destruction.

————I'll be even with 'em, quoth I, for I'll put the precise sum into a piece of paper, and hold it ready in my hand all the way: "Now I shall have nothing to do," said I (composing myself to rest), "but to drop this gently into the post-boy's hat and not say a word."————Then there wants two sous more to drink—or there is a twelve sous piece of Louis XIV. which will not pass—or a livre and some odd liards to be brought over from the last stage, which Monsieur had forgot; which altercations (as a man cannot dispute very well asleep) rouse him: still is sweet sleep retrievable; and still might the flesh weigh down the spirit, and recover itself of these blows—but then, by heaven! you have paid but for a single post—whereas 'tis a post and a half; and this obliges you to pull out your book of post-roads, the print of which is so very small, it forces you to open your eyes, whether you will or no: Then Monsieur le Curé offers you a pinch of snuff—or a poor soldier shews you his leg—or a shaveling his box—or the priestess of the cistern will water your wheels—they do not want it—but she swears by her priesthood (throwing it back) that they do:—then you have all these points to argue, or consider over in your mind; in doing of which, the rational powers get so thoroughly awakened—you may get 'em to sleep again as you can.

It was entirely owing to one of these misfortunes, or I had passed clean by the stables of Chantilly————

————But the postillion first affirming, and then persisting in it to my face, that there was no mark upon the two sous piece, I opened my eyes to be convinced—and seeing the mark upon it, as plain as my nose—I leaped out of the chaise in a passion, and so saw every thing at Chantilly in spite.————I tried it but for three posts and a half, but believe 'tis the best principle in the world to travel speedily upon; for as few objects look very inviting in that mood—you have little or nothing to stop you; by which means it was that I passed through St. Denis, without turning my head so much as on one side towards the Abbey————

————Richness of their treasury! stuff and nonsense!—bating their jewels, which are all false, I would not give three sous for any one thing in it, but Jaidas's lantern—nor for that either, only as it grows dark, it might be of use.

Chapter 17

CRACK, crack—crack, crack—crack, crack—so this is Paris! quoth I (continuing in the same mood)—and this is Paris!—humph!—Paris! cried I, repeating the name the third time————

The first, the finest, the most brilliant—

The streets however are nasty.

But it looks, I suppose, better than it smells—crack, crack—crack, crack —what a fuss thou makest!—as if it concerned the good people to be informed, that a man with pale face and clad in black, had the honour to be driven into Paris at nine o'clock at night, by a postillion in a tawny yellow jerkin, turned up with red calamanco—crack, crack—crack, crack—crack, crack,—I wish thy whip—

——But 'tis the spirit of thy nation; so crack—crack on.

Ha!—and no one gives the wall!—but in the School of Urbanity herself, if the walls are besh-t—how can you do otherwise?

And prithee when do they light the lamps? What?—never in the summer months!—Ho! 'tis the time of salads.——O rare! salad and soup—soup and salad—salad and soup, *encore*——

——'Tis too much for sinners.

Now I cannot bear the barbarity of it; how can that unconscionable coachman talk so much bawdy to that lean horse? don't you see, friend, the streets are so villainously narrow, that there is not room in all Paris to turn a wheel-barrow? In the grandest city of the whole world, it would not have been amiss, if they had been left a thought wider; nay, were it only so much in every single street, as that a man might know (was it only for satisfaction) on which side of it he was walking.

One—two—three—four—five—six—seven—eight—nine—ten.—Ten cook's shops! and twice the number of barbers! and all within three minutes' driving! one would think that all the cooks in the world, on some great merry-meeting with the barbers, by joint consent had said—Come, let us all go live at Paris: the French love good eating—they are all gourmands— —we shall rank high; if their God is their belly—their cooks must be gentlemen: and forasmuch as the periwig maketh the man, and the periwig-maker maketh the periwig—ergo, would the barbers say, we shall rank higher still —we shall be above you all—we shall be [1]Capitouls at least—*pardi!* we shall all wear swords——

——And so, one would swear (that is, by candle light,—but there is no depending upon it) they continue to do, to this day.

Chapter 18

The French are certainly misunderstood:—but whether the fault is theirs, in not sufficiently explaining themselves, or speaking with that exact limitation and precision which one would expect on a point of such importance, and which, moreover, is so likely to be contested by us—or whether the fault may not be altogether on our side, in not understanding their language always so critically as to know "what they would be at"—I shall not decide; but 'tis evident to me, when they affirm, "That they who have seen Paris, have seen every thing," they must mean to speak of those who have seen it by day-light.

As for candle-light—I give it up—I have said before, there was no depending upon it—and I repeat it again; but not because the lights and shades are too sharp—or the tints confounded—or that there is neither beauty or keeping, etc. . . . for that's not truth—but it is an uncertain light in this respect, that in all the five hundred Hôtels, which they number up to you in Paris—and the five hundred good things, at a modest computation (for 'tis only allowing one good thing to a Hôtel), which by candle-light are

[1]Chief Magistrate in Toulouse, etc.

best to be seen, felt, heard, and understood (which, by the bye, is a quotation from Lilly)—the devil a one of us out of fifty, can get our heads fairly thrust in amongst them.

This is no part of the French computation: 'tis simply this,

That by the last survey taken in the year one thousand seven hundred and sixteen, since which time there have been considerable augmentations, Paris doth contain nine hundred streets; (viz.)

In the quarter called the City—there are fifty-three streets.

In St. James of the Shambles, fifty-five streets.

In St. Oportune, thirty-four streets.

In the quarter of the Louvre, twenty-five streets.

In the Palace Royal, or St. Honorius, forty-nine streets.

In Mont. Martyr, forty-one streets.

In St. Eustace, twenty-nine streets.

In the Halles, twenty-seven streets.

In St. Denis, fifty-five streets.

In St. Martin, fifty-four streets.

In St. Paul, or the Mortellerie, twenty-seven streets.

The Greve, thirty-eight streets.

In St. Avoy, or the Verrerie, nineteen streets.

In the Marais, or the Temple, fifty-two streets.

In St. Antony's, sixty-eight streets.

In the Place Maubert, eighty-one streets.

In St. Bennet, sixty streets.

In St. Andrews de Arcs, fifty-one streets.

In the quarter of the Luxembourg, sixty-two streets.

And in that of St. Germain, fifty-five streets, into any one of which you may walk; and that when you have seen them with all that belongs to them, fairly by daylight—their gates, their bridges, their squares, their statues - - - and have crusaded it moreover, through all their parish-churches, by no means omitting St. Roche and Sulpice - - - and to crown all, have taken a walk to the four palaces, which you may see, either with or without the statues and pictures, just as you choose—

——Then you will have seen—

——but, 'tis what no one needeth to tell you, for you will read of it yourself upon the portico of the Louvre, in these words,

[1]EARTH NO SUCH FOLKS!—NO FOLKS E'ER SUCH A TOWN AS PARIS IS! SING, DERRY, DERRY, DOWN.

The French have a gay way of treating every thing that is Great; and that is all can be said upon it.

CHAPTER 19

IN mentioning the word gay (as in the close of the last chapter) it puts one (*i.e.* an author) in mind of the word spleen—especially if he has any thing to say upon it: not that by any analysis—or that from any table of interest

---

[1]Non orbis gentem, non urbem gens habet ullam
————————————ulla parem.

or genealogy, there appears much more ground of alliance betwixt them, than betwixt light and darkness, or any two of the most unfriendly opposites in nature—only 'tis an undercraft of authors to keep up a good understanding amongst words, as politicians do amongst men—not knowing how near they may be under a necessity of placing them to each other—which point being now gained, and that I may place mine exactly to my mind, I write it down here—

SPLEEN.

This, upon leaving Chantilly, I declared to be the best principle in the world to travel speedily upon; but I gave it only as matter of opinion. I still continue in the same sentiments—only I had not then experience enough of its working to add this, that though you do get on at a tearing rate, yet you get on but uneasily to yourself at the same time; for which reason I here quit it entirely, and for ever, and 'tis heartily at any one's service—it has spoiled me the digestion of a good supper, and brought on a bilious diarrhoea, which has brought me back again to my first principle on which I set out—and with which I shall now scamper it away to the banks of the Garonne—

——No;—I cannot stop a moment to give you the character of the people —their genius—their manners—their customs—their laws—their religion— their government—their manufactures—their commerce—their finances, with all the resources and hidden springs which sustain them: qualified as I may be, by spending three days and two nights amongst them, and during all that time making these things the entire subject of my enquiries and reflections—

Still—still I must away—the roads are paved—the posts are short—the days are long—'tis no more than noon—I shall be at Fontainebleau before the king—

——Was he going there? not that I know—

CHAPTER 20

Now I hate to hear a person, especially if he be a traveller, complain that we do not get on so fast in France as we do in England; whereas we get on much faster, *consideratis considerandis;* thereby always meaning, that if you weigh their vehicles with the mountains of baggage which you lay both before and behind upon them—and then consider their puny horses, with the very little they give them—'tis a wonder they get on at all: their suffering is most unchristian, and 'tis evident thereupon to me, that a French posthorse would not know what in the world to do, was it not for the two words ****** and ****** in which there is as much sustenance, as if you gave him a peck of corn: now as these words cost nothing, I long from my soul to tell the reader what they are; but here is the question—they must be told him plainly, and with the most distinct articulation, or it will answer no end— and yet to do it in that plain way—though their reverences may laugh at it in the bed-chamber—full well I wot, they will abuse it in the parlour: for which cause, I have been volving and revolving in my fancy some time, but to no purpose, by what clean device or facete contrivance I might so modulate them, that whilst I satisfy that ear which the reader chooses to lend me—I might not dissatisfy the other which he keeps to himself.

——My ink burns my finger to try—and when I have—'twill have a worse consequence—it will burn (I fear) my paper.

——No;—I dare not—

But if you wish to know how the abbess of Andoüillets and a novice of her convent got over the difficulty (only first wishing myself all imaginable success)—I'll tell you without the least scruple.

CHAPTER 21

THE abbess of Andoüillets, which, if you look into the large set of provincial maps now publishing at Paris, you will find situated amongst the hills which divide Burgundy from Savoy, being in danger of an Anchylosis or stiff joint (the sinovia of her knee becoming hard by long matins), and having tried every remedy—first, prayers and thanksgiving; then invocations to all the saints in heaven promiscuously—then particularly to every saint who had ever had a stiff leg before her—then touching it with all the reliques of the convent, principally with the thigh-bone of the man of Lystra, who had been impotent from his youth—then wrapping it up in her veil when she went to bed—then cross-wise her rosary—then bringing in to her aid the secular arm, and anointing it with oils and hot fat of animals—then treating it with emollient and resolving fomentations—then with poultices of marsh-mallows, mallows, bonus Henricus, white lilies and fenugreek—then taking the woods, I mean the smoke of 'em, holding her scapulary across her lap—then decoctions of wild chicory, water-cresses, chervil, sweet cecily and cochlearia—and nothing all this while answering, was prevailed on at last to try the hot baths of Bourbon—so having first obtained leave of the visitor-general to take care of her existence—she ordered all to be got ready for her journey: a novice of the convent of about seventeen, who had been troubled with a whitloe in her middle finger, by sticking it constantly into the abbess's cast poultices, etc.—had gained such an interest, that overlooking a sciatical old nun, who might have been set up for ever by the hot-baths of Bourbon, Margarita, the little novice, was elected as the companion of the journey.

An old calesh, belonging to the abbesse, lined with green frieze, was ordered to be drawn out into the sun—the gardener of the convent being chosen muleteer, led out the two old mules, to clip the hair from the rump-ends of their tails, whilst a couple of lay-sisters were busied, the one in darning the lining, and the other in sewing on the shreds of yellow binding, which the teeth of time had unravelled—the under-gardener dressed the muleteer's hat in hot wine-lees—and a tailor sat musically at it, in a shed over-against the convent, in assorting four dozen of bells for the harness, whistling to each bell, as he tied it on with a thong.——

——The carpenter and the smith of Andoüillets held a council of wheels; and by seven, the morning after, all looked spruce, and was ready at the gate of the convent for the hot-baths of Bourbon—two rows of the unfortunate stood ready there an hour before.

The abbess of Andoüillets, supported by Margarita the novice, advanced slowly to the calesh, both clad in white, with their black rosaries hanging at their breasts—

——There was a simple solemnity in the contrast: they entered the calesh; and nuns in the same uniform, sweet emblem of innocence, each occupied a window, and as the abbess and Margarita looked up—each (the sciatical poor nun excepted) each streamed out the end of her veil in the air —then kissed the lily hand which let it go: the good abbess and Margarita laid their hands saintwise upon their breasts—looked up to heaven—then to them—and looked "God bless you, dear sisters."

I declare I am interested in this story, and wish I had been there.

The gardener, whom I shall now call the muleteer, was a little, hearty, broad-set, good natured, chattering, toping kind of a fellow, who troubled his head very little with the hows and whens of life; so had mortgaged a month of his conventical wages in a borrachio, or leathern cask of wine, which he had disposed behind the calesh, with a large russet-coloured riding-coat over it, to guard it from the sun; and as the weather was hot, and he not a niggard of his labours, walking ten times more than he rode— he found more occasions than those of nature, to fall back to the rear of his carriage; till by frequent coming and going, it had so happened, that all his wine had leaked out at the legal vent of the borrachio, before one half of the journey was finished.

Man is a creature born to habitudes. The day had been sultry—the evening was delicious—the wine was generous—the Burgundian hill on which it grew was steep—a little tempting bush over the door of a cool cottage at the foot of it, hung vibrating in full harmony with the passions—a gentle air rustled distinctly through the leaves—"Come—come, thirsty muleteer —come in."

——The muleteer was a son of Adam; I need not say a word more. He gave the mules, each of 'em, a sound lash, and looking in the abbess's and Margarita's faces (as he did it)—as much as to say "here I am"—he gave a second good crack—as much as to say to his mules, "get on"—so slinking behind, he entered the little inn at the foot of the hill.

The muleteer, as I told you, was a little, joyous, chirping fellow, who thought not of to-morrow, nor of what had gone before, or what was to follow it, provided he got but his scantling of Burgundy, and a little chit-chat along with it; so entering into a long conversation, as how he was chief gardener to the convent of Andoüillets, etc. etc., and out of friendship for the abbess and Mademoiselle Margarita, who was only in her noviciate, he had come along with them from the confines of Savoy, etc. etc.—and as how she had got a white swelling by her devotions—and what a nation of herbs he had procured to mollify her humours, etc. etc., and that if the waters of Bourbon did not mend that leg—she might as well be lame of both—etc. etc. etc.—He so contrived his story, as absolutely to forget the heroine of it—and with her the little novice, and what was a more ticklish point to be forgot than both—the two mules; who being creatures that take advantage of the world, inasmuch as their parents took it of them—and they not being in a condition to return the obligation downwards (as men and women and beasts are)—they do it side-ways, and long-ways, and back-ways—and up hill, and down hill, and which way they can.——Philosophers, with all their ethics, have never considered this rightly—how should the poor muleteer, then in his cups, consider it at all? he did not in the least—'tis time we do; let us leave him then in the vortex of his element, the happiest and most thoughtless of mortal men—and for a moment let us look after the mules, the abbess, and Margarita.

By virtue of the muleteer's two last strokes the mules had gone quietly on, following their own consciences up the hill, till they had conquered about one half of it; when the elder of them, a shrewd crafty old devil, at the turn of an angle, giving a side glance, and no muleteer behind them—

By my fig! said she, swearing, I'll go no further—And if I do, replied the other, they shall make a drum of my hide.—

And so with one consent they stopped thus—

CHAPTER 22

——GET on with you, said the abbess.

—Wh----ysh—ysh—cried Margarita.

Sh---a—shu-u—shu--u—sh--aw—shawed the abbess.

——Whu—v—w—whew—w—w—whuved Margarita, pursing up her sweet lips betwixt a hoot and a whistle.

Thump—thump—thump—obstreperated the abbess of Andoüillets with the end of her gold-headed cane against the bottom of the calesh—

The old mule let a f—

CHAPTER 23

WE are ruined and undone, my child, said the abbess to Margarita,—we shall be here all night—we shall be plundered—we shall be ravished—

——We shall be ravished, said Margarita, as sure as a gun.

Sancta Maria! cried the abbess (forgetting the O!)—why was I governed by this wicked stiff joint? why did I leave the convent of Andoüillets? and why didst thou not suffer thy servant to go unpolluted to her tomb?

O my finger! my finger! cried the novice, catching fire at the word servant—why was I not content to put it here, or there, any where rather than be in this strait?

Strait! said the abbess.

Strait—said the novice; for terror had struck their understandings—the one knew not what she said—the other what she answered.

O my virginity! virginity! cried the abbess.

—inity!—inity! said the novice, sobbing.

CHAPTER 24

MY dear mother, quoth the novice, coming a little to herself,—there are two certain words, which I have been told will force any horse, or ass, or mule, to go up a hill whether he will or no; be he never so obstinate or ill-willed, the moment he hears them uttered, he obeys. They are words magic!

cried the abbess in the utmost horror—No; replied Margarita calmly—but they are words sinful—What are they? quoth the abbess, interrupting her: They are sinful in the first degree, answered Margarita,—they are mortal—and if we are ravished and die unabsolved of them, we shall both—but you may pronounce them to me, quoth the abbess of Andoüillets—They cannot, my dear mother, said the novice, be pronounced at all; they will make all the blood in one's body fly up into one's face—But you may whisper them in my ear, quoth the abbess.

Heaven! hadst thou no guardian angel to delegate to the inn at the bottom of the hill? was there no generous and friendly spirit unemployed—no agent in nature, by some monitory shivering, creeping along the artery which led to his heart, to rouse the muleteer from his banquet?—no sweet minstrelsy to bring back the fair idea of the abbess and Margarita, with their black rosaries!

Rouse! rouse!—but 'tis too late—the horrid words are pronounced this moment—

—and how to tell them—Ye, who can speak of every thing existing, with unpolluted lips—instruct me—guide me—

CHAPTER 25

ALL sins whatever, quoth the abbess, turning casuist in the distress they were under, are held by the confessor of our convent to be either mortal or venial: there is no further division. Now a venial sin being the slightest and least of all sins—being halved—by taking either only the half of it, and leaving the rest—or, by taking it all, and amicably halving it betwixt yourself and another person—in course becomes diluted into no sin at all.

Now I see no sin in saying, bou, bou, bou, bou, bou, a hundred times together; nor is there any turpitude in pronouncing the syllable ger, ger, ger, ger, ger, were it from our matins to our vespers: Therefore, my dear daughter, continued the abbess of Andoüillets—I will say bou, and thou shalt say ger; and then alternately, as there is no more sin in fou than in bou —Thou shalt say fou—and I will come in (like fa, sol, la, re, mi, ut, at our complines) with ter. And accordingly the abbess, giving the pitch note, set off thus:

Abbess,   } Bou--bou--bou--
Margarita, } ———ger,--ger,--ger.

Margarita, } Fou--fou--fou--
Abbess,   } ———ter,--ter,--ter.

The two mules acknowledged the notes by a mutual lash of their tails; but it went no further—'Twill answer by an' by, said the novice.

Abbess,   } Bou-bou-bou-bou-bou-bou-
Margarita, } —ger, ger, ger, ger, ger, ger.

Quicker still, cried Margarita.
Fou, fou, fou, fou, fou, fou, fou, fou, fou.
Quicker still, cried Margarita.

Bou, bou, bou, bou, bou, bou, bou, bou, bou.

Quicker still—God preserve me; said the abbess—They do not understand us, cried Margarita—But the Devil does, said the abbess of Andoüillets.

CHAPTER 26

WHAT a tract of country have I run!—how many degrees nearer to the warm sun am I advanced, and how many fair and goodly cities have I seen, during the time you have been reading, and reflecting, Madam, upon this story! There's Fontainebleau, and Sens, and Joigny, and Auxerre, and Dijon the capital of Burgundy, and Chalons, and Mâcon the capital of the Mâconese, and a score more upon the road to Lyons—and now I have run them over—I might as well talk to you of so many market towns in the moon, as tell you one word about them: it will be this chapter at the least, if not both this and the next entirely lost, do what I will—

—Why, 'tis a strange story! Tristram.

————Alas! Madam, had it been upon some melancholy lecture of the cross—the peace of meekness, or the contentment of resignation—I had not been incommoded: or had I thought of writing it upon the purer abstractions of the soul, and that food of wisdom and holiness and contemplation, upon which the spirit of man (when separated from the body) is to subsist for ever—You would have come with a better appetite from it—

—I wish I never had wrote it: but as I never blot any thing out—let us use some honest means to get it out of our heads directly.

————Pray reach me my fool's cap—I fear you sit upon it, Madam—'tis under the cushion—I'll put it on—

Bless me! you have had it upon your head this half hour.—There then let it stay, with a

Fa-ra diddle di

and a fa-ri diddle d

and a high-dum—dye-dum

    fiddle---dumb-c.

And now, Madam, we may venture, I hope, a little to go on.

CHAPTER 27

————ALL you need say of Fontainebleau (in case you are asked) is, that it stands about forty miles (south something) from Paris, in the middle of a large forest—That there is something great in it—That the king goes there once every two or three years, with his whole court, for the pleasure of the chase—and that, during that carnival of sporting, any English gentleman of fashion (you need not forget yourself) may be accommodated with a nag or two, to partake of the sport, taking care only not to out-gallop the king—

Though there are two reasons why you need not talk loud of this to every one.

First, Because 'twill make the said nags the harder to be got; and

Secondly, 'Tis not a word of it true.——*Allons!*

As for Sens—you may dispatch—in a word—"'Tis an archiepiscopal see."

——For Joigny—the less, I think, one says of it the better.

But for Auxerre—I could go on for ever: for in my grand tour through Europe, in which, after all, my father (not caring to trust me with any one) attended me himself, with my uncle Toby, and Trim, and Obadiah, and indeed most of the family, except my mother, who being taken up with a project of knitting my father a pair of large worsted breeches—(the thing is common sense)—and she not caring to be put out of her way, she stayed at home, at Shandy Hall, to keep things right during the expedition; in which, I say, my father stopping us two days at Auxerre, and his researches being ever of such a nature, that they would have found fruit even in a desert— he has left me enough to say upon Auxerre: in short, wherever my father went—but 'twas more remarkably so, in this journey through France and Italy, than in any other stages of his life—his road seemed to lie so much on one side of that, wherein all other travellers have gone before him—he saw kings and courts and silks of all colours, in such strange lights—and his re- marks and reasonings upon the characters, the manners, and customs of the countries we passed over, were so opposite to those of all other mortal men, particularly those of my uncle Toby and Trim—(to say nothing of myself) —and to crown all—the occurrences and scrapes which we were perpetually meeting and getting into, in consequence of his systems and opiniatry— they were of so odd, so mixed and tragi-comical a contexture—That the whole put together, it appears of so different a shade and tint from any tour of Europe, which was ever executed—that I will venture to pronounce—the fault must be mine and mine only—if it be not read by all travellers and travel-readers, till travelling is no more,—or which comes to the same point —till the world, finally, takes it into its head to stand still.——

——But this rich bale is not to be opened now; except a small thread or two of it, merely to unravel the mystery of my father's stay at Auxerre.

——As I have mentioned it—'tis too slight to be kept suspended; and when 'tis wove in, there is an end of it.

We'll go, brother Toby, said my father, whilst dinner is coddling—to the abbey of Saint Germain, if it be only to see these bodies, of which Monsieur Sequier has given such a recommendation.—I'll go see any body, quoth my uncle Toby; for he was all compliance through every step of the journey— Defend me! said my father—they are all mummies—Then one need not shave; quoth my uncle Toby—Shave! no—cried my father—'twill be more like relations to go with our beards on—So out we sallied, the corporal lend- ing his master his arm, and bringing up the rear, to the abbey of Saint Germain.

Every thing is very fine, and very rich, and very superb, and very mag- nificent, said my father, addressing himself to the sacristan, who was a younger brother of the order of Benedictines—but our curiosity has led us to see the bodies, of which Monsieur Sequier has given the world so exact a description.—The sacristan made a bow, and lighting a torch first, which he had always in the vestry ready for the purpose; he led us into the tomb of St. Heribald—This, said the sacristan, laying his hand upon the tomb, was a renowned prince of the house of Bavaria, who under the successive reigns of Charlemagne, Louis le Debonnair, and Charles the Bald, bore a great sway in the government, and had a principal hand in bringing every thing into order and discipline—

Then he has been as great, said my uncle, in the field, as in the cabinet— I dare say he has been a gallant soldier—He was a monk—said the sacristan.

My uncle Toby and Trim sought comfort in each other's faces—but found it not: my father clapped both his hands upon his cod-piece, which was a way he had when any thing hugely tickled him: for though he hated a monk and the very smell of a monk worse than all the devils in hell—yet the shot hitting my uncle Toby and Trim so much harder than him, 'twas a relative triumph; and put him into the gayest humour in the world.

——And pray what do you call this gentleman? quoth my father, rather sportingly: This tomb, said the young Benedictine, looking downwards, contains the bones of Saint Maxima, who came from Ravenna on purpose to touch the body—

—Of Saint Maximus, said my father, popping in with his saint before him,—they were two of the greatest saints in the whole martyrology, added my father—Excuse me, said the sacristan—'twas to touch the bones of Saint Germain, the builder of the abbey—And what did she get by it? said my uncle Toby—What does any woman get by it? said my father—Martyrdom; replied the young Benedictine, making a bow down to the ground, and uttering the word with so humble, but decisive a cadence, it disarmed my father for a moment. 'Tis supposed, continued the Benedictine, that St. Maxima has lain in this tomb four hundred years, and two hundred before her canonization—'Tis but a slow rise, brother Toby, quoth my father, in this self-same army of martyrs.—A desperate slow one, an' please your honour, said Trim, unless one could purchase—I should rather sell out entirely, quoth my uncle Toby—I am pretty much of your opinion, brother Toby, said my father.

——Poor St. Maxima! said my uncle Toby low to himself, as we turned from her tomb: She was one of the fairest and most beautiful ladies either of Italy or France, continued the sacristan—But who the deuce has got lain down here, besides her? quoth my father, pointing with his cane to a large tomb as we walked on—It is Saint Optat, Sir, answered the sacristan —And properly is Saint Optat placed! said my father: And what is Saint Optat's story? continued he. St. Optat, replied the sacristan, was a bishop—

—I thought so, by heaven! cried my father, interrupting him—Saint Optat!—how should Saint Optat fail? so snatching out his pocket-book, and the young Benedictine holding him the torch as he wrote, he set it down as a new prop to his system of Christian names, and I will be bold to say, so disinterested was he in the search of truth, that had he found a treasure in Saint Optat's tomb, it would not have made him half so rich: 'Twas as successful a short visit as ever was paid to the dead; and so highly was his fancy pleased with all that had passed in it,—that he determined at once to stay another day in Auxerre.

——I'll see the rest of these good gentry to-morrow, said my father, as we crossed over the square—And while you are paying that visit, brother Shandy, quoth my uncle Toby—the corporal and I will mount the ramparts.

CHAPTER 28

——Now this is the most puzzled skein of all—for in this last chapter, as far at least as it has helped me through Auxerre, I have been getting forwards in two different journeys together, and with the same dash of the pen—for I have got entirely out of Auxerre in this journey which I am writing now, and I am got half way out of Auxerre in that which I shall write hereafter—There is but a certain degree of perfection in every thing; and by pushing at something beyond that, I have brought myself into such a situation, as no traveller ever stood before me; for I am this moment walking across the market-place of Auxerre with my father and my uncle Toby, in our way back to dinner—and I am this moment also entering Lyons with my post-chaise broke into a thousand pieces—and I am moreover this moment in a handsome pavilion built by Pringello,[1] upon the banks of the Garonne, which Mons. Sligniac has lent me, and where I now sit rhapsodizing all these affairs.

——Let me collect myself, and pursue my journey.

CHAPTER 29

I AM glad of it, said I, settling the account with myself, as I walked into Lyons—my chaise being all laid higgledy-piggledy with my baggage in a cart, which was moving slowly before me—I am heartily glad, said I, that 'tis all broke to pieces; for now I can go directly by water to Avignon, which will carry me on a hundred and twenty miles of my journey, and not cost me seven livres—and from thence, continued I, bringing forward the account, I can hire a couple of mules—or asses, if I like, (for nobody knows me) and cross the plains of Languedoc for almost nothing—I shall gain four hundred livres by the misfortune clear into my purse: and pleasure! worth —worth double the money by it. With what velocity, continued I, clapping my two hands together, shall I fly down the rapid Rhône, with the Vivares on my right hand, and Dauphiny on my left, scarce seeing the ancient cities of Vienne, Valence, and Vivieres. What a flame will it rekindle in the lamp, to snatch a blushing grape from the Hermitage and Côte roti, as I shoot by the foot of them! and what a fresh spring in the blood! to behold upon the banks advancing and retiring, the castles of romance, whence courteous knights have whilome rescued the distressed—and see vertiginous, the rocks, the mountains, the cataracts, and all the hurry which Nature is in with all her great works about her.

As I went on thus, methought my chaise, the wreck of which looked stately enough at the first, insensibly grew less and less in its size; the

[1]The same Don Pringello, the celebrated Spanish architect, of whom my cousin Antony has made such honourable mention in a scholium to the Tale inscribed to his name.—*Vid.* p. 129, small edit.

freshness of the painting was no more—the gilding lost its lustre—and the whole affair appeared so poor in my eyes—so sorry!—so contemptible! and in a word, so much worse than the abbess of Andoüillets' itself—that I was just opening my mouth to give it to the devil—when a pert vamping chaise-undertaker, stepping nimbly across the street, demanded if Monsieur would have his chaise refitted—No, no, said I, shaking my head sideways—Would Monsieur choose to sell it? rejoined the undertaker—With all my soul, said I—the iron work is worth forty livres—and the glasses worth forty more—and the leather you may take to live on.

What a mine of wealth, quoth I, as he counted me the money, has this post-chaise brought me in? And this is my usual method of book-keeping, at least with the disasters of life—making a penny of every one of 'em as they happen to me—

—Do, my dear Jenny, tell the world for me, how I behaved under one, the most oppressive of its kind, which could befall me as a man, proud as he ought to be of his manhood—

'Tis enough, saidst thou, coming close up to me, as I stood with my garters in my hand, reflecting upon what had not passed—'Tis enough, Tristram, and I am satisfied, saidst thou, whispering these words in my ear, **** ** **** *** ******;—**** ** **—any other man would have sunk down to the centre—

—Every thing is good for something, quoth I.

——I'll go into Wales for six weeks, and drink goat's whey—and I'll gain seven years longer life for the accident. For which reason I think myself inexcusable, for blaming fortune so often as I have done, for pelting me all my life long, like an ungracious duchess, as I called her, with so many small evils: surely, if I have any cause to be angry with her, 'tis that she has not sent me great ones—a score of good cursed, bouncing losses, would have been as good as a pension to me.

——One of a hundred a year, or so, is all I wish—I would not be at the plague of paying land-tax for a larger.

Chapter 30

To those who call Vexations, Vexations, as knowing what they are, there could not be a greater, than to be the best part of a day at Lyons, the most opulent and flourishing city in France, enriched with the most fragments of antiquity—and not be able to see it. To be withheld upon any account, must be a vexation; but to be withheld by a vexation—must certainly be, what philosophy justly calls

VEXATION
upon
VEXATION.

I had got my two dishes of milk coffee (which by the bye is excellently good for a consumption, but you must boil the milk and coffee together—otherwise, 'tis only coffee and milk)—and as it was no more than eight in the morning, and the boat did not go off till noon, I had time to see enough of Lyons to tire the patience of all the friends I had in the world with it. I will take a walk to the cathedral, said I, looking at my list, and see the wonderful mechanism of this great clock of Lippius of Basil, in the first place—

Now, of all things in the world, I understand the least of mechanism—I have neither genius, or taste, or fancy—and have a brain so entirely unapt for every thing of that kind, that I solemnly declare I was never yet able to comprehend the principles of motion of a squirrel cage, or a common knife-grinder's wheel—tho' I have many an hour of my life looked up with great devotion at the one—and stood by with as much patience as any christian ever could do, at the other—

I'll go see the surprising movements of this great clock, said I, the very first thing I do: and then I will pay a visit to the great library of the Jesuits, and procure, if possible, a sight of the thirty volumes of the general history of China, wrote (not in the Tartarean, but) in the Chinese language, and in the Chinese character too.

Now I almost know as little of the Chinese language, as I do of the mechanism of Lippius's clock-work; so, why these should have jostled themselves into the two first articles of my list—I leave to the curious as a problem of Nature. I own it looks like one of her ladyship's obliquities; and they who court her, are interested in finding out her humour as much as I.

When these curiosities are seen, quoth I, half addressing myself to my *valet de place*, who stood behind me—'twill be no hurt if we go to the church of St. Irenaeus, and see the pillar to which Christ was tied—and after that, the house where Pontius Pilate lived—'Twas at the next town, said the *valet de place*—at Vienne; I am glad of it, said I, rising briskly from my chair, and walking across the room with strides twice as long as my usual pace—"for so much the sooner shall I be at the Tomb of the Two Lovers."

What was the cause of this movement, and why I took such long strides in uttering this—I might leave to the curious too; but as no principle of clock-work is concerned in it—'twill be as well for the reader if I explain it myself.

CHAPTER 31

O THERE is a sweet era in the life of man, when (the brain being tender and fibrillous, and more like pap than any thing else)—a story read of two fond lovers, separated from each other by cruel parents, and by still more cruel destiny—

> Amandus—He
> Amanda—She—

each ignorant of the other's course.

> He—east
> She—west

Amandus taken captive by the Turks, and carried to the emperor of Morocco's court, where the princess of Morocco falling in love with him, keeps him twenty years in prison for the love of his Amanda.——

She—(Amanda) all the time wandering barefoot, and with dishevelled hair, o'er rocks and mountains, enquiring for Amandus!—Amandus! Amandus!—making every hill and valley to echo back his name—

Amandus! Amandus!

at every town and city, sitting down forlorn at the gate—Has Amandus!—has my Amandus entered?—till,—going round, and round, and round the world—chance unexpected bringing them at the same moment of the night, though by different ways, to the gate of Lyons, their native city, and each in well-known accents calling out aloud,

Is Amandus $\Big\}$ still alive?
Is my Amanda $\Big\}$

they fly into each other's arms, and both drop down dead for joy.

There is a soft era in every gentle mortal's life, where such a story affords more pabulum to the brain, than all the Frusts, and Crusts, and Rusts of antiquity, which travellers can cook up for it.

——'Twas all that stuck on the right side of the cullender in my own, of what Spon and others, in their accounts of Lyons, had strained into it; and finding, moreover, in some Itinerary, but in what God knows—That sacred to the fidelity of Amandus and Amanda, a tomb was built without the gates, where, to this hour, lovers called upon them to attest their truths—I never could get into a scrape of that kind in my life, but this tomb of the lovers would, somehow or other, come in at the close—nay such a kind of empire had it established over me, that I could seldom think or speak of Lyons—and sometimes not so much as see even a Lyons-waist-coat, but this remnant of antiquity would present itself to my fancy; and I have often said in my wild way of running on—tho' I fear with some irreverence—"I thought this shrine (neglected as it was) as valuable as that of Mecca, and so little short, except in wealth, of the Santa Casa itself, that some time or other, I would go a pilgrimage (though I had no other business at Lyons) on purpose to pay it a visit."

In my list, therefore, of Videnda at Lyons, this, tho' last,—was not, you see, least; so taking a dozen or two of longer strides than usual across my room, just whilst it passed my brain, I walked down calmly into the *Basse Cour*, in order to sally forth; and having called for my bill—as it was uncertain whether I should return to my inn, I had paid it—had moreover given the maid ten sous, and was just receiving the dernier compliments of Monsieur Le Blanc, for a pleasant voyage down the Rhône—when I was stopped at the gate.

CHAPTER 32

——'Twas by a poor ass, who had just turned in with a couple of large panniers upon his back, to collect eleemosynary turnip-tops and cabbage-leaves; and stood dubious, with his two fore-feet on the inside of the threshold, and with his two hinder feet towards the street, as not knowing very well whether he was to go in or no.

Now, 'tis an animal (be in what hurry I may) I cannot bear to strike—there is a patient endurance of sufferings, wrote so unaffectedly in his looks and carriage, which pleads so mightily for him, that it always disarms me; and to that degree, that I do not like to speak unkindly to him: on the contrary, meet him where I will—whether in town or country—in cart or under panniers—whether in liberty or bondage—I have ever something civil to say to him on my part; and as one word begets another (if he has as little to do as I)—I generally fall into conversation with him; and surely never is my imagination so busy as in framing his responses from the etchings of his countenance—and where those carry me not deep enough—in flying from my own heart into his, and seeing what is natural for an ass to think—as well as a man, upon the occasion. In truth, it is the only creature of all the classes of beings below me, with whom I can do this: for parrots, jackdaws, etc.—I never exchange a word with them—nor with the apes, etc., for pretty near the same reason; they act by rote, as the others speak by it, and equally make me silent: nay my dog and my cat, though I value them both—(and for my dog he would speak if he could)—yet somehow or other, they neither of them possess the talents for conversation—I can make nothing of a discourse with them, beyond the proposition, the reply, and rejoinder, which terminated my father's and my mother's conversations, in his beds of justice—and those uttered—there's an end of the dialogue—

—But with an ass, I can commune for ever.

Come, Honesty! said I,—seeing it was impracticable to pass betwixt him and the gate—art thou for coming in, or going out?

The ass twisted his head round to look up the street—

Well—replied I—we'll wait a minute for thy driver:

—He turned his head thoughtful about, and looked wistfully the opposite way—

I understand thee perfectly, answered I—If thou takest a wrong step in this affair, he will cudgel thee to death—Well! a minute is but a minute, and if it saves a fellow-creature a drubbing, it shall not be set down as ill spent.

He was eating the stem of an artichoke as this discourse went on, and in the little peevish contentions of nature betwixt hunger and unsavouriness, had dropt it out of his mouth half a dozen times, and picked it up again— God help thee, Jack! said I, thou hast a bitter breakfast on't—and many a bitter day's labour,—and many a bitter blow, I fear, for its wages—'tis all— all bitterness to thee, whatever life is to others.—And now thy mouth, if one knew the truth of it, is as bitter, I dare say, as soot—(for he had cast aside the stem) and thou hast not a friend perhaps in all this world, that will give thee a macaroon.—In saying this, I pulled out a paper of 'em, which I had just purchased, and gave him one—and at this moment that I am telling it, my heart smites me, that there was more of pleasantry in the conceit, of seeing how an ass would eat a macaroon—than of benevolence in giving him one, which presided in the act.

When the ass had eaten his macaroon, I pressed him to come in—the poor beast was heavy loaded—his legs seemed to tremble under him—he hung rather backwards, and as I pulled at his halter, it broke short in my hand—he looked up pensive in my face—"Don't thrash me with it—but if you will, you may"—If I do, said I, I'll be d—d.

The word was but one-half of it pronounced, like the abbess of Andoüillets'—(so there was no sin in it)—when a person coming in, let fall a thundering bastinado upon the poor devil's cropper, which put an end to the ceremony.

Out upon it!

cried I—but the interjection was equivocal—and, I think, wrong placed too—for the end of an osier which had started out from the contexture of the ass's pannier, had caught hold of my breeches pocket, as he rushed by me, and rent it in the most disastrous direction you can imagine—so that the

Out upon it! in my opinion, should have come in here—but this I leave to be settled by

THE

REVIEWERS

OF

MY BREECHES,

which I have brought over along with me for that purpose.

CHAPTER 33

WHEN all was set to rights, I came down stairs again into the *basse cour* with my *valet de place*, in order to sally out towards the tomb of the two lovers, etc.—and was a second time stopped at the gate—not by the ass— but by the person who struck him; and who, by that time, had taken possession (as is not uncommon after a defeat) of the very spot of ground where the ass stood.

It was a commissary sent to me from the post-office, with a rescript in his hand for the payment of some six livres odd sous.

Upon what account? said I.—'Tis upon the part of the king, replied the commissary, heaving up both his shoulders—

—My good friend, quoth I—as sure as I am I—and you are you—

—And who are you? said he.——Don't puzzle me; said I.

CHAPTER 34

——BUT it is an indubitable verity, continued I, addressing myself to the commissary, changing only the form of my asseveration—that I owe the king of France nothing but my good-will; for he is a very honest man, and I wish him all health and pastime in the world—

Pardonnez-moi—replied the commissary, you are indebted to him six livres four sous, for the next post from hence to St. Fons, in your route to Avignon—which being a post royal, you pay double for the horses and postillion—otherwise 'twould have amounted to no more than three livres two sous—

—But I don't go by land; said I.

——You may if you please; replied the commissary—

Your most obedient servant—said I, making him a low bow—

The commissary, with all the sincerity of grave good breeding—made me one, as low again.—I never was more disconcerted with a bow in my life.

——The devil take the serious character of these people! quoth I——(aside) they understand no more of irony than this——

The comparison was standing close by with his panniers—but something sealed up my lips—I could not pronounce the name——

Sir, said I, collecting myself—it is not my intention to take post——

—But you may—said he, persisting in his first reply—you may take post if you choose——

—And I may take salt to my pickled herring, said I, if I choose——

—But I do not choose——

—But you must pay for it, whether you do or no.

Aye! for the salt; said I (I know)——

—And for the post too; added he. Defend me! cried I——

I travel by water—I am going down the Rhône this very afternoon—my baggage is in the boat—and I have actually paid nine livres for my passage——

C'est tout égal—'tis all one; said he.

Bon Dieu! what, pay for the way I go! and for the way I do not go!

——*C'est tout égal;* replied the commissary——

—The devil it is! said I—but I will go to ten thousand Bastiles first——

O England! England! thou land of liberty, and climate of good sense, thou tenderest of mothers—and gentlest of nurses, cried I, kneeling upon one knee, as I was beginning my apostrophe.

When the director of Madam Le Blanc's conscience coming in at that instant, and seeing a person in black, with a face as pale as ashes, at his devotions—looking still paler by the contrast and distress of his drapery—asked, if I stood in want of the aids of the church——

I go by Water—said I—and here's another will be for making me pay for going by Oil.

Chapter 35

As I perceived the commissary of the post-office would have his six livres four sous, I had nothing else for it, but to say some smart thing upon the occasion, worth the money:

And so I set off thus:——

—And pray, Mr. Commissary, by what law of courtesy is a defenceless stranger to be used just the reverse from what you use a Frenchman in this matter?

By no means; said he.

Excuse me; said I—for you have begun, Sir, with first tearing off my breeches—and now you want my pocket——

Whereas—had you first taken my pocket, as you do with your own people—and then left me bare a—d after—I had been a beast to have complained——

As it is——

—'Tis contrary to the law of nature.

—'Tis contrary to reason.

—'Tis contrary to the Gospel.

But not to this—said he—putting a printed paper into my hand,

Par Le Roy.

——'Tis a pithy prolegomenon, quoth I—and so read on
_ _
_ _
_ _

—By all which it appears, quoth I, having read it over, a little too rapidly, that if a man sets out in a post-chaise from Paris—he must go on travelling in one, all the days of his life—or pay for it.——Excuse me, said the commissary, the spirit of the ordinance is this—That if you set out with an intention of running post from Paris to Avignon, etc., you shall not change that intention or mode of travelling, without first satisfying the fermiers for two posts further than the place you repent at—and 'tis founded, continued he, upon this, that the revenues are not to fall short through your fickleness——

—O by heavens! cried I—if fickleness is taxable in France—we have nothing to do but to make the best peace with you we can—

And so the peace was made;

—And if it is a bad one—as Tristram Shandy laid the corner-stone of it—nobody but Tristram Shandy ought to be hanged.

Chapter 36

Though I was sensible I had said as many clever things to the commissary as came to six livres four sous, yet I was determined to note down the imposition amongst my remarks before I retired from the place; so putting my hand into my coat-pocket for my remarks—(which, by the bye, may be a caution to travellers to take a little more care of their remarks for the future) "my remarks were stolen"—Never did sorry traveller make such a pother and racket about his remarks as I did about mine, upon the occasion.

Heaven! earth! sea! fire! cried I, calling in every thing to my aid but what I should—My remarks are stolen!—what shall I do?—Mr. Commissary! pray did I drop any remarks, as I stood beside you?——

You dropped a good many very singular ones; replied he—Pugh! said I, those were but a few, not worth above six livres two sous—but these are a large parcel—He shook his head—Monsieur Le Blanc! Madam Le Blanc! did you see any papers of mine?—you maid of the house! run up stairs—François! run up after her—

—I must have my remarks—they were the best remarks, cried I, that ever were made—the wisest—the wittiest—What shall I do?—which way shall I turn myself?

Sancho Pança, when he lost his ass's furniture, did not exclaim more bitterly.

Chapter 37

When the first transport was over, and the registers of the brain were beginning to get a little out of the confusion into which this jumble of cross accidents had cast them—it then presently occurred to me, that I had left my remarks in the pocket of the chaise—and that in selling my chaise, I had sold my remarks along with it, to the chaise-vamper.   I leave this void space that the reader may swear into it any oath that he is most accustomed to—For my own part, if ever I swore a whole oath into a vacancy in my life, I think it was into that— *********, said I—and so my remarks through France, which were as full of wit, as an egg is full of meat, and as well worth four hundred guineas, as the said egg is worth a penny— have I been selling here to a chaise-vamper—for four Louis d'Ors—and giving him a post-chaise (by heaven) worth six into the bargain; had it been to Dodsley, or Becket, or any creditable bookseller, who was either leaving off business, and wanted a post-chaise—or who was beginning it— and wanted my remarks, and two or three guineas along with them—I could have borne it—but to a chaise-vamper!—shew me to him this moment, François,—said I—The *valet de place* put on his hat, and led the way —and I pulled off mine, as I passed the commissary, and followed him.

CHAPTER 38

WHEN we arrived at the chaise-vamper's house, both the house and the shop were shut up; it was the eighth of September, the nativity of the blessed Virgin Mary, mother of God—

—Tantarra-ra-tan-tivi—the whole world was gone out a May-poling— frisking here—capering there—nobody cared a button for me or my remarks; so I sat me down upon a bench by the door, philosophating upon my condition: by a better fate than usually attends me, I had not waited half an hour, when the mistress came in to take the papilliotes from off her hair, before she went to the May-poles—

The French women, by the bye, love May-poles, *à la folie*—that is, as much as their matins—give 'em but a May-pole, whether in May, June, July, or September—they never count the times—down it goes—'tis meat, drink, washing, and lodging to 'em—and had we but the policy, an' please your worships (as wood is a little scarce in France), to send them but plenty of May-poles—

The women would set them up; and when they had done, they would dance round them (and the men for company) till they were all blind.

The wife of the chaise-vamper stepped in, I told you, to take the papilliotes from off her hair—the toilet stands still for no man—so she jerked off her cap, to begin with them as she opened the door, in doing which, one of them fell upon the ground—I instantly saw it was my own writing—

O Seigneur! cried I—you have got all my remarks upon your head, Madam!—*J'en suis bien mortifiée*, said she—'tis well, thinks I, they have stuck there—for could they have gone deeper, they would have made such confusion in a French woman's noddle—She had better have gone with it unfrizled, to the day of eternity.

Tenez—said she—so without any idea of the nature of my suffering, she took them from her curls, and put them gravely one by one into my hat—

one was twisted this way—another twisted that—ey! by my faith; and when they are published, quoth I,—

They will be worse twisted still.

CHAPTER 39

AND now for Lippius's clock! said I, with the air of a man, who had got thro' all his difficulties—nothing can prevent us seeing that, and the Chinese history, etc., except the time, said François—for 'tis almost eleven—Then we must speed the faster, said I, striding it away to the cathedral.

I cannot say, in my heart, that it gave me any concern in being told by one of the minor canons, as I was entering the west door,—That Lippius's great clock was all out of joints, and had not gone for some years—It will give me the more time, thought I, to peruse the Chinese history; and besides I shall be able to give the world a better account of the clock in its decay, than I could have done in its flourishing condition—

—And so away I posted to the college of the Jesuits.

Now it is with the project of getting a peep at the history of China in Chinese characters—as with many others I could mention, which strike the fancy only at a distance; for as I came nearer and nearer to the point—my blood cooled—the freak gradually went off, till at length I would not have given a cherrystone to have it gratified—The truth was, my time was short, and my heart was at the Tomb of the Lovers—I wish to God, said I, as I got the rapper in my hand, that the key of the library may be but lost; it fell out as well—

For all the Jesuits had got the cholic—and to that degree, as never was known in the memory of the oldest practitioner.

CHAPTER 40

As I knew the geography of the Tomb of the Lovers, as well as if I had lived twenty years in Lyons, namely, that it was upon the turning of my right hand, just without the gate, leading to the Fauxbourg de Vaise—I dispatched François to the boat, that I might pay the homage I so long owed it, without a witness of my weakness—I walked with all imaginable joy towards the place—when I saw the gate which intercepted the tomb, my heart glowed within me—

—Tender and faithful spirits! cried I, addressing myself to Amandus and Amanda—long—long have I tarried to drop this tear upon your tomb—I come—I come——

When I came—there was no tomb to drop it upon.

What would I have given for my uncle Toby, to have whistled *Lillo bullero!*

CHAPTER 41

No matter how, or in what mood—but I flew from the tomb of the lovers—or rather I did not fly from it—(for there was no such thing existing) and just got time enough to the boat to save my passage;—and ere I had sailed a hundred yards, the Rhône and the Saône met together, and carried me down merrily betwixt them.

But I have described this voyage down the Rhône, before I made it—

—So now I am at Avignon, and as there is nothing to see but the old house, in which the Duke of Ormond resided, and nothing to stop me but a short remark upon the place, in three minutes you will see me crossing the bridge upon a mule, with François upon a horse with my portmanteau behind him, and the owner of both, striding the way before us, with a long gun upon his shoulder, and a sword under his arm, lest peradventure we should run away with his cattle. Had you seen my breeches in entering Avignon,— Though you'd have seen them better, I think, as I mounted—you would not have thought the precaution amiss, or found in your heart to have taken it in dudgeon; for my own part, I took it most kindly; and determined to make him a present of them, when we got to the end of our journey, for the trouble they had put him to, of arming himself at all points against them.

Before I go further, let me get rid of my remark upon Avignon, which is this: That I think it wrong, merely because a man's hat has been blown off his head by chance the first night he comes to Avignon,—that he should therefore say, "Avignon is more subject to high winds than any town in all France": for which reason I laid no stress upon the accident till I had enquired of the master of the inn about it, who telling me seriously it was so— and hearing, moreover, the windiness of Avignon spoke of in the country about as a proverb—I set it down, merely to ask the learned what can be the cause—the consequence I saw—for they are all Dukes, Marquisses, and Counts, there—the deuce a Baron, in all Avignon—so that there is scarce any talking to them on a windy day.

Prithee, friend, said I, take hold of my mule for a moment—for I wanted to pull off one of my jack-boots, which hurt my heel—the man was standing quite idle at the door of the inn, and as I had taken it into my head, he was someway concerned about the house or stable, I put the bridle into his hand—so began with the boot:—when I had finished the affair, I turned about to take the mule from the man, and thank him—

—But Monsieur le Marquis had walked in—

CHAPTER 42

I HAD now the whole south of France, from the banks of the Rhône to those of the Garonne, to traverse upon my mule at my own leisure—at my own leisure—for I had left Death, the Lord knows—and He only—how far behind me—"I have followed many a man thro' France, quoth he—but never at this mettlesome rate."—Still he followed—and still I fled him—but I fled him cheerfully—still he pursued—but, like one who pursued his prey without hope—as he lagged, every step he lost softened his looks—Why should I fly him at this rate?

So notwithstanding all the commissary of the post-office had said, I changed the mode of my travelling once more; and, after so precipitate and rattling a course as I had run, I flattered my fancy with thinking of my mule, and that I should traverse the rich plains of Languedoc upon his back, as slowly as foot could fall.

There is nothing more pleasing to a traveller—or more terrible to travel-writers, than a large rich plain; especially if it is without great rivers or bridges; and presents nothing to the eye, but one unvaried picture of plenty: for after they have once told you, that 'tis delicious! or delightful! (as the case happens)—that the soil was grateful, and that nature pours out all her abundance, etc. . . . they have then a large plain upon their hands, which they know not what to do with—and which is of little or no use to them but to carry them to some town; and that town, perhaps of little more, but a new place to start from to the next plain—and so on.

—This is most terrible work; judge if I don't manage my plains better.

Chapter 43

I HAD not gone above two leagues and a half, before the man with his gun began to look at his priming.

I had three several times loitered terribly behind; half a mile at least every time; once, in deep conference with a drum-maker, who was making drums for the fairs of Baucaira and Tarascone—I did not understand the principles—

The second time, I cannot so properly say, I stopped—for meeting a couple of Franciscans straitened more for time than myself, and not being able to get to the bottom of what I was about—I had turned back with them—

The third, was an affair of trade with a gossip, for a hand-basket of Provence figs for four sous; this would have been transacted at once; but for a case of conscience at the close of it; for when the figs were paid for, it turned out, that there were two dozen of eggs covered over with vine-leaves at the bottom of the basket—as I had no intention of buying eggs—I made no sort of claim of them—as for the space they had occupied—what signi-fied it? I had figs enow for my money—

—But it was my intention to have the basket—it was the gossip's inten-tion to keep it, without which, she could do nothing with her eggs—and unless I had the basket, I could do as little with my figs, which were too ripe already, and most of 'em burst at the side: this brought on a short con-tention, which terminated in sundry proposals, what we should both do—

—How we disposed of our eggs and figs, I defy you, or the Devil himself, had he not been there (which I am persuaded he was), to form the least probable conjecture: You will read the whole of it—not this year, for I am hastening to the story of my uncle Toby's amours—but you will read it in the collection of those which have arose out of the journey across this plain —and which, therefore, I call my

Plain Stories.

How far my pen has been fatigued, like those of other travellers, in this journey of it, over so barren a track—the world must judge—but the traces of it, which are now all set o' vibrating together this moment, tell me 'tis the most fruitful and busy period of my life; for as I had made no convention with my man with the gun, as to time—by stopping and talking to every soul I met, who was not in a full trot—joining all parties before me—waiting for every soul behind—hailing all those who were coming through crossroads—arresting all kinds of beggars, pilgrims, fiddlers, friars—not passing by a woman in a mulberry-tree without commending her legs, and tempting her into conversation with a pinch of snuff——In short, by seizing every handle, of what size or shape soever, which chance held out to me in this journey—I turned my plain into a city—I was always in company, and with great variety too: and as my mule loved society as much as myself, and had some proposals always on his part to offer to every beast he met—I am confident we could have passed through Pall-Mall, or St. James's-Street for a month together, with fewer adventures—and seen less of human nature.

O! there is that sprightly frankness, which at once unpins every plait of a Languedocian's dress—that whatever is beneath it, it looks so like the simplicity which poets sing of in better days—I will delude my fancy, and believe it is so.

'Twas in the road betwixt Nismes and Lunel, where there is the best Muscatto wine in all France, and which by the bye belongs to the honest canons of Montpellier—and foul befall the man who has drank it at their table, who grudges them a drop of it.

——The sun was set—they had done their work; the nymphs had tied up their hair afresh—and the swains were preparing for a carousal—my mule made a dead point—'Tis the fife and tabourin, said I—I'm frightened to death, quoth he—They are running at the ring of pleasure, said I, giving him a prick—By saint Boogar, and all the saints at the backside of the door of purgatory, said he—(making the same resolution with the abbesse of Andoüillets) I'll not go a step further—'Tis very well, sir, said I—I never will argue a point with one of your family, as long as I live; so leaping off his back, and kicking off one boot into this ditch, and t'other into that— I'll take a dance, said I—so stay you here.

A sun-burnt daughter of Labour rose up from the group to meet me, as I advanced towards them; her hair, which was a dark chestnut approaching rather to a black, was tied up in a knot, all but a single tress.

We want a cavalier, said she, holding out both her hands, as if to offer them—And a cavalier ye shall have; said I, taking hold of both of them.

Hadst thou, Nannette, been arrayed like a duchess!——But that cursed slit in thy petticoat!

Nannette cared not for it.

We could not have done without you, said she, letting go one hand, with self-taught politeness, leading me up with the other.

A lame youth, whom Apollo had recompensed with a pipe, and to which he had added a tabourin of his own accord, ran sweetly over the prelude, as he sat upon the bank—Tie me up this tress instantly, said Nannette, putting a piece of string into my hand—It taught me to forget I was a stranger —The whole knot fell down—We had been seven years acquainted.

The youth struck the note upon the tabourin—his pipe followed, and off we bounded—"the deuce take that slit!"

The sister of the youth, who had stolen her voice from heaven, sung alternately with her brother—'twas a Gascoigne roundelay.

VIVA LA JOIA!

FIDON LA TRISTESSA!

The nymphs joined in unison, and their swains an octave below them—

I would have given a crown to have it sewed up—Nannette would not have given a sous—*Vive la joia!* was in her lips—*Vive la joia!* was in her eyes. A transient spark of amity shot across the space betwixt us—She looked amiable!——Why could I not live, and end my days thus? Just Disposer of our joys and sorrows, cried I, why could not a man sit down in the lap of content here—and dance, and sing, and say his prayers, and go to heaven with this nut-brown maid? Capriciously did she bend her head on one side, and dance up insidious—Then 'tis time to dance off, quoth I; so changing only partners and tunes, I danced it away from Lunel to Montpellier—from thence to Pesçnas, Beziers—I danced it along through Narbonne, Carcasson, and Castle Naudairy, till at last I danced myself into Perdrillo's pavilion, where pulling out a paper of black lines, that I might go on straight forwards, without digression or parenthesis, in my uncle Toby's amours—

I began thus—

BOOK VIII

CHAPTER I

BUT softly—for in these sportive plains, and under this genial sun, where at this instant all flesh is running out piping, fiddling, and dancing to the vintage, and every step that's taken the judgment is surprised by the imagination, I defy, notwithstanding all that has been said upon straight lines[1] in sundry pages of my book—I defy the best cabbage planter that ever existed, whether he plants backwards or forwards, it makes little difference in the account (except that he will have more to answer for in the one case than in the other)—I defy him to go on coolly, critically, and canonically, planting his cabbages one by one, in straight lines, and stoical distances, especially if slits in petticoats are unsewed up—without ever and anon straddling out, or sidling into some bastardly digression—In Freeze-land, Fog-land, and some other lands I wot of—it may be done—

But in this clear climate of fantasy and perspiration, where every idea, sensible and insensible, gets vent—in this land, my dear Eugenius—in this fertile land of chivalry and romance, where I now sit, unscrewing my inkhorn to write my uncle Toby's amours, and with all the meanders of Julia's track in quest of her Diego, in full view of my study window—if thou comest not and takest me by the hand—

What a work it is likely to turn out!

Let us begin it.

CHAPTER 2

IT is with love as with Cuckoldom—

But now I am talking of beginning a book, and have long had a thing upon my mind to be imparted to the reader, which, if not imparted now, can never be imparted to him as long as I live (whereas the comparison may be imparted to him any hour in the day)—I'll just mention it, and begin in good earnest.

The thing is this.

That of all the several ways of beginning a book which are now in practice throughout the known world, I am confident my own way of doing it is the best—I'm sure it is the most religious—for I begin with writing the first sentence—and trusting to Almighty God for the second.

'Twould cure an author for ever of the fuss and folly of opening his

[1]*Vid.* p. 457.

495

street-door, and calling in his neighbours and friends, and kinsfolk, with the devil and all his imps, with their hammers and engines, etc., only to observe how one sentence of mine follows another, and how the plan follows the whole.

I wish you saw me half starting out of my chair, with what confidence, as I grasp the elbow of it, I look up—catching the idea, even sometimes before it half way reaches me—

I believe in my conscience I intercept many a thought which heaven intended for another man.

Pope and his Portrait[1] are fools to me—no martyr is ever so full of faith or fire—I wish I could say of good works too—but I have no

Zeal or Anger—or

Anger or Zeal—

And till gods and men agree together to call it by the same name—the errantest Tartuffe, in science—in politics—or in religion, shall never kindle a spark within me, or have a worse word, or a more unkind greeting, than what he will read in the next chapter.

CHAPTER 3

——BONJOUR!—good morrow!—so you have got your cloak on betimes!—but 'tis a cold morning, and you judge the matter rightly—'tis better to be well mounted, than go o' foot—and obstructions in the glands are dangerous— And how goes it with thy concubine—thy wife,—and thy little ones o' both sides? and when did you hear from the old gentleman and lady—your sister, aunt, uncle, and cousins—I hope they have got better of their colds, coughs, claps, tooth-aches, fevers, stranguries, sciaticas, swellings, and sore eyes.

——What a devil of an apothecary! to take so much blood—give such a vile purge—puke—poultice—plaister—night-draught—clyster—blister?— And why so many grains of calomel? santa Maria! and such a dose of opium! periclitating, pardi! the whole family of ye, from head to tail—By my great-aunt Dinah's old black velvet mask! I think there was no occasion for it.

Now this being a little bald about the chin, by frequently putting off and on, before she was got with child by the coachman—not one of our family would wear it after. To cover the mask afresh, was more than the mask was worth—and to wear a mask which was bald, or which could be half seen through, was as bad as having no mask at all—

This is the reason, may it please your reverences, that in all our numerous family, for these four generations, we count no more than one archbishop, a Welch judge, some three or four aldermen, and a single mountebank—

In the sixteenth century, we boast of no less than a dozen alchemists.

CHAPTER 4

"IT is with Love as with Cuckoldom"—the suffering party is at least the third, but generally the last in the house who knows any thing about the matter: this comes, as all the world knows, from having half a dozen words for one thing; and so long, as what in this vessel of the human frame, is

[1]*Vid.* Pope's Portrait.

Love—may be Hatred, in that—Sentiment half a yard higher—and Non-sense——no, Madam,—not there—I mean at the part I am now pointing to with my forefinger—how can we help ourselves?

Of all mortal, and immortal men too, if you please, who ever soliloquized upon this mystic subject, my uncle Toby was the worst fitted, to have pushed his researches, thro' such a contention of feelings; and he had infallibly let them all run on, as we do worse matters, to see what they would turn out—had not Bridget's pre-notification of them to Susannah, and Susannah's repeated manifestoes thereupon to all the world, made it necessary for my uncle Toby to look into the affair.

CHAPTER 5

WHY weavers, gardeners, and gladiators—or a man with a pined leg (proceeding from some ailment in the foot)—should ever have had some tender nymph breaking her heart in secret for them, are points well and duly settled and accounted for, by ancient and modern physiologists.

A water-drinker, provided he is a professed one, and does it without fraud or covin, is precisely in the same predicament: not that, at first sight, there is any consequence, or shew of logic in it, "That a rill of cold water dribbling through my inward parts, should light up a torch in my Jenny's—"

—The proposition does not strike one; on the contrary, it seems to run opposite to the natural workings of causes and effects—

But it shews the weakness and imbecility of human reason.

——"And in perfect good health with it?"

—The most perfect,—Madam, that friendship herself could wish me—

"And drink nothing!—nothing but water?"

——Impetuous fluid! the moment thou pressest against the flood-gates of the brain—see how they give way!——

In swims Curiosity, beckoning to her damsels to follow—they dive into the centre of the current—

Fancy sits musing upon the bank, and with her eyes following the stream, turns straws and bulrushes into masts and bowsprits—And Desire, with vest held up to the knee in one hand, snatches at them, as they swim by her with the other—

O ye water-drinkers! is it then by this delusive fountain, that ye have so often governed and turned this world about like a mill-wheel—grinding the faces of the impotent—bepowdering their ribs—bepeppering their noses, and changing sometimes even the very frame and face of nature—

If I was you, quoth Yorick, I would drink more water, Eugenius—And, if I was you, Yorick, replied Eugenius, so would I.

Which shews they had both read Longinus—

For my own part, I am resolved never to read any book but my own, as long as I live.

CHAPTER 6

I WISH my uncle Toby had been a water-drinker; for then the thing had been accounted for, That the first moment Widow Wadman saw him, she felt something stirring within her in his favour—Something!—something.

——Something perhaps more than friendship—less than love—something—no matter what—no matter where—I would not give a single hair off my mule's tail, and be obliged to pluck it off myself (indeed the villain has not many to spare, and is not a little vicious into the bargain), to be let by your worships into the secret—

But the truth is, my uncle Toby was not a water-drinker; he drank it neither pure nor mixed, or any how, or any where, except fortuitously upon some advanced posts, where better liquor was not to be had—or during the time he was under cure; when the surgeon was telling him it would extend the fibres, and bring them sooner into contact—my uncle Toby drank it for quietness sake.

Now as all the world knows, that no effect in nature can be produced without a cause, and as it is as well known, that my uncle Toby was neither a weaver—a gardener, or a gladiator—unless as a captain, you will needs have him one—but then he was only a captain of foot—and besides, the whole is an equivocation—There is nothing left for us to suppose, but that my uncle Toby's leg—but that will avail us little in the present hypothesis, unless it had proceeded from some ailment in the foot—whereas his leg was not emaciated from any disorder in his foot—for my uncle Toby's leg was not emaciated at all. It was a little stiff and awkward, from a total disuse of it, for the three years he lay confined at my father's house in town; but it was plump and muscular, and in all other respects as good and promising a leg as the other.

I declare, I do not recollect any one opinion or passage of my life, where my understanding was more at a loss to make ends meet, and torture the chapter I had been writing, to the service of the chapter following it, than in the present case: one would think I took a pleasure in running into difficulties of this kind, merely to make fresh experiments of getting out of 'em—Inconsiderate soul that thou art! What! are not the unavoidable distresses with which, as an author and a man, thou art hemmed in on every side of thee—are they, Tristram, not sufficient, but thou must entangle thyself still more?

Is it not enough thou art in debt, and that thou hast ten cart-loads of thy fifth and sixth volumes still—still unsold, and art almost at thy wit's ends, how to get them off thy hands?

To this hour art thou not tormented with the vile asthma that thou gattest in skating against the wind in Flanders? and is it but two months ago, that in a fit of laughter, on seeing a cardinal make water like a quirister (with both hands) thou brakest a vessel in thy lungs, whereby, in two hours, thou lost as many quarts of blood; and hadst thou lost as much more, did not the faculty tell thee—it would have amounted to a gallon?——

CHAPTER 7

——But for heaven's sake, let us not talk of quarts or gallons—let us take the story straight before us; it is so nice and intricate a one, it will scarce bear the transposition of a single tittle; and, somehow or other, you have got me thrust almost into the middle of it—

——I beg we may take more care.

CHAPTER 8

MY uncle Toby and the corporal had posted down with so much heat and precipitation, to take possession of the spot of ground we have so often spoke of, in order to open their campaign as early as the rest of the allies; that they had forgot one of the most necessary articles of the whole affair; it was neither a pioneer's spade, a pickaxe, or a shovel—

—It was a bed to lie on: so that as Shandy Hall was at that time unfurnished; and the little inn where poor Le Fever died, not yet built; my uncle Toby was constrained to accept of a bed at Mrs. Wadman's, for a night or two, till corporal Trim (who to the character of an excellent valet, groom, cook, sempster, surgeon, and engineer, superadded that of an excellent upholsterer too), with the help of a carpenter and a couple of tailors, constructed one in my uncle Toby's house.

A daughter of Eve, for such was widow Wadman, and 'tis all the character I intend to give of her—

—"That she was a perfect woman—" had better be fifty leagues off—or in her warm bed—or playing with a case-knife—or any thing you please—than make a man the object of her attention, when the house and all the furniture is her own.

There is nothing in it out of doors and in broad daylight, where a woman has a power, physically speaking, of viewing a man in more lights than one —but here, for her soul, she can see him in no light without mixing something of her own goods and chattels along with him—till by reiterated acts of such combination, he gets foisted into her inventory—

—And then good night.

But this is not matter of System; for I have delivered that above—nor is it matter of Breviary—for I make no man's creed but my own—nor matter of Fact—at least that I know of; but 'tis matter copulative and introductory to what follows.

CHAPTER 9

I DO not speak it with regard to the coarseness or cleanness of them—or the strength of their gussets—but pray do not night-shifts differ from dayshifts as much in this particular, as in any thing else in the world; That they so far exceed the others in length, that when you are laid down in them, they fall almost as much below the feet, as the day-shifts fall short of them?

Widow Wadman's night-shifts (as was the mode I suppose in King William's and Queen Anne's reigns) were cut however after this fashion; and if the fashion is changed (for in Italy they are come to nothing)—so much the worse for the public; they were two Flemish ells and a half in length; so that allowing a moderate woman two ells, she had half an ell to spare, to do what she would with.

Now from one little indulgence gained after another, in the many bleak and Decemberly nights of a seven years' widowhood, things had insensibly come to this pass, and for the two last years had got established into one of the ordinances of the bed-chamber—That as soon as Mrs. Wadman was put to bed, and had got her legs stretched down to the bottom of it, of which she always gave Bridget notice—Bridget, with all suitable decorum, having first opened the bed-clothes at the feet, took hold of the half-ell of cloth we are speaking of, and having gently, and with both her hands, drawn it downwards to its furthest extension, and then contracted it again side-long by four or five even plaits, she took a large corking pin out of her sleeve, and with the point directed towards her, pinned the plaits all fast together a little above the hem; which done, she tucked all in tight at the feet, and wished her mistress a good night.

This was constant, and without any other variation than this; that on shivering and tempestuous nights, when Bridget untucked the feet of the bed, etc., to do this—she consulted no thermometer but that of her own passions; and so performed it standing—kneeling—or squatting, according to the different degrees of faith, hope, and charity, she was in, and bore towards her mistress that night. In every other respect, the etiquette was sacred, and might have vied with the most mechanical one of the most inflexible bed-chamber in Christendom.

The first night, as soon as the corporal had conducted my uncle Toby up stairs, which was about ten—Mrs. Wadman threw herself into her arm-chair, and crossing her left knee with her right, which formed a resting-place for her elbow, she reclined her cheek upon the palm of her hand, and leaning forwards, ruminated till midnight upon both sides of the question.

The second night she went to her bureau, and having ordered Bridget to bring her up a couple of fresh candles and leave them upon the table, she took out her marriage-settlement, and read it over with great devotion: and the third night (which was the last of my uncle Toby's stay) when Bridget had pulled down the night-shift, and was assaying to stick in the corking pin—

—With a kick of both heels at once, but at the same time the most natural kick that could be kicked in her situation—for supposing * * * * * * * * * * * * * to be the sun in its meridian, it was a north-east kick—she kicked the pin out of her fingers—the etiquette which hung upon it, down—down it fell to the ground, and was shivered into a thousand atoms.

From all which it was plain that widow Wadman was in love with my uncle Toby.

CHAPTER 10

MY uncle Toby's head at that time was full of other matters, so that it was not till the demolition of Dunkirk, when all the other civilities of Europe were settled, that he found leisure to return this.

This made an armistice (that is, speaking with regard to my uncle Toby —but with respect to Mrs. Wadman, a vacancy)—of almost eleven years. But in all cases of this nature, as it is the second blow, happen at what distance of time it will, which makes the fray—I choose for that reason to call these the amours of my uncle Toby with Mrs. Wadman, rather than the amours of Mrs. Wadman with my uncle Toby.

This is not a distinction without a difference.

It is not like the affair of an old hat cocked—and a cocked old hat, about which your reverences have so often been at odds with one another—but there is a difference here in the nature of things—

And let me tell you, gentry, a wide one too.

CHAPTER 11

Now as widow Wadman did love my uncle Toby—and my uncle Toby did not love widow Wadman, there was nothing for widow Wadman to do, but to go on and love my uncle Toby—or let it alone.

Widow Wadman would do neither the one or the other.

—Gracious heaven!—but I forget I am a little of her temper myself; for whenever it so falls out, which it sometimes does about the equinoxes, that an earthly goddess is so much this, and that, and t'other, that I cannot eat my breakfast for her—and that she careth not three halfpence whether I eat my breakfast or no—

—Curse on her! and so I send her to Tartary, and from Tartary to Terra del Fuego, and so on to the devil: in short, there is not an infernal niche where I do not take her divinityship and stick it.

But as the heart is tender, and the passions in these tides ebb and flow ten times in a minute, I instantly bring her back again; and as I do all things in extremes, I place her in the very centre of the milky-way—

Brightest of stars! thou wilt shed thy influence upon some one——

—The deuce take her and her influence too—for at that word I lose all patience—much good may it do him!—By all that is hirsute and gashly! I cry, taking off my furred cap, and twisting it round my finger—I would not give sixpence for a dozen such!

—But 'tis an excellent cap too (putting it upon my head, and pressing it close to my ears)—and warm—and soft; especially if you stroke it the right way—but alas! that will never be my luck—(so here my philosophy is ship-wrecked again).

—No; I shall never have a finger in the pie (so here I break my meta-phor)—

Crust and Crumb

Inside and out

Top and bottom—I detest it, I hate it, I repudiate it—I'm sick at the sight of it—

'Tis all pepper,
 garlick,
 staragen,
 salt, and
 devil's dung—by the great arch-cook of cooks, who does nothing, I think, from morning to night, but sit down by the fire-side and invent in-flammatory dishes for us, I would not touch it for the world—

—O Tristram! Tristram! cried Jenny.

O Jenny! Jenny! replied I, and so went on with the twelfth chapter.

CHAPTER 12

——"Not touch it for the world," did I say—
Lord, how I have heated my imagination with this metaphor!

CHAPTER 13

Which shows, let your reverences and worships say what you will of it (for as for thinking—all who do think—think pretty much alike both upon it and other matters)—Love is certainly, at least alphabetically speaking, one of the most

A gitating
B ewitching
C onfounded
D evilish affairs of life—the most
E xtravagant
F utilitous
G alligaskinish
H andy-dandyish
I racundulous (there is no K to it) and
L yrical of all human passions: at the same time, the most
M isgiving
N innyhammering
O bstipating
P ragmatical
S tridulous
R idiculous—though by the bye the R should have gone first—But in short 'tis of such a nature, as my father once told my uncle Toby upon the close of a long dissertation upon the subject—"You can scarce," said he, "combine two ideas together upon it, brother Toby, without an hypallage" —What's that? cried my uncle Toby.

The cart before the horse, replied my father—
—And what is he to do there? cried my uncle Toby—
Nothing, quoth my father, but to get in—or let it alone.
Now widow Wadman, as I told you before, would do neither the one or the other.
She stood however ready harnessed and caparisoned at all points, to watch accidents.

CHAPTER 14

The Fates, who certainly all foreknew of these amours of widow Wadman and my uncle Toby, had, from the first creation of matter and motion (and with more courtesy than they usually do things of this kind), established such a chain of causes and effects hanging so fast to one another, that it was scarce possible for my uncle Toby to have dwelt in any other house in the world, or to have occupied any other garden in Christendom, but the very house and garden which joined and laid parallel to Mrs. Wadman's; this, with the advantage of a thickset arbour in Mrs. Wadman's garden, but planted in the hedge-row of my uncle Toby's, put all the occasions into her hands which Love-militancy wanted; she could observe my uncle Toby's motions, and was mistress likewise of his councils of war; and as his un-suspecting heart had given leave to the corporal, through the mediation of Bridget, to make her a wicket-gate of communication to enlarge her walks, it enabled her to carry on her approaches to the very door of the sentry-box; and sometimes out of gratitude, to make an attack, and endeavour to blow my uncle Toby up in the very sentry-box itself.

CHAPTER 15

IT is a great pity—but 'tis certain from every day's observation of man, that he may be set on fire like a candle, at either end—provided there is a sufficient wick standing out; if there is not—there's an end of the affair; and if there is—by lighting it at the bottom, as the flame in that case has the misfortune generally to put out itself—there's an end of the affair again.

For my part, could I always have the ordering of it which way I would be burnt myself—for I cannot bear the thoughts of being burnt like a beast—I would oblige a housewife constantly to light me at the top; for then I should burn down decently to the socket; that is, from my head to my heart, from my heart to my liver, from my liver to my bowels, and so on by the meseraic veins and arteries, through all the turns and lateral insertions of the in-testines and their tunicles to the blind gut—

—I beseech you, doctor Slop, quoth my uncle Toby, interrupting him as he mentioned the blind gut, in a discourse with my father the night my mother was brought to bed of me—I beseech you, quoth my uncle Toby, to tell me which is the blind gut; for, old as I am, I vow I do not know to this day where it lies.

The blind gut, answered doctor Slop, lies betwixt the Ilion and Colon—
In a man? said my father.
——'Tis precisely the same, cried doctor Slop, in a woman.——
That's more than I know; quoth my father.

CHAPTER 16

——AND so to make sure of both systems, Mrs. Wadman predetermined to light my uncle Toby neither at this end or that; but, like a prodigal's candle, to light him, if possible, at both ends at once.

Now, through all the lumber rooms of military furniture, including both of horse and foot, from the great arsenal of Venice to the Tower of London (exclusive), if Mrs. Wadman had been rummaging for seven years together, and with Bridget to help her, she could not have found any one blind or mantelet so fit for her purpose, as that which the expediency of my uncle Toby's affairs had fixed up ready to her hands.

I believe I have not told you—but I don't know—possibly I have—be it as it will, 'tis one of the number of those many things, which a man had better do over again, than dispute about it—That whatever town or fortress the corporal was at work upon, during the course of their campaign, my uncle Toby always took care, on the inside of his sentry-box, which was towards his left hand, to have a plan of the place, fastened up with two or three pins at the top, but loose at the bottom, for the conveniency of holding it up to the eye, etc. . . . as occasions required; so that when an attack was resolved upon, Mrs. Wadman had nothing more to do, when she had got advanced to the door of the sentry-box, but to extend her right hand; and edging in her left foot at the same movement, to take hold of the map or plan, or upright, or whatever it was, and with out-stretched neck meeting it half way,—to advance it towards her; on which my uncle Toby's passions were sure to catch fire—for he would instantly take hold of the other corner of the map in his left hand, and with the end of his pipe in the other, begin an explanation.

When the attack was advanced to this point;—the world will naturally enter into the reasons of Mrs. Wadman's next stroke of generalship—which was, to take my uncle Toby's tobacco-pipe out of his hand as soon as she possibly could; which, under one pretence or other, but generally that of pointing more distinctly at some redoubt or breastwork in the map, she would effect before my uncle Toby (poor soul!) had well marched above half a dozen toises with it.

——It obliged my uncle Toby to make use of his fore-finger.

The difference it made in the attack was this; That in going upon it, as in the first case, with the end of her forefinger against the end of my uncle Toby's tobacco-pipe, she might have travelled with it, along the lines, from Dan to Beersheba, had my uncle Toby's lines reached so far, without any effect: For as there was no arterial or vital heat in the end of the tobacco-pipe, it could excite no sentiment—it could neither give fire by pulsation—or receive it by sympathy—'twas nothing but smoke.

Whereas, in following my uncle Toby's forefinger with hers, close thro' all the little turns and indentings of his works—pressing sometimes against the side of it—then treading upon its nail—then tripping it up—then touching it here—then there, and so on—it set something at least in motion.

This, tho' slight skirmishing, and at a distance from the main body, yet drew on the rest; for here, the map usually falling with the back of it, close to the side of the sentry-box, my uncle Toby, in the simplicity of his soul, would lay his hand flat upon it, in order to go on with his explanation; and Mrs. Wadman, by a manœuvre as quick as thought, would as certainly place hers close beside it; this at once opened a communication, large enough for any sentiment to pass or repass, which a person skilled in the elementary and practical part of love-making, has occasion for—

By bringing up her forefinger parallel (as before) to my uncle Toby's—it unavoidably brought the thumb into action—and the forefinger and thumb being once engaged, as naturally brought in the whole hand. Thine, dear uncle Toby! was never now in its right place—Mrs. Wadman had it ever to take up, or, with the gentlest pushings, protrusions, and equivocal compressions, that a hand to be removed is capable of receiving—to get it pressed a hair breadth of one side out of her way.

Whilst this was doing, how could she forget to make him sensible, that it was her leg (and no one's else) at the bottom of the sentry-box, which slightly pressed against the calf of his—So that my uncle Toby being thus attacked and sore pushed on both his wings—was it a wonder, if now and then, it put his centre into disorder?

——The deuce take it! said my uncle Toby.

CHAPTER 17

THESE attacks of Mrs. Wadman, you will readily conceive to be of different kinds; varying from each other, like the attacks which history is full of, and from the same reasons. A general looker-on would scarce allow them to be attacks at all—or if he did, would confound them all together—but I write not to them: it will be time enough to be a little more exact in my descriptions of them, as I come up to them, which will not be for some chapters; having nothing more to add in this, but that in a bundle of original papers and drawings which my father took care to roll up by themselves, there is a plan of Bouchain in perfect preservation (and shall be kept so, whilst I have power to preserve any thing), upon the lower corner of which, on the right hand side, there is still remaining the marks of a snuffy finger and thumb, which there is all the reason in the world to imagine, were Mrs. Wadman's; for the opposite side of the margin, which I suppose to have been my uncle Toby's, is absolutely clean: This seems an authenticated record of one of these attacks; for there are vestigia of the two punctures partly grown up, but still visible on the opposite corner of the map, which are unquestionably the very holes, through which it has been pricked up in the sentry-box—

By all that is priestly! I value this precious relic, with its stigmata and pricks, more than all the relics of the Romish church—always excepting, when I am writing upon these matters, the pricks which entered the flesh of St. Radagunda in the desert, which in your road from Fesse to Cluny, the nuns of that name will shew you for love.

CHAPTER 18

I THINK, an' please your honour, quoth Trim, the fortifications are quite destroyed—and the bason is upon a level with the mole—I think so too; replied my uncle Toby with a sigh half suppressed—but step into the parlour, Trim, for the stipulation—it lies upon the table.

It has lain there these six weeks, replied the corporal, till this very morning that the old woman kindled the fire with it—

——Then, said my uncle Toby, there is no further occasion for our services. The more, an' please your honour, the pity, said the corporal; in uttering which he cast his spade into the wheel-barrow, which was beside him, with an air the most expressive of disconsolation that can be imagined, and was heavily turning about to look for his pickaxe, his pioneer's shovel, his picquets, and other little military stores, in order to carry them off the field—when a heigh-ho! from the sentry-box, which being made of thin slit deal, reverberated the sound more sorrowfully to his ear, forbad him.

——No; said the corporal to himself, I'll do it before his honour rises to-morrow morning; so taking his spade out of the wheel-barrow again, with a little earth in it, as if to level something at the foot of the glacis—but with a real intent to approach near to his master, in order to divert him—he loosened a sod or two—pared their edges with his spade, and having given them a gentle blow or two with the back of it, he sat himself down close by my uncle Toby's feet, and began as follows.

CHAPTER 19

It was a thousand pities—though I believe, an' please your honour, I am going to say but a foolish kind of a thing for a soldier—

A soldier, cried my uncle Toby, interrupting the corporal, is no more exempt from saying a foolish thing, Trim, than a man of letters—But not so often, an' please your honour, replied the corporal—my uncle Toby gave a nod.

It was a thousand pities, then, said the corporal, casting his eye upon Dunkirk, and the mole, as Servius Sulpicius, in returning out of Asia (when he sailed from Aegina towards Megara), did upon Corinth and Piraeus—

—"It was a thousand pities, an' please your honour, to destroy these works—and a thousand pities to have let them stood."——

——Thou art right, Trim, in both cases; said my uncle Toby.——This, continued the corporal, is the reason, that from the beginning of their demolition to the end—I have never once whistled, or sung, or laughed, or cried, or talked of past done deeds, or told your honour one story good or bad—

—Thou hast many excellencies, Trim, said my uncle Toby, and I hold it not the least of them, as thou happenest to be a story-teller, that of the number thou hast told me, either to amuse me in my painful hours, or divert me in my grave ones—thou hast seldom told me a bad one—

—Because, an' please your honour, except one of a King of Bohemia and his seven castles,—they are all true; for they are about myself—

I do not like the subject the worse, Trim, said my uncle Toby, on that score: But prithee what is this story? thou hast excited my curiosity.

I'll tell it your honour, quoth the corporal, directly—Provided, said my uncle Toby, looking earnestly towards Dunkirk and the mole again—provided it is not a merry one; to such, Trim, a man should ever bring one half of the entertainment along with him; and the disposition I am in at present would wrong both thee, Trim, and thy story—It is not a merry one by any means, replied the corporal—Nor would I have it altogether a grave one, added my uncle Toby—It is neither the one nor the other, replied the corporal, but will suit your honour exactly—Then I'll thank thee for it with all my heart, cried my uncle Toby; so prithee begin it, Trim.

The corporal made his reverence; and though it is not so easy a matter as the world imagines, to pull off a lank Montero-cap with grace—or a whit less difficult, in my conceptions, when a man is sitting squat upon the ground, to make a bow so teeming with respect as the corporal was wont; yet by suffering the palm of his right hand, which was towards his master, to slip backwards upon the grass, a little beyond his body, in order to allow it the greater sweep—and by an unforced compression, at the same time, of his cap with the thumb and the two forefingers of his left, by which the diameter of the cap became reduced, so that it might be said, rather to be insensibly squeezed—than pulled off with a flatus—the corporal acquitted himself of both in a better manner than the posture of his affairs promised; and having hemmed twice, to find in what key his story would best go, and best suit his master's humour,—he exchanged a single look of kindness with him, and set off thus

THE STORY OF THE KING OF BOHEMIA AND HIS SEVEN CASTLES

THERE was a certain king of Bo--he——

As the corporal was entering the confines of Bohemia, my uncle Toby obliged him to halt for a single moment; he had set out bare-headed, having, since he pulled off his Montero-cap in the latter end of the last chapter, left it lying beside him on the ground.

——The eye of Goodness espieth all things—so that before the corporal had well got through the first five words of his story, had my uncle Toby twice touched his Montero-cap with the end of his cane, interrogatively— as much as to say, Why don't you put it on, Trim? Trim took it up with the most respectful slowness, and casting a glance of humiliation as he did it, upon the embroidery of the forepart, which being dismally tarnished and frayed moreover in some of the principal leaves and boldest parts of the pattern, he laid it down again between his two feet, in order to moralize upon the subject.

——'Tis every word of it but too true, cried my uncle Toby, that thou art about to observe—

"Nothing in this world, Trim, is made to last for ever."

——But when tokens, dear Tom, of thy love and remembrance wear out, said Trim, what shall we say?

There is no occasion, Trim, quoth my uncle Toby, to say any thing else; and was a man to puzzle his brains till Doom's day, I believe, Trim, it would be impossible.

The corporal, perceiving my uncle Toby was in the right, and that it would be in vain for the wit of man to think of extracting a purer moral from his cap, without further attempting it, he put it on; and passing his hand across his forehead to rub out a pensive wrinkle, which the text and the doctrine between them had engendered, he returned, with the same look and tone of voice, to his story of the king of Bohemia and his seven castles.

THE STORY OF THE KING OF BOHEMIA AND HIS SEVEN CASTLES, *Continued*

THERE was a certain king of Bohemia, but in whose reign, except his own, I am not able to inform your honour—

I do not desire it of thee, Trim, by any means, cried my uncle Toby.

——It was a little before the time, an' please your honour, when giants were beginning to leave off breeding:—but in what year of our Lord that was—

I would not give a halfpenny to know, said my uncle Toby.

——Only, an' please your honour, it makes a story look the better in the face——

—'Tis thy own, Trim, so ornament it after thy own fashion; and take any date, continued my uncle Toby, looking pleasantly upon him—take any date in the whole world thou choosest, and put it to—thou art heartily welcome——

The corporal bowed; for of every century, and of every year of that century, from the first creation of the world down to Noah's flood; and from Noah's flood to the birth of Abraham; through all the pilgrimages of the patriarchs, to the departure of the Israelites out of Egypt—and throughout all the Dynasties, Olympiads, Urbeconditas, and other memorable epochs of the different nations of the world, down to the coming of Christ, and from thence to the very moment in which the corporal was telling his story—had my uncle Toby subjected this vast empire of time and all its abysses at his feet; but as Modesty scarce touches with a finger what Liberality offers her with both hands open—the corporal contented himself with the very worst year of the whole bunch; which, to prevent your honours of the Majority and Minority from tearing the very flesh off your bones in contestation, "Whether that year is not always the last cast-year of the last cast-almanac"—I tell you plainly it was; but from a different reason than you wot of——

—It was the year next him—which being the year of our Lord seventeen hundred and twelve, when the Duke of Ormond was playing the devil in Flanders—the corporal took it, and set out with it afresh on his expedition to Bohemia.

THE STORY OF THE KING OF BOHEMIA AND
HIS SEVEN CASTLES, *Continued*

In the year of our Lord one thousand seven hundred and twelve, there was, an' please your honour——

—To tell thee truly, Trim, quoth my uncle Toby, any other date would have pleased me much better, not only on account of the sad stain upon our history that year, in marching off our troops, and refusing to cover the siege of Quesnoi, though Fagel was carrying on the works with such incredible vigour—but likewise on the score, Trim, of thy own story; because if there are—and which, from what thou hast dropt, I partly suspect to be the fact—if there are giants in it——

There is but one, an' please your honour——

'Tis as bad as twenty, replied my uncle Toby—thou should'st have carried him back some seven or eight hundred years out of harm's way, both of critics and other people: and therefore I would advise thee, if ever thou tellest it again——

—If I live, an' please your honour, but once to get through it, I will never tell it again, quoth Trim, either to man, woman, or child—Poo—poo! said my uncle Toby—but with accents of such sweet encouragement did he utter it, that the corporal went on with his story with more alacrity than ever.

THE STORY OF THE KING OF BOHEMIA AND
HIS SEVEN CASTLES, *Continued*

THERE was, an' please your honour, said the corporal, raising his voice and rubbing the palms of his two hands cheerily together as he began, a certain king of Bohemia—

—Leave out the date entirely, Trim, quoth my uncle Toby, leaning forwards, and laying his hand gently upon the corporal's shoulder to temper the interruption—leave it out entirely, Trim; a story passes very well without these niceties, unless one is pretty sure of 'em—sure of 'em! said the corporal, shaking his head—

Right; answered my uncle Toby, it is not easy, Trim, for one, bred up as thou and I have been to arms, who seldom looks further forward than to the end of his musket, or backwards beyond his knapsack, to know much about this matter—God bless your honour! said the corporal, won by the manner of my uncle Toby's reasoning, as much as by the reasoning itself, he has something else to do; if not on action, or a march, or upon duty in his garrison—he has his firelock, an' please your honour, to furbish—his accoutrements to take care of—his regimentals to mend—himself to shave and keep clean, so as to appear always like what he is upon the parade; what business, added the corporal triumphantly, has a soldier, an' please your honour, to know any thing at all of geography?

—Thou would'st have said chronology, Trim, said my uncle Toby; for as for geography, 'tis of absolute use to him; he must be acquainted intimately with every country and its boundaries where his profession carries him; he should know every town and city, and village and hamlet, with the canals, the roads, and hollow ways which lead up to them; there is not a river or a rivulet he passes, Trim, but he should be able at first sight to tell thee what is its name—in what mountains it takes its rise—what is its course—how far it is navigable—where fordable—where not; he should know the fertility of every valley, as well as the hind who ploughs it; and be able to describe, or, if it is required, to give thee an exact map of all the plains and defiles, the forts, the acclivities, the woods and morasses, thro' and by which his army is to march; he should know their produce, their plants, their minerals, their waters, their animals, their seasons, their climates, their heats and cold, their inhabitants, their customs, their language, their policy, and even their religion.

Is it else to be conceived, corporal, continued my uncle Toby, rising up in his sentry-box, as he began to warm in this part of his discourse—how Marlborough could have marched his army from the banks of the Maes to Belburg; from Belburg to Kerpenord—(here the corporal could sit no longer) from Kerpenord, Trim, to Kalsaken; from Kalsaken to Newdorf; from Newdorf to Landenbourg; from Landenbourg to Mildenheim; from Mildenheim to Elchingen; from Elchingen to Gingen; from Gingen to Balmerchoffen; from Balmerchoffen to Skellenburg, where he broke in upon the enemy's works; forced his passage over the Danube; crossed the Lech—pushed on his troops into the heart of the empire, marching at the head of them through Fribourg, Hokenwert, and Schonevelt, to the plains of Blenheim and Hochstet?——Great as he was, corporal, he could not have advanced a step, or made one single day's march without the aids of Geography.——As for Chronology, I own, Trim, continued my uncle Toby, sitting down again coolly in his sentry-box, that of all others, it seems a science which the soldier might best spare, was it not for the lights which that science must one day give him, in determining the invention of powder; the furious execution of which, reversing every thing like thunder before it, has become a new area to us of military improvements, changing so totally the nature of attacks and defences both by sea and land, and awakening so much art and skill in doing it, that the world cannot be too exact in ascertaining the precise time of its discovery, or too inquisitive in knowing what great man was the discoverer, and what occasions gave birth to it.

I am far from controverting, continued my uncle Toby, what historians agree in, that in the year of our Lord 1380, under the reign of Wencelaus, son of Charles the Fourth—a certain priest, whose name was Schwartz, shewed the use of powder to the Venetians, in their wars against the Genoese; but 'tis certain he was not the first; because if we are to believe Don Pedro, the bishop of Leon—How came priests and bishops, an' please your honour, to trouble their heads so much about gun-powder? God knows, said my uncle Toby—his providence brings good out of every thing—and he avers, in his chronicle of King Alphonsus, who reduced Toledo, That in the year 1343, which was full thirty-seven years before that time, the secret of powder was well known, and employed with success, both by Moors and Christians, not only in their sea-combats, at that period, but in many of their most memorable sieges in Spain and Barbary—And all the world knows, that Friar Bacon had wrote expressly about it, and had generously given the world a receipt to make it by, above a hundred and fifty years before even Schwartz was born—And that the Chinese, added my uncle Toby, embarrass us, and all accounts of it, still more, by boasting of the invention some hundreds of years even before him—

—They are a pack of liars, I believe, cried Trim—

—They are somehow or other deceived, said my uncle Toby, in this matter, as is plain to me from the present miserable state of military architecture amongst them; which consists of nothing more than a fossé with a brick wall without flanks—and for what they gave us as a bastion at each angle of it, 'tis so barbarously constructed, that it looks for all the world—Like one of my seven castles, an' please your honour, quoth Trim.

My uncle Toby, tho' in the utmost distress for a comparison, most courteously refused Trim's offer—till Trim telling him, he had half a dozen more in Bohemia, which he knew not how to get off his hands—my uncle Toby was so touched with the pleasantry of heart of the corporal—that he discontinued his dissertation upon gun-powder—and begged the corporal forthwith to go on with his story of the King of Bohemia and his seven castles.

THE STORY OF THE KING OF BOHEMIA AND
HIS SEVEN CASTLES, *Continued*

THIS unfortunate King of Bohemia, said Trim,—Was he unfortunate, then? cried my uncle Toby, for he had been so wrapt up in his dissertation upon

gun-powder, and other military affairs, that tho' he had desired the corporal to go on, yet the many interruptions he had given, dwelt not so strong
upon his fancy as to account for the epithet—Was he unfortunate, then,
Trim? said my uncle Toby, pathetically—The corporal, wishing first the
word and all its synonimas at the devil, forthwith began to run back in his
mind, the principal events in the King of Bohemia's story; from every one
of which, it appearing that he was the most fortunate man that ever existed
in the world—it put the corporal to a stand: for not caring to retract his
epithet—and less to explain it—and least of all, to twist his tale (like men
of lore) to serve a system—he looked up in my uncle Toby's face for assistance—but seeing it was the very thing my uncle Toby sat in expectation
of himself—after a hum and a haw, he went on—

The King of Bohemia, an' please your honour, replied the corporal, was
unfortunate, as thus—That taking great pleasure and delight in navigation
and all sort of sea affairs—and there happening throughout the whole kingdom of Bohemia, to be no sea-port town whatever—

How the deuce should there—Trim? cried my uncle Toby; for Bohemia
being totally inland, it could have happened no otherwise—It might, said
Trim, if it had pleased God—

My uncle Toby never spoke of the being and natural attributes of God,
but with diffidence and hesitation—

—I believe not, replied my uncle Toby, after some pause—for being inland, as I said, and having Silesia and Moravia to the east; Lusatia and
Upper Saxony to the north; Franconia to the west; Bavaria to the south;
Bohemia could not have been propelled to the sea without ceasing to be
Bohemia—nor could the sea, on the other hand, have come up to Bohemia,
without overflowing a great part of Germany, and destroying millions of
unfortunate inhabitants who could make no defence against it—Scandalous! cried Trim—Which would bespeak, added my uncle Toby, mildly,
such a want of compassion in him who is the father of it—that, I think,
Trim—the thing could have happened no way.

The corporal made the bow of unfeigned conviction; and went on.

Now the King of Bohemia with his queen and courtiers happening one
fine summer's evening to walk out—Aye! there the word happening is
right, Trim, cried my uncle Toby; for the King of Bohemia and his queen
might have walked out or let it alone:—'twas a matter of contingency,
which might happen, or not, just as chance ordered it.

King William was of an opinion, an' please your honour, quoth Trim,
that every thing was predestined for us in this world; insomuch, that he
would often say to his soldiers, that "every ball had its billet." He was a
great man, said my uncle Toby—And I believe, continued Trim, to this
day, that the shot which disabled me at the battle of Landen, was pointed
at my knee for no other purpose, but to take me out of his service, and
place me in your honour's, where I should be taken so much better care of
in my old age—It shall never, Trim, be construed otherwise, said my uncle
Toby.

The heart, both of the master and the man, were alike subject to sudden
overflowings;—a short silence ensued.

Besides, said the corporal, resuming the discourse—but in a gayer accent —if it had not been for that single shot, I had never, an' please your honour, been in love—

So, thou wast once in love, Trim! said my uncle Toby, smiling.

Souse! replied the corporal—over head and ears! an' please your honour. Prithee when? where?—and how came it to pass?—I never heard one word of it before; quoth my uncle Toby:—I dare say, answered Trim, that every drummer and serjeant's son in the regiment knew of it—It's high time I should—said my uncle Toby.

Your honour remembers with concern, said the corporal, the total rout and confusion of our camp and army at the affair of Landen; every one was left to shift for himself; and if it had not been for the regiments of Wyndham, Lumley, and Galway, which covered the retreat over the bridge of Neerspeeken, the king himself could scarce have gained it—he was pressed hard, as your honour knows, on every side of him—

Gallant mortal! cried my uncle Toby, caught up with enthusiasm—this moment, now that all is lost, I see him galloping across me, corporal, to the left, to bring up the remains of the English horse along with him to support the right, and tear the laurel from Luxembourg's brows, if yet 'tis possible— I see him with the knot of his scarf just shot off, infusing fresh spirits into poor Galway's regiment—riding along the line—then wheeling about, and charging Conti at the head of it—Brave! brave, by heaven! cried my uncle Toby—he deserves a crown—As richly, as a thief a halter; shouted Trim.

My uncle Toby knew the corporal's loyalty;—otherwise the comparison was not at all to his mind—it did not altogether strike the corporal's fancy when he had made it—but it could not be recalled—so he had nothing to do, but proceed.

As the number of wounded was prodigious, and no one had time to think of any thing but his own safety—Though Talmash, said my uncle Toby, brought off the foot with great prudence—But I was left upon the field, said the corporal. Thou wast so; poor fellow! replied my uncle Toby—So that it was noon the next day, continued the corporal, before I was exchanged, and put into a cart with thirteen or fourteen more, in order to be conveyed to our hospital.

There is no part of the body, an' please your honour, where a wound occasions more intolerable anguish than upon the knee—

Except the groin; said my uncle Toby. An' please your honour, replied the corporal, the knee, in my opinion, must certainly be the most acute, there being so many tendons and what-d'ye-call-'ems all about it.

It is for that reason, quoth my uncle Toby, that the groin is infinitely more sensible—there being not only as many tendons and what-d'ye-call-'ems (for I know their names as little as thou dost)—about it—but moreover ***—

Mrs. Wadman, who had been all the time in her arbour—instantly stopped her breath—unpinned her mob at the chin, and stood upon one leg—

The dispute was maintained with amicable and equal force betwixt my uncle Toby and Trim for some time; till Trim at length recollecting that he had often cried at his master's sufferings, but never shed a tear at his own—was for giving up the point, which my uncle Toby would not allow—'Tis a proof of nothing, Trim, said he, but the generosity of thy temper—

So that whether the pain of a wound in the groin, (*caeteris paribus*) is greater than the pain of a wound in the knee—or

Whether the pain of a wound in the knee is not greater than the pain of a wound in the groin—are points which to this day remain unsettled.

CHAPTER 20

THE anguish of my knee, continued the corporal, was excessive in itself; and the uneasiness of the cart, with the roughness of the roads, which were terribly cut up—making bad still worse—every step was death to me: so that with the loss of blood, and the want of care-taking of me, and a fever I felt coming on besides—(Poor soul! said my uncle Toby)—all together, and please your honour, was more than I could sustain.

I was telling my sufferings to a young woman at a peasant's house, where our cart, which was the last of the line, had halted; they had helped me in, and the young woman had taken a cordial out of her pocket and dropped it upon some sugar, and seeing it had cheered me, she had given it me a second and a third time—So I was telling her, an' please your honour, the anguish I was in, and was saying it was so intolerable to me, that I had much rather lie down upon the bed, turning my face towards one which was in the corner of the room—and die, than go on—when, upon her attempting to lead me to it, I fainted away in her arms. She was a good soul! as your honour, said the corporal, wiping his eyes, will hear.

I thought love had been a joyous thing, quoth my uncle Toby.

'Tis the most serious thing, an' please your honour (sometimes), that is in the world.

By the persuasion of the young woman, continued the corporal, the cart with the wounded men set out without me: she had assured them I should expire immediately if I was put into the cart. So when I came to myself—I found myself in a still quiet cottage, with no one but the young woman, and the peasant and his wife. I was laid across the bed in the corner of the room, with my wounded leg upon a chair, and the young woman beside me, holding the corner of her handkerchief dipped in vinegar to my nose with one hand, and rubbing my temples with the other.

I took her at first for the daughter of the peasant (for it was no inn)—so had offered her a little purse with eighteen florins, which my poor brother Tom (here Trim wiped his eyes) had sent me as a token, by a recruit, just before he set out for Lisbon.——

——I never told your honour that piteous story yet—here Trim wiped his eyes a third time.

The young woman called the old man and his wife into the room, to shew them the money, in order to gain me credit for a bed and what little necessaries I should want, till I should be in a condition to be got to the hospital—Come then! said she, tying up the little purse—I'll be your banker—but as that office alone will not keep me employed, I'll be your nurse too.

I thought by her manner of speaking this, as well as by her dress, which I then began to consider more attentively—that the young woman could not be the daughter of the peasant.

She was in black down to her toes, with her hair concealed under a cambric border, laid close to her forehead: she was one of those kind of nuns, an' please your honour, of which, your honour knows, there are a good many in Flanders, which they let go loose—By thy description, Trim, said my uncle Toby, I dare say she was a young Beguine, of which there are none to be found any where but in the Spanish Netherlands—except at Amsterdam—they differ from nuns in this, that they can quit their cloister if they choose to marry; they visit and take care of the sick by profession—I had rather, for my own part, they did it out of good-nature.

——She often told me, quoth Trim, she did it for the love of Christ—I did not like it.——I believe, Trim, we are both wrong, said my uncle Toby—we'll ask Mr. Yorick about it to-night at my brother Shandy's—so put me in mind; added my uncle Toby.

The young Beguine, continued the corporal, had scarce given herself time to tell me "she would be my nurse," when she hastily turned about to begin the office of one, and prepare something for me—and in a short time—though I thought it a long one—she came back with flannels, etc. etc., and having fomented my knee soundly for a couple of hours, etc., and made me a thin basin of gruel for my supper—she wished me rest, and promised to be with me early in the morning.——She wished me, an' please your honour, what was not to be had. My fever ran very high that night—her figure made sad disturbance within me—I was every moment cutting the world in two to give her half of it—and every moment was I crying, That I had nothing but a knapsack and eighteen florins to share with her—The whole night long was the fair Beguine, like an angel, close by my bedside, holding back my curtain and offering me cordials—and I was only awakened from my dream by her coming there at the hour promised, and giving them in reality. In truth, she was scarce ever from me; and so accustomed was I to receive life from her hands, that my heart sickened, and I lost colour when she left the room: and yet, continued the corporal (making one of the strangest reflections upon it in the world)—

—"It was not love"—for during the three weeks she was almost constantly with me, fomenting my knee with her hand, night and day—I can honestly say, an' please your honour—that * * * * * * * * * * once.

That was very odd, Trim, quoth my uncle Toby.

I think so too—said Mrs. Wadman.

It never did, said the corporal.

CHAPTER 21

——But 'tis no marvel, continued the corporal—seeing my uncle Toby musing upon it—for Love, an' please your honour, is exactly like war, in this; that a soldier, though he has escaped three weeks complete o' Saturday night,—may nevertheless be shot through his heart on Sunday morning—It happened so here, an' please your honour, with this difference only —that it was on Sunday in the afternoon, when I fell in love all at once with a sisserara—It burst upon me, an' please your honour, like a bomb— scarce giving me time to say, "God bless me."

I thought, Trim, said my uncle Toby, a man never fell in love so very suddenly.

Yes, an' please your honour, if he is in the way of it—replied Trim.

I prithee, quoth my uncle Toby, inform me how this matter happened.

——With all pleasure, said the corporal, making a bow.

CHAPTER 22

I HAD escaped, continued the corporal, all that time from falling in love, and had gone on to the end of the chapter, had it not been predestined otherwise—there is no resisting our fate.

It was on a Sunday, in the afternoon, as I told your honour.

The old man and his wife had walked out—

Every thing was still and hush as midnight about the house—

There was not so much as a duck or a duckling about the yard—

—When the fair Beguine came in to see me.

My wound was then in a fair way of doing well—the inflammation had been gone off for some time, but it was succeeded with an itching both above and below my knee, so insufferable, that I had not shut my eyes the whole night for it.

Let me see it, said she, kneeling down upon the ground parallel to my knee, and laying her hand upon the part below it—it only wants rubbing a little, said the Beguine; so covering it with the bed-clothes, she began with the fore-finger of her right hand to rub under my knee, guiding her fore-finger backwards and forwards by the edge of the flannel which kept on the dressing.

In five or six minutes I felt slightly the end of her second finger—and presently it was laid flat with the other, and she continued rubbing in that way round and round for a good while; it then came into my head, that I should fall in love—I blushed when I saw how white a hand she had—I shall never, an' please your honour, behold another hand so white whilst I live—

—Not in that place; said my uncle Toby—

Though it was the most serious despair in nature to the corporal—he could not forbear smiling.

The young Beguine, continued the corporal, perceiving it was of great service to me—from rubbing for some time, with two fingers—proceeded to rub at length, with three—till by little and little she brought down the fourth, and then rubbed with her whole hand: I will never say another word, an' please your honour, upon hands again—but it was softer than satin—

—Prithee, Trim, commend it as much as thou wilt, said my uncle Toby; I shall hear thy story with the more delight—The corporal thanked his master most unfeignedly; but having nothing to say upon the Beguine's hand but the same over again—he proceeded to the effects of it.

The fair Beguine, said the corporal, continued rubbing with her whole hand under my knee—till I feared her zeal would weary her—"I would do a thousand times more," said she, "for the love of Christ"—In saying which, she passed her hand across the flannel, to the part above my knee, which I had equally complained of, and rubbed it also.

I perceived, then, I was beginning to be in love—

As she continued rub-rub-rubbing—I felt it spread from under her hand, an' please your honour, to every part of my frame—

The more she rubbed, and the longer strokes she took—the more the fire kindled in my veins—till at length, by two or three strokes longer than the rest—my passion rose to the highest pitch—I seized her hand—

—And then thou clapped'st it to thy lips, Trim, said my uncle Toby— and madest a speech.

Whether the corporal's amour terminated precisely in the way my uncle Toby described it, is not material; it is enough that it contained in it the essence of all the love romances which ever have been wrote since the beginning of the world.

CHAPTER 23

As soon as the corporal had finished the story of his amour—or rather my uncle Toby for him—Mrs. Wadman silently sallied forth from her arbour, replaced the pin in her mob, passed the wicket-gate, and advanced slowly towards my uncle Toby's sentry-box: the disposition which Trim had made in my uncle Toby's mind, was too favourable a crisis to be let slipped—

—The attack was determined upon: it was facilitated still more by my uncle Toby's having ordered the corporal to wheel off the pioneer's shovel, the spade, the pick-axe, the picquets, and other military stores which lay scattered upon the ground where Dunkirk stood—The corporal had marched—the field was clear.

Now, consider, sir, what nonsense it is, either in fighting, or writing, or any thing else (whether in rhyme to it, or not) which a man has occasion to do—to act by plan: for if ever Plan, independent of all circumstances, deserved registering in letters of gold (I mean in the archives of Gotham)—it was certainly the Plan of Mrs. Wadman's attack of my uncle Toby in his sentry-box, by Plan—Now the plan hanging up in it at this juncture, being the Plan of Dunkirk—and the tale of Dunkirk a tale of relaxation, it opposed every impression she could make: and besides, could she have gone upon it—the manœuvre of fingers and hands in the attack of the sentry-box, was so outdone by that of the fair Beguine's, in Trim's story—that just then, that particular attack, however successful before—became the most heartless attack that could be made—

O! let woman alone for this. Mrs. Wadman had scarce opened the wicket-gate, when her genius sported with the change of circumstances.

—She formed a new attack in a moment.

CHAPTER 24

——I AM half distracted, Captain Shandy, said Mrs. Wadman, holding up her cambric handkerchief to her left eye, as she approached the door of my uncle Toby's sentry-box—a mote—or sand—or something—I know not what, has got into this eye of mine—do look into it—it is not in the white—

In saying which, Mrs. Wadman edged herself close in beside my uncle Toby, and squeezing herself down upon the corner of his bench, she gave him an opportunity of doing it without rising up—Do look into it—said she.

Honest soul! thou didst look into it with as much innocency of heart, as ever child looked into a raree-show-box; and 'twere as much a sin to have hurt thee.

——If a man will be peeping of his own accord into things of that nature —I've nothing to say to it—

My uncle Toby never did: and I will answer for him, that he would have sat quietly upon a sofa from June to January (which, you know, takes in both the hot and cold months), with an eye as fine as the Thracian[1] Rhodope's beside him, without being able to tell, whether it was a black or blue one.

The difficulty was to get my uncle Toby, to look at one at all.

'Tis surmounted. And

I see him yonder with his pipe pendulous in his hand, and the ashes falling out of it—looking—and looking—then rubbing his eyes—and looking again, with twice the good-nature that ever Galileo looked for a spot in the sun.

——In vain! for by all the powers which animate the organ—Widow Wadman's left eye shines this moment as lucid as her right—there is neither mote, or sand, or dust, or chaff, or speck, or particle of opaque matter floating in it—There is nothing, my dear paternal uncle! but one lambent delicious fire, furtively shooting out from every part of it, in all directions, into thine—

—If thou lookest, uncle Toby, in search of this mote one moment longer —thou art undone.

CHAPTER 25

An eye is for all the world exactly like a cannon, in this respect; That it is not so much the eye or the cannon, in themselves, as it is the carriage of the eye—and the carriage of the cannon, by which both the one and the other are enabled to do so much execution. I don't think the comparison a bad one; However, as 'tis made and placed at the head of the chapter, as much for use as ornament, all I desire in return, is, that whenever I speak of Mrs. Wadman's eyes (except once in the next period), that you keep it in your fancy.

I protest, Madam, said my uncle Toby, I can see nothing whatever in your eye.

It is not in the white; said Mrs. Wadman: my uncle Toby looked with might and main into the pupil—

Now of all the eyes which ever were created—from your own, Madam, up to those of Venus herself, which certainly were as venereal a pair of eyes as ever stood in a head—there never was an eye of them all, so fitted to rob

[1] Rhodope Thracia tam inevitabili fascino instructa, tam exactè oculis intuens attraxit, ut si in illam quis incidisset, fieri non posset, quin caperetur.—I know not who.

my uncle Toby of his repose, as the very eye, at which he was looking—it was not, Madam, a rolling eye—a romping or a wanton one—nor was it an eye sparkling—petulant or imperious—of high claims and terrifying exactions, which would have curdled at once that milk of human nature, of which my uncle Toby was made up—but 'twas an eye full of gentle salutations—and soft responses—speaking—not like the trumpet stop of some ill-made organ, in which many an eye I talk to, holds coarse converse—but whispering soft—like the last low accents of an expiring saint—"How can you live comfortless, Captain Shandy, and alone, without a bosom to lean your head on—or trust your cares to?"

It was an eye—

But I shall be in love with it myself, if I say another word about it.

—It did my uncle Toby's business.

Chapter 26

There is nothing shows the character of my father and my uncle Toby, in a more entertaining light, than their different manner of deportment, under the same accident—for I call not love a misfortune, from a persuasion, that a man's heart is ever the better for it—Great God! what must my uncle Toby's have been, when 'twas all benignity without it.

My father, as appears from many of his papers, was very subject to this passion, before he married—but from a little subacid kind of drollish impatience in his nature, whenever it befell him, he would never submit to it like a christian; but would pish, and huff, and bounce, and kick, and play the Devil, and write the bitterest Philippics against the eye that ever man wrote—there is one in verse upon somebody's eye or other, that for two or three nights together, had put him by his rest; which in his first transport of resentment against it, he begins thus:

"A Devil 'tis—and mischief such doth work
As never yet did Pagan, Jew, or Turk."[1]

In short, during the whole paroxysm, my father was all abuse and foul language, approaching rather towards malediction—only he did not do it with as much method as Ernulphus—he was too impetuous; nor with Ernulphus's policy—for tho' my father, with the most intolerant spirit, would curse both this and that, and every thing under heaven, which was either aiding or abetting to his love—yet never concluded his chapter of curses upon it, without cursing himself in at the bargain, as one of the most egregious fools and coxcombs, he would say, that ever was let loose in the world.

My uncle Toby, on the contrary, took it like a lamb—sat still and let the poison work in his veins without resistance—in the sharpest exacerbations of his wound (like that on his groin) he never dropt one fretful or discontented word—he blamed neither heaven nor earth—or thought or spoke an injurious thing of any body, or any part of it; he sat solitary and pensive with his pipe—looking at his lame leg—then whiffing out a sentimental heigh ho! which mixing with the smoke, incommoded no one mortal.

[1] This will be printed with my father's *Life of Socrates*, etc. etc.

He took it like a lamb—I say.

In truth he had mistook it at first; for having taken a ride with my father, that very morning, to save if possible a beautiful wood, which the dean and chapter were hewing down to give to the poor[1]; which said wood being in full view of my uncle Toby's house, and of singular service to him in his description of the battle of Wynnendale—by trotting on too hastily to save it—upon an uneasy saddle—worse horse, etc. etc. . . . it had so happened, that the serous part of the blood had got betwixt the two skins, in the nethermost part of my uncle Toby—the first shootings of which (as my uncle Toby had no experience of love) he had taken for a part of the passion—till the blister breaking in the one case—and the other remaining—my uncle Toby was presently convinced, that his wound was not a skin-deep wound—but that it had gone to his heart.

CHAPTER 27

THE world is ashamed of being virtuous—My uncle Toby knew little of the world; and therefore when he felt he was in love with widow Wadman, he had no conception that the thing was any more to be made a mystery of, than if Mrs. Wadman had given him a cut with a gap'd knife across his finger: Had it been otherwise—yet as he ever looked upon Trim as a humble friend; and saw fresh reasons every day of his life, to treat him as such—it would have made no variation in the manner in which he informed him of the affair.

"I am in love, corporal!" quoth my uncle Toby.

CHAPTER 28

IN love!—said the corporal—your honour was very well the day before yesterday, when I was telling your honour the story of the King of Bohemia —Bohemia! said my uncle Toby---musing a long time---What became of that story, Trim?

—We lost it, an' please your honour, somehow betwixt us—but your honour was as free from love then, as I am—'twas just whilst thou went'st off with the wheel-barrow—with Mrs. Wadman, quoth my uncle Toby— She has left a ball here—added my uncle Toby—pointing to his breast—

—She can no more, an' please your honour, stand a siege, than she can fly—cried the corporal—

—But as we are neighbours, Trim,—the best way I think is to let her know it civilly first—quoth my uncle Toby.

Now if I might presume, said the corporal, to differ from your honour—

—Why else do I talk to thee, Trim? said my uncle Toby, mildly—

—Then I would begin, an' please your honour, with making a good thundering attack upon her, in return—and telling her civilly afterwards— for if she knows any thing of your honour's being in love, before hand—

---

[1] Mr. Shandy must mean the poor in spirit; inasmuch as they divided the money amongst themselves.

L—d help her!—she knows no more at present of it, Trim, said my uncle Toby—than the child unborn—

Precious souls!——

Mrs. Wadman had told it, with all its circumstances, to Mrs. Bridget twenty-four hours before; and was at that very moment sitting in council with her, touching some slight misgivings with regard to the issue of the affairs, which the Devil, who never lies dead in a ditch, had put into her head—before he would allow half time, to get quietly through her *Te Deum.*

I am terribly afraid, said widow Wadman, in case I should marry him, Bridget—that the poor captain will not enjoy his health, with the monstrous wound upon his groin—

It may not, Madam, be so very large, replied Bridget, as you think—and I believe, besides, added she—that 'tis dried up—

—I could like to know—merely for his sake, said Mrs. Wadman—

—We'll know the long and the broad of it, in ten days—answered Mrs. Bridget, for whilst the captain is paying his addresses to you—I'm confident Mr. Trim will be for making love to me—and I'll let him as much as he will—added Bridget—to get it all out of him—

The measures were taken at once—and my uncle Toby and the corporal went on with theirs.

Now, quoth the corporal, setting his left hand a-kimbo, and giving such a flourish with his right, as just promised success—and no more—if your honour will give me leave to lay down the plan of this attack—

—Thou wilt please me by it, Trim, said my uncle Toby, exceedingly—and as I foresee thou must act in it as my *aide de camp*, here's a crown, corporal, to begin with, to steep thy commission.

Then, an' please your honour, said the corporal (making a bow first for his commission) we will begin with getting your honour's laced clothes out of the great campaign-trunk, to be well aired, and have the blue and gold taken up at the sleeves—and I'll put your white ramallie-wig fresh into pipes—and send for a tailor, to have your honour's thin scarlet breeches turned—

—I had better take the red plush ones, quoth my uncle Toby—They will be too clumsy—said the corporal.

CHAPTER 29

——Thou wilt get a brush and a little chalk to my sword—'Twill be only in your honour's way, replied Trim.

CHAPTER 30

——But your honour's two razors shall be new set—and I will get my Montero-cap furbished up, and put on poor lieutenant Le Fever's regimental coat, which your honour gave me to wear for his sake—and as soon as your honour is clean shaved—and has got your clean shirt on, with your blue and gold, or your fine scarlet—sometimes one and sometimes t'other—and everything is ready for the attack—we'll march up boldly, as if 'twas to the face of a bastion; and whilst your honour engages Mrs. Wadman in the parlour, to the right—I'll attack Mrs. Bridget in the kitchen, to the left; and having seized the pass, I'll answer for it, said the corporal, snapping his fingers over his head—that the day is our own.

I wish I may but manage it right; said my uncle Toby—but I declare, corporal, I had rather march up to the very edge of a trench—

—A woman is quite a different thing—said the corporal.

—I suppose so, quoth my uncle Toby.

CHAPTER 31

IF any thing in this world, which my father said, could have provoked my uncle Toby, during the time he was in love, it was the perverse use my father was always making of an expression of Hilarion the hermit; who, in speaking of his abstinence, his watchings, flagellation, and other instrumental parts of his religion—would say—tho' with more facetiousness than became a hermit —"That they were the means he used, to make his ass (meaning his body) leave off kicking."

It pleased my father well; it was not only a laconic way of expressing—but of libelling, at the same time, the desires and appetites of the lower part of us; so that for many years of my father's life, 'twas his constant mode of expression—he never used the word passions once—but ass always instead of them—So that he might be said truly, to have been upon the bones, or the back of his own ass, or else of some other man's, during all that time.

I must here observe to you the difference betwixt

My father's ass

and my hobby-horse—in order to keep characters as separate as may be, in our fancies as we go along.

For my hobby-horse, if you recollect a little, is no way a vicious beast; he has scarce one hair or lineament of the ass about him—'Tis the sporting little filly-folly which carries you out for the present hour—a maggot, a butterfly, a picture, a fiddlestick—an uncle Toby's siege—or an any thing, which a man makes a shift to get a-stride on, to canter it away from the cares and solicitudes of life—'Tis as useful a beast as is in the whole creation—nor do I really see how the world could do without it—

—But for my father's ass——oh! mount him—mount him—mount him —(that's three times, is it not?)—mount him not:—'tis a beast concupiscent—and foul befall the man, who does not hinder him from kicking.

CHAPTER 32

WELL! dear brother Toby, said my father, upon his first seeing him after he fell in love—and how goes it with your Ass?

Now my uncle Toby thinking more of the part where he had had the blister, than of Hilarion's metaphor—and our preconceptions having (you know) as great a power over the sounds of words as the shapes of things, he had imagined, that my father, who was not very ceremonious in his choice of words, had enquired after the part by its proper name; so notwithstanding my mother, doctor Slop, and Mr. Yorick, were sitting in the parlour, he thought it rather civil to conform to the term my father had made use of than not. When a man is hemmed in by two indecorums, and must commit one of 'em—I always observe—let him choose which he will, the world will blame him—so I should not be astonished if it blames my uncle Toby.

My A—e, quoth my uncle Toby, is much better—brother Shandy—My father had formed great expectations from his Ass in this onset; and would have brought him on again; but doctor Slop setting up an intemperate laugh—and my mother crying out L— bless us!—it drove my father's Ass off the field—and the laugh then becoming general—there was no bringing him back to the charge, for some time—

And so the discourse went on without him.

Every body, said my mother, says you are in love, brother Toby,—and we hope it is true.

I am as much in love, sister, I believe, replied my uncle Toby, as any man usually is—Humph! said my father—and when did you know it? quoth my mother—

—When the blister broke; replied my uncle Toby.

My uncle Toby's reply put my father into good temper—so he charged o' foot.

CHAPTER 33

As the ancients agree, brother Toby, said my father, that there are two different and distinct kinds of love, according to the different parts which are affected by it—the Brain or Liver—I think when a man is in love, it behoves him a little to consider which of the two he is fallen into.

What signifies it, brother Shandy, replied my uncle Toby, which of the two it is, provided it will but make a man marry, and love his wife, and get a few children?

—A few children! cried my father, rising out of his chair, and looking full in my mother's face, as he forced his way betwixt her's and doctor Slop's— a few children! cried my father, repeating my uncle Toby's words as he walked to and fro.

—Not, my dear brother Toby, cried my father, recovering himself all at once, and coming close up to the back of my uncle Toby's chair—not that I should be sorry hadst thou a score—on the contrary, I should rejoice—and be as kind, Toby, to every one of them as a father—

My uncle Toby stole his hand unperceived behind his chair, to give my father's a squeeze—

—Nay, moreover, continued he, keeping hold of my uncle Toby's hand— so much dost thou possess, my dear Toby, of the milk of human nature, and so little of its asperities—'tis piteous the world is not peopled by creatures which resemble thee; and was I an Asiatic monarch, added my father, heating himself with his new project—I would oblige thee, provided it would not impair thy strength—or dry up thy radical moisture too fast—or weaken thy memory or fancy, brother Toby, which these gymnics inordinately taken are apt to do—else, dear Toby, I would procure thee the most beautiful women in my empire, and I would oblige thee, *nolens volens*, to beget for me one subject every month—

As my father pronounced the last word of the sentence—my mother took a pinch of snuff.

Now I would not, quoth my uncle Toby, get a child *nolens volens,* that is, whether I would or no, to please the greatest prince upon earth—

—And 'twould be cruel in me, brother Toby, to compel thee; said my father—but 'tis a case put to show thee, that it is not thy begetting a child —in case thou should'st be able—but the system of Love and Marriage thou goest upon, which I would set thee right in—

There is at least, said Yorick, a great deal of reason and plain sense in Captain Shandy's opinion of love; and 'tis amongst the ill-spent hours of my life, which I have to answer for, that I have read so many flourishing poets and rhetoricians in my time, from whom I never could extract so much.

I wish, Yorick, said my father, you had read Plato; for there you would have learnt that there are two Loves—I know there were two Religions, replied Yorick, amongst the ancients—one—for the vulgar, and another for the learned;—but I think one Love might have served both of them very well—

It could not; replied my father—and for the same reasons: for of these Loves, according to Ficinus's comment upon Velasius, the one is rational—

—the other is natural—

the first ancient—without mother—where Venus had nothing to do: the second, begotten of Jupiter and Dione—

—Pray, brother, quoth my uncle Toby, what has a man who believes in God to do with this? My father could not stop to answer, for fear of breaking the thread of his discourse—

This latter, continued he, partakes wholly of the nature of Venus.

The first, which is the golden chain let down from heaven, excites to love heroic, which comprehends in it, and excites to the desire of philosophy and truth—the second, excites to desire, simply—

—I think the procreation of children as beneficial to the world, said Yorick, as the finding out the longitude—

—To be sure, said my mother, love keeps peace in the world—

—In the house—my dear, I own—

—It replenishes the earth; said my mother—

But it keeps heaven empty—my dear; replied my father.

—'Tis Virginity, cried Slop, triumphantly, which fills paradise.

Well pushed, nun! quoth my father.

Chapter 34

My father had such a skirmishing, cutting kind of a slashing way with him in his disputations, thrusting and ripping, and giving every one a stroke to remember him by in his turn—that if there were twenty people in company —in less than half an hour he was sure to have every one of 'em against him.

What did not a little contribute to leave him thus without an ally, was, that if there was any one post more untenable than the rest, he would be sure to throw himself into it; and to do him justice, when he was once there, he would defend it so gallantly, that 'twould have been a concern, either to a brave man or a good-natured one, to have seen him driven out.

Yorick, for this reason, though he would often attack him—yet could never bear to do it with all his force.

Dr. Slop's "Virginity," in the close of the last chapter, had got him for once on the right side of the rampart; and he was beginning to blow up all the convents in Christendom about Slop's ears, when corporal Trim came into the parlour to inform my uncle Toby, that his thin scarlet breeches, in which the attack was to be made upon Mrs. Wadman, would not do; for that the tailor, in ripping them up, in order to turn them, had found they had been turned before—Then turn them again, brother, said my father, rapidly, for there will be many a turning of 'em yet before all's done in the affair—They are as rotten as dirt, said the corporal—Then by all means, said my father, bespeak a new pair, brother—for though I know, continued my father, turning himself to the company, that widow Wadman has been deeply in love with my brother Toby for many years, and has used every art and circumvention of woman to outwit him into the same passion, yet now that she has caught him—her fever will be passed its height—

—She has gained her point.

In this case, continued my father, which Plato, I am persuaded, never thought of—Love, you see, is not so much a Sentiment as a Situation, into which a man enters, as my brother Toby would do, into a corps—no matter whether he loves the service or no—being once in it—he acts as if he did; and takes every step to show himself a man of prowess.

The hypothesis, like the rest of my father's, was plausible enough, and my uncle Toby had but a single word to object to it—in which Trim stood ready to second him—but my father had not drawn his conclusion—

For this reason, continued my father (stating the case over again)—notwithstanding all the world knows, that Mrs. Wadman affects my brother Toby—and my brother Toby contrariwise affects Mrs. Wadman, and no obstacle in nature to forbid the music striking up this very night, yet I will answer for it, that this self-same tune will not be played this twelve month.

We have taken our measures badly, quoth my uncle Toby, looking up interrogatively in Trim's face.

I would lay my Montero-cap, said Trim—Now Trim's Montero-cap, as I once told you, was his constant wager; and having furbished it up that very night, in order to go upon the attack—it made the odds look more considerable—I would lay, an' please your honour, my Montero-cap to a shilling—was it proper, continued Trim (making a bow), to offer a wager before your honours—

—There is nothing improper in it, said my father—'tis a mode of expression; for in saying thou would'st lay thy Montero-cap to a shilling—all thou meanest is this—that thou believest—

—Now, What do'st thou believe?

That widow Wadman, an' please your worship, cannot hold it out ten days—

And whence, cried Slop, jeeringly, hast thou all this knowledge of woman, friend?

By falling in love with a popish clergywoman; said Trim.

'Twas a Beguine, said my uncle Toby.

Doctor Slop was too much in wrath to listen to the distinction; and my father taking that very crisis to fall in helter-skelter upon the whole order of Nuns and Beguines, a set of silly, fusty, baggages—Slop could not stand it—and my uncle Toby having some measures to take about his breeches—and Yorick about his fourth general division—in order for their several attacks next day—the company broke up: and my father being left alone, and having half an hour upon his hands betwixt that and bed-time; he called for pen, ink, and paper, and wrote my uncle Toby the following letter of instructions:

My Dear Brother Toby,

What I am going to say to thee is upon the nature of women, and of love-making to them; and perhaps it is as well for thee—tho' not so well for me—that thou hast occasion for a letter of instructions upon that head, and that I am able to write it to thee.

Had it been the good pleasure of Him who disposes of our lots—and thou no sufferer by the knowledge, I had been well content that thou should'st have dipped the pen this moment into the ink, instead of myself; but that not being the case—Mrs. Shandy being now close beside me, preparing for bed—I have thrown together without order, and just as they have come into my mind, such hints and documents as I deem may be of use to thee; intending in this, to give thee a token of my love; not doubting, my dear Toby, of the manner in which it will be accepted.

In the first place, with regard to all which concerns religion in the affair—though I perceive from a glow in my cheek, that I blush as I begin to speak to thee upon the subject, as well knowing, notwithstanding thy unaffected secrecy, how few of its offices thou neglectest—yet I would remind thee of one (during the continuance of thy courtship) in a particular manner, which I would not have omitted; and that is, never to go forth upon the enterprise, whether it be in the morning or the afternoon, without first recommending thyself to the protection of Almighty God, that He may defend thee from the evil one.

Shave the whole top of thy crown clean once at least every four or five days, but oftener if convenient; lest in taking off thy wig before her, thro' absence of mind, she should be able to discover how much has been cut away by Time—how much by Trim.

——'Twere better to keep ideas of baldness out of her fancy.

Always carry it in thy mind, and act upon it as a sure maxim, Toby—"That women are timid": And 'tis well they are—else there would be no dealing with them.

Let not thy breeches be too tight, or hang too loose about thy thighs, like the trunk-hose of our ancestors.

—A just medium prevents all conclusions.

Whatever thou hast to say, be it more or less, forget not to utter it in a low soft tone of voice. Silence, and whatever approaches it, weaves dreams of midnight secrecy into the brain: For this cause, if thou canst help it, never throw down the tongs and poker.

Avoid all kinds of pleasantry and facetiousness in thy discourse with her, and do whatever lies in thy power at the same time, to keep from her all books and writings which tend thereto: there are some devotional tracts, which if thou canst entice her to read over—it will be well: but suffer her not to look into *Rabelais,* or *Scarron,* or *Don Quixote*—

—They are all books which excite laughter; and thou knowest, dear Toby, that there is no passion so serious as lust.

Stick a pin in the bosom of thy shirt, before thou enterest her parlour.

And if thou art permitted to sit upon the same sofa with her, and she gives thee occasion to lay thy hand upon hers—beware of taking it—thou canst not lay thy hand on hers, but she will feel the temper of thine. Leave that and as many other things as thou canst quite undetermined; by so doing, thou wilt have her curiosity on thy side; and if she is not conquered by that, and thy Ass continues still kicking, which there is great reason to suppose—Thou must begin, with first losing a few ounces of blood below the ears, according to the practice of the ancient Scythians, who cured the most intemperate fits of the appetite by that means.

Avicenna, after this, is for having the part anointed with the syrup of hellebore, using proper evacuations and purges—and I believe rightly. But thou must eat little or no goat's flesh, nor red deer—nor even foal's flesh by any means; and carefully abstain—that is, as much as thou canst, from peacocks, cranes, coots, didappers, and water-hens—

As for thy drink—I need not tell thee, it must be the infusion of Vervain and the herb Hanea, of which Aelian relates such effects—but if thy stomach palls with it—discontinue it from time to time, taking cucumbers, melons, purslane, water-lilies, woodbine, and lettuce, in the stead of them.

There is nothing further for thee, which occurs to me at present—

—Unless the breaking out of a fresh war—So wishing every thing, dear Toby, for the best,

I rest thy affectionate brother,   WALTER SHANDY.

CHAPTER 35

WHILST my father was writing his letter of instructions, my uncle Toby and the corporal were busy in preparing every thing for the attack. As the turning of the thin scarlet breeches was laid aside (at least for the present), there was nothing which should put it off beyond the next morning; so accordingly it was resolved upon, for eleven o'clock.

Come, my dear, said my father to my mother—'twill be but like a brother and sister, if you and I take a walk down to my brother Toby's—to countenance him in this attack of his.

My uncle Toby and the corporal had been accoutred both some time, when my father and mother entered, and the clock striking eleven, were that moment in motion to sally forth—but the account of this is worth more than to be wove into the fag end of the eighth volume of such a work as this.—My father had no time but to put the letter of instructions into my uncle Toby's coat-pocket—and join with my mother in wishing his attack prosperous.

I could like, said my mother, to look through the key-hole out of curiosity —Call it by its right name, my dear, quoth my father—

And look through the key-hole as long as you will.

A Dedication to

A GREAT MAN

Having, *a priori*, intended to dedicate *The Amours of my Uncle Toby* to Mr. ***—I see more reasons, *a posteriori*, for doing it to Lord *******.

I should lament from my soul, if this exposed me to the jealousy of their Reverences; because *a posteriori*, in Court-latin, signifies the kissing hands for preferment—or any thing else—in order to get it.

My opinion of Lord ******* is neither better nor worse, than it was of Mr. ***. Honours, like impressions upon coin, may give an ideal and local value to a bit of base metal; but Gold and Silver will pass all the world over without any other recommendation than their own weight.

The same good-will that made me think of offering up half an hour's amusement to Mr. *** when out of place—operates more forcibly at present, as half an hour's amusement will be more serviceable and refreshing after labour and sorrow, than after a philosophical repast.

Nothing is so perfectly amusement as a total change of ideas; no ideas are so totally different as those of Ministers, and innocent Lovers: for which reason, when I come to talk of Statesmen and Patriots, and set such marks upon them as will prevent confusion and mistakes concerning them for the future—I propose to dedicate that Volume to some gentle Shepherd,

> Whose thoughts proud Science never taught to stray,
> Far as the Statesman's walk or Patriot-way;
> Yet simple Nature to his hopes had given
> Out of a cloud-capp'd head a humbler heaven;
> Some untam'd World in depths of wood embraced—
> Some happier Island in the watry-waste—
> And where admitted to that equal sky,
> His faithful Dog should bear him company.

In a word, by thus introducing an entire new set of objects to his Imagination, I shall unavoidably give a Diversion to his passionate and love-sick Contemplations. In the mean time,

I am

THE AUTHOR

BOOK IX

Si quid urbaniusculè lusum a nobis, per Musas et Charitas et omnium poëtarum Numina, Oro te, ne me malè capias.

CHAPTER I

I CALL all the powers of time and chance, which severally check us in our careers in this world, to bear me witness, that I could never yet get fairly to my uncle Toby's amours, till this very moment, that my mother's curiosity, as she stated the affair,—or a different impulse in her, as my father would have it—wished her to take a peep at them through the key-hole.

"Call it, my dear, by its right name," quoth my father, "and look through the key-hole as long as you will."

Nothing but the fermentation of that little subacid humour, which I have often spoken of, in my father's habit, could have vented such an insinuation—he was however frank and generous in his nature, and at all times open to conviction; so that he had scarce got to the last word of this ungracious retort, when his conscience smote him.

My mother was then conjugally swinging with her left arm twisted under his right, in such wise, that the inside of her hand rested upon the back of his—she raised her fingers, and let them fall—it could scarce be called a tap; or if it was a tap—'twould have puzzled a casuist to say, whether 'twas a tap of remonstrance or a tap of confession: my father, who was all sensibilities from head to foot, classed it right—Conscience redoubled her blow—he turned his face suddenly the other way, and my mother supposing his body was about to turn with it in order to move homewards, by a cross movement of her right leg, keeping her left as its centre, brought herself so far in front, that as he turned his head, he met her eye—Confusion again! he saw a thousand reasons to wipe out the reproach, and as many to reproach himself—a thin, blue, chill, pellucid crystal with all its humours so at rest, the least mote or speck of desire might have been seen, at the bottom of it, had it existed—it did not—and how I happen to be so lewd myself, particularly a little before the vernal and autumnal equinoxes—Heaven above knows—My mother—madam—was so at no time, either by nature, by institution, or example.

A temperate current of blood ran orderly through her veins in all months of the year, and in all critical moments both of the day and night alike; nor did she superinduce the least heat into her humours from the manual effervescencies of devotional tracts, which having little or no meaning in them, nature is oft-times obliged to find one—And as for my father's example! 'twas so far from being either aiding or abetting thereunto, that 'twas the whole business of his life to keep all fancies of that kind out of her head—Nature had done her part, to have spared him this trouble; and what was not a little inconsistent, my father knew it—And here am I sitting, this 12th day of August 1766, in a purple jerkin and yellow pair of slippers, without either wig or cap on, a most tragicomical completion of his prediction, "That I should neither think, nor act like any other man's child, upon that very account."

The mistake in my father, was in attacking my mother's motive, instead of the act itself; for certainly key-holes were made for other purposes; and considering the act, as an act which interfered with a true proposition, and denied a key-hole to be what it was——it became a violation of nature; and was so far, you see, criminal.

It is for this reason, an' please your Reverences, That key-holes are the occasions of more sin and wickedness, than all other holes in this world put together.

——which leads me to my uncle Toby's amours.

CHAPTER 2

THOUGH the corporal had been as good as his word in putting my uncle Toby's great ramallie-wig into pipes, yet the time was too short to produce any great effects from it: it had lain many years squeezed up in the corner of his old campaign trunk; and as bad forms are not so easy to be got the better of, and the use of candle-ends not so well understood, it was not so pliable a business as one would have wished. The corporal with cheery eye and both arms extended, had fallen back perpendicular from it a score times, to inspire it, if possible, with a better air—had Spleen given a look at it, 'twould have cost her ladyship a smile—it curled every where but where the corporal would have it; and where a buckle or two, in his opinion, would have done it honour, he could as soon have raised the dead.

Such it was—or rather such would it have seemed upon any other brow; but the sweet look of goodness which sat upon my uncle Toby's, assimilated every thing around it so sovereignly to itself, and Nature had moreover wrote Gentleman with so fair a hand in every line of his countenance, that even his tarnished gold-laced hat and huge cockade of flimsy taffeta became him; and though not worth a button in themselves, yet the moment my uncle Toby put them on, they became serious objects, and altogether seemed to have been picked up by the hand of Science to set him off to advantage.

Nothing in this world could have co-operated more powerfully towards this, than my uncle Toby's blue and gold—had not Quantity in some measure been necessary to Grace: in a period of fifteen or sixteen years since they had been made, by a total inactivity in my uncle Toby's life, for he seldom went further than the bowling-green—his blue and gold had become so miserably too strait for him, that it was with the utmost difficulty the corporal was able to get him into them; the taking them up at the sleeves, was of no advantage.—They were laced however down the back, and at the seams of the sides, etc., in the mode of King William's reign; and to shorten all description, they shone so bright against the sun that morning, and had so metallic and doughty an air with them, that had my uncle Toby thought of attacking in armour, nothing could have so well imposed upon his imagination.

As for the thin scarlet breeches, they had been unripped by the tailor between the legs, and left at sixes and sevens—

—Yes, Madam,—but let us govern our fancies. It is enough they were held impracticable the night before, and as there was no alternative in my uncle Toby's wardrobe, he sallied forth in the red plush.

The corporal had arrayed himself in poor Le Fever's regimental coat; and with his hair tucked up under his Montero-cap, which he had furbished up for the occasion, marched three paces distant from his master: a whiff of military pride had puffed out his shirt at the wrist; and upon that in a black leather thong clipped into a tassel beyond the knot, hung the corporal's stick—My uncle Toby carried his cane like a pike.

——It looks well at least; quoth my father to himself.

CHAPTER 3

My uncle Toby turned his head more than once behind him, to see how he was supported by the corporal; and the corporal as oft as he did it, gave a slight flourish with his stick—but not vapouringly; and with the sweetest accent of most respectful encouragement, bid his honour "never fear."

Now my uncle Toby did fear; and grievously too; he knew not (as my father had reproached him) so much as the right end of a Woman from the wrong, and therefore was never altogether at his ease near any one of them —unless in sorrow or distress; then infinite was his pity; nor would the most courteous knight of romance have gone further, at least upon one leg, to have wiped away a tear from a woman's eye; and yet excepting once that he was beguiled into it by Mrs. Wadman, he had never looked steadfastly into one; and would often tell my father in the simplicity of his heart, that it was almost (if not about) as bad as talking bawdy.——

——And suppose it is? my father would say.

CHAPTER 4

She cannot, quoth my uncle Toby, halting, when they had marched up to within twenty paces of Mrs. Wadman's door—she cannot, corporal, take it amiss.——

——She will take it, an' please your honour, said the corporal, just as the Jew's widow at Lisbon took it of my brother Tom.——

——And how was that? quoth my uncle Toby, facing quite about to the corporal.

Your honour, replied the corporal, knows of Tom's misfortunes; but this affair has nothing to do with them any further than this, That if Tom had not married the widow—or had it pleased God after their marriage, that they had but put pork into their sausages, the honest soul had never been taken out of his warm bed, and dragged to the inquisition—'Tis a cursed place—added the corporal, shaking his head,—when once a poor creature is in, he is in, an' please your honour, for ever.

'Tis very true; said my uncle Toby, looking gravely at Mrs. Wadman's house, as he spoke.

Nothing, continued the corporal, can be so sad as confinement for life— or so sweet, an' please your honour, as liberty.

Nothing, Trim—said my uncle Toby, musing—

Whilst a man is free,—cried the corporal, giving a flourish with his stick thus—

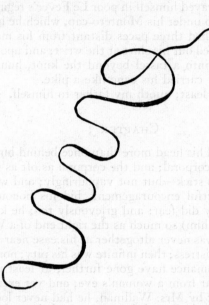

A thousand of my father's most subtle syllogisms could not have said more for celibacy.

My uncle Toby looked earnestly towards his cottage and his bowling-green.

The corporal had unwarily conjured up the Spirit of calculation with his wand; and he had nothing to do, but to conjure him down again with his story, and in this form of Exorcism, most un-ecclesiastically did the corporal do it.

CHAPTER 5

As Tom's place, an' please your honour, was easy—and the weather warm —it put him upon thinking seriously of settling himself in the world; and as it fell out about that time, that a Jew who kept a sausage shop in the same street, had the ill luck to die of a strangury, and leave his widow in possession of a rousing trade—Tom thought (as every body in Lisbon was doing the best he could devise for himself) there could be no harm in offering her his service to carry it on: so without any introduction to the widow, except that of buying a pound of sausages at her shop—Tom set out— counting the matter thus within himself, as he walked along; that let the worst come of it that could, he should at least get a pound of sausages for their worth—but, if things went well, he should be set up; inasmuch as he should get not only a pound of sausages—but a wife and—a sausage shop, an' please your honour, into the bargain.

Every servant in the family, from high to low, wished Tom success; and I can fancy, an' please your honour, I see him this moment with his white dimity waistcoat and breeches, and hat a little o' one side, passing jollily along the street, swinging his stick, with a smile and a cheerful word for every body he met:—But alas! Tom! thou smilest no more, cried the corporal, looking on one side of him upon the ground, as if he apostrophized him in his dungeon.

Poor fellow! said my uncle Toby, feelingly.

He was an honest, light-hearted lad, an' please your honour, as ever blood warmed—

—Then he resembled thee, Trim, said my uncle Toby, rapidly.

The corporal blushed down to his fingers' ends—a tear of sentimental bashfulness—another of gratitude to my uncle Toby—and a tear of sorrow for his brother's misfortunes, started into his eye, and ran sweetly down his cheek together; my uncle Toby's kindled as one lamp does at another; and taking hold of the breast of Trim's coat (which had been that of Le Fever's) as if to ease his lame leg, but in reality to gratify a finer feeling—he stood silent for a minute and a half; at the end of which he took his hand away, and the corporal making a bow, went on with his story of his brother and the Jew's widow.

CHAPTER 6

WHEN Tom, an' please your honour, got to the shop, there was nobody in it, but a poor negro girl, with a bunch of white feathers slightly tied to the end of a long cane, flapping away flies—not killing them.——'Tis a pretty picture! said my uncle Toby—she had suffered persecution, Trim, and had learnt mercy—

—She was good, an' please your honour, from nature, as well as from hardships; and there are circumstances in the story of that poor friendless slut, that would melt a heart of stone, said Trim; and some dismal winter's evening, when your honour is in the humour, they shall be told you with the rest of Tom's story, for it makes a part of it—

Then do not forget, Trim, said my uncle Toby.

A negro has a soul? an' please your honour, said the corporal (doubtingly).

I am not much versed, corporal, quoth my uncle Toby, in things of that kind; but I suppose, God would not leave him without one, any more than thee or me—

—It would be putting one sadly over the head of another, quoth the corporal.

It would so; said my uncle Toby. Why then, an' please your honour, is a black wench to be used worse than a white one?

I can give no reason, said my uncle Toby——

——Only, cried the corporal, shaking his head, because she has no one to stand up for her——

——'Tis that very thing, Trim, quoth my uncle Toby,—which recommends her to protection—and her brethren with her; 'tis the fortune of war which has put the whip into our hands now—where it may be hereafter, heaven knows!—but be it where it will, the brave, Trim, will not use it unkindly.

——God forbid, said the corporal.

Amen, responded my uncle Toby, laying his hand upon his heart.

The corporal returned to his story, and went on—but with an embarrassment in doing it, which here and there a reader in this world will not be able to comprehend; for by the many sudden transitions all along, from one kind and cordial passion to another, in getting thus far on his way, he had lost the sportable key of his voice, which gave sense and spirit to his tale: he attempted twice to resume it, but could not please himself; so giving a stout hem! to rally back the retreating spirits, and aiding nature at the same time with his left arm a-kimbo on one side, and with his right a little extended, supporting her on the other—the corporal got as near the note as he could; and in that attitude, continued his story.

CHAPTER 7

As Tom, an' please your honour, had no business at that time with the Moorish girl, he passed on into the room beyond, to talk to the Jew's widow about love—and his pound of sausages; and being, as I have told your honour, an open cheery-hearted lad, with his character wrote in his looks and carriage, he took a chair, and without much apology, but with great civility at the same time, placed it close to her at the table, and sat down.

There is nothing so awkward, as courting a woman, an' please your honour, whilst she is making sausages—So Tom began a discourse upon them; first, gravely—"as how they were made—with what meats, herbs, and spices"—Then a little gaily,—as, "With what skin—and if they never burst—Whether the largest were not the best?"—and so on—taking care only as he went along, to season what he had to say upon sausages, rather under than over;—that he might have room to act in—

It was owing to the neglect of that very precaution, said my uncle Toby, laying his hand upon Trim's shoulder, that Count De la Motte lost the battle of Wynendale: he pressed too speedily into the wood; which if he had not done, Lisle had not fallen into our hands, nor Ghent and Bruges, which both followed her example; it was so late in the year, continued my uncle Toby, and so terrible a season came on, that if things had not fallen out as they did, our troops must have perished in the open field.——

——Why, therefore, may not battles, an' please your honour, as well as marriages, be made in heaven?—My uncle Toby mused—

Religion inclined him to say one thing, and his high idea of military skill tempted him to say another; so not being able to frame a reply exactly to his mind—my uncle Toby said nothing at all; and the corporal finished his story.

As Tom perceived, an' please your honour, that he gained ground, and that all he had said upon the subject of sausages was kindly taken, he went on to help her a little in making them.—First, by taking hold of the ring of the sausage whilst she stroked the forced meat down with her hand—then by cutting the strings into proper lengths, and holding them in his hand, whilst she took them out one by one—then, by putting them across her mouth, that she might take them out as she wanted them—and so on from little to more, till at last he adventured to tie the sausage himself, whilst she held the snout.——

——Now a widow, an' please your honour, always chooses a second husband as unlike the first as she can: so the affair was more than half settled in her mind before Tom mentioned it.

She made a feint however of defending herself, by snatching up a sausage: —Tom instantly laid hold of another—

But seeing Tom's had more gristle in it—

She signed the capitulation—and Tom sealed it; and there was an end of the matter.

CHAPTER 8

ALL womankind, continued Trim, (commenting upon his story) from the highest to the lowest, an' please your honour, love jokes; the difficulty is to know how they choose to have them cut; and there is no knowing that, but by trying, as we do with our artillery in the field, by raising or letting down their breeches, till we hit the mark.——

——I like the comparison, said my uncle Toby, better than the thing itself—

—Because your honour, quoth the corporal, loves glory, more than pleasure.

I hope, Trim, answered my uncle Toby, I love mankind more than either; and as the knowledge of arms tends so apparently to the good and quiet of the world—and particularly that branch of it which we have practised together in our bowling-green, has no object but to shorten the strides of Ambition, and intrench the lives and fortunes of the few, from the plunderings of the many—whenever that drum beats in our ears, I trust, corporal, we shall neither of us want so much humanity and fellow-feeling, as to face about and march.

In pronouncing this, my uncle Toby faced about, and marched firmly as at the head of his company—and the faithful corporal, shouldering his stick, and striking his hand upon his coat-skirt as he took his first step— marched close behind him down the avenue.

——Now what can their two noddles be about? cried my father to my mother—by all that's strange, they are besieging Mrs. Wadman in form, and are marching round her house to mark out the lines of circumvallation.

I dare say, quoth my mother—But stop, dear Sir—for what my mother dared to say upon the occasion—and what my father did say upon it—with her replies and his rejoinders, shall be read, perused, paraphrased, commented, and descanted upon—or to say it all in a word, shall be thumbed over by Posterity in a chapter apart—I say, by Posterity—and care not, if

I repeat the word again—for what has this book done more than the Legation of Moses, or the Tale of a Tub, that it may not swim down the gutter of Time along with them?

I will not argue the matter: Time wastes too fast: every letter I trace tells me with what rapidity Life follows my pen; the days and hours of it, more precious, my dear Jenny! than the rubies about thy neck, are flying over our heads like light clouds of a windy day, never to return more—every thing presses on—whilst thou art twisting that lock,—see! it grows grey; and every time I kiss thy hand to bid adieu, and every absence which follows it, are preludes to that eternal separation which we are shortly to make.——

——Heaven have mercy upon us both!

CHAPTER 9

Now, for what the world thinks of that ejaculation—I would not give a groat.

CHAPTER 10

MY mother had gone with her left arm twisted in my father's right, till they had got to the fatal angle of the old garden wall, where Doctor Slop was overthrown by Obadiah on the coach-horse: as this was directly opposite to the front of Mrs. Wadman's house, when my father came to it, he gave a look across; and seeing my uncle Toby and the corporal within ten paces of the door, he turned about—"Let us just stop a moment, quoth my father, and see with what ceremonies my brother Toby and his man Trim make their first entry—it will not detain us, added my father, a single minute":— No matter, if it be ten minutes, quoth my mother.

——It will not detain us half one; said my father.

The corporal was just then setting in with the story of his brother Tom and the Jew's widow: the story went on—and on—it had episodes in it—it came back, and went on—and on again; there was no end of it—the reader found it very long—

—G—help my father! he pished fifty times at every new attitude, and gave the corporal's stick, with all its flourishings and danglings, to as many devils as chose to accept of them.

When issues of events like these my father is waiting for, are hanging in the scales of fate, the mind has the advantage of changing the principle of expectation three times, without which it would not have power to see it out.

Curiosity governs the first moment; and the second moment is all economy to justify the expense of the first—and for the third, fourth, fifth, and sixth moments, and so on to the day of judgment—'tis a point of Honour.

I need not be told, that the ethic writers have assigned this all to Patience; but that Virtue, methinks, has extent of dominion sufficient of her own, and enough to do in it, without invading the few dismantled castles which Honour has left him upon the earth.

My father stood it out as well as he could with these three auxiliaries to the end of Trim's story; and from thence to the end of my uncle Toby's panegyric upon arms, in the chapter following it; when seeing, that instead of marching up to Mrs. Wadman's door, they both faced about and marched down the avenue diametrically opposite to his expectation—he broke out at once with that little subacid soreness of humour which, in certain situations, distinguished his character from that of all other men.

CHAPTER 11

——"Now what can their two noddles be about?" cried my father—etc.——

I dare say, said my mother, they are making fortifications—

——Not on Mrs. Wadman's premises! cried my father, stepping back—

I suppose not: quoth my mother.

I wish, said my father, raising his voice, the whole science of fortifications at the devil, with all its trumpery of saps, mines, blinds, gabions, faussebrays and cuvetts—

—They are foolish things—said my mother.

Now she had a way, which, by the bye, I would this moment give away my purple jerkin, and my yellow slippers into the bargain, if some of your reverences would imitate—and that was, never to refuse her assent and consent to any proposition my father laid before her, merely because she did not understand it, or had no ideas of the principal word or term of art, upon which the tenet or proposition rolled. She contented herself with doing all that her godfathers and godmothers promised for her—but no more; and so would go on using a hard word twenty years together—and replying to it too, if it was a verb, in all its moods and tenses, without giving herself any trouble to enquire about it.

This was an eternal source of misery to my father, and broke the neck, at the first setting out, of more good dialogues between them, than could have done the most petulant contradiction—the few which survived were the better for the cuvetts—

—"They are foolish things"; said my mother.

——Particularly the cuvetts; replied my father.

'Tis enough—he tasted the sweet of triumph—and went on.

——Not that they are, properly speaking, Mrs. Wadman's premises, said my father, partly correcting himself—because she is but tenant for life—

—That makes a great difference—said my mother—

—In a fool's head, replied my father—

Unless she should happen to have a child—said my mother—

—But she must persuade my brother Toby first to get her one—

—To be sure, Mr. Shandy, quoth my mother.

—Though if it comes to persuasion—said my father—Lord have mercy upon them.

Amen: said my mother, *piano.*

Amen: cried my father, *fortissimè.*

Amen: said my mother again—but with such a sighing cadence of personal pity at the end of it, as discomfited every fibre about my father—he instantly took out his almanac; but before he could untie it, Yorick's con-

gregation coming out of church, became a full answer to one half of his
business with it—and my mother telling him it was a sacrament day—left
him as little in doubt, as to the other part—He put his almanac into his
pocket.

The first Lord of the Treasury thinking of ways and means, could not
have returned home with a more embarrassed look.

CHAPTER 12

Upon looking back from the end of the last chapter, and surveying the
texture of what has been wrote, it is necessary, that upon this page and the
three following, a good quantity of heterogeneous matter be inserted to
keep up that just balance betwixt wisdom and folly, without which a book
would not hold together a single year: nor is it a poor creeping digression
(which but for the name of, a man might continue as well going on in the
king's highway) which will do the business—no; if it is to be a digression, it
must be a good frisky one, and upon a frisky subject too, where neither the
horse or his rider are to be caught, but by rebound.

The only difficulty, is raising powers suitable to the nature of the service:
Fancy is capricious—Wit must not be searched for—and Pleasantry (good-
natured slut as she is) will not come in at a call, was an empire to be laid at
her feet.

——The best way for a man, is to say his prayers—

Only if it puts him in mind of his infirmities and defects as well ghostly as
bodily—for that purpose, he will find himself rather worse after he has said
them than before— for other purposes, better.

For my own part, there is not a way either moral or mechanical under
heaven that I could think of, which I have not taken with myself in this
case: sometimes by addressing myself directly to the soul herself, and arguing the point over and over again with her upon the extent of her own
faculties—

—I never could make them an inch the wider—

Then by changing my system, and trying what could be made of it upon
the body, by temperance, soberness, and chastity: These are good, quoth I,
in themselves—they are good, absolutely;—they are good, relatively;—
they are good for health—they are good for happiness in this world—they
are good for happiness in the next—

In short, they were good for every thing but the thing wanted; and there
they were good for nothing, but to leave the soul just as heaven made it: as
for the theological virtues of faith and hope, they give it courage; but then
that snivelling virtue of Meekness (as my father would always call it) takes
it quite away again, so you are exactly where you started.

Now in all common and ordinary cases, there is nothing which I have
found to answer so well as this—

—Certainly, if there is any dependence upon Logic, and that I am not
blinded by self-love, there must be something of true genius about me,
merely upon this symptom of it, that I do not know what envy is: for never
do I hit upon any invention or device which tendeth to the furtherance of

good writing, but I instantly make it public; willing that all mankind should write as well as myself.

——Which they certainly will, when they think as little.

CHAPTER 13

Now in ordinary cases, that is, when I am only stupid, and the thoughts rise heavily and pass gummous through my pen—

Or that I am got, I know not how, into a cold unmetaphorical vein of infamous writing, and cannot take a plumb-lift out of it for my soul; so must be obliged to go on writing like a Dutch commentator to the end of the chapter, unless something be done—

—I never stand conferring with pen and ink one moment; for if a pinch of snuff, or a stride or two across the room will not do the business for me— I take a razor at once; and having tried the edge of it upon the palm of my hand, without further ceremony, except that of first lathering my beard, I shave it off; taking care only if I do leave a hair, that it be not a grey one: this done, I change my shirt—put on a better coat—send for my last wig— put my topaz ring upon my finger; and in a word, dress myself from one end to the other of me, after my best fashion.

Now the devil in hell must be in it, if this does not do: for consider, Sir, as every man chooses to be present at the shaving of his own beard (though there is no rule without an exception), and unavoidably sits over-against himself the whole time it is doing, in case he has a hand in it—the Situation, like all others, has notions of her own to put into the brain.——

——I maintain it, the conceits of a rough-bearded man, are seven years more terse and juvenile for one single operation; and if they did not run a risk of being quite shaved away, might be carried up by continual shavings, to the highest pitch of sublimity—How Homer could write with so long a beard, I don't know—and as it makes against my hypothesis, I as little care —But let us return to the Toilet.

Ludovicus Sorbonensis makes this entirely an affair of the body (ἐξωτερικὴ πρᾶξις) as he calls it—but he is deceived: the soul and body are joint-sharers in every thing they get: A man cannot dress, but his ideas get clothed at the same time; and if he dresses like a gentleman, every one of them stands presented to his imagination, genteelized along with him—so that he has nothing to do, but take his pen, and write like himself.

For this cause, when your honours and reverences would know whether I writ clean and fit to be read, you will be able to judge full as well by looking into my Laundress's bill, as my book; there was one single month in which I can make it appear, that I dirtied one and thirty shirts with clean writing; and after all, was more abused, cursed, criticised, and confounded, and had more mystic heads shaken at me, for what I had wrote in that one month, than in all the other months of that year put together.

——But their honours and reverences had not seen my bills.

Chapter 14

As I never had any intention of beginning the Digression I am making all this preparation for, till I come to the 15th chapter—I have this chapter to put to whatever use I think proper—I have twenty this moment ready for it—I could write my chapter of Button-holes in it—

Or my chapter of Pishes, which should follow them—

Or my chapter of Knots, in case their reverences have done with them—they might lead me into mischief: the safest way is to follow the track of the learned, and raise objections against what I have been writing, tho' I declare beforehand, I know no more than my heels how to answer them.

And first, it may be said, there is a pelting kind of thersitical satire, as black as the very ink 'tis wrote with—(and by the bye, whoever says so, is indebted to the muster-master general of the Grecian army, for suffering the name of so ugly and foul-mouthed a man as Thersites to continue upon his roll—for it has furnished him with an epithet)—in these productions he will urge, all the personal washings and scrubbings upon earth do a sinking genius no sort of good—but just the contrary, inasmuch as the dirtier the fellow is, the better generally he succeeds in it.

To this, I have no other answer—at least ready—but that the Archbishop of Benevento wrote his nasty Romance of the Galatea, as all the world knows, in a purple coat, waistcoat, and purple pair of breeches; and that the penance set him of writing a commentary upon the book of the Revelations, as severe as it was looked upon by one part of the world, was far from being deemed so, by the other, upon the single account of that Investment.

Another objection, to all this remedy, is its want of universality; forasmuch as the shaving part of it, upon which so much stress is laid, by an unalterable law of nature excludes one half of the species entirely from its use: all I can say is, that female writers, whether of England, or of France, must e'en go without it—

As for the Spanish ladies—I am in no sort of distress—

Chapter 15

The fifteenth chapter is come at last; and brings nothing with it but a sad signature of "How our pleasures slip from under us in this world!"

For in talking of my digression—I declare before heaven I have made it! What a strange creature is mortal man! said she.

'Tis very true, said I—but 'twere better to get all these things out of our heads, and return to my uncle Toby.

Chapter 16

When my uncle Toby and the corporal had marched down to the bottom of the avenue, they recollected their business lay the other way; so they faced about and marched up straight to Mrs. Wadman's door.

I warrant your honour; said the corporal, touching his Montero-cap with his hand, as he passed him in order to give a knock at the door—My uncle Toby, contrary to his invariable way of treating his faithful servant, said nothing good or bad: the truth was, he had not altogether marshalled his ideas; he wished for another conference, and as the corporal was mounting up the three steps before the door—he hemmed twice—a portion of my uncle Toby's most modest spirits fled, at each expulsion, towards the corporal; he stood with the rapper of the door suspended for a full minute in his hand, he scarce knew why. Bridget stood perdue within, with her finger and her thumb upon the latch, benumbed with expectation: and Mrs. Wadman, with an eye ready to be deflowered again, sat breathless behind the window-curtain of her bed-chamber, watching their approach.

Trim! said my uncle Toby—but as he articulated the word, the minute expired, and Trim let fall the rapper.

My uncle Toby perceiving that all hopes of a conference were knocked on the head by it——whistled *Lillabullero*.

CHAPTER 17

As Mrs. Bridget's finger and thumb were upon the latch, the corporal did not knock as oft as perchance your honour's tailor—I might have taken my example something nearer home; for I owe mine, some five and twenty pounds at least, and wonder at the man's patience—

—But this is nothing at all to the world: only 'tis a cursed thing to be in debt; and there seems to be a fatality in the exchequers of some poor princes, particularly those of our house, which no Economy can bind down in irons: for my own part, I'm persuaded there is not any one prince, prelate, pope, or potentate, great or small upon earth, more desirous in his heart of keeping straight with the world than I am—or who takes more likely means for it. I never give above half a guinea—or walk with boots—or cheapen toothpicks—or lay out a shilling upon a band-box the year round; and for the six months I'm in the country, I'm upon so small a scale, that with all the good temper in the world, I outdo Rousseau, a bar length—for I keep neither man or boy, or horse, or cow, or dog, or cat, or any thing that can eat or drink, except a thin poor piece of a Vestal (to keep my fire in), and who has generally as bad an appetite as myself—but if you think this makes a philosopher of me—I would not, my good people! give a rush for your judgments.

True philosophy—but there is no treating the subject whilst my uncle is whistling *Lillabullero*.

——Let us go into the house.

CHAPTER 18

CHAPTER 19

LILLI BULLERO

Lively

Lilli bul-le-ro

Lilli bul-lero bullen a la. Le-ro le-ro, lil-li bul-le-ro,

Le-ro le-ro, bullen a la, Le-ro le-ro, lil-li bul-le-ro, le-ro le-ro, bul-len a la.

CHAPTER 20

____ * * * * * * * * * * * * *
* *.____

—You shall see the very place, Madam; said my uncle Toby.

Mrs. Wadman blushed—looked towards the door—turned pale—blushed slightly again—recovered her natural colour—blushed worse than ever; which, for the sake of the unlearned reader, I translate thus—

"L—d! I cannot look at it—

What would the world say if I looked at it?

I should drop down, if I looked at it—

I wish I could look at it—

There can be no sin in looking at it.

——I will look at it."

Whilst all this was running through Mrs. Wadman's imagination, my uncle Toby had risen from the sofa, and got to the other side of the parlour door, to give Trim an order about it in the passage—

* * * * * * * * * *—I believe it is in the garret, said my uncle Toby—I saw it there, an' please your honour, this morning, answered Trim —Then prithee, step directly for it, Trim, said my uncle Toby, and bring it into the parlour.

The corporal did not approve of the orders, but most cheerfully obeyed them. The first was not an act of his will—the second was; so he put on his Montero-cap, and went as fast as his lame knee would let him. My uncle Toby returned into the parlour, and sat himself down again upon the sofa.

——You shall lay your finger upon the place—said my uncle Toby.—I will not touch it, however, quoth Mrs. Wadman to herself.

This requires a second translation:—it shows what little knowledge is got by mere words—we must go up to the first springs.

Now in order to clear up the mist which hangs upon these three pages, I must endeavour to be as clear as possible myself.

Rub your hands thrice across your foreheads—blow your noses—cleanse your emunctories—sneeze, my good people!—God bless you—

Now give me all the help you can.

CHAPTER 21

As there are fifty different ends (counting all ends in—as well civil as religious) for which a woman takes a husband, she first sets about and carefully weighs, then separates and distinguishes in her mind, which of all that number of ends is hers: then by discourse, enquiry, argumentation, and inference, she investigates and finds out whether she has got hold of the right one—and if she has—then, by pulling it gently this way and that way, she further forms a judgment, whether it will not break in the drawing.

The imagery under which Slawkenbergius impresses this upon the reader's fancy, in the beginning of his third Decad, is so ludicrous, that the honour I bear the sex, will not suffer me to quote it—otherwise it is not destitute of humour.

"She first, saith Slawkenbergius, stops the ass, and holding his halter in her left hand (lest he should get away) she thrusts her right hand into the very bottom of his pannier to search for it—For what?—you'll not know the sooner, quoth Slawkenbergius, for interrupting me—

"I have nothing, good Lady, but empty bottles"; says the ass.

"I'm loaded with tripes"; says the second.

——And thou art little better, quoth she to the third; for nothing is there in thy panniers but trunk-hose and pantofles—and so to the fourth and fifth, going on one by one through the whole string, till coming to the ass which carries it, she turns the pannier upside down, looks at it—considers it—samples it—measures it—stretches it—wets it—dries it—then takes her teeth both to the warp and weft of it.

——Of what? for the love of Christ!

I am determined, answered Slawkenbergius, that all the powers upon earth shall never wring that secret from my breast.

Chapter 22

WE live in a world beset on all sides with mysteries and riddles—and so 'tis no matter—else it seems strange, that Nature, who makes everything so well to answer its destination, and seldom or never errs, unless for pastime, in giving such forms and aptitudes to whatever passes through her hands, that whether she designs for the plough, the caravan, the cart—or whatever other creature she models, be it but an ass's foal, you are sure to have the thing you wanted; and yet at the same time should so eternally bungle it as she does, in making so simple a thing as a married man.

Whether it is in the choice of the clay—or that it is frequently spoiled in the baking; by an excess of which a husband may turn out too crusty (you know) on one hand—or not enough so, through defect of heat, on the other —or whether this great Artificer is not so attentive to the little Platonic exigencies of that part of the species, for whose use she is fabricating this— or that her Ladyship sometimes scarce knows what sort of a husband will do—I know not: we will discourse about it after supper.

It is enough, that neither the observation itself, or the reasoning upon it, are at all to the purpose—but rather against it; since with regard to my uncle Toby's fitness for the marriage state, nothing was ever better: she had formed him of the best and kindliest clay—had tempered it with her own milk, and breathed into it the sweetest spirit—she had made him all gentle, generous, and humane—she had filled his heart with trust and confidence, and disposed every passage which led to it, for the communication of the tenderest offices—she had moreover considered the other causes for which matrimony was ordained—

And accordingly *

The donation was not defeated by my uncle Toby's wound.

Now this last article was somewhat apocryphal; and the Devil, who is the great disturber of our faiths in this world, had raised scruples in Mrs. Wadman's brain about it; and like a true devil as he was, had done his own work at the same time, by turning my uncle Toby's Virtue thereupon into nothing but empty bottles, tripes, trunk-hose, and pantofles.

Chapter 23

Mrs. Bridget had pawned all the little stock of honour a poor chambermaid was worth in the world, that she would get to the bottom of the affair in ten days; and it was built upon one of the most concessible *postulata* in nature: namely, that whilst my uncle Toby was making love to her mistress, the corporal could find nothing better to do, than make love to her—"And I'll let him as much as he will," said Bridget, "to get it out of him."

Friendship has two garments; an outer and an under one. Bridget was serving her mistress's interests in the one—and doing the thing which most pleased herself in the other: so had as many stakes depending upon my uncle Toby's wound, as the Devil himself—Mrs. Wadman had but one—and as it possibly might be her last (without discouraging Mrs. Bridget, or discrediting her talents) was determined to play her cards herself.

She wanted not encouragement: a child might have looked into his hand —there was such a plainness and simplicity in his playing out what trumps he had—with such an unmistrusting ignorance of the ten-ace—and so naked and defenceless did he sit upon the same sofa with widow Wadman, that a generous heart would have wept to have won the game of him.

Let us drop the metaphor.

Chapter 24

——And the story too—if you please: for though I have all along been hastening towards this part of it, with so much earnest desire, as well knowing it to be the choicest morsel of what I had to offer to the world, yet now that I am got to it, any one is welcome to take my pen, and go on with the story for me that will—I see the difficulties of the descriptions I'm going to give—and feel my want of powers.

It is one comfort at least to me, that I lost some fourscore ounces of blood this week in a most uncritical fever which attacked me at the beginning of this chapter; so that I have still some hopes remaining, it may be more in the serous or globular parts of the blood, than in the subtle *aura* of the brain—be it which it will—an Invocation can do no hurt—and I leave the affair entirely to the invoked, to inspire or to inject me according as he sees good.

THE INVOCATION

Gentle Spirit of sweetest humour, who erst did sit upon the easy pen of my beloved Cervantes; Thou who glided'st daily through his lattice, and turned'st the twilight of his prison into noon-day brightness by thy presence—tinged'st his little urn of water with heaven-sent nectar, and all the time he wrote of Sancho and his master, didst cast thy mystic mantle o'er his withered stump,[1] and wide extended it to all the evils of his life——

[1] He lost his hand at the battle of Lepanto.

—Turn in hither, I beseech thee!—behold these breeches!—they are all I have in the world—that piteous rent was given them at Lyons——

My shirts—see what a deadly schism has happened amongst 'em—for the laps are in Lombardy, and the rest of 'em here—I never had but six, and a cunning gipsy of a laundress at Milan cut me off the fore-laps of five—To do her justice, she did it with some consideration—for I was returning out of Italy.

And yet, notwithstanding all this, and a pistol tinder-box which was moreover filched from me at Sienna, and twice that I paid five Pauls for two hard eggs, once at Raddicoffini, and a second time at Capua—I do not think a journey through France and Italy, provided a man keeps his temper all the way, so bad a thing as some people would make you believe: there must be ups and downs, or how the deuce should we get into valleys where Nature spreads so many tables of entertainment.—'Tis nonsense to imagine they will lend you their voitures to be shaken to pieces for nothing; and unless you pay twelve sous for greasing your wheels, how should the poor peasant get butter to his bread?—We really expect too much—and for the livre or two above par for your suppers and bed—at the most they are but one shilling and ninepence halfpenny—who would embroil their philosophy for it? for heaven's and for your own sake, pay it—pay it with both hands open, rather than leave Disappointment sitting drooping upon the eye of your fair Hostess and her Damsels in the gate-way, at your departure—and besides, my dear Sir, you get a sisterly kiss of each of 'em worth a pound—at least I did—

—For my uncle Toby's amours running all the way in my head, they had the same effect upon me as if they had been my own—I was in the most perfect state of bounty and good-will; and felt the kindliest harmony vibrating within me, with every oscillation of the chaise alike; so that whether the roads were rough or smooth, it made no difference; every thing I saw or had to do with, touched upon some secret spring either of sentiment or rapture.

—They were the sweetest notes I ever heard; and I instantly let down the fore-glass to hear them more distinctly—'Tis Maria; said the postillion, observing I was listening——Poor Maria, continued he (leaning his body on one side to let me see her, for he was in a line betwixt us), is sitting upon a bank playing her vespers upon her pipe, with her little goat beside her.

The young fellow uttered this with an accent and a look so perfectly in tune to a feeling heart, that I instantly made a vow, I would give him a four-and-twenty sous piece, when I got to Moulins—

——And who is poor Maria? said I.

The love and pity of all the villages around us; said the postillion—it is but three years ago, that the sun did not shine upon so fair, so quick-witted and amiable a maid; and better fate did Maria deserve, than to have her Banns forbid, by the intrigues of the curate of the parish who published them—

He was going on, when Maria, who had made a short pause, put the pipe to her mouth, and began the air again—they were the same notes; yet were ten times sweeter: It is the evening service to the Virgin, said the young man—but who has taught her to play it—or how she came by her pipe, no one knows; we think that heaven has assisted her in both; for ever since she has been unsettled in her mind, it seems her only consolation—she has never once had the pipe out of her hand, but plays that service upon it almost night and day.

The postillion delivered this with so much discretion and natural eloquence, that I could not help deciphering something in his face above his condition, and should have sifted out his history, had not poor Maria taken such full possession of me.

We had got up by this time almost to the bank where Maria was sitting: she was in a thin white jacket, with her hair, all but two tresses, drawn up into a silk-net, with a few olive leaves twisted a little fantastically on one side—she was beautiful; and if ever I felt the full force of an honest heart-ache, it was the moment I saw her—

—God help her! poor damsel! above a hundred masses, said the postillion, have been said in the several parish churches and convents around for her, —but without effect; we have still hopes, as she is sensible for short intervals, that the Virgin at last will restore her to herself; but her parents, who know her best, are hopeless upon that score, and think her senses are lost for ever.

As the postillion spoke this, Maria made a cadence so melancholy, so tender and querulous, that I sprung out of the chaise to help her, and found myself sitting betwixt her and her goat before I relapsed from my enthusiasm.

Maria looked wistfully for some time at me, and then at her goat—and then at me—and then at her goat again, and so on, alternately—

—Well, Maria, said I softly—What resemblance do you find?

I do entreat the candid reader to believe me, that it was from the humblest conviction of what a Beast man is,—that I asked the question; and that I would not have let fallen an unseasonable pleasantry in the venerable presence of Misery, to be entitled to all the wit that ever Rabelais scattered —and yet I own my heart smote me, and that I so smarted at the very idea of it, that I swore I would set up for Wisdom, and utter grave sentences the rest of my days—and never—never attempt again to commit mirth with man, woman, or child, the longest day I had to live.

As for writing nonsense to them—I believe, there was a reserve—but that I leave to the world.

Adieu, Maria!—adieu, poor hapless damsel!—some time, but not now, I may hear thy sorrows from thy own lips—but I was deceived; for that moment she took her pipe and told me such a tale of woe with it, that I rose up, and with broken and irregular steps walked softly to my chaise.

——What an excellent inn at Moulins!

CHAPTER 25

WHEN we have got to the end of this chapter (but not before) we must all turn back to the two blank chapters, on the account of which my honour has lain bleeding this half hour—I stop it, by pulling off one of my yellow slippers and throwing it with all my violence to the opposite side of my room, with a declaration at the heel of it—

—That whatever resemblance it may bear to half the chapters which are written in the world, or for aught I know may be now writing in it—that it was as casual as the foam of Zeuxis his horse; besides, I look upon a chapter which has only nothing in it, with respect; and considering what worse things there are in the world—That it is no way a proper subject for satire—

—Why then was it left so? And here without staying for my reply, shall I be called as many blockheads, numskulls, doddypoles, dunderheads, ninnyhammers, goosecaps, joltheads, nincompoops, sh--t-a-beds—and other unsavoury appellations, as ever the cake-bakers of Lernè cast in the teeth of King Garangantua's shepherds—And I'll let them do it, as Bridget said, as much as they please; for how was it possible they should foresee the necessity I was under of writing the 25th chapter of my book, before the 18th, etc.?

——So I don't take it amiss—All I wish is, that it may be a lesson to the world, "to let people tell their stories their own way."

The Eighteenth Chapter

As Mrs. Bridget opened the door before the corporal had well given the rap, the interval betwixt that and my uncle Toby's introduction into the parlour, was so short, that Mrs. Wadman had but just time to get from behind the curtain—lay a Bible upon the table, and advance a step or two towards the door to receive him.

My uncle Toby saluted Mrs. Wadman, after the manner in which women were saluted by men in the year of our Lord God one thousand seven hundred and thirteen—then facing about, he marched up abreast with her to the sofa, and in three plain words—though not before he was sat down—nor after he was sat down—but as he was sitting down, told her, "he was in love"—so that my uncle Toby strained himself more in the declaration than he needed.

Mrs. Wadman naturally looked down, upon a slit she had been darning up in her apron, in expectation every moment, that my uncle Toby would go on; but having no talents for amplification, and Love moreover of all others being a subject of which he was the least a master—When he had told Mrs. Wadman once that he loved her, he let it alone, and left the matter to work after its own way.

My father was always in raptures with this system of my uncle Toby's, as he falsely called it, and would often say, that could his brother Toby to his process have added but a pipe of tobacco—he had wherewithal to have found his way, if there was faith in a Spanish proverb, towards the hearts of half the women upon the globe.

My uncle Toby never understood what my father meant; nor will I presume to extract more from it, than a condemnation of an error which the bulk of the world lie under—but the French, every one of 'em to a man, who believe in it, almost as much as the Real Presence, "That talking of love, is making it."

——I would as soon set about making a black-pudding by the same receipt.

Let us go on: Mrs. Wadman sat in expectation my uncle Toby would do so, to almost the first pulsation of that minute, wherein silence on one side or the other, generally becomes indecent: so edging herself a little more towards him, and raising up her eyes, sub-blushing, as she did it—she took up the gauntlet—or the discourse (if you like it better) and communed with my uncle Toby, thus:

The cares and disquietudes of the marriage state, quoth Mrs. Wadman, are very great. I suppose so—said my uncle Toby: and therefore when a person, continued Mrs. Wadman, is so much at his ease as you are—so happy, Captain Shandy, in yourself, your friends and your amusements—I wonder, what reasons can incline you to the state—

—They are written, quoth my uncle Toby, in the Common-Prayer Book.

Thus far my uncle Toby went on warily, and kept within his depth, leaving Mrs. Wadman to sail upon the gulf as she pleased.

——As for children—said Mrs. Wadman—though a principal end perhaps of the institution, and the natural wish, I suppose, of every parent—yet do not we all find, they are certain sorrows, and very uncertain comforts? and what is there, dear sir, to pay one for the heart-aches—what compensation for the many tender and disquieting apprehensions of a suffering and defenceless mother who brings them into life? I declare, said my uncle Toby, smit with pity, I know of none; unless it be the pleasure which it has pleased God—

A fiddlestick! quoth she.

Chapter the Nineteenth

Now there are such an infinitude of notes, tunes, cants, chants, airs, looks, and accents with which the word fiddlestick may be pronounced in all such causes as this, every one of 'em impressing a sense and meaning as different from the other, as dirt from cleanliness—That Casuists (for it is an affair of conscience on that score) reckon up no less than fourteen thousand in which you may do either right or wrong.

Mrs. Wadman hit upon the fiddlestick, which summoned up all my uncle Toby's modest blood into his cheeks—so feeling within himself that he had somehow or other got beyond his depth, he stopt short; and without entering further either into the pains or pleasures of matrimony, he laid his hand upon his heart, and made an offer to take them as they were, and share them along with her.

When my uncle Toby had said this, he did not care to say it again; so casting his eye upon the Bible which Mrs. Wadman had laid upon the table, he took it up; and popping, dear soul! upon a passage in it, of all others the most interesting to him—which was the siege of Jericho—he set himself to read it over—leaving his proposal of marriage, as he had done his declaration of love, to work with her after its own way. Now it wrought neither as an astringent or a loosener; nor like opium, or bark, or mercury, or buckthorn, or any one drug which nature had bestowed upon the world—in short, it worked not at all in her; and the cause of that was, that there was something working there before—Babbler that I am! I have anticipated what it was a dozen times; but there is fire still in the subject—allons.

Chapter 26

It is natural for a perfect stranger who is going from London to Edinburgh, to enquire before he sets out, how many miles to York; which is about the half way—nor does any body wonder, if he goes on and asks about the Corporation, etc.--

It was just as natural for Mrs. Wadman, whose first husband was all his time afflicted with a Sciatica, to wish to know how far from the hip to the groin; and how far she was likely to suffer more or less in her feelings, in the one case than in the other.

She had accordingly read Drake's anatomy from one end to the other. She had peeped into Wharton upon the brain, and borrowed [1]Graaf upon the bones and muscles; but could make nothing of it.

She had reasoned likewise from her own powers—laid down theorems—drawn consequences, and come to no conclusion.

To clear up all, she had twice asked Doctor Slop, "if poor Captain Shandy was ever likely to recover of his wound—?"

——He is recovered, Doctor Slop would say—

What! quite?

Quite: madam—

But what do you mean by a recovery? Mrs. Wadman would say.

Doctor Slop was the worst man alive at definitions; and so Mrs. Wadman could get no knowledge: in short, there was no way to extract it, but from my uncle Toby himself.

There is an accent of humanity in an enquiry of this kind which lulls suspicion to rest—and I am half persuaded the serpent got pretty near it, in his discourse with Eve; for the propensity in the sex to be deceived could not be so great, that she should have boldness to hold chat with the devil, without it—But there is an accent of humanity—how shall I describe it?—'tis an accent which covers the part with a garment, and gives the enquirer a right to be as particular with it, as your body-surgeon.

"—Was it without remission?—

"—Was it more tolerable in bed?

"—Could he lie on both sides alike with it?

"—Was he able to mount a horse?

"—Was motion bad for it?" *et caetera*, were so tenderly spoke to, and so directed towards my uncle Toby's heart, that every item of them sunk ten times deeper into it than the evils themselves—but when Mrs. Wadman went round about by Namur to get at my uncle Toby's groin; and engaged him to attack the point of the advanced counterscarp, and *pêle mêle* with the Dutch to take the counterguard of St. Roch sword in hand—and then with tender notes playing upon his ear, led him all bleeding by the hand out of the trench, wiping her eye, as he was carried to his tent—Heaven! Earth! Sea!—all was lifted up—the springs of nature rose above their levels—an angel of mercy sat beside him on the sofa—his heart glowed with fire—and

---

[1] This must be a mistake in Mr. Shandy; for Graaf wrote upon the pancreatic juice, and the parts of generation.

had he been worth a thousand, he had lost every heart of them to Mrs. Wadman.

——And whereabouts, dear Sir, quoth Mrs. Wadman, a little categorically, did you receive this sad blow?—In asking this question, Mrs. Wadman gave a slight glance towards the waistband of my uncle Toby's red plush breeches, expecting naturally, as the shortest reply to it, that my uncle Toby would lay his fore-finger upon the place—It fell out otherwise—for my uncle Toby having got his wound before the gate of St. Nicolas, in one of the traverses of the trench opposite to the salient angle of the demi-bastion of St. Roch; he could at any time stick a pin upon the identical spot of ground where he was standing when the stone struck him: this struck instantly upon my uncle Toby's sensorium—and with it, struck his large map of the town and citadel of Namur and its environs, which he had purchased and pasted down upon a board, by the corporal's aid, during his long illness —it had lain with other military lumber in the garret ever since, and accordingly the corporal was detached into the garret to fetch it.

My uncle Toby measured off thirty toises, with Mrs. Wadman's scissors, from the returning angle before the gate of St. Nicolas; and with such a virgin modesty laid her finger upon the place, that the goddess of Decency, if then in being—if not, 'twas her shade—shook her head, and with a finger wavering across her eyes—forbid her to explain the mistake.

Unhappy Mrs. Wadman!

——For nothing can make this chapter go off with spirit but an apostrophe to thee—but my heart tells me, that in such a crisis an apostrophe is but an insult in disguise, and ere I would offer one to a woman in distress—let the chapter go to the devil; provided any damned critic in keeping will be but at the trouble to take it with him.

CHAPTER 27

My uncle Toby's Map is carried down into the kitchen.

CHAPTER 28

——AND here is the Maes—and this is the Sambre; said the corporal, pointing with his right hand extended a little towards the map and his left upon Mrs. Bridget's shoulder—but not the shoulder next him—and this, said he, is the town of Namur—and this the citadel—and there lay the French—and here lay his honour and myself—and in this cursed trench, Mrs. Bridget, quoth the corporal, taking her by the hand, did he receive the wound which crushed him so miserably here.——In pronouncing which, he slightly pressed the back of her hand towards the part he felt for—and let it fall.

We thought, Mr. Trim, it had been more in the middle,—said Mrs. Bridget—

That would have undone us for ever—said the corporal.

——And left my poor mistress undone too, said Bridget.

The corporal made no reply to the repartee, but by giving Mrs. Bridget a kiss.

Come—come—said Bridget—holding the palm of her left hand parallel to the plane of the horizon, and sliding the fingers of the other over it, in a way which could not have been done, had there been the least wart or protuberance—'Tis every syllable of it false, cried the corporal, before she had half finished the sentence—

—I know it to be fact, said Bridget, from credible witnesses.

——Upon my honour, said the corporal, laying his hand upon his heart, and blushing, as he spoke, with honest resentment—'tis a story, Mrs. Bridget, as false as hell—Not, said Bridget, interrupting him, that either I or my mistress care a halfpenny about it, whether 'tis so or no—only that when one is married, one would choose to have such a thing by one at least—

It was somewhat unfortunate for Mrs. Bridget, that she had begun the attack with her manual exercise; for the corporal instantly * * * * *
* * * * * * * * * * * * * *

Chapter 29

It was like the momentary contest in the moist eye-lids of an April morning, "Whether Bridget should laugh or cry."

She snatched up a rolling pin—'twas ten to one, she had laughed—

She laid it down—she cried; and had one single tear of 'em but tasted of bitterness, full sorrowful would the corporal's heart have been that he had used the argument; but the corporal understood the sex, a quart major to a terce at least, better than my uncle Toby, and accordingly he assailed Mrs. Bridget after this manner.

I know, Mrs. Bridget, said the corporal, giving her a most respectful kiss, that thou art good and modest by nature, and art withal so generous a girl in thyself, that, if I know thee rightly, thou would'st not wound an insect, much less the honour of so gallant and worthy a soul as my master, wast thou sure to be made a countess of—but thou hast been set on, and deluded, dear Bridget, as is often a woman's case, "to please others more than themselves—"

Bridget's eyes poured down at the sensations the corporal excited.

——Tell me—tell me, then, my dear Bridget, continued the corporal, taking hold of her hand, which hung down dead by her side,—and giving a second kiss—whose suspicion has misled thee?

Bridget sobbed a sob or two—then opened her eyes—the corporal wiped 'em with the bottom of her apron—she then opened her heart and told him all.

Chapter 30

My uncle Toby and the corporal had gone on separately with their operations the greatest part of the campaign, and as effectually cut off from all communication of what either the one or the other had been doing, as if they had been separated from each other by the Maes or the Sambre.

My uncle Toby, on his side, had presented himself every afternoon in his red and silver, and blue and gold alternately, and sustained an infinity of

attacks in them, without knowing them to be attacks—and so had nothing
to communicate—

The corporal, on his side, in taking Bridget, by it had gained considerable
advantages—and consequently had much to communicate—but what were
the advantages—as well as what was the manner by which he had seized
them, required so nice a historian, that the corporal durst not venture upon
it; and as sensible as he was of glory, would rather have been contented to
have gone bareheaded and without laurels for ever, than torture his master's modesty for a single moment—

—Best of honest and gallant servants!—But I have apostrophized thee,
Trim! once before—and could I apotheosize thee also (that is to say) with
good company—I would do it without ceremony in the very next page.

Chapter 31

Now my uncle Toby had one evening laid down his pipe upon the table,
and was counting over to himself upon his finger ends (beginning at his
thumb) all Mrs. Wadman's perfections one by one; and happening two or
three times together, either by omitting some, or counting others twice
over, to puzzle himself sadly before he could get beyond his middle finger
—Prithee, Trim! said he, taking up his pipe again,—bring me a pen and
ink: Trim brought paper also.

Take a full sheet—Trim! said my uncle Toby, making a sign with his
pipe at the same time to take a chair and sit down close by him at the table.
The corporal obeyed—placed the paper directly before him—took a pen,
and dipped it in the ink.

—She has a thousand virtues, Trim! said my uncle Toby—

Am I to set them down, an' please your honour? quoth the corporal.

—But they must be taken in their ranks, replied my uncle Toby; for of
them all, Trim, that which wins me most, and which is a security for all the
rest, is the compassionate turn and singular humanity of her character—I
protest, added my uncle Toby, looking up, as he protested it, towards the
top of the ceiling—That was I her brother, Trim, a thousand fold, she could
not make more constant or more tender enquiries after my sufferings—
though now no more.

The corporal made no reply to my uncle Toby's protestation, but by a
short cough—he dipped the pen a second time into the inkhorn; and my
uncle Toby, pointing with the end of his pipe as close to the top of the sheet
at the left-hand corner of it, as he could get it—the corporal wrote down the
word
HUMANITY----thus.

Prithee, corporal, said my uncle Toby, as soon as Trim had done it——
how often does Mrs. Bridget enquire after the wound on the cap of thy
knee, which thou received'st at the battle of Landen?

She never, an' please your honour, enquires after it at all.

That, corporal, said my uncle Toby, with all the triumph the goodness of
his nature would permit—That shews the difference in the character of the
mistress and maid—had the fortune of war allotted the same mischance to

me, Mrs. Wadman would have enquired into every circumstance relating to it a hundred times—She would have enquired, an' please your honour, ten times as often about your honour's groin—The pain, Trim, is equally excruciating,—and compassion has as much to do with the one as the other—

—God bless your honour! cried the corporal—what has a woman's compassion to do with a wound upon the cap of a man's knee? had your honour's been shot into ten thousand splinters at the affair of Landen, Mrs. Wadman would have troubled her head as little about it as Bridget; because, added the corporal, lowering his voice, and speaking very distinctly, as he assigned his reason—

"The knee is such a distance from the main body—whereas the groin, your honour knows, is upon the very curtain of the place."

My uncle Toby gave a long whistle—but in a note which could scarce be heard across the table.

The corporal had advanced too far to retire—in three words he told the rest—

My uncle Toby laid down his pipe as gently upon the fender, as if it had been spun from the unravellings of a spider's web—

—Let us go to my brother Shandy's, said he.

CHAPTER 32

THERE will be just time, whilst my uncle Toby and Trim are walking to my father's, to inform you that Mrs. Wadman had, some moons before this, made a confident of my mother; and that Mrs. Bridget who had the burden of her own, as well as her mistress's secret to carry, had got happily delivered of both to Susannah behind the garden-wall.

As for my mother, she saw nothing at all in it, to make the least bustle about—but Susannah was sufficient by herself for all the ends and purposes you could possibly have, in exporting a family secret; for she instantly imparted it by signs to Jonathan—and Jonathan by tokens to the cook as she was basting a loin of mutton; the cook sold it with some kitchen-fat to the postillion for a groat, who trucked it with the dairy maid for something of about the same value—and though whispered in the hay-loft, Fame caught the notes with her brazen trumpet, and sounded them upon the housetop—In a word, not an old woman in the village or five miles round, who did not understand the difficulties of my uncle Toby's siege, and what were the secret articles which had delayed the surrender.——

My father, whose way was to force every event in nature into an hypothesis, by which means never man crucified Truth at the rate he did—had but just heard of the report as my uncle Toby set out; and catching fire suddenly at the trespass done his brother by it, was demonstrating to Yorick, notwithstanding my mother was sitting by—not only "That the devil was in women, and that the whole of the affair was lust"; but that every evil and disorder in the world, of what kind and nature soever, from the first fall of Adam, down to my uncle Toby's (inclusive), was owing one way or other to the same unruly appetite.

Yorick was just bringing my father's hypothesis to some temper, when my uncle Toby entering the room with marks of infinite benevolence and forgiveness in his looks, my father's eloquence rekindled against the passion—and as he was not very nice in the choice of his words when he was wroth—as soon as my uncle Toby was seated by the fire, and had filled his pipe, my father broke out in this manner.

CHAPTER 33

――THAT provision should be made for continuing the race of so great, so exalted and god-like a Being as man—I am far from denying—but philosophy speaks freely of every thing; and therefore I still think and do maintain it to be a pity, that it should be done by means of a passion which bends down the faculties, and turns all the wisdom, contemplations, and operations of the soul backwards—a passion, my dear, continued my father, addressing himself to my mother, which couples and equals wise men with fools, and makes us come out of our caravans and hiding-places more like satyrs and four-footed beasts than men.

I know it will be said, continued my father (availing himself of the Prolepsis), that in itself, and simply taken—like hunger, or thirst, or sleep—'tis an affair neither good or bad—or shameful or otherwise.—Why then did the delicacy of Diogenes and Plato so recalcitrate against it? and wherefore, when we go about to make and plant a man, do we put out the candle? and for what reason is it, that all the parts thereof—the congredients—the preparations—the instruments, and whatever serves thereto, are so held as to be conveyed to a cleanly mind by no language, translation, or periphrasis whatever?

――The act of killing and destroying a man, continued my father, raising his voice—and turning to my uncle Toby—you see, is glorious—and the weapons by which we do it are honourable.—We march with them upon our shoulders—We strut with them by our sides—We gild them—We carve them—We in-lay them—We enrich them—Nay, if it be but a scoundrel cannon, we cast an ornament upon the breech of it.――

――My uncle Toby laid down his pipe to intercede for a better epithet—and Yorick was rising up to batter the whole hypothesis to pieces—

—When Obadiah broke into the middle of the room with a complaint, which cried out for an immediate hearing.

The case was this:

My father, whether by ancient custom of the manor, or as impropriator of the great tithes, was obliged to keep a Bull for the service of the Parish, and Obadiah had led his cow upon a pop-visit to him one day or other the preceding summer—I say, one day or other—because as chance would have it, it was the day on which he was married to my father's housemaid—so one was a reckoning to the other. Therefore when Obadiah's wife was brought to bed—Obadiah thanked God—

—Now, said Obadiah, I shall have a calf: so Obadiah went daily to visit his cow.

She'll calve on Monday—on Tuesday—on Wednesday at the farthest—

The cow did not calve—no—she'll not calve till next week—the cow put it off terribly—till at the end of the sixth week Obadiah's suspicions (like a good man's) fell upon the Bull.

Now the parish being very large, my father's Bull, to speak the truth of him, was no way equal to the department; he had, however, got himself, somehow or other, thrust into employment—and as he went through the business with a grave face, my father had a high opinion of him.

——Most of the townsmen, an' please your worship, quoth Obadiah, believe that 'tis all the Bull's fault—

—But may not a cow be barren? replied my father, turning to Dr. Slop.

It never happens: said Dr. Slop, but the man's wife may have come before her time naturally enough—Prithee has the child hair upon his head?—added Dr. Slop—

—It is as hairy as I am; said Obadiah.—Obadiah had not been shaved for three weeks—Wheu--u----u--------cried my father; beginning the sentence with an exclamatory whistle—and so, brother Toby, this poor Bull of mine, who is as good a Bull as ever p—ssed, and might have done for Europa herself in purer times—had he but two legs less, might have been driven into Doctors' Commons and lost his character—which to a town Bull, brother Toby, is the very same thing as his life—

L—d! said my mother, what is all this story about?——

A Cock and a Bull, said Yorick—And one of the best of its kind, I ever heard.

THE END